# The Love at LAST SERIES

BOOKS 1 - 3

## KATERINA SIMMS

# Reading Order

Book One:
The Last Heartbeat

Book Two:
The Last Place You Look

Book Three:
The Last in Line

# The Last Heartbeat

LOVE AT LAST, BOOK 1

The Last
HEARTBEAT
LOVE AT LAST BOOK ONE
KATERINA SIMMS

# Description

**Work brought them together, love kept them intertwined.**

Four years after unimaginable tragedy, Agathe Santos knows that hope is for losers and so is love. Work has become her greatest escape.

CEO Luke Tindall wants a wife, a family, a love that will last. He might have hired Agathe to save his company and deal with his goofy brother, but from the very first meeting, he has desired far more than her sharp wit and tireless work ethic. If only her past wasn't such a big secret. If only that secret wasn't a wound she didn't want healed.

But even as Agathe can no longer deny her feelings for Luke, love is not something she thinks she deserves. Now she must brave her boldest choice yet: lose Luke forever, or lose the one thing that makes her life worth living.

*For fans of slow-burn, heat-with-heart romance.*

**Keep reading to curl up with this soul-stirring romance today!**

# Chapter One

*Oh, God. This is it. I'm going to die in this field.*

Agathe Santos snapped her clouded gaze to the arrow lodged in the gum tree behind her, nock still quivering. Her heart squeezed, and she fought an urge to be sick. *Holy hell!* This wasn't how her night of "partying" was meant to end! As medieval and whimsical as death by arrow point sounded, she wanted to stay firmly alive and in modern times.

Her blood still coursed at the high-pitched *whoosh* that had skimmed past her ear. The smell of midnight dampness rising from the ground, she spun around now to fully realize the freaking arrow had only just missed her head.

A sudden chill surged through her veins. The loss of her contact lenses meant she couldn't see shit, all because the mismanaged fire pit at Uncle Raymond's annual family reunion forced her to rub smoke from her eyes, knocking her lenses loose. Worst still, the family reunion was one she would've gladly missed for the fifth year running.

"Who's there?" Her voice cracked, and her next breaths exploded past her lips on a series of heavy pants.

Despite her squinting, no one stepped through the night, and her active imagination conjured thoughts of a vigilante marksman with lunatic tendencies. Perhaps a person searching isolated fields for someone to murder at arrow point. That someone being her.

Her stomach clenched and threatened to spill her half-digested pinot from the party. If only she could see clearly. If only she hadn't been so eager to earn another four years of freedom from her family's sympathetic looks and questions about her well-being....

And sure, her Argentinean relatives meant well, but unlike them, she wasn't in a hurry to forget.

Dammit. She should have just stayed in Melbourne. This was what she got for traipsing out to the sticks and listening to people who complained about her long work hours. *What the hell did they know? They weren't the ones getting shot at.*

The sleepy town of Roseford was no place for a city-loving woman like her.

If only she'd ignored the pressure to socialize. If only she hadn't misplaced her cabin key. Maybe then she wouldn't be the poor sap fumbling through this endless expanse of overgrown grass on a near-freezing autumn night, with some crazy lurking nearby....

A silhouette appeared in the farthest reaches of her vision. A masculine figure bounded toward her. She unlocked her knees, ready to fall. Ready to plead for her life.

"Are you okay?" His voice echoed toward her. A strong voice. One that held a refined and rumbling English accent, electrifying the edges of her nerves.

Her world froze, but she forced a shaky nod, refusing to appear weak. Refined accent or not, the silhouette's verbal show of concern didn't lull her.

The backs of her eyes ached, and she squinted for more detail. Pale skin glowed through her defective vision. Thick, espresso-dark waves curled over a square hairline. And an archery bow dangled from the tips of his long, brawny fingers.

Her muscles turned to loose jelly, and she waited for an apology. Some sign he wouldn't hurt her. All she got was the crunch of leaves under his feet and the pale man moving closer.

"What the hell are you doing out here?" His rough tone halted her heavy breaths.

With near-perfect detail now, his full, dark brows furrowed, his bottle-green eyes glinting in the moonlight.

"Keys." She waved her tiny, black handbag with so much vigor the entire contents clanged to the ground. Vying for mercy, she offered a cutesy cringe while a jittery sensation ran through her body. "I lost my keys out here earlier today, and now I'm locked out of my cabin."

Her hollow tone lit an imaginary fire in her chest, awakening her natural tendency for defense. She'd spent four years wishing she was anything but alive, so now that her existence seemed at genuine risk, who was she to back away? Or, in other words, maybe she had room to push her luck.

So, she jutted her chin and threw down her challenge. "And what the hell are *you* doing out here?"

She stared him down, or more precisely up, since her five-foot-seven inches didn't compete with his six-foot-something build.

He returned a heated glare, one she imagined could set water to fire if he concentrated hard enough. One. Two. Three times, he blinked, his attention flicking over her body, inciting a sharp prickle to rake over her skin.

Maybe she shouldn't have tested this madman's conviction.

Maybe she *did* want to live after all.

Just having that desire added churning to her queasy belly.

"I own the main house across the field." He stabbed a thumb over his shoulder, the main house indeed in that direction. "That makes me your weekend host. I couldn't sleep, so I came out here for a walk and some archery."

She drew her shoulders back and turned toward the arrow-pierced tree. *Archery?* Who in the age of high-speed internet and self-driving cars still did archery?

Maybe that arrow had hit her after all. Maybe her sanity had finally snapped. Or maybe what she experienced was some tragic, Robin Hood-themed hallucination.

She patted the side of her head and found no signs of blood. *Pity.* She'd have to settle for being just plain out of her ever-flipping mind.

She spun back to Pale Man, and despite her tormented past, or maybe because of it, her usual sass bubbled past the edge of her buckling restraint. "You need to work on your aim. And can I suggest any future practice not be at one in the morning *or* aimed at my head?"

He narrowed his eyes and waited a long beat. "I'll keep your suggestion in mind."

Cold night and lost key be damned, her nerves weren't strong enough to deal with this man's too few words and pointy glares. She'd sleep on her cabin's veranda if she had to or find some other place to hide. Anything to avoid more minutes struggling to *not* pitch her guts at the feet of her socially awkward weekend host.

Unable to keep from sticking it to him one last time, she tilted her chin up and spoke. "Well, if you're done trying to kill me, I'll go now."

"I'm not trying to kill you." His words were tight and deliberate. "And you haven't found your keys. Where will you sleep?"

His pinched scowl looked more annoyed than murderous, and still, her bravado fled, dragging her voice down to a croaky whisper. "If you're not trying to kill me, then drop the bow. You're scaring me."

Tension slid from his face, smoothing out the wrinkles across his forehead and around his eyes. Just as quickly, his fingers sprang open, and the bow thudded onto the leaf-covered grass.

"I'm sorry. I didn't think...." He shrugged the carry case of arrows off his shoulder, his voice dimming with a husky edge before he took one long step forward. "Let me make it up to—"

"Stop." She shot her hand out, the sudden reflex sending her off-kilter so that she stumbled.

Though his apology and lack of weapons made him distinctly less threatening, a sudden coldness hit her with swift violence. She resented the shiver this man brought to her bones. The hard impact of what had happened, of how badly this could have gone. Her pinging nerves made her want to curl up in a ball. Worse still, she couldn't understand why she even cared about the risk he'd posed to her safety.

He stopped, as asked, and an ashen look of abject hopelessness took over. "I'm going to turn around now. You were right. I should go."

His mouth compressed, accentuating the sharp corners of his jawline, but despite his promise to leave, he didn't move.

His attention fell to the ground, and he frowned. "I must have gotten my dates mixed up. I've only just taken over this property, and I promised the previous owners I'd honor their final few cabin bookings."

The skin over his strong cheekbones tightened in stark contrast to his full, wide mouth. Even through her dazed thoughts, she weighed up his harder features in difference to his other, softer ones. Those contradictory features drew out a level of interest she had no business feeling.

First, there was the dark stubble shadowing his chin, then his wind-ruffled hair looked soft enough to make her want to reach out and touch him. *You know, just to confirm that softness.* A softness at odds with his tall, thick, masculine frame....

"If I'd known you'd be here, I would have stayed at my main home in Melbourne." Those green eyes relaxed, and his general aura of danger eased too. "I never meant to ruin your weekend. Again, I'm sorry."

Her focus dropped to his black leather sports jacket over a casual blue flannel shirt. Even his clothes hinted at approachability. Though his unwavering stare seemed to ponder her stillness, she weighed up the cost of trusting his story. Experience had taught her that the price of misplaced trust could be soul-crushing.

The subtle light in his eyes had her relaxing just a little, that light hinting she'd be a heavy-handed shrew to continue her habit of bringing bitterness and dread to every surprise encounter, even if he didn't know of her tendency to do that.

"If you are who you say you are" —she gave a tight nod, recalling her reason for being in this creepy, dark field— "then you'll have a copy of my cabin key."

"It's in my front pocket." He held a stiff stance, both hands raised in a gesture of innocence. "I'm afraid to move. You know, in case you freak out again."

She flattened her tone. "You shot an arrow at my head. If you ask me, my 'freaking out' was downright low-key."

He paused before giving a small, casual shrug. "You're right. Though I didn't know you'd be here, so...."

She rolled her eyes. "Just give me the key already."

"You believe me now?" His tone mirrored her dry response.

She opened and closed her fingers, unwilling to reveal anything about her "beliefs."

"The key, please."

He pulled a bundle of keys from his front shirt pocket and ever so slowly detached one. "At least let me walk you to your door. As you now know, it's not the best idea to wander around out here alone."

Despite her outstretched hand, he wrapped his fingers around the key in quick possession.

Screw this guy and his attempt to coddle her. She was a grown-ass human being, fully capable of walking seventy yards to her cabin door. Even if it was cold. And dark. And she'd already managed to get shot at.

"I'll walk myself, thanks." She nodded to her open palm, indicating she still wanted that key. "Besides, you're out here wandering alone too. What's the difference?"

She used her glare to provoke him into pointing out that being a woman made her somehow fairer game for arrow-wielding loonies.

He did no such thing, returning her glare with the press of his chiseled jaw, a small muscle there ticking under his stubble. "For someone stranded in a field, you sure are rude." He snatched back his hand and pulled the key from her reach. "And technically, this is my key. You lost yours. Remember, Agathe?"

Her eyelids pulled wide, and she inched back a little. "You know my name?"

"Yeah." He huffed out a laugh. "And just to prove myself again, I know your name because it was next on the list of expected guests."

She balled her hands into fists at her sides, anything to keep from launching herself at him for the key whilst simultaneously eviscerating his smug grin. "So you have a knack for names but not dates?"

"Aren't you glad?" His gaze bounced around her face, eyes glinting in a way that said he found her more comical than daunting. "Otherwise, I'd still be in Melbourne, while you'd be sleeping on the cold ground tonight, rather than that cozy four-poster king bed I so graciously left in your cabin. It's much nicer than the one I'm lumped with in the main house, you know."

Her insides inexplicably fluttered at his mention of her bed, much less that he'd at any point been anywhere near it.

"Way to spin almost killing me to your favor." She grumbled, staring down at the ground because a distinct heat worked its way through her cheeks. "Now, you keep mentioning this key, but I still don't see it in my hand."

"You're right, I'm stalling"—he paused, but she still refused to look at him—"mostly because… *Sos la mesa más bella que he conocido.*"

She snapped her attention up to him and stumbled back a half-step. *Was this man fully jacked, or what?*

"Sorry, but I don't understand what you mean." She shook her head, her mind still reeling.

"Pardon me." He grinned wider. "I thought with a surname like Santos, you might speak Spanish."

"Yeah, I speak Spanish." She straightened, wiping her damp palms against the front of her oversized, sage cardigan, a laugh attempting to bully its way free. *Idiot.* "But you just called me the most beautiful table you've ever met."

The pale man's cheeks flushed red against his, what she'd decided was delightfully ivory-cream skin, his jaw unmissably slack. She bit her lower lip, unwilling to allow any signs of her amusement to encourage him.

"I meant '*mujer*', as in 'woman'. Not '*mesa*', as in 'table'." His smile grew to impossibly large proportions, where perfect white teeth stoked a stealthy, tingly sensation within her. *Looks like I don't need the extra encouragement, either.* "God, I bungled that one up. I don't know whether to feel happy or embarrassed that you understood."

Despite the corny pickup line, her devious heart fumbled, stirring a once long-dead desire to try to make someone feel better about their mistake.

She lowered her gaze and frowned, her thoughts grating over another painful reminder. *When was the last time I let a man seduce me?*

The excruciating answer was *never*. Or at least as close to never as humanly possible if six years was some measure of never.

She lifted her attention to his flawless smile and those welcoming green eyes, where his analytical gaze held an intelligent air. An intelligence not so easily defined. Meanwhile, his hard-set jaw—with tension that seemed almost habitual—gave the impression of a man difficult to fool.

She could lie to him. Show him her indifference. But he'd see through her act, wouldn't he?

Heat washed over her face and neck, her tummy clenching at the needling suspicion he *already* saw past her bluster. Even as her body, with its prickly nerves and hot flashes, made up its own mind on how she felt about this his flirtations, her *actual* mind still urging her to leave him here in this field.

Sure, his potential as a deranged murderer had faded, but a different kind of danger surfaced. His interest felt way too good, his light teasing awakening a long-dormant desire. He made her feel something—anything—and her sheer lack of apathy did *not* bode well.

So, perhaps Prince Charming here, with his shaky grip on the Spanish language, had a point. Maybe she did have more in common with an inanimate table than any red-blooded woman. At least, that's what she wanted. And in a world where not even her divorce registered as a real loss, where she'd become numb to men and their advances, maybe her life really didn't have room for anything more than shuffling through her dark and tragic memories.

Yeah, she had no room in her life for Prince Charming, especially when getting attached would mean surrendering the last thing in her life to hold any significance. The one person who'd trusted her completely. The one person she'd failed.

*Elsie.*

Still, maybe she took his flirting way too seriously. He'd complimented her, not proposed. Maybe she could start by answering the questions his interest posed. Was she ready to let a man flirt with her? Touch her? Had she atoned enough to deserve a trace of pleasure and distraction?

She drew a hard breath, her face scrunching into what she assumed was a pained grimace. If she did want to test whether the years really had corroded her down to nothing more than a mass of cells, minus any real shred of womanhood, she had yet more to consider.

The man's piercing gaze maintained an open invitation, his

unyielding stare leaving no doubt his words on her beauty went beyond empty flattery.

He wanted her.

That open wanting stirred a heat in her lower belly, alerting her to a totally illogical truth.

*She wanted him, too.*

# Chapter Two

"If it puts you at ease…." Luke held out his hand and waited for Agathe's dark-brown gaze to fuse with his. "My name's Luke."

He couldn't help but steal another look at her. Her captivating hair, a mix of deep chocolate and fine, sandy-blonde streaks, fluttered in the night breeze. Her deep-bronze skin, along with her delicate facial features, gave off a forest-nymph aura. Mysterious and birdlike. Slight and elegant…even if she did wield a strong portion of snark. Meanwhile, the air cracked around her like high-voltage lightning, her narrowed gaze dropping to his outstretched hand.

"I'd say it's nice to meet you"—she reached out all the same, her slender fingers curling around his, a fragile heat trailing from her soft skin—"but under the circumstances, I'd be lying."

Despite a natural desire to laugh at her cynical reply, his gut clenched, and sickness rocked his insides. The gloom in her eyes reminded him that he'd almost shot her. That a decade in the British military would have counted for nothing if his earlier arrow hadn't gone astray.

He pulled his hand back and rubbed his palm over the scruff of his two-day re-growth. Crossbow practice should have been safe at this ungodly hour and on his own land, but if Agathe had been hurt... *Or worse....*

Her split-second rustle of movement had made him veer his aim and saved them both. The gum tree he'd shot would recover, but she wouldn't have.

He swallowed at the thick lump in his throat and vowed he'd used his bow for the very last time. Firearms practice had gone long ago, it wasn't as though he was in the service anymore, so he could live without archery, too. "If there's anything I can do... Please, let me make amends."

Her dark stare washed over him, then lingered on his chest. The slow inspection sent a hot sting through his body, and he breathed deeply, working hard to maintain focus.

Only a fool would assume she had the same salacious thoughts invading her mind, but he was clearly one goddamn fool. Why else had he impulsively voiced his attraction to her?

Her dragging silence now shook him to the core. It brought focus to the growing gloom in her befuddled stare and highlighted something intrinsically different about Ms. Agathe Santos. Something greater than natural beauty and bronzed features. Or snark.

If nothing else, the drawn-out silence made him pray to a heaven he didn't believe in that she might share a small bit of pull toward him, too, like maybe she wanted this moment to linger a while longer.

"The key should be enough." A deliciously husky whisper poured from her lips, and she held out her hand again, gaze sweeping the surrounding bushland while her pupils pooled. "And maybe you can walk me back to my door after all."

Her attention slammed into him, detonating an imaginary explosion deep within his ears. He reached out and handed her the key, stifling an urge to wrap his hand around hers again and not let go this time. "Thanks for trusting me."

Trust. *There, he said it.* Now he had no choice but to make good on his unspoken promise not to creep her out any more than he already had.

He peered down at her scattered belongings on the ground and told the surge of blood through his body to calm the fuck down. She needed help, not some randy stranger breathing down her neck.

"Feel free to keep the spare key." He knelt and collected the fallen items from her purse.

"Are you sure?"

"Yeah." He stood and handed her purse back.

Her frown eased, and a small light entered her eyes. The cold air nipped at his cheeks, and he turned away, homing in on his task of leading her back to her cabin, anything to distract from the hormones inflicting hell on his body.

But even as he stalked ahead, he weighed the reality here. This woman had to be somewhere around her mid-twenties, with years of partying and maturing ahead of her. He, on the other hand, had just turned thirty-six and had lost all interest in short-term flings.

He needed mature.

Someone to settle down with.

He yearned for the comfort and consistency of a lifelong partner.

Not that Agathe would be interested in him, anyway. Not a younger and beautiful woman like her, one sporting a restless energy and dreams that probably went far beyond an uncomplicated life, complete with children and shared domestic bliss.

He took a few steps onto the cabin's front veranda and, for some inexplicable reason, paused in the doorway, cursing his inability to summon something witty to say.

So, he said nothing.

She peered up at him, her features set in an already familiar frown. "I'll continue the key-finding expedition tomorrow morning before I catch my train back to Melbourne."

He stuffed his hands into his jeans pockets, halting his desire to reach out and reassure her. "You're not about to get in trouble over a lost key. This is my place now, so I'll find the key soon enough or change the locks if I don't."

Her shoulders dropped. "Thank you. And I'm sorry."

Her attention held a gentler stare, eyes lacking their hardened edge and carrying a soft sheen that hinted at an unfathomable hope. So he offered a half-hearted smile, mirroring her softening but telling himself to let this woman be. "You have a nice night, Agathe."

He turned away. If he were lucky, sanity would return once he'd found his house and some sleep. Alone. In his own bed.

"Luke."

The shaky clip of her voice held him at the veranda's edge. He squeezed his eyes shut and sighed an expletive. His name from her lips made a shiver of need wash over him, and he had little choice but to spin around and give her his focus.

"I don't know how to say this. I…" She wrapped her arms around the elbows of her green cardigan, the flared sleeves pulled over her fingertips, her gaze darting about his face, and her cheeks suddenly flushed. "Please don't leave."

An invisible force hit him square in the chest, one that had him glaring at the cabin's door, pulse racing at the possibility of some unseen threat because surely this woman didn't have any other reason to want *him* to stay with her. "Is something wrong?"

The quick shake of her head had luscious waves falling about her face. "No. Actually, yes." She lifted her cheeks in a tight grimace. "I guess this is where I invite you in for coffee, even though we both know coffee isn't the real reason for the invitation."

While his feet stayed fixed to the veranda, something deep within him jolted, stealing away his next breath, his pulse thundering loud in his ear. Time stopped, though not such a bad thing since he needed a moment to replay what she'd just said.

Her suddenly pale lips hinted at him hearing right, that this cagey woman had just propositioned him for sex. *Actual sex!* Another rush of thoughts swarmed his mind and killed any chance of him making any sense of her offer.

An inner voice told him to keep his distance. Clearly, one of them wasn't thinking straight, and he couldn't decide which one. Keeping his distance would have been the sensible thing to do, but his legs worked of their own volition and walked him toward her, his mouth adopting an uncharacteristic need to talk. "I'm not sure that's what you want."

The scent of sunflowers and rain, sweet and watery, floated off her beautiful dark skin. Diverting his senses to something other than this alluring woman, he pressed his eyes shut and inhaled the smell of smoky gum trees. Only his efforts weren't enough, not when light footsteps thudded closer.

He reopened his eyes to *her* blinking back up at him, those deepbrown pupils reeling him in again. "I'm not completely sure either, but it's time, and I need to do this."

His chest muscles bunched at her mixed response. *What am I supposed to do with that?*

She lifted a hand and rested it on his shoulder. Pure, instinctual need prompted his own hand around her slender waist.

"Excuse me if I'm used to a little more enthusiasm." Despite those words and his doubts, his thumb stroked her cardigan's soft, thin wool, his touch designed to coax her closer, to possess her. A bastard move if ever there were one.

She shook her head, and her fingertips tracked a slow line down his neck. "I *do* want this."

Her lowered voice dripped with promise while her careful touch drifted over his throbbing pulse, igniting a heat that engulfed his body. And still, he had no idea what mystical turn of events had provoked this stunning creature into his arms or what he should do about it.

He frowned at the small crease between her brows. "There'll be no regrets?"

She gave a small shake of her head, her eyes glistening, less hesitant now, more a hint at vulnerability. "No regrets. I just don't know how to start."

The innocence in her statement didn't match his initial sense of her, though the confession did stir his blood. She was less an impulsive fun-seeker and more a lost soul searching for the comfort of another.

"Then let me help." He brushed his lips to hers, though even his line about help was a lie. He wanted her, pure and simple and selfish as that.

Her fingertips dug into his shoulder, and her lithe frame curved like a delicate bundle of softness against his much larger frame. He stroked his palm over the tense muscles at her lower back, those muscles easing and urging him to escalate the light graze of lips into something more profound and all-consuming.

Hungry passion took over, and the fever in her kiss rose to match his, each fine sweep of her tongue a simple miracle that turned his body impossibly hard. Though he fought the burning instinct to have her right there on the cold veranda floor, her quiet groan plucked at his restraint.

Agathe Santos was something else altogether. A gift. Maybe a reward. A sure contradiction to the stable, sensible man he sought to be. She reduced him down to pure and present pleasure, his dreams of home and family damned. The only real justification he gave for his actions now was that he'd visited hell and endured the worst humans could offer. Maybe he'd cut himself some slack this one time.

The truth was, with each passing second, he cared less about why Agathe here had fallen into his arms, only that she made his heart thud and made him feel more alive than he had in years. And God help him. He didn't want a one-night stand, but he *did* want to watch as desire filled her dusky eyes and those exquisite lips called his name.

Over and over and over again.

# Chapter Three

Agathe's heart thundered against her ribcage, a wild drumbeat that must have journeyed all the way from her chest and into the gorgeous man kissing her. She held firm to him, her fingers trembling, while the scent of citrus and leather and something raw and masculine melted her from the inside out. She had no idea why, but she needed this exchange. Now. With Luke.

His tongue swept hers, hard and commanding. No one had ever kissed her with such intensity, like she had his full attention, like he truly wanted *her*. Most frightening of all was the skin-tingling sense that when she let him into the cabin, this man would know exactly what to do to make her body sing.

His hands tangled in her hair, and he tilted her chin up, demanding better access. She gave him just that, and a guttural groan rumbled through his chest.

Luke was a force, his sharp breaths matching the fevered thrum of her heart. The hard surface of his pectoral muscles barely dented under her touch, and a new wave of urgency had her responding with a needy whimper. He didn't have the body of a polished city gym rat. His unyielding firmness was not the kind any bench press or kettlebell could produce. What she held in her arms were wide shoulders and solid planes, a grand example of uncompromising strength and hard work.

Everything about him, from his thick forearms to his possessive kiss, spoke of rugged masculinity. Someone who'd maybe led a rough life. Well, she knew a few things about life's hard knocks, so maybe, just maybe, she'd found the perfect candidate to eclipse her sorrows.

His lips gentled against hers, and he gave off the energy of a tame lion, his brawny fingers through her hair, wielding a proficient light caress. Tiny shards of pleasure effervesced from the nape of her neck down, and she shelved the need to scrutinize this guy's story in favor of tugging at the buttons of his flannel shirt.

His tongue brushed her teeth, rewarding her bravery. The subtle taste of him brought a shiver to her body and enlivened her stilted heart. *Holy flying monkeys.* Maybe this really could work. She'd have one night free from the demons in her head.

A slow moan rumbled through his chest and turned into a playful laugh, his hands dragging lower to the curve of her ass, where he lifted her off her feet and pinned her against the cottage wall.

The decisive move sent sensual heat searing through her veins, and she wrapped her thighs around his narrow hips, loving the sensation of lumpy, weathered boards digging into her back, that mild discomfort keeping her mind on the present and far from the past.

Soon, they'd soon be inside the cabin. Soon, they'd be having sex. Even though she'd always been cautious, right now, she didn't even care. As long as this smoking hot man made the last four years disappear.

She arched into him, appealing for more. Giving her what she wanted, he slid his hand under her skirt and rested his large palm on her outer thigh. Heat gathered between her legs. *Soon. She needed him soon.*

A desperate cry broke from her throat, and she plucked at the final clear plastic buttons on his shirt. The rise and fall of his honed pecs filled her vision now, and her fingers hit his abs' beautifully rippled surface, all while the catch of his breath fueled her excitement.

For one brief moment, she was more than unfortunate Agathe Santos. She was a sex goddess. Ready to give as good as she got. A woman who bucked against the bulge at the front of this man's pants, demanding more, not too shy to voice her desperation.

He wrenched his lips away, chest heaving and breathing labored. "Holy hell, Agathe."

She gave a rough groan. "You should know, most Latinas don't take well to descriptions of hell as holy."

His soft chuckle brushed her cheek, but he ground against her, his bare palms running up and down her thighs, sending sparks of desire over her skin and igniting a hot sensation between her legs. "You should know, you do a piss-poor impression of a religious person."

She laughed, then startled. *Since when did she laugh?*

"You might be right." She buried the joy, choosing not to focus on its meaning.

He pressed his forehead to hers, silent until she locked gazes with him. "Tell me again you want this."

She forced her stare not to veer. "I do. I want this."

*Though not you, exactly. Just the escape.*

The hard press of his lips found hers again, suggesting a need to hurry, and her pulse raced at how quickly things had progressed. At least the overhead porch light was off, and the low visibility would obscure her overwrought reactions if this whole "having sex" thing got too much. She wanted to believe he wouldn't notice her struggle but doubted that very much. He didn't seem the type to let anything slip by unacknowledged.

He leaned in, and his erection pressed into her again. He wasn't small and she hadn't slept with anyone in years. Her heart squeezed because sex with Luke would hurt.

Her heart didn't just clench at his size alone, the power imbalance here set her off too. The promise in his touch. The passion in his kiss, even as his hungry lips softened her further. Then there was his general confidence and ease… *He had so much more on her when she had close to zero.* It had been so long. Her spirit was so completely broken. The unfamiliar idea of relinquishing control hurt more than she could bear.

A pain-filled whimper fell from her lips, and her muscles froze.

He froze, too, and, just as quickly, pulled his lips away.

That simple cry revealed too much, all while another unintended sob broke loose.

Since she'd already well and truly fucked this whole thing up, she lashed a hand over her mouth and tried hard to keep quiet.

"Please." The weak plea squeezed through her fingers. "Don't stop."

The corners of her eyes stung, but she gripped her legs around his hips in an attempt to hold him there. His backing away would only confirm that any kind of pleasure wasn't for a woman like her. She glanced up at the heavily shadowed veranda roof and swore.

Luke lowered her to the ground and stepped back. "I have to. You're not totally into this, and now, neither am I. And please, don't cry. You've done nothing wrong."

His heavy breaths signaled his difficulty in stopping, but the fact that he did stop, the fact he reached to stroke her face in an understanding gesture, snapped some metaphorical bungee cord within her.

She jerked away from him and back to the reality of her stagnant life. For a second there, she'd glimpsed escape, but someone like her didn't deserve an escape.

"I'm not crying, and don't give me your pity." She frowned at the lax edges around his eyes, then ran her angry gaze over his exposed chest. "There's only one thing I want from you."

He merely jutted his chin toward her hand. "You're shaking."

She tucked her hand behind her back, but he still reached out and pressed something cold and metallic into her palm.

"And if I don't end this now, you'll be crying soon enough." His analytical glare held her for a beat, and a muscle over his jaw ticked. "Go inside and look after yourself before you persuade me to do something we'll both regret."

She peered down at the cabin key in her hand, a key she must have passed back to him during their exchange. By the time she lifted her gaze, his back was turned, and his heavy footfalls took him down the aged veranda steps.

Just as he disappeared into the darkness, she sank against the cabin wall, the calm landscape ahead not at all reflecting her feelings. Her thoughts were less *charming Roseford woodland* and more *desolate dystopian desert.* A place where cold-blooded snakes and violent sand-storms eroded her frazzled grasp for freedom.

*How dare she try to move on!* The only sanity-saving concession here was that she'd never have to face Luke Whatever–the–rest-of-his-name-was again. She'd return to Melbourne tomorrow, reprise her usual role as an icy and sexless workaholic, and once more, her life of stable misery would go on.

~

The next morning, Agathe dragged her small suitcase out onto the veranda, hauling the cabin door closed behind her. An empty envelope sat clutched under her armpit, and she pulled it out, dropping the key inside, fulfilling the previous owner's instructions to leave the key under a potted plant at the veranda's edge. Assumedly, Luke would be over later to pick it up, and if luck worked in her favor, she'd be far from the cabin long before then.

She knelt before the designated shiny, blue ceramic plant pot atop the bumpy wood boards, only to lift the pot and find a folded white card waiting underneath.

Her heartbeat snagged, and she paused, momentarily unwilling to touch the card. *I know who this is from.* Long seconds passed before she released a sigh and sat cross-legged on the cold boards, resigning herself to unfolding, then reading the note.

*Agathe,*

*The spare key was in the field, not far from where we met last night.*

She peered ahead to the hilly terrain and early autumn leaves. Rusty hues were bright against the chilly morning fog, the tension in her muscles a reminder of last night. As bad as things had been, at least Luke's key recovery erased one tiny portion of her guilt.

*I can't stop thinking about last night.*

She snorted out a sardonic laugh. *Yeah, because he thinks I'm outright unhinged!*

*Despite how things ended, I'd like to get to know you. So, if you feel the same, my number is at the end of this note.*

She frowned at that last line. Why would he want to know more about a clusterfuck like her? Maybe he was a masochist. Or someone incapable of knowing what was good for them. Maybe she was the one who needed to stay away. Heck, her own self-destructive tendencies were hard enough to deal with without adding another person's problems to the mix.

*Please cancel your taxi and come to the main house. I'll foot the bill if the driver's waiting by the time you get this note. I'm leaving for my home in Melbourne today, too. I'll give you a lift, and we can talk.*

*Please,*

*Luke*

She pressed her hand to her chest and tried to catch her breath. Did this attractive, seemingly stable man hope a shared road trip would provide some on-road entertainment at her expense?

*No. That wouldn't be it.*

His restraint last night hinted at a decent guy. Probably too decent for her. And he'd been right to stop at her first sign of distress. In the clarity of day, she did regret what had almost happened.

The man was smoking hot and, given his home in Melbourne and estate in Roseford, probably very loaded, too. He didn't need a walking disaster like her defacing his perfect life. Besides, she'd learned long ago that getting attached to others opened her up to a kind of heartbreak near impossible to survive.

So, she couldn't accept his offer of a ride. Wouldn't be calling him, either. No matter how intrigued she was to know his story, too.

She left his card where she'd found it and stood. Maybe he didn't seek entertainment at her expense, which meant he might just be a great guy willing to look past her freak-out last night. Maybe he possessed genuine pity or, worse, affection for her. And still, she didn't dare to dream that big.

*Leave the poor, nice man alone. I deserve to languish in my misery.*

Her nerves tingled beneath her skin, and before she could second-guess her decision, she took her first steps off the veranda. Luke had glimpsed past her carefully maintained façade. That meant he knew too much.

If she let things go further with him, he'd likely have questions, and he sure as heck didn't need to know her story. Not when even *she* didn't want to know her story.

As much as the dull pain in her chest begged otherwise, leaving was her only option.

She heaved her suitcase down the brick path leading to the cabin's low-wire front gate, ready for when her taxi arrived. One day she'd forgive herself for last night's slip-up and for messing around with poor and well-intended Luke. Soon, any recollection of their almost night together would fade. Just like most other memories did. Other memories, just not the ones involving Elsie.

# Chapter Four



*Three months later*

Agathe jolted at the high-pitched wail of her cell phone ringing. An air-raid siren probably wasn't the best choice for a ringtone, even though the awful sound did mean she never missed a call.

She scavenged through her brown leather work satchel and ignored the sea of black-clad professionals crammed onto her city-bound tram and pitching annoyed glares at her. Their dark office attire was typical Melbourne corporate wear and not all that dissimilar to her own clothes, even if her current doom-and-gloom color palette hadn't always been her style.

A little breathless from her fraught rummaging, she pressed the phone to her ear.

"Hello?"

"Are you at the client's building yet?" Sue Hatchman's clear-cut tone sliced through the receiver.

Agathe brushed non-existent fluff from the collar of her aubergine silk blouse. "I'm just about to step off the tram."

A small lie, but one her senior manager would never know about.

"Good. I'm glad I got you before you walked in." Sue's abrupt tone hinted at having other things to do, which in truth, she always did. "Just wanted to wish you luck and remind you that Tiluma Technology is a huge, new client for us. We need you to go above and beyond to encourage a long-term partnership. Do you understand? You have to shine for me, Agathe, especially since you're the one who convinced me to vouch for your ability to handle this post."

Kind of Sue to use the word *convinced* when Agathe had, in fact, begged, sucked up, and manipulated her way into getting the higher-ups at Slate and King to let her singlehandedly manage this project, all because a middle-management position had opened up, and she *wanted* that promotion.

Besides, Tiluma Technology was a moderate eighty-person setup with a few minor efficiency issues. There was no need to enlist extra help since she didn't doubt she could kick the small company up another level and claim all the glory. So, just as Sue Hatchman took a chance on an inexperienced Agathe three years ago, this gamble, too, would pay off.

"You have nothing to worry about." Agathe stared out the tram's windows, already envisioning that in mere months, her photo would grace the halls at Slate and King's head office, the new middle manager, just one rung below Sue. "Give me a few weeks. I can handle Tiluma."

Sue, the woman with enough power to demote, fire, re-purpose, and reward Agathe, let out an appeased sigh. "Good. Just don't make me look bad in front of the other seniors, okay?"

Almost every spare minute of Agathe's free time was dedicated to her job. A symptom of having little else in her life, though at least work provided something to keep her going—the one area in which she always shone and *never* failed. The one place she still mattered.

The tram halted with a ding, and its doors swung open.

Sue had nothing to worry about.

"You won't regret this. I promise." Agathe raced to shuffle out with her fellow commuters and ended the call.

She paused on the sidewalk and trekked her gaze skyward to the three-story building with the modest, red-brick façade. A building that cowered beneath the surrounding monolithic glass skyscrapers on either side, a deceptive image since Tiluma's reputation stood strong as a tech start-up to look out for.

Despite being just a few years old, the company specialized in viral joke apps and raked in a solid fifty million a year. That being said, Tiluma's upward progression had stalled lately. Hence she'd been hired to figure out why.

She sidled up to the building's glass doors, doors that didn't budge even though she shoved at the brushed metal handle.

"Hello?"

She startled at a disembodied voice, the tinny sound coming from a speaker to her left. *That's right.* Most tech firms liked to keep tight security, what with all their computers and innovative prototypes being hot property to those looking to deal in stolen hardware or profitable new ideas.

"Hi." Her voice came out wispy and flustered. "I'm, um… Agathe Santos. Your management consultant from Slate and King."

"Oh, right. Cool." Party-like screaming wafted loud in the speaker's background, and the door clicked before swinging open automatically. "Come on in."

She marched through, her black high heels padding on the slate-gray carpet. Trendy, raw-brick corridor walls surrounded her on either side while the sound of gleeful squealing grew louder, causing her to stop in her tracks. The crescendo of noise was akin to a bunch of overly excited kids engaged in a summer water fight.

She tilted her head and listened harder, nerves jangling at how odd all of this seemed. Then again, Tiluma was a company based on humor. Perhaps rowdiness was part of the deal? Perhaps this was no more than an extra vibrant office party? And really, she had her own tasks to focus on, starting with making a good first impression.

She powered on and rounded a corner through a glass-walled corridor and some large windows glowing up ahead. The lack of plaster here created a fresh and open feel, lightening her mood as she trod onward in search of someone in charge.

The rounding of another corner brought her to a hub of commotion. A man with a beautiful face and shaggy blond hair bounded toward her, his expression lit with a giant grin. She smiled at his approach, at the way his smile played up a masculine cleft at the edge of his chin.

Despite the oversized, frat-boy clothing, her breath caught on his soft, blue eyes. His handsome face, paired with his robust build, echoed the appearance of another rugged man she'd met months ago in the woods of Roseford.

She darted her gaze to a lady screaming past with whipped cream in her hair. *What the heck?*

Next came a man clutching a huge slice of chocolate cake, his animated chuckle forcing her to focus on even more details. On the mess. On the people around her. Some laughed. Some huddled in corners, far from happy. This scene was more chaotic than fun.

The screams over the intercom suddenly made sense, and her chest squeezed. This was no cheerful office party. This was an all-out food fight.

She snapped her focus to the beautiful stranger standing before her, her heart rate climbing. He held a ham and cheese sandwich poised at her shoulder level, and his lopsided grin hinted that he clocked her new understanding.

His beauty turned less enchanting, instantly menacing. He reached out and pressed the ham sandwich into her shoulder, the slow, squelch of bread and deli meat meshing in the fibers of her gray jacket.

"I stab you with a sandwich." His eyes lit anew, and his grin grew impossibly wide, though his joy only opened a hollow sensation in her tummy. "You are now infected with ham and cheese disease."

He let go and gave a theatrical laugh before the shaggy pest loped away like a goofy Labrador.

The sandwich fell to her feet, and she peered down at her food-stained outerwear, pure confusion and shock ricocheting through her body. Why would someone do this to her? To a person who they'd never met?

The slow movement of blood through her veins gave way to a hot rise of anger, her movements jerky as she dug through her work-satchel and mumbled obscenities. At least her favorite silk blouse survived the ordeal, but not even that small win would keep her from eventually hunting down the blond sandwich attacker.

She shifted away from the pandemonium and took a seat atop a row of tables against a far wall, dabbing a tissue at her gray jacket while keeping an eye out for future attacks.

Her gaze locked with a scowling man seated at her right, his white shirt smudged with what looked like red jelly, though she chose to focus less on what wasn't working and more on his carefully gelled hair and smart, black-rimmed glasses.

"Agathe Santos." Seeking to offer a sense of camaraderie, she shot a hand out and smiled.

His frown eased, and he took her hand. "Daniel Ari. Engineering manager."

Embracing the reprieve of a positive exchange, she turned toward him. "Ari? I'm going to take a wild guess and say you're Sri Lankan."

He laughed and swept a hand over his face and torso, gesturing at his pitch-black hair and his skin a shade darker than her own. "You mean the rest of me didn't give that away?" He offered a genuine grin now. "My real surname's Ariyanayagam. Ari is just easier for most folks around here to pronounce. You're our new management consultant, right?"

"I'm supposed to check in with Max Tindall." She gave a weak laugh because "checking in" clearly wasn't going all that smoothly. "But it's nice someone else here is expecting me."

Daniel's smile faded, and he turned, jutting his chin out toward the man who'd "stabbed" her with a sandwich. "That's Max Tindall. Consider yourself checked in."

Her face turned slack, and she bit back a need to blurt out the words, *"Holy shit!"* Within seconds, a distinct heaviness pressed down on her chest, making her next breaths difficult to draw.

"Max Tindall, as in Tiluma's second-in-charge, as in the chief technical officer?" She shook her head, trying to clear a rush of thoughts, and for the first time in her career, hoping she misunderstood. *"That's* Max Tindall?"

"Yep." Daniel gave a slow nod, his lips pressed together in a look of sympathy. "Though you forgot to add, 'the CEO's little brother.'"

"Holy shit." Her shoulders slumped with sudden resignation, and she skimmed her focus over the frantic scene ahead. A number of employees had now escaped.

*Why would anyone allow this level of disarray?*

Her jaw slackened, and the next words fell out. "I can only imagine what your CEO is like."

Daniel patted a hand over hers as though he sensed her fleeting resolve. "He's a decent guy, really, just in over his head with running things. Max is a law unto himself, and we're yet to figure out how to rein him in."

She reeled back just in time for a Vietnamese rice paper roll to hit the floor at her feet. Suddenly, foreseeing Tiluma being slapped with an employee harassment lawsuit didn't seem such a stretch. Someone needed to fix this. And given her job, that someone would be her.

"Max couldn't have done all this alone." She kicked a piece of shredded carrot off her shoe and gestured to the mass of exploded food around them. "Who helped him?"

"Me." Daniel gave a defeated shrug. "Apparently…"

She dipped her chin and eyeballed his clean-cut appearance, along with his rounded shoulders. Paired with the apprehensive trail of his voice, he wasn't an obvious contender for a die-hard troublemaker.

He gave a sheepish smile and jutted his chin in the direction of a petite redhead huddled in a corner with an inordinate amount of food clinging to her navy-blue blazer. "I put together a surprise birthday party for Caroline over there. Everyone was supposed to bring a plate of food, you know, to eat, not to throw. But then Max traipsed in with his funny-guy shtick, and this happened."

Daniel gestured to the chaos before him.

Hoping some lighter topic might make this guy feel better, Agathe raised a brow. "So, Caroline's your girlfriend?"

"I wish. But look at her. She won't want anything to do with me after today." He stared back a Caroline, the woman dabbing a paper napkin to her cake-saturated blazer, the action pointless with the magnitude of the mess.

"Given her attempts to save her outfit"—Agathe nudged him with her shoulder, again, offering hope—"I'm going to guess Caroline's an optimistic and persistent sort. She's not about to let a little cake ruin her chances at love."

Daniel dipped his chin and gave her a disbelieving glower. Okay, so her offer of hope failed to land on target.

"Well." Ready to make her awkward exit, she slapped her hands on the tabletop on either side of her. "It's about time I—"

A white blur whizzed past her lower periphery, making fast contact with her tummy. Her mouth dropped open at a piece of half-melted brie clinging to her jacket.

*What the…?*

She shot to standing. Her last shred of control was gone. This was war, though, against whom she didn't yet know.

The cheese unstuck and plunked to the floor, and a growl tore from her throat. Set to finding the cheese culprit and making them pay, she fixed her sights forward and scanned the crowd. Once she found her assailant, she'd go straight to the top, to whomever supposedly ran this sideshow.

Her gaze fused with a set of familiar green eyes—not the cheese thrower—that guy took one look at the overwhelming man staring at her and fled out of sight. No, these dazzling eyes belonged to someone else—someone a heck of a lot more frightening. And though hard to admit, a damn sight more attractive. Someone who made her world spiral and tilt…

A sick feeling rocked her belly, and her ribcage turned impossibly tight. Suddenly, her work at this office seemed less straightforward.

Those dazzling eyes belonged to a man she thought she'd never see again. Or, more precisely, *hoped* she'd never see. A man she'd met three months ago. In Roseford. A man she hadn't quite had the pleasure of having sex with because she'd freaked the fuck out and left him no choice but to bail on her.

And then, even as he'd expressed a desire to still know her, of course, she'd bailed on him.

Luke Whatever-the-rest-of-his-name-was….

Her shoulders sank. Her skin tingled. Those narrowed and incredulous eyes were unmistakable.

Up until now, she'd justified her quiet escape from Roseford as being for the best, but the heat in his stare made her second-guess her choice to ignore him. Sure, given her circumstances, she'd had no other option but to walk away. And still, she had regrets.

With her career being the one thing she could control—the one thing that gave her existence a sole scrap of meaning, the thing that forced her out of bed when grief offered a perfect reason to stop trying altogether—Luke's presence warned he was somehow enmeshed with her work at Tiluma.

Back at Roseford, he'd seen her weak, vulnerable, damaged—nowhere near as together as she liked to present. He'd seen her verge on breaking and knocked back a chance at no-strings sex just to spare her wellbeing. As sucky as her logic seemed, she resented his kindness and ability to unearth so many of her buried emotions.

So, he didn't just risk her professionalism now. He jeopardized her entire way of being. And what she resented most of all—more than the knowledge she *still* felt something for him—was that walking away from him this time wouldn't be so easy.

Convinced his heart might have just stopped beating, Luke rubbed a hand over his chest until a solid *thunk thunk* pulsed against his finger-tips. While his heart still worked, the reality of who stood before him sank in, forcing his heartbeat to race ever faster.

A smile wobbled the corners of his lips and lifted his confusion. Agathe Santos might have given him a miss all those months ago, but she sure as hell stood mere yards from him now—her dark eyes unblinking—a stunned deer stuck in the path of an eighteen-wheeler.

A million nagging questions ravaged his mind, mostly over why she'd stumbled at the prospect of making love with him that night, as well as why she hadn't let him drive her home the next day, but then his attention snagged on Daniel Ari beside her and Luke's thoughts hooked onto something else.

Maybe she'd never been as free to see him as he'd assumed.

His chest clenched at the memory of her silent exit, and he

narrowed a glare at Daniel placing a hand on her shoulder, the man leaning in and whispering something in her ear.

Was Daniel her reason for being in this office today? Had she come here to visit *him*?

Luke shelved his suspicion and swayed his focus to the disheveled room at large, several employees staring gape-mouthed at him....

Even that distraction didn't cool his temper, and a low growl rumbled up from the base of his throat due to the unnecessary waste of food splattered all over his walls, carpets, furniture, and staff... Did these people have no concept of poverty or hunger? The moral responsibility of having access to so much food?

He snapped his gaze to his younger brother and charged ahead, stopping only when he came close enough to press a firm hand to Max's shoulder, fingers aching to shake some sense into him once and for all. "Fix this disaster."

Max's cheeks flushed, and he had the sense to bow his head and nod. He looked like a child who'd tried to behave only to fall victim to impulse. Not an unusual thing in Max's case. "I've done it again, haven't I?"

Though the muscles at Luke's jaw eased, he couldn't go so far as to offer comfort, so he simply replied, "We'll talk later."

And they *would* talk, just not here. Despite being a poor decision-maker, Max didn't deserve public humiliation.

Max nodded again, and Luke turned away. Most employees had ceased staring and peeled back to their desks. Meanwhile, Agathe merely stood where he'd left her, her ashen frown only a little reduced from earlier.

The food smudges on her demure gray jacket made the skin over his face heat and tingle, the contents of his stomach roiling every time he thought too deeply about what had just occurred. No matter her reasons for being here, her welcome to his office shouldn't have included a hell-walk through utter disrespect and disorder. No one deserved this literal mess, least of all woman with so many jagged edges and so much open vulnerability.

He strode ahead and stifled his anger, along with an urge to fire whoever had dared launch food at her, only stopping when he came to Daniel. "Mind if I talk to Agathe alone?"

Daniel shrugged, already standing. "Sure thing."

The man strolled across the room, and Luke latched his focus on Agathe, his eyes stinging from the fiery glare she lobbed his way, even as he spoke first. "Why are you in my office?"

She jerked back, two deep grooves etched between her brows. "*Your* office?"

Her gaze flitted about his face. As if seeing him anew. As if computing a multitude of possibilities. As if weighing up a not-so-hidden compulsion to run… Only for her ensuing shrug to form a poor attempt at indifference.

"I'm a management consultant on hire here. I'm supposed to offer advice on this company's current problems, though any novice could see what those problems are." She waved a hand over her ruined outfit and scoffed. "A full-blown exorcism would do more to fix this mess than any service I could provide. Is this place always such a disaster?"

Despite her cutting assessment, as though she didn't yet know his role at Tiluma, he barely held back a laugh. "So, I should fire you and call a priest?"

Hinting that the word "fire" sparked renewed understanding of her rank, paleness once more drained her warm complexion. Still, he needed her fearless approach. Her unabashed digs and dark quirks gave him reason to believe she'd fit in well at this office.

So, unbeknownst to her, he would not let her go. Even if his unsuccessful history with this woman still warned that he would struggle to keep her from running again.

# Chapter Five

*Luke Tindall… CEO.*

Agathe blinked at the sign on the frosted-glass door and nodded slowly to herself, her mouth falling into a sudden dry and speechless gape. Of course, this little factoid about Luke fit with the usual run of shitty events to befall her life. Of course, Luke didn't just work at Tiluma. He had to be *the* CEO. And when he'd asked her to continue their conversation in his office, he'd meant literally, *his* office. Anything less than the man behind her almost-sexcapade being the owner of this entire, goddamn, multi-million-dollar company would mean her run of lifelong bad luck had ended. And heavens knew *that* couldn't happen.

With a glint in his maddeningly attractive green eyes, he peered down at her. "Are you okay?"

She held back a low growl. *Don't rub it in. Don't you dare make me feel worse for turning you down!*

She lifted her chin in a signal he should go on—that she was just fine—even though her heart thundered a wild beat. *Shit. Shit. Shit. Shit. Shit.*

He let out a heavy sigh and pushed through the glass door, leaving it open for her to trudge in behind him. The sudden quiet churned at her tummy, and she hated the way she'd already checked out his ass on the way in. A firm ass that conjured thoughts of other firm body parts. Body parts that, just months ago, she'd wanted way too close to her own.

She'd researched Tiluma. Knew the CEO was named Luke Tindall and that the first two letters of the company's name came from his surname, Tindall, and the next letters, a combination of his and Max's first letters stuck together. Ti-lu-ma. Tindall, Luke, Max. *Gosh, I'm denser than a brick.*

Then again, no internet search had turned up any photos of Tiluma's elusive CEO. *Of course not.* So, she'd never connected Luke Tindall, "CEO," with the hot but unattainable "Luke" she'd abandoned in Roseford. Ten points to this guy's parents for giving him the most generic name ever. At least with the name Agathe, no one in this country ever confused her with anyone else.

Tiluma being a tech firm and all, she'd assumed its CEO would be a stereotypical wiry nerd. But then, she knew the classic saying about assuming, and here she was, making an *ass* of herself. Doubly stupid of her to assume fortune would arbitrarily start cutting her breaks now. Fuck her life.

The enticing scent of citrus, spice, and man invaded the air marked for her current breath, and pretending not to notice, she plunked herself on a leather seat opposite his desk. Just to add to her air of indifference, she slung her bag onto the ground beside her with a loud thud.

If he hadn't noted her annoyance yet, he would see it soon. And since he hadn't given his last name in Roseford, he deserved her atti-tude now. This unexpected and undesirable encounter was just as much his fault.

His commanding stare held her as he sat on a black leather chair behind his dark wood desk. "You can't quit this job."

His decisive tone jolted her clear of her mental rant, the furrowed determination across his brow propelling her back to their almost-night together, to her pressed against that cabin wall, and his fingers curled around her thigh. There'd been panic, just like she panicked now, the icy chill through her veins solidifying an urge to defy his request and leave his office.

*He knows too much.*

He held up a hand as though he read her desire to escape. "I've seen that look before. You've got those wide, deer-in-headlights eyes again."

Her fingers clawed into the chair's armrest, not willing to question what he meant, her heart pounding at his observation. "We can't work together."

She had a professional image to maintain. A job to do. And would achieve neither in the same office as this man.

"We can't?" He paused, allowing the question to hang through a heavy silence. "If you're scared I'll abuse my power, we've already established I'm more than capable of controlling myself. Canceling an assignment on your first day won't good look to your employer."

Taking the chance to ignore what "controlling himself" had entailed the last time they'd met, she huffed out a short laugh and pointed at the various stains on her beloved jacket. "After what I just walked in on, I'm sure my 'employer' will understand."

His eyes blazed with an indecipherable heat, attention dipping to her ruined garment before he's lips did an unconvincing curl at the corners, and he gave an easy shrug. "It's just a little cake."

She narrowed her eyes and flattened her tone. "It's the ham and cheese sandwich your *brother* accosted me with, actually. That, and someone else's brie…."

Despite her yearning to leap from her chair and wrap her scrawny fingers around his thick, lumberjack neck, she opted to continue abusing her chair's armrest with her painful clawing.

He raised both hands in an overt gesture of surrender. "Again, I'm sorry. I'd say things like food fights don't happen around here often, but I'd be lying. So, clearly, we need your help."

"I'd rather not." The tension in her hands didn't abate, though she forced a casual shrug. "I'm sure my company can arrange a competent replacement."

He leaned forward in his chair, the movement a little too abrupt. "No. It has to be you. Your boss will assume you're thin-skinned. That's not who you are, is it? Agathe?"

She paused for a moment, allowing the issue at hand to roll around in her head, along with her current hate for him, only for his genuine concern now to dull the edge of her animosity.

"My manager knows me better than you do." She mumbled those hollow words, not totally believing them. "She won't think less of me if I step away."

*Lies. Lies. All lies.* Sue would be pissed. But so be it if lies would get her out of this arrangement. Even as the first throat-clenching signs of guilt seeped in, another thought struck her, a thought connected to his stubborn insistence she remain. "Did you track me down through my work?"

His shoulders trembled over a quick laugh. "Do you mean, did I hire you in the hopes of seducing you?"

While his cheeks rose with a poorly hidden smirk, her cheeks burned. Though his mocking made her want to get up and leave, the word *seduce* did other things to her entirely. Made her pulse race and brought her back to their night in Roseford. To his hands all over her body, her hands all over him.

She flicked her gaze up, attention threatening to drop to where the giant desk obscured his narrow hips and any view of his....

*Nope. Don't even think it. Not even to myself.*

Sweat gathered on her palms, and his eyes glinted, his gaze sweeping over the length of her body as though he'd read her wayward mind.

"In light of our interesting first meeting"—his Adam's apple bobbed, as though he took a second to recall the not-so-fun part about that night—"you made your feelings known when you left. So, no, there was no point looking for you. My PA hired your firm, and I had no idea who you worked for. I had no clue you'd be the consultant to show up today."

The intensity in his glare ebbed down to his hands pressed flat on his desk, as though her rejection that night still hurt, a sign he didn't totally hate seeing her now but didn't quite know what to make of her presence, either.

A tiny tremor worked its way through her muscles, and she huddled deeper into her chair, that tremor perhaps belonging to shame.

He took a swift breath and leaned back, his chair creaking a little as he did so. "Anyway, you're right. It's none of my business if you want to go." He grabbed the phone to his right and stabbed at the keypad. "Though, I can only imagine how your manager will feel about a direct call from Tiluma's CEO."

He instructed his PA to connect him to Sue, the woman Agathe had guaranteed success to not an hour ago. Meanwhile, Agathe pretended she didn't care, sticking out her foot and focusing on the limited details of her black high heels.

She'd fought so hard to get to where she was now—working on her first solo project and on a sure path to a promotion. The years of pushing through a job that provided her sole source of relief. The daily, painstaking effort to excel. So much about this moment contradicted all she'd sought to achieve.

Maybe he was right. Maybe she *was* unnecessarily throwing away her chance. This begged the question, was she really just going to sit here and let something as small as one regrettable night ruin it all?

*Fuck, no!*

She snapped her gaze to the phone still pressed to his ear. He was right about something else. She *would* look thin-skinned, and she couldn't back out now. Even if working with him would make her time at Tiluma a living hell. Even if she still questioned why he cared enough to convince her to stay.

Hadn't she endured far worse? She could endure the conflict of being around a man who made her hormones run wild while the rest of her just plain wanted to run.

"Hang up." Having not expected the hard delivery of her blurted demand, she pressed her lips together to keep from contradicting herself.

Luke frowned before the wrinkles on his forehead eased, and he very slowly lowered the phone. Meanwhile, she narrowed another glare at him, letting him know she didn't appreciate his obvious toying with her. "Why are you so insistent I stay?"

He eased back into his chair, far too comfortable with this confrontation. "I believe you're what this office needs."

She rolled her eyes and then focused on him. "I think we've established you don't know me."

"Call it a hunch, based on three decades of unique life experience." His stare hardened, strong fingertips drumming a rapid beat over the glossy surface of his desk. "My instincts tell me you're up for the challenge."

"I challenge myself plenty already." The snark in her reply held a calmness she didn't actually feel, though "fake it till you make it" had become her life motto, so what difference would another "fake" be?

And yes, she did challenge herself plenty. Every day, in fact. Every time she rolled out of bed and made good on her promise to get on with her life.

"Fine." He paused his drumming, his focus growing more intense. "One more challenge won't make much of a difference to you, will it?"

"Maybe not, but I still question your 'instincts.'" She offered a shrug, set on making him pay for his assumptions. "The way I see it, more than your beliefs on what I can contribute to this office, you're still angling to finally get into my pants."

He leveled a blank stare before his eyes glittered, stunning and annoyingly endearing, as he pressed a knuckle over his lips and over a small chuckle. "Do I have to remind you that I was the one who backed away last time? *You're* the one who wanted to continue. *You're* the one who wanted in *my* pants."

Despite the strain drawing at her chest, she ticked one corner of her lip upward, ignoring his ability to kick the legs out from under her argument. "Details. And just to be clear"—she hardened her expression and dragged her body forward in her seat—"I don't like being strong-armed into working here. My choice to stay is tentative. If I don't like Tiluma—if I don't like you—I *will* leave."

Luke's gut hollowed at the defiant jut of Agathe's jaw, even though he did his utmost to mirror her rebellion. If he had his way, this stubborn-headed woman's skepticism would shift, and soon, he'd find the space to let go of his own unaffected air.

"Don't think of my ultimatum as strong-arming." He smiled, hiding the roaring emotions churning through his stomach. She had that soul-shattered look again. A look he'd seen a thousand times before. That same pained stare many of his army buddies held, the ones who returned home whole in every way but in their minds.

That look made him regret not letting her leave Tiluma as she'd asked, though he, too, could be stubborn. And in this case, he hoped his stubbornness would be for the greater good.

"Think of this as a trial." He shrugged, certain someone as intelligent and headstrong as Agathe could be lured with a challenge. Though those rich, brown eyes deepened in color, and her forehead creased as if she needed added reason to ease her doubt. "Stick around for a week. Observe my staff. Interview anyone you like. Figure out where our troubles lie, and if by Friday you don't think you can help, I'll send you back to Sue with a glowing appraisal."

Her jaw stiffened some more, and she crossed her arms over her chest. "So, five business days, that's it?"

He nodded, trying desperately not to stare at her honey-tinged lips, lips he'd had the honor of kissing and would trade his entire company just to do so again… Only, for keeps this time.

She dipped her chin and lifted a single shoulder in an easy shrug. "Sure. Fine. I can do that."

A massive weight rose from his chest, and his lungs filled with life-giving air. Five days to figure this woman out, a dream compared to his three months of having absolutely nothing but silence.

He hadn't lied about not looking into her life. But by God, he'd wanted to. There'd been something about her that night. An electricity. A glow that only shone brighter because of her surrounding darkness. He couldn't quite explain why he felt that way about her, only that Agathe drew at him, and he wanted to know why.

So, five days….

Five days to find some answers.

Five days more than he thought he'd ever get with her again.

"And if you still choose to leave, there won't be any hard feelings." He swallowed against the bunched muscles in his throat and worked to keep his neutral air through the bald-faced lie. "You won't work all that closely with me, and you can set your time here for as long as you think necessary." The occasional flit of her gaze over his face hinted at her need to figure him out, too, a need that raked a sharp prickle over his skin and added an unshakeable rasp to his voice. "I don't know how much more accommodating I can be."

She straightened, stare darkening anew, a sign her general caginess had a lot to do with whatever torment went through her head, though his words succeeded in convincing her the power balance here shifted a little in her favor. "I appreciate your efforts to keep me."

He nodded and took an extra moment to observe her, three months of curiosity briefly satisfied. "A week, then."

"And we keep things strictly professional." Her attention bore into him. A dare for him to defy her.

Then again, he wanted to take her professionalism, scrunch it up, and throw it in the trash, just so he could set the whole damn thing on fire and be certain her reasons for distance couldn't return. She had a right to be wary.

"I can keep my distance." The words fell from him, more a self-reminder to play this her way, at least for a while.

Agathe Santos would be his happy distraction amidst the toil and drudgery of work. He wouldn't overstep. He'd settle for adoring her from afar.

She pushed herself out of her chair, standing in still silence for a long time, her returned stare giving the impression she utilized some hidden ability to rifle through his thoughts.

Heat stirred at the base of his stomach, spreading low and lighting the knowledge that he liked being the center of her focus. Even if she did only care to look at him long enough to second-guess his motivations.

"You didn't have your PA on the line just then, did you?" Her jaw took on a hard set, as did her eyes.

His world stilled for a fearful beat before his chest heaved, and he buried the irrational storm of laughter fighting to break free. "I needed to force an answer from you."

Her fingers curled into soft fists at her sides, and her lips formed a thin line, only for one corner to tick upward in an audible click. "Nice one. I should have figured it out earlier." She closed her eyes and shook her head, more to herself than to him, as though she saw the humor in his ploy. "Anyway, I'd better go."

She twisted toward the door, and her sudden looming exit lit a burning need in him—more precisely—an urgent desire to settle the details in something that had niggled at him since their first meeting.

"Agathe?"

His voice had her lashing her focus back to him while he fought an urge to get up and meet her where she stood.

"That night outside your cabin. When we almost...." Her gaze veered away, and he paused, sensing his next words would damage their established truce.

*Infatuation and curiosity. When it comes to her, they get the best of me.*

But if he held back now, if she decided to leave by week's end, he might not get another chance alone with her. "You said it was time. What did you mean by that?"

Her skin paled, and a resolute silence took over. A silence that suggested she might run from Tiluma, after all.

"You said you wouldn't pry." Her husky tone confirmed his fear about her second thoughts, and her gaze didn't budge from his, her wounded frown berating him for trying to learn more.

Seeking to buoy her already dented opinion of him, he kept his tone sure. "I'm sorry."

*Time to divert the topic. Time to return to what brought her here, to begin with.*

So, he straightened and schooled his expression into something that hopefully looked a whole lot less invested. "My PA is next door to the left, and her name's Emily. She can give you a scan card to enter the office as you wish, and she's also your best starting point for any questions about the company."

Agathe's eyes held a stony edge, but her shoulders rounded, and she eventually nodded. "Okay. Thank you."

Her slow turn from him spoke of the energy this whole exchange drew from her. Even the door's light click in the wake of her exit reverberated a slew of sentiments he couldn't quite untangle.

He'd gotten her to agree to stick around, but her reluctance and refusal to address their past left him with nothing more than a hollow victory—all while he'd bet his entire wealth that a mutual spark still glowed somewhere beneath her evasion.

He'd never been a weak-willed man, but she'd been compelling enough in Roseford to have him stray from his dreams of a long-term relationship. All for a fleeting night in her arms. And yet there'd been more to his motives that night than sheer and impulsive lust.

Agathe Santos had felt a connection, too. Long enough to step away from her doubts in an attempt to hook into him. Though she'd been the one to start things, he could be the strong one here and not stop until he had a chance to explore the irrefutable chemistry between them.

# Chapter Six

A familiar five-beat tap sounded at Luke's office door, and he glanced up from the financial report laid out on his desk, his hands balled into fists on either side of the paper stack, the distinctive knock belonging to his brother.

"Come in."

The door swung open and narrowly missed a collision with the wall behind. Soon, Max moseyed in with his habitual loping gait and a wide grin. "Hello, brother."

That bright tone stoked the fireball already raging in Luke's chest. "What do you want?"

Max slapped a hand over the base of his throat and put on a grand performance of being offended. "What makes you think I want anything?"

"Because I know you, and you're standing in my office." Luke straightened, his posture stiff and a couple of inches taller than before his brother's entrance. "You don't come in here unless you want something."

Max offered a shrug, then plunked down in the same chair Agathe had sat in three days prior. "Fair call. Why are you looking so serious, anyway?"

Luke held up a sheet from the pile in front of him, then counted the seconds before Max's disinterest in anything company-related kicked in. "Financial run-down. We're still at a profit, but our gains have slowed."

Max cringed, though not convincingly, leaving Luke to rue the fact he never got to be the carefree sibling. "Here's hoping the newbie consultant can sort out our circus, huh?"

Luke took a deep breath but held off on the exhale. Agathe's presence at Tiluma was too new to have made a dent in the company's problems, much less offer any clues on what to make of her. "She's not a newbie, and I hope you've apologized for the way you treated her the other day."

Max cringed again, this time for real. "Sheesh. Yeah, I did. I still feel terrible about that."

"You *should* feel terrible. You threw food at her and who knows how many others on our staff." He glared, a familiar reaction to his brother lately, somehow doubting Max ever regretted anything he did. "Now, why are you here?"

"There's not much happening today, and I was hoping I could take the afternoon off to work on my shoulder."

Luke peered down at his papers, wishing his lack of attention might drive his brother away or at least provide the ability to turn Max down. "You took an entire morning off three days ago."

"But my injury's been playing up something awful lately, and I need to go to the beach." Max rustled in his chair.

Luke lifted his gaze to Max rubbing his shoulder, his drawn and pleading look plucking at what he knew to be Luke's deeply embedded guilt. "The answer is no. And who swims in the ocean in late autumn, anyway?"

"You know the weather's never stopped me before." Max paused his rubbing. "Melbourne's cold snaps are tame compared to York's."

*True.* Melbourne winters were a million times more bearable than York. The summers were warmer, too. Still, Luke grumbled an obscenity and returned his focus to the report. "Join a gym and go after work like a normal person. I need all hands on deck. The Ernest Schneider meeting will be on us soon."

"Come on, man." Max groaned and flopped back onto his chair with a heavy thud. "This office is killing me, and Daniel can cover while I'm gone. You know I'm not much help with the whole Schneider thing, anyway."

The heat in Luke's chest exploded, and he slammed his flat palms to his desk, shooting his brother a volcanic scowl. Ernest Schneider was Tiluma's first big break in years. Tiluma needed some serious investment dollars, and it also needed to expand to doing more than just joke apps. More than anything, the company still wasn't stable enough for Luke to step back—something he'd wanted to do for the longest time.

That's where Ernest Schneider came in.

He had money and a far-reaching reputation. If Luke ever hoped to stand a chance at enjoying his life again, then Max's constant ball-and-chain act needed to stop.

Attempting to come across as more reasonable and less irate, Luke softened his expression and tone. "Max, you're already skating on thin ice. Your constant dipping out of the office doesn't motivate the people who have to work under you."

With company growth came increased pressure. He would have to deal with Max in a more serious way since brotherly love and responsibility could only keep tripping Luke up for so long. As CEO, he'd need to put his foot down, and soon.

But then, despite all good intentions, he'd been the very reason for his little brother's failure—the one to erase his chance at greatness—to bring an end to the one thing to bring Max the most joy. And his brother had shed literal blood.

If not for guilt, if not for brotherly ties, then Tiluma would be spared Max's ham-fisted tendencies. Yet another thing for Luke to feel guilty about.

He wanted Tiluma's enduring success. Wanted happy staff who loved working at his quirky tech firm. Only now, what he wanted came into direct conflict with what he feared. Failing his family.

In his world, a work-life balance did not exist. That "balance" poised on the tip of an earthquake-affected mountain, so ready to fall. As much as he wanted success, success would likely only come at the expense of abandoning Max. Of depriving his younger brother of any purpose he might have found within the very business he'd inspired. Tiluma.

Max's jaw remained slack in the wake of Luke's refusal to let him ditch his work.

"Please, Luke, have mercy, just for today." He clasped both palms together in a hammed-up plea. "I'll give you perfect attendance for the next two weeks. Promise."

Luke crossed his arms and leaned in. "Perfect attendance for three months. Nothing less."

Max's eyes flared, the request near impossible for the likes of this younger Tindall.

"Ah. Okay." More silence before he gave a resolute nod. "Sure. I can do that."

Luke wasn't naive enough to believe the promise. He'd be amazed if Max lasted a week, but at least this provided a hold-over on his brother while he tried to formulate a better plan for Max's life. "Square things with Daniel before you leave."

Max clapped his hands and rubbed them together while hissing out an excited, "Yesssss."

Next, he leaped from his chair and marched for the door, only to stop just before opening it. "Oh, and I almost forgot. There's a lunchtime meeting. Daniel's unlikely to cut it, so I'll need you to cover."

Luke raised a brow, a gesture designed to tell Max he'd pressed his luck enough already.

"Come on, man. It's a cruisy lunch meeting, and you'll have an excuse to put away the papers and eat something for a change. Besides, I get the feeling that Agathe bird wanted to talk to someone more senior than Daniel. You'd be an upgrade on either of us."

Adrenaline zinged through Luke's body, and his pulse sped at the mere mention of Agathe's name, forcing him to clamp his teeth together just to keep from agreeing too fast.

He had a chance to speak with her again. A sit-down lunch, of all things. In other words, as near to a miracle as he'd ever encountered.

Sure, she wouldn't be thrilled to see him, but he sure as hell wanted to see her.

"Fine. Go." He returned his attention to his paperwork and pretended to be somewhere between bored and bothered, not for a second trusting Max with the slightest clue about his feelings for Agathe. "I'll take the meeting."

~

"You've ruined my fucking life."

Agathe jolted at Jenny's harsh words, the woman slamming the cell phone she'd been speaking into on Tiluma's long breakroom table.

The clear glass teapot in Agathe's grasp shook right along with her hand and white chrysanthemum buds sloshed about inside. Jenny let out a holler and doubled over onto a seat, her head coming to rest in the crooks of her folded arms.

A torrent of muffled sobs broke from under Jenny's crumpled form, and Agathe locked her knees, peering around the empty room in numb refusal to move from her spot. Even if she had interviewed this woman just days ago and thought her nice enough, Agathe had long ago lost her ability to console others.

Many years ago, rushing over to comfort Jenny would have been just Agathe's thing, but not anymore. These days, tears were banned—from herself, from anyone—much less a web developer she'd met only once before. Sure as glue stuck to paper, her acceptance of tears died with her desire to show any interest in other people's dramas.

Hoping someone, anyone, would come to deal with the emotional woman, she placed her teapot on the nearby counter and held strong to her decision to never again hug anyone's pain away. Many had tried on her, and none of that worked. She sure as heck was not going to fake a talent for suturing emotional wounds. Especially not with useless platitudes.

Daniel powered in, his constricted gaze already passing judgment on Agathe's numb inaction.

"Jenny?" He pressed a hand to the sobbing woman's shoulder. "Jenny, are you okay?"

Jenny lunged and dragged him into a forced embrace, her sobs heavier against his bowed neck, the rest of his tall, lanky frame curved forward like a severely bent palm tree.

*Yeah, no thanks.*

Agathe would take Daniel's judgmental stares over folding herself in two for a hug she didn't even want, much less soothe Jenny's mumbling about a boyfriend, five years, and him ditching her "to expand his horizons."

The crying grew louder, and all Agathe could do was take a relieved breath and focus on her upcoming meeting with Max Tindall. A cold response? *Okay, sure.* But Agathe would swap her grief with Jenny's any day. Grief over a fickle dude who'd done Jenny a favor when he'd *noped* his excuse-making ass out of her life. Far greater sorrows existed beyond a failed relationship. Jenny had dodged a bullet.

Meanwhile, Agathe had bigger problems to wrangle. Having spent three days interviewing employees about Tiluma's issues, most problems pointed to Max, and now she was minutes away from stepping into a potentially heated meeting with the man.

She blinked away her concerns and focused on Daniel patting Jenny's shoulder. "You've been working hard lately. Why don't you take the afternoon off?"

Jenny gave a quick nod.

Just as predicted. *Crisis averted.*

Daniel's soft and even-keeled approach offered more comfort than Agathe could have invoked, making her feel even better about her earlier lack of intervention.

She collected her teapot and two glass teacups and readied to leave the room. All going well, her fancy meeting would soften the blow she meant to deal Max. They'd share a lovely chat in the small meeting room down the hall, sip chrysanthemum tea, fill up on the mini Chinese banquet she'd arranged, and then maybe if luck worked in her favor, he wouldn't lose his cool when she hit him with the truth of his lackluster work at Tiluma.

The guy seemed fun-loving and nice enough, but many nice guys turned explosive when faced with the evidence of their professional incompetence. So, she'd be clear, quick, and encouraging. Avoid angering Tiluma's CTO and, therefore, his brother, Luke.

"Oh, Jen." Agathe startled at Max's bright lilt, the man himself striding across the open-plan breakroom. Aiming to be invisible, she backed against the counter, though Max thankfully focused on Daniel and made a soft tutting sound with his tongue against his teeth. "Daniel, no. One afternoon won't do. She looks wrecked enough to need two weeks off, at least." He pouted and sat next to Jenny, lashing an arm around her shoulder and then rubbing vigorously. "We'll call it compassionate leave, okay, Love? I know how much you liked that guy."

Daniel's jaw swung open. "I know Jen's upset, but we need—"

"Look at her." Max pointed at Jenny.

Jenny blinked at Daniel, her eyes red and watery, while she sniffed.

Daniel stood silent and shook his head out of seeming disbelief.

The blatant disregard for his advice gave the room a heavy air, though the whole exchange offered great insight into how things worked—or didn't work—in this office. Agathe shuffled in her spot and considered stealthily side-stepping the hell out of this damn-awkward exchange.

Quiet seconds passed, and Daniel's attention switched from Jenny to Max, his stare pinched and flinty. "We don't have time or staff to spare. We need Jen's skills to be ready for Ernest Schneider's visit in two weeks."

Max tutted again. The sound was extra annoying this second time around.

"Daniel, dude, have a heart." He turned to Jenny and tilted his head toward the exit. "Away with you, young lady. Come back when you're feeling better."

In her rush to escape, Jenny scraped her chair against the timber floor, quick to scurry out of the room with Max in her wake.

Agathe drew close to Daniel and lowered her mini collection of teaware to the table beside him. Truth be told, she enjoyed the sense of independence that came with working solo at Tiluma. As much as she avoided awkward emotional displays, the staff were friendly and fun, and the company's problems were an engaging challenge. She especially loved having sole reign over how those problems were corrected.

Not even Luke's weighty presence dissuaded her. Sure, there were moments when his proximity got all too distracting, chiefly, the odd occasion his cagey stare met hers and breathing became difficult. But he made good on his promise to maintain a healthy distance, and all in all, she loved how this dream opportunity unfolded.

Daniel held a flat stare, one that seemed to question her lingering presence. "I don't want any tea if that's what you're here for."

She shrugged, offering what she hoped was a sympathetic smile. "The tea's not for you. It's for Max."

"Why does Max deserve tea?" Daniel straightened, a frown dragging at his expression. "Has he wheedled you into acting as his PA now?"

She imagined Max probably did clown his way into getting people to do his bidding, but not her. "Don't look so devastated. I have a meeting with him in five minutes."

She settled down on the seat beside Daniel, vowing to spend no more than two of those five minutes here. "I'm about to tell Max what everyone in this office is too scared to say."

Daniel tilted his head to one side. "You are, are you?"

She nodded, a light thrill working up her spine. She was getting things done, just as she'd been hired to do, and maybe her upcoming discomfort would do some good.

Daniel gave a tight laugh and pointed to the exit. "No, you're not. There's no way you have a meeting with Max. He's just left for the day. And before you ask, yes, it is common for him to waltz out of here and forget he has something to do."

"What?" A tight pressure compressed around her chest, and she glanced in the direction of where Max's exit. "He's *gone*?"

Daniel gave an apologetic shrug. "Yep. Took the afternoon off and, as usual, left me to run the show. Alone."

She tapped her palm to her forehead, a move designed to keep her from losing her calm. "Why on Earth does Luke allow him to skip out like that?"

"Family ties, maybe? We've all, at some point, fallen victim to

Max's snap decisions or his failure to pass on a message or complete a task. And if you do talk to Luke about Max, don't expect him to listen. Others have tried. Nothing ever comes of it."

She gave a small growl under her breath and waited for her cool to return. "Never mind speaking to Luke. At this point, I'd settle for just being able to talk to Max about Max."

She stared down at her decorative teapot, deflated that her efforts would go to waste and that her rare moment of enthusiasm had met the same fate. Her attention shifted to the man beside her. With no hurry to return to the meeting room, she'd at least use this chance to gain more insight into Tiluma. "Who's Ernest Schneider? Why's the upcoming meeting with him such a big deal?"

Daniel huffed out a resigned breath as if he'd already given up hope on that endeavor, regardless of what it meant for this company.

"Ernest Schneider is a superstar tech investor. Other investors flock to wherever he sinks his money. But..." Daniel drew out a pause, perhaps pondering how to convey his next words. "The man's eccentric and resides in some remote castle in Germany. He's freakishly hard to get an audience with, and he *hates* traveling. So, you see why his looking into Tiluma is an outright miracle. We won't be the only Australian company he scopes out while here, either, and still, his interest alone is a huge win for our future projects."

She took a second to mull over what she'd heard versus what she'd learned about how this company ran. "And let me guess, there are only two ways this could go?"

"Yep." Daniel tapped at his temple, a sign he figured they shared the same concerns. "Either he'll invest, and others will rush to follow, or he'll opt out, and word will spread that he turned us down. Confidence in Tiluma's value will slide, as will our chances of finding future investors."

She ran a finger over the teapot's warm glass lid, her thoughts stuck on how she and Daniel were bind buddies. Both had a short deadline to get Tiluma into shape, and both had little real control over curtailing the impending car crash this company hurtled toward.

She narrowed her gaze, the skin over her face taut from frustration. "All because the two people in charge refuse to get their act together."

Daniel laughed. "If you value your job, you won't put it exactly like that to either of them."

Though her heart thudded wildly, she grinned and rose to her feet, determined to throw all she had into doing her job, into saving this company. "I better go pack up the meeting room. While I'm at it, I'll think of ways we can meet this Schneider deadline."

"Good luck." Daniel gave a light-hearted scoff, one that said, *You'll need it,* but she reached for her teapot and marched for the meeting room all the same.

She'd have her portion of lunch and mull over the Schneider issue while she ate, maybe box up Max's abandoned helping and offer it to the other employees to take home. A kind gesture to prove to herself not all was lost.

If she found a way to make Tiluma appealing to a seasoned investor like Ernest Schneider, the partners at Slate and King would have no choice but to reward her talent. She'd have her promotion and be the next rising star amongst her peers.

After all, Max could dodge her for only so long. She *would* catch up with him. And when she did, she'd make sure he saw just how much his thoughtless actions and inactions affected those around him. After that, she'd whip him into shape. If frank words and retraining weren't enough, she'd have harsh words for Luke, letting him know this dysfunctional duo would ruin this company and the people who relied on its existence.

Of course, she'd omit the bit where she also wouldn't let him ruin her chance at getting ahead.

The closed meeting room door stood before her, and she pressed an elbow down on the handle, the metal lever giving way so that the door swung open. Just as quickly, her gaze hooked on the tall, pale, and infuriatingly handsome man waiting for her. His instantly grave presence suggested that, in more than work, he would always find a way to unravel her best-laid plans.

# Chapter Seven

Agathe's hand went limp—the one holding the teapot—and tea spilled free from the spout and lid all the way down to the hem of her slate-gray pencil skirt. All too soon, hot water stung her knee and hit the floor with a humiliating *plop*.

"I… Err…" She kicked a splatter of tea from the rounded tip of her black high heel and pretended her heart didn't do a sickening dance beneath her ribcage, ignoring the prickle of her mildly scalded skin. Luke's green eyes stared right back at her, his broad set taking up far too much space in this tiny meeting room. "Sorry about the carpet."

He lunged forward, which only made her jolt back in response, spilling more tea.

"Please don't burn yourself." He shot out a hand and grasped the teapot's handle, fingers encasing hers, causing a hot ball of need to explode in her tummy. *As if she wasn't burning enough.*

She loosened her fingers and let him ease the teapot out of her shaky grip.

"You've put in a lot of effort for a meeting with my brother." He set the teapot down on the meeting room table and turned back to her, his jaw firm under a frown.

She stared at the lunch she'd carted over from the Chinese restaurant two doors down, arranged with painstaking care about the table. He was right. She *had* invested a lot of effort into this meeting, and now that he stood here, not his brother, this setting did feel far too intimate.

"Max is the second most powerful man here." She flicked a strand of hair from her face and forced her focus back to Luke, her act of indifference hiding the dull ache filling her chest. "I figured he wouldn't like what I have to say, so—"

"So, you thought feeding him would help?" The outer corners of his lips trembled, like he wanted to laugh, only to bring the small muscles under control and pitch forth a renewed look of questioning.

Was he mocking her? Maybe just amused? Maybe she'd genuinely impressed him with her efforts. Still, she tightened her jaw and crossed her arms, deciding she'd rather appear pissed than stupid.

He stepped closer. Close enough to resurrect the memory of her pressed between him and a cabin wall. One half-step forward now, and their bodies would make contact once more.

"I… uh…" The skin over her neck warmed, and she prayed a blush wouldn't expose her true feelings for this man, the thrilling shudder zipping down her spine something she'd never experienced before. She needed to divert her thoughts before any more impulses took over, and she became the one leaning into him. "I only just learned Max canceled. I came here to pack all this away."

A sharp citrusy scent hugged her in a tide of delicious memories, that scent delivered with the light musk of Luke's own skin. She wanted more. More *him*. But had her reasons for keeping space between them. So, she cleared her throat with a futile hope the action would have a similar effect on clearing her mind.

The banquet across the table now seemed like evidence of her pitiful need to impress, and she tried not to look there, which meant keeping her attention mostly on Luke and his astute stare. As always, he seemed to know too much. And what he'd probably gleaned was her work meant more to her than it should, which in turn revealed something about what she lacked in her life.

Though he kept a quiet presence, his gaze swept her face, his large frame looming—most definitely trying to see into her thoughts while leaving her to fear that he might actually succeed. "Max was somewhat prepared this time. He sent me here to fill in."

The tenderness in his tone, that he didn't tease her efforts, even the sense that he seemed to acknowledge her reticence… warmth bloomed and spread through her torso, warmth encasing her heart, more a cage than the comforting blanket any other woman might have experienced.

Caution compelling her to the safety of her professional armor, she drew a sharp breath and turned for the nearest seat.

*Have this meeting with Luke, then get on with my day.*

She stopped in her tracks, then snapped her gaze back to the man. *What was she doing?*

"No." She frowned at him, expressing her annoyance. At him. At herself. Even as she'd walked away from him, she'd played out an unconscious impulse to follow his every command. "I set up this meeting with an express need to speak to Max. Not you."

His brow ticked upward, and he dipped his chin, a skeptical man. "Did you tell him that, or did you plan on simply launching into an appraisal of his work? He seemed under the impression this would be more of a general meeting."

Strain drew at her cheekbones, and she narrowed her eyes, holding back an irrational desire to hiss at him. "Or maybe he knew exactly what I wanted to say and bailed?"

He peered down and nodded to himself. "That could also be true. He did seem desperate to leave."

His attention met her again, his eyes giving off warmth, the rest of him skirting the table until his hands rested on the back of the chair opposite her. "Please, just sit. I still want to hear what you've learned so far."

A ringing silence stretched between them, a silence that held her suspended between wanting to leave and wanting to stay. Though she mirrored his stance and clutched the back of her chair, no doubt looking far less in control than him. "I thought you planned on keeping your distance?"

"Seems fate—and Max—had a different plan." He rounded his

chair and sat, his hands pressed to the table. "Agathe, I'm clear on the other side of this table and have every intention of keeping my hands to myself. We're both here now. I might as well hear what you have to say."

His smooth expression hinted at a ploy, his confident gaze raising her temperature. He'd mentioned controlling his hands, not that he lacked the desire to use them, and that knowledge alone added to the heat in her cheeks.

Still, he *was* the CEO. Her temporary boss. He owned this company and had every right to her early findings. His positive feedback would also be instrumental to her bid for a promotion.

She let out a sigh and practically threw herself into her chair, the hydraulics hissing under her forceful approach. "Fine. Let's do this."

The soft smile lines around his eyes eased as though he'd hoped for more enthusiasm. "Great. We'll develop some professional chemistry. Nothing more."

And there he went again. *Chemistry.* Was he stoking her imagination on purpose? Lobbing a reminder of their brief magnetism when in each other's arms? Or maybe *she* was the problem, the one who couldn't control the rapid-fire beat of her heart or her pathetic tendency to turn everything he said into an innuendo.

"Let's get one thing straight." She leaned forward and stabbed a finger in his direction. Innuendo and raging attraction aside, she took her job seriously and would treat this man with the same direct honesty she did any other client. "You asked for an outside opinion, and I have one that comes with the unedited truth. I don't have the same risks your employees do. I don't need to tiptoe around you. So, I hope you're ready for what I have to say about how this company operates."

Luke bit back a sigh of enthusiasm, his focus glued to Agathe's fiery dark stare, while his inner emotions bounced somewhere between turned on, impressed, and a touch defensive.

"I'd appreciate your honesty." Needing a break from her intensity, he reached out and divided the two teacups between them. The pretty glass set a contrast to her prickliness.

Meanwhile, the carefully arranged display of spring rolls, barbecue pork, and king prawns across the table offered more proof yet of how much she'd invested in this meeting.

"I know you're no fool, Mr. Tindall." She slumped back, her gaze fixed on his hand pouring her tea. The deflated look suggested disappointment at his lack of retaliation. "You probably know what I'm about to say."

His name from her mouth sent tingles through his body, and he forced his focus on her downturned gaze and lack of eye contact. If she felt anything for him, she hid it well.

She leaned over and pulled out a clipboard, ignoring the empty plate he'd set before her and choosing work before food. Not that he minded. Her busyness allowed an opportunity to take in her tousled hair and flurry of sandy-blonde streaks—where thick waves broke free of her messy bun, framing her face's fine bone structure. The entire time, his hand ached to reach out and touch her.

Her gaze flicked up to him, and he fought the urge to look away. Though her rich, dark-chocolate glare struck at full force, he reciprocated with a message that he didn't mind her catching his admiration.

His heart racing faster than a hollow-point bullet, he continued his act of being unaffected, breaking the stalemate with the pretense of loading his plate with food and returning to her statement about him not being a fool. "What gave me away?"

Her lower lip jutted, and thick, black lashes pressed closer together in a squinted scowl. Sure enough, she detested his toying. "Do you want to hear what I have to say or not?"

"Sorry." He swatted a hand, the casual gesture a promise he'd try to remain on track, even if the blood currently rushing to his lower regions brought him pain. "I've got a lot on my mind."

Like, he wanted to take those pouted lips of hers and kiss her until she softened to his will, he sure as taxes would do the same for her. Then again, did Agathe even do soft?

*Oh yes. Yes, she did.*

He'd experience that softness. Her gentle moans. Her body melded into his. The effects of which haunted him with months of need to finish what they'd started....

Then again, thinking about ravaging her was a hell of a lot nicer than addressing what she had to say next because he sure knew what Ms. Santos had to say. He just didn't want to hear it.

"Your brother is detrimental to this company."

*Bingo.*

Just as he'd thought.

He slumped back and huffed out a heavy breath, the impact of her verbal sledgehammer reverberating through his mind. "You got right to the point, didn't you?"

She sent him a glower. "Max is a huge liability. I'd be neglecting my role here if I wasn't honest about the fact that he's unwittingly dismantling Tiluma's success from the inside out."

A weighty silence filled the room. She wanted a reply, but all he could do was peer down at the Singapore noodles on his plate. Neither of them had touched any food, and each for different but justifiable reasons.

She cleared her throat, and even though he couldn't see her, he sensed her satisfaction at overcoming her first hurdle. "My initial observations are that Max is underperforming. He also holds an unwarranted high-rank position in this company. His severe lack of management skills, and experience, undermines your more talented staff, and that alone has created discord across multiple teams."

Despite the loud pounding sound in his ears, he lifted his head and shot her a deadpan expression. "That's a long list of displeasure. No wonder Max gave you the slip."

She rolled her eyes and went about forking a minuscule serving of noodles onto her plate, providing him extra seconds to stew.

"Your team spent months working on the Myers Rigged app. A simple undertaking that still hasn't launched." All too settled in her slow dissection of his efforts at running this company, she peered at the food on her plate, depriving him of her attention. "I get a huge sense of animosity over how long this project is taking."

A weak sensation spread through his chest, but he found the energy to grumble a reply. "I'm aware of the lapsed deadline."

The Myers Rigged app was Tiluma's new big project, a play on the hugely popular Myers Briggs personality test. The app spat out hilarious but slightly insulting results. Instead of a user being grouped as an *Introverted, Sensing, Thinking, Perceiving* type, the app would label them an *Antisocial, Unfeeling, Over-analytical, Robot.* There was even a cute, angry robot graphic to go with the results.

"Yet, by all reports, Max continues to come up with tangent ideas and add-on features." Agathe's rebuttal, along with her matter-of-fact tone, chipped again at his waning appetite. "The app isn't progressing, and the delay has Tiluma bleeding money."

His teeth clenched in protest to the truth, the dull pain in his jaw spreading to his head, buzzing with all the clichés. Honesty was a bitter pill to swallow. The truth *did* bloody hurt. In this case, it was also mortifying. "I know all that, too."

The flailing app. His employees' suffering. This astute woman relayed all of Tiluma's issues. All this while he couldn't defend his actions due to an obligation to keep his reasons for saving Max private.

Sickening nausea churned his stomach. It filled him with a growing sense of dread and sorrow. When Tiluma had issues, *he* had issues; and he looked weak and indecisive when he was anything but.

*Except for where my brother is concerned.*

"Look at me." Her gentle yet firm tone stole at his brooding, and he obeyed. The depth in her eyes and the softer edges to her expression somehow made him feel like an even bigger asshole. "Luke, the app is just one example. That food fight a few days ago angered a lot of people. From what I've heard, antics like that aren't uncommon in this office."

A forceful pressure squeezed at his throat, and his fingers pressed into the table. She'd taken a risk in confronting him, and she'd been professional and compassionate about it. As much as he hated this conversation, he couldn't begrudge her or her approach, so he rewarded her risk with an honest reply. "No, they're not, but I can't simply fire or demote Max, either."

Her shoulders eased a little like her sympathy for him deepened even more. "Because he's your brother?"

Yes, but she didn't know the whole story.

Max was the one who deserved her compassion the most.

If not for Luke, Max's life would have taken a different path, and his aimlessness now would not exist. So, Luke *owed* his brother protection, or at the very least, time to find his way.

Other people relied on Luke to safeguard Max, too—their sister Sophie. The two were closer in age, and her relationship with Max was also closer. A natural at caring, she needed to focus on completing her final year at university, *not* worrying about how her oafish brother got along.

And then their mother relied on Luke, as well. After a lifetime of work and raising children, then the grief of losing their dad three years ago, she deserved to relish her senior years, deserved time to be with her friends back in Scarborough. So, though no real agreement existed, Luke held an unspoken responsibility to keep the family peace so she wouldn't have to.

Agathe's hand paused across the table as if she fell just shy of reaching for him. He wished she would. Wished he could. But he settled on clawing his fingers into the table to keep from bridging the distance for her.

He'd promised to keep his hands to himself, hadn't he?

"Tiluma's foundation is built on fun." The new huskiness to her voice somehow added a sultry edge to a talk about work. "I get that Max might think his sense of humor falls in step with keeping an entertaining workplace, but some of your employees are downright miserable. Their willingness to stay hangs by a thread." She grimaced, returning her hand to her side. Her stare soon fused down to the table as if to second-guess her words and actions. "Most people here just want to do their jobs. They take their careers seriously, and Max's brand of *fun* makes that nearly impossible."

Though he had no desire to sacrifice his innocent staff in exchange for saving his brother, he was still backed into a corner with no escape. "While I acknowledge Max lacks certain skills, this company owes a lot to his contributions."

"I understand his ideas are a cornerstone to many of Tiluma's best apps. I do. But did he ever even work in an office before his current CTO role?" She sent out a casual stare and waited in complete silence for an answer, her question a sure sign she knew she had him.

He dipped his chin and used his glower to warn her to ease off. Yes, she had a point, but he wasn't stupid, and he had his reasons.

"Max and I have discussed his need to extend his range." Even as he stared her down, he couldn't hold back his appreciation for her sharp mind and ability to go toe to toe with him. "It's fair to give him time to adjust."

She tilted her head to one side and reeled back. "Tiluma is four years old. How much training has he had in that time? How many chances will you give him before you decide he simply isn't cut out for this industry?"

"I'll give him as much time as he needs."

"Look, I get the whole family ties thing, but ties only work if you're not bringing each other down. Max bailed out of this meeting for a reason, and he dropped you in it instead. That's not the actions of a fair person. He's not good at his job, and you both know it."

Despite the bunching of his abdominal muscles and the knowledge that she was yet again right, he shrugged. "And as I said, Max is worth having around. I have to give him a chance."

"No." She held out a hand in a gesture for him to stop. "Enough excuses. He's had plenty of chances and seemingly failed every one."

A searing heat filled his chest, and for the first time since meeting this woman, he fought the urge to stand and leave her. "You want me to fire him?"

"Nooooo." Her gaze slid to the side, her dragged-out reply a deliberate attempt at poorly hidden sarcasm. "Max might be an ideas man, but he shouldn't run your entire tech department. Daniel deserves that job. In the meantime, Max needs a major demotion, extensive training…." Her voice dropped to a near-inaudible mumble. "A complete attitude shift…."

Fingers curling and opening, he leveled a scowl her way while working through her snarkily delivered list of demands.

In truth, he'd considered all the options she'd offered before. He'd just always been too busy to organize any training, or as she'd said, made excuses so as not to hurt his brother with that plan, much less a demotion. He'd also thought it a low and impersonal act to let any other staff member handle the issue.

So here he sat now, the fruits of his inaction hanging before him in the form of Agathe's burrowing stare. "You don't ask for much, do you?"

Her gaze did a gentle dip to her plate. "I'm not the one asking. Your employees are."

Her hushed tone… that she mentioned his employees and that she was merely the bearer of their dissatisfied message… He reached for his fork, intending to play casual, while his stomach clenched in a warning he wouldn't be eating just yet.

"Tiluma is Max's company too. We started this together." His grip tightened around the fork, leaving him to wonder which would snap first, the fork or his fingers? "You don't understand my predicament."

"Maybe I don't." She gave him a direct stare that said she at least attempted some compassion. "There's no way I can know what your family situation is, but you're paying me to do a job, and this is me doing it. Now, it's your turn. Keep this ship and its crew together. Otherwise, Max won't be the only one failing at his job description."

She pushed some noodles into her mouth and chewed, still shooting him an unwavering stare, one that dared him to contradict her.

Unfortunately, he couldn't.

"Fine." He bit the insides of his cheeks and held onto a growl. "I'll see Max gets some management training. Though I'm still not sold on demoting him."

Her expression turned flat, unimpressed, a clue that his offer for Max's training didn't appease her in the slightest. "He also needs a stiff talking-to. I could—"

"No." He shook his head, his voice a stiff warning for her to not overstep. "I'll do that too."

She dipped her chin and eyed him from under her lashes, her challenging look a reminder of how much he sometimes liked her attitude, even, or maybe especially when directed at him. "Okay, but if you don't talk to Max, I will. It might be your job to keep this ship together, but right now, it's mine to push it back on course, and I don't intend to fall short on my end of this bargain."

He gave her a flat look, one that said, *I hear you. Can you cool it now?*

She rolled her eyes. "Fine. I'll hold back for now."

She ripped a page from her clipboard and extended it toward him. "Here's a list of recommended training programs. I suggest Max start immediately."

He took the paper but decided to save looking over it for later. Right now, he had something or someone else he wanted to focus on. "Are you always so hard-nosed about your work?"

She squinted in a not-so-serious scowl. "Always and without fail. And you're paying me to be hard-nosed, so don't be such a crybaby." Her lips curled ever so slightly, both the lips and the sly curl dropping his heartbeat to a low thunder. A woman in her element. A woman with so many hidden layers, both light and dark. "Besides, Max's antics won't help your chances with Ernest Schneider. I take those high stakes seriously."

Luke took a bite of food, somehow impressed she had the guts to call him a crybaby, something no one within these walls would ever do. *Was it even possible to be turned on by an insult?* Also, she'd learned about the Schneider meeting. Guts and initiative. What wasn't there to like?

The pulsating heat through his groin suggested he liked just about all he knew of her. Perhaps being CEO and getting his way too often—having people always tread so lightly—didn't suit him. Her insult-infused doses of reality, and her professional confidence, appeared to be everything his overly-pampered ego craved.

Wanting to prolong this exchange, he circled back to her comment about the Schneider meeting. "What high stakes, exactly?"

"You need Schneider, and I want Tiluma to do well since I'm also" — she peered down, her lashes fluttering as though she'd lost the ability to look at him directly—"I'm angling for a promotion at Slate and King."

Her gaze lifted, her throat bobbing with a nervous swallow, the skin over her cheekbones taut in a beseeching, strained smile. "Luke, you have a great staff with great potential, and I need your help as much as you need mine. Trust my advice, okay? Trust my advice and work with me here."

He sat silent, his pulse loud in his ears, for the first time feeling the wondrous sensation that this woman needed him for something. *Anything.* But even as he weighed her plea, he wished she'd shown as much spirit and fight the night he'd held her in his arms. He wished that her request extended beyond work.

At least for now, though, he could do this one thing for her. "I'll do my best. Just promise you won't speak to Max yet."

She pushed a loose lock of hair behind her ear and gave a small nod, her pursed lips a hint that she may have expected more resistance from him but appreciated he had none.

An inordinately long silence lingered, one that was easy to endure, though he tensed with a need to avoid breaking the spell with any sudden movements. "Is the heavy stuff over now?"

Given the intimate space, his voice felt overly loud, but she nodded anyway, her lack of words suggesting she, too, didn't know how the peace pact changed things between them.

He peered down at his plate and pondered this subtle softening in her. "Can I ask a personal question?"

"We promised not to get personal, remember?" Her quick reply and weighty tone added tension to the room.

He lifted his head and offered a big smile as though smiles alone could tame her. "It's not *that* kind of personal."

She wrinkled her nose as if to say, *Really?* But all she verbalized was, "Okay."

He leaned far across the table, pressing one hand into the timber surface and using the other to reach for her. She gave a small jolt, her gaze widening as his fingers caught a loose lock of hair framing her face.

He rubbed his thumb over the silken strands, pretending to feel nothing special. "Is this a convincing dye job, or are the blonde streaks natural?"

A slow grin crumpled up her cheeks, and her relieved laughter cracked out.

"Firstly"—she reached for his hand and slid her hair from his grasp —"didn't anyone ever teach you it's rude to touch a woman's hair?"

Despite the question, her raised brow hinted she took no real offense, and then there was the fact she still held his hand as she spoke again. "My mother's Irish-Australian, and my dad's Afro-Argentinean. The color's a natural result of my eclectic genetics. Oh, and the blonde gets paler after some hours in the sun."

The corners of her lips lifted even higher, her dark eyes twinkling with a previously unseen lightness. Her seductive joy stirred his blood and eviscerated the strain in his chest. So much so his words got away from him, despite a need to keep the conversation simple. "Your genetics aren't eclectic. They're perfect."

She rolled those sultry eyes but still continued the exchange. "How about you? What's with the posh accent?"

He laughed, never before thinking of himself or his accent as *posh*. The entire time, her fingers remained curled over the back of his palm, leaving him to wonder if she meant to touch him or had merely forgotten herself.

"York, England. I'm Scarborough-born." He kept his voice bright, never once imagining he'd be able to share easy banter with her. If they'd been anywhere else but this office, he would have rounded the table, pulled her into his arms… anything to gain access to more of her. "Max and I arrived in Melbourne three years ago, but my mother and sister still live in the U.K."

She lifted her chin, her gaze holding on him for a long length of easy silence.

A distinct need grew within him, a need for something further, a need her quiet appraisal carved deeper and deeper until he was forced to hold back from reaching out to stroke a thumb over her high cheekbones…. To caress her burnished-bronze skin or maybe even taste her delicate pink lips again.

No matter what message her light touch now sent, even he knew the moment could be so easily broken, not just with his touch, but what he might also say.

He wanted to reveal the ways she upended his life. How he didn't mind because he was more alive now than in so many recent years. She was a question, the answer less important than the value she added to his days just by merely being in them.

He wanted to share the dumb and clichéd truth of just how beautiful she was to him—in every moment—especially this one. That she made him wish things could be different. That his heart beat heavier even for the distance this ill-placed table forced between them.

Her face twisted, and she snatched her hand back as though she caught her mind wandering too.

"Don't." She shook her head, clear strain drawing her shoulders upward. A woman who'd read his desires and rejected each one. "This job is all I have, Mr. Tindall, and there's nothing else in this world that I want."

He winced at her weak whisper and her choice of words, and the formal use of his name.

And still, he understood.

As the person in the position of power, he had a duty to respect her choice to keep him in his place. Away from her.

She blinked down, and loose bits of hair shrouded her face, her next breath a thin rattle. "I never thanked you for stopping what almost happened between us in Roseford. I was wrong to think I could indulge in something more, and you were right. I would have regretted us sleeping together."

The word *regret* reverberated through his skull, and his stomach hollowed, her gratitude contradicting his sense of unfinished business, while the sad glow to her eyes made his heart twist in place.

Something was fundamentally broken within her, maybe something neither she nor anyone else could fix, but even that hypophysis seemed too fatalistic. He'd seen people pick themselves up. Dust themselves off. He'd *been* one of those people.

"Let me help you." His lips pressed together, the words sounding as short-sighted and arrogant as they probably were.

Even if something had hurt her so critically that she'd shut her heart inside a steel cage and thrown away the key, his role wasn't to fix her.

She stood and swiped her clipboard from the table. "Thank you, but you can't, and I need to go."

She marched for the door but paused before opening it.

"You wanted to know what I meant when I said it was time." She peered down at the floor, her cheeks dull and her shoulders slumped. "The truth is, there can never be a *time* for someone like me."

Her insurmountable pain made his ribcage squeeze in sympathy for her, but even as she did the wise thing and left, his next tight breaths urged him to not let her go.

# Chapter Eight

That night, Agathe huddled deeper into her couch, the brown leather crackling beneath her. She tugged the hood of her baggy, white sweater over her head and created a barrier between her and her television, a multi-colored patchwork cushion hugged to her chest. But no amount of warmth or comfort could defrost the glare she aimed at her favorite romantic comedy.

Her insides coiled, and she tried to blink away the sting in her eyes, but that didn't help. This was her go-to movie for a small slice of romantic escapism on a bad day. *Not tonight.* Tonight, the shots of semi-naked bodies and hungry kisses made her want to scream, her earlier lunch with Luke eviscerating her ability to envisage her own redemption in the movie's heroine. No, that heroine's icy defenses and hers weren't the same. Agathe most definitely held a more impermeable frost.

And the laid-back hero? Tonight, he seemed downright unimpressive. Tonight, he did nothing to spark her interest. That Hollywood smile. Those glittering blue eyes. Both underachieving features compared to the attractive green sparklers she encountered on a daily freakin' basis at work.

She slumped back and closed her eyes, releasing a low growl.

Would she ever know peace again?

Even just the hellish sort of peace she knew before Luke came along. She shouldn't have revealed so much to him today. Shouldn't have let his charm weaken her resistance. Even though he *always* weakened her resistance, case in point, her habit of over-sharing around him.

She opened her eyes and tossed aside her general lack of care for tonight's movie in favor of grinning at the television hero in the throes of declaring his love. At least the sappy ending contrasted with life's overall tragedy… or just *her* life.

*How in Hades do I face Luke again?*

Nearly sleeping together in Roseford already almost did her in, and today's shared admiration, followed by the mutual googly eyes and tender sentiments… working at Tiluma would be awkward as hell. Perhaps even hellish enough to make her burst into actual flames every time she got anywhere near her hot-as-jalapenos boss….

The movie credits rolled, and she hit the "off" button on the remote on her glass coffee table. Of course, just like her sappy rom-com movie, some buried corner of her heart wanted a happily ever after ending. *Whether she deserved that was another issue.*

Her mind paused on Roseford, on her moment of desperation, the night they'd met, opening a window to what she wanted, but couldn't have. Well, if that night *had* opened a window, windows were also designed to be closed, so maybe she could find a way to do just that. *Right now.* Maybe owning up to the one yearning she couldn't outrun would make all her wishful thoughts disappear. Her yearning for *Luke.*

Time to admit she didn't know herself as well as she thought. Because, for reasons she couldn't understand, this man had a hold on her, and perhaps her constant denial only made her desires burrow deeper and deeper into her subconscious.

That had to be it.

So, an admission of her feelings might set her free.

Seeking comfort, she wrapped a hand around the baroque-style lovers painted on the side of her favorite porcelain teacup, the romantic scene eliciting another scowl, though her proceeding sip of warm tea still soothed.

The first step. Break Luke's spell. By the goddess, she wanted to break that damn spell. She'd start by speaking aloud what she'd avoided up until now.

"I want Luke Tindall."

The admission rang through her empty living room, and she slammed her eyelids shut, her ribcage suddenly overly tight. Despite her private surroundings, the echo of those verbalized raw needs left her feeling exposed. Just imagining how flakey she looked made her want to vomit a little in her mouth.

Still, for once, being alone was something she could wholeheartedly embrace as a cure for her problem.

"I want Luke so bad my loins just might burst into a lust-fueled bonfire."

She tried hard not to chuckle at the cliché.

*Okay, maybe this whole confession thing isn't total wretchedness.*

"I want to get laid, and I want Luke to be the one I get laid with."

Wild heat swept her face and lifted her heartbeat to a solid thump, that admission cutting a little too deep.

*Still, don't stop just yet.*

She tried again. Adding her most candid confession yet.

"I want one small release from this never-ending misery. I want to forget...."

Her body ached, her nerves shredded, all while her heart hollowed and a new thought plagued her.

*What have I done?*

She flung her eyes open and fought the new sting there. Don't cry. Not over this. Not over the inability to get over anything. *Ever.* Not over *him.*

Sure, today's events came as a reminder of the emptiness in her life, of how little hope rendered, but at least strength lived there in her admission. She'd attempted to rewrite a portion of her aimless existence. For that, at least, she could be proud.

She could never jeopardize the *one thing* she held most dear. Not for anyone. Not for lust or love. Not when each moment of unintended happiness took her further and further away from Elsie.

Hopefully, her feelings for Luke would subside now.

They had to. They simply *had* to.

Unchecked feelings meant danger. They meant risk-taking. Spontaneity. Sex. And all of that could lead to genuine love and adoration when she couldn't afford either.

So, too much relied on her staying just as she was.

Aloof. Alone. Unloved.

# Chapter Nine

"Hard at work, I see."

Agathe stopped scratching her pen over her notebook and stared up at Daniel standing over her at the large and otherwise empty conference room table. He nodded at her notebook riddled in black ink, or more precisely, her saccharine etching of a dolphin leaping into the air.

She shrugged, the boredom of waiting having caught her. "Got to get my creative kicks somehow."

He plunked into the seat beside her while more people filtered into the room, their expressions neutral despite the intense quiet.

"Have you run out of people to grill already?" He flipped his laptop open, and she laughed, still scanning the room of now mostly filled seats, all except the two empty chairs designated for Max and Luke.

"No grilling today. I'm here to observe group dynamics. By the way, what's on this meeting's agenda that requires so many people?"

Daniel nodded out to the room, a room six times bigger than the intimate space she'd shared with Luke yesterday. "All-hands-on-deck management meeting. We present our general progress reports gaining a collective understanding of where the company's at in the lead-up to the Schneider visit."

She tapped her pen's cold, metallic tip to her lips and took a moment to think. "And how do you feel about the company's current trajectory?"

"Personally" —Daniel leaned in, his voice dropped to a whisper— "I don't believe there's any way to prepare for Ernest Schneider. The man's obsessed with cleanliness. You should see the list of requirements his PA sent through, and there's this rumor he once destroyed a company after a fly landed in his assistant's glass of sparkling mineral water. I mean, how do you avoid something as unpredictable as a fly entering a building, much less landing in someone's drink?"

She wanted to laugh but cringed instead, about to ask where Max and Luke were, only for the room's chatter to die off.

Luke marched through the already open glass double doors, quick to take his place at the table's head. A flurry of activity erupted around her. Papers rustled, laptops opened, and chairs creaked as people sat taller. She waited, her focus on the door in anticipation of Max, but he didn't show.

She switched back to Luke's gaze, the turbulent green of his eyes locked to hers. Cheeks hot and heart pounding, she glanced down at her closed notebook... the same heat from her face traveling down to her lower belly.

*Hormones. Just hormones. That, and Luke being the male equivalent of an ovulation starter kit.*

She wanted to chuckle at that thought. Did such an ovulation starter kit even exist? If it didn't, maybe she'd just come up with his next business venture. All he had to do was find a team of scientists who could extract whatever about him sent her once-hesitant ovaries into hyperdrive.

A suppressed chuckle broke from her lips, and Daniel turned to her, one brow raised in a silent question.

She waved a hand in a dismissive gesture aimed at convincing him to drop whatever suspicions ran through his nerdy brain, but the corners of his eyes crinkled with a subtle smile. His way of saying he'd let nothing go.

Luke used his commanding tenor to call for everyone's attention, his next string of words causing a deluge of blood to rush her ears, his distracting effect on her body overwhelming any power to grasp what he said.

Next, his marketing manager stood and began speaking about some campaigns Agathe had heard about during her employee interviews but knew little of. For the most part, she wasted long minutes working double-time to control her breathing and retrain her mangled focus on her job.

She'd started this day with a list of goals to fulfill. With a drive to succeed and exceed, her feelings for Tiluma's CEO would complicate all of that, and so, she needed to get her act together and lose her deepened emotions from yesterday's meeting... She needed to stop drowning in her thick, soupy haze of conflicted arousal.

Daniel nudged her with an elbow, and she startled, his face scrunched in her direction. "What's with you two today?"

*Shit! Fuck! Poop!*

*Daniel noticed.*

"Nothing. Nothing is with us." She shook her head repeatedly and flipped through her notebook, a feeble action since this was a new book, and most pages were blank.

"Your far-off expression tells me your mind is on another planet altogether, and Luke keeps giving you looks, too. You have no real role in this meeting, so he shouldn't be looking at you at all. And..." Daniel slanted closer. "Is that sweat on your temples?"

She slapped a hand to her hairline, her palm indeed slightly damp. *Damn, Daniel!* "No. It's just warm in here."

"Really, now?" He huffed out a subdued laugh. "So much for Melbourne being weeks from winter, and this room's better than adequate air-conditioning."

"Fine. Luke's pissed about our talk yesterday." She ground the lie through gritted teeth. "As you predicted, Max never showed up for that meeting, but Luke did, and I gave him a piece of everyone's mind. He didn't take it well. Do you think anyone else has noticed he's annoyed with me?"

She forced herself to send Daniel a pleading look, her face hot from her dishonesty, her stomach sinking because she saw no other way.

Daniel's attention held a long few seconds, and her stomach sank even more. His brown eyes eventually softened, though the grin he extended didn't. Perhaps she was a worse liar than she thought. "No. Everyone's too absorbed in their own stuff."

"Agathe."

She started, her gaze darting to Luke, who stared at her from across the room. A distinct cold hit her body, but she straightened and nodded to acknowledge him.

"I wanted to thank you for your suggestions regarding Max." His bottom lip sat fuller than the top, an oh-so-tempting detail she shouldn't have noticed, especially not with an entire room staring her way. "As some might have already noticed, my brother isn't at this meeting. And yes, I know his unexplained absence isn't all that unusual…."

A few brave people took up the challenge and chuckled, the pause, unfortunately, allowing her spare seconds to admire the stretch of his powder-blue shirt over the steep contours of—what she knew from experience—were well-honed pectoral muscles.

"As of today"—his voice jolted her back to reality—"Max is taking a management training course, which means he'll be out of the office two days a week for a month." Luke turned to Daniel. "Daniel will fill in on the days Max is away."

She turned to the man beside her, her right hand now locked in a painful grip around her pen. "You knew? You knew about Max's training? You were only humoring me."

Daniel's eyes glistened, and laugh lines and dimples formed around his mouth. "Sure did, and sure was. Even a complete social novice could tell Luke wasn't the slightest bit 'pissed' about your meeting yesterday."

Though Daniel's revelation said nothing between her and Luke was all that covert, Luke's grin trained on her as if some intimate secret lingered between them. "Thanks to everyone's honest feedback and Ms. Santos' advice, Max is getting the help he needs. I ask that everyone gives him support and patience through his learning phase."

All the managers nodded, and some turned to her to offer an appreciative smile. Her heart thudded at the public salute, but Daniel's arrogant smirk dampened her joy. "You know, Luke was adamant that not another day passed without Max starting one of the courses you suggested. It's amazing. All our years of trying, and then Ms. Santos enters the building, and our human resources department almost implodes in the mad rush to secure Max a spot."

She grimaced and shifted her focus to Luke giving her another of those "hot looks" Daniel pestered her about. *Oh, hell!* Luke's quick glance made her thoughts fall back to last night's self-confession. A confession that was not strong enough to cast out her feelings for him. Maybe she *was* in over her head.

Maybe she needed the help of a priest or a witch doctor. Heck, anyone who could expel the complex sensations awakening in her body. Watching Luke take charge of this room, shining in his powerful role, praising her… Between the want in his eyes and the scrutiny in Daniel's, she had nowhere to look. She had no escape.

So, she stared ahead and kept her expression blank, hoping the emotionless mask would erase the sudden chill spreading through her body. The worst thing possible had happened. *Luke Tindall had listened to her.* He'd acted on her advice. He'd endorsed her skills before a room full of people—people whose opinions mattered to her and her career.

Worse still, he was everything but the arrogant, pushy, self-absorbed CEO she wanted him to be. He was downright likable and made hating him more impossible than ever…. Right when hating him was what she needed most.

Daniel cleared his throat, but only loud enough for her to hear, before he leaned in and whispered in her ear, "Still want me to believe there's nothing between you two?"

Luke paused at the row of cubicles where Agathe's temporary desk sat up ahead. Office chairs cluttered the space, and the multiple glowing computer screens made him regret treating her like any other consultant by not giving her a private office.

Most of his employees were still out to lunch, but a tall, blond doofus of a man stood next to her desk. *Max.* As much as Luke loved his brother, the guy had a lot to atone for, and his presence now added to Luke's irritation.

He took a slow breath and continued on to Agathe, a brown gift bag hooked on the ends of his fingers. *His own attempt at atonement.*

Max's focus stayed downcast on her, and he rubbed the back of his neck, his ashen complexion paired with an atypical somber frown.

"Thanks for taking the time to hear me out." He took a step back and almost bumped into Luke, who now stood at Agathe's desk, too. Max's gaze bounced from Luke to Agathe before his eyes widened. "Oh, I'll… ah… leave you both to it."

Luke gripped his brother's shoulder and held him in place. "Shouldn't you be at training right now?"

As usual, Max's tense look made a quick shift to a jovial smile. "They let me out for lunch, you know. But I'm heading back now, promise. I just wanted a few words with Agathe."

Luke gave no more than a stiff nod, and Max strode away. Meanwhile, Agathe's silent attention lingered on Max, and when she finally did focus on Luke, her eyelids narrowed, and her lips pursed. "Why are you here?"

His fingers tightened around the brown paper bag's handle. Though he had other reasons for seeking her out, the pained look on his brother's face, coupled with the fact he'd trekked across multiple city blocks to see her—a woman he'd avoided at all costs—seemed worth questioning. "First, tell me why Max was here."

She ticked one corner of her lip upward, the face version of a shrug. "He wanted to apologize for ditching my meeting yesterday."

"He did?" Breath burst past Luke's lips, falling just short of an incredulous laugh.

"Yeah, I know. Though I thanked him, I also told him his staff needed apologies and promises of improved behavior more than I did. Amazingly, he agreed." She pinned him with another stare, brows raising in a *go-figure* sort of manner. "Turns out Max is all right after all, and whatever you said to him must have struck some sore point. I actually have a speck of hope he'll change."

Luke didn't know how to respond to her lack of faith in his ability to keep his brother in check. Then again, he had failed on that front for four years now, so maybe he needed to take her doubts on the chin and move on.

Still, even with Max not being a nuisance for a change, Luke's lips strained into a probable frown. He did want Agathe's faith in him. Faith, and a whole lot more. "I take it that's your version of a thank you?"

She offered a surprisingly easy smile. "As close as you're going to get."

Briefly dumbstruck at her lighter response—or maybe awestruck—he gave a slow nod.

The smile on her face, the one she so rarely used, lit up the darkness in her eyes like the moon on a cloudless night, and that smile made the ache in his own heart pop and fade, a thousand tiny fireworks vanishing into space.

"I wanted to talk to you about our conversation the other day." He paused. While yesterday's meeting had been enlightening, it hadn't ended as well as he'd hoped, and a gap stretched between them that he wanted to close. "Something didn't sit right with me."

Even as she maintained a neutral gaze, her forehead wrinkled and pinched. "You mean, the part where I said more than I should have?"

She dipped her chin, daring him to lead into yet another tense exchange.

"I wouldn't put it that way. You didn't reveal *that* much. You only added minor detail to what I'd already gleaned from you. I'm sure you'll be happy to know that I'm still as confused as ever." He reached out and dropped the gift bag to her desk, her eyelids widening. "I wanted to give you this."

She glanced at the bag but didn't touch it. Another silent beat passed before she spoke. "A gift?"

He nodded, then jutted his chin out in a gesture for her to open it.

But she leaned back in her chair and distanced herself from the peace offering. "I take it you buy gifts for all your employees?"

He shrugged, even though the firm accusation in her tone indeed bothered him. "If one of my employees came to me with a personal issue… Yeah, I might."

"I didn't come to you for that reason, and you know it. In fact, you came to me when I was expecting Max, remember? And…" She pressed her fingertips over her eyes, the quick drop of her shoulders a hint she caught the heat in her tone. "Look, I'm sorry. It wasn't your fault about Max. What I mean is, everything I said yesterday just sort of… slipped out."

The upward, apologetic twist in her tone had him blowing out an exasperated breath, his mind reeling at this woman's ability to transition through so many moods in one conversation.

"Intentional or not, I can't pretend I didn't hear what I did." Sensing her need for a break from his drilling for information and vowing not to press her anymore, he jutted his chin to the paper bag again. "Open it, so you'll at least know what it is."

Though she reached for the bag, her gaze stayed on him and a reluctant smile curled her lips through a small growl. "Fine, but let's make this clear, I don't like pity gifts."

She pulled a see-through box from the bag, and her smile dropped. A clear glass teacup now rested in her hand. His chest rose with light exhilaration, and he needed to know her feelings about his gift.

He'd stopped by a boutique on his way to the office that morning, buying the cup because he figured she'd appreciate the painted vines and delicate, white, jasmine flowers twisting up the sides.

"You've been watching me." Her dark stare didn't leave the cup, and her voice was a hollow whisper. "And you decided I liked tea things from our brief meeting yesterday."

He shrugged with a casualness he didn't possess, working hard to pretend he didn't notice the furrowed pain lingering on her brow. "Was I wrong? I know almost every detail about this company. The glassware you brought to yesterday's meeting doesn't belong to Tiluma's kitchen. It must have been yours. I also saw the way your fingers clawed into the table when I poured tea like you worried I'd drop your precious teapot, even though you were the one to spill tea all over yourself and the meeting room carpet."

Her lips clenched as though she suppressed a smirk, but what drew him most was the ever-so-slight tremble of her fingers as she turned the cup around and inspected its sides. "I don't like that you've been watching me."

Her words remained breathy and small, like a child sharing their fear of monsters in the dark.

"You were sitting right across from me. I had nowhere else to look." Nor could he have looked elsewhere, even if he'd wanted to. The truth was, he hung on every second of every moment with this woman. And yes, he noticed everything about her.

Hoping she might understand, he stuffed his hands in his pockets and softened his tone. "I figured you were down on yourself. You might appreciate a kind gesture."

She huffed out a tight laugh. "Well, that's one way to look at it, but what gets me is, you saw a small moment of panic and somehow decided I valued teacups?"

"You don't give much away, Agathe, so that 'small moment' spoke volumes."

Her direct stare also spoke volumes, mostly about her reluctance, though her overall expression did ease.

"Good." He gave her an unaffected smile. "So, consider yourself lucky I talked myself down from buying the entire tea set."

A small chuckle escaped her, and she lowered the cup, staring at it as though she held winter's first and most precious snowflake—not that it ever snowed in Melbourne. "My own mother hasn't noticed I like teacups."

Not wanting to offend her, he tried not to laugh—though a sense of pride blossomed in his chest, sending wisps of lightness throughout his body. That lightness faded in the dazed sheen invading Agathe's eyes, leaving behind a wish that she would just open up to him.

"Hey." He used the abrupt word to capture her focus. "You're not the only one with a past."

Though she gave a shaky nod, her shoulders rounded, and she shut him out further.

Just as his statement implied, he'd been through tough times too, and though he had no idea what her "tough times" were, he figured it'd help her to know someone saw her. *And that someone was him.*

"If ever you want to talk, I'm happy to talk, too. I'll even share my past with you. I promise it's not pretty." He smiled, hoping to offer a sense of camaraderie through his humor, as well as a direct offer of help before he nodded to the teacup. "And if it makes you feel any better, I'm not trying to buy you with trinkets. There's nothing personal or pity-filled about that gift."

He meant the part about not buying her off, but there *was* something personal about his gift, and he *did* intend to win her over. Not with stuff, but with kindness and hope, along with time for her to notice this unmistakable connection.

She released a quick breath and then cleared her throat as though shaking off some baffled state.

"Okay. Well." She shot to standing, cup held high in a strained salute. "Thanks."

He watched her turn and power away, his regret less centered on her hurried escape—one of many thus far—more on watching his good intentions count for nothing. All because of her stalwart need to cling to whatever secrets held her prisoner.

Then again, he had something in his favor—an ability to get her talking, even if her confessions came only in dribs and drabs. He could cling to his optimism with the same bull-headedness she used to cling to secrets, and he'd formulate a plan. He'd get through to her. Disrupt her current state of normal and push her out of the shadows. And he'd do all that far sooner than Ms. Santos could ever expect.

# Chapter Ten

Agathe tucked her laptop into her work satchel and turned her mind to the darkening sky outside, the day over, while Melbourne called. She loved these cool autumn nights, the way the streets wound down after a busy workday, only to welcome excited theatergoers onto the wide, shop-lined pavements each evening.

She'd step out there soon, too, the city alive and on full display with whirring trams and delectable scents wafting out from bustling restaurants. If she were truly lucky, she'd see her favorite Peruvian band busking the streets. She'd give them a few minutes and offer a handful of coins before her journey home, where warm tea and a scandalous book awaited.

A dull *thoong* disrupted her exit, and she turned her attention to the building's courtyard, the sound repeating and akin to a blunt object hitting metal. Next came the muffled song of children's laughter.

*Strange.*

Her heart swelled, and she squinted at the large glass wall showcasing the yard. Though the yard had a basketball hoop, she'd never witnessed anyone actually using it. Only now she did, and the vision of Luke—with his sincere grin pointed at two children sitting cross-legged on a timber bench near him—caused the muscles in her throat to tighten.

She swallowed at the constriction just as he spun from the children and slung a clean shot through the hoop. *Of course, the man has game... in more ways than one.*

She scoffed at her pathetic longing and twisted around, set to escape out the main door and onto the street, anywhere far from Luke. Only then she second-guessed herself and peered over her shoulder at him, his focus catching hers as though instinct guided him to look at that exact moment. *Shit.*

His smile dropped, and he allowed the ball to bounce aimlessly behind him. Meanwhile, she briefly forgot she wasn't all that religious and lowered her chin to mutter a silent prayer. If heaven existed, no one up there would be interested in helping her, but now wasn't the time to think about the Great Blue Yonder.

She peered back up, where he still watched her and for some unexplainable reason, she stared right back. His hair sat ruffled from his running, the sleeves of his fitted charcoal shirt rolled up to expose strong forearms, while his first three collar buttons opened to reveal yet more strength there.

He looked undeniably sexy and infuriatingly approachable—two things she didn't need him to be right now.

Would she be rude to still turn and walk away? Sure, she'd caught his gaze, but he'd caught her attitude more than once now, and maybe she was best to let him think her a naturally cold woman.

*He was kind to you today... and pretty much every other day.*

*He doesn't deserve 'cold.'*

More curse words filled her mind, and she released a low growl. *Fine.* She'd at least say something about going home and offer a 'friendly' goodbye. Content with her plan, she gave a fortifying nod and marched on, the two children quick to turn their little faces toward her at the courtyard door's pitchy creak from her push at its handle.

The oldest child, a girl around six years old, and the boy, about four, beamed bright enough to rip a hole right through her already shredded heart.

"Are you here to play basketball?" The girl's question came with a distinct lisp, her missing front teeth distorting her words.

Agathe shook her head, and her pulse thudded loud in her ears. She avoided children at the best of times. They had a way of making her limbs turn weak and her heartbeat and mind teeter on the brink of overdrive—like maybe she might actually explode and little pieces of her would scatter into the atmosphere.

But since these kids weren't just passing by, she couldn't avoid them, and their cheerful stares invited her into whatever world they'd built with Luke. If only she'd chickened out of this interaction when she'd had the chance....

The girl's gappy smile expanded. "Good, cos Luke's hogging the ball, and he won't let anyone else play."

"Hey." Luke pushed his heavy stare from Agathe and gave the girl a playful scowl. "Your dad gave me orders not to let you two get grubby before he takes you out to dinner. You should thank me for keeping you out of trouble."

His subtle frown returned to Agathe, but unlike the comical one he'd given the girl, this frown hinted he'd seen her reticence around the children. Because, of course, Luke noticed everything.

"Don't be silly, Luke." The little boy wrinkled his nose, his eyes squinting with unfettered mischief. "Daddy won't be mad. Just a little play, please?"

Luke leaned in with features drawn in fake intimidation. "Maybe not, but your mum will be, and I'm *definitely* not messing with her."

As if to rise to the challenge, the little boy dipped his chin low, and his bright, blue gaze skipped over to Agathe. "Are you Luke's girlfriend? Tell him to share."

Agathe's mouth dropped open, but she failed to summon a reply. The best she could do was fix a wide-eyed and beseeching glare Luke's way, even though she'd been ungrateful earlier and didn't deserve his saving.

The door creaked again, and a middle-aged, balding man poked his head through. "Claire. Dylan. Time to go."

He smiled at Agathe and threw an appreciative wave Luke's way. The kids leaped from their seats and ran with loud giggles to their dad, the girl giving her little brother a small shove amidst their race. "Mum told you to stop asking people that."

The boy shoved her back. "Well, she *could* be his girlfriend...."

The glass door slammed shut, and the children left, leaving Agathe to stare at Luke in stunned silence.

Tram wheels screeched from the streets outside Tiluma's not thick or high enough red-brick walls, the sharp, metallic grind filling in where conversation failed. Heck, even the tall maple to her right conspired against her, adding a loud rustle.

"I...umm..." Her voice cracked, and she rolled her shoulders back to compensate for sounding like a gawky teenager. "I'm sorry for the abrupt exit before."

Luke kept his unbroken attention glued to hers. "You don't need to apologize, and you don't need to worry about legging it away from me."

She chuckled at his *legging-it* comment. "I knew you'd say something along those lines."

The tension across his face eased, and he lowered his shoulders, an invisible wall dropping between them. "Am I that predictable?"

She nodded, second-guessing her next words. "Predictably nice. Yeah."

Her husky tone made her want to wince, but the enlivened zing of adrenaline rushed through her and claimed first place on her list of worries. As always, she couldn't decide whether to throw herself at him or run in the opposite direction.

He strode a few yards away, his steps slow and confident, before retrieving the ball and stopping in front of her again. "Is that the crux of your problem with me? I'm too nice?"

A derisive laugh broke from her, but even though she so desperately wanted to do otherwise, she forced herself to maintain eye contact. If nothing else, he deserved her honesty. "Seems to be."

He quirked a brow but said nothing, bouncing the ball a few times as if the repeated sound might break her.

*Well, it did.* And she let out a resigned sigh, conceding that perhaps she owed him a more detailed explanation. "You did something thoughtful, and my natural reaction was to turn all 'ice queen' on you.

I get it. I'm a deeply flawed human being. So much so that even my 'thank you' wasn't all that genuine. I'm sorry, okay? What more do you want from me?"

He narrowed his eyes at her as though the question of "what he wanted from her" made him think, but then he bounced the ball again and twisted his body toward the net. He took a shot at the hoop, and once again, the ball sailed through with a sharp *swish*.

"No." He rounded back on her. "You acted with suspicion, and given our past encounters, I don't blame you."

His gaze skated around her face, features relaxed and all too accepting when a defensive glare would have put her more at ease.

Lost on what to do with his compassion, she said nothing, allowing him time to race away, retrieve the ball, and return, her reply surfacing once she held his full attention again. "I think it's obvious my problems run deeper than the few misunderstandings we've had."

His constricted stare from earlier came back, analytical, his eyes still somehow lit with humor. "Oh, yeah. On many levels."

A mischievous grin curled his lips, a grin that backed his claims of not really minding her problems. *If only he knew.* Then again, if he *did* know, he'd run a mile from her.

*Isn't that what I want, anyway?*

True. And still, she stayed; her hands curled at her sides, the strain in her body a common reaction to this man and his constant stillness, as if him just being here could bait her into explaining.

And because she already figured he could read her mind, she added, "I'm *not* getting into my private life with you."

He didn't even flinch at her growled delivery, and to be honest, a tucked-away corner of her didn't believe her statement either. She couldn't shut up around him.

He pressed the ball between his hands, his long fingers stretching and hugging a large portion of the bumpy orange surface, his focus unwavering.

"I don't expect you to." His ensuing shrug brought attention to the wide span of his shoulders. "Your mistrust says about as much as any confession, as does all the effort you've invested into keeping me away.

So, from what I'm seeing, it's the chemistry between us that's really got you spooked."

A smug grin took over his face, and her tummy clenched, her entire body caught somewhere between denial and attraction.

"There's nothing between us. No connection. Certainly no 'chemistry.'" She locked her arms into stiff rods at her sides. "We settled that on the day I agreed to work here."

He shook his head, his face losing all humor. "No. We agreed to not act on what's between us. I never once said no chemistry or feelings existed. They most definitely do. You know it, too."

He drew closer, his steadfast gaze insisting his statement was a clear fact and not a point open for debate. Hoping to keep from growling, she bit the insides of her cheeks; but he tilted his head to one side and analyzed her further.

"If I'm wrong, then you wouldn't be stonewalling me right now."

She threw her hands open on either side of her, gesturing to the world at large. "How am I stonewalling? I'm literally standing here, wanting us to get along. I'm *not* stonewalling you."

"Really?" He scoffed and spun, tossing the ball at the hoop, the third clean shot since she'd come out to see him. But, this time, he didn't chase the ball. He let it fall and roll away.

"You talk a lot"—he turned back to her, his breath a light pant from his long-range throw—"but you don't reveal a damn thing, and your silence serves a purpose."

Even though her mind scrambled for the right words to shut down his accusation, her shoulders stiffened from the sense that *maybe* he was right.

A great part of her *did* want to be known by someone outside her own head, but her sanity relied on keeping her deeper thoughts locked away. She'd invested years of hard work and sacrifice in establishing a sacred fortress of secrecy and, thus, protection. She sure as hell wouldn't reveal those secrets to a man she'd met wandering through some fields in Roseford. The fact that he was essentially her boss only made keeping to herself an even wiser choice.

Besides, if she ever did unleash every hurt and emotion overrunning her soul, the deluge of *stuff* would never stop flowing. The outpouring of grief would drown her and anyone reckless enough to get too close. So, yeah, keeping her stuff private was the right thing to do…for everyone.

"Am I the only one who makes you this defensive?" His voice jolted her from her thoughts, his strained frown pulling his jaw into a hard line.

She hugged her arms around herself and gave a reluctant nod. "Yeah. Pretty much."

*And I won't endure yet another cataclysmic downfall in growing feelings for you.*

*Not when the last defeat still remains more than I can take.*

"Hmm…" He chased after the ball again, leaving her hanging.

Now, she made a point of wearing her own frown. "*Hmm…what?*"

"Like I said." He bounced the ball a couple of times and then lobbed it at the hoop. "Chemistry." The ball missed its target by miles. He swung back to her with a broad and boyish smile, hinting he'd missed the shot on purpose. "You feel something for me, and that terrifies you."

*No shit, Sherlock.*

But she shook her head and took a slow step back. "No."

His eyes sparkled brilliant, all emerald and light—like a man hiding a winning lottery ticket in his pocket, even though Luke Tindall didn't need any extra money. "It sure isn't your professional obligations holding you back, Agathe."

Though his voice gentled, her heartbeat climbed, as though in a race to outrun his growing adoration… or maybe even her own….

"You know"—he grabbed the ball again, both brows raised to her— "I'd never snitch to your boss if things didn't work between us."

"I don't care what you'd do." She stuck out her chin, her tone hollow because, actually, she did care. She cared too much. "I don't want 'things' to work between us. I don't want them to even start."

He dipped his chin, his light-hearted glance saying, *Come now, you don't fool me.*

Even her stubborn silence couldn't budge the smooth serenity from his face, though her silence did seem to prompt him to speak again. "You don't strike me as someone with a poor judgment of character,

Agathe. In fact, your job demands an ability to see through people's façades. We've spoken enough times now, and you've interrogated my staff enough to have a good inkling of who I am. On top of that, I've seen the way you stare at me when you think I'm not looking...."

That last embarrassing observation struck a small inferno in her chest, but she took a deep swallow and plastered on her most sarcastic tone. "And what stare is that?"

His eyes glistened anew, his gaze unwavering, suggesting that, unlike her, he didn't mind being caught looking. "The same hungry stare you gave me all through yesterday's meeting. Your eyes go wide, and you don't blink all that much. It's a terrified-but-intrigued expression like you're dying to find out what it would be like to not turn me away for a change. To be fair, I can't stop wondering the same about you."

Her ribcage compressed hard around her lungs, and her world came to a grinding halt.

*How mortifying.*

While he'd been busy watching her every reaction, she'd repaid his efforts by looking like a heavy-breathing lurker. She clearly wasn't as stealthy with her staring as she'd thought!

She cleared her throat and schooled her overheating face into a flat expression, holding firm to her argument because she had no other freaking choice. "My job also demands I keep it in my pants."

He held still for a beat before his chest trembled, and then the light staccato of a merry chuckle came tumbling from his lips. "Let's cut a deal, then. I'll help you keep it in your pants if you tell me the real reason you're shutting me out."

She jerked back, new tension pressing heavily on her brow. "You *don't* have as much power of attraction over me as you think you do."

"I don't believe that"—he shrugged, lips pressed into an unconvinced flat line—"I'd even go so far as to say what you feel is more than just attraction."

He prowled closer, his gaze blazing, a man with enough sexual charge to turn her muscles into metaphorical jelly.

Truth be told, she burned to re-experience that scintillating kiss he'd given her in Roseford. And as usual, Luke, with his ability to crawl into her brain and rifle through every one of her salacious thoughts, had his own things to say about Roseford.

"I have as much power as I did the night we met. Maybe more." His smile rose another degree, tinged with humor, as though she presented some kind of fun challenge. "And I'm almost certain I could recreate those conditions right now."

He loomed over her, his added height and intoxicating scent of citrus and spice exuding a physical clout that made her hold up a hand as a guard between their bodies. "Don't come any closer."

But even those words couldn't stop her conviction from sinking. She wanted to reach out and hitch her lips to his, to let 'chemistry' run its course.

His gaze smoldered with desire, but just as she commanded, he stayed put. "Tell me why you're holding back."

His respect for her wishes endeared, yet another thing that angered and worked against her. "I don't have to tell you anything."

He leaned down, bringing his lips closer to what she desired, but refused to acknowledge.

"You want this, too."

His voice held a sultry rumble that snaked through her body, scattering her thoughts and awakening senses she didn't know she had.

Oh, yes, she *wanted* this.

Wanted him.

The flutter of heat washing over her said as much. As did the uncontrollable moisture pooling between her legs.

"Luke." She meant to back away again, but her legs refused to oblige as if they'd rather wrap around his waist than walk her out the door. "Please."

His words, his closeness, his hot breath against her cheek… each small detail broke her down to weak need. Even her "please"—designed as a *please, don't*—sounded more like a pleading *please, do.*

The lines of concern over his forehead smoothed out. He knew he had her. "I won't touch you, Agathe. Not unless you ask me first."

"Then step back." She flinched at her soft, twisting whisper, the strongest voice she could produce in light of his hold on her.

He shook his head. "I won't do that either."

"Maybe you're right. Maybe this isn't all about my job, but"— she eased back, the effort of doing so akin to prying two super magnets apart—"nothing can happen here."

*Fuck my life!*

He took a step closer, filling the space she'd just made. Shock zinged through her body, and an icy-sharp pain took hold. What was he doing? Why was he so insistent on affecting her? Her heart thundered so hard in her chest that she might just keel over at his feet.

"Then, at least tell me why." His beautiful stare refused to let her go. "I want you. You want me. Why am I the one in the dark? At least ease my misery a little and fill me in on what's happening here."

*What's happening?* She opened her mouth, ready to argue that her reasons were none of his business, but her voice cracked, and her throat dried. No words could make him understand. So, no words came.

She'd promised herself time and time again there'd be no more tears, and explaining would bring those. If she cried now, she wouldn't stop. Her years of learning to tame that tide would be for nothing. So, she simply couldn't let this man break her, not when Elsie had already done just that.

And she'd more than broken Agathe. She'd downright destroyed her.

"I'm not free." She blinked up at him, vowing to provide just enough information to make him step away—her tone thankfully clearer now, despite the swell of tension drawing at her belly. "And you're asking for more than I can give."

He jerked back, his face suddenly rigid at providing the distance she'd fought for. "'Not free?' As in, you're seeing someone? Or... *Married?*"

She blinked again, sharp urgency emerging as a stab of pain emanating midway through her chest. The downcast shock on his face left her heartbeat turning savage. Unable to lie, her usual evasion hadn't worked, so maybe the truth would.

"I'm not married. Not anymore." She cringed at the sting of that admission. "And it's all my fault."

# Chapter Eleven

Luke kept his feet rooted to the ground, even as Agathe marched for the door, seconds from leaving. He wanted to be strong, to let her go—*but dammit*—he couldn't. Her fingers curled around the steel door handle, and adrenaline rushed through his veins, lunging him forward until his hand slammed onto the door's thick glass.

"Stop."

She startled, and her pupils dilated to wide, black pools; but her shock wasn't enough to stop him from shifting to trap her between him and the exit. He couldn't recall the last time he'd been so unshakably serious. He wouldn't let her run.

He expected her anger, for her to shove him away and run—but her next reaction was far more heart-wrenching, and she sagged against the glass wall behind her—her attention cast downward while an unfocused sheen clouded her eyes.

He let his hand fall from the door, her dejection making room for him to trust she'd stay put. "I don't understand."

She'd been married and then divorced. *How?*

This wasn't the usual path of a young, professional woman in Melbourne. And what about her claim that she'd caused the divorce?

A deluge of possibilities brought a frown to his face. "Did you cheat? Lie? Steal? What about being previously married would prevent you from moving on now?"

His insides churned with each empty second, and yet, all she gave was a renewed and silent flaring of her eyes. Her attempt to run, and now her silence, left him questioning whether she was simply flippant toward love.

Maybe marriage hadn't mattered all that much to her. Maybe *that* lack of care brought her to his side in Roseford… and now. But she'd turned him down, hadn't she? So, maybe not so flippant. Maybe some other deep secret….

That she was severely damaged in some way and therefore unavailable, as she warned.

That he should have listened to her warnings from the very beginning.

Or worse, that he wasn't enough to eclipse the legacy of some ex-husband.

"No. Nothing like that." Her lips pressed into a firm line denoting doubt, and she pulled back. "Henry and I…We were an odd match, to begin with, but we treated each other well enough."

Her frown dipped down again, shutting her off from him once more.

*Henry.* Her ex-husband's name made her story seem evermore, awfully real.

She'd shared an entire life with some other guy, a fact that shouldn't have bothered Luke but, for some reason, did. The ache expanding in his chest begged for answers. A morsel of redeeming truth to pin on this woman. A sign his instincts about her goodness weren't all wrong. "Then why run a mile at the idea of being with someone else?"

A heavy sigh spilled from her, the scrunch of her brow mirroring his own pain. "The story hurts too much to tell, and let's be honest, there'd be no payoff if I did talk. My confusion when it comes to you isn't a positive sign of my potential. So, excuse me if I've sent some mixed signals. I'm sorry, Luke. I really am sorry."

*Some mixed signals?* She'd outright asked him to sleep with her in Roseford. No "signal" could be clearer than that. At least her admitted confusion established that his hopes of having her weren't based on complete delusion.

So, *hope* had him breaking his vow not to touch her, his new vow being to make her confront whatever doubts raged within.

"Look, I'm interested in you. More than interested." He took her face in his hands. "And I know you feel at least something for me. Otherwise, you wouldn't have cared about that goddamn teacup or coming out here to apologize."

He tried his best to slow his urgent delivery, a pink tinge rising in her cheeks and wild shadows intensifying the depth of her eyes. "I might not know your story, Agathe, but I trust my instincts. They tell me you're someone worth knowing and getting to know. Make no mistake, I don't want to stop at this being just a business relationship. Can you tell me that's not what you want, too?"

Her blush faded, and a breathy creak broke from her. "I...I want that too." Her gaze dropped to his chin, implying that even just voicing her wishes stole something from her. "But you won't stop at just learning about me, will you? You'll want more. You'll want everything."

He remained silent. His attempts at being gentlemanly dwindled when it came to Agathe because she was right. He couldn't hold back. He'd want more than just a few glimpses of who she was away from this office. "No. I won't stop there."

She slipped out of his hold and pressed a hand over her throat, rubbing as if that might provide relief, though her pained expression said it didn't work. "No, you won't. And you're right. There *is* something between us. Something I can't seem to fight, no matter how much I should. I want to act on my feelings, too, Luke, but all I can do is act. I have no space for feelings, do you understand?"

Her focus snapped to him, a little startled, a little drained.

"Agathe." He meant to say more, but no other words flowed.

She lifted a hand and gestured for him to stop speaking anyway, her eyelids squeezed shut.

"I have limits, Luke. I..." When her eyes reopened, a renewed strength smoothed the once-hollow planes of her face. "I can't give you what you're asking for. I can't give details or any true portion of myself. I don't *want* to talk. Got it?"

He nodded, hoping if he stayed silent and provided time for her to direct the fragile energy between them, then maybe she'd allow another small glimpse of hope.

"But I…" Her breath shook, and her lips pressed closed in a struggle to finish that sentence.

So, he stepped near. "Tell me."

From this closer position, the familiar scent of sunflowers and rain washed over him while she patted a hand over her chest where her heart was. "I can't give you this, Luke." She lifted the same hand and lay it gently on his cheek. "But I can give you this."

With that, she rose to her toes and pressed her lips to his.

Even as his hands found a life of their own and captured her waist. Even as he pulled her into him and drove the kiss deeper. He understood. *Perfectly.*

She couldn't give him her heart. Couldn't give him her story. But she offered her body as a compromise. A remedy for what would otherwise end as an unexplored attraction. A remedy he knew within his heart would only serve as temporary relief.

Because he wouldn't stop at an attraction. Nor at the physical. But, at least for now, he would settle and take whatever she gave. Because he simply couldn't risk losing her to someone else. Or worse…risk not having her at all.

# Chapter Twelve

A shock of electricity ran down Agathe's spine, and Luke's fingers slid down her back, leaving her mind and body to muddle in the wake of her rash decision. The soft warmth of his strong and indulgent caress made her press into him even more. Despite all her earlier protests, she offered herself as a willing sacrifice—some sex-starved crazy woman, because that's exactly what she was—illogical with need.

This kiss had been three months in the making when she'd let no man touch her in years. So really, nothing about her choice was rash. Her skin tingled at how she'd initiated this moment, which pointed to how badly she wanted release from her physical captivity. Now, her body responded with a sigh and a rush of all-encompassing heat, opening her heart to unfamiliar soaring ecstasy.

*Oh, but this relief won't last.*

Yes, she knew that as much as she knew her own name, but the sheer possessiveness in Luke's embrace made any future regret seem a small trade. First, she would have a sweet release. She would taste a moment of long-dreamed-of oblivion.

She ran her hand down the front of his fitted shirt, testing the firmness of his prominent pecs and flat abdomen. Strength incarnate. His lips meshed with hers, and every so often, his tongue would sweep her mouth, claiming her. So vital. So alive. A man offering a promise of the delicious escape to come.

But then, he wrenched away, and her heart immediately stumbled—the sudden loss was a warning that if he couldn't ease her constant heartbreak, nothing else would.

"Let's take this back to my place." His stare searched hers like he fully expected her to say no.

Well, he was right, and she shook her head—not wanting to risk losing her nerve on the drive to wherever he lived—or adding personal touches in staging this interaction at either of their houses. She had no wish to pursue intimacy.

"Fine." He frowned, eyes darkening. "My office, then."

She nodded and allowed him to grip her hand and pull her along. His wide steps meant she half-jogged to keep up through the overly bright lights of Tiluma's empty corridors. Occasionally, he'd turn, and the heat in his stare would send needy shivers through her body, his office door now looming yards away.

*This is it.*

He pressed a palm to her lower back and wrenched the handle open, urging her into the room, the door too quick to click behind her. Even though she had zero desire to run, his flick of the lock jolted her with a sense of finality.

Taking hold of her hand, he padded back a few steps toward a chocolate leather couch. Her knees locked in refusal to move. "No. Not there."

Even the couch was too intimate. She wouldn't lie with him. Wouldn't have him surround her with anything akin to warmth or tenderness. All she wanted was raw. Basic. Non-binding.

*Sex.*

So, she pointed her chin toward his desk. "There."

He gave her the same dissatisfied glower as when she'd refused to let him take her home.

"Agathe," he growled, a warning that he wanted something beyond a meaningless screw.

*Well, too bad.*

For all she cared, he could fuck her till she forgot her own name. In fact, she wanted just that, *without* the risk of emotional attachment.

She leveled a resolute stare, only for his frown to deepen, but she refused to let his disapproval sway this decision. She wouldn't lie to him. Wouldn't let him believe he could fall for her. He was a good man. One who deserved so much more than the nothingness she could offer.

"The desk or nothing." She crossed her arms and allowed him time to think it over. "And while we're stopping for air, you better have protection because—"

He caught her in his arms and hoisted her up, quick to wrap her legs around his waist, the action forcing her to latch to his shoulders instinctively. "Is this what you want?"

Breathless from the fire in his stare and the heat of his body, she nodded.

"And just to be clear"—his lips loomed close to hers—"I have protection."

He crashed forth a devouring kiss. Rougher, needier, and more urgent than before.

She moaned, allowing her body to relax and revel at getting what she wanted and how she wanted it. His power, hers to direct. *Harsh passion, with little risk.* She'd failed one child. She wouldn't fail another, and Luke's vigilance meant she could let go with less chance of getting knocked up anytime this century.

His hands cupped her ass, and he took a few steps to the desk, the hard surface quick to cool the mostly-bare skin of her thighs. She peered down at the polished woodgrain and only then saw her skirt hiked high enough to put her lacy black underwear on full display.

"Happy now?"

She lifted her attention to his sly grin, a grin that darkened his stare. Despite her list of demands, he wasn't at all an unwilling participant.

She smiled, glad to play the unaffected vixen. "Oh. Very."

"Damn you, Agathe." He buried his face in her neck and nipped at the tendon just below her ear.

An easy laugh broke free of her, and she leaned back, raking her fingers through his thick, brown waves. "Damn me to hell."

His fingers swept up her back, and he found the ends of her hair, tugging back to expose her throat. His rain of endless kisses there sent blades of awareness throughout her body, her next soft moan designed to spur him on.

Yanking away the light material of her underwear, he left her bare and open to his touch while the crisp crinkle of him unrolling a condom filled her ears.

He took her quickly and in one solid, smooth glide—that first thrust forcing her to battle against his size and her years of sexual deprivation. She clenched hard around him, and he held still as if he knew to provide time for the ache within her to ebb.

Moments later, his thrusts started. Slow. Each careful but deliberate movement increased her arousal.

Distancing her torso from his, she leaned back until her elbows pressed into the desk; and he rode her faster, his force and urgency drawing from her a cry. Everything he gave was what she'd asked for and more.

From here, she saw everything. The strain on his face from the physical effort of pounding into her. The strain of delaying his release. Then the beautiful ripple of muscle as his movements revealed an unrelenting command over her body.

How could this one act take her light years from what the old Agathe would have wanted? Or maybe it was less about the "act" and more about the man himself. *Sex and Luke.* Her new medicine for a life she otherwise couldn't stand?

Oh, but she *could* stand this.

The pressure of his increasing pace. The intensity of his stare pinned on her. Her rising pleasure was so gratifying she slammed her eyes shut and relished each life-affirming thrust. Her thighs clenched around him, and her hips lifted to relish every last inch.

Though her heart screamed for something more—something intimate, with emotional connection—there were no guarantees she'd experience anything like this again. So this would be enough.

Tight ferocity took over his face, and he dug his capable fingers into her waist. She cried out to the ceiling and once more blocked his deep, emerald gaze.

That gaze and its pleading promise. That he *could* give her sweet and personal if only she'd let him. His fluid movements testified to his ability. *To his spirit. To his feelings for her…*

But her broken heart only needed distraction and lust. The temporary bliss of a lover.

Nothing more.

She surged forward, and he caught her with the skill of a man who knew how to read his lover. A man who was hiding tenderness behind all he did to her now. *What a pity for him.*

Wrapping her in his arms, he pulled her in, her one relief from the compassion in his hold being that he buried his face against her shoulder, thus breaking eye contact. She bucked against him, urging him to finish because her climax approached fast. She wanted to release—her chance to forget—but her encouragement only forced his great, green stare back to her.

He held the wide and soft gaze of a man treading emotional waters.

"No." She near choked on the word, but his stare confirmed that being with her meant something to him.

Unlike her, he didn't pretend to go through the motions, and his sincerity chipped at her denial. This had grown beyond mindless fucking.

She liked Luke. Genuinely liked him. Everything she'd seen said he could be far more than just this short burst of passion. But, no matter how much his beseeching gaze awakened, this short burst of passion was all she could offer. No matter how lonely she'd let herself become. No matter what, she turned away. *This* would have to be enough.

He pressed his forehead to hers and punished her with his anguished glare, obliging her to witness what she did to him. "Too late."

He pumped her with earth-shattering urgency and speed, and she didn't have time to ponder his husky whisper, her breath rising with each overwrought thrust. And those eyes. Those sad and powerful eyes confirmed what they both knew. He'd succeeded. He'd made her *feel.*

White hot arousal tore through her body, and she threw back her head, giving in to desire until her emotions frayed like a row of overly tight stitches, splitting, unraveling, her every last restraint ripped.

*Pluck went those stitches.* With the reminder of just how much she missed being loved. The feeling of inherent safety. Like maybe she belonged.

She folded against him, savoring his warmth, and another thread tore.

*Pluck.* The reminder of how much she'd missed having someone hold her. Touch her.

She cried out but didn't cry, even though the urge was there. Tears were more than she deserved, as were the ripples of ecstasy skating through her body.

*Pluck.* The sensation of him swelling, his heat spilling within her.

She shuddered, and every part of her plunged into unlimited bliss —her body igniting on a cellular level—pure physical joy smashing a seismic chasm through every last layer of long-held control.

That same joy stole at her breath. Invaded her innate cynicism. That joy shook the ground of who she'd become, while Luke's arms encased her in a tight embrace that suggested he knew he'd broken her in some deep way.

Through her staggered breaths and fading trembles, her shattered boundaries began to rebuild, and she pushed him back, her attention glued down to the fine-grain lines of his desk because she'd lost the ability to hold his gaze.

"Thank you."

Her cold gratitude slammed the door on whatever intimacy he'd otherwise glimpsed.

"Agathe."

She offered nothing but avoidant silence.

The sound of his resigned sigh filled the room, and he withdrew, even as she fought an unspoken need to keep him inside her. Meanwhile, her forehead throbbed from a sustained glower.

"Here." Next came rustling and the scratch of a pen over paper, then his hands engulfing hers. "Take this."

She peered down at the folded yellow Post-it note he'd pressed into her palm. "What is it?"

His prolonged pause cut through her daze, and she finally lifted her attention to him again. "My address."

"Why?"

*Why would I ever want or need his address?*

Severity dragged on his unabashed frown, and he added, "Because next time, we do this at my house."

<h1 style="text-align:center">Chapter Thirteen</h1>

A new day and Agathe pushed through Tiluma's corridors, her attention low on the slate-gray carpets, while loose tendrils of hair acted as a veil about her face. Despite Luke giving her his address last night, she had no plans to use it, much less get personal with him ever again. Mostly, her greatest wish was to finish her day without bumping into him.

The raucous sound of a dog's bark bounced down the corridor, and she paused at the distinctive musk of canine. Gross curiosity spurred her gaze higher, and she quickened her pace.

Ahead in the break area, twenty or so Tiluma employees gathered, expressions an array of delight and despair, while approximately ten dogs of differing sizes and breeds scampered about Max. She paused at the edge of the action for a long minute, her hands balled into fists and jaw clamped shut to keep from swearing.

"What's all this?" Despite her desire to hold back, her voice took on a life of its own, cutting clear across the group and surprising even her.

Deciding to run with her brash delivery, she gathered her wits and strode over to Max.

"Oh, Agathe. I'm glad you're here." He smacked her on the shoulder like he figured her some kind of old friend. She wasn't his friend. In fact, right about now, she didn't even want to be his co-worker. "My first day at management training was incredible. I thought I'd implement one of my new team-building ideas right away. Look…"

He gestured to the room at large as if she hadn't already pushed her way through the canine pandemonium, his jovial grin still growing. She turned and cringed at one particularly mangy-looking terrier. The scraggly beast lay on its back, rubbing its filthy fur against the carpet.

"By bringing a pack of wild dogs to work?" She paired her unenthused flat tone with an incredulous wince directed Max's way.

He laughed and slapped her shoulder again while she tried not to splutter against the forceful, awkward gesture. He pointed to the mangy terrier, the one assaulting the carpet. "That one's just tagging along for a bit, but the rest have owners. I sent a company-wide memo out last night inviting everyone to bring their dog to work. You know, to boost morale."

Returning his attention to her, he tucked his hands into his pockets and rocked back on his heels. Meanwhile, a sick feeling somersaulted through her stomach, the mangy terrier now licking its crotch, forcing her to restrain a need to dry heave. "Did you clear all this with human resources first?"

He waved his hand in a flippant gesture and made a *pfft* sound with his lips like *she* was the irrational one here. "Where's the spontaneity in that?"

The last shred of her control twisted and threatened to snap, but she took a slow and centering breath and counted to ten, vowing not to pepper her next sentences with expletives.

"Good team building isn't about spontaneity, Max. There's effective planning and knowing how to read your crowd, too, you know?" Her voice rose, and she bit her lower lip to keep from saying more.

*Shit.* If she didn't reel herself in, she might actually lose her temper.

She pointed to the wider office, at confused employees and their befuddled gapes. "Can't you see, not everyone here is having a good time? Did you even bother to check if anyone here has an allergy to or fear of dogs? Did you check if Tiluma's current building lease allows animals on the premises?"

She leaned forward, elbows locked at her sides, her entire body stiff with barely leashed anger. Sure, her dark mood wasn't all Max's fault, but how could one person be so damn inept? "Did you check if Tiluma's insurance covers dog-related injuries, say, if one of these dogs goes feral and bites someone? Heck, did you even stop to weigh up whether dogs in the office might actually hinder productivity at a time when Tiluma *really* needs to get its ass into gear?"

Save for a few awkward throat clearings and the shuffle of the more discreet employees peeling away, a deathly quiet swept the room.

The queen of cool professionalism had lost her crown.

Then again, having sex with Luke probably had a lot to do with both her irritability and sunken professionalism.

"No. I didn't do any of that." Max blinked at her, his washed-out complexion and husky tone pulling her from her own mounting disaster and onto his.

"Look, I'm sorry." She closed her eyes and rubbed a finger between her strained brows, trying really hard not to feel completely shit about herself. "I'm being too harsh on you, but can you please just sort this mess out? And just…just get human resources to help you next time you have a *spontaneous* idea, okay?"

She opened her eyes and leveled him with what she hoped was a softer stare. His shoulders slumped as he spoke again. "Sure thing. I'm sorry about this, too. I really am. Are you okay?"

She held up a hand in a sign for him to just deal with the issue and spare her the questions. She'd had enough of those from his brother. "I'm fine, but before I let you off the hook"—she pointed to the mangy terrier—"where on Earth did you find that thing?"

"He's, umm…He's from the alleyway next door." Max's sheepish grin bent into a wobbly grimace. "I pass him every day on the way to work and figured he might like a break from the cold outside. I was surprised he even let me catch him today. He usually just scampers off. Do you think he likes me?"

She clamped a hand over her mouth and, this time actually did swear. Bless Max's well-meaning and far-too-childish heart, but who in heck brought a stray dog into work?

"Oh God, I'm going to be sick." She spun away and pressed a hand to her tummy, not sure how much she dramatized her disgust while weighing up the myriad of diseases the stray may have brought in. So, really, she wasn't being dramatic at all. "Just deal with him too, okay? Call the nearest no-kill shelter and get him out of here."

She stormed away, quitting Max's dog-themed circus, hating that he bore a strong enough resemblance to Luke to make her realize that breaking her dry spell last night had been her dumbest idea ever. Hopefully, this day was young enough that things could only get better, that work would provide her usual numb escape.

Head bowed, she powered on as the list of potential formal actions anyone might file against Tiluma at Max's stunt played in her mind. Her desk sat just a few cubicles ahead, and she aimed to get there fast. Only now, her quick pace worked against her because she slammed head-first into a tall wall of unrelenting muscle.

She bounced back, her head snapping up in time to see Luke with his usual shadowy glare, while an instinctive "Holy fuck!" fell from her mouth out of sheer shock.

And because of that shock, she reverted to defense and returned his glare with extra hasty words thrown in. "Control your brother."

Luke didn't so much as blink, but he did narrow his stare at her, making her feel small. "I'd rather control you."

She jerked back, the sudden move at least distancing her by a couple of steps. "What does *that* mean?"

"It means," he lowered his voice to a tense whisper, quiet enough that no one else around could hear, "your lashing out at Max has little to do with his dumb-ass idea, so maybe try some of your own advice and reel yourself in a little."

She rolled her eyes, giving that claim the dismissal it deserved. "I care about this job. I have a promotion to snare. We had a deal, *remember?* If you can't straighten Max out, then I will."

She took a wide step and tried to push past, but he whipped out a hand and stopped her escape. "I've done everything you asked, haven't I? And you care about your job a little too much."

His lashing tone and unyielding stare seemed to refer to more than just her gripe with Max. He, too, was pissed about last night, but his reasons were completely different from hers. Last night was his compromise. He wanted more. The entire time he'd made love to her, she'd felt that to her bones. She'd hurt him, yes. And she'd hurt herself. But they were adults here, and she refused to shoulder the blame alone.

"I care about my job too much?" She tilted her head toward the backdrop of his brother and the dogs, suggesting Luke needed to care a whole lot more. "What sort of a misogynistic ego trip is that?"

*Screw Luke.* Actually, she'd already done that, *but damn him to a flea-infested island with Max's alley strays!* He didn't get to dictate how she ran her career, much less her personal life. He didn't get to be yet another person on her case about her work ethic. She refused to dim her efforts to make anyone feel better about the path she walked.

"I'm going to do you one last kindness and gloss over the probable truth that you would never say anything so asinine to one of your male employees." She pushed her chest forward and lifted her chin in a defiant stance. "I'll also assume your true gripe here is based on jealousy, that you don't care enough about your job, and neither does your brother. I'm trying my darndest to make this company work, so it won't be on me when all your lack of care blows up in your face."

His face turned ashen, and his jaw slightly slack. Metaphorical alarm bells clanged in her ears, her muscles coiling with impossible strain. This burning anger. Her harsh honesty. All of it pulled her from her usual state of anesthetized loneliness.

Her closeted knuckle-dragger, dressed as a refined CEO, he'd changed things. He'd broken her daily drudgery and cracked her façade.

*Damn Luke, and damn him again. What is happening to me?*

Whatever he'd done, she outright hated him now, so she peered down at his hands still wrapped around her upper arms. "Let me go."

She shook him off and didn't spare him a glance as she marched for the meeting rooms along the far right wall, quick to slam the door shut and barricade herself inside the smallest one.

She would ditch her cubicle for the day. Hide here, away from public view and away from Luke. But first, she'd wait for the overwrought tremble in her limbs to subside.

Seeking a moment of calm, she sat on a chair and dropped her forehead to the desk, her breath fogging the polished hardwood now pressed to her nose. She could have stayed like that for hours. Could have basked in this room's silence where her heartbeat slowed, and her thoughts fell into focus...if not for the loud *snap* of a door handle and the violent crash of the door itself swinging open.

# Chapter Fourteen

A tight band squeezed around Luke's head, not a surprise since the intimacy from last night ended with Agathe bounding away like a proverbial scared rabbit. And now, in this meeting room, she had that same frightened look—her wide eyes expressing a desire to hide, to preserve her emotional walls over any concern for her physical safety.

His hands strained with a need to reach for her, but he kept his arms at his side and his hands to himself. Up until now, showing her goodwill hadn't gotten him far. He'd hoped that last night would sustain him. That time would convince her he had more to offer than sex and distraction. That he could help her through whatever held her back. That he was someone worth the risk of falling in love with...

"We need to talk." Despite his words, he needed more than just talk. He needed to shake something, *preferably her prickly temper* if tempers could be shaken. He needed his sanity back. He needed her honesty.

If only he'd forced this conversation last night rather than torture himself with an entire evening and morning stewing over thoughts of her and the impossibility of this situation.

Her red-rimmed stare pointed his way, constricted and holding heat. "No. You need to leave me alone."

She lowered her forehead back to the table as though she honestly believed he'd let this exchange end here. Not a chance.

He pressed his jaw tight and embraced the dull pain emanating through to his teeth. His life had been in peril countless times, but she, more than any warzone, had an increased ability to crush each and every one of his future dreams.

But the warzones had taught him that bad situations could be reversed and some dreams recaptured. Sometimes, giving up wasn't an option, and neither was surrendering his hopes of one-day finding stability and a family.

Agathe and her mayhem might have momentarily trampled over all his previous wishes, but he was *still* capable of pursuing what he wanted. "You had no place reprimanding Max. You certainly didn't need to do it in front of the entire office."

"And I'll apologize to him." Her voice muffled against the table before she lifted her head and gave a casual shrug. "But your brother's acting like a tool, and that's an indisputable fact."

Angry fire licked the walls of his already churning stomach, and he drew a slow inhalation, searching for calm. Sex or not, she needed to quit insulting Max.

"Why don't you tell me how you really feel?" He tilted his head to one side, remembering he was the CEO here. *He'd* hired *her*. She didn't run this show. "And why don't you try saying that to Max's face?"

She narrowed her gaze again and spat out a hard scoff. "Why don't you start taking your company's issues seriously?"

"Because you're taking my job seriously enough for both of us."

The corners of her lips curled as though she found humor in his reply, but the increasingly familiar heat in her stare said she wasn't done cross-lecturing him. "Funny. I don't think you appreciate just how much Max's stunts are nudging Tiluma toward trouble. You need just one pissed employee to drop a lawsuit, and Tiluma's reputation is ruined. Just one. And I can tell you now, *Luke Tindall*, you have far more than one standing right outside this meeting room."

She stabbed a finger a the door, the truth in her statement a damp and heavy blanket to his simmering rage. But then....

"You don't know the first thing about my brother." He kept his words slow and deliberate, and he leaned forward to crowd her space. "Give him time. At least until he receives the training *you* suggested."

"Neither of you has the luxury of time." She mirrored his stance, angling in, her dark scowl counteracting his attempt to intimidate. "Schneider's visit is in a month, and I'll be checking in on other clients at Slate and King all next week. I won't be around to babysit progress here. I can't hold Max's hand while he develops basic people skills. And let me save you some future heartache with the truth now, your brother has zero chance of putting on a decent show in time. Meanwhile, your whole tech team is suffering, and for a damn tech company, that's downright inexcusable." She lowered her chin, her glare sharp as knives and equally pointed. "Don't you think someone as savvy as Schneider will notice the deficit?"

He curled his fingers at his sides, the skin over his knuckles overly tight, a stab of shame piercing his pride. Or maybe not so much shame, but the knowledge that she was right. "I'll handle Max. We'll get Daniel to cover with Schneider."

"And that's another thing." The shadow of a smirk twisted her mouth as though she'd thought through any excuses he might make and had a list of replies already imprinted on her brain. "I don't think you realize just how much Daniel does to compensate for your one weak employee or how lucky you are to have that man. It's a miracle he's stuck by Tiluma this long."

Her eyes glinted like she got a kick out of knocking him down a peg or two. Meanwhile, her previous claim about Daniel deserving Max's position reduced his heart rate to a thudding beat.

Maybe it would be a matter of time before his brother lost the CTO role. Maybe there was only so much covering Luke could do for Max. But truth be told, he wasn't standing here now because of Max. He was here because of Agathe.

The subtle shift of her gaze away from his said she knew as much, which was why he spoke again. "We need to talk about last night."

But she returned her attention to him and shook her head. "In the light of day, in this office, last night never happened."

He delayed any protest, but only so long as to push past the sting of her words. "You're the one who insisted the action happen right here, *in* this office."

"Yeah, and I can promise you there'll be no repeat action."

An incredulous laugh broke from him, and he took a few calculated steps to her side, leaning in close to her ear. "I doubt that very much."

She leaned back a bit and turned her head to glare at him. "You're full of yourself, you know that?"

He gave a smirk, one even he didn't fully believe, and didn't so much as blink at her annoyed tone. "I do know. In fact, I'm so full of myself that I'll make you a promise."

"Oh, yeah?" She rolled her eyes in an *I'm-already-bored* expression. "What promise?"

"That I'll figure out what your deal is soon enough, and when I do, there'll be no escape for you, Ms. Santos."

Her perfect jawline formed a slight tremble before she barked out a short but fake laugh. "What are you going to do? Lock me up in the secret set of dungeons you have installed under this building?"

He folded in his lower lip, biting back a laugh. Her rebuff should have hurt, but it was such a sarcastic, *Agathe* thing to say, so he couldn't help but toy with her right back. "And you do a weak job at playing dumb, Agathe, but you *know* I won't need to lock you up. I plan to have you. I mean *body and soul*, have you. And there'll be a day when I'll know everything there is to know about you, Ms. Santos. When there'll be no more avoiding me."

She rolled her eyes again and dragged out a groan. "Oh, okay, so not a dungeon, but more like setting up outside my house with a pair of binoculars?"

Though he warred between wanting to laugh again and wanting to growl at her frustrating humor-based deflection. He held the silence instead, all the while waiting for her sarcasm to settle and her full attention to return to him.

And it did—with a vengeance. The miracle of time added a subtle shiver to her breath as her deep stare held his, her fingertips curling above the timber tabletop. His years of military and boardroom experience read Ms. Santos' rising nerves. That she hid secrets on top of secrets and emotions, she struggled to withhold.

"I don't need to spy on you, Agathe." He dropped his tone, once again expressing his disappointment. "You'll tell me in your own time."

He affected her, no doubt about it. Only, she had no clue what to do with him. And even with all her avoidance, a large portion of his dented pride clung to his having any impact on her at all.

He focused down on her crossed legs under the table, her foot bouncing back and forth, a jittery move that gifted him a chance to share his observation. "Your fear is showing."

She paused her foot bouncing while her gaze held dead-still on him, like he'd hit the nail on the head and she searched for another channel for denial.

"Yeah, I am afraid." Her near-whispered tone admitted defeat. They'd come too far last night for her to contradict anything. "So, maybe you could give me the space I've asked for?"

She shot to her feet and snatched up her leather satchel, lifting her chin in a gesture that blocked him out again.

His blood raced. He refused to be *blocked*. Somehow, he'd make her stay. Make her push past whatever held her back. Maybe he wasn't the world's biggest romantic, but he recognized something in her worth keeping. Worth fighting for. Goodness and vulnerability she seldom acknowledged. And then there was the fact that she wanted him just like he wanted her.

Or, at least…he hoped so.

He took a step toward her, but she held up a hand and motioned for him to stop, a weary smile dominating her expression. "Too bad you can't control everything, huh?"

He frowned but pushed down the boiling swell of defense threatening to break free of him. "I'm not trying to control you. I'm trying to help."

"Yet another thing I don't want."

"And yet you still need it." He reached out and stroked her arm, her attention snapping down to his hand, her eyelids flaring. "You're a mess, Agathe. You've admitted that yourself. If all my presence does is push you toward dealing with your issues, then maybe that's enough reason for me to stick around."

She released a sardonic laugh. "How about you start with your own problems?"

He didn't respond. Because, well, she had a point. But also, unlike her, his problems didn't stop him from pursuing a promising relationship.

The skin around her eyes bunched, suggesting she grew tired of waiting for his answer, and so she moved to speak again. "Did you ever think of the alternative? The one where I confront my *mess*, and I lose what little sanity I have left? How many times do I have to remind you that you know almost nothing about me?"

The tilt of her head and the dip of her voice implored him, that sad plea spurring him to speak again. "About as many times as I have to remind you that I've seen enough to know you're not going to crack while trying to get better."

Her face stilled and seemed to lose a shade of color. He stepped closer, as close as possible without touching her, a hurricane of emotions rattling his heart and pushing him to place sincerity in his next words above all else. *She has to believe me. Our future depends on it.*

"You're strong, Agathe." He paused along with her halted breath, one that fought to reject his words and proximity. "If you don't believe me, just look at how hard you dispute my decisions when others tiptoe away."

Moisture gathered at the lower rims of her eyes, and the muscles at her cheekbones bunched and trembled. But as always, he assumed that whatever she said next wouldn't be half of what she felt. "I've been treading water for so many years, I can barely drag myself through each day. I don't want to be strong, Luke. I can't take anyone else along, much less down, with me. Do you understand?"

His heartbeat slowed. Not what he'd expected. And he was almost certain he didn't want to know where she went next with this. "I do."

"Good." She peered down and nodded. "Then you know not to rest your hopes on me."

He lifted his hand and stroked the back of his fingers to the velvet softness of her cheek. To his surprise, she leaned into him, the slight movement suggesting she craved his support. "I think I will try anyway. If you've felt this way for years, maybe it's time to do something about it. Maybe it's time to stop treading water and swim." He tilted his mouth down, amazed when she lifted hers, his pulse quickening even as his lips met hers.

*Yet another surprise.*

This kiss was something else entirely. A soft, sweet promise. Though, whose promise exactly remained anyone's guess.

He pulled back, still intending to continue the embrace for a while longer, or at least for as long as she would let him, but first, he had one last sentiment to share. "And you should also know, Agathe. There's no way in hell I'm giving up on you."

*Chapter Fifteen*

A week later, Agathe stood outside of Tiluma's building again, her work satchel slung over her shoulder, while she puffed warm breath into her hands. The wintery afternoons had reached peak bitterness, and the Irish side of her blood failed to win over her sun-loving, Afro-Argentinean roots. Melbourne's blistering summers couldn't come fast enough.

She tapped her card to the building's security scanner and waited for a click to signal she could enter, all while releasing a silent wish that her return to this office would give her immunity from Luke Tindall's gravitational pull. Her week away had involved visiting old clients and reviewing their progress, but her reprieve from Tiluma couldn't last forever. So, here she was again, back at the site of her heart's conflict.

The click came, and the glass doors slid open. She bowed her head and pushed forward, steeling herself against the knowledge that Sue Hatchman waited inside.

True to form, Sue stood ahead in the break area, fulfilling her duty to gather information for Agathe's performance review. With her hip leaned against a bench, she fixed a smile on Daniel seated at the lunch table, no doubt having already grilled the man on Agathe's work so far.

"Ah! Speak of the devil." Sue's gray-blue eyes shone, offering at least one positive sign.

"I guess being the devil, I should be glad that people are talking about me?" Agathe forced a good-humored smile and ambled closer.

"That you should." Sue gave Daniel a regretful cringe. "A genuine pleasure to speak with you, Mr. Ari. You don't mind if I disappear with Agathe for a quick chat, do you?"

"I have to get back to work, anyway." Daniel groaned and stood. "As you know, we're all under the gun."

He gave Agathe a stealthy elbow nudge of encouragement on the way out, soon disappearing amidst the office's sea of pale blue desks and black roller chairs. Meanwhile, Agathe's tummy squeezed tight, and nausea took over, though she did her best to keep her expression light and follow Sue's confident strides away from the break area.

This was Agathe's first solo gig. Though she'd probably already screwed up with her public outburst over Max's "Bring Your Dog to Work Day," and then there was the fact she'd slept with Luke....

*Holy shit. I'm a walking, talking catastrophe!*

Sue's hands-on performance appraisal couldn't have come at a more God-awful time.

"You've made quite an impact here." Sue's voice cracked through Agathe's anxious wanderings.

*How much does Sue know?*

*How long till I get fired?*

Agathe peered down at her feet, her footsteps small and sheepish, though maybe that sheepishness came from the fact that her boss now led her toward the same meeting room she and Luke had last fought and then kissed for long minutes after. Her body had damn-near burst into flames then. Now, it did again, but for a whole other reason.

"Everyone sings your praises." Sue glided through the door and then lowered herself into a chair, swiping her cropped silver hair from her forehead, while Agathe took a seat opposite her manager. "One employee described you as 'a wrecking ball, but in a good way.' You've identified quite a few issues, as well as taken strong steps to rectify them, though I hear there's a rather dire deadline coming up."

"Yes." Agathe locked her gaze forward and forced her teeth together to keep from gnawing on her lower lip. "An investor meeting with Ernest Schneider. It's meant to be an informal chance for him to mingle and ask questions, but what with the unusual requests his office keeps sending, the meeting seems anything but casual. Then there are the unfinished projects he'll likely ask about, the stagnant profits, the obvious management issues... Someone as perceptive as him will notice something's not right here, and everyone is feeling the pressure."

Sue leaned in, her glare taking on a glacial hardness. "Do you think you can get Tiluma to pull it off?"

"Honestly?" Agathe huffed out a deep sigh, and her posture slumped. "I'm not sure."

Sue kept her elbows on the desk. "It would look mighty good for you if they did."

"I know." Agathe gave a rueful smile, the odds still stacked against her. "A miracle turnaround is what I'm aiming for."

"As for Luke Tindall"—Sue leaned back, expression lightening once again—"I'm impressed he's given your advice so much personal attention."

Heat rushed through Agathe's face. "I know it's unusual for a CEO to even interact with consultants, but—"

"Don't look so panicked. I get it. Mr. Tindall is a CEO who gets involved on all levels of his company. Heck, I was a little stunned when he asked to speak directly to me about your input. His direct approach means good things for you, as well as Slate and King's relationship with this company." Sue extended a hand and patted the table. "And you can relax. Luke loves your work."

The swelling in Agathe's throat expanded, and her thoughts switched to her last encounter with him. How she'd laid into him about Max. How he'd laid right back into her about her disastrous life, then offered hope, along with a kiss and more tenderness than she deserved.

And now he'd taken it upon himself to give her a glowing review. What was she supposed to do with that?

Something about his gentle approach dug at her core and skated past her years of built-up defenses, all while dredging up a well of sunken emotions. She didn't want to *swim,* as he'd urged. She wanted to lash out. She wanted to cling to her old patterns with fierce loyalty and take his constant provocations as another reason to run.

To run away from him.

But damn him and damn her. Every time she *did* seek to run, a soft voice in her head asked who she'd be if she let go of all the guilt. If her endless list of emotional and psychological wounds no longer stopped her. *Imagine that.*

But she couldn't imagine, much less justify, a life where her inner demons didn't give chase. Not while Sue stared at her. Actually, not ever. Her wounds were healed into permanent scars. Her life disfigured beyond repair. And maybe that was just how she preferred things to stay....

"Luke had nice things to say about me?" Her question came as a croaky whisper, one meant to divert her darker thoughts, one infused with unexpected and highly annoying curiosity.

Sue shrugged, her focus a little too strong for comfort and lighting a fear that the woman could see into Agathe's brain. That she knew exactly what went on in there.

*Nothing good. Nothing good, for sure.*

"He mentioned you're a hard taskmaster. Though, that *is* what he's paying you for...."

Agathe nodded her understanding and sought to steer the conversation away from Luke. "And what are your thoughts on my work so far?"

"You've made great progress." Sue held a matter-of-fact tone. "And I do hope you and Tiluma can rise to the Schneider challenge for everyone's benefit, but especially yours."

Sue pressed her hands to the table and stood, patting Agathe's shoulder on her way out. Soon, Agathe sat alone in this room, her tummy twisted in imaginary knots and the clock on the wall stating a time of just past five p.m.

A steady stream of employees filed past the open door while Daniel sat much farther away with Caroline at the break area's table again. Agathe abandoned the meeting room and marched over to the couple, a captivating pile of multi-colored fabric and a rustic-looking toy owl positioned on the table before them. "What's all this?"

Caroline clutched a patch of sky-blue material and a pair of fabric scissors, her wide and frazzled stare pinned to Agathe. "I'm part of the company's bi-weekly sewing group, but since Tania quit last week, we're like the blind leading the blind."

"What Caroline means is…." Daniel gave Caroline a kiss on the cheek, their connection having clearly deepened since the food fight. "She's now in charge and needs to produce a model toy owl for the group to copy. She's not sure she can follow the sewing pattern, much less finish the owl by tomorrow's lunch meeting."

Caroline rolled her pale-green eyes. "It's just not happening. Either there's something wrong with the pattern, or I can't make this work."

Agathe offered a sympathetic smile. "It looks like you handled the owl well enough."

Caroline laughed and held up a mangled miniature jacket. "The owl is Tania's doing, but there's no chance I'll get this jacket done in a year, much less by tomorrow."

"There goes our date night." Daniel slumped back.

Caroline offered him a gentle pat on the cheek. "Oooh, honey, I'm sorry."

Agathe's chest muscles drew tight, and she turned away from the show of affection in favor of the thin, paper sewing pattern unfolded on the table.

"That looks simple enough." She pointed to the pattern.

The cutesy stare-off between Daniel and Caroline broke, and Caroline straightened. "You can read that?"

Agathe nodded. "As easily as I can read the time. I used to be a…."

*Wait.* No one here needed to know about her past.

So, she cleared her throat and pretended to analyze the pattern again, taking a seat next to Caroline and hoping the move would distract her from asking any questions. "I used to do a lot of crafts.

Why don't you two clear out, and I'll get this done? It won't take me long."

"Really?" Caroline's jaw dropped open, her eyes glistening like she was about to cry. "You'd do that?"

"Only if you tell me why Tiluma has a craft group when none of you are any good at crafts." She grabbed some scissors from the table and got to cutting a whole new piece of blue cloth.

"We're an enthusiastic bunch, who genuinely want to learn, but Tania was the knowledgeable one who held us together. Then she broke out in a whole-body rash after Max's 'Bring Your Dog to Work Day.' Mind you, this was after her handmade skirt got a permanent blueberry jam stain during that food fight. So, she just up and left without warning." Caroline jumped to her feet, arm already hooked around Daniel's, and quick to lean her head to his shoulder with a wistful sigh.

"After all Max put her through, management wasn't brave enough to insist on her completing her notice period. Anyway, so here we are, leaderless. Our group might be a clueless bunch, but we have fun, and that's worth sticking together for. Only…umm, Agathe"—she gave a tight grimace—"seeing as we *are* leaderless, would it be too much trouble to ask you to join us just for tomorrow's lunch? You know, to show us what to do?"

Agathe dipped her chin and switched a glare between Daniel and Caroline's beaming faces, just a little jealous of what appeared to be a simple and supportive relationship.

*If only simple and supportive was something that I could do.*

If only the daggers of her past didn't hang over her head like a permanent threat. Though, past aside, she'd didn't wish anyone a dose of her daily loneliness and misery.

"Go." Her grumble was so half-hearted that Caroline beamed with the correct assumption that Agathe would, in fact, swing by to lead the craft group tomorrow. "You two look like this office is the last place you want to be."

Caroline's eyes lit up, and she hunched down, offering Agathe a rushed hug. "Thank you. Thank you. You've saved my skin."

Caroline hurried out with Daniel, leaving Agathe once again alone, though this time, surrounded by sewing needles and spools of colored thread. She released a sigh and turned to her work satchel, digging out her seldom-used, gold-rimmed glasses. Her contact lenses were retired earlier in the afternoon. Back when she'd believed her day was almost done.

Glasses now perched on the bridge of her nose, she lined up and pinned the cloth to the pattern. For the first time in years, her mind stilled with the monotony of crafting, but the office lay quiet. Too quiet. A strong reminder of why she'd stopped with this flowery craft crap years ago.

A still mind opened her to the hollows in her life, and right now, her thoughts fixated on just how much she enjoyed Tiluma's staff and its laid-back culture.

Worst of all, it's enigmatic CEO.

And yeah, she did like Luke. Not only in an *I want to lick chocolate sauce off your body and worship at your temple* way, but in a far more disturbing sense where his words and encouragement made her want to change. Though she didn't feel capable of change, she also didn't want to keep avoiding him—something she did with most other pleasurable facets of her life.

Her hand paused, and she lowered her sewing. Yes. She *did* enjoy every aspect of Luke Tindall. Even the bickering.

"That was a really nice thing you just did."

*Holy heck!* She startled and snapped her gaze to Luke, cold shock still threading through her veins as though her mere thoughts of him had conjured him into this room. He leaned against the archway some yards back, with his hands stuffed casually into his pockets and a pleased smirk curling his lips.

She swallowed and flitted her attention to the wall clock. "Please don't tell me you've been standing there a whole hour?"

Despite her flat tone, her heart dropped to a plodding beat. This was her first sighting of him in a week, and for all her frustrations, it might as well have been a year.

The distance should have been good for her, but now he stood there —his tantalizing lips eased to an affectionate grin—her tingling skin awakened her to the sad truth that she'd missed him all along.

"No, I was answering emails in the next room when I heard your exchange with Daniel and Caroline." He pulled his hands from his pockets and sauntered over. "I gave you an hour's head-start before I came out to bother you."

*Bother her?* Yes, he did bother her. *Bother, and fluster, and beguile…*All the other extra British-sounding words that probably also rolled so effortlessly off his overly skilled tongue, with its all-too-alluring accent.

She fiddled with the fabric, cheeks hot over her wayward mind and the sense he'd caught her doing something extremely stupid, which he kind of had.

His eyes crinkled in the corners, and his beam grew bigger. "I would have come out sooner if I'd known you were wearing those glasses."

She touched a fingertip to the gold frames. "Are they that bad?"

He huffed out another laugh. "Oh no, the exact opposite. You should wear them more often. You look…"

He focused a sharp stare her way but didn't finish his sentence.

"What?"

"Hot." He lowered his brow, a sullen look taking over. "Sorry. That's not an acceptable thing to say in our current location."

A smile cracked past her attempt to seem unaffected. "I'll accept your unacceptable description, anyway."

When had she ever felt *hot,* much less had someone who was *actually* hot described her as such? *Never.* That's when. So, heck yes, she'd accept the portrayal. In fact, maybe she could pull out her phone and ask Luke to say the word again while she hit record. Get him to say it extra low and slow because, frankly, *that* would be hot. After that, she could replay his enticing thoughts about her until her dying day.

Her skin was still on fire in the wake of his compliment. She tied the end of a thread and then cut her needle free. Next, she rose from her chair in an attempt to escape.

"I'm finished." She needed to go before she started believing her delusions or, worse, tried to randomly rub up against the delectable man who'd called her *hot.*

His eyes sparkled, and he leaned against the table beside her, blocking her attempt to leave.

*Shit.*

Maybe she wasn't the only one unable to control their urges.

"I have to admit." He toyed with a fabric scrap on the table to his side. "I'm a little jealous of how happy you sound every time I catch you talking to Daniel."

She plunked her butt back down and scowled half-heartedly at his now-piercing stare. "That's because Daniel isn't trying to marry me."

Luke threw back his head and laughed, a full-bodied chuckle belonging to a man who didn't hold back.

"Now who's getting ahead of themselves?" His expression dropped along with his gaze, which landed on his fingers and the fabric scrap. "And maybe Daniel's not interested because he's figuratively blind."

He quirked one side of his lip in a rueful expression. "And deaf." His stare lifted and bore into hers with a deadpan glaze. "And very, very stupid."

He let loose with a huge grin, one that added extra sparkle to his eyes.

*Well, isn't someone here a closet comedian?*

She shook her head and, in spite of her efforts not to, laughed at his dorky humor. "We both know Daniel is far from stupid."

"In this area, he must be." Luke brushed a leg against hers, and a flood of warmth filled her belly. "You have a beautiful laugh, Agathe. You should use it more often."

She rolled her eyes and put on a flat tone, even though his words brought comfort to the spot where her heart lived. "Don't get used to it."

Even though he blocked her exit, she extended her hands and collected stray fabric, advancing her plan to leave.

Someday soon, she'd move on from her work at Tiluma. She'd have no reason to see Luke and be free of his suggestions of a future together, even though she'd told him time and time again none could exist.

And he, too, would move on.

She had no doubts about that.

He'd find a more plausible lover.

The only other alternative would be allowing him into her world—

a world he would reject if he knew about her past. *If he knew who she really was.*

She slid the final scraps into the paper bag and only then worked up the courage to look at him again. He pinned her with an imploring stare as though he searched for clues she hadn't meant her comment about him not getting used to her laugh.

His rounded eyes exuded hope, all too adoring, and seeming to say, *but I want to get used to that laugh.*

Her heart kicked, hinting a desire for the light, bubbly feeling of regular laughter, too—as well as Luke's attention and a chance at normalcy and love. And then there was the freedom to mirror his longing. Oh, she'd do anything to have that. To give him something that looked more like happiness and less like evasion.

But then there came the fear that she couldn't do any of it. That the earth would crumble beneath her feet, and even just *wishing* for laughter would implode her already shaky stability. At least for her, dreaming was a fool's game, and she couldn't forget that.

As if he heard every syllable of her hopelessness, Luke frowned and still extended a hand. To her surprise, her palm shot up instinctively and filled his.

"Come on, it's late." He gave her his light smile and tugged her closer. "I'll drive you home."

# Chapter Sixteen

Agathe slid into her temporary cubicle at Tiluma and cringed at the squeak of her chair beneath her. The nerve-grating sound added to the heaviness already dragging at her tummy. Today, she'd need every last ounce of strength to survive the next eight hours of work.

She had plans to observe employees, get updates from anyone willing to talk, and corner Max to check on how his management training progressed. All while fighting an overwhelming urge to crack because all she really wanted to do was curl into a ball and cry.

The gnawing in her stomach grew while the tight band around her ribcage crushed her next breath—that discomfort having surfaced the very moment she'd woken this morning—deepening now that the date on the calendar to her left glared back. *June twenty-third.*

That date siphoned her every last drop of energy. She'd known it was coming but blocked it out anyway. Every June twenty-third left her so broken that she'd spend the rest of her year rebuilding, trying to forget, only for this day to swing by again and all too fast.

*The day I lost Elsie.*

Sickness wound through her belly, and she pressed her hands to her diaphragm, working hard at each breath. Last year was the first time she'd pried herself out of bed and actually made it to work. Every year before that had involved three days at home, just trying to purge her revived grief.

This year, though, she'd regressed. And even as she sat at her desk, staring at her blank computer screen, her legs twitched with a need to run all the way back to her home in South Yarra. To hide again and maybe never come out.

What a strong contrast to yesterday. She'd been so happy talking to Daniel and Caroline. Even Luke's presence had filled her with delight. He'd given her hope. The glimpse of a life complete with friends and a future worth anticipating. For one brief evening, she belonged.

But today…

*Today was Opposite Day.*

Today her heart slowed and threatened to stop beating altogether. Worse still, she didn't care all that much if it did because a still heartbeat brought the prospect of seeing her Elsie again….

*But would she even want to see me?*

Agathe leaned her head back against her chair, hoping a short break would push her through her clouded state. Even though she couldn't pause for long. Someone would see. They'd stop and ask questions. Was she okay? Could they help? Which would only draw more attention and tip her over the edge into the icy depths of an unwanted breakdown.

A high-pitched giggle pulled her attention. The loud excitement of a young boy. Though she refused to look.

"Agathe!" Two childish voices yelled in unison from across the office. "Hey, Agathe!"

She pressed her eyes shut and swore under her breath, willing herself to straighten. Of course, Dylan and Claire, the two children from the courtyard weeks ago, ran toward her. Claire wore a red-tartan school uniform, and Dylan khaki shorts and a blue T-shirt.

Claire gave a rapid and enthusiastic wave, her scrawny legs charging her forward. "Agathe, guess what?"

She didn't get to make her big reveal before her tiny ankle clipped the corner of a cubicle, and she pitched forward. Her arms flailed through her thudding crash to the rough-spun, blue carpet.

Agathe's hand clapped instinctively over her mouth, and her legs propelled her to the sobbing child.

"Oh, honey." She enveloped Claire in a protective hug, though a line of blood seeped thick and fast from the girl's knee. "I have tissues and Band-Aids in my bag. Just breathe and relax. I'll sort this out, okay?"

Claire gave a quick nod and pressed her lips together, seeming to want to hold her emotions together now that Agathe had her. Meanwhile, Dylan stood nearby, mouth agape and arms hanging loose at his sides. On her scramble toward her desk, Agathe reached out and gave his hair a reassuring scruff. Quick to next dig through her bag, she soon returned to a bewildered Claire.

"Here." She handed Claire a folded tissue, those brilliant blue eyes staring back at her, an embodiment of innocent fear. "Just press the tissue down firmly on your knee. And since you have a spare hand, here's another tissue for your eyes."

Agathe surrendered yet another tissue and ran her shaky fingers over Claire's forehead, removing loose hair from her face and offering comfort.

Claire gave a wobbly giggle. "Thanks."

"Don't mention it." Agathe unwrapped a Band-Aid. "Can you tell me where your dad is?"

Claire's face crumpled, and her sobs started anew. "I don't know. He told us to wait at his desk while he gave Luke something and that he'd be back to take me to school and Dylan to daycare. Oh no, he'll be so mad when he finds out we ran away."

"Hey, trust me, he'll be glad just to see you're okay." Agathe pressed a hand to Claire's cheek. "Anything less than that, and he'll have to deal with me."

She offered a smile and pulled the tissue away from Claire's knee. The bleeding had slowed, but they both hissed at the size of her wound.

"Looks like we'll need two Band-Aids here." Trying to make light of the accident, Agathe chuckled and began pressing the bandages down.

Claire's upturned stare gathered more tears, but she gave a shaky grin and threw her arms around Agathe's shoulders. "You sound just like my mum."

A fruity hint of children's shampoo infiltrated her senses and cut down to her core. The shampoo smelled like the strawberry one she'd once used on Elsie. That fragrance was forever imprinted on Agathe's memory.

She leaned back and forced herself to let go. Forced herself not to confuse the girl before her with the one she'd buried long ago. Forced herself to remember why she avoided children at all costs….

Four. Long. Years.

Four years to this very day.

Of course, Claire had to be around the same age as Elsie. Well, the age she would have been had things not gone so tragically wrong.

So, of course, Claire's presence stung like a molten branding iron pressed to Agathe's skin.

She had to get away.

A sharp sob broke from her, and she whipped her head around to find a small crowd gathered, witnessing the aftermath of Claire's fall. Witnessing Agathe's rise of emotion.

Claire's dad charged through the crowd. His eyes flared, and words rushed in an anxious apology. A razor-edged pain twisted in Agathe's chest as he bundled Claire up and whisked her away, Dylan trailing not far behind.

Luke broke through the huddle next, and his presence only intensified the rush of emotion blurring Agathe's senses.

"Are you okay?" He crouched before her, his breaths panted, and his gaze swept over her in a clear sign that he read her panic.

Though she scrambled for a reply that refused to come, her attention slipped to an employee to her left—an older guy she didn't recognize, his brows pushed together in yet more concern, his hyper-focus glued to the unwanted tears pushing from her eyes and down her cheeks.

She slapped a hand to her face and then pulled her damp fingers away to see the water gathered there.

*Don't crack. Don't crack. Whatever you do, Agathe, just don't crack.*

She rarely cried and never, ever, in front of others.

Luke's stare called to her focus again, his ever-darkening eyes belaying the dawn of new questions.

*He wants to know.*

She was startled at that thought and stood, quick to push past him and the overbearing crowd. Except, some people didn't move away fast enough, so she plowed right through them, her heart so constricted she didn't fully register the pain of each impact, much less know if she'd escape this building without falling into a useless heap.

And all the while, a persistent voice chanted in her head.

*Hold it together. Hold it together. Don't fall apart.*

*Especially not in front of him…*

Agathe's escape from Tiluma came minus a plan, and by late afternoon, she sat alone on a bench at the edge of the city's most uninhabitable location on a cold day. Albert Park Lake. Where the frigid water matched her stricken mood perfectly.

The icy wind nipped at her face, slapping her hair against already stinging cheeks. She couldn't go home. Not to a place that contained all the best and worst of her life, either kind of memory, not one she could take just right now. Perhaps, she should have moved out years ago, but moving meant letting go of the remnants of her daughter that still lingered in those walls, and *letting go* was a final step she both failed at and refused to take.

Hours of scattered rain had fallen about her in light mists. She huddled and endured each downpour, probably looking every bit irrational, her attention fixed on the lake's pewter surface and the flint-colored cityscape reflected across the water.

Seven hours of watching. Of avoiding glimpses of the lakeside cafes and the happy people inside. The bitter outdoors was a more likely friend. Also isolated and hiding secrets…

She willed a hard and deep breath and welcomed the chilled sting in her lungs, the pain another apt confirmation of what went on inside. But her fingers hurt from the cold, and she squeezed her hands into fists on her lap. Anything to stop the tears and reminders of a fast-approaching nightfall. She'd need to leave. Even if she didn't want to. Her coat was too thin to spare her from the evening's harsher attack.

Pure instinct brought her to standing. If she couldn't stay here. If she couldn't go home. There was somewhere else she could be. Somewhere to maybe ease the impossibly heavy feeling in her heart. All she needed to do was dig through her satchel for a once-discarded Post-it note.

Pretty soon, her fingers clipped a sharp edge of paper as though some subconscious part of her brain maintained a secret log on the note's location. One easy tug and the paper sat between her fingers, and Luke's address stared up at her.

What did she have to lose in seeing him again? She'd already lost everything that mattered. Just a twenty-minute stroll, and she'd be at his house. If he'd left the office on time, she wouldn't have to be alone.

Maybe the guilt from that first time wouldn't haunt her again. Even if it did, guilt from pleasure trumped grief from tragedies past. So, to hell with dealing with her mess. To hell with promises to never sleep with him again. And to hell with her fear of forgetting Elsie.

Clearly, that pain wasn't going anywhere. Luke made for a decent distraction. All Agathe had to do, was put one foot in front of the other and start walking.

# Chapter Seventeen

Luke froze at the sight of Agathe standing on his doorstep, his grip on the door so tight, a dull pain radiated through his fingers. Her clothes were drenched, and her shoulders rose and fell with sharp, panted breaths that left puffs of cloudy vapor around her.

"Agathe." He whispered her name and stepped aside. Her tangible neediness stretched across the threshold and wrapped his heart in a tangle of barbed panic. "Come in. You're cold."

Her focus dropped to his chest, and she swallowed. "I'm not looking for you to be nice to me."

Of course not. *Had she ever?*

Her attention met his again, a little more stoic though still very much wide-eyed. The wobble of her jaw through her chattering teeth only added to the sense of poorly concealed fragility. When she'd run from his office earlier, he'd entertained the idea of maybe never seeing her again, not once predicting she'd turn up to his door looking cold and pale.

He reached out and pulled her in, her wet clothes quick to shed droplets on his wood floors. "Wait here a second."

He turned and bolted for the bathroom, ripping a thick towel off the heated rack and throwing it over his shoulder before returning to her shivering side. He pried her arms from around her waist, her gaze darting around, as he pulled her bag off her shoulder and dropped it with a thud to the floor. Next, he shucked off her useless blazer, which revealed her black wool sweater sodden underneath.

"What happened?" His brow grew tight. *Had she come here just to tell him she was leaving?*

Despite his question, she merely stood there, her lashes fluttering, allowing him to undress her. His warmer fingers caught the hem of her sweater, the skin at her waist cold. She flinched at his touch as though she only now fully registered what he did. He'd planned to wrangle her sweater off to make room for the towel, but her focus latched on him, and he lost all will to move.

Gazes locked in a prolonged silence. He could have sworn she held her breath the entire time and that a trace of color returned to her cheek. Her reaction made him ache to pull her closer. It hinted that maybe she wanted the same, too. The next beat confirmed his suspicions, her eyelids drifting shut while she leaned in and rested her head on his chest.

He did nothing but hold her there for the longest time, savoring the rise and fall of her slowed breaths through her back. Not even the cold dampness of her clothes bothered him. The only thing that mattered was this simple exchange. That Agathe let him in.

He could hold her like this forever, or at least until the chill from her body eased, and she let him get her something warmer to wear. She seemed so small and not her usual formidable self. While holding her made his heart quicken and his mouth dry.

But the little spell between them broke with the stiffening of her muscles. She reeled back and out of his hold, her expression hard, like maybe she'd caught herself enjoying the tender moment a little too much. "Just hand me the towel. I can do this myself."

He frowned and dared to step forward, reclaiming the ground she'd put between them. "Why are you here?"

Despite his desire to strongarm her into accepting his help, he gave her the towel and honored her desire for space.

Still, even as she shivered before him, her stare drilled into him. "You told me the next time would be at your house."

Her narrowed pupils pleaded with him to catch on fast.

*No way.* His shoulders slumped. *She had to be joking.*

"Can we talk about this first?"

She shook her head and pushed past him. Deeper into his house. "No talking. No niceties. No explanations." She gazed around the spacious interior to the numerous original, abstract paintings on his white walls, mouth ever so slightly agape. "Cool place. Let's get started."

She tugged off her sweater, one sleeve at a time, the groan she released directed at the wet fabric clinging to her skin.

He stepped forward. "Here, let me help."

But she sent a fiery glare over her shoulder and shook her head, her wet waves snapping about her face. So, he stayed put.

The sweater eventually gave up and hit the ground with a splat. She dabbed the towel at her skin and then kicked off her brown ankle boots, each one landing with a loud *thunk thunk.*

The image of her stripping brought a lump to his throat, and despite the tingling awareness rushing through his veins, he spoke again. "We can't do this."

The inferno in her glare said otherwise, and his surging hormones agreed, even though her heightened emotional state meant he almost certainly couldn't follow through.

"You want to help me?" She stalked toward him, her hand tugging at the towel draped over her shoulder—slowly, deliberately, pulling it away—before the bit of cloth hit the floor. "Still wanna play the good guy?" She dipped her chin and upturned a smoldering stare at him. "Then be a good guy and fuck me."

The air stilled, and everything within him paused. His breath included. Her brash command tilted his world, condescending and somehow still seductive.

"Your ambush here isn't exactly fair."

She gave an unconvincing shrug. "This isn't about being fair. This is about getting what we want."

His attention danced over the slight curl of her lip, past her delicate cheekbones, and up to her dark-chocolate eyes. His stirring nerve endings begged him to take her right now, but another voice inside him said that would be too easy. That he needed the reasons behind her searing demands, first.

So, he reached out and stroked her cheek, unable to resist touching her beautiful skin, so many shades darker than his own. "You're upset, and you've got more fairness in you than you let on. I'm not taking advantage of you."

She jerked her head to one side, moving from his touch. "You infer qualities that I don't have."

Her fingers wrapped around his wrist, and she slid his palm over the gentle curve of her hip, one brow raised in a wicked dare, drowning his concerns in a sea of desire.

"Why are you suddenly so desperate to jump my bones?" The question came out rough and croaky, and he hated having to question this at all. Having to fight his need to look after her, to warm her, his entire body screaming a contradiction for him to just shut up and do as demanded.

She lifted her lips higher and gripped his hand, sliding his palm up until his fingertips grazed the underside of her bra-covered breast.

*She wants to kill me with longing.*

"Do I need a reason?" Her eyes glinted. "Have you looked in a mirror lately?"

Though her compliment made his heart beat harder, he knew enough to recognize the diversion and locked his arm, preventing her from moving his hand any higher.

He needed a clear mind and the truth. *Now.* Before he did something they'd both regret....

"This won't happen unless you tell me what's wrong."

She lifted onto her toes and hummed, the low rumble emanating from deep within her long and graceful throat, her skin there glistening in its semi-damp state. Her hum turned to a low purring moan, and she darted out her tongue, indulging in a slow and seductive lick of his lips.

His length grew within his pants, a harsh reminder that she had the upper hand here.

"You see?" She leaned back and pinned him with an evil, all-knowing grin. "We both agree. This will work just fine."

She turned and sauntered away, certain that his base desire would win. The distance should have given him relief, but the scent of flowers, woman, and rain hit him straight between the eyes, proving her right.

Averting his gaze was too hard a task, especially now that she leaned back against his living room wall, her dainty foot propped against the white plaster, her hand lifted as she ran a finger down the dip between her breasts.

"You can join me now, Mr. Tindall." Her position gave him a full view of her scarlet bra, the shred of sheer lace revealing her pebbled nipples underneath and teasing him further. And heaven help him, her sinful smirk filled him with limitless promises of what was to come. "Or, I can start without you?"

His cock stiffened, and a hot sensation zipped up his spine. *Damn her.* Even though he locked his legs in place, she turned each of his breaths hollower than the last.

With every passing moment, she upped the stakes, unzipping her slacks and allowing the black material to pool at her feet. Her actions turned his erection impossibly hard and made him yearn for release. Whatever she did next risked eviscerating his one and only bargaining chip. Withholding sex.

He curled his hands into firm fists at his sides and fought for restraint. If he caved, he'd lose the end game, and she'd never reveal a damn thing after that.

Her fingers skimmed the front clasp of her bra, and he charged forward. "Don't."

He grabbed her wrists, but her knowing smile curved higher still. "Mr. Tindall?"

He bent and collected the towel from the floor, shoving it into her non-bra-clasping hand. "Cover yourself, Agathe."

How dare she resort to blatant manipulation.

Now, she hugged the towel to her chest, and her shoulders slumped forward, eyes pooling in a look of shock. "I need this. Please don't make me beg."

No matter how tempting the idea, he didn't want her under these conditions, especially not when her softened plea cooled his temper and arousal.

His heart shifted at her blinking up at him, all mocking gone from her eyes and replaced with open vulnerability. "Just do this. Don't ask any questions. And…I'll explain later. Okay?"

She hooked a hand to the gray, fleecy material of his waistband and pulled him nearer. He groaned at the extra closeness, but the gentle kiss she brushed over his lips truly undid him. Though he fought to step away, her palpable need held him in place.

Breaking the kiss, he kept his forehead on hers. "Agathe. Talk. Please."

Her cold, spindly fingers cupped his face, reminding him once again she'd come here out of despair. That reminder squeezed his chest in a seeping sort of pain, his eyes closing at the sound of her whispered plea. "Fuck me first. And maybe then."

He pulled back and searched her gaze, wanting this. Desperately. Maddeningly. Label him a dirty bastard, but he loved the idea of doing her until they were both shaking and senseless. But just as before, that wouldn't be enough. And he and Agathe had opposite goals.

She didn't want him to make love to her. Not tenderly, not with any real affection. While even that fell short of what he wanted most. His ultimate prize. *Her.*

She'd walked here, through wind and rain, looking for a cathartic experience. He'd do everything he could to give her just that. To give himself a little something, too. Bond her closer. Draw out her truth. He had to get this right so he stood a chance of learning more and finally making her his.

"No maybes." He pressed his hand to her lower back, pulling her in. "Promise me."

As if she read the fine print in his demand, a tremble entered her breath. He'd do as she wished, but only in exchange for the truth.

Though her brown stare moved about his face, she gave a hurried nod. "I will. I promise."

He pressed his lips to hers, sealing the deal, only to release her long enough to get this strange deal started. "Okay, then tell me what you want."

# Chapter Eighteen

Agathe swallowed at the muscles bunching in her throat while her heart drummed a wild and mysterious beat. Fear or fearlessness? She couldn't decide, but she'd spent months running from Luke, only to run *to* him tonight. And now, as she pondered his question about what she wanted, her soul whispered for her to let go of every boundary and rule. To capture this chance and allow herself a true moment of freedom.

"I want to lose myself."

Though her brazen response had her clamping her jaw shut, his focus stayed fixed, stern, and silent.

*Had she said the wrong thing?* Despite all appearances, her pulse thundered through her earlier lewd show. Maybe she'd made a fool of herself. Maybe she was best to leave. Only, now he offered a stiff nod as if awaking from a daze.

"Stay here. I'll be right back."

Her focus darted around the room, and he jogged away, leaving cold loneliness to envelop her. Farther ahead, a light clicked on in the same room he'd disappeared to earlier when retrieving her towel. Gleaming white tiles peeked through an open door revealing a bathroom, soft rustling sounds breaking across the mostly quiet space.

The light clicked off, and he stepped back into view. Her tummy fluttered, and she hugged her arms around her bare waist in defense against the room's chill and her self-consciousness at being near-naked.

He bounded back and outstretched a hand. "Hold this."

Instinct had her reaching out, the square foil packet of a wrapped condom soon resting in her open palm. Her breath hitched at how excruciatingly real her deal with him got, and still, faint hope kept her from running.

His lips tugged wider as though he noticed her concern. "I'm going to need my hands. You won't."

Her interest tweaked at his words, and the lump in her throat gave way to an excited tingle, one that washed over her body and eviscerated the chill from her misadventure in the cold. His hand rose to encase hers, closing her fingers around the small packet, while his other hand skimmed up her opposite arm, lighting an explosion of sensations all the way up to her collarbone.

Those long, strong fingers. They unleashed a sweet dance of feather-light touch, his thumb stroking the front of her throat while she tilted her head back, and so submissively let him.

She meant to smile at that, at her actually letting go. Only, his hungry mouth crashed over hers, possessing and melting her into his embrace.

*Sweet peaches, this man would ruin her.* But she wanted more. Wanted everything he might give.

His rock-hard erection prodded her belly, reminding her of what she wanted most, both reward and punishment for her seducing him. But she insisted on focusing on the reward. That his hard length could spur her on. That, for once in her life, she held some command over a man that any woman would crawl over broken glass to be with.

And right now, she wanted him just as exposed as her.

So she reached down and balled the hem of his hooded sweatshirt, only for him to grab her wrists and stop her hurried attempt to undress him. "You wanted to lose yourself. So let go and let me do this."

His fierce stare held. A challenge. A dare. A litany of questions. Could she really do this? Could she really surrender to somebody else? To *him*?

But he was right. She *had* asked for this, and now he stood before her, willing to provide. Only now, her unruly pulse prompted a need to slip into old habits.

*Whoa…Ease up. Just enjoy.*

A sharp breath slipped into her lungs, and she gave a shaky nod, vowing not to ruin this. The tension around his eyes relaxed, and he stepped back, removing his sweatshirt and then tugging away the rest of his clothes. Before long, he stood there fully naked and beautiful. All broad male and frighteningly powerful.

His manhood stood thick and proud, promising escape. The kind she'd literally run here to claim. Meanwhile, her heart fluttered at his slow, confident steps closer, that easy prowl lighting her desire to melt into a puddle at his feet.

His next touches started at her neck, where hot breath and light kisses landed on her skin, only to travel lower. Over the crest of her shoulder. Lower still, to the soft flesh just above her breast.

A hiss of breath pushed past her lips, and her limbs turned suddenly weak. Soon, he knelt before her, a toughened warrior bowed at a temple's steps, his brawny hands cradling the sides of her ribcage, a man paying homage to some goddess far beyond Agathe's actual worth.

"You're perfection." His large hands engulfed her bra, cupping and lifting her.

The heat from his touch seeped deep into her bones, and she squeezed her eyes shut and pretended that she deserved his praise. That she deserved to feel so unabashedly sensual and alive.

His lips rose to the slight swell of flesh just above her bra, where he landed yet more kisses before his tongue swept her skin, forcing her head back to the wall with a groan.

Her reaction only encouraged him, his hard breaths adding coolness to his slightly damp trail of kisses on her chest, his hand quick to pop the clasp of her bra. His hold claimed her freed breasts, his thumbs a rough and scintillating contrast to her sensitive nipples, even more so now that his soft lips worshiped the space of her lower belly.

Everything about him. Everything about this moment. Made her feel like a small bird trapped within a lion's paw, blissfully unaware or unperturbed of the risks that lay ahead.

*Screw risk and screw overthinking. She felt damn good right now, and that's all that mattered.*

She sighed again and allowed the sexual pressure within her to rise, her breath exhaling on a needy whimper. He tugged away at her underwear, and the light fabric rasped over her hips. Once again, his earlier comment filled her mind, the one about perfection.

"Can I taste you?"

She startled at the request and snapped her attention down to his brilliant green gaze staring up at her. She swallowed hard and nodded, willing herself to hold strong, to just enjoy. His tender kiss hit her upper thigh—less a tease, more a promise—then he hooked her left leg over his shoulder and proceeded to brand her delicate flesh.

His tongue at her sensitive folds sentenced her to blind arousal, obliterating the pain that had brought her here, to begin with. A man who was unapologetically masculine and strong. His lips at her bud drew her next gasp. Though her legs buckled, he merely caught her and pinned her harder to the wall.

Heart swelling, she surrendered to his touch, a hushed moan escaping while steady, wet heat flowed from her core. And still, his hot mouth took her in until her breaths heaved and her muscles tingled. Her climax drew so near and promised sweet oblivion.

"Patience." He pulled back, his fingers taking over where his mouth had been. Slower. More maddening in pace. She groaned her protest and bucked against him, searching for that euphoric dive so cruelly pried away.

"We have a deal. I'm going to keep it"—he slid her leg from his shoulder and rose, quick to kiss the corner of her jawline, as he whispered low toward her ear—"first, you'll need to turn around. I want to be inside you when you come."

Arousal surged and forced her next sigh, despite the fact he barely touched her. This man, all class and control in the office, *goddammit*, when he got her alone, he morphed to pure sex in human form.

The scent of citrus and burgeoning sex filled her senses, and she did as asked, turning until nothing but the cream-colored wall filled her vision. The pressure of his hand spanned her shoulder blades, tilting her forward until her torso met with the cold plaster.

Her ass jutted out and was completely exposed, she couldn't see what was happening behind her, but the crinkle of the condom wrapper gave a strong clue. Even as heat surged between her legs, she sucked in a panicked breath.

She'd never let anyone take her like this, not against a wall and with so many lights on. She'd always been a missionary position girl, romantic to the core, with a tendency toward being shy. But that was then. This was *now*. And despite who she'd once been, or maybe because of it, she wanted this. Wanted this as if she'd planned these exact conditions all on her own.

*Or maybe this man already knows me too well....*

Thoughts like that risked her backing out, so she focused on each new and exciting sensation. Of him leaning over her, hands gliding down each of her arms until his fingers interlaced with hers at the wall, his gentle command for her to hold still and embrace his close contact. The head of his cock nudged at her entrance, and he shifted his left hand to her hip, steadying her, entering her in one long, smooth stroke.

A tight moan surged up her throat, bringing with it a desperate plea. "More. Please."

She pressed into him, demanding just that. His movement. Her release. Her head bent forward to embrace the wall's cold kiss at the edge of her hairline.

"Soon." His taut whisper matched the grip of his hand.

Even his restraint drew a reaction, her prickling nerves unfurling a dance of tingles up her spine and into her entire body. So she groaned and clenched around him, the penalty for what he did to her. Except, his surging length only stretched, filled, and punished her back.

"Goddammit, Agathe." He hissed and buckled against her, like he, too, burned with frustration. "Let me do this."

His hand snaked around her, and he held her still, his fingers soon finding the center of her arousal while he unleashed a series of harsh thrusts. One after another, her rough breaths burst from her lungs, making it impossible for her to keep up with him, to hold back the climax rolling through her like a violent avalanche. He pounded harder. Relentless. A hint that he sensed her imminent peak and worked to offer exactly what she needed.

And just like that, her body shook, and her worries capsized. Now, all that surfaced was the simmering awareness of wanting and getting, her lack of thought a broken needle on a compass she'd never wanted to follow anyway. All she had was the feeling of his hands and his thrusts, those unforgiving caresses so exquisite she cried out her release.

The feeling of being lost and adrift wasn't so bad, after all. Beautiful nothingness stretched out far before her, and she shuttered her eyes to welcome that weightless pleasure. The pure freedom only Luke delivered.

Oh, and she wanted to thank him, so she screamed out his name, embraced his next hard buck, and handed over more control. No other man had ever had this effect on her. Even his kisses on her shoulder offered a sense of tender calm amidst this storm. As did his torn whisper of her name, as he swelled and released within her.

All too quickly, a sliver of cold infiltrated the warmth he offered. The moment over. None of this real. She couldn't truly have him.

Or *this*.

Her heart clenched. Fierce. Distraught. And a sob ricocheted throughout her chest, surfacing as a pained cry.

Her? Cry? *Never.* But she buried her face into her bent arm at the wall, her ribcage jolting under an attack of sobs she couldn't hold back. He was most definitely someone worth keeping, but *she* wasn't.

She never cried, but she sure did now. Huge, fat, undeniable tears. And one name played on her mind.

*Elsie. Always Elsie.*

The more that name circled her thoughts, the more her inner world crumbled.

Luke withdrew and spun her around. She dizzied before her gaze locked on his.

He'd fulfilled his end of the bargain, and now she'd have to honor her share. Even if her heart cracked at the agony of what would come next. The shame. The heartache. Every exhausting detail brought her to the point of encroaching on her client's, Luke's, personal space and begging him to fuck her. All so she could delay sharing her God-awful story. One she hadn't touched in four years.

As much as she sought to hide, he cupped her cheeks and forced her to look at him, his gaze doing a panicked dance about her face. "Please. Just tell me."

For all the pain that overran her now, he might as well have been twisting a dull knife into her heart. All that remained was to rip out the blade.

"I…" She worked past a sob, allowing her proverbial blood to flow.

*God. She couldn't breathe.*

"I have a daughter. Her name is Elsie."

# Chapter Nineteen

Agathe pressed her hand over her diaphragm and struggled to breathe, the sex-induced flush on Luke's cheeks draining to sheet white. His gaze swept over her bare tummy as if searching for evidence of her past motherhood, but she'd been young, and her body quick to bounce back almost completely. Aside from a couple of faded stretch marks on her breasts, there was no way to know she'd ever carried a child. Though in many ways, she wished Elsie had left behind more scars.

She waited for him to make the next move. His silence was unnerving, though she crossed her arms over her chest, fearful he'd look there next. She'd endured many deep disappointments in life, but if this man shunned her over Elsie, much less the minor imperfections to her body from carrying her child, she'd quit Tiluma tomorrow and never speak to him again.

"You have a daughter." His hollow tone echoed a numb repetition of what she'd already said.

He turned his muscular back to her, blowing a quick puff of air past his lips and scruffing his dark waves with one hand, quick to collect his dove-gray sweatpants from the floor.

Her tummy clenched at his sudden absence, his current vague silence and non-reaction torturing her more than angry words could.

"We really need that talk." When he turned back to her, still hitching up his pants, the deep creases on his forehead denoted something somber. "Sit."

He reached for a powder-blue blanket draped over an armchair and then handed it to her. Though she accepted the offering and tugged the blanket onto her shoulders, she kept her head bowed and said nothing on her way to the sand-colored leather couch. An empty pause dragged out as she waited for him to join her, hinting that maybe he now saw the logic in the limits she'd set for this relationship.

He'd stop expecting more from her than just sex. He'd see she was too much work. Too fragile. Maybe she should have had this conversation sooner.

As though he wanted to give her space or wanted to put some symbolic distance between them, he took a seat on the smaller couch to her left. Either way, he sat with his knees spread, elbows leaned forward, and his undivided attention burrowed her way. "Talk."

Her gaze flittered away, eventually settling on the thick, knitted blanket pooled in her lap. "I don't know how to start."

"You have a daughter. Her name is Elsie." That name had her lifting focus to his brows pressed in a firm line. "Where is she now?"

Her stomach pitched, and she hugged the blanket tighter to her chest. The very last thing she cared to think about was where Elsie lay now.

"You remember how I said my ex-husband and I were an odd match?" She pressed her eyes closed and shook her head, barely able to face this topic, much less look at Luke's dire frown as she did so. "We met at university toward the end of my degree. Henry was a business lecturer, and I studied art therapy. He was fifteen years my senior and his work kept him busy. Even though we hardly ever saw each other and had no major permanent plans, we dated on and off for over a year."

She opened her eyes and shrugged. "I was young. He seemed so worldly and intelligent. You get the drift…."

Not wanting to see the disappointment in Luke's eyes, she peered down and offered more of her story. "I was a year out of university and working a job I loved when I fell pregnant. Completely unplanned, but we were forced to rethink the nature of our relationship."

Though a sick feeling churned in her belly, she set her attention back to Luke, his eyes wider than before. "So, you had a shotgun wedding?"

His satiric choice of words. His open look of disbelief. His response signaled curiosity over judgment, and the frost around her heart thawed enough for a small laugh to slip through. "Of course, if I had my time again, I'd do things differently, but yes. Henry was from a well-known publishing dynasty and on the verge of taking over from his father. He had a reputation to uphold and endless rivals to pacify. They would have taken our story and torn us to shreds on every major platform. He'd no longer pass as a reliable and responsible business-man, and as a young woman of color, the public commentary would be extra nasty toward me. Gold digger. Jokes about me winning the lottery…He meant well. We both did."

Luke held a long pause, his jaw straining through a scowl. "You don't mean Henry Roth from Paper Planes Publishing?"

She nodded.

He slumped back with a sigh and scrubbed a hand over his face. "Shit."

A cold sensation washed over her. "You know him?"

"We've met a few times." He raised one shoulder, a not-so-casual shrug. "Tiluma advertises through Paper Planes all the time."

"Oh, shit." She peered away, her words mirroring his, a guilty heat consuming her face. "I'm sorry."

"Don't be. Unless you're about to tell me Henry did something heinous? In which case, I might have to hurt him back…." His stare pinned her, genuinely requesting an answer.

Her mouth wavered from speechlessness since she'd never once considered this man might be protective of her. So, all she mustered was a hurried shake of her head.

He settled back, the tight draw of his shoulders releasing. "Your past won't affect how I deal with him in the future."

She nodded to herself and vowed to move on, to focus less on his undeserved concern over her and more on completing this transaction of sex for words. "Henry was abroad when Elsie was born. He worked overseas a lot by that point, but he flew back as soon as he could. The Roths saw to it that I had all the professional help I needed, but after a month of nannies and midwives prying and intervening, I dismissed everyone."

Luke's overly focused expression turned lax, so she set about helping him understand. "You spend the years before being a parent carving out your individual identity, and then suddenly, this tiny person enters your life, and everything you once knew burns down. It's sobering. Scary. Your entire future revolves around the whims of an unwieldy, loud, and helpless child, but they're utterly vulnerable, the most vulnerable they'll ever be, and they need you. So, what do you do? You vow to love them as much as you possibly can. To the very last heartbeat, but—" Her voice caught, and she paused to rein in her pain. "Yours, not theirs. And you never go back to who you were before. No matter what happens next. And you never, ever expect to see a day when they're not with you anymore."

Raising Elsie had been exhausting, but even now, having regained her nights of unbroken sleep and more time to herself than she knew what to do with, she'd give anything just to return to her days with her little girl.

"Elsie was by no means an easy baby. Henry was gone much of the time, and I dealt with every tantrum, tear, tooth, and cold on my own" —she paused to clear the lump swelling in her throat—"but she gave the best hugs and never wanted anything more than to be with me. She was my entire universe, and I was hers. I lived for the squeals of laughter and her sleepy face at night, those droopy eyelids and pouted lips, her sandy-blonde curls wrapped around my fingers as she slept. To the outside world, I was just a mum, but I'd never worked harder, and no other job was ever more important or fulfilling as that one."

Luke shuffled forward again, his expression soft but eyes narrowed. "Agathe. Tell me what happened to Elsie."

She swallowed and looked down at her hands, lungs burning against her already tight ribcage. The mere fact he asked meant he knew this story didn't end well.

"Elsie was two. I was twenty-three." She sucked in a breath, one that hurt as it went down. "We were enjoying the sunshine and searching for rainbows after a burst of heavy rain, out on a quiet back street in South Yarra, when I took out my phone, ready to take some photos of her, and…." She blinked, and new tears spilled down her cheek. "I heard the sound every parent dreads."

She peered up at Luke's stooped posture and his hands clasped together so tight white pressure points formed on his knuckles. Meanwhile, her jaw trembled with the effort of merely forming her confession. "One minute, my baby was picking dandelions on the nature strip, just blowing fluff about and having a good time; the next, she's crying out, *'Mummy!'* and I lift my head in time to see the quick flash of a white delivery van hydroplaning on the wet road toward her. It jumped the curb, but I couldn't get to her. I saw…I saw my baby go under."

She doubled over, and a loud wail tore through her chest. She couldn't go on. Not with this story. Not with the memory of that sickening thud. The sound of her baby's shrieking cry. How, seconds later, Elsie lay in her arms, limp and drenched in blood.

Rustling sounds pierced her despair, and strong arms swept her up. Luke pulled her into him. The pressure from his embrace felt almost painful, but that pain was enough to drown out some of her darker thoughts.

"My baby cried in my arms." A violent shiver rocked through her body, one that seemed to emanate from her bones, her voice cutting loose with another soul-wrenching sob. "She cried, *Mummy, ouch.* Just one long, loud cry. All she wanted was for me to fix the pain, but I was completely useless. I couldn't do anything. I couldn't fix anything. I hadn't even been looking when that van first started to spin out of control."

Oh, the guilt. The guilt consumed her every single time she remembered. She pressed the heel of her hand to her chest and rubbed hard, trying but failing to find some kind of comfort.

Her heartache simply wouldn't ease. In all honesty, it never truly had. So, she rocked back and forth, struggling against Luke's hold as he kissed the top of her head. "By the time the ambulance came for her,

her lips had turned deep blue. The wait mustn't have been more than a few minutes, but watching her slowly slip away made it seem like hours. Then came the pandemonium of the ER, followed by five slow fucking hours waiting for my baby to die."

She scrunched her face, welcoming the spill of more tears. "I watched her die, Luke, all while wanting time to hurry so she'd no longer hurt. All while wanting to hear one more laugh or feel one more squeeze of her tiny fingers around mine. And all I'm left with now are photos, a few personal items, and the memory of her laid out on that hospital bed." She peered up at him but registered little beyond the deluge of water spilling from her eyes.

"So, you want to know where Elsie is?" The tension in her throat made controlling her pitchy and desperate tone impossible. "She's in the ground. She's in the ground. And I couldn't stop it."

# Chapter Twenty

Luke waited for the heaving in Agathe's shoulders to subside, her face swollen and marked from more tears than he'd witnessed from anyone in a long time. Not since the war zones. Not since the aftermath of rebel bombings. Not since fathers digging graves and mothers crying over the limp bodies of their babies. He'd seen it all. The consequences of war were etched on his brain. But even those scenes differed from this. They didn't involve someone he quickly fell in love with.

His heart twisted, and his soul ached for her. *Holy shit!* Of course, she'd avoided him. Of course, she'd flipped out when Claire had fallen over. He couldn't erase her devastation. Couldn't fix the agony she had relived. The best he could do was offer his support and be with her through her pain. A pain she'd be certain to carry forever.

She sagged back onto the couch, and he released her from his hold, a cold stillness washing over her face. "So now you know. Elsie is dead, but she wasn't supposed to die, and I wasn't supposed to outlive her. And today… today is the anniversary of her death."

A hard breath pushed through him, his emotional reserves running near empty. *How much more tragic could her story get?*

"That explains a lot." He wrapped his hand around hers and squeezed. "Agathe, there's nothing I can say except that I'm sorry."

She nodded, slow and steady. "At least you're not trying to find some sort of silver lining. There is none. Not for this. Not even when Henry gifted me the house at the end of our sham marriage. Certainly not when the van driver killed himself out of sheer guilt. That happened just prior to his court date for culpable driving charges. And the note he left..." She paused, lip trembling as she lifted her gaze to him, like she couldn't bring herself to go into further detail, her eyes red-rimmed and her cheeks sunken. A woman spent from grief. "I've tried to find that silver lining. I've tried everything. But nothing makes it better. *Nothing*."

New tears welled in her eyes, adding weight to his heartbeat. He wanted to help, but, as she'd said, there was no helping this. All he could do was hope his presence alone would make some difference.

So, he pressed her open palm to his lips, the scent of sunflowers floating off her delicate wrist like dawn after a gloomy night, and kept his voice low as he spoke again. "Sometimes it hurts more to try to fix the unfixable."

She peered down at her hand cradled in his, her thick eyelashes fluttering, while she nodded in seeming understanding, or maybe, appreciation. "Months after Elsie died and Henry left, people invited me to socialize. My old job heard about what had happened, and they invited me to return as an art therapist at the children's hospital. I even had offers to date again."

She huffed out an incredulous laugh, and her face tilted up to him in a look of apology, though for what, he didn't know. Maybe she figured he didn't appreciate so much honesty?

But hearing her story was everything he'd wanted all along.

"It was as if I was expected to go on like becoming Elsie's mother never happened. Like I was supposed to return to all the things I'd let go of before she came along. To the mundanities of being social, to falling in love, to making other people's children happy and watching them flourish and grow like mine never would." She shook her head, and her chest heaved with a wayward sob. "I couldn't do it."

That sob heralded her renewed rocking, the tension around her mouth signaling an attempt to suppress more wild emotion, all while saying something more. Something like, *I still can't do it. I still can't move on.*

A bitter taste coated his tongue, and he swallowed back the swell of burning bile. What she'd said about her inability to fall in love. Did that still apply? Had that admission been meant specifically for him?

*How can I ever dare to compete with the memory of a dead child?*

He rubbed a thumb over the back of her hand, bringing her focus back to him. Back to helping her get this story out. Because right now, helping her was more important than what he wanted. God knew she'd probably sat in her misery for years, holding onto her feelings until they eroded every last scrap of joy.

"Tell me what you did next." His words came in an unexpectedly husky tone, and the strain around her eyes dropped like she sensed his regard for her rules on life.

And even then, he was far from pleased, more like crestfallen on her behalf and hopeless on his own.

"Despite many people's advice, I kept the house. I couldn't imagine a new family moving in. I couldn't let go. Elsie's sad ending was a brief part of our joyful years together." She gave a rueful smile, head shaking almost sheepishly. "For a long time, I lived in a sort of mental darkness and refused to leave the house. Refused to even eat most days. And when the van driver hung himself, I only sank deeper. So many thought my life would improve because of his death, but all I saw was another life ruined, that I wasn't the only one scarred with guilt. I never wanted anyone else to die. Not Elsie. Not even him."

"You felt guilty?" Despite the tragedy regarding the driver, his thoughts latched onto her self-confession. "Don't tell me you think you could have prevented her death?"

Puffy bags rimmed her eyes along with the purple bruises visible under her skin. Even though she maintained the conversation, she looked exhausted. "I should have protected Elsie. I should have never let her get ahead of me. Should have never reached for my phone. No matter how many times we'd done that walk, I should never have assumed she'd be safe enough."

He shook his head, steeling his tone for what he had to say next. "No.

What happened to Elsie could have happened a million other ways. Heck, when I was in primary school, a speeding car veered off the road and smashed through our classroom wall, right over where a bunch of us would have been sitting had it not been the school holidays. Elsie might still be here if the road hadn't been wet or if that deliveryman had been in less of a hurry. But you're not a superhero, Agathe, and an extra split second to intervene might have only meant you went under that van right along with her. No amount of vigilance or feeling bad will mean you'll outrun, control, or predict every misfortune. I've seen enough go wrong to know. No one gets it right one hundred percent of the time."

Her jaw slackened, and her brows pressed together. She held a long pause before speaking again. "What do you mean? What have you 'seen?'"

He patted her hand, wanting to keep the focus on her. "That's a story for later, but what I want to know is how you eventually got yourself out of that house and working again?"

She kept her attention on him for a long moment as if trying to read his mind in the wake of her evaded question, or perhaps because she still very much lived in that house, only she maintained a convincing impression of a mostly functional person.

"I had no choice." She shrugged, her attention skittering away, her voice soft and cautious. "Bills needed to be paid, and my health suffered from not getting out enough. Not eating. One day, I woke to realize Elsie would have wanted me to find a way to go on. And that's still the only thing that keeps me going."

She peered down and interlaced her fingers through his, the action sending immediate comfort to the rest of his body. "So, I picked a job I thought I could be good at, one that gave me distraction and purpose, something competitive and challenging. Something that kept me far away from children and reminders of Elsie."

"Until today." His brain felt overly full in his head, the same date of Elsie's death, and then how Claire's fall would have brought Agathe face-to-face with her fears.

There'd been blood and tears and a child who needed help. He couldn't imagine the torment that moment dredged for her.

But she released a sharp laugh before a sorrowful smile ruled her lips. "Yeah. Until today."

"About today"—he gave her hand another gentle squeeze and wore a sympathetic smile on his face—"for what it's worth, you were amazing with Claire. Even as her dad carried her away, she kept looking back at you with awe in her eyes."

Agathe's gaze held still on his, her pupils widening while her ribcage jerked, and the occasional lingering sob broke through. He'd meant well, but his compliment seemed to overwhelm her and perhaps even highlighted what she lacked in her life. Someone to care for. Someone to love. Someone like Elsie.

*Someone not him.*

And still, he reminded himself that this wasn't about *him*. That reminder left him feeling completely delusional for ever even entertaining the thought he had a chance.

"You've got that look again. The same one you had when you noticed everyone watching today. Like you're..." He pressed his jaw shut, unsure if his next words would make things worse. "Like you're falling apart on the inside."

She released another sardonic laugh, and unexpected light seemed back in her eyes. "You just described how I feel ninety percent of the time. Only, I usually do a better job of hiding it."

He reached up and cupped his spare hand to her cheek, only for her entire body to go taut.

"While I'm on the topic of observations..." Not wanting to make her uncomfortable, he took his hand away. Her reaction confirmed his long-held theory about her. "You also have problems accepting acts of warmth."

"Thanks for pointing that out." She gave a tight laugh but hooked a hand around the arm he'd dropped away from her. An act of apologetic affection. "You really know how to make a person feel better."

He offered a genuine laugh now, thankful for these moments of light amongst the dark. "You know that's exactly what I'm trying to do though, right?... Make you feel better....even if my approach is sometimes a bit too pushy."

She looked down and nodded as she smiled. "Yeah, I know you

mean well, but I've grown comfortable in my reclusion. So, when someone like you comes along, my issues seem more pronounced. You make it hard for me to push you away." Though she gave another constricted laugh, her gaze reconnected with him, and her grip on his hand tightened. "While not fully understanding what you're asking of me. But you know now. And there are times when I'm with you, and I feel so trapped."

Never wanting to make her feel that way, his stomach lurched, and instinct had him reaching to stroke a thumb over her cheek, his anguish softening when she nuzzled into his touch. "I'm sorry."

Maybe he'd been wrong to pursue her. Maybe he was best to step away. But then, she threw enough signs to hint that she did, in fact, crave his presence.

"More surprisingly, there are times like tonight. Like before…" Her cheeks flushed, and she pointed to the wall where he'd fucked her to literal tears. "When I feel completely free."

His entire body stilled, and his heart swelled, seeming to fill whatever space remained in his chest. Her blatant confirmation was so unexpected, even if he'd already sensed she used sex to run from her pain.

Though he related to her form of escape, he'd come to a point in his life where he wanted more.

So, he drew a slow breath, setting his mind to changing the subject. Regardless of his *wants*, they came a distant second to her general well-being. "Everyone at the office is worried about you. Some of us thought you might never return."

She gave a sigh, her shoulders dropping. "I'll be back tomorrow."

He shook his head and held an unyielding stare. One that hopefully let her know not to argue. "No, you'll be back when you're ready. And you're not ready, Agathe, not by a long mile. I'll call Sue in the morning and make sure she knows everything's covered until you return."

Now, she was the one shaking her head, albeit in a fierce protest from side to side. "Don't you dare tell Sue. I'll be back tomorrow. I need to be. I need to work."

*No, she didn't.*

She just knew no other way of surviving. Work was her crutch, but one that held a great deal of potential to leave her burned out and more broken than ever. She needed to learn another way, though just accepting a well-earned day off would be a first step.

Once again, she looked like a scared deer. This was a woman dealing with the misfortune of losing a child, plus the brutal trauma of watching the whole thing happen. So, recalling how he'd once thought her similar to the soul-shattered warriors he'd served with, the pieces now fit, and he had a far clearer understanding of this woman. Agathe *was* soul-shattered. Scared, too.

But the only person who could set Agathe free was Agathe, and all he could do was provide support while continuing his search for hope.

Like tonight.

Tonight offered hope.

A sign that maybe he wasn't so screwed after all.

"Stay here with me tonight." He paused, a little surprised at his offer, the new shadows in her already dark eyes signaling a fear he so desperately wanted to chase away. That love with him didn't have to hurt. "Just let me hold you. You don't have to be alone."

# Chapter Twenty-One

Agathe hugged a warm paper cup of coffee in her hands, her attention gliding over a decorated shop window within the grand Block Arcade. Once her favorite shopping spot, the high, stained-glass ceilings and intricate mosaic floor alone were worth visiting. This Melbourne icon was a perfect model of Victorian-era design and classic Italian architecture.

For too long, she'd denied herself beauty and leisure, but thanks to Luke's insistence, today's day off had her indulging a pastime she'd neglected since before Elsie's birth.

A light tingling spread throughout her body on this, a completely atypical day, and after an entire night cuddled up to the most heart-stirring man she'd ever met.

She felt gratified. A little content. And the sight of a rich purple silk scarf had her feeling even better.

The scarf popped with silver paisley leaves, and feathery tassels dangled from each end. The material itself looked soft and delicate, and her fingertips itched to reach through the glass and stroke it. Where she'd once lived for flamboyant designs and striking colors like this, her current wardrobe consisted of only dark and neutral hues. Even if she never felt right wearing the scarf, she'd have it all the same, its presence in her wardrobe perhaps enough to boost her mood and confidence.

Fearing the small unfurling of joy within, she clasped her coffee cup harder and hoped for the queasiness in her tummy to subside. *Is this what moving on feels like?*

For the first time in years, she had a taste of life beyond her usual daily drone. Luke reigned over far more than just her body. He controlled her hope, too. A hope she hadn't wanted, much less knew existed.

But he also had a seat at the center of her inner world. The one place Elsie still lived on.

So, her shoulders slumped with her heavy sigh while her thoughts flipped between the scarf and her more terrifying thoughts. Of Luke's skilled handling of yesterday's outburst. His calm. His ability to knock over her biggest obstacle—her belief that no man would accept her past—when so much of her grief survived on the ugliness of her history and the futility of her future.

But he'd *hugged* her through her tears. *Invited* her to stay. *Convinced* her to take a day off.

*What the hell has he done to me?*

She pressed her coffee cup to her lips and took a sip to muffle the small voice in her head reminding her of her months of unused leave. That she could take many more days off if she so wished. Rest a little. Live out her unrealized dreams of seeing the world....

*Shut up, Agathe. Stop it. Right now!*

The dark, bitter taste of coffee hit her tongue again, and she sought refuge in the passing of other rugged-up shoppers. Her sex-fueled ambush of Luke last night landed her with a challenging dilemma, one where she didn't want to think about why she'd agreed to spend the night, much less the ease of their casual chat over breakfast. She'd even complimented him on his just-woke-up face, his deliciously ruffled hair…his sexy-as-hell deep morning laugh.

Yeah, none of that lusty musing belonged to her.

Weirdest of all, today was the easiest day she'd had in years. Like she'd endured an evening of turmoil, only to wake to unfamiliar normalcy, again lighting the fear that Luke had cracked something open within her, with zero chance of her mending the break.

But she rolled her eyes now and told herself to get a grip, to stop overthinking the whole Luke thing. To embrace the distraction before her and find her wallet.

So, she dug around in her small purse, only for a light *ding* to alert her to a message on her phone. She peered deeper into her bag, the mocha-colored silk lining glowing from the screen, which displayed one far-too-heavenly name. *Luke.*

Of course, he'd text just as she planned to forget him.

Still, she pulled out her phone and read the message.

LUKE

It's past time for a proper date. Meet me at Tiny Tokyo's after work?

Though a smile pushed at her lips, she sank back and punched out a hurried reply.

I can't.

Her mouth slid open at her abrupt response. Then again, this was the day off she should have taken yesterday instead of pushing herself to the point of breaking and ending up on his doorstep.

A date? Really? Dates meant talking and intimacy. They meant being *seen*. She'd had enough of that already. How much more did he want? How much more did she *have*?

Deciding he deserved more than a two-word rejection, she typed again.

I'm sorry, is that bad?

Ding.

No. Not at all.

I'm enjoying the day to myself.

That she even explained herself, when she'd always planned on ending things with him eventually....

Her phone dinged with another reply.

> It's fine. I'm happy for you. Really. Just enjoy your day, okay?

Her pulse gathered, and a lump caught in her throat. Why did it mean so much to know he was happy for her, that he even tried to comfort her when she'd just passed up a date with him?

*He was good to me when he could have been a total exploitative asshole, which is what I was prepared for. I was prepared to ditch him. Now I don't know what to do.*

The stupid voice in her head was right, which made her frown at her phone, frown at her preference for indifference over kindness.

Her phone pinged again.

> Tomorrow, then? :)

She jerked her chin back, a spluttering laugh breaking through. While surprise ebbed, her heart strained, and she whispered to herself. "Damn you, Luke. Why are you so annoyingly understanding?"

And with that, a sudden flood of sadness weighed heavy on her. He didn't give up—probably a good thing, being a CEO and all—but his tenacity meant she couldn't keep him at bay forever. Not after last night. Not after he'd refused to take advantage of her. Not after he'd accepted and supported her through a gut-wrenching recount of her last moments with Elsie.

She'd need to turn him down eventually, but for now, she inexplicably worked up the courage to run her fingers over the touch screen. If he could show grit, then so could she. She'd find a middle ground. Something she could live with. Something more like her recent style.

> Fine. Tonight. Your place. Sex. No date. ;)

# Chapter Twenty-Two

The scent of sex and summer flowers lingered in the air, and Luke ran a knuckle down Agathe's upper arm, admiring the warm tone of her skin against his paler complexion. Her head lay across his shoulder, and she smiled up at him, sated in his bed.

"Go on that date with me." His voice was hushed and heavy, and he kissed the top of her hair, a gesture more intimate than he usually enacted, but he needed to indulge in a rare moment of affection.

She groaned and turned to bury her face against his neck. "Why?"

*Because I might be in love with you.*

He couldn't share his true thoughts, so he let out a soft chuckle, deciding not to get too insulted by her protest. "Because I want to get to know you outside of this bed."

She laughed, and her breath brushed his skin. "You've known me in other places too. Your office desk, the living room wall, and then there's your shower not a half hour ago."

Another laugh rumbled through his chest, despite her avoiding his request.

"Fine." He swept a sandy-blonde strand off her shoulder. "I want to talk to you away from this bed, or any walls, or showers. I want us to meet somewhere public for a conversation over dinner."

She let out a sigh and rolled back so her gaze hit the ceiling.

"I can't." The afterglow of vigorous sex dimmed on her rosy cheeks. "No. I can't."

A dull pain bunched in his chest, and he reined in his own groan of frustration. He'd half-expected that answer, but her rejection hurt all the same. "Because you're scared of letting me get closer?"

She shook her head, deep lines appearing between her brows. "No. Okay, yes. But mostly because I'm not right in here." She patted her chest, indicating her heart. "Or in here." She pointed to her head. "You told me to deal with my mess, and I thought I was improving, but yesterday showed just how far I am from ever being a complete person."

"I don't believe that." He wrapped his fingers around the same hand she'd used to point out all the places she needed work. "Yesterday was a step forward."

Her gaze danced around his face. "You think so?"

He shrugged, drawing from all that life had taught him about recovering from adversity. "Some things get worse before they get better. You've gone through a lot of change lately. Upheaval is expected."

She dipped her chin, peering up at him through narrowed eyes. "Change? You mean, because of you?"

"You said yourself, it's been a while since you've been with a man. I believe no amount of convincing would have brought you to me if a small corner of your heart hadn't been looking for something more."

She stared at him for a long time, her dark eyes gaining a depth he couldn't quite discern, though at least the lines on her forehead relaxed. Maybe some of what he said broke through.

"Something, as in a relationship?" Her eyes shone overly bright, outright daring him to confirm that's what he meant.

Well, she definitely had some magical hold over him, but not enough to deem him completely senseless.

A smile crept past his lips, and he worked hard to hide its full force. "Something could mean whatever you want. Whatever you feel is missing in your life. But a woman as smart as you would know my stance when it comes to relationships."

"Smooth save there, Romeo." She returned her stare to the ceiling. "But I can't decide what I want when it comes to anything."

"Well then, while you decide"—he hugged her closer, his thumb stroking the curve of her shoulder, her skin like living silk compared to his—"how about I tell you a story about myself?"

She jerked her focus back to him, mouth dipping into a frown. "A story?"

"I know more than a few intimate truths about you now." He squeezed her shoulder, his way of reassuring her everything would be okay. "It makes sense that I share, too."

"I don't know about that. We're pushing too far past the limits of this relationship."

He laughed. "I think we crossed more than a few limits against my living room wall, not to mention my desk, shower, and now this bed, remember?"

She gave him a playful slap on the forearm. "Hey, you know that's not what I meant."

"I know." Kissing her forehead, he hoped each warm gesture he offered would, over time, accumulate enough to melt away her distrust. "But my story has a point, and you should hear me out. I know you better than you think."

Her eyes glinted, amused and perhaps a little unbelieving. "Really, now?"

"Really." He took a deep breath and sank back into his pillow, preparing to share one of his darkest memories. A memory that dragged on him every time he conjured it up. A memory that shaped much of the life he lived now.

"I haven't always been Luke Tindall, up-and-coming CEO of a successful tech firm. I grew up the shy kid who routinely ditched playing with others to wander alone in the woods back in York. I liked solitude. I liked exploring wild places and getting into scary situations. To those who knew me, it was no surprise when I became a soldier and then a sniper."

Agathe let out a gasp and leaned away. "You were in the military? You shot people? You *killed* people?"

He gripped her shoulder, imploring her to hear him out. Though the slack expression on her face made his insides churn. He'd received similar reactions before, which was why he so very rarely talked about his past. "Guys who terrorized villages and targeted the vulnerable. They took hostages, raped, murdered, and worse, Agathe. Every clean shot I made saved many more lives than I took. I might have many regrets, but I don't regret a thing I did as part of my service."

Her eyes eased off from their open alarm, and her entire body held an unnatural stillness. Long seconds passed before she gave a stiff nod for him to continue.

He took a deep breath. At least she'd partly accepted that detail of his former life, though she'd probably need more time to truly come to terms with it. "For many years, I didn't need people to survive. I loved being alone in remote locations. I'd spend days and weeks alone, away from base camp, deep in enemy territory. My career required me to be cold and a loner and I excelled at my job. Thrived on it, even."

He shook his head, remembering the stoic, stubborn, detached young man he'd been. To this day, he still struggled to find a middle ground between his regimented past and his permissive present. The very reason he let Max run a little too free.

"And then, just as my military contract ended, the war also ended." He let out a rigid laugh, recalling the disorientation of it all. "I got shipped home from Iraq, back to normal civilization, back to living within the confines of a simple house in Scarborough. I didn't adjust well to the luxury of modern amenities and the suffocating pressure of well-meaning people dropping by to check on me. I couldn't go back to my job, but I couldn't stand my new life, either."

He turned to Agathe, once more relating to her disconnected existence without her child, how a life-altering event could make being with and relating to *normal* people near impossible. "I'd find myself roaming the streets at night, taking those familiar detours into the forest from my childhood. I half-searched for peace and solitude, while a darker side of me hoped to find trouble. Anything to break the monotony and provide any kind of purpose."

He paused to weigh up how much to tell her, then decided some details could wait.

"And then Max ran into his own troubles, so he and I started

Tiluma. After some initial, unexpected success, we took a risk and moved the company to far-flung Australia, where he and I could escape our old familiar surroundings. And where, for a while there, the money and status in our new country suckered me in. I spent two years as a slave to superficial rubbish. I used all the networking jaunts and cashed-up parties as a crutch to survive, even though Tiluma could succeed without them." He shrugged, still one hundred percent glad he'd given up on that particular part of his life. "And so, I pulled the plug on attending any needless publicity or socializing events, and I became known as a reclusive CEO."

Agathe's eyes sparkled up at him like maybe she'd found something for herself in his story. "And let me guess. That's why I found you roaming about in Roseford? You were on one of your aimless night walks, looking for trouble."

He didn't bother to stifle his smirk and gave her chin a playful tap with the knuckle of his thumb. "And for once, I'd say I succeeded in finding it."

She glared as if to say, *you've got to be joking.* "More like your wayward arrow succeeded.... Or nearly failed, depending on if it had actually struck me."

"In hindsight, I don't completely regret my poor aim that night." *It led me to you.*

A cold wave of reality swelled through him. The arrow might have led him to her, but whether he would get to keep her was another issue. "But, yes, I bought the Roseford property because I wanted an escape from the city. I needed opportunities to think and to disappear. To revisit my past and re-evaluate my place in the world. I think, to varying degrees, everyone does sometimes."

Her attention slipped back to the ceiling. "I have the opposite problem." Her voice rasped like it struggled to move through her throat and whatever else she refused to let go of. "I don't want to think. I'm not interested in meeting the woman I've become since...."

Her jaw pressed shut, and she blinked blindly ahead.

He knew what she meant.

*Since Elsie died.*

He lifted his opposite hand and turned her to face him. "Agathe, there's no person alive who isn't a complex mix of good and bad. And trust me, you're nowhere near all bad."

Her throat bobbed with a sharp swallow.

He continued anyway, certain she needed to hear a few home truths. "You're strong but more than a little lost. You also give yourself more blame than you're due. You worry about tripping at the first shove in the wrong direction. I've been there. You've most certainly been there, broken and fragile. It's why you avoided letting me in. I get it." He stroked his thumb over her trembling lower lip, her gaze darting and watery and seeming to fight to stay on him. A hint that maybe she preferred to hide away than confront his words. "But unlike the day you lost Elsie, this time, you're not alone."

She opened her mouth, but silence engulfed whatever she'd planned on saying. Seconds passed, and she frowned. "I'll manage. I enjoy being alone."

Her husky tone made him less inclined to believe her, and he shook his head. "No. No, you don't. You've become accustomed to it. There's a difference."

Her facial features set into a façade of hard, straight lines. "Because you clearly know me better than I know myself, right?"

"No. Because I see you." He stroked his knuckle over her chin again, willing her to relax. "And if you had a permanent mirror in front of you, you'd know what I'm talking about. It's rare to see this face of yours looking at peace."

He extended his fingers and caressed her cheek. Their gazes locked in a silent challenge for her to prove to him that his touch right now had no effect on her aversion to ease up.

She huffed out a breath and turned away, taking herself from his reach. "Okay, fine. Maybe it's just that I *want* to enjoy being alone, but I don't, and I'm trapped between holding onto grief and trying to find some quality of life." She turned her head back to him as though her candor came as a surprise even to her. "I'm exhausted. I want to stop running. And more than ever, I'm scared of what relaxing would mean for me. For Elsie."

"Because you think being happy would mean leaving her behind?" His heart ached. He'd seen similar fear from his military friends. The fear of moving on. He didn't want this for her. But maybe that fear was downright unavoidable.

Her gaze softened, and she gave a tiny nod.

"I'm afraid that moving on would involve pretending the past never happened." Her lips formed a rigid half-smile like that admission truly hurt. "Happiness feels like selling out."

He pushed his palm into hers and gave a gentle squeeze before kissing the back of her hand. "What if I said we could be in this together? That you could start with me?"

"How?" She kept her tone flat. "By sleeping with you some more?"

His chest trembled with an uncontrolled laugh. Sometimes her ingrained skepticism had hilarious perks.

"No, but you're welcome to do that too." He unleashed a big smile, set to lead her away from all things dark and past-related. "Challenge yourself to accept a few of those acts of warmth I talked about. Stop fighting everything so much. Especially me. And best of all, bring a change of clothes to the office tomorrow because we're going on that date."

# Chapter Twenty-Three

The booths at Tiny Tokyo's were literally tiny, the tight seating arrangement forcing Agathe's knees to rub against Luke's under the table. The intimate space, along with the knee rubbing, shouldn't have been a problem. They'd rubbed far more intimate parts before, but her tummy stirred and sank all the same because nothing about this date felt natural.

Luke's alluring grin spread. Watching him now, she longed to be away from this staring competition, one punctuated by food and dim lighting. To be, instead, in his bedroom, giving him something else entirely to smile about.

"Thanks for staying back to help set up for Schneider's meeting tomorrow." His long fingers stroked the tips of hers on the table. "You didn't have to."

She shrugged, prying her gaze off his mouth long enough to poke a chopstick at a piece of salmon sashimi in front of her. "You were my date, and I had to wait around, anyway. Also, others helped too. I would have looked like a slacker if I didn't join in." He cut forth with a laugh. She gave her nose a playful wrinkle in response. "Besides, I'm going to win some major professional brownie points when Tiluma nails this. Promotion, here I come."

She peered up to find his brows raised and his eyes narrowed. An expression marked with a true challenge. "We both know that's not the only reason you stayed back. Just like there was no real reason to step up when Caroline needed help with that toy owl. No reason other than you being nicer than you make out."

A smile wobbled the corners of her lips, but she kept her tone emotionless either way, not yet sure about how much significance to place on this date. "Really?"

"Yeah. You're nice, and you also like working at Tiluma. Admit it."

"No." She pointed a finger at him. "You're the *nice* one, remember? I'm the flaming car wreck, voted most likely to explode."

He choked a little on a laugh. "You're also a fraud."

"Well, thank you, that's the kindest thing anyone has ever said to me." Her shoulders shook with an involuntary tremble, and just like that, a deep chuckle broke out. She took a second to calm down, then decided she could afford to open her heart to him a little, even if just in a joking manner. "And you're a really sweet guy when you bother to put the effort in."

Pine-green flecks twinkled in his eyes, and the skin at the corners creased with his beam. Even in the low light, she swore he wiped away a laughter-induced tear. "*Lo intento. Sono asqueroso después de todo.*"

She fell back in her seat and clutched at her stomach, uncontrollable laughter spreading a dull pain through her abdomen. *Oh goodness, the man doesn't know when to give up on a language he clearly can't master.* Even worse, she was in a densely packed restaurant, so she felt compelled to restrain her noise level. "Did you really mean to say, 'I do try. You are disgusting after all?'"

His cheeks paled, and he clapped a hand over his mouth. Though, to be honest, she was impressed to note that much past the water in her eyes.

"I'm so sorry." He gave his head a slow shake, indicating he needed a second to take in the carnage. "That's not at all what I meant. I meant to say, 'You are amazing, after all.' Now I'm too scared to even attempt anymore Spanish to correct myself."

"I think you meant *asombroso*, not *asqueroso*." She waved a hand in a gesture of forgiveness, her heart thudding with how much fun she had around him. "The words share some similar letters but have completely different meanings. Props for trying, though."

Coming on this date raised the stakes, numbering her days spent shying away from his sympathetic looks, jovial looks, and, worst of all, his hot looks. This date suggested she'd have to be bolder and more open to his company, all while avoiding the closeness he wanted that she couldn't give. Then again, life had already hurt her too much. There wasn't much more damage he could do. So, she could afford the risk of a close friendship with him.

Friendship, yes. But love? *Definitely not.*

Worst-case scenario, the Schneider meeting tomorrow would distract her from Luke and her swelling heart. If the meeting went well, Tiluma would no longer need her, and her relationship with Luke would gain extra space.

*Tread carefully. Remember what I used to say, "Things will never be okay."*

Her throat dried, and her cheeks burned. She had enough regret to cool her joy without being so actively sour, but then again, maybe the sour served a purpose.

If she stuck to her limits, he'd tire of her and move on of his own accord.

She wouldn't have to break two hearts.

Just her own.

She reached out and took hold of his fingers, her attempt at participating in the relationship he seemed so set on trying. "Thanks for asking me here tonight."

*There.* Her first real go at thawing the ice. Initiating non-sexual contact *and* a compliment. *You go, girl!*

His fingers stilled over her hand. "And thanks for clearing your busy schedule for me."

Her cheeks pulled and mirrored his grin, likely cracking her otherwise worried glower, though his look soon stiffened.

"What is it?" She frowned, narrowing her focus on him.

"Given how honest you've been with me, there is something I want to share with you." He let go of her hand. "My biggest regret."

She sunk back and reached for a much-needed sip from her water glass. *So much for escaping regrets.*

A large part of her wished to remain ignorant, to just enjoy her night, but then the last few years had made her extra sensitive to red flags, and her earlier hope retreated like a spooked horse searching for a gate. Maybe she did need to know after all. Even if she didn't *want* to.

She took a huge gulp of water and tried to play cool. "You told me about your war past. I don't expect anything more."

He shook his head while a muscle ticked at his jaw. "I need you to understand who I really am, if not for personal reasons, then for professional."

His stare constricted on her, and her appetite waned.

*What is he getting at?*

"Tomorrow is a huge deal. If things don't pan out, if you end up regretting ever working with me, then I want you to understand why I couldn't just get rid of Max."

A sense of foreboding snaked a path of sickness through her tummy, yet the thin sliver of hope this man gave her fought back. "Max is improving, and Daniel will wrangle him if things get out of hand tomorrow. You have nothing to worry about. I'm sure the Schneider meeting will be a success. You really don't have to..."

His broad shoulders sagged, and a dull sadness shadowed his eyes as he peered up to the scarlet silk wall hanging to her right. "You don't know Schneider as I do. He's meticulous and has crushed companies a million times better prepared than Tiluma. A whole lot of things could go wrong tomorrow."

Luke waited long seconds for the groove between Agathe's brow to ease. Only it didn't. She might have started this date nervous, then happy, but now, all signs of her brief confidence slipped away. All because of his need for transparency.

"What a lot of people in Australia don't know about Max is that his big dream was to be a competitive open-water swimmer. It was every-thing he'd worked toward for the best part of a decade." He tried to rush the explanation, hoping to move on quickly so her laughter might return. That sweet, rare sound had come to mean so much to him, but then again, so did revealing these details of his past.

He couldn't coax her into a relationship without having her really know him, a main reason for this date, after all. And heaven knew he damn well wanted to know everything about her, too. "Max and I spent our childhood racing each other in the waters off Scarborough. It didn't matter what the conditions were. We competed against just about anything, though he kicked my ass every time. If things hadn't gone bad, if I hadn't screwed up his life, he could have been one of the world's best swimmers. You remember I told you how I returned from war restless?"

Her pupils darkened in what was a likely mix of confusion and worry, and still, she nodded. Hoping to ease her concern, he reached out and squeezed her hand.

"Well, in my despair, I took Max down with me." Not wanting to see judgment in her eyes, he swallowed and then lowered his gaze. "I was in one of my moods. The silence in my house drove me mad, and I couldn't sit still any longer. So, I called Max and asked if he wanted to come on a simple hike through North York National Park. I was desperate to relive our old times together, back before our father died and my future got murky. Back before life got complicated."

He scowled at the cherry-black table surface, tight shame pulling through his chest and down into his abdomen, the image of that familiar rugged coastline as fresh as ever. "Except I was so out of my skin to chase some kind of thrill that by the time Max arrived at my house, I'd packed the climbing equipment and planned an adventure he didn't seem all too eager on."

Agathe's fingers curled around his, vying for his attention. "But you made Max go anyway?"

Though he still refused to look up, he imagined her gaze offering gentle support. Not that he deserved any. "Max never said as much, but I saw apprehension in his eyes. Just like everyone else, he didn't want to upset the irritable war veteran, so he agreed to go rock climbing anyway. I'm sure it was his way of helping me, and he did help, just at a much higher cost than I would have ever asked for."

She leaned in, and she gave a pointed stare, her gaze mirroring his in a look of hard focus. "What happened?"

He looked toward the red wall hanging again, its embroidered depiction of a Japanese countryside failing to soften the invisible pressure crushing his chest. "The weather that day was wild and windy. A whole lot of rain had fallen the night before, and there were enough signs to know we shouldn't have climbed the cliff."

"Oh, Luke..." She pulled her fingers from his and pressed them to her mouth. "But you did, didn't you? You climbed the cliff?"

He nodded, the swell of nausea sloshing around inside his belly and burning up his throat.

"We did." He reached out for her hand again, needing extra strength, needing to urge her to still like him once this story ended. "And just as I climbed to safety at the top, I turned to see Max halfway up, a large chunk of rock face crumbling beneath his hand and taking him a hundred feet down with it."

Agathe sucked in a sharp breath, and her hand clutched him as if she, too, scrambled not to fall. "Max fell?"

Just as more food arrived, a tingling heat overran his face. He paused long enough for the waiter to set down their plates and step out of earshot. "Yeah, and obviously survived, only because he happened to land on a scarce patch of shoreline not dotted with rocks. But he sustained a career-ending shoulder injury. One that left him the suddenly aimless one, and I, the one with an instant drive to put things right."

Her mouth fell open and flailed for a beat. "And that's why you started Tiluma? To give Max a new direction?"

"In a roundabout way, yes, but I'm starting to think there's no putting this right." He eyed his food, and his stomach churned at the thought of eating anything. Besides, he wanted to get this story out and done with. To see what kind of damage it would do to her perception of him. "Our first app was based on a joke Max made about wanting some game to take his frustrations out on. Something with some poor sap he could throw downstairs, swing hammers at, and make more miserable than he was."

Despite the general frat-boy nature of Tiluma's products, he stifled a cringe at how inappropriate this topic seemed for a date.

Even though he'd never planned on being the CEO of a joke app company, to this day, he still worked at maintaining the gentlemanly manner his parents toiled so hard to instill in him—this whole operation still not suiting his personality, though Tiluma more than paid his bills and gave Max some semblance of purpose. "So, I took whatever money I'd saved during my military service and hired a software developer to make the totally depraved app Max had in mind. It was meant as a gift. Or maybe an apology. No one ever expected it would become so popular."

Agathe's hand paused halfway to her chopsticks, and her entire face illuminated with a knowing grin. "You're talking about the Sam Splat app."

He smiled, undeservedly proud she knew the name of his first-ever app. "Yes. Max has this knack for coming up with ridiculous ideas that hit a chord with the public. We ran with his wild concepts time and time again and gained more and more success with each attempt."

She dipped her chin and peered at him through upturned eyes. "We all know Max has brilliant ideas, but his ability to implement or manage them…."

He huffed out a laugh. At least she took his story in stride. "I know, and in those early days, I was the one who managed most things while Max was in charge of creative input. Only, Tiluma grew too fast, and I couldn't be his dedicated minder anymore."

"So then, why position him in such an ill-fitting role?" She slid a piece of teriyaki chicken into her mouth. Soon enough, her forehead smoothed as though a lightbulb flicked on in her mind. "You felt guilty about his accident and wanted him to play a key part in the company you created together."

The unexpected comfort in this exchange had his muscles weakening as he nodded. "Guilt. Regret. Everything in between…I'd snatched potential greatness from him once before. I needed to give him something to feel good about. So, I couldn't have him playing a background role at Tiluma."

"You're a great brother, Luke, and your love for Max has achieved the near impossible." She reached out and squeezed his hand, her tender gaze extending a jolt of electricity. Being the center of her attention never failed to get to him, and his heart rushed its next few beats. "You built a multi-million-dollar company, and you get to work together every day. Isn't that enough? How much more do you think you owe him?"

He cleared his throat, her encouragement mixed with those hard-hitting questions, leaving him scrambling for something to say. "I don't know, but as kind as your words are, they're not completely true. I ruined his life."

She gave a shrug and refocused on her meal. "You can't know that for sure. Athletes get injured all the time."

"Well, in that case…." Finally feeling relaxed enough to eat again, he picked up his chopsticks and poked at the rice on his plate. "I didn't need to fast-track his retirement."

Her eyelids flared in a way that seemed to say, *now see here, you!* and she pointed her cutlery at him. "No. You diverted his course. That's all."

He gave a laugh. "You and I know Tiluma isn't where Max shines. He could have been a great swimmer, and I took that away from him."

She leaned back into the leather bench behind her with a sigh. "You give yourself too much credit, Luke. As much as Max and I clash, he's got a good heart, and I know he'd never blame you for what happened. You've warded away his sorrows with a steady job, creative input, and a big, fat company share. Anyway, he's still young, and you don't know what sort of stepping stone Tiluma will be until he moves on to the next great thing."

He sat quietly for a moment, pondering the optimism in her new perspective and the softness in her delivery.

*Softness.* He'd intrinsically known she possessed the propensity, but only in the last few days did he glimpse her ability to offer comfort with any kind of consistency. Her aptitude to finally say something nice about Max suggested her once-crippling caginess had faded.

One thing was for sure. The night she'd run to him had changed *everything*.

So maybe he could convince her to make room for him after all.

"I have my future planned out." *And I want you to be part of that future.* His sentiments now seemed to come from somewhere far outside himself. "I have clear direction on where I want to go. Max deserves to have a similar purpose."

She held up her hands in a resigned gesture. "Trust me, plans are overrated, and they don't always pan out. Perhaps Max is content with his ad hoc existence. I know I would be in his position."

"I don't believe that." He coupled his sure tone with pinning his attention on her, a silent command that she not look away. "Plans offer hope, Agathe. They make life worth living. That's what Max deserves. That's what everyone deserves."

*Especially you.*

Her stare turned rigid, as did the set of her jaw. She lowered her chopsticks at a glacial speed, her whole unaffected act evaporating. "And when plans don't pan out, life becomes unbearable. No one deserves *that*."

His heart rattled, and he gritted his teeth against the knowledge that life had done a tragic number on this woman. By association, it had done a number on him too. Worst still, he had no idea how to pull her free, only that he had to try.

"When plans don't work out, you make new plans." He held perfectly still, his unmoving stare designed to weaken her evasion.

She took a sharp breath and momentarily broke eye contact, seeming exasperated and anguished but too proud to admit to either. "Since we're on the subject of plans, what are yours? Get your bank account to a billion dollars and retire to the Caribbean?"

Sending a message that he didn't love her sarcasm, he picked at his food and veered his gaze to take the sting out of this standoff. Old habits die hard, and right now, Agathe looked for a fight.

He didn't want a fight. He wanted to see her thrive. Wanted to see her happy. And wanted to be the reason for it all. Lastly, he wanted to make her his. "No. As I said, money makes life easier, but having done without it before, money isn't the source of all contentment. Nor can it buy what I want most."

Her lips lifted, and a wicked glint flashed in her constricted eyes.

"Oh, yeah? And what do you want most? An endless supply of crossbows and sweatpants?"

She sought to make him laugh, to once again deflect from the discomfort of facing her issues, but he didn't so much as blink. From battlefield to boardroom, he'd honed principles that couldn't be dented, and her humor now felt more like a slap than a joke. Especially when his future with her hung in the balance.

So, he didn't want jokes, nor did he want sarcasm, and when it came to the things he *did* want, he couldn't back down. Not when what he wanted most was her.

"I've lived in a nice house for years now, but it's been a damn long time since I've lived in a home." Her jaw slackened like she saw where he was headed with this. *Good.* No amount of sidestepping could stop him, and he curled his hands on the table, intensifying his stare on her dark gaze. He'd make her see. He *had* to. "I want a wife, Agathe. I want children. And one woman to share everything with. Every victory and every heartbreak. I want forever. And when I find that woman, I'm not letting her go. Not ever. And not for anything."

*And I've found her. I'm almost sure that woman is you.*

Silent seconds passed, and her complexion dulled while her shoulders rounded forward. "Wasn't this meant to be a casual date?"

He flinched. That she'd caught the serious subtext in his words. That her remark blasted a big, fucking hole into the casual pretense of this date. That his spirit of honesty bludgeoned her with his desire for commitment, marriage, and family.

As if the story of his past hadn't been enough, he'd needed her to know about his dreams too. So now, he couldn't take back what he'd shared, and even then, another part of him didn't want to.

"You know what I want, Luke?" Her pupils turned from wide, deep pools into laser-sharp pinpricks, and she lifted her posture into a poker-straight position. "I want you to take me home. I'm done here."

# Chapter Twenty-Four

Red, yellow, and green streetlights flicked past Agathe's rain-splattered window, the multi-colored flashes adding to the aggravated shouts stuck on a loop in her head. *Damn Luke. Damn him and his big mouth.*

She stared ahead, refusing to look at him, refusing to fall apart in his presence. At least, not again. He'd wielded his desires like a weapon, as if he had a natural right to stoke any kind of fire in her. *Well, screw him. He doesn't.* And so what if he wanted marriage and kids? She'd had both and wanted neither.

*Why am I so angry?*

The question startled her into looking at him, into forgetting she shouldn't be looking at all. His attention stayed ahead, fingers white-knuckled around the steering wheel, lips squeezed so tight they blanched.

He'd crossed a line, her future with him perishing the moment he mentioned the two things she absolutely didn't want or need. And yet, his silence offered something different, a sign he either cared about her reaction a little too much or perhaps not at all.

Her heart clenched at that thought, mostly because she couldn't obscure the deeper understanding that he did, in fact, care. He cared a lot, and his affection alone chipped away at her need to run.

Leaving him was inevitable, and his confession tonight only hurtled that end ever faster her way. If she stayed, she could just see herself caving to his dreams at the expense of her own. Even if her dreams only consisted of staying exactly as she was.

But back to the question. *Why am I so angry?*

Because she'd known from the beginning he'd be a family kind of guy, and she'd been stupid to tuck that detail away for the sake of momentary pleasure.

Luke was down to earth. Understanding. *Nice.*

A nice man who used to kill people. *Don't forget that.*

Just like her, he wasn't all he seemed. Another contradiction on a relationship a hell of a lot more complicated than she'd bargained for.

Then again, maybe he was just further along when it came to healing from his past. Not that her past was something she could ever heal from.

Either way, she'd become foolishly attached to him and demanded things he'd been reluctant to give. *No-strings-attached sex. Shame on her.* From day one, he'd had no place in her life, his damage nowhere near as ingrained as hers. She lacked the strength to take on the weight of what he truly wanted. Marriage. Children. *Love.* Argh!

And now the toll bells rang.

*But tell me, why am I so angry?*

Because there'd been a time when she'd had all that he wanted. Happiness. Luck. A future filled with hope. And then, she'd lost everything.

And just like a starving child crying outside a candy store window, his provocations now made her want more when wanting was a dangerous gamble. When wanting asked her to relive her pain-riddled past with a whole new family.

*Why am I always so damn angry?*

She was divorced with a dead kid. *That's why.*

Did she need another goddamn reason?

She pulled her gaze from him and forced a sharp breath. He'd spoken of forever like the promise of forever was something she could give. But she'd told him all about Elsie. He should have known. Forever didn't exist, not for her.

Tears prickled her eyes, and her throat clogged.

She had to get home. Had to get out of this stifling car.

"Are you okay?"

She closed her eyes, her heart straining against his concern.

Even as she sought to hate him, he delivered more unjustified kindness.

She gave a shaky nod and uttered a weak, "Yep."

His manner around her made her wish she could be the ideal woman he spoke of when all she could be was *this* woman. The one who fell short. The one who fell apart. The one with thick tears streaming down her face.

So, she swiped at her cheek and removed any evidence of sadness, her chest burning because all she'd ever had was *pretending*. Pretending she could do it all and that nothing hurt. Pretending she didn't care that the years would eventually leave her behind.

She clung to the charade of not caring, especially now, when this glimpse of him, of what she could never have, stung like all hell.

"Agathe?"

She flung her eyelids open and turned to find him staring at her, her pulse spiking in response because he'd killed the engine, and a quick glimpse out her window revealed they'd arrived at her house.

"Let me walk you to your door."

The warmth in his tone forced her eyes shut again. She could do this. All she had to do was make it to her front step and utter one word.

She'd be honest with him, tell him they had no future. Chances were he already knew. But maybe, just one last time, she'd pretend to be someone else. Someone whole.

She used whatever speck of will she had left to reopen her eyes and reach for her door handle, where her first step outside had the evening's cold wind permeating her thin, black sweater.

The ground on her journey to her front door glittered with recent rain, and Luke joined her there, for a short while not speaking, though his gaze darted over her face with taut and intense scrutiny. "You're bothered by what I said at the restaurant."

She shivered and hugged her arms around her ribcage, the miserable weather insignificant compared to the emotions swirling through her mind. "You're welcome to have your own dreams, Luke."

A frown dragged at his features, but his soft gaze washed over her before he nodded slowly. "You should go inside. You're cold."

He spun away, swifter than expected, and before she could stop, her hand shot out and hooked around his elbow. "No."

Her shaky tone had her snapping her mouth shut. The cool, black leather of his sports jacket pressed to her fingers. She couldn't let him go. Not before uttering what she'd meant to say all along. "Stay."

All too slow and gradual, he turned to face her, for a long time merely looking, while the repetitive *drip, drip, drip* of water from her tile roof proved torture to her ears.

An icy gust continued to lap her face, the needle-sharp sensation prodding her to speed this whole God-awkward exchange along. "Stay. Please."

His brow dipped at the center, but aside from that, he gave little away. "Why?"

"Because." She sighed at his unreadable stare, her heart sinking because, once more, she used his kindness against him. All because she wasn't ready to let him go. All because she wanted one final test to make sure she couldn't do this relationship thing that seemed to matter so much to him. "I need your help. I want you to touch me with all the gentleness you can muster."

The strain around his eyes eased, but his posture remained stiff, and he shook his head. "This is a bad idea."

"I know, but I can't do this without you." She took her hand off him and fidgeted with her sweater sleeves. "I need to know if I can accept those acts of warmth you say I struggle with. Maybe you need to know too."

The tension at his jaw returned, as did the hard press of his lips. "I opened my heart to you at the restaurant, and you've been acting strange ever since."

"Please." A distinct heaviness, like a bucket full of ball bearings, settled in her gut and weighted her tone. She couldn't lie, but she couldn't make any promises, either. "Just for tonight."

"Jesus, Agathe." Her name pushed past gritted teeth, and he

rubbed the back of his neck. "At what point have I well and truly entered self-punishment territory?"

"I don't have the answer to that." She bounced where she stood, warding off the cold, warding off every conflicted emotion pinging around within her, all while pinning him with her most desperate stare.

A low growl rumbled up his throat, and he stepped closer, cupping her cheek while his beautiful green gaze searched hers. "Tonight, then. But Agathe, I hope you know exactly what you're asking of me."

The door clicked behind Luke, and he softened at the neat coziness within Agathe's home, a place unexpectedly elegant, with off-white decor and surprising splashes of color. The Victorian dwelling's classic red-brick and easy interior design didn't match the hardened woman she pretended to be.

The real Agathe had class, kindness, and character, all hidden behind a thick layer of prickly defense. But tonight offered him a chance to break past her stony walls.

She pressed into him now, fingers raking through his hair, while her lips found his. A string of languid and blissful kisses poured from her, and his body sighed with pleasure while his mind flicked back to her desperation outside.

*This moment, right now, feels like our last.*

He wanted to be wrong. After all, she *had* asked for warmth, for gentleness, for what he'd wanted to give her all along. So, he scooped her up and wrapped her legs around his waist, whispering his plans to the shell of her ear. "Bedroom?"

Her lips engaged with the side of his neck, and she pointed blindly behind her to a set of cream-colored stairs, where he soon charged forward and then up. A door sat ajar, with a king-sized bed visible inside.

Blue light filtered from the window inside this room, and he entered, lowering her to the pillowy sheets, engraving every last detail of her on his mind. The way her blonde-brown tresses fanned out around her, the wide-eyed expression she sent his way like she too sensed the end loomed near.

An awareness of time slipping by brought an ache to his bones that, really, this was her stepping away. And still, he looked for a sign. *Something* to indicate he read her wrong, that she did truly feel for him, at least a hint of what he did for her. A sign she shared his life's direction. Or at least, she *could* be his in time.

Ambushing her with his dreams at dinner had been his compromise. If he pushed and demanded her cooperation, she'd run. Most definitely, she'd run. But if he did and said nothing, nothing would happen. He would never be more than a placeholder for her pain.

And maybe this moment now would be more of the same, but he'd offer her everything, plus his unrushed silence and hope *he* and their time together thus far would be enough. That the intimacy in this exchange would speak volumes of his love for her, his motivations here not altogether selfless.

For all he would give, he wanted something back.

He wanted his love returned.

# Chapter Twenty-Five

Agathe's skin tingled at the sweet, soft kisses Luke feathered all over her neck, his body one sumptuous, hot blanket over hers. If this were just the start of his acts of warmth, she'd be a puddle of molten woman by the time he was done.

He tugged away her clothes, and his followed soon after. Everything about tonight seemed unfamiliar—lighter, and heavier all at once —his unrushed silence speaking volumes that he'd fallen for her and wanted the same in return.

She closed her eyes, pretending to not see his need. Pretending proved impossible when his touch pulled at her dwindling emotional reserves, and his quiet adoration made her feel like a heroine from a Greek tragedy. A heroine searching the underworld for her lost love, only to be dragged back to a shadowy place where love didn't exist.

Because Elsie had taken all traces of love with her. To *her* underworld. To wherever it was departed children went. And Agathe had been barred from that place forever, perhaps barred from experiencing love, too, as long as she lived on this Earth and her daughter didn't.

Luke's hand slid from her knee and up her inner thigh. She sucked in a breath. Her propensity to love may or may not have survived, but her body sure as hell still knew how to respond.

He parted her and exposed her sex. His light caress there caused her to writhe against him. Heat poured over the anguish-driven chill in her bones, and sweet pleasure swallowed her like a gentle wave stroking the shore. She liked that image. *A gentle wave.* Gentle, like the sultry kisses he trailed from her navel to her neck. She could be that wave. Calm and non-thinking. Luke could be her shining sun. His light could illuminate her darker depths. The first spark of life in a place once thought barren.

The rock-hard press of man against her had her arching right back into him and pleading. "I want you now."

His answer came on the fluid glide of his generous length within her, his mouth on hers, as he filled and stretched. Each new thrust delivered hot tingles that ran through her veins. Just like that, he fulfilled his promise of pleasure, and her world expanded, shook, and glowed.

Soon, happiness and joy danced behind her closed eyes, painting a vibrant world where death didn't exist. A world where belonging and tenderness was hers again, where she and Luke grew old together, with a grown-up Elsie there through it all. *Imagine that.*

"Luke." His name fell from her on an indulgent cry, her heart breaking and singing all at once.

"I've got you." His husky whisper filled her ears, his hands cupped her face, and his beautiful gaze poured a silent wish in through the cracks of her ruined heart. A wish for trust. A wish for her to be his.

The crack inside her pulled wider, tearing her defenses down one painful inch at a time, leaving her breathless in the best kind of way. Lighting a longing for this moment to last forever. His every deliberate movement within her brought the truth she'd denied all along.

He did have her. In so many ways, he had her.

Tears trickled down her temples, and as much as she tried, she couldn't bring herself to close her eyes again. To shut him out.

"More," her voice quivered, and his gaze fused with hers. His unshakable stare implored her to feel, like he wouldn't grant her more until she did. There'd be no quick release. Not when he wanted her. *Body and soul.*

Pupils wide and full of wonder, he brushed his fingertips over her cheek in a series of light and lingering touches—a man entangled in a precious, priceless, fleeting moment—while truth be told, she couldn't claim to be far from that either.

In all her time of knowing him, he'd provided so much. A safe place to talk and a willingness to meet her right where life dumped her. While she'd rarely taken time to appreciate all that giving. She owed him her vulnerability. And, maybe, she owed herself, too.

So, she allowed her muscles to relax and arched into him, taking what he offered and giving of herself too. *Honestly. Wholeheartedly.* Until a shimmer of need burst from her center and awakened every inch of her body, daring her to ask for things she didn't deserve... Tenderness. Security. Devotion.

Luke's gaze answered in return, seeming to say, *"You can have all of me. Just give me your heart. Your trust. Your future."*

She sank further, clamping her thighs around his hips and demanding more. More sensation. More release. Every muscle in her body shook until surrender and release converged into one, unbuckling the last of her reservations.

His hard thrusts drew from her a desperate cry, and she clung to his shoulders, intense pleasure breaking within her, violent and all-encompassing and far beyond anything she'd ever felt before.

A guttural moan wrenched from deep within her, one that urged him to surrender right along with her. As always, he gave, his lips finding hers again, as though he drank her in, growing within her, in a vow she would not experience this alone.

Another wave of satisfaction swallowed her, and he reached his own peak, swelling, and shuddering, his beautiful emerald gaze exuding this moment's inescapable magnitude. Only for the glow there to dull in the ebb.

"This isn't enough, is it?" His voice rang rough and ragged, and he drew back, his features wrinkled and taut. "Agathe, it's not enough."

The hole in her heart tore wider, spilling a deluge of unfulfillable promises. She had no words of undying love. No offer of a bright future. Hell, she couldn't even predict how she'd get through tomorrow. Or the next day. Or the next...

So. No. This wasn't enough. But not because of Luke. Because no amount of wanting could manifest all the things she lacked. Sex was all she had. *She* wasn't enough.

The only fair course of action would be to find a kind way to let him go.

*But how?*

Eyes squeezed tight to hold back her tears, she pressed her forehead to the heat of his shoulder. How long had it been since she'd cried so often, if at all?

This man had turned her into an open wound, weeping and pained. In just being *him*, he'd gotten to her. He'd made her want to stay.

But he had standards. Ones she couldn't meet. He'd get tired of waiting for her to level up, of never getting the brand of love and compassion she just didn't possess. If she didn't end this, he'd leave. No doubt about that.

"Agathe," his quiet words rattled against his hard breaths. "I want to mean something to you."

She blinked up at his pleading gaze, that imploring and direct stare proof of what being with her cost him. And because of that proof, she clamped her jaw to keep from talking, to keep from speaking words that would damage them both. Words she had no place saying.

*Oh, but you do mean something to me.*

No relationship could flourish with her. She couldn't drag him down to her level. She couldn't waste his time. Or let him get further invested. Or break his heart.

*You mean more than I ever intended. So much more. If I could, I would cut away the pain and be the woman you need. But I can't. I just can't.*

She *was* her pain. Elsie *was* her pain.

And cutting away the pain would mean cutting away her daughter.

She also couldn't lie. Couldn't say he meant nothing.

Because now, against all odds, *she loved him.*

Loved him enough to see the cold and tragic truth. Her love wasn't enough. So, her greatest kindness would be to say nothing. To let silence be her answer.

~

The adoring glimmer in Agathe's eyes clouded, and her cheeks hollowed, her numb expression forcing Luke's heartbeat to shrink to a labored thud. He pressed his eyes shut and fought for composure. His next breaths so hard to come by.

Her body had only just stopped shuddering around him, yet her vacant stare offered all the answers he needed.

All the *wrong* answers.

Despite what he'd hoped, her invitation into her house wasn't any kind of welcome step forward—his effort to learn if he meant something to her was met with gaping silence. Her earlier request for tenderness was nothing more than a bitter goodbye.

He rolled onto his back and hooked an elbow over his eyes, willing his thoughts to slow into a bogus impression of calm. He needed to escape. Needed space from her emotionless gaze. Needed to disappear to somewhere a heck of a lot less painful than here.

"I'm sorry," her voice came in a soft whisper. Not enough. Definitely not enough.

His stomach constricted. He didn't want a damn apology. Not another reminder that her past held her captive. No matter how much he loved her or how desperate he wanted that love returned, he needed to accept one sore truth. She *couldn't* love. Maybe never would love.

Though he already regretted his impatience, the light touch of her fingertips to his forearm left him surging up to the edge of the bed, where he sat with his back to her, depriving her of any chance to look at his face. "I need to clean up. Is that the bathroom over there?"

He pointed to a door to his left but didn't wait for a reply, launching himself forward, too emotionally raw to linger in her bed.

Tonight cost him. It cost him dearly. She'd asked for warmth and softness, then repaid him with literally nothing. Sure, he understood why, but he also didn't have to love the result.

The door he'd pointed to did lead to a bathroom, and he pushed through before closing the door behind him and resting his hands on the white stone vanity. There, he glared into the mirror, analyzing the dark shadows and wary lines over his forlorn face. The man staring back at him wasn't one he easily recognized. This was the haunted man he'd left behind the day Max tumbled down that cliff, that man forcing a new Luke to step forth and step up.

*What have I done?*

He'd made a frantic fucking fool of himself, that's what. But then, nothing could have made him say no. Not when she'd looked at him with her wide and pleading eyes, her expectant stare conveying a desire to try. Had she genuinely thought she could conjure the ability to be what he needed? Or had she outright lied to him? And still, he couldn't completely blame her because his own stupid weakness had plunged him into disenchantment, too.

*Idiot!*

She never pretended to be anything less than one massive fucking risk. Why hadn't he believed her? *Why?* He, of all people, knew not all risks paid off. He'd encountered enough emotionally scarred individuals. Some recovered from hardship. Some didn't. Of those who didn't, the people closest to them paid the highest price.

So, his moment of reckoning with Agathe had arrived. Even if he ached for her, even if he would possibly *always* ache for her, he needed to step away. He couldn't stick around forever and play her emotional whipping boy.

Her moments of sunlight were too few and far between. Whatever help he offered didn't work, and his continued presence seemed to only cripple her ability to deal with her problems. She needed to sink or swim. On her own, this time.

Hating to admit defeat, he groaned and turned on the tap, the sting of her brush-off still too fresh in the air.

*I have no other choice.*

He cleaned off and waited for his more turbulent emotions to pass, a heavy sigh escaping him as he turned and marched back into the bedroom.

She sat bolt upright in the bed, the cream-colored bed sheet clutched at her chest as if linen could hide his memories of what she looked like underneath. "Luke?"

"I need to go." He tugged on his pants, avoiding any glimpses of her deep frown. "We have a big day tomorrow."

"Luke," her voice twisted and pleaded again. "Stop. Just wait a minute."

"Why?" He set about buttoning his shirt, fingers not as coordinated as he wanted, fucking up his shot at a clean escape. "Do you even care about having any kind of future with me?"

He waited a beat, hating the harshness in his tone, not meaning to hurt her, but hell, he wasn't able to hold back either. Her mouth hung open, but no words came out. Maybe he should stop. Maybe he should shut his mouth and just go home. But screw it, she'd crushed his hopes with every tenderness given, only ever leading him down a long path of rejection. "This is cut and dried, Agathe. I shouldn't have walked through your front door tonight."

God, he needed to get away from here. Needed to think. He felt deceived. Felt like a fool. Even if she'd never intended either. He refused to look at her on his quick stride to her bedroom door, didn't pause on his way down her stairs, or when the icy night air hit his cheeks in cold solidarity.

Everything about tonight told him not to hold on anymore. Over and over and over again, all he could hear was that he should give up.

That loving Agathe Santos hurt too damn much.

*Chapter Twenty-Six*

Agathe clung to her morning coffee, the heated paper cup offering none of its usual comfort on her tram ride to work. Last night left her shaken to the core. Today's upcoming Schneider visit left her scattered and lost. This meeting meant everything, her giant career leap, and a golden promotion, even though moving onto bigger things meant leaving Tiluma.

Her tummy hollowed at the impending loss. She didn't have the same connections with her colleagues at Slate and King as she did at Tiluma. Even with Luke's now-rightful anger, the thought of leaving his office still made her feel sick.

*Or maybe it's because I'll never see him again?*

Her phone rang in her hand, and she frowned at the name on her screen. "Hello?"

"Agathe." Sue's direct tone cut through. Unfortunately, this woman never missed an important event. "I wanted to wish you luck for today. Is everything in order for a successful meeting?"

She scrubbed a hand over her forehead and weighed up how much honesty to give. "Luke has his doubts." Her gut churned at mentioning his name, much less that his doubts weren't limited to just his company. "But I'm confident we can put on a competent show."

Sue clicked her tongue, followed by a weighty sigh. The woman never took well to anything less than guaranteed success. "Let me guess, the brother's still a wild card?"

"Yeah." Agathe huffed out a breath, at the same time blowing a loose strand of hair from her cheek. "But he's improving."

"Well, let's hope you've made a deep enough impact to pull this off. I don't need to remind you how a win here will look in regard to any promotion."

Agathe gritted her teeth. "No. All good. I understand."

"Great." Sue's tone brightened. "Then give me a call when Schneider leaves. I want to know how it all went."

Agathe hung up and took a long swig of her coffee. The tram dinged, and she turned to her left, her stomach now sinking for a whole other reason. Tiluma's building stood just outside her window, a huddle of employees gathered with dumbstruck gazes glued to the office door.

The tram's brakes sent forth an ear-piercing screech, and she surged out of her seat, eager to know what the huddle was all about. Her first steps onto the street brought her to the side of a red and gray van parked on the double-wide sidewalk, an area usually reserved for pedestrians only.

Daniel stood nearby, and she grabbed his arm, his face a wall of tight aggravation. "What's happened?"

He pointed to the van on the curb. Only then did she notice the giant cockroach painted on the side. "We have cockroaches?"

She sure as hell had never seen any.

Daniel shook his head. "Fleas."

She reeled back. "Wait? What? No. You can't be serious."

Her recently consumed coffee churned in her stomach, especially as Daniel's expression hardened. He *was* serious. "Remember Max's impromptu *Bring-Your-Dog-to-Work Day*?"

She pressed a hand over her face, her skin there suddenly cold. "Holy fuck! Not the mangy stray?"

Daniel nodded. "The fumigation process takes five hours, and the toxic gasses need at least another twenty-four hours to settle before anyone can enter the building."

A shiver worked up her spine, and her lungs struggled for a clear breath. The Schneider meeting would be canceled. Tiluma's reputation would be ruined, as well as her hopes for a promotion.

She focused on Daniel again. "How did we not know about this before today?"

"Apparently, we did." Luke sidled up to her, his voice dull, as if something all too meaningful had been wrenched from his life, leaving behind just a husk of who he'd been the day prior.

*Please let it be the fleas, not last night's awful departure.*

His sunken cheeks and ashen complexion, a major feat given his already light skin, made her throat feel all thick and dry. His gray tinge aged him by about ten years.

"That disgruntled employee you warned me about?" He shrugged, shoulders settling into a defeated slump she'd never witnessed on him before. "Yeah, that became a reality. The landlord got an anonymous complaint. We were given notice about the fumigation and a chance to change the date, but when I wasn't available, the message fell to Max."

Her stomach muscles clenched, like bracing to ward off a sucker punch to the gut, but no amount of bracing stopped the impact of this truth. "And the date change never happened because Max never passed on that message."

Luke shook his head. "No. He didn't. And now I have to call Schneider and cancel today's meeting."

An inferno spiked in her tummy, and her hands formed into tight fists at her side. She wasn't one to give up, but the fumigation process had begun, leaving no escape route here. But what stung most was that this disaster could have been prevented. If only she'd intercepted that angry staff member. If only she'd insisted on more in-office help for Max, or heck, that someone else take over his job until he proved he could handle even the smallest bit of responsibility. One thing was for sure. Her *sink-or-swim* approach had turned into one big, fucking mass drowning.

She turned to Luke, perhaps for no other reason than to fill the all-consuming silence ripping shreds off her insides. "Any idea who the disgruntled employee was?"

Luke let out a sigh. "Daniel tells me Tania, Max's former PA, was bent out of shape about the dog day. But who knows? I'm sure there's more than one disgruntled employee to sift through." He looked about, eyes clouded and jaw set, the chaos around him seeming to outweigh any hurt from last night. Why would he still speak to her now? "And I wouldn't blame them."

Four men in puffy, white protective suits trudged past, and groups of employees broke from the huddle, probably going home. The whole point of Ernest's meeting was to show him how well the office ran. Except, now there was no office. *What the hell would she tell Sue?*

Hot frustration seared through her chest, and her muscles fused into a painful strain all over. "And what will you do about Max now?"

Luke dipped his chin, his narrowed stare a slow warning. "Agathe. Don't."

She jerked her chin higher. Screw warnings and screw his tough CEO act. Where was that toughness in all the years Max had so silently dismantled this company? Besides, she'd issued her own damn warnings. *Numerous times…* And now her chance at a promotion evaporated before her very eyes.

"Don't what?" She glared at him with all the fire she could muster, which turned out to be a lot of fucking fire because she'd reached her limit with this man and the flaming disaster her life had become since meeting him.

"You know my reasons for keeping Max." His eyes flared, voice tight, signaling he expected her to keep his secret about the cliff fall.

And still, her head flung back in an uncontrolled and incredulous laugh. "You mean that, unlike every other person in your employ, Max gets a free pass and the undeserved glory of being second in charge? Yeah, I know." She thrust her hands out to her sides, gesturing to the scene around them. "How's that working for you?"

"Agathe." His tone sank to a growl. "Stop."

"Why? So you can continue with your misguided sense of duty to a full-grown man?" She tilted her head to one side and raised a brow in a challenge. "For Christ's sake, Luke. What you do impacts so many more people than those living in your little family bubble. Hell, just as a start, there are your employees and *their* families…."

His glare burned forward, and a muscle ticked at his jaw. "You think I don't know that?"

"No, I don't. You damn well don't act as if you do. So, maybe it's time someone told you." She ground her statement and pushed each word through gritted teeth. "Max may be quirky. Lazy. Absentminded. But he's no fool." She jabbed a finger at Luke. "But *you*, on the other hand…." She jabbed again, unleashing her full frustration. "You're the rampaging idiot who toyed with a hundred livelihoods just to ease your own pitiful guilt."

He jolted back as if she'd given him a physical slap. "You've crossed a line."

"What are you going to do?" Beyond caring, she twisted one corner of her lip into a sardonic smile. "Walk out on me?"

Oh, she went there.

Suddenly aware she'd yelled loud enough for everyone to hear, she turned to the crowd of gape-mouthed employees, any privacy between her and Luke demolished. But again, her mounting rage meant she shrugged off even that slip-up.

For so long, grief had been her stable ground. For a short time, Luke replaced that grief. He nudged her toward her own crumbling cliff's edge, toward hope and happiness, toward an emotional plunge she couldn't survive. And worst of all… *He'd left her.*

Left her with the real prospect of many more years of fear and solitude now that she knew what it was to have love. Now that she had no direction. He'd replaced her sense of security with hollowness. He'd left her with no safe place to turn. But then again… *Of course, he'd left.*

An ever-expanding lump formed in her throat, along with the knowledge that she was a complete and utter lost cause, incapable of love. This breakup was on her. She'd pushed him away too many times. Though, even with that understanding, logic and reason weren't always well paired, and she couldn't forgive him for holding her to her bluff.

"I get that Max is family. That there are different rules for him." Her voice cracked, and she paused to allow time to recover now that her rage had descended into drowning sorrow. "You forgive his every mistake, only to abandon me in my vulnerable moment. Can you see why it hurt me to see you leave last night?"

Someone in the crowd let out a gasp, wrenching her attention to a middle-aged woman with her hand wrapped around a stunned-looking man's arm beside her.

Willing to let the near strangers enjoy the show, Agathe turned back to Luke. Crowd or not, she needed to have it out with him, once and for all.

His lips dipped to a frown, and his cheeks held a distinct strain. "What difference would my staying have made? All I wanted was to hear that you cared, so don't tell me you figured your silence wouldn't hurt me too. You knew it would."

His focus stayed on her only a moment more until he slid his stare to his employees, and his cheeks fell slack, a sign some deep realization hit him square in the chest. "Don't I get to have a few human needs? All of this…." His stare met her again, though he lifted his hands to the people around him, to his building overrun with fumigators traipsing past. "I never planned for any of this, but I carry the burden every day. At what point do I get to stop worrying about everyone else and go after what I want?"

Her shoulders dropped, and sickness rocked her insides again while her ears rang with a sudden hypersensitivity to the crowd and noises around her. She'd been so busy licking her own wounds she'd at no point noticed his.

And he'd tried to warn her.

With Tiluma being only a few years old, he'd been tossed into the role of CEO with little to no experience, and he'd probably been treading water ever since. And the wife and children he'd dreamed of having? Maybe they were the extent of what he'd wanted all along. Before the stress of fixing Max. Of running a company and having a million obligations filling his to-do list.

And now… Now the Schneider meeting was a bust, and Luke's crestfallen face forced the awareness that this would be their last encounter. She'd tried to believe she could hold down a relationship. *But who was she kidding?* Too much bad blood passed here. And she was too broken. Luke had put up with a lot of her bullshit, and she'd been wrong to forget how much he'd done.

There was no way they could work together after today.

So, now he stood before her, shoulders tense, his entire form locked in a rigid stance. All while he awaited an answer.

*At what point do I get to stop worrying about everyone else and go after what I want?*

Her thoughts sank to Elsie, to those dark-blonde curls framing her angelic hazel eyes. The mental image alone sent her heart into an unstable flutter.

And right then, Elsie provided the answer. The reason why this exchange could only ever end with two people parting ways.

*At what point do you stop worrying about others?*

She closed her eyes, and her heart slowed to a plodding beat. In the chaos of her emotions, emotions that swung from one extreme to another, her daughter offered a smile—her delicate, pink lips and smooth, round cheeks, for once less haunting and more reassuring.

*Mumma's sweet, little peach.*

She'd endure any torture just to kiss that tiny face one last time.

She'd give everything. Literally, *everything*, to have Elsie walk this earth again. Would trade places without a second of a doubt.

Now, she opened her eyes to Luke stepping forward, but she shot out a hand, begging him to give her just one more moment of space. "Wait."

He paused, and a cry clawed at the base of her throat, her tears springing free from a small trickle to an escalating thick stream. "If you're truly lucky, Luke, the answer is *never*."

She drew toward him, for once wanting to be the one to reach out and pull him into what she'd decided would be their final embrace. "I hope you'll always have someone to worry about. It really is the best feeling in the world."

More tears fell, none that she could control. She turned her face into the warmth of his neck and clung to him. Grasping at her last chance to savor his support, she offered a heartfelt truce before she once more went out into the world alone.

The only person she'd worried about in the last four years had been herself. For a moment there, someone else had captured her focus. And while his light scent soothed, and his large body calmed her torrid emotions, she wasn't whole, and he wasn't Elsie.

He pulled back, and his fraught gaze danced around her face as if aware her actions equaled a final goodbye.

"Call Schneider." She did a one-eighty turn and powered away, finishing what he'd started last night, and what she should never have entered into in the first place.

The gawping crowd parted, and she kept her head bowed, but a pair of strong and somehow familiar hands grabbed at her shoulders. Not Luke. *Max.*

He stood with the crowd at his back, his face sporting the same ashen tone as his brother's.

"Don't do this to him." His blue eyes widened to a plea. "Don't leave Luke because of me."

Cold shock ran through her veins, and she locked her muscles in place to keep from running. Since when did Max approach anything with any kind of cognizance or gravity?

She hugged her arms around her and bounced on the spot again, forcing her feet to remain in this place. "I'm not leaving because of you."

He flicked his gaze to where Luke most likely stood, a frown weighing his expression. "I've never seen that look on his face before. If you go, you'll break his heart."

All breath seemed to leave her lungs since Max confirmed that she did, in fact, manage to torture anyone unfortunate enough to get sucked into her miserable orbit.

"I'll do worse if I stay." She unlocked her arms and slid back, breaking Max's hold. Her only comfort was that, at least now, she could say she'd done the right thing. She'd ended Luke's torture. "Go, look after your brother, okay?"

Her heart hammered, and she turned, jogging away before Max could say anything else to convince her to stay. Desperate to disappear around the nearest corner, she got as far as the next building before a black limousine slowed beside her, and a tinted back window rolled down.

She stopped in her tracks. A shock of white hair and a wrinkled face appeared from beyond the glass. Weathered gray eyes glared at the disturbance out front of Tiluma. *Schneider.* An hour early. *Of course, he'd be early.*

He turned and glowered at her, her face likely tear-stained, puffy, and red.

A quick beat passed before the window slid closed, and the car pulled away.

# Chapter Twenty-Seven

"I wondered when this would happen."

Sue Hatchman's lips formed a flat line, her tight expression similar to a headmistress ready to scold a wayward pupil. Agathe sank deeper into her chair, attention swerving to a cloudless Melbourne sky outside the private office window at Slate and King.

Though her tummy gave a heavy kick of guilt, she cleared her throat and dove into the discussion. Whatever happened next wouldn't do much to further dent her current status of being a shitty person. "What would happen?"

Sue gave a calculated shrug. "You'd crack."

Though Agathe had already counted on adding losing her job to her mudslide of recent fuckups, she blinked and reeled against a sudden inability to conjure words. "You saw yesterday coming?"

"Sure." Sue wove a pointed finger through the air, gesturing to the world at large. "Though, what with the whole public display outside Tiluma, getting involved with Luke Tindall, Schneider falling through so cataclysmically…I never predicted you'd implode on such a grand scale." She leaned forward in a clear bid for total attention. "But then again, it's kind of typical that most people crack at a crucial point in their career. You were so close, Agathe. So close. I had hoped you wouldn't end up being like *most people*. Not when you were weeks away from becoming a key figure here at Slate and King."

The air was thick with disappointment, and Sue shook her head.

Agathe's insides contracted and wrung, and her posture bent along with her already lowered self-worth. Hearing her utter failure verbalized hurt on a whole other level than merely just thinking about it.

"And now?" she whispered, not sure she wanted to hear the answer.

"And now, I don't know. It takes years to build the trust we handed to you, and you blew it all away." Sue lifted her hands. "I got a call from Tiluma's human resources manager. They're worried about you. To be frank, so am I."

Agathe sagged in her chair. The phone call and Sue's pointed stare only confirmed her greatest flaws had become public knowledge.

Sue sighed. "I don't know what to do with you. I could lecture you on reliability, on not hooking up with a client, on your need to lighten up...but you're not incompetent, Agathe. You know all this already. What I will say, though, is that you've now made your problem my problem, which leaves me with a giant mess to clean up on top of my already heavy workload."

Agathe peered down at her hands folded in her lap, feeling even shittier now, like gum stuck to the underside of Sue's shoe.

"Agathe." Sue's stern tone demanded Agathe look at her again. "While I'm amazed Tiluma even wants to work with anyone from this office again, not only do I have to summon a replacement for you at Tiluma, but I have to grapple with the knowledge that I vouched for you, and you made me look inept in front of the board. And still, I spent much of this morning fighting tooth and nail to see you don't get fired." She huffed out a sigh, shaking her head. "I don't even know why I did that."

Agathe straightened in her chair. "I'm not fired?"

Sue gave a flat stare. "No."

Agathe reeled back, her fingers clawing into her thigh. "But why? Why not?"

Sue rolled her eyes, a begrudging sign against having to admit the following. "Because I convinced the board that firing long-standing staff in the clear throes of emotional distress would be a public relations nightmare. Besides, the mention of a potential lawsuit alone was enough to make them take a step back. And…as I said, I had a feeling you'd crack one day. In some ways, I blame myself."

Sue's explanation confirmed that everyone really did think Agathe an unhinged timebomb waiting to explode, and in Sue's case, the observation had been a long-standing one proven true. Agathe buried her face in her hands and groaned, wondering if she wore her emotional scars like a giant tattoo on her forehead.

How many of her colleagues noticed? Did everyone secretly tip-toe around her?

Seeking more answers, she kept her face buried and said, "Am I really that obvious?"

"You've always walked around this office with a dark cloud hanging over your head. You worked so tirelessly, and yes, at times it did cross my mind that you punished yourself with a heavy workload." Sue paused and let out a sigh. "On some level, I figured you couldn't keep it up forever."

Agathe took a centering breath. Her heart was pained with just how much Sue noticed and that, perhaps, she didn't deserve a second chance at keeping this job. "I hooked up with a client. That would have to be an inexcusable offense, right?"

Sue shrugged. "While no one here is pleased with your involvement with Mr. Tindall, Tiluma's H.R. manager conveyed Luke's direct request that you don't lose your job. In fact, it was a condition of keeping them as a client."

A sharp, burning sensation sheered through Agathe's nerve endings. Her entire body was left in shock while she took a deep gulp against each memory of all she'd done to hurt him. And he still looked out for her? *Even now.*

This new revelation confirmed just how much she simply did *not* deserve his love.

Luke belonged to someone else. Someone better. Someone more equipped to handle a relationship. No matter how much his name remained on a loop in her head, she'd made the right choice in leaving him behind. At least she could say her troubles stemmed from a need to save a life—Luke's—rather than mourn one.

She crossed and uncrossed her legs and, when that failed to offer any comfort, forced herself to focus on Sue. "Where do we go from here?"

"Well." Sue sank back in her giant office chair as if the worst of this conversation had ended. "You take some time off. Let the dust settle around what happened yesterday while you sort yourself out. Meanwhile, I'll put out the fires left in your wake."

Agathe's heart stammered at losing work as her crutch. Even for just a little while. Even though this was the best-case scenario. She did need time off. Time to figure out what to do next. Because if she were truly honest, this job no longer covered over the cracks in her life. The long hours and high-pressure clients only distracted from a wound no amount of over-scheduling healed. In the meantime, that unattended wound festered and spread, harming those who bothered to extend her any care.

Maybe time away would propel her toward something different.

Maybe she'd find a life where the emotional void of Elsie's death and the bittersweet ache of Luke's absence hurt a little less. Where ghosts didn't haunt, and love caused no damage.

She swallowed against another thought that the last four years warned that a day of healing and peace might never come. That some tragedies were so brutal nothing would fade the scars left behind.

Luke had been right. And she had to try.

She'd sought him for a reason. A subconscious effort to push for change, never quite sure if those changes were any good for her. But given the battered state of her heart, all the carnage left behind, she'd clearly sought a change in all the wrong ways.

A spark of hope lit the uncertainty in her soul, and she turned to Sue. "How much time do I have off?"

"A month." Sue frowned as though she were looking for clues on whatever went through Agathe's head.

"I have a lot of unused leave." Agathe paused and gnawed on her lower lip, her near termination limiting the amount of wriggle room at her disposal. Still, she'd need more than a month. "Can we make it three?"

She threw a pleading sort of cringe. Though Sue glared, the tension around her eyes soon settled. "Fine, I can probably swing that. Three months it is."

Resigned to her murky fate, Agathe pushed out of her chair and thanked Sue before leaving.

Goodbye, promotion.

Goodbye, perhaps, to her entire career.

In just twenty-four hours, her life had flipped upside down, her existence something akin to a Dali painting smashed together with an Edvard Munch. Her hands pressed to her cheeks in a silent howl like "The Screamer," her new world a surreal wasteland like those dismal melting clocks.

She had three months. Three months to sort through all she'd learned. Three months to unpack what her time with Luke had been about. And three months to decide what to do next.

Luke opened his front door to Max waiting on the other side. Not the person he'd hoped for, his shoulders immediately sinking. The strain on his brother's face garnered the quickest of glances before he turned to storm down the hall, leaving the door wide open for Max to follow.

*The visitor Luke wanted most would likely never cross his path again.*

Hiding his disappointment but not his dull tone, he called out behind him. "Want a beer?"

"Yeah, a beer would be great." The front door clicked shut, and Max soon joined him at the kitchen counter. "About the other day—"

Having spent two days actively avoiding Max and perhaps not one hundred percent ready to see him, Luke cut him off intentionally, jamming a beer bottle into his brother's hand. "Here."

Max stared back, unblinking. "Ah. Thanks."

A nervy silence followed, and Luke pressed his bottle to his lips, indulging in a long pull of cold, bitter beer. Thanks to his brother and his never-ending string of stunts, Tiluma's future lay in ruins. Luke hadn't yet allowed staff back into the office, and any day now, he expected a pile-up of resignations on his desk.

So much hard work had gone to waste, and so many people remained rightfully mad to see the Schneider opportunity fall through. Morale was at an all-time low. Worst still, all of this could have been avoided.

And then there'd been that sorrowful scene with Agathe....

A thudding pain knocked around in Luke's head, a warning his brain teetered on the edge of being overwhelmed. Meanwhile, Max rolled his unopened beer bottle between his hands, hips leaning casually against the white marble counter like he had no care in the world.

"An apology would be nice right about now." Luke stared at his brother.

Max stilled and then straightened his posture, cheeks hollow and color faded. "Yeah, I'm sorry. I'm shit at my job, and I've screwed up Tiluma for everyone."

Wanting to add guilt to Max's discomfort, Luke pointed his bottle in an accusatory manner. "*You* should have been the one to call Schneider and explain. You're just damn lucky it would have looked like an insult and a cop-out if I hadn't been the one to talk to him."

Not that any explanation would sway Schneider toward ever looking Tiluma's way again....

Max's gaze dropped to the ground, and he shook his head. "I know. I'm sorry about that too." He placed his unopened beer on the counter and lifted his attention. "But I can fix this."

Luke spat out a brash laugh. "You've got to be joking. You made everyone at Tiluma look ridiculous. We're an industry joke now. No investor will come within a mile of our office. How the hell do you think you can fix this?"

"I've spent two days making calls and managed to get hold of Bret Lowell, and—"

"You mean the infamous party boy, rich kid with the idiotic TV commercials?" Luke dipped his chin, shooting Max a resolute glare, unable to scrub the mental image of Bret Lowell dressed as a koala while hawking his latest electrical appliances sale. "No. Hell no."

Max maintained a stern frown and crossed his arms in an added show of defense. "I met him the other week while out on the town. He's actually very clever, and he could—"

"No." Luke reveled in his short reply, a good shield against his past pattern of entertaining Max's harebrained business acumen. "No more help."

Max drummed his fingers on the counter, his jaw stiff, the rest of him unmoving. But only until he shrugged and pitched forth a lopsided smile. "Agathe was right. I'm not suited for the CTO role. I quit."

"You what?" Luke's fingers loosened on the bottle in his hand, and he lowered the glass to keep from dropping it.

"I quit." Max shrugged again, his posture suddenly more relaxed as if those two words released him from a world of anguish. "I want to scale back and enjoy the money we've made. I don't want to play out some role I just happened to fall into, and the CTO gig is just too much pressure. So, I'm going to step back and figure out what I *really* want to do with my life. Besides, you know Daniel deserves the position way more than I do."

Heat rose through Luke's chest, along with a new kind of anger mixed with jealousy that Max found it so easy to cut professional ties and move on with his life. A luxury Luke didn't have.

"So, you're just going to leave me to run Tiluma on my own?" He scoffed, struggling to reign in his crackling temper. "A reputation-damaged Tiluma, at that!"

Max's expression hardened. "You run this show alone, anyway, and you just said you don't want my input anymore."

Cold, hard truth dowsed Luke's temper, making room for his truer feelings. "But we're a team."

Max swiped up his beer bottle and twisted the top, the lid soon making a cracking sound. "No. We're brothers. And right now, Tiluma is getting in the way of that. Since it's the only aspect of this job I ever enjoyed, I'll offer app ideas from time to time if that's what you want, but other than that, I need to go."

Luke sank back and plunked his weight onto a nearby stool. "Tiluma won't be the same."

"No. It won't." Max took a sip of his beer and shrugged. "It'll be better. We both know that."

"I wouldn't go that far."

Max huffed out a staggered laugh. "No, your guilt won't let you, but it's still true."

Luke paused at yet another mention of his guilt, Agathe's similar sentiments from the other day confronting him once again.

"Your guilt is another thing Agathe was right about." Max took another drink, his stare fixed ahead. The statement made Luke's stomach lurch like his brother had dug into his thoughts and wrenched out the painful bits. "I know you started Tiluma to make up for my accident, but that was years ago, and you've helped me for way too long. You don't owe me anymore. In fact, you never did. And since I don't want any part in destroying your life, I'm setting us both free."

"You had a promising future, and I ruined it."

Max gave an adamant shake of his head. "I have more money and stability than any swimming career could have ever provided. *You* did that too. You've punished yourself enough and paid me back ten times over. I mean, yeah, you basically talked me into throwing myself off a cliff, but…." He chuckled, then cleared his throat, scrubbing a hand over his chin until a more sober expression took over. "I know you were messed up at the time, Luke, and that you didn't mean anything by it. And look, we both turned out well in the end."

Luke veered his attention to the glossy counter beneath his right hand, the cold stone seeping a clarifying chill through to his palm. He couldn't recall the last time they'd spoken so candidly. Truth be told, he missed this. He missed just being Max's brother and not his boss. Against all odds and his clownish character, Max made an accurate point.

"That's pretty much what Agathe said, too." He turned his attention back to Max, his voice roughened and stomach pained with the sting of his more recent and bitter memories.

Max took a seat next to him. "About Agathe—"

Luke held up a hand, signaling for him to stop right there.

Max shook his head, eyes glittering. "Dude, will you stop interrupting me? Hear me out on this one."

Luke gave him a narrowed side glare. "You know, for someone here to apologize, you sure are damn bossy today."

"I'm allowed to be." Max sent forth a huge grin. "I quit, remember? From here on out, you're just my grouchy older brother."

Luke raised a brow, amused and annoyed at the same time. "You forget there are two people involved here, and Agathe made her decision."

"Yeah, and I might not have a reputation for being the brightest person ever, but I saw the look on her face when she walked away." Max's forehead creased as if he pleaded for Luke to really listen. "She cares about you, and that counts for something."

Luke did his best to rein in his frustration, even though it rose like hot lava all the same. "She also walked away. She stone-cold left."

"She didn't walk. She ran away heartbroken." Max leaned in, leaving Luke nowhere to escape. "And did you see her tears? There was nothing *stone-cold* about her exit. Take this from someone with more reason to dislike her than you do. Someone she's been hard on from day one. Being hard isn't the same as being straight-up unkind, and she's never been that. Everyone at the office loved her. Some are more upset about her leaving than Schneider falling through."

Luke slumped forward and pressed his palm to his forehead, Max's unlikely praise of Agathe offering more evidence that a good woman had slipped from his grasp. But what else could he do? He'd loved her. Invited her into his world. And none of it stopped her from leaving.

"When I asked if I meant anything to her…." He eyed his brother, his voice husky at the memory of how this whole landslide started. "She said nothing. She committed to nothing."

Max scoffed and gave his head a slow and incredulous shake. "Man, you must put in some serious effort to be this bleeding stupid. She had no obligation to stroke your fragile ego. Can't you see? The woman thought herself too damaged for a relationship, and so she broke her heart and yours just to protect you from the heartache of having her around."

Luke squinted, shooting Max what he hoped passed as a skeptical look. But Max just rolled his eyes again and threw an expletive in under his breath. "Jesus flippin' Christ, Luke. She didn't want to leave.

She just didn't want to drag you down with her. Any pea-brained numbnuts could see that. Of course, she cares about you. Hell, I'd say she probably loves you, too." He paused, like he awaited a reply, then swore under his breath again when he got none. "Leaving was her ultimate sacrifice, you idiot."

Luke jolted. He hadn't been called an idiot since he'd been about sixteen years old and an actual idiot, but for the second time in as many days, that word hit him with direct and blunt force. First, when Agathe had called him out for *toying with a hundred livelihoods*, and now Max.

Having had enough and wanting to be alone, Luke rose from his seat. "Time for you to go."

Max blinked up at his brother but otherwise didn't move. "Only if you promise you'll get your shit together and get Agathe back."

Luke prowled forward, each tense step twisting his dwindling patience tighter and tighter. "I'll think about it."

"If you don't do something, I swear on our sister's psych degree that I will."

Luke gave a half-hearted glare, at least glad Max hadn't sworn on their mother's life or something, still not taking his brother's threat all that seriously. "I said I'd think about it. Now, get out of my house."

Getting Agathe back wouldn't be as simple as Max made out. She wanted her distance, and far be it from him to get in the way of those wishes.

"Fine, I'll go." Max stood, eyes glinting like he relished the idea of maybe having influenced his older brother in some way. "But is everything good between us now?"

His smile grew like he knew Luke would never cut him out over anything as small as money or business. The little jerk also knew that his insightful rant about Agathe succeeded in turning this supposed apology on its head. But then again, Max wouldn't be Max without his lively quirks. And Luke loved his younger brother.

He gave Max a playful shove on the shoulder and expedited his journey out the front door. "I'll think about that too."

# Chapter Twenty-Eight

*Two months later*

Agathe peered out the train's scuffed window, the *click-clack* of metal wheels setting her heart to a high flutter. Roseford Station loomed just ahead, with its red-tile roof hovering above a black asphalt platform. She veered her gaze to her phone in her hand, half to deny her arrival, half to browse the list of recent messages sent from Luke:

> We need to talk.

> I can't stop thinking about you.

> I'm an idiot.

She frowned at that last one, so unlike him, but perhaps an indication he wasn't doing so well these days. He hadn't contacted her in two months, but over the past two weeks, she'd received five messages. Five messages she hadn't responded to, even though she'd put herself on this train to see him.

> Please, Agathe. I'm a pain in the ass without
> you, and everyone around me is struggling.

The wording in that message seemed a little off too, but some people didn't handle breakups well. Maybe Luke was one of them. True enough, she'd had more than her fair share of *moments* over the years and found relief in knowing she wasn't the only unstable person in this extinct relationship.

> I'll be in Roseford this weekend. Alone. Please
> come see me. I'm sorry for all the messages,
> but I need closure. I won't bother you anymore
> after this.

The finality of that last message left her miserable for days and prompted her to catch this train. It was a glimpse into his emotions following her abrupt exit. She'd broken her heart in walking away, but he'd been the one blindsided. She'd known her true motives. He hadn't. She owed him this visit. She owed him an explanation.

Besides, she'd essentially used him for sex and walked away. The guilt over her actions tore shreds off her every night, and the chance of a civil face-to-face encounter fueled her journey. She had to heal the rift. Had to have the frank exchange she'd never given him. The one he now asked for.

And if the encounter went badly, she'd catch a cab to Uncle Raymond's, perhaps reacquaint herself with his booze collection and cheer herself up. The man was also a killer cook, so it wouldn't be a wasted weekend.

Her family had been right from the start. They'd done nothing wrong, and she'd reached a point in her recovery where she wanted to let them into her world again. What they hadn't been right about was the timing.

But now, after two months of therapy and hard-won self-healing, she looked at her future through a different lens. For the first time in years, she had moments where just being alive was enough.

The train ground to a halt, and she jumped to her feet, gathering her one bag and hurtling out the sliding door where she willed her nerves to give her heart a break. This visit wasn't just about closure or healing. She needed to finish what she'd started. She needed to see Luke. Needed to know he was okay. Heck, maybe *need* wasn't the right word. Maybe she just plain *wanted* him….

*But I ruined every hope months ago….*

Hope. Ha! What a ridiculous word. She chuckled that even her therapist pushed for her to find hope in just about everything, to embrace the possibility of positive outcomes as if hope were the key to *living* versus being merely alive.

Part of her therapy meant learning to make positive thoughts a near-natural compulsion, but try as she had, she wasn't convinced that would ever happen. Still, her pessimism no longer stopped her altogether. So maybe she made progress all the same.

*And what positive light can I cast on my current predicament?*

Hmmm…well…Luke *had* asked for this meeting, so there was that. In fact, he'd asked to talk numerous times. It wasn't like she showed up in Roseford uninvited.

A yellow cab waited outside the station, the only one in the designated taxi rank. She waved at the driver, a woman in her mid-forties, who gestured for her to jump on in.

"Where to?" The woman peered through the rearview mirror, her blue eyes lively, as though she had no worries and no real hurry.

"Ninety-three North Road." Agathe buckled her seatbelt.

The car picked up speed, and her pulse raced faster than the vehicle she rode in, the same vehicle entering the main road. This meeting with Luke marked two months of soul-searching and time spent alone. She'd done the things he'd said she needed to all along. She'd adopted a slower pace. A pace that mostly brought on one ugly day after another.

There'd been days upon days where she raged and got lost in her anger, where she let her house fall into neglected disarray. Days where she cried until her eyes were so swollen they refused to open, and she pretty much lived in her bed and ate microwaved leftovers. Days where she'd been reduced to a weak puddle of sobbing woman, folded on her bathroom floor. And there were days when she felt nothing, where she didn't regret ending things with Luke at all. Not when the reflection in her mirror showed a puffy-eyed and bedraggled representation of all she'd kept inside.

She'd needed those days.

Needed to battle against her dependence on distraction—the distraction she'd created with work, and then Luke, and then sex with Luke. She'd needed to stop. To face her past *alone*.

And then, one day, the rage lifted. As did the sadness.

Little by little, she felt better.

And as much as her healing remained a work in progress, she'd developed skills for handling her grief. She found herself wanting to make space for those who cared about her. *To accept acts of warmth.* Just as Luke had said. But all of that had been impossible back when she'd believed herself unworthy of kindness.

She scoffed, loud enough for the taxi driver to give her a frown through the rearview mirror. While Agathe had found some peace, she'd alienated all who cared, and now she had a lot of atoning to do.

What hope did she have that her family would want her back?

And what about Luke?

Rocks crunched under the taxi's tires, drawing her attention to a narrow path and a wide veranda to her right. Her chest tightened, and she struggled for the next few breaths.

*For frig's sake, get it together. I have to be here whether I want to or not.*

After all that had happened, she couldn't simply ignore Luke or pretend he meant nothing. That his presence had made no impact on her life.

He'd been the impetus to her sorting herself out, while she'd mostly just messed with his heart. For that alone, she needed to dust off her bravery.

A green metal letterbox peered back at her, the number ninety-three announcing Luke's rural home. She dug through her large, yellow tote bag and searched for money to pay the driver.

"Do you mind waiting until I give you a signal to leave?" She handed the driver more cash than due. "I don't know if anyone will be home or how long this will take."

The driver gave a jovial laugh and waved the wad of notes in the air. "Sure thing."

Agathe pushed her door open and slid out onto the gravel path. Her few steps to Luke's veranda felt like a slow death march, her heart thundering with each labored step.

Just then, a familiar, hollow feeling opened within her chest. The same feeling plagued her after each soul-baring counseling session. There'd been months of solitude, of unearthing regret, pain, and bitterness, but she'd also learned.

She held her fist to the pine-green door, ready to knock, steeling herself for whatever happened next.

~

Luke glared at his laptop screen, unable to focus on the dry content of yet another financial report. Why he'd brought his work to a relaxing weekend in Roseford, he didn't know. Maybe he'd known his troubles would follow him because, frankly, that's all they'd done for the last two months straight. Follow and taunt.

Maybe, he wasn't so different from Agathe after all. Both used work to chase away darker thoughts. Then again, unlike Agathe, he failed to maintain focus and muddled through his hours with little done.

He groaned and buried his head in his hands, the public showdown with Agathe having changed so much, including how everyone at Tiluma saw him. Since Max's exit and Daniel's promotion, some things did improve, but not enough to hide Luke's struggle against major professional and personal upheaval.

His employees now gave him prolonged stares twisted with sympathy. He fumbled through tasks he'd found easy just months ago. He was indecisive while merely cruising through a blander version of his previous life, and he had no idea how to break this exhausting and insidious loop.

Determined to take advantage of his property's surrounding bushland, he stood and abandoned the report on his desk. He'd promised himself a weekend of exercise, solitude, and an end to his moping. The time had come to put action to that promise. Time for a run.

He marched toward his front door, even though he'd been on a hundred runs since Agathe left, and none worked to set him free. It didn't help that Max wouldn't get off his case about rekindling what was now a well and truly faded relationship. His insistence added weight to Luke's tendency to engage in daily death stares with his phone, willing himself to disregard her wishes and call her anyway.

He swung open his front door and pinned his gaze high to the patchy blue-gray sky behind the sway of multiple slender gum trees up ahead. Quick to push himself forward, he slammed straight into something sizeable and solid on his landing.

He peered down at a woman bouncing backward and away from his chest, to her slender figure flailing and then landing in a loud and cracking heap on the timber veranda. Long nutmeg and sand-colored hair fell in a tangled mess about her face.

*Nutmeg and sand-colored hair?*

*It couldn't be...*

"Luke?" The pile of person pushed her hair from her face, and her small, surprised voice slammed into him with the force of a freight train.

Everything within him halted—his breath, his thoughts, his desire to move—all he could do was stare.

Wide, dark eyes mirrored his shock. His nymph-woman with her warm, brown skin and delicate features. She glowed against the backdrop of spring flowers along his path, her beauty as devastating and painful as her absence.

He settled back on his heels, chest tight, fingers clawing into the doorframe. "Agathe? You're here?"

Despite her crumpled state at his feet, she peered up at him, the once-strained muscles around her eyes visibly relaxed. Not in a momentary way, but as if this were who she was now. As if she merely returned to him from some serene holiday, having finally found peace.

He should have reached out to her, apologized for slamming into her, or at least offered to help her stand. Only, he couldn't move past her presence, and his mind and body refused to work as he wished.

She held up her phone, gaze not veering from his, not even for a second. "I got your messages."

"Messages?" He reeled back a little.

"The... ah..." Her face paled. "The messages you...." She scrambled to her feet, her attention on her phone before she flicked her gaze back up to him. "Oh, shit. You didn't send any messages, did you?"

He shook his head, slow, because his mind still raced to piece this whole scene together.

Nothing made any sense. Not seeing her. Nothing of what she said. Then again, her pale cheeks made her appear equally confused. *What is she talking about? Messages? What messages?*

He stepped aside and opened his door wider, an automatic reaction, really, since he was yet to decide whether to feel elated or annoyed to have her here. She'd ditched him, after all, and in front of all his staff. And still, his life was lacking without her, and he wanted to hear what she had to say. "Come in."

She stepped back and swung her wild gaze around to where a yellow cab waited at the end of his path. "Oh no, I can't. I'm so sorry. I don't know what's happened, but I've clearly bothered you, and I should leave now."

She turned away and began walking, though her gaze stayed on him a moment longer, and her chin trembled in a hint she needed one last glimpse.

"Wait." He lunged out but stopped short of actually touching her. His breath staggered, and his voice a hard and desperate plea. "Show me the messages."

Her bewildered stare lingered for a quiet beat before her brows dipped, and she extended her phone to him. "This is really embarrassing."

He flicked through the list of bizarre texts he'd supposedly sent, all while calculating how he might rewrite the script on her last, hurried escape. There were details he wanted to clarify before she ran from his life again.

He frowned and lifted his gaze to her. "The number's mine, but do you really think I'd call myself a pain in the ass?"

One corner of her lip quivered, and she dipped her focus, a sign that maintaining seriousness proved too hard a task. "I thought you might have gone a little post-breakup crazy."

He stared at her growing cringe and reddened cheeks but handed the phone back. "These were all sent on weekends."

She lifted her attention again and flicked hair from her eyes. "So?"

"So, the times and dates link to Max's visits to my house. He must have used my phone to message you, then deleted the evidence on my end before I could notice."

Her face fell slack. "What tech-savvy guy doesn't lock his phone?"

"One who doesn't care too much for sports." He bit back a smile, enjoying the way her gaze darted around his face, and uncertainty hollowed the space beneath her cheekbones. "Max and I have been hanging out a lot lately. I check work emails on my phone while he watches games. I must have wandered away a few times and left my phone unlocked in his presence."

She tilted her head to one side as though she didn't believe his theory. Or perhaps she simply didn't *want* to believe. Because that would mean she'd trekked all the way to Roseford for a man who hadn't sought her out. But oh, how he'd wanted to. So very much.

"And you're sure Max is the only person who could have sent those messages?"

His heart skipped at the hint she might actually want him to have been the one who'd sent those texts.

"The Max theory is the only one that makes sense. He's also the only person who knew I'd be here this weekend." That and the ratbag had gotten fed up with Luke's refusal to contact Agathe and made good on his vow to take matters into his own hands. Luke paused, another thought entering his head. "And why would I call myself an idiot?"

A grin flicked across her mouth, and the color of her irises seemed to grow a richer brown. "Yet another message that seemed a little odd."

She clamped her mouth shut again, shoulders trembling, the little witch restraining a laugh.

He leaned his weight forward and studied her closely, her tiny changes ones he'd thought impossible. She carried a lightness, her eyes sparkled with an ease he'd never seen in her before, and her smile... Her smile seemed to spring from a place way deep within, where once that smile had mostly been just a series of joyless reflexes playing out across her face.

He wanted to close the space between them. To place his lips at each corner of her glorious grin. To make up for her months of absence until he'd had his fill.

*But I don't have that right anymore. She left me, remember?*

"I'm sorry about this mix-up." The lines over her cheekbones smoothed, this action alone far more open and less defensive than the woman he'd known. "You didn't ask me here. You deserve your privacy. I'm going to leave."

She turned again, and his heart gave a tug. He couldn't let her go. Not yet. Not again.

His feet worked of their own accord and took him a giant step forward, his voice ringing out before common sense intervened. "You're here now. Stay."

She spun around, her glance striking him, then hitting the floor.

"Oh right, I forgot." He sank back on his heels, feeling like a fool. "You're the one who walked away last time. Of course, you don't want to stay."

She blinked up at him again as though fighting some conflict in her head. "I do. It's just...."

He waited for her to finish her sentence, but she seemed to lose that ability. Meanwhile, his breath labored under the weight of what he should have asked the second she'd appeared at his door. "Why are you here?"

Her lower lip momentarily disappeared between her teeth. "I wasn't happy with how I left things. I can't say I had any other option but to leave, but I agreed with what I thought was your request for closure."

A molten fire ignited in his chest, tension drawing at his muscles. He jammed his hands into his pants pockets and ground out his next words. "So you're here to say goodbye again, just in a different way?"

She was right, though. Her first exit could have included time for him to ask all the questions still ravaging his mind, but then, maybe they could have also come up with a compromise to her leaving. One where he wised up to doing things differently with her, perhaps something that involved him being less protective of his needs, with more space for her to decide how she felt.

He relaxed his shoulders and set his goal to not riling her, to obtaining those answers he'd wanted all this time. To learn what thoughts ran through her head. To find out if she'd truly only come here to close the book on what they'd shared.

Her gaze shifted about his face as if still searching for the right answer to her being here. Her non-reply tore at his patience, but a lack of patience had gotten him into this mess in the first place. So, he jutted his chin to the waiting taxi and focused on how much he didn't want her to leave. How he'd been too hard on her that first time. And yet, she'd still traveled all the way here to see him today.

"Is the taxi leaving?"

She peered over her shoulder. "I asked the driver to wait."

"In case I told you to leave?"

She shrugged. "Or, you know, you simply weren't home."

He jerked back at the smart-aleck reply, and a short laugh busted loose.

*What has happened to Agathe?*

The cold breeze skated her scent of sunflowers and rain to him, and the bright fragrance alone delivered a familiar sense of homecoming, her softer expression stirring hope.

Maybe she *had* changed.

Maybe he could be different too.

So, with that thought in mind, he focused on her barely perceptible smile, the one that made his heart lurch and fueled his next words. "Tell the cab to go. You're staying."

# Chapter Twenty-Nine

A frown dragged at Agathe's lips while Luke held his door open and made room for her to enter. She spun around and waved the taxi away, not all that sure she'd made the right choice. The sinking in her heart said she'd just waved goodbye to her only chance at escape.

She turned back to Luke just as his jaw set firm, and his gaze burrowed into hers. "Come on in."

While her life had gotten easier, his heavy tone indicated just how much she'd hurt him. He stepped aside, and she bowed her head, avoiding an extra glimpse of the deep lines marking his forehead.

The door clicked shut behind her, and her stomach roiled anew. Her entrapment looked more real now, while a long list of things to say scrolled through her mind, with nothing seeming quite right. The more she thought about what they'd shared and what she'd thrown away, the less she knew how to approach this conversation. Hell, she had zero idea what went through Luke's mind, and until she did, she couldn't decide which of her wishes to commit to words.

Did she want to apologize?

*Yes.*

To throw herself at his mercy and beg for re-entry into his life?

*Maybe.*

Was she anywhere near entitled to that?

*Hell, no.*

And even if she got that second chance, could she provide the love and consistency he deserved? *Who friggin' knew?*

A sudden tight pain twisted in her gut, the details of his living room blurring behind her fractured focus. All she saw was his weathered gaze studying her from a few feet away, followed by the understanding that, for the first time in months, they stood alone. *Together.*

The ache of seeing him radiated through her torso. She'd missed him. Missed *this.* The comfort of having him near. Amongst all the uncertainty, her desires held true. She wanted back into his world.

Her diaphragm hitched under a stalled breath, and her tummy constricted with a quick surge of nerves. There was no knowing if she'd get this next bit right, but as surely as she loved her daughter, she loved Luke too and was staring at her last chance to claim him.

The problem was she no longer had free rein with him. She had no right to reach out verbally, touch, or hug him anymore. The wall between them felt so expansive she couldn't even share a line of open banter. So much had passed, so much time and trauma, all largely her fault. Her only hope was that he'd understand.

She'd needed to leave him, that much had been certain, but her recovery came at the cost of love. And without that time away, she would never have opened to one certain truth. *That her love for Luke could exist on its own.*

As a love so different from the bond she shared with Elsie.

Not a replacement, but in addition to what she held for her daughter.

Perhaps that's where she'd always been wrong. She *did* love Luke. Months of missing him said as much. Only, she'd believed all forms of love or happiness would erode her link with Elsie. Agathe had taken far too long to recognize that punishing herself was no way to uphold Elsie's memory. And punish herself, she had.

All that remained now was a frozen inability to function in Luke's presence. Because she'd punished him too. Her regret ran so deep she could only stand here, speechless and unable to move, drinking in the bewildering image of him before her.

*Enjoy the view. Who knows if or when I'll see him again.*

Her hands balled at her sides, her body reduced to an aching lump of hurt. The wariness in his eyes made her want to purge every wild emotion rushing through her bloodstream.

"I…" Heavy doubt held her back, but she swallowed hard and forced herself to speak some more. "I should apologize for my abrupt exit the last time."

Echoing silence enveloped her and made her mouth dry, his unshifting stare making her heart sink anew. Her words sounded empty. *Pathetic.*

His stormy stare reflected a turbulent sea of emotions, one she wanted to flinch from, even though she held utterly still, leaving room for his reply. "And what about the public humiliation in front of my entire office?"

She cleared her throat and lowered her head, having once believed hope her greatest enemy and now seeing that maybe she'd been right. "Not my brightest moment."

He took a loud breath in, followed by a weighty sigh. "If I were a smarter man, I would have seen your exit coming."

She stifled an urge to snap her focus up, her shame and fear so thick she couldn't bring herself to look at him again. "And if I were a smarter woman, I would have left an opening for me to return."

Her stomach churned, and she waited for him to say or do something. *Anything.*

His shoes made a series of thuds against the floor, thuds that grew louder. She squeezed her eyes shut, hoping he wouldn't touch her. If he did, she'd break for sure.

"Agathe." The soft rumble of his voice melted her insides. "Look at me."

She squeezed her eyelids tighter and shook her head. *No, if you give me hope only to turn me down, there'll be no going back.*

Losing Elsie had left her heart in pieces, and she had no idea what pain would swallow her whole if she lost this man again. For good this time.

His familiar scent of citrus and man drifted over her, jolting her senses. What a strange reaction, coupled with the feeling of home-coming and the knowledge that Luke now held the power to crush her.

"Agathe." A hint of humor uplifted his tone.

Surely, she looked like a petulant child refusing to face up to some major blunder. In other words, she looked like the complete and utter wimp she actually was.

Another rustle came, and a knuckle pressed beneath her chin, tilting her face upwards. Her heart fluttered, and like a clamshell fighting to stay shut, she squeezed her eyelids tighter.

"Look at me." His voice dropped to a gentle whisper, similar to a man coaxing an injured animal. A man himself injured and aching. "Don't make me kiss you."

Her eyes flung open, and her jaw dropped wide. She reeled back, her desire for him somehow roaring amidst her bare shock. "Why would you do that?"

He shrugged, a triumphant grin lighting his face. "I figured the prospect would get you to look at me. It worked, didn't it?" His smirk sank, and his affected stare returned. "And because kissing you is all I've thought about since you walked away. That, and maybe I should have disregarded your wishes and searched for you, anyway."

Legs wobbly at what she heard, she shook her head. "That wouldn't have worked."

His strong fingertips slid to the curve of her neck, enlivening her body with a light tingling. "I know."

She did all she could to not lean into his touch and focused all her effort on her next words. "I thought you'd be angry at me."

His gaze dipped. "I was."

"I'm sorry."

His thumb rubbed the tendon along her neck, and he remained quiet for a while, the intimate gesture sending tendrils of warmth throughout. "I'd beg you to stay, but I'm not sure that would be fair."

"Because I'm a mess?"

"Is that still true?"

Suppressing a swell of emotion, she pursed her lips, her mind dizzying at every effort she'd poured into her two months of recovery.

"I don't know." Everything was still so new, so untested, her life only now just knitting back together.

She peered at his collarbone, at the hollow of his throat peeking above his crewneck t-shirt. A sob surged up her throat, and she swallowed hard to bury it—so close to everything she never knew she wanted, and yet so far. "I'm starting to consider the chance there might be hope for me, but I still can't give you any promises. I know you want promises. Someone who can stay."

Perhaps this was his turn to ditch her.

"Then let me admit that I'm a mess too." He drew his face in closer, and her heart hammered. "And that promises mean a whole lot less these days, now that I know I'm more whole with you in front of me than I've been in these last two months without you."

Her muscles sagged at the significance of his words. They suggested that her hope wasn't so misguided after all.

His brow eased, and unmistakable sincerity entered his expression. "Come back to me."

A heavy breath, one she had no idea she'd been holding on to, fell from her and took away the strain in her chest. *He still wants me. And yet…*

She pulled her hand away from his shoulder. "I can't come back."

His posture stiffened.

She shook her head and held back a need to smack her own forehead. Her ham-fisted choice of words only made this worse.

"What I mean is, I can't return when I was never really yours." She shot him a look she hoped conveyed an apology.

He narrowed his eyes, clearly confused.

"Oh, sugar, let me try that again. I mean, I never truly gave myself to you in the first place." She sank back. His pinched glare settled. *There. That's better.* "I don't blame you for getting frustrated with me or wanting answers. It wasn't your job to wait around for me, just as much as I couldn't hurry along my healing for you. I held back, and you lost patience. I get it. That was the natural flow of things between us at the time. I didn't handle my emotions, so they handled me instead."

"Agathe." He tilted his head to one side as though analyzing the subtext of her words and pleading with her all at once. "You flipped out. Everyone does. You needed to get your life in order, which was more than understandable. And if I had a choice between keeping you in a broken state or letting you go to work on yourself, as much as it would pain me to watch you leave, I'd let you go every time."

Despite the sting of his honesty and her need to look away, she forced her gaze to stay on him. "I broke whatever we had before it had a chance to begin. I'll always be sorry for that."

"No. You did what was best for you and what you thought would be best for me. You should be proud of that. I am. And I'm sorry, too. I shouldn't have pushed for more. Not when I knew, on every level, you weren't in a place to start anything."

Her heart sank, and the sickness from earlier resurfaced. No matter how she approached this, whatever she had to offer might never be enough. "I'm still not sure I'm ready to start anything with you. Only that I *want* to start something. Does that make sense?"

He drew near, nodding. "I don't expect anything more than us taking this one day at a time. Can you handle that much?"

"Luke." His name came as a whisper. She couldn't stand the idea of letting him sell his dreams short for her sake. "You want a wife and children when I'm nowhere near ready for that. I'm not sure I ever will be. I can't risk failing another child, and I can't ask you to give up a future that clearly means a lot to you. One day you'll resent me for holding you back."

Her voice cracked, and tears prickled her eyes. Meanwhile, Luke's smile fell.

She pressed her jaw shut, awaiting his answer or maybe the sure rejection coming her way.

"If I've learned anything, it's that I want you more than I want any hypothetical family." His hand rose, and his thumb stroked her jawline. "And you could never fail at love, Agathe. It's not in your genes. Just like you didn't fail with Elsie. You loved that little girl. And the troubles you have now, bear witness to that love. What happened to her was a tragic accident, but she wasn't alone. You were right there with her, holding her, watching over her. I bet you were the best mother a kid could hope for, and Elsie died knowing you unequivocally cherished her."

His hand gripped her upper arm like he offered strength and yet more hope. Agathe could feel her muscles turning weak, all as her mind churned with a need to rein in her burgeoning tears while processing his words.

"And if we do happen to travel down the path of marriage and children"—he stroked her face some more as if coaxing her to focus on him—"just know whatever family we create will be different from what you had. I'll never leave you to deal with life alone. Every joy or sorrow will be shared, even if that means flying you and any child to wherever my work takes me or, failing that, canceling any out-of-town meetings." His pupils dilated, and he leaned in as if imploring her to believe him. "No matter what happens, Agathe, if you let me, you'll always be the center of my world."

She choked back a fearful sob. His promises cut deep. Promises that raised the stakes and gave her yet more things to lose. How could he offer all those things? How could he be so damn sure?

"I'll ruin this too."

He shook his head. "No. You won't."

Her leg muscles coiled like they prepared to run. To spare him the giant sacrifice he wanted to make. "My heart's too broken. I still have so much baggage to sort through. My past will resurface, and I'll—"

"Listen to me. You won't." His fingers applied more pressure to her upper arm, imploring her to listen and stay. "Your past is your story. It's who you are. It will always be there. I don't want you any other way, you hear me? I'm a grown man, Agathe. One capable of confronting my own choices. It's not your job to save me from a relationship with you. You've tried that, and look where it got us. We're both bloody miserable and apart."

His strong tone resonated through the air, and all she could do was stare, her world completely still and quiet. He'd crushed her last protest and, what's more, displayed zero doubts. As always, he drew out her every truth and flaw and rewarded her with support and acceptance. And though she'd walked into this encounter secretly hoping to win him back, he was the one trying to convince her.

So, maybe he had a point. Maybe he *could* handle whatever she threw at him. Maybe her only task was to accept what he offered and hold him to that challenge.

Mood lifting, she raised her arms and hooked them behind his neck, tucking her head just under his chin while her body sank against his. "Don't let me go."

He took in a deep breath and pulled her closer, instant warmth seeping through her muscles and down into her bones. "Never."

A long silence lingered while she absorbed this moment and the steadfast feel of him. "Can I have that kiss now?"

Soft laughter tore through her chest, and she stared up to the light of a thousand emeralds glinting in his eyes. No matter where life took her, no matter what she did, Elsie's memory would always be there. No amount of self-inflicted misery would take that away.

So maybe it *was* time for Agathe to be happy.

To live. To love. To squeeze everything she could from the life she had, and her daughter didn't.

She owed Elsie that. She owed Luke.

*She owed herself.*

Luke's lips touched hers, gentle as a brush of silk, with shared passion rising as a swell of emotion hot and wild in her chest. *She'd be okay.*

She had inner strength and the lessons of her past.

She wasn't alone anymore.

She had *Luke.*

# Epilogue



*One year later*

Agathe lowered the small bouquet of light-pink peonies into a metal vase beside the white marble headstone, certain Elsie would have loved these flowers.

She could imagine Elsie now, pulling out a single bloom and plucking petals just so she could watch them flutter to the ground. Heavy tears rolled down Agathe's cheeks, and she sniffed back a sob, her fingertips pressed to the cool earth as if she were reaching for her little girl. "Happy birthday, sweet child."

Her gaze swept out to the rows of graves under the soft spring sun, the cloudless sky so different from the gray day she'd lost Elsie. Since then, everything had changed in equal contrast.

A strong pressure landed on her shoulder—Luke's hand—and he huddled down beside her. "Are you okay?"

His attention danced around her face before he extended a thumb to wipe the tears off her cheeks. How on earth had she gotten so lucky? She nodded, and his soft kiss connected with her forehead, the gentle warmth filling her with comfort.

He turned to the headstone, his long fingers making contact with the name depressed in glittering gold. *Elsie Roth.* A heart-shaped rose quartz lay embedded in the stone, an iridescent reminder of the young soul resting underneath. "Happy birthday, Little Miss."

He patted the stone as though Elsie stood before him, and he patted her head. Agathe's heart tugged, and tears sprang anew. If only these two had met. *Just once.* Elsie would have loved Luke.

Agathe rose to her feet and swiped at her face. These days her eyes had a hair-trigger for springing leaks, her emotions never far from the surface. Then again, her crying wasn't such a bad thing, not after years of holding back. "Let's go."

Luke stood and hooked a hand around her elbow, his tall figure looming over her. "Hang on a minute, not just yet."

His eyes sparkled like green glass under a bright midday sun, his jaw pressed in a granite line and signaling he had something to say.

Conjuring a million dreadful scenarios, she frowned, some habits having stuck around, as in her general pessimism. "What is it?"

He blew out a forceful sigh. "You'll either think this is a brilliant idea, or you're going to run to the car and make me walk home."

Her lips twitched with a smile, but the mystery in his words kept any overflow of happiness at bay. "Just tell me."

He peered down and gave a surrendering sort of nod, then reached behind him and pulled out an envelope from under his sports jacket. "I got Elsie a birthday present."

Agathe's heart stumbled, and her cheeks contracted into an even bigger grin. "You got her a card?"

"It's more than that." He nodded at the envelope. "Open it."

She grabbed the envelope and ran a shaky finger under the closed flap. A glittery pink card soon sat in her hand, looking completely unlike anything Luke would pick out, with its white dancing unicorns and a multi-colored rainbow.

Tears sprung anew, and she tried to focus past the water in her eyes. "What is this? I don't understand."

Her hand met with the hollow at her throat, her fingers brushing the purple scarf she'd bought when she thought she'd never again feel liberated enough to wear anything so vibrant.

Luke stepped forward and cupped his hands to her elbows, taking some of her weight while she tried not to fold to a pile on the lawn.

"Thanks to your advice, Tiluma has succeeded in ways I couldn't have imagined. In a strange way, Elsie tore us apart, only to bring us back together, and because of her, we're stronger now."

He nodded at the quiet grave, its white marble glowing like a mini celestial being watching over them. "I once said that she was lucky to have you as a mother, to have you there in her last hours, but I also know a lot of children don't have that." He turned to the envelope. "I want the extra profits we've made as a result of your changes to go to a new program for seriously ill children in foster care. They'll get the best help money can buy, and we'll fund programs to provide things such as magic shows, assisted day trips, and in-hospital entertainers. Max is in on the idea, too, though I suspect we could save money on clowns and just send him into the wards instead."

A laugh broke through her tears, and she blinked up at Luke, her mind still reeling.

"I want these children to have as much joy in their lives as possible." His thumb traced gentle circles over her elbow, and his stare deepened. "As much joy as I know you gave Elsie every day."

She bent forward with a laughter-filled sob, the rapid assault of her heartbeat halting her ability to count just how many zeros were printed on the paper. She already felt lucky, but Luke's big-heartedness now exceeded her understanding.

She peered up at the sky and tried to compose herself, her thoughts spinning on how much he'd improved her life. How he'd encouraged her to open her own business, a city-based store dedicated to exotic teas and beautiful tea sets. Her years as a corporate consultant had given her more than a few invaluable business skills, and she loved her new venture.

He'd also been true to his word about keeping her close. Together, they'd been on numerous trips around the world. She'd even visited York to meet his mother and sister, Sophie.

And despite Luke's praise, she couldn't take full credit for Tiluma's new success. Max's suggestion of Bret Lowell as a new investor proved an unexpected stroke of genius. Bret's loony persona made a perfect fit for Tiluma's fun reputation, and that same loony persona brought great publicity. The fact Bret also hid an astute knowledge of all things profit-making meant the business went from strength to strength.

She dropped her attention back to Luke and shook her head. "This is too much."

"Donating this money is the right thing to do." He sent forward a gentle smile. "You've had to overcome a hell of a lot of trauma, Agathe, and I want to add some positivity back into the world in Elsie's name." He shrugged. "Besides, I have you, and you're everything I want and need. This money will do far more good to those children's lives than it will to mine."

She held her silence for a while longer before adding, "Why on earth would you think I'd make you walk home over this?"

He pulled her in closer, thick lines of tension scoring his face. "Flip the card."

She did as told, only to find a yellow diamond ring tied with a matching ribbon to the back.

Her knees buckled, but Luke caught her, his laugh prying her focus from the card. "I'm the one who's supposed to be on the ground right now, not you."

She found her feet, only for him to let go and lower himself to one knee before her. "Marry me?"

"Wait. What?" She slapped her hand over her mouth, her fingers shaking. "You want to marry me?"

His eyes glinted along with his giant grin. "Heck, yes. If you'll have me."

"But—" Meaning to ask again why he thought she'd make him walk home, her mouth merely slipped open, and her gaze caught on Elsie's grave, new understanding creeping in. "You thought I'd be upset about you proposing in a graveyard."

He glanced at Elsie's headstone. "If you say yes, she'll be my step-daughter. My family. I wanted her to be part of this, too." His attention returned to Agathe, and he intertwined his fingers with hers. "I want you both in my life forever. So please, say yes."

The trail of tears on her cheeks turned her face cold, but her chest burned in unison with the embers of emotion smoldering from within.

This man expanded her world beyond recognition, and if anything, she was the one who wanted to repay him.

She nodded frantically, breathlessness seizing her lungs while her mind whirred with an inability to process this moment. "Yes. Of course, yes."

He jumped to his feet and scooped her up in his arms. "I love you. I always will."

His lips caught hers in a forceful kiss. When he finally pulled away, she laughed, her forehead pressed to his. Her heart was so full of joy, and it strained against an undeniable truth, a truth she would *never* again keep to herself. "I love you too, Luke Tindall. Always. Forever. And under the strict condition that you guard me whenever your brother is holding a ham and cheese sandwich."

A laugh rumbled through his chest and against her body, his lips soon meeting hers in another brief kiss. "I promise. Now…" He leaned in and whispered into her ear, *"Déjame que te lleve a casa."*

She giggled. His Spanish, for once, was flawless. *"Sí, mi amor.* It'd be an honor to go home with you."

His SUV waited farther down the hill, and he placed her on the ground to begin the trek back. All the while, she suppressed a need to point out that his home was now her home and had been for six months.

Instead, she bested him in a different way, slipping her arm around his and resting her head on his shoulder. "By the way, we'll need a short engagement."

She smirked as they walked, awaiting the inevitable question.

"Why?"

"Because Elsie has a half-sibling due in late May, and I don't plan on being as big as a house when I walk down the aisle."

Luke stopped in his tracks and tugged at her arm, twisting her to face him.

His cheeks paled with what looked like a mix of shock and buried hope. "You're pregnant?"

New and happy tears sprang free from her eyes, and her shoulders shuddered from unrestrained laughter while she released a fast nod. His eyelids flared with unmistakable joy, and his wide grin shone brighter than any cluster of pearls. He hugged her tight and spun her around, raining a heavy series of kisses over her cheeks through his laughter.

They'd been careful, hadn't planned on conceiving a child—at least, not just yet—but a recent doctor's visit proved that's exactly what had happened. And while she'd thought that being pregnant would see her deepest fear realized, fear no longer ruled her world, and her heart only soared at this second chance.

Her love for Luke had nudged her into healing, into believing she deserved happiness and love. And now, a new life stretched out far ahead of her, filled with glorious memories of her years with Elsie. And that new life brimmed with redemption and family and a man so far beyond her wildest dreams. *A man who would stay at her side, in her heart.*

Now that she knew how to live again. How to love. Now that she finally knew peace.


THE END

# The Last Place You Look

LOVE AT LAST, BOOK 2

# The Last Place YOU LOOK

LOVE AT LAST **BOOK TWO**

## KATERINA SIMMS

# Description

**She wants a new life. He just wants to live. Love is found in the most unlikely place…**

Budding psychiatrist Sophie Tindall, on the run from her predictable life, escapes to the small Australian town of Roseford.

At just thirty-six years old, Orlando Piras is Roseford Aged Care's youngest resident. Once worldly and daring, his now regimented existence makes him a hostile thorn in everyone's side—especially when it comes to his new volunteer visitor—the annoyingly inquisitive Sophie Tindall.

But just like so much of his life, his true feelings for Sophie must remain a secret. Sweet, smart, beautiful, with a cruel ability to awaken hope, she's everything he's ever wanted, and now can't have.

Every day his condition worsens. And even as Sophie begins to see Orlando as the man to change her forever, she is the one with just three months to save his life.

*For fans of Me Before You and Archer's Voice.*

**Keep reading to indulge in this soul-stirring journey!**

# Chapter One

"Oh dear, I think you might be too qualified."

Sophie Tindall adjusted her smile at Warren, the seemingly sweet octogenarian with faded blue eyes and a grin that turned his paper-thin skin into a concertina.

"I hope not." Her attention skittered around the packed common room at Roseford Aged Care Facility. Maybe Warren was right. Maybe her decision to volunteer here *was* an odd choice. "I might have a medical degree, but I still have six years of psychiatry training to complete when I return home to the UK. There's always more to learn."

"Oh, don't get me wrong, dear, I'm glad you've been matched with me." He gestured to the other elderly residents and their volunteer visitors seated at the gray Formica tables around him, then shot her a wink, along with a chuckle. His rough-but-cheery demeanor reminded her of her late father. "I'm the envy of every other codger in here. I'm not complaining."

She returned his laughter and sent her gaze once more across the room. The hum of chatter ricocheted off the cream-colored walls, and the musky scent of people mixed with the light burn of antiseptic floor cleaner. She opened her mouth, about to thank Warren for the compliment, when her stare slammed into a set of deep, espresso eyes.

Her heart stammered, but she turned back to Warren, ignoring the rugged, younger man appraising her from across the room.

"You're doing me a favor, really." She widened her smile, the expression a strain against her hammering pulse. "I plan to use some of my free time in Australia to meet people from your demographic. You see, I want to specialize in geriatric psychiatry."

He clapped his hands in exaggerated delight, leaning back in his seat, oblivious to the beautiful stranger staring her down from behind him. "Ahh. So, I'm your guinea pig then?"

She nodded and chanced another look at *the starer*, a man perhaps in his mid-thirties, sitting next to a woman who appeared to be in her late sixties. She was a little on the younger side for an aged care resident, but it wasn't unheard of.

Sophie refocused on Warren, vowing to set *the starer* aside for now. "I hope you don't mind."

"Of course not." Warren interlaced his fingers over his generous belly. "I could listen to your lovely accent all day. Tell me, what part of the UK do you come from?"

"I live in London, but I'm Scarborough born and raised, sir."

The muscles behind her eyes hurt from fighting the compulsion to watch the man behind Warren again. The heat and mystery in the stranger's dark gaze called straight to the core of why she'd come to Australia. To live a little. To embark on an adventure.

*Oh, stop sugar coating this. I want to get laid!*

Electricity zipped up her spine, and she shivered at the blunt self-confession.

"Sir?" Warren huffed out a laugh, kindly eyes glittering anew. "Oh, you are a dear, but plain old Warren will serve just fine. We're soon-to-be-friends, aren't we?"

The tension dropped from her shoulders. He had a point; she was here to befriend him, and despite Mr. Dark and Mysterious staring her down—despite her inclination toward staunch professionalism—she could afford to relax a little.

She jutted her chin toward the self-serve tea station. "Say, how about I get us a cup of tea, and then we can get to know each other better?"

He gave a quick nod of approval. "I'll have a white with two sugars. Thanks."

She wrapped her fingers around the rough, crimson fabric on her chair's armrests and pushed herself to standing. "Coming right up."

Even as she walked, she sensed the sexy stranger's glare burn into her back. Or maybe it was more a *hope* than a *sense*. That those alluring, chocolate-noir eyes hadn't left her. That he followed her with as much intrigue as she had for him.

She approached the tea station, and her stomach clenched. She was a bonafide-nerd, someone who preferred books over booty calls. She had no place feeling excitement over this guy's notice. Nothing in her past prepared her for how to connect with a man as rugged and handsome as the one who'd wrenched her attention just minutes earlier.

His warm, olive skin and enigmatic gaze alone demanded notice, much less that coarse-but-still-sexy, indented scar along the top left of his forehead. She hadn't yet found the nerve to appraise his lips, though she figured when she did that they, too, would offer a promise of easy confidence and great sex.

A shiver worked up her spine at the word *sex*.

Okay sure, she was overanalyzing what were a couple of split-second glances, but overanalyzing was ingrained into her personality. Besides, her body recognized his intensity and hoped he'd maybe share a small degree of attraction toward her, too.

She filled two paper cups with boiled water and held one in her hand to warm her palm, leaving the other to sit on the table while the tea steeped. For so long, her life had consisted of one safe choice after another—anything to keep from rocking the foundations of trust she'd decimated amongst her family so many years ago.

But she'd tossed aside *safe choices* the day she decided to come to Australia.

Her thoughts looped over her reasons for being here. Those reasons were two-pronged. First, she'd wanted to embark on informal volunteer work while she had some rare time to do so. Second, she'd ended a four-year relationship with Hector Winthrop in order to escape the mundane life she'd built back at home. A life of predictable relation-ships and musty text books—a life now dedicated to playing catch-up on a great deal of personal discovery.

Any decent psychiatrist worth their salt needed life experience. And just like any decent psychiatrist, she also needed to make peace with her hang-ups—to do away with caution and find some freedom.

She would let life rough her up a little—or perhaps, again—but with a lot less carnage this time.

Maybe the sleepy town of Roseford wasn't the most daring place to start. But Luke, her tech CEO brother, had been kind enough to offer her free use of his country cabin. As a cash-strapped student, she'd jumped at the chance. From there, she'd been lucky to scrape together enough funds for plane tickets, a hire car, and a bit of spending money.

She already lived in a major city back home, so drew the line at residing under Luke's nose at his Melbourne home. And Roseford's big, community aged care facility, with its volunteer program, meant she could work on her people skills. So maybe living in the sticks would be a welcome change after all.

"Want to grab a drink?"

She jolted, stilling just in time to not pour hot tea on her black leggings.

Burnt umber eyes glinted mere inches from her own. Mr. Dark and Mysterious's gaze did a slow glide over her body. Like a man full of devious, delicious secrets. *Like a man imagining her naked.* Though what-ever he imagined probably didn't match the reality of what hid beneath her olive-green tunic—a pair of sensible, beige-cotton under-wear with a stupidly high waist.

She lowered her teacup to the table. "I. Ah. You're asking me out?"

Full lips curved higher. "I mean, not now. After the old timers clear off."

His soft rumble wafted over her like smooth butterscotch, and he stood a little too close. But even his close proximity added an air of natural intimacy.

*This guy.* With his dark scent of incense and sandalwood. He smelled like an ancient church. Sacred and arcane. Or maybe just a really manly soap. And even though his thick, inky curls sat a little scruffy, and his loose, gray sweat pants were a tad on the overly casual side, he still managed to resemble a sexy version of Lucifer—tall, with imposing physicality—minus the horns and gnashing teeth.

*This guy* probably enjoyed women clad in red lace and hot times, not a med student in high-waisted underwear and a bad case of repressed sexuality.

She took a sharp swallow at the lump in her throat and searched for her ability to reply. This would be her first, and maybe only, chance at exploring her wild-and-sexy side… *Do I even have a wild-and-sexy side?*

Then again, she'd taken risks on men in the past. Long ago. Before Hector—who'd been a whole other mistake unto himself…

"Are you sure?" Her brow tightened with the counterproductive question, but she couldn't stop from voicing her doubt. "You don't know the first thing about me."

*Why am I killing this exchange? I should throw myself at him. Just take whatever is on offer and say yes.*

"I thought the whole point of grabbing a drink was to get to know each other." He dipped his chin, and those deep brown eyes set forth a challenge—as if he knew more about her than she knew of herself. "But I'm happy to skip the drink and get straight to taking each other's clothes off, if that's what you'd prefer…"

His lip crept up on one side. She glanced away, face hot, heart thundering. Why hadn't she thought to splash out on some serious red lace lingerie *before* embarking on this trip?

"Um…" She cleared her throat, attempting to play cool. "Maybe let's start with that drink."

His eyes glinted, and he gave a quick nod, then turned away, calling over his shoulder, "Catch you later."

He spoke loud enough for everyone to hear. The older woman he'd been sitting beside glared at Sophie.

Sophie loaded herself with cups of tea and scampered over to Warren. His kindly eyes narrowed as she handed him his cup. "That boy is pure trouble. You'd be wise to stay away from him."

Sure, maybe Warren's heart was in the right place, and going on a date with a fellow volunteer held the potential to complicate things should they not get along, but Sophie was a beggar and couldn't afford to be choosey. Not when she'd found an incredibly attractive opportunity for adventure right here in Roseford. And if this opportunity worked out, she wouldn't have to bother with long trips to Melbourne just to get some action.

She waved a dismissive hand, a wave that said a strait-laced woman like her knew better than to engage in any trouble with a man like the one she'd just met. Gosh, she'd accepted a date from someone and hadn't even grabbed his name... Oh well, Warren had to be wrong; no one who was "pure trouble" would spend their time volunteering at an aged care facility.

"Never mind him." She refocused on Warren, leaning in. "Tell me about you."

Warren went on to explain about his life. She held a polite smile and nodded at his stories about his family and a long career in metal welding, which had eased off into a newfound passion for small-scale wire sculpturing, all the while dispersing her own input into the conversation.

Just as her pulse finally came down from her earlier excitement, her two-hour window with Warren ended, and in an instant, her pulse picked up again.

Mr. Dark and Mysterious would be waiting for her. She had a date with someone supposedly experienced in *trouble*. Someone who might be able to show her the way...

She stood and patted Warren's shoulder, promising to return with the other volunteers in two days' time.

*It's only a drink. I can do this. Or bail if I really can't.*

A care worker wheeled in a cart with blue lunch trays, while Sophie waited at the common room's exit, one of the last volunteers to leave. Only, her handsome stranger still sat amongst the tables and the other residents, while his elderly partner brushed past in a hurry to get out.

For a brief moment, a beautiful smile tugged at his soft-looking lips, but then he dipped his chin and those same lips curled into a wicked grin. She waited another few beats, expecting he'd stand and follow her out the door.

But he didn't.

Her body stiffened. She spun around to peer outside through the glass sliding doors, where the lady he'd sat next to ambled through the parking lot, then ducked into a white hatchback. The taillights flared red, and the car pulled away.

Sophie whipped back to her sexy stranger. Her stomach flipped. A care worker slid a lunch tray in front of him, his new flinty glower saying there'd be no drink.

She'd heard of young people taking up residence in nursing homes, but never before had she actually encountered one. It often took some injury, disability, or condition—something that required twenty-four-hour assistance—to land someone non-geriatric in a place like this. Often because there weren't enough places in more appropriate facilities, especially if someone lived rural. Rural, as in, Roseford.

Pain radiated through her chest, and her heartbeat throbbed loud in her ears; even worse was the burning in her cheeks and the sickening cramp in her tummy. She forced herself to turn and place one foot in front of another. To get the hell out of there.

The man she'd hoped would kick-start her sexy, new life wouldn't be "catching her later". *He wouldn't be going anywhere.* He wasn't even a volunteer. *He was a resident.*

# Chapter Two

That afternoon, Sophie sat alone at The Keeper's Arms, Roseford's only pub. The lighting was subdued and a subtle, but not completely unpleasant, smell of stale beer punctuated the air. Judging by the empty seats, the large venue was at half capacity.

She nursed a white wine on the table before her, and her bruised ego brought strain to her heart. At the very least, she deserved a break from making her own lunch and scrimping over every dollar she spent to be at this pub now.

Her embarrassing encounter at the home left her unfocused and regretful, with little idea of what had truly happened, or why that guy had picked her to torment. Her heart pounded at how much she'd failed at her first attempt at breaking from her boring existence in the hopes of finding a man.

She twisted the wine glass in front of her, the thin stem not quite as cold as the lump that nestled in her chest. A dazzling stranger had jumped at the chance to toy with her. To humiliate her. To chip away at her unstable confidence. Why? Why her? Did she look like a woman easily fooled? Clearly, she did.

The way his all-seeing stare had cooled to flat malice…

She swished the citrine liquid in her glass and then knocked back a big mouthful. Even the biting taste played on her dread. He'd banked on her naïvety. That she'd never pick him for a resident. A man in his thirties, much less mobile, much less seemingly mentally aware. *Jerk.*

She didn't know his name. Didn't know his story or his motivation. But sure enough, she wanted to hate him.

And yet... Something held her back from that very thing. Something about him plucked at her intrigue.

He didn't appear to have anything wrong with him... Well... Except for his not-so-charming personality.

She scoffed under her breath and shook her head at her stupidity. Maybe she hadn't moved quite as far from that innocent girl she'd once been, but she could start by letting the whole ordeal go. She'd come to this country for experience, and the dazzling jerk had given her just that—though not the positive encounter she'd hoped for.

Her lunch arrived, and she pushed a fry into her mouth, savoring the comfort of carbs whilst using her spare hand to reach for her phone. She needed to hear a friendly voice and had promised to call her best friend and housemate in London.

"Sophie!" Hannah Taylor's voice chimed in clear as a bell. "How are you doing? Meet anyone cute yet? Oh God, the house just isn't the same without you. Talk, girl. Tell me what's happening."

Tension slid from Sophie's body. Hannah was the least difficult person she knew—well, except for the whole being messy thing, and Sophie always having to clean up after her housemate, which did complicate her life more than needed. And then there was Hannah's strange passion for collecting charity shop handbags and leaving them all over their tiny apartment... "I'm fine, just settling in. Tell me how everything on your side of the pond is doing."

"Hmm. Well, not much going on, really. You've only been away a week. Oooo, but I'm sure you'll be devastated to hear that I saw Randal Berry leave his apartment with a new, leggy bimbo on his arm." Hannah giggled.

Randal Berry was their downstairs neighbor, a guy Sophie had a not-so-secret crush on. A crush spanning the entire six years she'd lived in the two-story building.

"Don't say that." She reached for her wine glass again, gulping down another sip of reality-obscuring liquid.

"What? The bit about Randal having a new girlfriend, or the part where she's a bimbo?"

"Both. But the bimbo part especially. It's beneath you. And she could be a nuclear physicist for all you know."

"Yeah, but she's totally not. Come on, Soph, you know Randal doesn't date anyone with an I.Q. higher than a potato."

Sophie pulled her wine from her lips and tried not to choke. Hannah did have a point. And Randal did have a type. Tall, athletic, blonde… not very bright… All the clichés and all the things Sophie wasn't, not with her medium brown waves and shorter than average build. He'd never go out with a visually standard nerd such as herself. Which was probably why she liked him. The man was unattainable. A relationship was never going to happen. Though really, she had no desire to change for a man, so she'd painted herself into a corner with that particular infatuation.

She cringed, and her earlier tension returned. Just today she'd tried to "aspire" again and here she sat, drowning her sorrow and using her best friend for distraction. A small wave of guilt took over, because there was one man that she'd forgotten in all her musing. *Hector.*

She'd dated Hector for far too long, in part because he seemed a safe bet. But she'd learned that a safe bet wasn't all that safe when life ticked over and mutual misery provided their only connection. They'd used each other as a crutch to shy away from taking any real risks. Not that her recent attempt at risk-taking had paid off, but at least she could say that for the first time in years she was trying.

"How's Hector?" She dipped another fry in sauce, pretending her friend could see the casual gesture as the intended diversion from a completely un-casual question.

"He dropped off a box of your things yesterday." Hannah's voice lowered, quieter than before. "To be honest, he seemed a little sad. He said he might shoot a message your way to see how you're doing."

A heaviness settled in her chest. Truth be told, she'd kind of blind-sided Hector with the whole break up, then jumped on a plane for a four-month rest from her years of study and long clinical hours. But even her exit, and his general immaturity when maturity mattered most, didn't stop her from wanting to see his life improve. Especially since he'd graduated with his computer science degree a full year ago and still hadn't landed a full-time job. "If you hear from Hector before I do, tell him I hope he's well."

Hannah released a heavy sigh. "Oh Soph, it's not your job to fix everyone's problems."

"I'm not *fixing*. I'm being polite."

Though she had to admit, guilt did have a lot to do with her politeness. She'd escaped London at the first viable chance; she'd used the double-whammy of Luke's engagement and the fact that his fiancée, Agathe, was pregnant, as an excuse.

"Fine, next time I see him, I *might* say something, but... Just so you know, I think you're giving him false hope, and this is totally going to bite you in the ass one day."

Sophie speared a chicken tender on her plate but waited before eating it. Hannah had already given her many huge lectures on no longer putting others' needs ahead of her own aspirations, and she wanted to avoid yet another one. "Maybe you have a point."

"Damn right, I do. There are boundaries to every relationship, Soph. Let Hector sort himself out." Hannah paused but released another sigh when Sophie didn't offer a rebuttal. "Anyway, tell me more about how Australia's treating you? Something other than 'I'm fine'."

"It's too early to say for sure." Sophie pressed the cold bulb of her wine glass to her forehead—a refreshing breather from the weight of this conversation, much less her earlier loss of pride with the guy from the care home. "I've moved into the cabin and started my first day volunteering at the local aged care." She made a point of omitting anything regarding The Jerk. "I'm working with a lovely man named Warren, who I'll visit every Wednesday and Friday."

"And aside from that, you'll be taking time to yourself, right?" Hannah had opposed Sophie's volunteer gig from the very beginning; said it would be mixing work with what should be a holiday. Of course, Sophie didn't see it that way. "I've only ever known a Sophie who works herself to the bone. I can't wait to see my friend get a good rest and a decent shag for a change."

Sophie startled, pulling the glass away from her forehead and a small amount of wine sloshed to the table. "I… Ahh… I'll try?"

Hannah let out a raucous laugh—one so robust it reminded Sophie why she called Hannah a friend in the first place. The woman had a way of keeping her on her toes, and pointing out when she'd sold herself short.

"You're blushing right now, aren't you? Oh, shit"—a car horn blared through the phone, half drowning Hannah out—"gotta go. Running late. I love you. And honey, work on not working, all right?"

The call ended before Sophie could reply, but Hannah's sentiments lingered. No amount of oddball shenanigans from an attractive aged care resident would keep her from what she wanted—the chance to restart her life. Nor would those shenanigans stop her from returning in two days and upholding her promise to see Warren again.

# Chapter Three

"You've got to be fucking kidding me."

Sophie blinked as The Jerk's words struck her harder than a sledge hammer to the face. Her mouth hung open, her worst nightmare unfolding before her very eyes.

Minutes prior, she'd entered Roseford Aged Care to a caregiver rushing toward her—the caregiver's blue eyes flared, her wide shoulders heaving as she relayed a rushed story of how Warren had passed away from an unexpected heart attack two nights ago. Sophie's own heart sank in the few seconds it took to absorb the shock of how a guy who echoed her father had also died in a similar fashion.

This detail brought back the day she'd received the call to return to Scarborough because "time was running out", only she'd arrived to her father's side an hour too late. His body was still warm. His spirit long departed.

So, she'd stood mere meters from the home's exit, reeling, her palm pressed to her aching chest, when the same caregiver ushered her deeper into the center. *"Not a problem, dear. We have a suitable replacement resident waiting for you."*

A lie!

There was nothing *suitable* about her new resident.

Now, she sat blinking, a hot sliver of anger blooming beneath her ribcage. This man was no resident. He was a sore thorn in her side–a burned piece of toast in a hurried attempt at breakfast. Except the toast had slipped from her fingers on her way out the door and landed butter-side-down on her doorstep, too germ-ridden to attempt eating... Or something like that.

Either way, she did *not* want to be partnered with this man and his perpetual deep brown stare.

Her attention slid to his lips; her politer nature made her question if he'd really just dropped the f-bomb upon seeing her. Definitely not because those lips still sat undeniably full and enticing. Surely lips that looked like that didn't swear?

She drew a slow breath and grappled with the shock of her predicament, then took a second to glare at the caregiver who'd delivered her to this menace of a man. Hopefully, the glare mirrored The Jerk's sentiments of, "You've got to be fucking kidding me", but the caregiver only grimaced and disappeared out the common room door.

Sophie turned back to her tormentor; the small scar at the top of his forehead adding to his diabolical bully act.

*I should get up. I should just go.*

But her fingers dug into her chair's textured armrests, and a deeper voice whispered that any self-respecting psychiatrist would at least try to figure this guy out.

If anything, a unique learning opportunity sat right in front of her.

Most patients in aged care were just that. *Aged.* People who'd lived long, full lives. Everyone, especially staff, knew to expect death. When someone like Warren died, as sad as his parting was, there was also the knowledge that he'd had a lengthy chance to achieve his dreams. But that wasn't the case with the guy seated before her. He was young with a temper. That temper alone offered clues that maybe he wasn't done with life.

And even if he wouldn't make being around him easy, maybe Sophie could still help. No one got into medicine for *easy*. And she knew a thing or two about vulnerability and skepticism, so maybe she could try to learn what The Jerk's deal was. Though she'd probably need to start with not referring to him in her thoughts as "The Jerk".

Besides, she'd made a vow to be braver in life, and now that chance presented itself, she couldn't let this smart mouth break her down. His past toying might be on the vanilla side of what she'd encounter one day, anyway.

She tilted her head back and glared down her nose at him, making it clear she'd sized him up and wouldn't be intimidated. "Yeah, well… I'm not so eager to see you either, but here we are."

The muscles in Orlando's face tightened, and a wayward glare slipped through his attempt at an unruffled smirk. *Who knew Miss Neat and Nerdy had an attitude?*

He'd long regretted the home's director, Candice Olsen, badgering him into participating in this half-baked volunteer program. But then, he still held a deep need to get out of the center occasionally—to escape the sight of wrinkled skin and urinary drainage bags—to engage with the outside world.

And in order to do that, he needed more funding. He needed a dedicated carer. Which according to Candice, increasing his chances of that meant pretending he gave a shit about fitting in. Even though one look at him made it blindingly fucking obvious he didn't fit in.

He pushed past his usual fatigue and brain fog and refined his smirk on Miss Neat and Nerdy, then dropped his voice to a low rumble. "You were eager enough to see me last week. Very eager, as I recall."

Nerdy's face went rigid, and her ivory-eggshell skin turned paler still.

He'd seen that look a million times over. She wanted to tell him to fuck off. Well, good. He'd honed a knack for convincing people to leave him the hell alone. Or to at least give him a bit of space. And any minute now, Miss Nerdy would play right into his hand.

She cocked her head to one side, her pretty lips forming a soft smile. "You want me to get angry at you. You want me to leave."

Her steady tone embodied sweet control; and the ever-present tension in his jaw relaxed for a brief second. This wasn't how his attempts at prodding anger usually went.

Miss Nerdy's light green eyes glittered. She thought herself clever. Like she'd conjured the weakest piece of advice from some book titled *Psychology 101*—some shit about mirroring his emotions—and figured she'd be special enough to get through to him.

He brought tension back to his jaw. Just because this woman deluded herself into believing the world less of a shitty place for having her in it, didn't mean he owed her any kind of proof of that belief.

"Congratulations. I hope you didn't need a degree to help you figure out the bleeding fucking obvious, but just to aid you with the next step, maybe you could make good on your observation and leave."

Miss Nerdy's face didn't shift an inch, the soft-looking skin over her freckle-dusted cheekbones remained perfectly still. "No. I think I'll stay just to tick you off."

She, and her small frame, all five-foot nothing of her, sat defiant and firm.

He frowned deeper for noticing.

Granted, this woman showed more pluck than he'd credited her for, but funding be damned, he didn't need another do-gooder digging into his life.

He'd had and missed his chance at being known. His last chance had disappeared the day his ass landed back in Roseford. In this care facility. He didn't want one more person asking him to do things he didn't care to do. To talk about things he didn't want to remember. As if his life wasn't already its own special variety of fucked up.

His chest muscles bunched, and his stomach churned, just enough to remind him not to show Miss Nerdy how much she'd already ticked him off.

"Fine." He crossed his arms and sat back, making it clear he wouldn't make this pleasant. "You must be one of those women who enjoys a little punishment."

He made a show of looking her up and down, keeping his gaze extra slow and creepy. The corners of her eyes creased with another self-satisfied smile, and her expression only brightened—like the intended creepiness in his gesture went right over her head.

Not the reaction he'd hoped for.

She looked the picture of innocence, the floaty, pale yellow tunic she wore atop black jeans and brown knee-boots adding to that effect, as if she belonged on the cover of *Earthy Provincial Magazine*. If such a magazine existed.

She settled in her seat, mirroring his posture—yet another thing she must have picked up from *Psychology 101*—though Miss Nerdy's oblivious nature meant maybe she wasn't that clued in after all.

Her green eyes fused with his, more serious now. "Why'd your last volunteer quit? Did your charming personality scare her away?"

He gave a little shrug and buried a need to chuckle at her dig. He'd never been one to intentionally hurt or embarrass others, except to maintain what little personal space still remained to him, which Miss Nerdy wanted to infringe on. So, he wouldn't mislead Miss Nerdy into thinking he'd co-operate. Better to crush her dreams now and send her on her way. Just like the last lady.

"Not exactly."

"What then?"

He shrugged again. "She was a sore loser."

"Oh?"

He put on his best smirk, leaning over the pale gray table between them, reeling her in, setting Miss Nerdy up for a mighty fall. "She didn't think I could get you to agree to a date."

Miss Nerdy's cheeks sank before defensiveness kicked in, and she narrowed her eyes. "I know that's not what happened, but good attempt at covering up just how repellent other people find you." Her gaze dropped to her hands, betraying a smidgeon of shame over her lashing out. "Why did you ask me out on a date, anyway?"

His stomach clenched at her whispered tone. He'd noticed her pain last week too, the second his lunch tray landed on the table in front of him, and she'd realized he wouldn't be leaving with her as promised. Right then, she'd witnessed everything she needed to know about him. About the ridiculous shit-show called his life.

He gave a loud sigh and waited for her attention to return to him.

No point apologizing. He didn't want her to like him. Any *like* she might have would only be an offer of charity.

"Just wanted to see if I still had it in me." He gave her a wink, though his jest held more truth than he admitted. "Thanks for the confidence boost."

A small muscle over her jaw ticked. Perfect. The last thing he needed was another person convinced they could affect anything akin to positive change in him. There was nothing positive about where he was headed.

"That was a cruel trick." She maintained a death stare, despite her choked voice.

"Life is cruel. Get used to it."

Her face held momentary tension, before she looked back down at her hands and shook her head. "I don't know why you're here, but I know they wouldn't put a person like you in a place like this unless living in the outside world was impossible." She lifted her gaze, expression softening with something resembling sincere compassion. "Your life can't be easy. I can see why you view the world as cruel. You're right, it can be."

A ball of angry heat ignited in his chest; his breath surged, harsh and hot. People rarely voiced their observations. They sure as shit never presented those observations with any sort of kindness—usually only as a rage-filled explanation of why he'd turned into one giant pain in the ass.

But then, he didn't want kindness. Didn't want compassion. He sure as heck didn't want Miss Nerdy's wrath-inducing empathy.

He knew how to deal with opposition at every turn. What to do with people's anger when he didn't fall on his knees in gratitude for help that he had zero option but to accept. Yet...

He jutted out his chin. His abrasiveness counted for nothing with this woman, and his head hurt more than usual—probably her fault too. Well, maybe a blunt order would work. "What's your name?"

Miss Nerdy maintained her peaceful smile. "My name's Sophie. And what about y—"

"Right, Sophie. I want you to leave."

Her expression fell, and bonafide hurt turned her pupils into wide pools. He'd seen that look on her before. *The moment she'd learned the home was his home.*

She glanced about the room, as if she cared what the others thought of her and this scene. Her stare landed on him again, her mouth agape and ready to question, but he refused to let her question anything. Just because she could come and go as she pleased didn't mean he had no power. "Leave. Now."

"Orlando."

He jolted.

Shelley, the soft-headed staff member who'd delivered this insufferable woman to him, broke his stare-off. She stood over his left shoulder and let out an exasperated sigh. "I hope he's not giving you trouble, Miss Tindall."

He trained his attention back on Miss Nerdy, refusing to reward Shelley's interruption.

Sophie blinked, though to her credit, her stare did not part from his either.

"Orlando?" A small, sarcastic smile crept across her face—as if she took great joy in learning his name. "He's no trouble at all." Her attention stayed eerily glued on him, though she spoke to Shelley. "In fact, he's all charm. Really. However, it might have been helpful to know you'd be partnering me with such a *remarkable* resident."

"I. Ah…" Shelley released a nervous chuckle. "Candice told me you're on track to be a psychiatrist one day. I thought you'd… appreciate the challenge?"

Orlando's muscles pulled taut.

*A psychiatrist? Hell no!*

That was the absolute last thing he needed.

No wonder this woman had latched onto him and refused to let go. *Fuck.* She probably saw him as the ultimate "fixer upper". Not old and decrepit. Not like the other losers in this home. Though unbeknown to her, just as bloody doomed.

Her gaze bore into him, her chin raised as if his dissatisfaction pleased her to no end. He mouthed the word, *leave.*

She gave a smirk, followed by a nod as if to say, *fine.*

The air shifted as she stood, and brought the scent of daisies and spring flowers because, of course, Miss Nerdy would smell sweet like a meadow full of delightful spring blooms.

She turned to Shelley. "It was nice to meet you." Then looked down at him—both literally and figuratively, her eyes glinting once more. "Orlando, I'll see you next week."

# Chapter Four

Sophie stalked toward the Aged Care center's exit, only for her feet to spin her in a hard right turn down the corridor, toward an office she'd visited back when she'd first signed up to be a volunteer.

She stopped and stared at a closed door, her mind racing with the wild hope that Orlando hadn't noticed her detour. The name "Candice Olsen" hung on a sign before her, the job description "Center Director" underneath. Her hand worked of its own accord, and her knuckles connected with the door's glossy white wood.

Despite the volunteer gathering's chatter farther up the hall, her loud knock reverberated around the fluorescent-lit corridor—or maybe her nerves simply heightened her senses to every sound around her.

"Come in." The muffled female voice called from the other side.

She looked about, checking to see if anyone witnessed her out of character master stroke of daring, then seized a last second of calm before pushing the door open.

A woman in her early forties peered up from her desk; a woman Sophie had met briefly weeks ago. She had medium-length hair in the most stunning shade of bright copper.

"Hi." Sophie paused for a mere second, doubting her action. "I'm sorry to bother you, Ms. Olsen, I'm Sophie Tindall. We met—"

"Yes. Yes. Come in." Candice beckoned with her hand, her bright blue stare serious but not unwelcoming. She was likely busy and in a rush to know what Sophie wanted. "I remember you."

She pointed at a chair across from her. Sophie did as directed and took a seat. "I've just been placed with Orlando, and I was hoping you could spare a few minutes to talk."

Candice sank back in her seat and let out a heavy sigh, hands coming away from the laptop in front of her. "And let me guess, you want to be placed with someone else?"

"I'm not sure if you're aware, but he's not exactly the most welcoming resident."

Candice spluttered a small laugh void of any real joy. "Oh, I'm aware, but if it makes you feel any better, he misbehaves the same for everyone."

Sophie gave a slow nod, still pondering how best to serve her thoughts out loud. "Orlando needs help." And though some of his words hurt, she knew enough to understand the people most likely to strike out were also often the ones concealing the most damage. "I have no desire to be partnered with anyone else just yet, but thank you for offering."

Candice's chin jerked back.

Sophie, on the other hand, noticed that she hadn't taken a healthy breath since the moment she'd first sat in front of Orlando. She took that big breath now and exhaled on her explanation. "I understand there are limits to what you can tell me, but if there's anything you can share about him, anything that might make my job as his volunteer easier… I'm in Australia for four months, and I don't want to waste time muddling my way with him. So, I'd appreciate any and all of your help."

Candice broke with a genuine smile—one that brought a sparkle to her eyes and hinted at cunning—as if she knew Sophie's reluctance to leave would be exactly what Orlando didn't want but perhaps desperately needed.

"You mean you're not running for the hills? His last three volunteers gave up after barely one session, two at best."

Sophie shook her head. "He's not exactly my ideal candidate, but running away won't be helpful to his wellbeing or my reasons for taking this placement."

Candice extended a long, contemplative look, her wheelie chair creaking as she leaned even farther back. "Then I guess I better make good with compelling you to stick around." Her face eased. "I can't get into too much detail, especially since so much of Orlando Piras's condition remains a mystery. In my layman's understanding, he's somewhere on the neuromuscular impairment spectrum, with behavioral and cognitive issues limited to his episodes. No memory loss, no impaired judgment, no lowered attention span, or delusions outside of his episodes.

"He has some general fatigue and brain fog most days. Mobility-wise, he can manage well enough most days, prefers to stay active in the center gym. We've added a few extra pieces of equipment to encourage this, as lack of movement after an episode might mean losing his ability to move in totality. Our grounds are extensive enough for simple exercise and fresh air, but his episodes are when he really needs us. That's when he forgets who he is and fails to function as any normal thirty-six-year-old man would. There are particular times during his episodes when he's a danger to himself and others."

Sophie thought back to Orlando, to the harshness in his eyes, the sheer size of him…

"So, he's violent?"

Candice shook her head. "No. Not at all. Not intentionally, anyway. We wouldn't have him here among our residents if that were the case. Let's just say you wouldn't want him driving a car or at home alone when one of his episodes hits. He can't fend for himself in any way. And I'll be honest with you, Miss Tindall, Orlando's family is well known and loved in this town. I know Orlando sticks out at this center, but Roseford is one of those towns that looks after their own, and he wouldn't be here if he didn't have to be. And trust me, everyone has pulled a lot of strings to afford him a place at our community-owned center and around people who know him. His attitude might wear on us from time to time, but our residents and staff still want him around."

Sophie frowned. She couldn't imagine what made Orlando likable enough that so many people would shift and bend to accommodate him, but perhaps, as Candice had said, the blind acceptance was a symptom of a tight township.

Sophie's mind already went to piecing together this man and his condition—though the details remained vague enough to make it hard to draw any clear conclusions. Her volunteer status meant she had no real right to pry into what tests he'd undergone, specialists he might have seen, or even the duration or course of his illness, much less his prognosis.

She had no other option but to turn to what she *could* do—what her current role entailed—enriching Orlando's life. Maybe if she got him to ease up on the *sealed-fortress-of-doom* persona, he'd offer the information she needed to *truly* help him.

"Is there any way you see me breaking through to him?" She refocused on the woman ahead, her mind already forming a rough game plan. "Anything he needs that the center can't provide?"

Candice nodded, as though she admired Sophie's train of thought. "Yes, actually. Orlando's government funding was cut drastically months ago, and because of this, his dedicated carer is only funded for a couple of visits a week and only for a couple of hours. That's not enough to take him out for much more than a walk around the block or a coffee down the road if they're really quick." Ms. Olsen shrugged. "Our staff is pressed enough for time and can't dedicate too much attention on any one resident. He used to get full days out, and his overall mood has taken a huge hit since those stopped."

Sophie's tummy did a small flip, the impossibility of Candice's suggestion already sinking in. "You want me to take him out? I'm allowed to do that?"

Her and Orlando on an outing together? She just couldn't see that happening.

Candice nodded. "Granted, if you can get him to agree first."

Sophie gave a shaky laugh. "I'm almost certain he'd rather see me jump in the nearest lake and never return."

Candice leaned forward, elbows rested on her desk, gaze set in a pointed stare. "Sophie, Orlando will never admit it, but he needs help. He needs purpose and things to be passionate about—despite the degenerative nature of his condition. You might not be in Australia for long, but you're the first volunteer who hasn't spoken one word to him and run in the opposite direction. The fact you cared enough to knock on my door…" She paused, allowing the silence to speak for itself. "You sure can't make him feel much worse than he currently does. Orlando isn't our easiest resident, but he's not irrational, either. If you keep showing up, he'll notice. And what he does with your continued presence is anyone's guess, but it's up to you to stick it out to see what happens."

# *Chapter Five*

"You didn't tell me you're a psychiatrist."

The muscles along Sophie's spine squeezed in response to Orlando's narrowed stare and the way he'd practically spat the word *psychiatrist*, as though she might as well have been a *parking inspector* or *evil overlord*.

"That's because I'm not a psychiatrist." She fought back a need to return his scowl, doubt scrubbing at her decision to visit him again.

Befriending this man was about as easy as befriending a death adder. Scrap "befriending", she'd settle for him simply not scowling. Clearly, his low opinion of her hadn't softened since their last meeting.

"I have a medical degree, but I'm yet to specialize in psychiatry, which is what I intend to do next. Besides, we never got to the point of swapping pleasant small talk. Remember? Nor were you welcoming enough to ask what I do. How was I supposed to tell you anything about myself?"

He unleashed a harsh squint, scowl shifting from mean to mocking. "So that's your schtick? Find a pet project here until you can unleash yourself on some real patients."

"Not exactly. The medical degree means I can already be 'trusted' with 'real patients' if that's what I choose to do." She leaned one elbow on the table between them, a casual gesture to weaken his attempt to diminish her qualifications. "But what I really want is to specialize in old-age psychiatry. This volunteer position is about getting to know the demographic I plan to work with."

His voice cracked under a burst of laughter. A few residents in near proximity turned and glared at him. "And then you got lumped with the dumpster-fire young guy. How's that for meeting your 'demographic'?"

"Well. Yes." She sunk back, a pit of shame opening up in her belly.

Despite being the person in the power position here, this man made her feel smaller than a gnat. And still, she was the one with the ability to get up and leave if she wanted to. Orlando couldn't. He had little control and possibly resorted to grasping at hers.

"Warren would have been perfect, but it seems he had other plans. I should make it clear though, my volunteer work isn't about me fixing anyone. I'm here to understand the issues and lives of whoever I'm partnered with." She looked him up and down. Maintaining her composure. With his good looks and the cocky attitude, appealing to his vanity might work. "And I wouldn't exactly call you a 'dumpster-fire.'"

She offered a soft smile.

He returned a flat stare. "What about a walking disaster? Or a clusterfuck?"

Okay. So, her niceties didn't move him. "Is that how you see yourself?"

"Is that you psychoanalyzing me?"

"No." She mirrored his blank stare. "This is me attempting to have a normal, human conversation."

An uncomfortable silence drew out, and his emotionless stare lingered. "And how's that going?"

"I think we both know, not very well." She focused on the large windows to her right—taking a momentary break from the standoff. An extensive garden waited outside, edged in rose bushes and fruiting trees. The tranquil image offered a reminder that few discomforts—including this encounter—lasted forever.

She willed her attention back to him, vowing to tough out his resistance. To test her grit. She'd dealt with worse than this man.

A satisfied smirk broke the hard line of his lips. "So, ask to be reassigned."

She leaned in, matching his innate intensity with a glare of her own. "One thing you should know about me, I don't give up."

And every desire to surrender stoked a decades-old fire within her, a fire built on mistakes she still needed to make up for. Mistakes when it came to herself. Mistakes when it came to others. Mistakes she couldn't let define her forever. Even if that meant not letting a small volunteer role such as this get the best of her. She'd help this man, even if helping meant sticking around just so he could mouth off at her.

She could take a bit of attitude.

She'd worked too damn hard to give up so early.

Orlando shrugged. Maybe he didn't care, but the mild dart of his gaze said her presence did rattle him.

"Orlando." His attention snapped back to her. "Rather than resist this, wouldn't it benefit you to just go with the exchange? Perhaps we could help each other—"

"Sophie, honey." He slanted forward, gaze smoldering and dark. She saw through his wolfish act—but the heat in that stare, the heat focused solely on her—sent butterflies through her middle either way. "There's nothing in this world I want from you."

The spell in his eyes burst quicker than a balloon held to a flame. She sucked in a breath. Still… She could fix this. "I know about your funding cut. I have a hire car while I'm living in Roseford. If you'd prefer, I could take you out for—"

Laughter broke from him again, and he slumped back into his chair. "Wow, you really are keen to go on that date with me, aren't you?"

*Arrogant prick.* She glared at him. Was she even allowed to think of him as an *arrogant prick*? Hadn't she just vowed to stop calling him The Jerk, even if only in her own head?

Sure, she'd heard worse about patients from more senior doctors, but that didn't make their negative approach right, nor did it give her license to stoop to judging a patient weathering a hard time. That said, Orlando's ribbing definitely upstaged anything her brothers ever dished out—and that was saying something. And sure, he had a right to feel sore about his life, but that didn't mean she had to let him treat her badly.

Sophie gave a slow shake of her head and fell just short of *tutting* at him. "One minute you're beating yourself up, next you're back to being God's gift to women." She took a drawn-out pause for no other reason than to make him wait. "Orlando, honey, I wish you'd make up your mind."

The smile on his face froze, but even that didn't slow him down much. "Since you seem to know all about my funding, I'm going to take a punt and guess you went straight to the top and spoke to Candice?"

"Yeah, I did. I take this role seriously."

"Right. Well. You're acting like a horny-as-fuck stalker. So, lay off the seriousness." His gaze bore into her. "I'm not interested in your help."

Shock waves ran through her body at the "horny-as-fuck" line. She might have traveled across the world to live a little, but that was more about gaining experience than being *horny*. Not that any of that was this guy's business… "Even if my help means more freedom than you've had in months?"

"The answer's still no."

"Explain to me why."

His crinkled scowl did a swift scan over her. "I don't have to explain shit to you, Miss Neat and Nerdy. Or are you confused because your text books never gave you a game plan on how to deal with a person like me?"

*Neat and Nerdy.* Though she'd always figured she gave off a "clean cut" impression, her heart still squeezed at the mockery in his tone. He knew less of her than she knew of him. He couldn't understand the origins of where "neat and nerdy" came from.

She waited for her composure to return. For her heart rate to settle and the hollow in her middle to fill back up again. Hoping to force something from him other than defiance. Hoping to hit a nerve as he'd done to her so many times already. "So, you figure you're a losing hand, and you might as well give up altogether?"

He scoffed out a hard laugh. His elongated stare made it so she could almost hear the wheels of thought turn over in his head, as he calculated the severity of his next blow. "Losing hand? More like losing my mind. You know, I'll be long dead before you nab your first boyfriend. What are you, twelve? But you can call the death sentence I'm living a 'losing hand' if that makes you feel better about nosing around in my business."

"I'm twenty-eight." The words fell limp out of her mouth, while the other words *death sentence* pinged around in her skull with no exit point for release. "I'm just small." There she went again, spewing useless phrases. Meanwhile, she struggled to wrap her thoughts around how a man so commanding could also be supposedly dying. "You don't have to carry the burden of what you're dealing with on your own."

Pathetic reply but better than her last two attempts.

He let out another tight laugh. "Nice try, but no."

She squeezed her eyes shut. Vexed. Down. Out of her depth. "Why even participate in the volunteer program if you won't let me help?"

She reopened her eyes; he merely held her stare, though a small muscle ticked in his jaw. The creases on his forehead and cheekbones seemed to soften for a second there. Maybe he did care about his impact on her.

He turned his head and broke eye contact. "Drop it, Nerdy."

The hanging silence revealed little more than the ironic, cheerful mumble of other volunteers and their partners around her. Orlando's pointed stare returned to her face—not so cheerful—and her heartbeat thudded loud in her ears.

His silence spoke louder than words. His harsh approach indicated there was more to discover. Like he had a story. A mountain of hidden pain. And no miracle placation could win him over. So maybe she'd have to come to terms with being no different from every other volunteer who'd left.

She wanted to leave this surly man too. Leave him right here where he sat. But she couldn't. Not just yet. What if Candice was right? What if he needed a friend more than he let on?

"I…" Though she spoke mostly to herself, her voice rasped on a brittle sound. "I want to help."

What more could she do? He gave her nothing.

His hard glare softened once more. Maybe, for the briefest second, he doubted his approach. "I know. But you can't."

She opened her mouth, ready to ask for a proper chance. To plead with him to ease up on her just a little. But all her possible words died on her tongue.

Orlando's posture snapped into a poker-straight position. His eyes flashed wide, panic-filled, and so dissimilar to the stoic man she'd encountered twice already—like he'd lost control of all movement— like confusion swallowed all his confidence.

Every muscle on his face pinched. Split-second desperation filled his gaze. And his deep-chocolate stare lost all depth. His eyes glazed over. His warm, olive skin paled.

The common room's thick, eucalyptus-scented air clogged her throat. She lunged for him—shook his arm—but hard layers of muscle and bone failed to respond. She turned. Searched for help. A large, male nurse bolted toward her in wide, loping strides.

"It's happening again."

Sophie's jaw loosened. She spun back to Orlando. A goofy grin pulled his mouth wide like a clown tripping on acid.

He was gone, missing in a place inside his own mind, a place no one else could follow.

# Chapter Six

Electricity coursed through Sophie's legs. *Run.* Not the instinct of a would-be psychiatrist. But logic had fled.

Beads of sweat formed over Orlando's forehead, while her skin prickled with panic. This man was having an episode, and in his moment of need, her mind drew a blank.

His fingers trembled; the slow but constant tremor spread to his arms with increasing violence. Within seconds, his entire torso shook, and a childish laugh broke from him. Then he shrieked.

Volunteers and residents turned. A security guard she'd noticed on a couple of occasions joined the nurse, and both men hooked their fingers under Orlando's armpits.

"Come on, Buddy. Let's get you to your room while you can still walk." The nurse lifted him to his feet. Untrue to character, Orlando followed without protest. The nurse leaned forward and peered around Orlando's broad chest to address the security guard. "We'll sedate him there."

Sedate? Why? Did this man pose a risk? Sophie jumped to her feet. Overcome with an unexplainable drive to protect.

"Kayla." Orlando's high-pitched cry tore across the room. He sounded like a lost child. His frightened stare pointed at her. "Kayla. Come with me. Please."

She glanced around, and the entire room stared at her, their collective gaze asking, *What will you do next?*

A sick sensation rushed her body. Orlando thought *she* was Kayla. *But who was Kayla?*

She clenched her eyes shut. The urge to run resurfaced. Her chest constricted under the mounting stress. Maybe she'd made another mistake. Maybe she didn't belong here after all. Maybe his problems were more than she could handle…

*And I call myself a doctor?*

She shuddered against the question.

Where was her fight?

She had to find her professional grit and help this man. For herself. For *him.*

"Kayla." Orlando's face disappeared around a corner, twisted and pained. "Please. I'm scared."

Her left foot moved of its own accord, propelling her forward and across the room, making the decision for her. "Hang in there. I'm right behind you."

By the time she caught up, he already lay sprawled across a single bed in a sparsely furnished room, a moss-green wool blanket beneath him.

"Kayla." He panted in heavy breaths and reached out a shaking hand, the rest of his body convulsing. The security guard kept one hand pressed to Orlando's chest, the other held to his now bare upper thigh, pinning him while the nearby nurse readied a syringe.

Despite the poison Orlando had served her earlier, she stood at his shoulder and took the hand he held out to her. "I'm here."

He needed her. Now. And she had a moral duty to be there for him.

The strength of his fingers wrapped her palm, and he tugged her in. She stumbled and almost collided with the security guard.

"Stay." Orlando's wild eyes darted around her face. "Please stay."

She swallowed on a ball of emotion and nodded.

The nurse administered the sedative via intramuscular injection straight into his thick thigh. Orlando's eyes squeezed shut, and he shuddered, resisting what was happening to him in this small way.

She rubbed her thumb over the back of his hand. "I'm not going anywhere."

She kept a soft whisper, and her cheeks burned at her overwrought reaction. As if she'd never seen a man sedated before, much less performed a few sedations herself. As if she'd never seen someone with a neurological disorder. She had. Many times over. She'd done placements at several major hospitals... *So why was this man different?*

His hold on her eased. She refocused on the details of his face—his eyes still closed but lacking strain, his cheeks slack and void of expression. The drugs had worked, more effectively and quicker than she'd expected. *He slept.*

She jerked her head up and sought out the nurse, who was busy covering Orlando's lower half with the green blanket. "What did you use on him?"

The security guard stepped back and gave her a direct line of sight with the male nurse. "Ketamine, ma'am."

"Ketamine?" She frowned. "Isn't that a bit much? He wasn't violent. He didn't resist you. Wouldn't Midazolam have been better?"

The nurse's soft smile returned, the security guard already on his way out the door. "I know, ma'am, but we have orders. Orlando doesn't get violent, but he gets distraught. He, himself, prefers the Ketamine over Midazolam as it means less prolonged drowsiness, and he doesn't have to wait out the episode. What you just witnessed was mild. His bigger reactions in the past have been frantic to say the least. The potential for accidental harm to himself or staff increases if we let an episode continue."

"I don't mean to criticize, but it sounds as though his episodes aren't all that managed."

"Yes, ma'am." The nurse's gaze shifted to a nearby wall, as though he weighed up how much to tell her. "If we played by the rules, Orlando would be on constant behavior-modifying drugs, but when we did that, he was pretty zoned out and even more miserable than he is these days. You might not agree, but the staff here decided we were happy to manage him as is. It's a big facility, we make room for him, and as you saw, he's mostly compliant. Even though he's a cranky type, we consider him family here, and he does stuff for us by way of the occasional maintenance job or whatever else he keeps himself busy with. He's a team player in his better moments."

Sophie turned back to Orlando with his deceptively calm face. So much about what she'd heard about him through others didn't connect with the moody man she'd met—including what Candice had said about the other residents wanting to accommodate him—even though Warren had also warned her about him being "trouble".

And since she was thinking about things Candice had said… "Candice mentioned Orlando's condition is degenerative."

The nurse nodded, proceeding to snap off his blue plastic gloves. "That's the assumption. Young people in his position don't tend to have long life expectancies. If not due to their condition, then from the medication, or just the day-to-day emotional wear of being in a home."

Sophie took a moment to consider what life would be like for someone in Orlando's position. Candice had said he needed to get out more. That the lack of outings affected his mood, much less the physical ramifications of being cooped up inside day in, day out, away from anyone his own age.

She turned to the nurse again, thankful to have yet another person to grill about Orlando, since the man himself wasn't all that forthcoming. "Is he always scared during an episode?"

The nurse gave a soft chuckle. "No, ma'am. Sometimes he passes out cold. Sometimes he acts like a happy-go-lucky kid. It seems he's reverting back to something, you know? But with episodes like today's, he starts off afraid and spirals into pure terror. Once that happens, he's near unstoppable. We have to control the episodes early. He was lucky you were here, miss. I don't know who Kayla is, but he seemed to look to you and settle some. I think you took the edge off."

She buried the name Kayla in her memory—both the desperation with which Orlando called it and the fact he'd used that name on her. *Why? And why her?* Somehow, she'd have to find a way to weasel that bit of information out of him.

The nurse made soft rustling sounds behind her. "If you need any help, press the buzzer on the side table there, and someone will arrive soon. Otherwise, I'll be back later to check on him."

She nodded her thanks and kept her attention on Orlando, fingers returning to the back of his brawny hand. The warmth of his skin slowed her galloping heart and stilled her enough to take in more details in his near-empty room.

Most long-term patients tended to personalize their rooms in some way, either with photographs or knick-knacks from their former lives. But Orlando's room had none of that—just a bigger-than-standard TV on a chest of drawers in the left corner, a small stereo on a table to the right. No photos. No knick-knacks. Not even a left-out item of clothing to show he even lived here.

The lack of stuff seemed important. Like he denied his existence at the center or perhaps refused any memory of his former life.

And what sort of life had he had, anyway?

She studied his face, those stormy eyes closed to reveal little more than a row of thick, black lashes—those eyes for once at ease. His dark olive skin still sported a sheen of sweat, but his breathing had at least settled.

And despite his peaceful exterior, she doubted this man ever found peace. Not under the weight of what she assumed was forced bravery. Not with all that buried emotion. His stony act signaled he didn't care, though from how others spoke of him, a different Orlando existed altogether.

He cared a lot and about a lot of things. But he'd had years to practice apathy.

His wide-eyed fear during his episode, the raw pain as he'd called her Kayla… all told a story.

Kayla. He cared about her, too.

Sophie could only imagine what it took to be him. Almost ten years older than her, but if not for his condition, with decades of life ahead of him. So then, a life deteriorating in a nursing home, and a man with little to no hope of ever returning to who he'd once been.

He was right about his younger age putting him outside of her target demographic, but her help didn't come with an age limit. She'd signed up for a career in care, and sometimes that care entailed dealing with an impending end. And whether Orlando expressed it or not, he needed her. Needed someone to not give up on him.

# Chapter Seven

"Kayla." Orlando's voice crackled on the name, his throat dry and brittle like fallen leaves. "Kayla, you still there?"

His head throbbed. He wanted to see, but his heavy eyelids kept fluttering closed. He groaned, turning his head to his left. Honey-sable hair and eggshell, pale skin flashed before his eyes. His eyelids snapped closed again.

Not Kayla. She had auburn hair and a deep tan.

A cold chill ran through his body. He forced his eyelids open again. Ivory skin. Sea-green eyes? *Shit!* Definitely not Kayla. The cold chill morphed into a burning ache—one that coursed through his veins, poisoning his daydream.

*Idiot, Kayla's dead. I live in the old folks home now.*

Shit. Shit. Shit. Shit. The burning in his veins intensified. He hadn't heard or uttered the name Kayla in decades. Why now?

A groan rumbled deep in his chest, the sedatives always too slow to wear off. The reality of who sat beside him sank in. *Sophie.*

"What are you doing here?" Gravel wore at his throat, though the pain at least distracted from the knowledge this woman had watched him lose all sense of himself.

"You were in a bad way." Her hand brushed his arm, and an

enlivened shiver ran through his entire body—her soft tone sounded measured and intolerably comforting. "I didn't want you to wake alone."

He let out a rough laugh, then coughed when that didn't feel so good.

As if he didn't wake up alone every other day—episode or not.

She pressed a cool glass to his lower lip, ignoring his attempt to laugh off her presence. "Here, drink."

Chilled water coursed over his tongue, trickling down his raw throat like a blissful balm. He drank, slowly, fighting the urge to chug the whole damn glass. Experience had taught him not to over indulge, that would bring nothing but nausea and vomiting, and this poor woman had seen enough.

He scowled at her, still sipping, questioning his need to spare her, much less categorizing her as poor when he normally considered her just a plain old pain-in-the-ass.

She kept the glass to his lips a little longer as if she understood his need for caution. A memory of smoke-filled air circled his thoughts. *His former life.*

The sting of sun beat down on him. The protection and torture of his heavy coat. His hands stained black. Tall gum trees impersonating ghosts, hundreds of years of growth gone up in literal flames. Before him stood a graveyard of burned-out giants, stretched as far as the eye could see. But then came the pure relief of throwing off his helmet. Of removing his mask. The choking smell of scorched earth, dry air, and timber. Followed by that first sip of water…

He pulled away from Sophie and the glass, and then sank back into his pillow, eyes shut to block out the haunting memory. "Thank you."

But even his small show of gratitude hurt.

He couldn't go back—the past as much a scar on his soul as his illness. Though a knotted sensation worked through his core now, and a far more recent realization rose to the surface.

*What exactly did I do during this latest episode?*

His eyes flung open, and he stared at Sophie. Kayla's name still singed his lips, and her presence filled the room like yet another ghost. "You can go now."

He couldn't be certain if he'd meant the words for Kayla or Sophie, but he didn't need to turn to the woman beside him and see pity on her face.

"I will. Soon." Her even tone matched her neutral expression, and she showed no judgment. "I just want to know you're okay first."

The knotting in his belly unfurled, releasing his sense of shame, only to make room for hot anger. Her willingness to stick around annoyed him more than the idea she might flee in disgust. "I'm fine. You can go."

"Who's Kayla?"

The direct question hit him swift as a slap. He squeezed his eyes shut and whispered an obscenity. "None of your business."

Her chair scraped against the carpet. He opened his eyes to her standing over him. "Fair enough. I just hope you know I mean well. I'll be back in two days as per the volunteer schedule. If you're feeling up to it, we can talk then."

The fire within him roared, and he scowled his contempt. Even her white cotton tunic taunted him like some kind of flag of innocence, the kind of untouchable goodness he couldn't measure up to, even on his best day.

He shifted against the wool blanket on top of him, the one scratching and irritating the skin of his belly through his thin t-shirt. The light from the open window shone too bright.

He hated having his window open. Who'd opened his bloody window?

Even the rose bushes outside, with their pink and yellow blooms, seemed too cheery, too pink–their overly sweet aroma in the air a sharp invasion of an outside world he couldn't access. A world he no longer belonged to.

And the woman before him was much, much worse.

That pleading gaze… The one she'd used just moments before he'd blacked out. A look that had brought him idiotically close to accepting her help… Everything about *her* was just too suffocating to his already limited sense of personal space.

"As I recall…" He caught the flinty edge to his voice and went with it. "You were ready to slap me minutes before I spazzed out. Now what? You saw a hint of how fucked up my life is and you feel sorry for me?" Miss Nerdy's pupils dilated, black pools surrounded by crystal green waters. As if recovering from an episode didn't pain him enough, now he had to add the guilt of hurting her to his current misery. "If it weren't for Candice's nagging about my need for more funding, I wouldn't be putting myself through this volunteer program, do you understand? Heck, the funding isn't much motivation anymore, so cut it out with your puppy dog eyes and wrangling me into talking to you. Nothing you have to offer will make my life any less aimless than it already is."

Her jaw hung open for a moment, before she clenched it shut again. "I'm not here to cure your condition. I don't even know all that much about it. All I want is to improve your quality of life in any way you'll let me."

He snapped his gaze away from her and stared up at the ceiling. "Well, you can't, and I don't want you to. So go."

"You want to get out more." Her voice held a stern edge now as she regained her defenses and rose to the argument. "I can help you with that."

"After what you just witnessed?" He huffed out a short laugh, refusing to look at her. "You still want to take me out? Are you insane?"

"I'm a doctor, remember?" She paused, as if she figured he needed a moment for that information to sink in. As if he could forget. As if he hadn't encountered enough well-meaning doctors. "I'll get the home to give me the run down on the best course of action should you have an episode. Ms. Olsen seems to think it's doable. All I need is your consent."

"Well, you don't have it." He glared at the ceiling and tried not to growl.

She'd clearly taken time to think this through. And even though he should have jumped at the chance to get out, a deeper part of him still resisted. "In fact, given what you've seen and that you're a psychiatrist, I'd say you're taking this role way too seriously."

She crossed her arms in his peripheral vision, her white tunic shifting—calling for his attention, though he tried not to conjure up the mental image of how the fabric might bunch and dip between her small and perky breasts.

He squeezed his eyes shut again, making it appear as though he wanted to block her out—not a total lie—though, really, he'd just annoyed himself. How had he already noted she had small, perky breasts?

*Because I can't help myself. She's young, and beautiful, and smart, and puts up with my bullshit. I'm one low-life, dirty bastard. That's for sure!*

Well, clearly two years surrounded by oldies hadn't killed off his last shred of virility. Though, damn Sophie even more for jolting that particular aspect of his past back to life.

He turned to her, her arms still folded in seductive confirmation of how he'd figured she'd appear—her pinched stare, along with her petite but solid build, reminiscent of a feisty, little dancer.

*My tiny dancer.*

He shuddered, recoiling at the desire to stake any kind of claim over this woman. To call her *his*. She wasn't his. Not by any stretch of any mile. And the challenge in her stare made him want to prove her wrong for ever trying to help him. The very sight of her compact figure looming over him in his bed made him want to pick her up and have his way with her. To prove he wasn't the helpless soul that life seemed set on making him.

*Fuck.*

She tilted her head to one side. "What about me makes you uncomfortable?"

*Fuck again.* Wrong question, lady. Wrong timing too. Not with where his thoughts wandered...

He turned his attention back to the ceiling, even more disgusted with himself, even more confused. Why now? Why did his libido surge back to life now? And why with this damn woman?

He frowned ahead. "Everything about you makes me uncomfortable."

"Okay. Fine. I'll be back in a couple of days. Until then, you can either think of somewhere you'd like to go, or I'll come up with something myself. And..." She huffed out something similar to a sigh, mixed with a groan, as if reluctant to offer her next words. "And if I truly do make you uncomfortable, then I promise to keep my mouth shut the entire time we're out. At least that way, we'll both get to enjoy some freedom without the bickering."

His stomach hollowed at one particular word. *Freedom.* That word embodied everything he'd wanted in recent years, doled out so casually from this woman's lips. She clearly took her freedom for granted. Though he couldn't blame her. So had he.

And yet. She offered freedom, at the expense of her ability to scour for more information, a compulsion probably near impossible for this well-meaning do-gooder.

"I know doctors are said to have a God complex." He kept his attention away from her. "But you take your deity status to a whole other level."

She released a soft laugh, one that skated over his skin in light tingles. "You're welcome to think what you want. In fact, I'd say your skepticism is a natural response."

"Thanks for the validation." And simply because she'd made his skin tingle... "But you should know I plan to have you removed as my volunteer."

"Sure. I mean, you doing the ditching would be a nice departure from volunteers walking out on you, right?" The door knob creaked, alerting him to her impending exit. "So, you make that request, and I'll await the call telling me not to come. Otherwise, I'll swing by in two days to pick you up."

# Chapter Eight

"Is this a biker bar?" Sophie perched on the edge of a bar stool at Hell Cat Tavern and cringed at all the leather-clad, bearded dudes dispersed in small groups around the dingy space. The sour stench of stale beer and sweat surrounded her, probably permeating the cotton of her favorite beige tunic.

It was just before noon on a Friday, and some of the guys appeared more bedraggled than others, as if they'd continued their drinking session from the night before. Orlando sat beside her, his large palms cupping a giant mug of beer, while he gave her an exaggerated shrug in reply. "Could be a biker bar. I've never really noticed." He turned his attention to the room and released an audible sigh. "Ahhh. I've missed this place. You were right about getting out more. I feel better already." He spun his darkened gaze back to her, eyes narrowed, as though he knew just how out of place she felt. "And wait till we check out Teasers later on. You'll love it there."

Teasers was a strip club, and his stare dared her to backtrack out of her promise to take him wherever he wished.

In her two days spent fretting over this man's power to fire her as his volunteer, she hadn't once considered he'd try to use her offer of help as a form of torture. Maybe she'd just been so glad to simply not get fired that she'd blanked out on his true nature. *Silly woman.* Then again, maybe he really was into biker bars and strip clubs, and this was what he simply wanted to do. Though an unexplainably optimistic part of her brain still refused to accept that notion as fact.

She took a deep breath, meaning to release a sigh, but instantly regretted her decision. The stink of sweat and beer assaulted her nostrils again, and her stomach twisted in revolt. Either way, biker bars or sweat stench aside, she wouldn't break. She'd stick out her promise to Orlando. After all, she'd wanted more life experience, and here she was getting some.

"I'm sure Teasers will be lovely." She tilted her chin and sipped at her orange juice—orange juice she'd needed to convince the barman three times not to add hard liquor to. "And you're right. You do look happier, and I'm glad our arrangement works for you."

She offered Orlando an easy smile, withholding her judgment in exchange for embracing his venue of choice. He ticked an eyebrow. As if her optimism annoyed him. "Watching you try to fit in here brings me happiness. You're not exactly a 'Hell Cat' kind of girl."

She gave a strained laugh, sweeping her gaze over the room until her focus landed on a biker seated with his back to her. Bum crack and hair spilled from the space between his tight leather vest and his even tighter leather pants. She cringed, half expecting his pants to explode and someone in his near vicinity to lose an eye from a wayward metal button or something. Though she hoped not. That would mean she'd have to roll up her sleeves and administer first aid, which meant even more bad things for her favorite beige tunic.

"You're right." She flicked her gaze back to Orlando, eager to forget the impending leather pants disaster. "I'm not a 'Hell Cat' kind of girl, but I'm willing to make sacrifices. I understand how being stuck in the care facility day in, day out might turn you into a grouch."

"Or maybe I'm just an asshole." He gave her a deadpan stare. "Did you ever think of that? Maybe I'm an asshole who really loves checking out strip clubs and women with big boobs?"

He gave the room a casual glance as if he hadn't just said the word boobs. But then her face heated, his unnerving attention stopping at her not-so-big chest.

"Sure." She shrugged, convinced he was messing with her. "But I figured taking you out couldn't make you more of an asshole."

His expression turned flat again, and he drew out a silence.

Her stomach churned, so she spoke once more. "Can I ask you something?"

He turned back to his beer, giving the impression he'd finished messing with her for the time being. "I can't promise I'll answer."

When he wasn't busy scowling, his side profile revealed lips that curved so beautifully upward and a well defined jaw beneath a thick, dark layer of stubble. If she didn't know him, she'd describe him as *masculine perfection*, but she did know him, so the best she could conjure was *attractive trouble maker*.

She sighed, getting on with the task of trying to help him. "Why are you in an aged care facility? Surely some better suited housing situation could be arranged for someone your age?"

He remained silent, this time tilting his beer in the palm of his hand, inspecting its foamy surface. "I lost my job some years ago due to my condition and had no more money left after my last hospital internment. I needed immediate care, and Roseford Aged Care is close to where my next of kin lives." He shrugged. "The center was willing to take me."

"Oh?" She settled back a little, the lack of snark in his reply an encouraging sign. "So, you have family here? Have you always lived in Roseford?"

His gaze darted over in a sidelong glare. He said nothing.

"Okay." She bit her lower lip, unable to keep from pushing her luck. "But if you *do* have family in the area, could they also assist in taking you places?"

He pulled his attention from her. Quiet. Focused down on his beer again.

"I get visits. That's enough." His voice was a mix of gruff, soft control. "I don't expect anyone to burden themselves with whether I might spaz out while I'm away from the center. I still don't know why you bothered."

She cringed at his harsh use of the words "spaz out", but at least she'd gotten him to divulge something about himself. How long till she could get him to discuss his condition? His current treatments, tests, and prognosis? She'd encountered so many cases during her placements where patients languished simply because they didn't have the right specialists or care. Maybe Orlando was one of these people. Maybe at the very least, she could act as a temporary medical advocate.

His glare eased, and his deep chocolate gaze lingered on her face in an unreadable expression. "My turn."

She jolted out of her train of thought. "Sorry? What?"

His sly grin returned. "My turn to ask a question."

Her shoulders drew tight. She wanted to say no, but…

He gave a small chuckle as if her discomfort amused him. "Let me guess, being a psychiatrist and all, you figured you'd ask all the questions and I'd just sit here like a good little boy and tell you all my sad stories."

"I'm not a psychiatrist. And that's not what I thought."

That last part wasn't one-hundred-percent true. He was right. She'd never really considered sharing anything personal about herself.

He tilted his beer at her. "Not a psychiatrist, *yet*. And you forgot about the part where I'm not your patient. This is supposed to be a two-way exchange, remember?"

She gnawed her lower lip once more, gaze accidentally sliding back to the biker's butt-crack again. A sudden shudder ran up her spine, and she turned to Orlando. "Okay, fine. Ask."

His eyelids narrowed, as if readying himself to analyze every detail of how she responded to whatever he said next. "Why would a woman like you choose to live out her life in a safe little bubble?"

The muscles on her face turned involuntarily lax, and her heart sunk in her chest. "What are you talking about? A 'woman like me'? What bubble?"

*Am I really so obvious?*

And what other things had he learned about her from their limited exchanges? Hadn't he been too busy with his own distant brooding? Gosh, why was she so rattled? Why wouldn't her mind quit firing one question after another? Which, ironically enough, was yet another question.

He turned away from her, attention fixed forward, as though he could hear the confusion pinging around in her head. "I mean, you'd be a smokin' hot woman if not for the potato sack clothing and uptight personality."

She tipped her chin down, mouth agape at her loose-fitting tunic over steel gray leggings and knee-length boots. Okay, maybe she could see how her beige top resembled a potato sack, but had he really just insulted her favorite tunic?

"I'm not uptight, you're just too much of a prickly bastard to let me relax long enough for you to get to know me." He whipped his gaze back to her, but her mouth had run away from her and wasn't ready to stop. "And let me get this straight. You've decided from my choice in clothing, I must be a closeted nun?"

"Am I wrong?"

This time her mouth didn't gape so much as waver. She snapped her jaw shut, refusing to succumb to his attempt to shame her. "No, you're not, but I'm working on it. And you know, maybe sometimes looks aren't what they seem." She flicked a loose strand of hair from her face. "Happy now?"

"No. You haven't answered my question." He placed his beer on the counter and leaned back. "If I'm not wrong, then what's with the sheltered act?"

"It's not an act. Some people are introverts."

"Yeah, some people." His all-knowing smile sent a shudder of doubt through her belly. "But that's not the whole story with you, is it?"

"I don't know what you're talking about."

He didn't respond right away, which in and of itself added discomfort. His deep gaze seemed to search for some kind of confirmation before he nodded, as if he'd found his answer despite her avoidance. "I've seen fear and confusion on enough faces to see it in yours too."

The weight in her tummy turned into a mammoth boulder nestled low in her gut. He spoke of fear, something she had in spades. Fear of failing. Fear of falling short. Like she was doomed either way, whether she made a go of her life or not. Maybe that's where the confusion part of his remark kicked in. Because most days, she doubted the decisions she made. And she might be one to linger back, but no fear or confusion had ever stopped her. At least, not forever. The fact she'd come on this holiday proved she could take risks. Which reminded her, she really did need to ease up on Orlando's problems and return to her mission of finding a man. Maybe then she'd stay occupied long enough to worry less about her not-so-elderly resident.

Still, there was one positive to his shocking insight—his statement offered a clue to the life he'd once had. The one where he'd "seen fear and confusion on enough faces". What did he mean by that? Though something about his confession made her feel more settled in his presence. She doubted much could ever surprise him.

She blinked, using the cold glass in her hand as a distraction. She did owe him some sort of clarity. "I've watched others mess up their lives simply because they didn't tread carefully enough. I don't want to make those same mistakes."

Orlando didn't need to know that *their lives* was actually *her life*. She'd never come close to talking about this. Not with her ex, Hector. Not with her best friend, Hannah. What would they think if they knew the truth? One thing was for sure, they'd never see her the same again.

So perhaps the transient nature of her relationship with Orlando offered a pleasant kind of false courage. Even if she did find herself mostly responding to him in indirect riddles.

"And an entire life can pass while you're busy treading carefully." He offered a wry smile. "I've seen plenty of that too."

"Are you speaking from personal experience?"

"Just the opposite. Though personal experience might mean messing around too much led me to the same result. So maybe you're right about not treading carefully." He paused to release a heavy sigh. "Anyway, we were talking about you. Who are these 'others' you mention, the ones who apparently messed up their lives?"

She broke eye contact and feigned interest in the various colorful bottles of liquor behind the bar. If this man had taught her one thing, it was that answering undesirable questions with silence constituted acceptable currency within the parameters of this relationship.

"Right." He spoke with a grumble, before casually slapping a hand to the counter. "I've had enough of this charade." He shot to standing. "Let's go."

"What? Already?" She frowned, her thoughts snapping to her cringe-worthy next task of going to Teasers. "You're not going to finish your beer?"

He laughed, eyes glittering a little too much for her comfort. "If you haven't noticed, I haven't taken a single sip of my beer. I'm not dumb enough to add alcohol to all the meds I'm on."

She peered down at his full glass sitting on the counter. "Why did you ask to come to this bar then? Didn't you want to relive 'the good old days'?"

The scar at the top of his forehead crinkled as he smiled. "I've never been to this bar in my entire life. And as far as I know, Teasers doesn't exist." He pulled a navy-blue jacket over his shoulders. "But as I said, watching you try to fit in here sure did bring me a great deal of happiness."

# Chapter Nine

Hilltop on High was Roseford's most popular cafe, famous for its rustic look and cozy high tea service. Three-tier cake stands with floral country-kitsch patterns stood on most tables, while their occupants sipped from matching kitsch teacups. Sophie sat at a table on the back patio; the wide, wrap-around area unsurprisingly reflecting the cafe's name in that it perched atop a big hill overlooking a picturesque scene of Roseford's rolling hills.

Her laptop sat propped open before her, while the summer sun heated her skin. She dragged her gaze away from the view of gum trees waving in the breeze and a glass-like lake winking from the valley's base. Back to her latest research. Or anti-research, since she used the cafe's complimentary WIFI to browse a local dating site that Luke's fiancée Agathe had urged her to try.

"You know they have phone apps for that now?"

Cold shock zipped up her spine, and she squeezed her eyes shut—needing a moment for shame to subside before she could face the voice's owner. Though she maintained a tight cringe, she opened one eye and peered up at Candice Olsen. "Thanks, I tried, but the cheapo phone I took with me traveling doesn't support any kind of newfangled software."

Candice gave a warm smile. "Don't look so pained, it must be difficult being young and single in a far-flung town like Roseford." She pointed to the seat across from Sophie. "Mind if I sit?"

"Make yourself comfortable." Sophie snapped shut her laptop and welcomed the opportunity to wrangle more information out of someone about Orlando.

"This place is always a little crazy in the warmer months. Thanks for sharing your table." Candice lowered herself into the chair and placed a little sign with her order number down beside her. She leaned forward, fingers interlaced. "I heard you witnessed one of Orlando's episodes."

Sophie paused; her mild progress with him at Hell Cat had somehow faded his episode to the background of her mind a little. That small experience gave her more to associate with him than his condition had. Or maybe he'd spoken to her for a few minutes without any disdain and blindsided her with the things he'd noticed about her that most people didn't.

"Yes." Her mouth remembered Candice sat watching her, even if her brain hadn't. "Though I can't claim to know much more about his condition than I did before."

"Well…" Candice flopped back in her seat and dropped a sigh. "All I can say is what you saw was minor."

Sophie focused on her closed laptop and disappeared into her thoughts for a moment. "I did ask him why he wasn't in a different facility, given his age and care requirements. All I got was that he needed ongoing help, and he didn't want his family taking on his burdens."

"Often there aren't the right resources when a young person experiences a life-changing injury similar to Orlando's. A lack of options may mean they can't stay in their own home and aged care is the only solution." Candice gave a tiny shrug; the structured seams of her moss-green blazer gave her shoulders a square shape. "Orlando wasn't lying about not wanting to be a burden on his family. He has a younger brother who has a successful career interstate, and though his elderly mother lives in Roseford, she's in no condition to handle a guy as big as him when he's in the throes of a bad episode. I can understand why he doesn't want her looking after him."

Sophie maintained her silence, unsure whether to ask for more information or shut up and count herself lucky. She now knew Orlando had a brother interstate and his mother lived in the area… and one other potential detail…

She leaned forward, daring to plow for more evidence. "Orlando is in care because of an injury?"

"That's the assumption, yes. Though a few other factors cloud any real certainty."

Candice's order arrived at the table—a chicken sandwich and espresso—and Sophie waited so the woman could enjoy a first sip of coffee. Her attention wandered in the silence, to Orlando and his little stunt at the biker bar. The way he'd toyed with her, gotten her to take him to a place he had no interest in visiting beyond watching her twist in discomfort. Yes, he'd been a little more open to confiding in her, but he'd toyed with her all the same.

"I want to help him." Her cheeks burned with what might have been a blush, as if she'd offered up some deep, dark desire rather than a concerned volunteer's basic impulse to look after her resident. "But he doesn't want my help. He wants to make my life hell."

Candice let out a short laugh and lowered her coffee, as if she feared her laughter might make her spill her hot beverage. "I wouldn't go that far. He seems to actually like you."

"No, no, that can't be right." The heat in her cheeks released, only to give way to a series of quivers in her belly—a visceral protest against the notion Orlando might *actually like her*. "He threatened to fire me the other day. And yesterday, he made me take him to a dingy biker bar, where he proceeded to laugh at my discomfort. I'm pretty sure he finds great joy in making me want to quit."

"Hmmm… Yes." Candice skimmed a forefinger over her coffee cup handle and nodded to herself. "Actually, he did tell me the other day that he wanted you gone, but I guilted him into reconsidering."

Sophie released a shaky chuckle, thinking back to his non-guilt-ridden shenanigans at the bar—his fake beer drinking and the fake desire to visit a strip club afterward. "Guilt? Is Orlando even capable of that emotion?"

"Sure is. I told him how much the volunteer program meant to you—that getting booted would reflect badly on your study and future work placements." Candice took a big bite of her sandwich and chewed, as if convincing Orlando of anything was a non-event to her.

"B...But that's not entirely true. I already have my degree. Volunteer work is completely irrelevant in relation to my career. As far as anyone would be concerned, this is purely a recreational pursuit."

"Yeah, he said something similar, but I fudged the details a little, you know. I said that having international experience on your resumé will look better than none at all, and that's why you signed up to volunteer in the first place. That you're hugely over-qualified, and you could be enjoying your holiday, so given how far you've traveled to work with someone, he better not disappoint you."

Sophie's jaw hung loose and her face felt bloodless. Not only had Candice twisted the truth to a painful degree, but Orlando had been close to dismissing her after all. *Then*, by some crazy miracle, he'd taken pity on her. Not that she needed his pity. But the fact someone as guarded as him even *felt* pity, much less toward her...

Her nerves were a live wire sparking and flailing, and she reached for her cup of tea in the hopes she might find some kind of calm.

Candice's stare bore ahead. "You're judging me right now, aren't you?"

"A little, yeah. I'm not sure I want to work with a resident who's been manipulated into working with me."

"My little white lie benefited everyone, didn't it? Orlando now has someone to take him out—I don't think you understand how huge that is. You got to keep your volunteer placement. And I got my most unwilling resident out of the center for a couple of hours. Even my staff were happy, since he was decidedly less difficult for the remainder of the day. So, I'm calling this a win."

Sophie peered around the large cafe with its packed tables and cacophony of chatter and clinking cutlery. The smell of sugary cakes from the kitchen mingled with the hill's fresh grassy scent. Her gaze skimmed nearby faces, only to land on Candice's again, just as a new realization struck.

Yes, the cafe was busy, but it wasn't *that* busy. There were more than a few empty tables left.

"There's more to you being here than needing a table, isn't there?" She waited as Candice's complexion dropped to an ashen shade. "You care about Orlando, and there's something more specific than his outings that you're worried about."

Candice broke eye contact, shoulders suddenly rigid as her earlier nonplussed attitude evaporated. "Young people in care require so much more community access. In particular, they need people close to their own age. People like you. All I want is for Orlando to receive help while he still can."

"Because his condition is degenerative?"

"That's the assumption." She returned her gaze to Sophie. "But no, it's because he requires so much more than someone to simply walk him to his room and sedate him when his episodes are at their worst. It's the aftercare that's a literal soul-crusher—when he needs physical rehabilitation and a heck of a lot of intervention." Candice's fingers tightened around her blue floral coffee cup, as though she held back a tide of frustration. "Speaking as one professional to another, in the last year alone, he's had two major episodes. Both left him immobile for months on end. His body simply forgets how to walk, how to move; though he recovers oddly quicker than most accident victims, so I guess that's where the belief comes from that this is more neurological than physical. Either way, each time he has to relearn how to do so many things all over again."

Sophie's lungs compressed, her next breath hard to take. No wonder she struggled to get him to engage with the outside world. "He essentially has to start from scratch with every major episode?"

"Yes. And no one knows quite why his brain reacts the way it does, just that he's in the strange position where his condition isn't bad enough to have him take up a hospital bed, but it's prohibitive enough that he needs constant help."

Sophie let her gaze wander toward the hills, with their sunlit pastures intersected by low wire fences. A few of her prior thoughts on

Orlando clicked into place. Why he was always so grumpy. Why he always seemed ready to check out of life.

*Imagine having to start over and over and over again...*

Candice rested a flat palm to the table, beckoning for Sophie's attention. "I know he's not easy, but I choose to focus on his ability to get back up after each and every set back. I don't know how he does it, but I do wonder how much longer we can keep convincing him to try. There's so much more going on in that man. So much more than the bad temper he puts on show.

"Something's changed in him lately, and I'm worried. More worried about him than any other resident in my care. And trust me, I'm doing all I can to make the place livable for him—bending so many rules—making so many allowances. And everyone else in this town feels for Orlando too. Do you think anyone here would put up with his stuff if there wasn't a sense of looking out for our own?" She peered down at her hand on the table and winced. "He's losing his spark, Sophie, and I'm getting really worried we might lose him completely. Not to his illness, but to himself."

Sophie's mind ground to an immediate halt, and the clash of cafe sounds seemed to stop around her. Nothing but the beat of her own rushing heart filled her ears. Coldness filled her veins as if her blood itself lost all heat. Soon, a great shiver ran up the sides of her ribcage, and her entire body shuddered in response. She knew exactly what Candice meant about losing Orlando to himself. And the gravity of that meaning cut bone-deep.

She didn't want to believe it. She didn't want to imagine someone as stubborn and unassailable as him taking his own life. But she'd tended to enough suicide attempts during her hospital residencies to know these things could be unpredictable.

She fought to locate her words—but words didn't come. Men were statistically more effective when it came to suicide attempts. They had a knack for finding permanent, and often more gruesome, results. But the one thing she'd heard time and time again—families and friends often had no idea the patient had lost their will to live.

Anyone in her field understood that even the most resilient people could falter under life's curveballs. And just like illness, depression didn't discriminate.

She caught Candice's eye, her pulse still fast. "Orlando needs a psych assessment."

"It's been done. Whatever he said to the psychs, they decided he was of sound enough mind and didn't present anything inconsistent with someone in his position. He's never made an actual attempt at ending his life, and he refused any offer of further help." Candice sent forth a tight glare. Maybe she figured Sophie hadn't been listening, or that her statement hung doubt over Candice's ability to provide care. "There was only so much pushing I could do. Why do you think he was pissed about your dreams of becoming a psychiatrist? He thought I'd planted you to spy on him."

Candice leaned back in her chair as she awaited Sophie's reply. New ease slid across her face, hinting that she'd finally released a great weight off her shoulders, only for that weight to shift right onto Sophie.

A dull pain radiated down her back, the force and magnitude of Orlando's situation, and now her own, settling in. Heck, she couldn't even be sure Candice's assumption on his mental state was all that correct. He'd passed his psych assessment after all. Either way, she couldn't tell him what she knew. Not yet, anyway. Any progress she'd made with him was too fresh with too little trust established. He'd only push her away. For good this time.

And suddenly this unplanned meeting felt too complicated and too much to bear.

This tranquil Australian holiday didn't seem quite so calm after all.

She stood and lifted her laptop along with her, her appetite for tea and dating websites gone. She couldn't even decide whether to thank Candice for the forewarning—or berate her for not leaving the information about Orlando's mental state trapped firmly in its box.

"I'm sorry." Candice's brows pushed together in seeming remorse as if she saw that this conversation wasn't wholly appropriate or appreciated. "I only told you because I need you to stick it out with Orlando until I can at least sort more funding for him—or until I can think of something else to keep him distracted. I know it's a lot to lump on a volunteer. I'm only asking you to do what you can, within the limited months you have, because of your academic background, because Orlando seems receptive to you, and because I believe you can open some windows of possibility for him. Please. Just be the friend he needs right now. Okay?"

# Chapter Ten

Orlando drummed his fingertips over the gray Formica table, as the care workers wheeled in the last few residents. The drumming reverberated in his ear. *Thrum. Thrum. Thrum.* Until abrupt recognition made him stop.

*I'm nervous? What the fuck is that about?*

He took a deep breath and forced the tension from his shoulders. What was there to be nervous about? Nothing except the daunting truth that talking to Sophie Tindall somehow injected new interest and cheer into his day. Interest and cheer. Two sentiments long absent in his world. As if her visits kept him going.

*Well, what a scary thought. Fuck, I'm pathetic.*

A burst of laughter erupted out of him, and an elderly woman nearby shot forth a judgmental glare.

Maybe he *was* pathetic. *Stupid too.*

Any enthusiasm he had for Sophie wouldn't hold back his miserable fate.

*She's a distraction. Nothing more. Got it?*

Yes, his decline would arrive soon enough. He had to remember that. No point getting too invested in this woman.

He gazed around the room, at all the frail bodies with trembling fingers and papery skin. His peers. Though some days, he had even less control over his body than most of this poor lot. Chances were, maybe a few would outlive him.

"Eager to see Sophie today?" Shelley stepped into his view with her smug grin, no doubt pleased her harebrained attempt to match him with Sophie had lasted this long.

He jutted his chin toward the giant brown cardboard box in her hands, ignoring her invasive question. "What's that?"

Her grin widened, and she reached into the box. A smaller, glossier carton landed on the table in front of him.

"Puzzles. For today's session. I'm sure you'll love it." Her overly bright tone denoted sarcasm. She'd been around long enough to know he never showed enthusiasm for anything, much less puzzles.

He scowled, his muscles heavy under the usual effort of working past his lethargy.

"Oh, I love puzzles!" A genuinely happier, distinctly British voice cut in. Sophie appeared from behind Shelley.

Orlando's cheeks lost all rigidity, his scowl hiding at the sight of Sophie's beaming smile.

"At least one of us does." He'd meant to grumble the words, but only managed muffled dissatisfaction. Some unexplainable corner of his conscience didn't want to dull her joy.

Shelley winked at him, she'd noticed his muted response, then turned away to distribute more puzzles. Sophie plonked into the seat opposite him and her large, brown handbag hit the ground beside her.

"Nawww, two kittens. I love kittens." She leaned over the table, gawking at the puzzle box, a little too close for his comfort. The fresh scent of spring flowers jumbled his senses.

She lifted her gaze, bringing the most stunning view of sparkling hazel eyes—green pools streaked in umber and gold—too close to his face. "It's only one-hundred pieces, but both kittens are gray, so that might add some fun complexity."

Her innocent passion kicked his heart against his ribcage and lightened his lethargy. He wanted to laugh but didn't. "I know I've called you Miss Nerdy before, but could you at least try not to prove me right?"

She rolled her eyes, darting her hands out and prying the box open. "I forgot who I was talking to, Mr. Sour Lemons."

He opened his mouth, ready to insult her back, but nothing happened. Again came that rising need to laugh, almost as if just having her near was enough to momentarily melt away years of anger and bitterness. He lost all desire to fight her at the sight of those spindly fingers making fast work of flipping the upside-down puzzle pieces.

So, he joined in, keeping quiet as he turned any piece so the cardboard backs stayed down, and the mottled colors peeked up. Occasionally, he dared to lift his gaze and her eyes rewarded him with a glint. As if simple things like cat puzzles really did bring her joy.

His heart stumbled again.

*Damn. Damn her.*

He'd done enough damage to everyone who came into contact with him already; he couldn't bring this woman down too. Besides, what the hell was he thinking? Sophie hadn't shown any romantic interest in him whatsoever. Not since that first meeting, where she'd accepted his offer of a date. Not since finding out he was a resident. Not since he'd continually proved to her what a grade-A asshole he was.

And why *would* she be interested? Hell, why would he? No good would come from letting his emotions run wild here.

He shifted pieces around, avoiding any eye contact. "You're looking extra chipper today. Did some cute boy ask you to the social?"

*Fuck.*

Even when he tried, he couldn't help but give her shit, much less attempt to gather something of her personal life. He'd grown used to rubbing people the wrong way. The mere fact he wanted to rub this woman in any way, much less *every* way—right and wrong—meant he didn't know how to stop tormenting her.

She separated an edge piece from the others and put it aside. Her gaze rose to him, and the corners of her eyes creased with a cheeky grin. "No. You might refer to me as being twelve, but I'm a bit too old for socials. These days my excitement levels require a little more action than a slow dance and an awkward kiss."

His cheek muscles slackened, and his brain shorted for a reply. She paused and then laughed. "I didn't think it'd be so easy to put a look of shock on your face."

He gave a slow shake of his head and returned his attention to the puzzle. "I didn't expect you'd open our conversation with a commentary on your sex life."

He forced his thoughts from what sort of *action* might actually arouse her excitement, just as his hand brushed hers over a puzzle piece.

Her skin was about a million times softer than his and a few shades paler too, while her small stature and Britishness nudged his mind to all things soft, feminine, and classic. The smell of freshly brewed black tea. New cut flowers on a bedside table. Crisp morning light over pristine white bedsheets. A naked Sophie laid out on those bedsheets…

Instant heat spread through his chest and electricity coursed through his extremities. His heart didn't just kick, it seesawed on the edge of exploding.

He snatched his hand back but too late.

Her stare slammed into his, pupils wide and mouth agape. Maybe she'd felt the same surge of electricity. The same shock of need. And if she didn't, then why did she blink at him? So silent. So still.

Her eyelids fluttered some more, and her attention slid down to the table. Neither one spoke. Neither one of them acknowledged the awkward gravity. Which was fine by him.

"So, in light of our biker bar adventure last week…" She kept her head down, gaze firmly averted. "Maybe you could suggest somewhere you'd actually want to visit next time?"

"A lake." He cleared his throat and made himself form a more substantial sentence, though his hands ached to reach out and swipe the light tendrils of sable hair fallen from her ponytail and framing her face. "On the outskirts of town. I haven't been there for a while. Years even. I want to go there."

The lake bordered the back paddock of his childhood home, a deeply personal place where he and his now-dead father had once upon a time spent hours fishing and talking shit together. Those long-lost hours meant even more to him now—now that only one of them still survived. At least, for the moment …

To Sophie's credit, she'd witnessed one of his episodes and not run screaming into the night. She'd even endured his farce adventure to that dive biker bar. So, maybe he could trust her with the lake too.

"Sounds like an adventure." Her bright tone brought him back to the moment. "How about next week?"

He nodded, not intending much of a reply given where his thoughts went now. But then memories of the lake and his dad were always hard to escape once he got thinking on them, and he couldn't handle that pain, so he made a joke instead. "Just be sure to wear sunscreen. Next week will be a hot one, and you Brits are like vampires."

She gave him a crinkled scowl, as if she didn't quite understand, so he offered up his punchline. "Can't handle direct sunlight."

A loud crack of laughter erupted from her—one the circled around the room. He peered around to find residents and volunteers alike wide-eyed and slack-jawed, as though he and Sophie had suddenly become the nuisance kids in class, and no one believed he'd made the woman beside him laugh rather than cry.

He turned back to her and nearly startled at the genuine chuckle rumbling through his chest. He picked up a puzzle piece, vowing not to overthink his reaction, joining the piece to the few she'd already assembled.

Just as that piece fell into place, his stomach churned, and a strong burning smell entered his nostrils. A smell of charred food. Headache-inducing. Eggy. Like stove gas…

And something else… Something… Something similar to singed cloth.

A fire alarm shrieked. Loud. Painful. His chest constricted. Skin prickled.

*That smell.* So overwhelming. Like a tidal wave arching over him, seconds from crashing down.

*The sound.* Familiar. Terrifying. The wail frayed his nerves. His control stripped. It told him to go. So his body worked of its own volition, using what little energy he had to launch him into survival mode. He scrambled to the floor, panic and memory converging as one. The reaction mimicked one of his episodes. *But different.* At least he didn't disappear into his mind.

No. His mind sparked and fired under a barrage of commands. Instinct and action took him over. He grabbed Sophie and dragged her down with him, then barked out an order. "Get down. Stay down."

# Chapter Eleven

"W…w…what's happening?" Sophie's knees collided with the hard linoleum floor, instant pain radiating up her legs. She wanted to cry out but didn't have the time. Orlando's hand hooked under her armpit, and he dragged her along on all fours toward the doorway.

"Smell that?" He gave a half-yell, gaze wide and hyper-alert.

She turned her head to her right, then upward—where residents, volunteers, and staff shuffled out the door in calm compliance with the fire alarm. Her wrists already hurt from crawling, something no one else did. "You mean like someone burnt lunch?"

Everyone peered down at her. Many snickered as they left.

Orlando's attention darted around the room.

"And hear the alarm? This is serious." He huddled, head ducked at the common room's archway, hand held up for her to stop behind him. "Listen. Stay low. Okay? The air's cleaner down here. The gas won't get us so much as the lack of oxygen from the smoke, so you need to stay low. Do you understand?"

He peered around, as if blind to all the people scraping past. She sniffed at the air. No gas smell, no visible smoke, but the open fear in his eyes forced her to nod and play along.

An announcement mumbled over the home's speaker, something

about a small fire in the kitchen. Already extinguished. No huge deal. But residents might prefer to go outside for fresh air while staff worked on clearing the smoke smell and switching off the wailing fire alarm.

"The men. Where are they?" Orlando knelt back and looked about him, as if he hadn't heard the announcement. "They should be here."

"What men? Orlando, what men?" She reached out and put a hand on his shoulder. Maybe if he felt her, he'd return from whatever world he'd lost himself in.

"The fire crew. Don't worry, we'll be okay. I'm sure they'll be here any minute." He put his hand over the one she held to his shoulder and patted. Her heart twisted from his show of concern amidst his panic. He seemed to be having some kind of flashback, perhaps a post-traumatic-stress reaction. Something with more physical and mental control than what she'd witnessed with his episode. "In the meantime, I'll get you out safe, and then I'll run back in for the others."

He used his spare hand to swipe at the sweat beading on his forehead, and it was then she decided to let him have this moment, to not embarrass him with the reality of what was really happening.

The alarm went silent. But still, Orlando didn't seem to notice. His breaths panted hard and fast, and he pushed beyond the common room door, around the corner, and motioned for her to follow.

As people filed back in, she and Orlando crawled out, and she yielded to his world. He crawled along, looking back every so often as if to check that she was okay. Even in distress. Even in this moment where he believed his life in danger. He worked to protect her.

A pair of white nurse's shoes stopped inches from Sophie's fingers on the floor. She tipped her head back and craned her neck. Shelley stood over her, head slowly shaking as if to ask, "What the hell are you two doing?" But Sophie held a hand up, signaling for Shelley to stay quiet, to let Sophie handle this.

Shelley frowned but nodded anyway, then retreated.

Orlando's alert control seemed telling in itself. His considered movements hinted at experience. Like he knew his way around an emergency. Like he'd done this before and relived some kind of ingrained trauma where survival trumped flipping out.

He pointed a strained smile her way, an offer of reassurance. "We're almost there. Can you make it a little farther?"

She nodded. Quiet. Overwhelmed at this glimpse at who he might have been outside the home's protective walls and the ones he'd built around himself. A tight lump swelled in her throat. *Poor Orlando.*

Even as he struggled now, she felt completely safe. If this situation were real, he'd still be looking out for her. That first unnerving time they'd met, she'd recognized something in him. His intense stare. His overpowering masculinity. His stillness. For all his problems, this man still held a moral code and maintained a sense of honor.

They reached the sliding doors, and only then did he stand, offering a hand to help her up too. Her knees stung in painful protest, and she peered down at her red palms, cringing at all the germs she'd just encountered on the center's floor. Not that she had much time to cringe, because he grabbed her wrist and hurried her into the parking lot.

Wind whipped her hair about her face, and the lot was full of volunteer's cars. He looked about again before pinning her with a soft stare, where dark circles shadowed his eyes. He appeared truly strung out, even more than normal. "They're not here yet. I hope you don't mind. I have to go back inside. I have to help the others. Dammit. I thought these days were behind me."

He let go of her and turned, but she launched forward and recaptured his hand. "Stop. You don't have to go."

He peered at the home's doors. Uncertain. A man fighting a battle within. *Stay here in safety with her, or risk his life going back in.* His gaze latched onto hers. "They're in there. I don't have any other choice. I have to go back."

Still, everything about his rounded shoulders and hollow tone said, *"But I really don't want to."*

In his mind, he'd just saved her. Maybe it was time she ended his torture. Maybe it was time she repaid this perceived rescue.

She pulled him closer and cupped both her hands over his clenched fingers, encasing his hand.

"It's over. Everyone is safe." She held his gaze, keeping her tone and touch soft.

Sweat drenched the front of his navy-blue shirt, but she reached out and pressed her palm to his chest, repeating the words. Her hands offered sensory distraction—her words pleaded for him to believe her. She wanted to offer escape from the demons in his head and strength where his currently faltered. "It's over. Everyone is safe. Including you."

His brow creased with deep lines, a sign he concentrated hard on what she'd said. The firm set of his jaw released, he broke eye contact, and his gaze shifted to the center's open doors, cheeks relaxing as if he finally saw what she did. No fire. No smoke.

"It's over?"

She held his hand tighter and offered what she thought he might need to hear. "Yeah, you're okay. You're safe."

His stare snapped back, eyelids widened, while his black pupils grew large. Two jerky breaths lifted and fell beneath his ribcage, like a shattered man jolted from a dream, working double time to dam his emotions.

His reaction prompted her to take a risk, to wrap her arms around him in yet another offer of comfort. She expected him to fling her away. To call her irrational. But she also expected he'd had more than his fair share of abandonment. So maybe she needed to be brave. And maybe he needed something different.

Moments passed, and he didn't fling her away. He didn't call her irrational.

He merely paused slightly before his body sunk against hers, and his arms engulfed her in a reciprocated embrace.

Her heart swelled and strained, as he shook in her hold, heavy breaths brushing the small hairs along the nape of her neck. And she clung to him, absorbing this vastly different Orlando—someone she hadn't encountered up until now–someone he probably didn't let *anyone* encounter.

*Don't get too used to this. This moment will end. He'll go back to being the hardheaded man I'm used to.*

She took a long breath and shelved the reminder, savoring his solid warmth and uncharacteristic openness. She could appreciate the hardheaded man. The hardheaded man had a good reason for being. That hardheadedness protected him. The hardheadedness likely kept him alive.

"It's okay. It's okay," she whispered and patted his back. For all he'd been through. For this glimpse at his former life—a life no doubt worlds away from the one he lived now.

She repeated the words until she'd convinced herself he might believe them, even though he offered no confirmation of his own. This man, strong and vital, shaking in her arms—the result of constant physical setbacks and psychological scars.

What it must take to be him, to wake every day. A young man trapped in an old man's life.

To miss out on so much stuff that most people took for granted, with no remedy in sight.

For a brief moment, earlier today, she'd rejoiced at seeing him in a cheerier mood; like maybe Candice's suspicions—which had already been assessed and dismissed—really didn't hold much truth. Though Sophie had planned on asking him some subtle questions, that plan had been shot to pieces and replaced with a starker reality.

No wonder Candice feared for his mental state.

But now Candice wouldn't be the only one looking out for him. And even through Sophie's bewilderment, what she really felt was awe that he'd survived this far. That a different man existed when Orlando's defenses were down.

His shaking stopped, and he pulled back, but not enough to let her go. "Sorry about that."

She shook her head, unable to meet his gaze, her attention pinned to the dip at his throat. "What sort of a wanna-be psychiatrist would I be if I couldn't handle a little emotion?"

She tried for a reassuring smile, but her lip trembled, refusing to cooperate. Her reference to her work offered cheap deflection in exchange for his display of raw vulnerability—though she did need space and time to unpack what she'd seen.

She forced her gaze to meet with his. The color in his face hadn't returned, and he looked spent.

"Come on." She stepped out of his hold, a part of her wishing she didn't have to. "We'll start the slow walk back inside."

## Chapter Twelve

Sophie raced her fingertips over the keys of her laptop, her elbows digging into the glossy red timber of what she'd just been informed was a native Australian Jarrah wood dining table. She shelved any enthusiasm for the expensive slab of timber, and her brother's bragging, and focused on entering Orlando's full name into her web browser.

Agathe took a seat beside her. "I propose Sophie and I do a bit of shopping and sightseeing tomorrow. Let's say, from eleven onward? That will give her time to sleep in after bar-hopping with Max tonight."

Sophie tilted her screen down, trying not to draw attention to her search results and why she'd asked to access Luke's WIFI.

Max sauntered past, beer in hand, mischievous grin in place. "I hope you mean because we'll be getting in late rather than Sophie getting drunk. Otherwise, you clearly don't know this woman. You'd have to pin her down and hold her mouth open to get her to drink anything more than a couple of white wines."

Moments away from clicking a link that seemed to offer a lead, Sophie glared at her brother. "Hey, just because you're all for wild nights and puking into gutters, doesn't mean I have to be. I hate being drunk."

The constant whoosh of cars and city lights infiltrated from outside the double-story brick house in South Melbourne, a strong reminder she wasn't in Roseford anymore. And speaking of reminders, Max's words jogged her memory on why she didn't drink much, the true reason far more painful than the one she'd given. A reason her brother had probably long forgotten, though she never would.

He leaned his hips into the back of a chair across from her, smile still strong. "Yeah, cos you're a control freak, and you struggle to let go, my dear sister. But I'm going to try my damnedest to change that tonight."

"You don't have to try anything. I'll play along, I promise." She clicked the link and continued her farce of being only half invested in the screen before her.

Max meant well, but he'd accomplished world fame for partying and having no clue. About anything. Ever. And he clearly didn't have a clue about her. Though he was right about one thing. She did struggle to let go. And *letting go* had been one of her reasons for traveling abroad. Except, she'd abandoned that goal since meeting Orlando, so she'd do her best to let loose tonight. "As long as you promise not to —" Her gaze reconnected with her screen and a short gasp fell from her. "Oh…"

Agathe leaned over, her shoulder pressing into Sophie's. "Well, hello. Who's that? Is he someone you're talking to on that dating site I suggested? He's gorgeous."

Luke charged into the room, the bottle of wine he'd gone looking for in hand. He crowded in behind Sophie, yet another uninvited person staring at her laptop. "Hey, why are you using my precious WIFI to look up photos of "gorgeous" firemen?"

An icy chill washed over Sophie's skin. *Gorgeous* didn't sum up the man on her screen.

*Magnificent*, maybe.

*Every woman's wildest dream*, for sure.

But more heart stopping than any of that, the man staring back at her was Orlando. Yes, eyes twinkling and smile beaming, with zero cares in the world. *Orlando.*

He was an immaculate cliché of masculine beauty with his chiseled jaw, glossy black waves, his golden olive skin... Even the scar atop his forehead somehow added a human edge to his perfection... Though what held her frozen most was the attention-grabbing fireman's uniform. Not just because a set of perfectly sculpted, six-pack abs peeked out from his open jacket—though that didn't help her frozen state—but because the uniform confirmed a massive detail about his former life.

"He..." She swallowed, needing more time, unable to connect this man with the one who pretty much cussed her out at every meeting. But it was him. It was most definitely him. The shadows of this dream man still lingered in the Orlando she knew now. "He's my resident at the nursing home."

"No way." Max crowded in, too. "That's no geriatric geezer. That's, that's..."

She stared blankly ahead. "Orlando."

No. Not a geriatric at all.

She scrolled down the page to a photo of him posed beside a child at a community event. Rainbow balloons hovered on strings behind him, and he wore a wholesome smile. The article said something about him taking part in a "sexy" fundraising calendar for the local fire service.

She scrolled farther again. To another photo. *Holy hell.*

This time the heavy jacket was gone. Broad pectoral muscles accompanied his rippling abs. Smears of strategically placed black ash lay painted over his torso and thick biceps—a homage to someone vividly young and vital. A hero. *A firefighter.*

No wonder he'd freaked out at the alarm the other day.

She saw past the provocative photo long enough to make sense of their last encounter, of all the things he'd left behind, his past resurfacing at the first sign of smoke and fire alarms. The trauma he must have endured to react that way. The emotional scars he carried beneath the ones his condition already caused. He was a man who paid for the privilege of just staying alive.

And even as her brain absorbed the implications of the images before her, her body reacted. Skin warming. Heat pooling between her thighs. While a deep gnawing guilt grew in her gut.

Any attraction to this man wouldn't be right. There was nothing official about her role, but she'd made a promise as his volunteer. To help. Not ogle. And even as that promise crossed her mind, so did the visceral memory of his arms around her.

The man on her screen looked like a god, or maybe just an airbrushed version of what his job entailed. Someone beyond reach of anything or anyone. When the man she'd met was very much human.

"No wonder you've barely left Roseford." Max elbowed her in the shoulder.

"It's not as if he struts around the home looking like that." She gave him a playful shove back, a deceptive move in light of the roiling sickness within her. She stared at her screen, at eyes full of gleaming welcome. "In fact, I'd say there's next to nothing of this man left."

Except, of course, for that hint of *something*. The something as he'd near collapsed in her arms. A hint of inherent good. A man who'd tried to save her, to save others, at risk to himself. And maybe this hint formed another layer to his rage. Orlando was lightning trapped in a bottle. A force of nature bursting to fulfill a purpose. His once beautiful and strong body now a cage.

She closed the laptop, face hot, shame burning a hole in her chest. Another thought entered her mind. Researching his past had been a bad idea. She'd crossed a line. Orlando wouldn't be happy if he knew.

Max's devilish grin pulled her attention. She didn't want to know what he thought, so she peered up to Luke, who leaned over from behind her chair, face almost above hers. "I've seen that look on her face before. She's adopted another stray bird."

"Except this time, it's not a bird." Max wiggled his brows. "It's a sexy fireman with abs of steel."

"Stop it." She slapped Max's arm, hard enough to assert her seriousness, gentle enough not to hurt. "He doesn't flash his abs during my visits. And as far as I know, the six pack is another thing of the past."

*Why on earth am I even discussing Orlando's potential abs?*

And even in her protest, her treacherous mind pulled up the memory of his firm body pressed to hers—how Candice had said he exercised to keep himself sane—the intimate knowledge that at least something of those abs had survived…

*Damn. Damn. Damn.* Why couldn't she get her thoughts to behave?

Agathe waved her hands out in front of her, beckoning for attention. "Hang on a minute. Stray birds? What are you guys talking about?"

Luke gave his fiancée a light peck on the cheek and took a seat beside her. "We all grew up near a forest back in York. Occasionally, a local cat would bungle a kill, and Sophie would swoop in to save any injured animals. At least, she'd try. She'd drive everyone crazy with her latest find, get so invested, when ninety-nine percent of the time the poor little critters never made it."

She scowled at her brother. "Yeah, but occasionally one would. And it paved the way for my medical degree, didn't it? So, my 'investment' wasn't all for nothing."

"Yeah, and one-hundred percent of her finds would tweet or squeak up a storm all night, every night." Max pressed the heel of his hand to his forehead. "Man, I can't even count how much sleep I lost each time she brought home an injured stray."

A small chuckle escaped Luke's lips. "If it'd been up to Sophie, she would have skipped school and collected stray creatures every day."

Sophie slumped back in her chair. "Well, I didn't. And despite what you say, my education didn't suffer one little bit."

Luke peered around Agathe. "Soph, you know what we're getting at here. Do the best you can with this guy, but don't get too caught up."

"Who says I'm getting 'caught up'?"

Max crossed his arms, making it clear he didn't believe her attempt at indifference. "The fact that we haven't seen you nearly enough this trip. Or maybe the fact it's a Saturday night, and you're spending your time researching this guy rather than hitting the town with me already."

She pushed her laptop away and held both hands up in surrender. "Okay, fine. I get it. Let's go."

"Yes!" Max gave an excited hiss and turned to the kitchen counter, where he collected his dark gray sports coat from one of the bar stools. "I'll race you to the front door."

But later that night, against all warnings, Sophie didn't keep her thoughts off Orlando. The Ruby Room's loud dance music sent vibrations through her body, while the bar's swinging strobe lights flashed blue, yellow and red across the walls and roof. Max had disappeared to the men's room, so she rummaged through her purse which sat on the bar top.

The photo of Orlando actually smiling clung to her memory. She had a hunch, one she wanted to confirm. Her limited and expensive phone data allowed her to perform yet another internet search, while she ignored the fact she'd already spent two hours of her night *not* meeting people.

Her gaze darted about her phone screen, where one particular headline stood out amongst the blurs of blue and black text on a white background. Some article about a chemical fire.

*Bingo.*

She clicked on the link.

Orlando's name came up in the first paragraph.

"Hey there, beautiful." A bass-heavy voice interrupted her reading.

She focused on her phone for a split second longer, gathered some mention of Orlando hailed as a hero, something about being taken to hospital with minor smoke inhalation, before ripping her attention away and onto a cute guy standing before her, one hand rested on the bar, an amused smile on his face.

She gave him a quick half-smile back, before holding up a forefinger. "So sorry, just one moment."

She returned to her phone, aware that Max would never let her live down the uncharacteristic rudeness. Hopefully he wouldn't spot her trawling the internet over talking to the actual live human standing beside her.

"So, so sorry." She skimmed another article, not experiencing quite as much guilt as she should have.

This article was about the same fire, which had occurred three years prior. She got to the part where there'd been a lawsuit. Her eyelids flared.

Orlando had wanted compensation for his treatments, better care, and a deeper investigation into his condition… but then he'd dropped the lawsuit.

"Riveting reading, I assume?"

She peered up. Mr. Clean-cut-and-cute beamed another, wider, perfectly straight-toothed, blindingly white grin.

"Absolutely." She jammed her phone into her pocket and extended a hand to him. "Thanks for waiting. It's nice to meet you."

Clear blue eyes twinkled, and he took her hand. Her enthusiastic offer to shake seemed novel to him. To her defense, she wasn't up with the latest dating rules and sucked at playing cool. So maybe a handshake wasn't the done thing? She didn't know.

"Nice to meet you too." He turned her palm over and kissed the back of her hand. "Can I buy you a drink?"

Mr. Clean-cut-and-cute dripped charm by the bucketload; his pristine looks and unfettered smile gave the impression he'd never experienced a single dark moment in his life. She gave a quick nod. His light appeal was a welcome change from all things serious. All things Orlando.

She gave the handsome stranger her drink order and spent the next two hours talking to him, glad for the distraction. Glad she'd somehow attracted a man's attention, much less someone so well-put-together. All the while, she withheld her focus from Max, who hid in a far-off corner with a group of people he seemed to know, throwing her an occasional, encouraging thumbs-up.

By the end of the night, Mr. Clean-cut-and-cute gave her a peck on the cheek and his phone number. His name was Branden. An executive in some giant city-based company. A banker? Accountant? Lawyer… *Something…*

Honestly, she hadn't committed much of what he'd said to memory. Just as her brothers had warned, her one-track-mind struggled to focus on the charming guy or his pleasant retelling of his perfect life, even though she should have. Even though she had nothing against "perfect" or Branden.

Only, a different kind of perfection had her captured. The broken kind. Or as her brothers had put it, her "injured bird".

# Chapter Thirteen

Sophie killed the engine to her red hatchback, then leaned forward to peer through the rain at the warehouse and the giant, blue sign on the warehouse's side, the words "Aero Syntech" confirmed she'd stopped at the right place.

Her attention dropped to the passenger seat and a glossy pink cardboard bag containing the spoils of yesterday's shopping trip with Agathe. A few new clothes, but mostly lingerie—something other than beige or high-waisted—both of which she'd promised Agathe she'd ditch just in case she met and decided to go home with another charming Branden type.

Her cheeks heated every time she looked at that bag. She couldn't see herself having enough courage to wrangle an encounter with any man, much less wear the racy garments in front of anyone.

*But, oh, how I want to.*

She sank back in her seat and took a steadying breath, running over her questions thanks to a phone call she'd made that morning. A phone call that led to this one stop before heading back to Roseford.

Aero Syntech had been the chemical warehouse mentioned in the articles about Orlando's injury. She'd managed to arrange a private meeting with a guy named Sam. Though his role and what he knew about Orlando's case remained a mystery.

A loud knock boomed against her window. She jolted and turned to find a man in a heavy white lab coat and a clear rain poncho standing outside. Fat droplets of water streaked her window, adding to the nerve-wrenching, ominous vibe of this encounter.

"Sophie?" The man's steady question came with a short burst of foggy breath against her window's cold glass.

He was a good twenty years her senior, his glasses speckled with rain, and strands of sandy brown hair sticking out from his plastic hood, but plastered to his forehead.

She gave a hasty nod.

He stepped back, allowing space for her to open her door. "It's me, Sam. We haven't got long before my lunch hour is up. We should hurry."

She scrambled with her door, failing to pry the handle open on the first attempt.

Once again, she had poked around in Orlando's life, and who knew what this Sam guy had to say or whether this risk would pay off. She stepped out and shut the car door behind her. "Thank you for meeting me."

"I feel bad about what happened to your friend." Sam spoke against the loud rain, and he tipped his head to one side, indicating she should follow. He hurried through a gate in the long chain-link fence, toward the factory.

Meanwhile, gray-white clouds hovered far above, hitting her with a stinging, white glare, and she had to crane her neck just to compete with his tall, lanky build and make eye contact with the back of his head.

"You're not supposed to be here, understand? So, if anyone asks, you're an old friend of mine who's thinking about studying chemical engineering."

She clambered to keep up, a whipping wind adding to her bumpy sound as she spoke. "I can do that. Can you tell me what happened the day of the fire?"

"Sure. We had a couple of tradesmen repairing the building's exterior. Some of the inventory had been shifted around, when some numb-nuts stationed a pallet of experimental chemicals outside." Sam pointed to an area to the building's left, as if signaling where the incident had occurred. "A perfect concoction of high winds, high summer temperatures, nearby work setting off sparks, and drums and drums of highly flammable chems. You know what happened next."

Yeah, she knew what happened next, though it remained to be seen whether what he described had anything to do with Orlando's life-changing condition.

She sped up a little and got in stride with Sam. "But it was a relatively benign fire, right? Big blaze, but no casualties. Orlando was the only victim, and even he was out of hospital after a basic overnight stay."

"That's correct, and the warehouse admitted to holding more fuel load than it probably should have. I saw the huge plumes of chemical smoke and changing winds that day. Your friend worked one of the farther trucks minus a breathing apparatus, which I later learned is normal if not working too close up. But then the wind shifted and smacked him and a few others head-on with smoke."

"And that's where his injuries occurred?"

Sam gave a short laugh. "If you mean the smoke inhalation that landed him in hospital that night, sure. But the other stuff, the stuff he sued for? No. I can tell you now, he didn't get those here."

She glanced about, uncertain why this guy would agree to meet with her, only to reveal she'd hit a dead-end.

"And you'd know that, how?" She positioned herself next to a door and stopped walking. Maybe if Sam thought someone might catch them talking, he'd make quick with the details. Especially now that she realized she'd never clarified who Sam was exactly. "I'm sorry, what is your role at Aero Syntech, anyway?"

"Let's just call me a run-of-the-mill engineer. If you have access to Mr. Piras's court documents, then you'll figure out who I am soon enough. I testified at one of his hearings."

She crossed her arms and buried a growl; his vague reply made her think he was holding back. "About the court case, any idea why it got dismissed?"

"You don't know?" He jolted a fraction. "Insufficient evidence."

And just like that, the tables of suspicion turned. The vertical creases in the center of his forehead, along with his narrowed stare, implied he knew her presence here wasn't all above board.

She peered to her right, to a window on the door, wanting a chance to look inside without showing obvious signs of snooping. "I gathered that much, but the very fact you're standing here makes me wonder whether you agree with that judgment?"

Her shoulders sank as she leaned back and found the window was actually frosted over.

Sam gave a shrug. "It's the opposite, actually. Your friend sued the fire association for exposing him to toxic chemicals and Aero Syntech for having those chemicals improperly stored. And as I said, Mr. Piras was completely obscured in smoke with no breathing apparatus on. And because other unprotected firefighters caught the same cross winds and are doing just fine, the company had strong grounds to claim they weren't totally in the wrong. So again, insufficient evidence."

That sounded like bullshit reasoning to Sophie, and she wanted to say as much.

In her experience, each person's body was unique. Multiple people could be exposed to the same contaminant and react in vastly different ways. But then, antagonizing Sam would get her nowhere. He wasn't a judge. And no doubt Orlando's lawyer had sought medical counsel in deciding how far to push his case.

So far, Sam here was turning out to be a wasted trip.

"I'm going to need more details." She softened her tone, scrubbing any hint of rising frustration. "Why the secrecy over this meeting? Why are you meeting with me if you believe Aero Syntech is innocent?"

"Look, Ms. Tindall. I'm not just any engineer, I'm a chemical engineer." He pointed a thumb at the building beside him. "The suits in there would have a stroke if they knew I was talking about Mr. Piras without the presence of their high-priced lawyers. Not that they'd ever allow me to talk to some random off the street. I'm meeting you in good faith." He stuffed his hands into his white pockets, the tension across his forehead easing on a look of open concern. "Beyond what I saw that day, the other reason Aero Syntech called on me to testify was that I'm a key developer of the chem that burned in that fire."

"In other words, you're confident that whatever Orlando inhaled couldn't have caused his issues?"

Sam gave a lopsided smile, leaning in a little. "The chemical that burned that day is called TL-20. It's an experimental fuel that releases lower emissions when used in large commercial aircraft. Don't get me wrong, I don't recommend inhaling any kind of chemical smoke, but TL-20's fumes simply wouldn't cause the specific reactions Mr. Piras suffers from now. Lung damage. Sure. Cancer? Maybe after long periods of exposure. But not psycho-centric episodes. Not what I saw in the videos Mr. Piras's legal defense made me watch."

A frown dragged at his lips, and Sam turned unnaturally quiet. Perhaps whatever Orlando's lawyers had shown him still weighed heavy on his conscience. Maybe he wasn't just covering up for his employer after all. Maybe Sam's presence had more to do with sympathy than guilt.

He relaxed his shoulders and continued to yell over the rain. "I'm meeting you because I feel for Mr. Piras. He and his team stopped a fire that could have had a much worse outcome. They ran in when everyone else ran out. And if you're here to get help for him, then you're standing in the wrong place, and that means potentially everyone else around him is looking in the wrong places too. Which means you all need to regroup and start looking elsewhere."

She stifled an urge to share the news that it appeared no one looked in the wrong places because everyone had stopped looking altogether. Especially Orlando.

Still, she'd come here to help him. If she wanted to regain her holiday, much less her life, she needed to settle on a resolution. So far, that resolution involved doing as much as she could to get Orlando the right treatment. That way her overbearing investment in his life could end.

"How do I know this isn't an attempt to send me looking in the wrong direction?"

"Here." Sam dug around in his coat pocket, movements jerky. She'd crossed a line and really teed him off this time. He thrust a small notepad and pencil into her hand. "Give me your email address, I'll send you a list of TL-20's ingredients. If that's not putting my job on the line, I don't know what is. Find someone in the know, and they'll tell you that nothing in TL-20 would cause Mr. Piras's condition. Especially not from one exposure."

She peered down at the notepad jammed into her hand, her heart pounding at how much she'd overstepped her place in being here to begin with.

Max and Luke were right; she'd made this whole Orlando thing way bigger than intended and way too personal. Now poor Sam wanted to throw his career away to appease her curiosity. Yet, she'd come too far and knew too much to turn a blind eye. And if nothing else, she'd at least well and truly taken the plunge into her new world of being brave.

She scribbled her email address on the tiny page, face hot, shoulders drawing upward. "I'd appreciate it if you didn't tell anyone I met with you today. I really am trying to do the best by Orlando."

Sam outstretched a hand and retrieved the notepad. "Likewise. And good luck, Ms. Tindall." He wrenched the door handle down, and the industrial sounds of forklifts and various other machinery broke through. "I hope you find what you're looking for."

# Chapter Fourteen

"You look different."

Sophie whipped her attention over to Orlando seated beside her on the ground at the lake's edge, her skin tingling under the strong afternoon sun and that he'd noticed her floral sundress with the mustard-yellow background. "Yes. The dress is new."

She tucked her knees in and folded her arms over the top, her chest straining that she might have opened herself up to another one of his barbs. Still, even if one did come, she needed him in a good mood in order to learn more about his condition.

"You don't usually do color." His low and easy rumble somehow ensured that him noticing a change in her appearance didn't diminish his cool act one little bit. "I thought black, white, and beige were your thing."

She smiled over at him, squinting against the glare from the lake. "I wanted a change."

A small, gray stone sat nestled between his large fingers, and tiny flecks of dirt stuck to his skin. She could have sworn he mumbled something along the lines of, "You don't need to change," but she couldn't be sure.

She sharpened her attention on him. "Sorry, what was that?"

Maybe the jovial Orlando she'd witnessed in her internet searches would come out to meet her.

With one careless flick of his wrist, he tossed the stone into the lake and turned back to her. "I said, 'Good to see a change from the usual headmistress look.'"

Just like the stone he'd pitched into the water, her stomach sank, and she scowled for half a second. An awkward silence dragged, but she didn't even care. Orlando deserved more time to stew in the juices of his backhanded compliment.

The soft lapping water at her feet should have soothed, but each minuscule wave against her toes only advanced her anger. She had a mind to ask why he was so sour. Why he had to take his moods out on her—someone only seeking to help—and the one person willing to talk to him for any extended period of time. The one person who took him places. Who endured his bitterness. And, unlike the center staff, she wasn't even being paid for the *privilege* of minding him.

"I. Ah." His lowered voice snapped her thoughts back to him. "I should thank you for your help the other day."

His forehead creased with what she could only describe as a confused glower. Her mental tirade halted. His gratitude was the last thing she expected. Then again, he had a way of leading her into traps, so maybe she needed some caution.

"You *should* thank me, or you *want* to thank me?" She narrowed her eyes, still peeved at his earlier negative feedback. "There's a big difference, you know."

The muscles on his face released, and his haunted stare took on extra shadows, as if saying thank you wasn't second nature to him, but he'd push himself to say it, anyway.

"I want to thank you. You put up with a lot from me, I get it. And you handle stuff I figure most normal people have already run away scared from. Thank you."

A burst of heat exploded in her chest, and something unfurled from deep within her—something akin to an icy pond melting under extreme conditions, leaving only warm and welcoming waters.

"Nothing about you scares me." She cleared her throat, but she couldn't take back the husky whisper. "Does that make me abnormal?"

Nothing about his temperament or his condition *did* scare her, but there were other things about Orlando that shook her to her very foundation—the myriad of ways he could hurt her if she made the mistake of getting too close—the ways she could likewise hurt him.

His analytical stare held for a long and heart-stopping moment, until he eventually turned away. "That or you're foolishly brave."

"I think I'm none of that, but your gratitude is appreciated either way."

His gaze narrowed on the lake, giving the impression he didn't quite know what to reply or what to make of her. Though frankly, the confusion was mutual.

She took a deep breath, set on changing the subject. "Tell me about this place." She nodded out to the tall gum trees lining the water's edge and a well-worn jetty with a single tethered rowboat to her left. "Why did you want me to bring you here?"

He shrugged. "I came here a lot as a boy. Just wanted to pay the old place a visit."

A small bird perched on the edge of the rowboat, tiny gray tail swinging in a joyful side-to-side motion. Maybe if she got him to talk about the easier details of his past, there'd be room to broach the subject of her research and her plans to help him. "Roseford would be a nice place to grow up."

"In some ways it was, though I'd kinda always banked on a life away from here."

His shoulders drew a little in a begrudging sign that he expected her to ask for more detail, which was a good sign she should probably ask nothing. Besides, she already knew what his dreams had entailed. Where those dreams had led. Though Orlando had no idea she'd dug into his past. Or that she'd met with Sam at Aero Syntech.

She was yet to abandon her suspicion over the claim TL-20 had nothing to do with Orlando's condition. Sam was a chemical engineer, likely a damn good one too—but he wasn't a doctor. Heck, even if he had been. Even if Orlando's own lawyer had received advice from a doctor who agreed with Sam's ideas about TL-20—advice that had maybe pushed Orlando to drop his case—she'd seen firsthand that there were doctors, and then there were *doctors*. Each one had their own strengths and skill sets. And finding the right specialist care could make all the difference to Orlando's life.

"What about you?"

She startled at Orlando's question but stared ahead, the cool wind off the lake brushing her face and bringing with it the water's earthy-sweet scent. "You want me to tell you where I grew up?"

He scraped a patch of dirt with the heel of his brown leather boot. Maybe he too didn't expect the sudden interest in her life. "Yeah. What's with the accent?"

"York." She offered a gentle smile. "I grew up in York."

He faced her, wrists curving over his bent knees, long fingers pointed toward the ground. "And what does a childhood in York entail?"

"I guess it would be similar to life in Roseford. I grew up in a small town, only with a different landscape. I had the ocean and cliffs nearby, and the forest closer still. My younger years were magical, really."

He frowned, suggesting he'd grasped her positive assessment and still heard the somber notes underneath. "And you still left."

"I wanted to experience life away from my small town." Actually, she'd practically run from her small town, but she couldn't say that. It would be selfish to bog him down with her own sad tales. "I also wanted to study."

And she'd been great at study—making the most of city life, not so much.

"Right. So, you stepped out in search of excitement and"—Orlando let out a short chuckle—"decided to specialize in geriatric psychiatry?"

She shook her head at the irony. Geriatric psychiatry didn't seem all that glamorous or exciting to most, but there was a certain beauty in working with the elderly.

"My high school used to do this whole community linkage thing." She paused, making sure he'd understand she really did care about her job. For his sake, more than hers. That everything she did was because she wanted to see the people in her care do well. "Students would partner up with a resident at the local nursing home, not too dissimilar to the volunteer program here in Roseford. The lady I was paired up with was named May. The sweetest woman I'd ever met, with some of the saddest stories. The thing that really struck a chord with me most was how she'd lost her younger brother in a downed military ship during WWII. How half a century had passed, and her eyes still misted when she spoke of him, and how that very story would soon disappear with her own passing.

"Every week I had a meeting with living history, and it was an honor to bear witness to what she had to say. I'd never had much contact with elderly people before that point, but May changed my life. She made me want to do my bit to help make these people more comfortable, more heard in a world often in too much of a hurry to listen. Our society shifts in ways that repeat old mistakes over and over again, and I don't know—" She toyed with the hem of her dress, a lump forming in her throat. Would Orlando understand, or would he simply mock her as usual? Though to his credit, today his bitter appraisals were mostly absent. "I guess I figure if we all cared about our elders a bit more, maybe we wouldn't feel so isolated or aimless ourselves."

His focus honed in on her, and she wondered if maybe he knew she spoke partly about herself. The drawn-out silence put new strain in her muscles, and she refused to look at him in case anything she did tipped him off further.

"You make them sound like saints."

The tension in her body eased. If he noticed anything, he thankfully didn't let on. "I guess living in care, maybe you have a different opinion?"

He shook his head at the lake. "I try not to mingle with the locals."

"Why not?"

"The oldies don't tend to stick around long, if you know what I mean. My situation is depressing enough."

His subdued tone formed an uncomfortable ache around her heart, and she dropped her attention to her sandaled feet. "Right. Sorry."

She'd been stupid to overlook that detail. A detail no doubt more painful given he'd grown up around many of those residents, only to get a front row view to their decline. And of course, according to Candice, there was the added weight of how those same residents made allowances to ensure he received care at the center.

She rose to her feet, wanting to shake away the disquiet weighing heavy on her shoulders. "Is this fresh water?"

"Not sure I'd drink it." His voice settled behind her, but the shame of her blunder kept her from facing him. "Safe enough to swim in, though."

She closed her eyes to the soft breeze on her face and took a slow breath, the air sweet and smelling of sunshine and muddy earth. "I can't remember the last time my feet touched water, outside of a shower, of course."

Nowhere in the world could she see clear lakes surrounded by gum trees. No amount of time in this country would ever be enough to uncover the mysteries of its overwhelming, natural beauty. Just the other morning, a mob of gray kangaroos had decorated the wild grassland outside her cabin. They'd grazed in a heavy mist over the valley, and she'd awoken to peaceful magic all around—a secret dance of nature unfolding for her eyes only.

She kicked off her shoes and went about gathering the hem of her long dress, ready to test the water.

A shuffling sound from behind her pulled her attention to Orlando jumping to his feet.

"What are you doing?" His eyelids flared.

"I thought it might be nice to wade in a little. Why?"

He didn't answer, just sent her a flinty glare, that glare dropping to her exposed knees.

A quick laugh broke from her. "My shoes are the only thing coming off, trust me."

His gaze met hers again, brows bowing at the center. "This partnership is awkward enough without having to see your skinny ass."

Laughter tore through her again, but she turned away to sink her ankles into the water. "Nice to know you still noticed my ass despite my 'headmistress' clothing."

She chuckled to herself, imagining Orlando rolling his eyes behind her.

He didn't respond, so she left him to his silence, wading deeper now. The sensitive skin behind her knees tingled at the water's cool touch, sending a thrilling shiver through her body. "You know, you don't have to sit there scowling at me. You could always join me."

"I'm not sitting, and I'm not scowling."

She whipped around, heart thudding to see him standing in the water about three meters away. His heavy boots lay abandoned on the shore, and she opened her mouth to voice surprise. But his hands swept out in front of him, collecting the lake's surface until a light shower of water hit the front of her dress.

The cold impact sucked air from her lungs, and she gaped at her water-speckled dress.

A wave of instinctual laughter clashed with another instinctual drive to seek revenge. She swung her foot out and kicked water back at him, instant regret holding her in place as the giant spray slammed into his stone-blue, cotton shirt.

She expected a growl, for him to swear and retaliate and give her a serve of his usual stick-in-the-mud attitude. What she didn't expect was for him to laugh.

The joyful sound alone kept her off guard, and one huge, man-sized kick of lake water hit her square in the face. She let out a shriek and spluttered to expel water from her mouth.

Her hair hung in thick, soggy tendrils, plastered to her face and shoulders. Her dress clung to her body. But the afternoon air was warm, and Orlando's laugh kept her warmer still. The low rumble of it... The way his eyes lit with his wide smile. His jeans were wet from mid-thigh down, his fault from his backfired revenge. But that smile...

He held the same smile from his photos. The one from his past. A grin that beamed and brought light to his face. Genuine. Unfettered. Real. Energetic and amused. And not on a computer screen, but just meters away.

He smiled for *her*.

She had so many questions, starting with, when had that smile last made an appearance? But she refused to ruin the moment.

He spun away. Another laugh rose from his wide chest, and that laugh cracked the air, unabashed and spontaneous, as if he couldn't stop even if he wanted to. He was like a child playing in the rain, the lake one giant puddle to frolic in. The gleam in his eye lifted her, and before she knew it, her inner child soared too.

He doubled back toward her—as though he figured she'd wasted enough time. She squealed and ran in the opposite direction, but she wasn't fast enough.

Somewhere in the pandemonium, she dropped her hem in the water. Her legs tangled in the material. So much for trying to look stylish.

She tripped, her face inches from the water, only for a strong hand to grasp her elbow and pull her up.

Orlando drew her to him so swiftly, her forehead almost collided with his.

She puffed against more laughter. "I didn't know you had that in you."

"Neither did I." He paused, his gaze darting over her face.

A clump of hair clung to her forehead, obscuring her vision on one side. She moved to clear her eyes, trying hard not to focus on his tight grasp on her elbow or the blossoming heat filling the space between their bodies.

"I would have brought towels if I'd—" She lifted her attention to him staring at his hand at her elbow. One sharp lift of his chin, and his attention met hers.

"If I were any other man." The air between them prickled. "If I had any kind of future, I'd—" He clamped his jaw, not finishing that sentence.

"I...ummm..." Her heart thundered, and she had no idea what to say or do next, but when his gaze dropped to her lips, her senses locked further.

Did she want Orlando—with his haunted stare and undoubtable beauty—to kiss her? *Oh, yes.* Should she let him? *Hell, no.*

A kiss would mess up their professional partnership.

Sure, there were no strict rules about volunteers getting involved with residents. She'd even heard a story or two of senior marriages stemming from such introductions. For those in care, when it came to intimate relationships, it was vital to maintain as much privacy and autonomy as possible.

But more lay within her doubts than the way they'd met. She already struggled to distance herself from this man—her internet searches a case in point. She'd get attached.

She hadn't come to Australia to fall in love. Far from it. But she was the type to fall easily and fall hard—and that was without considering just how complex falling in love with someone in Orlando's position would be. So, maintaining her space would be for her benefit as much as his.

She'd be leaving in mere months. And his life remained complicated enough. As much as she wanted it, a kiss would be unfair.

And still…

*Oh goodness.*

Her tummy flipped.

She'd just weighed up the probability she'd fall in *love* with Orlando. She really needed to regain her grip.

"I researched you." The words shot from her mouth, her need to avoid any intimacy with this man landing her in a different kind of trouble.

He reeled back and let go of her arm. "You, what?"

"After your flashback the other day, I researched you. I know you were a firefighter. I know about your accident. I know about the lawsuit. I even visited Aero Syntech and spoke to an engineer there." Her body tensed.

*What am I even saying? Why am I saying it?*

Her stomach flipped again, for an entirely different reason than to run from her earlier attraction.

Dark anger burst in his eyes, his deep brown pupils seeming to turn black. But in her usual fashion, she couldn't stop rambling. Also in her usual fashion, she would not stop rambling until she'd obliterated every last chance he'd want to kiss her… Even though she still so desperately wanted him to. "I've made some phone calls. Depending on the replies, there's a small chance I can get you some help."

*There.* She sounded like a right clueless idiot. Even to herself. *Bravo, Sophie.*

Orlando blinked, and his teeth ground together, a ripple of muscle flexed and released over his jaw. Perhaps he sifted through all she'd said and couldn't make sense of any of it. "You dug up information on me?"

"Nothing that isn't already publicly available." She cringed. She really was a level ten clueless idiot. "You know what I do. Give me a chance to alleviate your situation."

"You dug up information on me, then turned up at Aero Syntech, and then made phone calls like a bonafide creeper?" He shook his head, stepping farther away; face contorting a little, as though the woman he'd potentially wanted to kiss had vaporized and turned into a toad. "I've had all the offers of help I can deal with. Nothing's worked. I don't need you doubling down on me too. That's not what this relationship is about."

A sick sensation spread through her gut, while his displeasure cast a heavy net around her shoulders, dragging her beneath the lake's surface.

"I'm not 'doubling down'. I'm not even asking you to do anything." She'd meant well. Really, she had. Even if his hardened features made it clear he didn't see her efforts quite so positively. "I've seen a number of cases turn around with the discovery of something that was previously missed. I want to make sure that's not you. If you'll just humor me, I'll—"

"You'll, what?" His features hardened. "You'll imply I haven't already thought about every possible scenario? As if my lawsuit tanking and being told I was clutching at straws wasn't humiliating enough? Do you even hear how condescending you sound right now?"

"I just thought—"

"Let me guess." His words cut forth, as if he couldn't hold back even if he tried. "You thought maybe your 'almost' psychiatry qualifications could be enough to fix me? Is that it?"

The weight of his accusation held her in place. Or maybe it was the kernel of truth that bothered her so.

She'd been arrogant to think she knew better than anyone else involved in his care. Or maybe some corner of her heart didn't believe that life could really be over for a man so otherwise strong.

His expression eased and a slight softness entered his glare. Maybe he too heard the harshness still reverberating around his words. "Sophie, I don't need another doctor. I need you to—"

He pressed the heel of his hand to his forehead and spun away, as if he second guessed whatever he'd meant to say.

"Tell me." She stepped forward but fell short of offering her touch.

"This is way more honesty than I've had in years." He kept his back to her, but his tone dragged husky. "For a second there, playing in the water, I felt like a man again. A man without a death sentence looming over his head. A whole man." His broad shoulders rounded, the rough-spin of his cotton shirt stretching over his back. He turned to her, dark clouds gathering in his eyes, despite the perfectly clear sky around him. "For one brief moment my problems disappeared, and then you jumped in with your own special brand of verbal castration. I don't need another doctor, Sophie. Do you hear me? I'm not some charity case who can't take care of his own shit. What I needed from you was an equal. At the very least, I needed a friend."

The word *friend* echoed in her skull, and the hollow in her stomach collapsed into a bottomless sinkhole. She'd failed him, indeed, over-stepped her mark; completely missed the simpler elements of what she should have provided from the very beginning—a meaningful connection with the outside world—a life for him beyond Roseford Aged Care's walls.

*Everything I'd started to give him already.*

But *enough* was rarely enough for her, and she'd underestimated the value of all the gradual softening she'd already drawn from him. She'd all but ignored his achievements thus far.

And she'd hurt him in the process.

She lowered her attention to the easy waves pushing at her sundress. "I'm sorry. I—"

She lifted her chin, owing him some direct eye contact and a decent look at her guilt as she apologized. He inched forward, like he planned to speak.

"Orlando?" A different voice called out from afar.

Sophie spun around to an older woman, perhaps in her mid-seventies, power-walking across the sandy bank. A path of golden yellow dust rose behind her, and she held a hand high in a quick and excited wave, a black Staffordshire terrier trotting along beside her.

Orlando frowned, rapt attention no longer on Sophie.

"Mum?"

<h1 style="text-align:center">Chapter Fifteen</h1>

"Why you here?" Orlando's mother spoke to him in a strong Italian accent, and Sophie sank back, a set of magnificent blue-green eyes glittering her way. "And who this?"

Orlando cleared his throat, cheeks relaxing though his brow was still tight, failing to completely obscure all signs of his earlier anger. "This is Sophie." He nodded toward her minus any eye contact, then made his way out of the water. She followed his exit, feeling less than worthy of his mother's attention. "She's my volunteer from the home. She's been deemed competent enough to take me out."

A slow grin widened on his mother's mouth, and she threw herself toward Sophie in an enthusiastic embrace. "Thank you for helping my boy. I so happy Orlando has a new friend his age." She backed away, her knobbly, bent fingers brushing wisps of hair from Sophie's face with a sense of motherly affection. Her care and warmth exuded from the quick glance she threw Orlando. "She's pretty, no?"

Orlando clenched his jaw, appearing to hold on to a need to remain polite. His mother didn't seem to notice the tension passing between her son and his "new friend". She peered back at Sophie. "You both come to my house. I live near. I feed you."

Sophie's muscles locked in protest. "Oh. No. I can't."

The staccato words were less gracious than she would have liked, but she really couldn't impose on Orlando's mother after having just disappointed him. And especially not in light of how deeply she'd already allowed herself to get pulled into his life.

"You take care of my boy, I take care of you." Orlando's mother grabbed Sophie's hands and drew her closer. "Please. I will also give you towels."

"Mum." Orlando spoke on a low growl. "She said, no."

His mother waved a hand in a dismissive gesture. "Where your manners, Orlando?" She hooked her arm around Sophie's and gave a sharp tug. "Sophie comes and so do you. It's Italian hospitality."

Sophie stumbled along, scooping up her sandals, her sincere moment of joy with Orlando long gone. She couldn't look back at him. Not to plead for help. She didn't deserve help. Nor could she put her foot down and hurt his mother by refusing to eat at her table.

Orlando trudged a few paces behind, the black Staffordshire terrier trailing farther still, as they crossed through a thick line of gum trees.

"My name is Marcella." His mother spoke in a bright whisper, though the scores of wrinkles on her forehead signaled a woman well versed in worry. "Orlando is in a temper, yes?"

Sickness turned within Sophie's tummy, her dress dripping water down her legs, adding discomfort as she walked along. Still she gave a shaky nod. "It's my fault."

Marcella held a momentary silence, as if assessing what exactly Sophie might have done to upset her boy.

"It will be okay." Marcella's decisive voice cut through, and she patted Sophie's hand. "Everything be better with food. Orlando's father take him to the lake for important talks as a boy." She lifted her posture along with her voice, including Orlando in the conversation. "It's nice he think to take you here too."

Sophie's skin prickled as Marcella insinuated she knew all too well that Sophie and Orlando had been embroiled in their own *important talk*—one they hadn't quite finished before Marcella showed up.

"Sophie's a grown woman." Orlando's grumble sliced through the hanging quiet. "You don't need to hold her hand."

Marcella peered over her shoulder. "With you in your temper, I do. You scare your friend. You make her upset already."

Cold guilt ran through Sophie's veins. She turned back to him, not exactly sure what she hoped to achieve, except perhaps a silent offer of apology. His tight stare spoke of anger, but his rolling silence said he would not rat her out to his mother about looking into his past.

His attention switched back to his mother. "Let her go. We're joining you. Isn't that what you wanted?"

"*Si, tesoro mio.*" Marcella let out a heavy sigh and released Sophie's hand.

A red brick house sat atop a small hill up ahead. The sky behind its corrugated-iron roof had already faded to a vibrant pink-orange with evening rolling in fast.

Marcella's dog brushed against Sophie's left leg, tongue lolling to one side as it peered up. She leaned down and scratched the dog's head. An ambush of licks drenched her palm in doggy slobber. She laughed. "Aren't you a beautiful one? What's your name?"

"Nero." Orlando's clipped tone sent her back to standing. The dog didn't seem to care. The sound of his name sent him darting toward Orlando, and in a well-synced series of steps, Nero leaped into his arms.

Marcella shrugged. "Nero was Orlando's. The dog live with me now."

Trust Orlando to name his dog after a fiendish Roman emperor.

A long hush took over, and they made it to Marcella's door. Marcella went inside and pointed Sophie toward the bathroom to wash the remnants of dog slobber off her hands and find a towel; meanwhile, Marcella went to the kitchen to call Roseford Aged Care and alert them that Orlando would be returning late.

Once back in the living room, Sophie overheard Orlando tell his mother he needed a rest. She rounded the corner to find the shadows beneath his eyes supported his claim, while Marcella wandered over to her son and touched his face with slow tenderness. "Go, rest. I will talk to Sophie."

Orlando opened his mouth, like he second-guessed leaving his mother alone with Sophie, but then he walked toward the door anyway.

He slowed beside her, voice a hushed whisper, eyes narrowed. "Don't use this as an opportunity to dig up more information about me." He sauntered out the door and called behind him, "I'll be back out in half an hour."

Marcella's blue-green eyes lit up, and she motioned for Sophie. "Come. Come. I'm excited to meet one of Orlando's friends."

"I'm not sure he'd count me as a friend right now." Sophie followed into the adjacent kitchen, heart heavy, overcome with a need not to allow her role in Orlando's life to bring Marcella too much hope.

"He likes you." Marcella opened a retro-looking, lipstick-red fridge —a fridge that matched an equally red oven set into blond, woodgrain cabinetry. "He's angry at you. But he likes you."

The sun disappeared behind a far line of trees through the kitchen window, turning the world outside a deep indigo hue. Meanwhile, Sophie sought conversation away from whatever Orlando may or may not feel for her. "Who's Kayla?"

Though Orlando had warned her not to ask questions about him, this one fell from her mouth before she could stop herself.

Marcella straightened, fridge door still gaping open. "Orlando told you about Kayla?"

Sophie shrugged a shoulder, chest constricting. "Not exactly. I was there when he had an episode, and he called me that name."

"He thought you were Kayla?"

She nodded, unnerved with the clear interest. "Who is she?"

"Kayla is Orlando's friend from when he was little." Marcella peered down, and for the first time, her face lost all excitement. She refocused on the open fridge door, silent, as though deliberating over what to say.

She eventually collected a bowl of salad greens and placed it in the center of the small dining table.

"Orlando, he care for Kayla a lot, you know? Many people not happy that our family come from a different country. We look different. Speak different. Orlando not fit in. But Kayla never worry about what others think. She was his only friend for a very long time, and because of her, other children begin to like him. They give him a chance. And because of that, then some parents accept our family too. And even though Orlando and Kayla know each other forever, when they are in high school, he had... What do you say... strong feelings for her."

For some inexplicable reason, Sophie felt her organs sag within her body, and the unease of that sensation took her to the dining table for a seat. Somehow though, she stayed fully invested in learning more about Orlando's past. About a little boy isolated for no other reason than he had olive skin and was born to a migrant family. And a solitary girl who came along with her brave brand of friendship.

And even though Sophie didn't know what it was to be excluded over race, she knew such experiences left marks on a child. Marks that often altered self-belief all the way through adulthood. Orlando undoubtedly hadn't forgotten his ill treatment. Chances were, his condition made up just part of why he acted like an outsider. Why he'd wanted a life away from Roseford.

She peered back at Marcella, wanting to know more. "And what happened when they were in high school?"

Marcella pressed a switch on her red kettle. Clearly, she had a love for all things scarlet.

"Eventually, they do start to date. Kayla loves Orlando, Orlando loves Kayla..." She paused, gaze glued to the tile floor. "They skip school one day and go to the beach. Kayla get stuck in the tide, but there's no one else but Orlando to help. But he can't save her. He didn't know how. They call it a rip tide. He didn't know you swim along the shore, not toward it. He too nearly died." She closed her eyes and sucked in a slow breath. "I think this is why he maybe want to be a fireman. Save people, you know? Why maybe he never want a serious relationship after that." Marcella snapped her eyes open and swatted a hand as if to shrug off the topic.

"Survivor guilt."

"Sorry?"

"Your description indicates he tried to make up for Kayla's death with his subsequent life choices." Sophie let out a sigh, while Marcella poured water from the boiled kettle into a large pot on the stove. "Though, it's hard not to wonder how different his life would be if

Kayla hadn't died. No firefighter. No accident. Maybe no neurological condition."

Marcella added a small palmful of salt to her boiling pot, though she managed to peer over at Sophie as she did it. "Orlando told you about the accident?"

Sophie shook her head. "I figured it out."

"I bet that make him happy." Marcelle laughed. Pasta went into her pot now. She shot Sophie a sudden sideways glance. "Oh. That is why he is mad with you. Yes?"

Sophie gave a sheepish smile. "I'm trying to help. He's not onboard with that idea."

Marcella dropped the empty pasta packet into a bin under the sink, renewed lightness crinkling the skin over her cheekbones. "You think you can help?"

"I don't know. I have a medical degree, but I'm as green as a doctor can get, though I have witnessed a few cases where further investigation helped." She lifted herself out of her seat and padded over to the counter for the bag of green beans Marcella had left out. "It's a long shot, but I doubt looking deeper into his treatments over the years will make Orlando's situation any worse."

Marcella stared in silence for a moment, her hand coming to rest over Sophie's. "Thank you. Orlando won't say it but I will." Her fingers curled around the back of Sophie's hand—fingers boney but her touch tender. "Someone else is trying to help my boy, this is very special to me. But if you don't mind, please don't talk to him about Kayla. It makes him sad." Her gaze stayed locked on Sophie's, sandy-brown brows releasing their tension. "You care for him. No?"

Heat washed over Sophie's torso, and she dropped her attention to the counter where Marcella's hand covered hers. Orlando would be royally pissed if he walked in right now.

She slipped her hand away and reached for a small knife on a nearby chopping block, deciding she would help top and tail the beans.

"Not like that. No." The breathlessness with which she spoke made it hard to believe her own lie.

She didn't know what she felt for him exactly. The more she learned about him, the more she wanted to know; the more her heart ached for him to let her in, the more she needed to distance herself.

And still, she'd been the one to shrink away when he'd eyed her lips less than an hour ago. He'd wanted to close the distance between them. She hadn't. But here she was again, asking questions. Getting too close. Her head ached from the merry-go-round of clashing thoughts.

Marcella set a red bowl beside Sophie for the beans in, though the woman's gaze stayed on her until she caved and offered returned eye-contact.

"Before his accident, Orlando had a lot of women. After his accident, I'm the only woman he sees." Marcella's continued flat expression resembled someone going through the motions of a story that hurt to retell. "For all the 'I love you', not one woman stayed. I don't blame them. My son ran out of money in the city and had to come back to Roseford. None of us knew what was wrong with him. We still don't. Only that it will maybe get worse. Maybe kill him." Her voice cracked on the last line, a woman doing her best to hold herself together. She gave a hard swallow, working at control, eyes red-rimmed, but dry of tears. "I'm his mother. It's no other woman's job to look after him. I stay. I want to stay. Mothers stay, you know?" Her thin fingers curled into the countertop, trembling. Her voice wobbled, too, and a tear finally trickled down her cheek. "If he could let me, I would go with him."

Sophie lowered the knife, her forearms limp under the weight of Marcella's words. *Go? Go where?* She frowned at Marcella's tear-streaked face, so happy minutes earlier.

Did she sense the same things Candice did? That Orlando might not want to live for much longer? Or was Marcella speaking more broadly about the possible degenerative nature of his condition?

Bile rose up Sophie's throat, but she swallowed it down, her own wave of emotion threatening to spill over. In another life, she'd come close to knowing just what Marcella did, but as fate would have it, she couldn't claim any personal experience of motherly love. Not like Marcella described. Not the sheer desire to follow a child to the grave if that were the only place that child could go.

Her shoulders sagged, and she gave a surrendering sigh before turning to Marcella and pulling the woman into her arms. Muffled sobs broke against Sophie's neck, but she held still, allowing the woman a moment to grieve.

Minutes passed before Marcella pulled back, gaze suddenly brightened. Maybe a good cry had been all she needed. "If Orlando were okay, you would be with him. No?"

Sophie shook her head with taut vigor. "I can't. I—"

"Orlando was always popular with women." An exuberant smile tugged at Marcella's cheeks, as if she wasn't all that interested in Sophie's explanation. She sniffed, using the back of her hand to swipe at another tear, before giving a soft chuckle. "He was always restless. A curse. I used to worry he would never settle down and give me grandchildren, but now I know there are bigger things to worry about than no grandchildren... Anyway, he never let any woman be a friend. Not after Kayla. You are special. I know this."

Sophie snorted out a laugh, then pressed a hand over her mouth to stop herself. "I'm sorry." A few seconds passed, and she mumbled through her palm. "I'm almost certain that right now he'd rather see me disappear under a moving bus than call me a friend."

If he'd been angry about her researching his past, heaven help her if he knew about this chat with his mother.

"I know my boy. And I like you too." Marcella took the idle knife off the counter and started on the beans Sophie had failed to complete. "If things were different, meeting you would bring me hope—"

"But there's nothing—"

"Let me finish." Marcella held up a hand, sending forth an insistent stare. "I know you say he not like you—maybe you believe that—but if I say nothing now, I will forever have regrets." Her pale cheeks showed the full weight of her wariness, and she returned to cutting beans as if she couldn't look at Sophie as she spoke. "Please don't break my boy's heart."

Sophie's jaw slid open, and for a few seconds, words refused to form in her brain. "I have no intention of getting involved with Orlando."

Marcella continued to hurriedly trim beans. "It's my job to love him, no matter what. Enjoy your time in this country. Find out what you can for Orlando's illness. But if you feel for him, let him go. Save yourself. Don't let my boy love you, only to watch you leave." Her words were rapid fire, and she shook her head as she spoke. She cut, strain and speed culminating in jerky, fevered movements. "You know about his condition. He cannot follow you. Get on with your life like any young woman should. His life is hard enough without watching more people leave. You will break him. You understand? Just like Kayla did. Maybe worse. Leave loving him to me." Her chin jerked up, her gaze latching onto Sophie's. "Please."

Sophie's blood coursed through her body at a wild and straining pace. Every muscle felt weak, and she wanted to fall into a pile on the floor—or maybe she wanted just to fall *through* the floor and disappear. Her mere presence had obviously made this woman's life worse than it had already been.

For the longest time, her mind blanked. Sure, she found Orlando attractive, but she'd never once entertained the idea of a relationship beyond her being his volunteer. Marcella's warnings and gray-tinged face spelled out why.

"I understand." Her mouth wobbled into a reassuring smile, while she vowed not to argue or offer excuses, even if Marcella's assumptions were way off. "Thank you."

"Thank you for what?"

Sophie swung around to find Orlando standing in the doorway, his attention switching between her and his mother.

"Your mum was giving me some advice about the locals." Sophie smiled at her cleverness, her claim not a complete lie since Orlando *was* a local. "How was your rest?"

He stared at her, the skin over his cheek bones taut, like he recognized her deflection but hadn't heard enough to press her on what had passed.

Marcella walked over to him and placed both hands either side of his face, forcing him to break his stare-off with Sophie. Her fingertips skimmed his cheeks, like a mother soothing a small child. Her son. Her son who required all the gentleness she could muster.

"Sit." She stroked his cheek with the pad of one thumb. "Food will be ready soon."

Orlando held his mother's gaze, expression unreadable. His tight jaw said he didn't appreciate the unmissable sorrow on her face, but the softened edges around his eyes betrayed his usual pretense that nothing got to him. That he never worried.

Orlando worried about Marcella.

# Chapter Sixteen

"My mother warned you to stay away from me, didn't she?"

Sophie maintained a hurried stride on her way back to the car, annoyed at Orlando's question and that he, with his longer legs, managed to trudge even farther ahead of her. If anyone was going to be pissed, it should have been her.

She hugged herself, the gesture not enough to fend off the cold night or the icy strong winds skimming off the lake. "What makes you think your mother warned me away?"

"I know my mother." His hands hung in curled fists at his sides.

"It's dark. I can barely see where I'm going." She frowned at his hulking physique and those long legs stalking farther and farther away. "Will you slow down already?"

He didn't slow down. He stopped completely. Then whipped around to give her the full intensity of his devilish, dusky glare. "Happy now?"

She drifted past, at least glad not to have to look at him. "I will be when we get to my car."

In truth, she couldn't blame his snappish mood, much less her own. Marcella's parting stare had held a vivid *remember what I told you* vibe and hadn't been at all subtle. Any chance of a pleasant goodbye had been shot to pieces. Orlando took one look at his mother, then at Sophie, and marched instantly off into the gloomy night.

The memory made her cringe, and she figured, despite the fact she'd gotten ahead of him, Orlando probably needed a break from people making decisions behind his back. So, she breathed in the lake's damp and muddy scent and dispensed the truth. "Fine. Yes, she did warn me. But I like your mother, and I understand why she did it."

No. Actually. The warning stung. And she'd felt no better than a child being slapped on the wrist for something she hadn't yet done. She understood, sure, but understanding and appreciating were two different things.

The thud of his feet grew louder, and he soon sidled up to her, though she tried to ignore him. "And what do you plan to do about her warning?"

She focused on the glittering water ahead—black, though speckled in moonlight—her tiny car a shadowy blob to the right. "Nothing. The warning was baseless."

A second of silence, save for their panting breaths, passed long enough for her to wonder if he'd speak again. "Why? Because Saint Sophie could never have feelings for Screwball Orlando?"

Her belly churned, and unease sent her state of mind further off-kilter. His blunt words failed to hide the low huskiness in his tone, a huskiness that suggested her reply might hold more importance than he let on. And maybe her tummy churned because she did have the feelings he spoke of, and his mere question hinted his awareness of that fact.

"Both your mother's warning and your question just now are redundant." She swallowed hard, hoping with all hope he wouldn't drill down on her need for denial. "I would never cross that line with you. Never."

He barked out a laugh. "Never is a strong word, one I'm not sure you'll be able to keep. And which line would you never cross exactly? The non-existent one between volunteers and patients?" He walked in stride with her now, close enough that his body heat caressed her left arm, the lightness in his tone in itself unnerving her. "You're the only one drawing lines, Saint Sophie."

She shot him a glare, only to witness the maddening view of his mischievous grin. Why did her need for caution always seem amusing to him?

"My work means something to me." She picked up her pace, her car not far now, though her feet sank into the long grass with its swishing, dense brush. "You're not serious about wanting to cross any lines with me. And don't call me 'Saint Sophie'. You don't know the first thing about me."

A growing rasp of grass behind her announced his fast approach. He soon positioned himself ahead, forcing her to a standstill. "But you know everything about me, given your research into my life and all. And that's fair?"

"You know why I did that."

She glared, shifting to get away from him. He sidestepped, stopping her, making it clear he wanted this conversation. Even if she didn't.

"What I find interesting, is how your professional integrity flies out the window when it comes to digging up my past, but despite whatever *you* think you know about me—" The devilish grin returned, eyes glinting against the moon. "Let's just say I don't need the internet to figure you out."

She rolled her eyes. Maybe if she let him talk, he'd let her and this conversation go.

"Fine." She huffed out a breath, theatrically bored. "Tell me what you know. It's cold, and I've more than earned the cup of Earl Grey tea waiting for me at home."

He scowled, clearly disapproving of her glib approach. "You're passive and indecisive. For the most part, you struggle to stand up for yourself. Worst of all, you look after other's needs without factoring in your own."

As much as she disliked what he had to say, his confident appraisal held a dangerous edge of truth.

"You think I'm naïve, don't you?" Tension bunched the muscles at her chest, making it harder for her to breathe against all his quips about her being a "nerd" and a "saint". How dare he fling her attempts to care for him in her face and use it to make her sound stupid and weak? "And let me guess, you think these attributes are also my fault?"

He lifted a palm to the sky, only confirming the statement, and stoking a need to find out about his other perceptions. "I'm sure you think your heart is in the right place."

She pressed her jaw tighter and held back on defending herself, if only for the moment. "Tell me what *you* think."

"I didn't ask you to look into my life. You either did it under the naïve impression you could help, or to satisfy your curiosity because you had more malicious reasons." He trained his heavy gaze on her, as if he saw every thought running through her head, analyzed it, then hung those thoughts out for all to see. He inched a little closer. That mere inch was enough to churn her guts anew. "I know which version I'd rather believe. In which case, you'd do better to protect your heart and not get so invested in things that will hurt you."

"Things that will hurt me? As in you?"

His smile crept up on one side, the rest of his expression flat. "I'm a losing bet, remember?"

She barked out a laugh, jabbing at his pumped-up certainty that she would ever get so invested in him. "I'm not looking to get involved with you, Orlando. Though I am glad you've noticed my commitment to your care. It's my job not to give up on people. And since my intention is to work with the elderly, pretty much every case I take on will end sooner rather than later. *Losing bet* or not, you don't need to worry about me getting hurt."

His eyes narrowed, but he remained silent, suggesting he didn't believe her future career would be her sole reason for meddling.

Perhaps he genuinely disliked being nothing more to her than a case. *Well, tough.*

She lifted her chin, ready to set him straight on the limits of this relationship. "It takes more strength to let others in than it does to keep your guard up. I acknowledge that must be exhausting for you, but all the flaws you point out in me lack perspective. Where you say I look after others at the expense of myself, another might say I'm hard-working and I enjoy a challenge."

He stared at her, unblinking. "Whoever said that is an idiot."

She locked her muscles in place. "Do you always have to be so rude?"

"On the subject of you and me? It seems so, yes."

"There is no 'you and me'."

A tiny smirk cracked his stony glower and he made a *tsk* sound. "Naïve. Or maybe it's denial?"

"You're being ridiculous."

She took a step forward, moving to leave.

He took a wide sidestep, halting her exit yet again.

His glower returned harder than ever, jaw set, like he'd had enough. "You really think my observations here are wrong? That I lack perspective? Well, I have a little perspective for you…" He drew nearer, the direct hold of his deep, dark pupils seeming to bore into her soul. Her heart thundered. The close proximity took up all her air and fanned whatever growing attraction she might have had, yet stifled, toward this man. "Where you demand gratitude for your help, I hate being treated like a spectacle. I'm not a puzzle for you to solve, Sophie. I'm not an experiment. I'm sure as heck not some animal in an exhibit for you to observe. Passive might be your 'thing', but it's never been mine."

Her heart squeezed. She let out an awkward crackle, before finding her voice. "That's not what I intended."

"Nevertheless, that's how you made me feel."

A gust of wind *whooshed* over the long grass. She peered down at her feet. The mere fact he talked about his feelings should have been a good sign, but those feelings entailed pain, and she'd been the cause.

"Not that long ago, I was an independent man with decades of life ahead of me." He paused, attention veering toward the lake, which seemed to stretch out forever into the night. "I have nothing now. Nothing except the same conversations with the same dying people at the home. The monotonous routine of every meal served at the same time every day, every day playing out almost the exact same way. Except for when I've had a bad episode.

"And then it's the need to have someone I barely know wipe me, bathe me, turn me over so I don't get bed sores. I can't even rely on the comfort of my own mind functioning as it should." He reached out and tipped her chin up, forcing her to see him. To see the reasons why he was rude and often grotesquely direct. "You want to know what makes me tick, Sophie? The answer is nothing. A person in my predicament doesn't waste their energy on dreams and desires. And you, in all your academic brilliance, should already know that. There was no point to your digging, and that's what makes you naïve."

He gave his head a slow and steady shake, not much different from a stern teacher scolding a child, though a muscle twitched in his cheek, belying his defenses weren't quite as impenetrable as she'd figured. "And no matter how much you might think I fail as a man, I deserved to know what you were up to. I have nothing, but I never once gave up my right to tell you to shove your job and your research."

His last words hit her like a hard slap to the face, so much so her skin burned of its own accord. He was right. She didn't deserve to be in the same space as him.

He'd deserved to know. And she deserved his take down now. She'd known that truth the second she'd carried out that internet search on him. She'd not only been naïve, but she'd been downright condescending in confessing her failure too.

She bit her inner cheeks, shame snaking its way through her insides and adding to her sense of unease. But even then, she still fought to be right, and she fought an urge to point out he would never have agreed to her help.

She'd come to Australia to rough her life up a little. To learn about herself… But now as she got her wish, she skulked away at the image reflected back.

"For what it's worth—" She forced herself to maintain eye contact, to offer a win in light of her mistakes. "I don't see you as a losing bet or an incomplete man. You were dealt an impossible hand, and I'm in awe you've held together as well as you have." She paused, hoping he'd take heart of what she had to say next, minus discovering another detail she had on him—Candice's hunch. "I hope you continue to do so for a very long time."

He gave a little flinch, his head tilting to one side, as if her words affected him, or maybe he'd gleaned her knowledge of his potential wish to end his life. Her heart squeezed. Her skin prickled. But ever so slowly, one corner of his lip curled up.

"So Mother was right." A light burst to life in his eyes. "You would if you could."

"I—" Her mouth wavered open and closed for a few seconds, delaying her ability to respond. "I didn't say that."

"See what I mean?" He turned on his heel, this time the first to head for the car. "Indecisive."

She stood stunned in his wake, attention glued to his back as she tried, but failed, to chase after him. She couldn't believe he'd turned the conversation on its head, but then again, this was Orlando. He took *heartfelt* and made it into a joke.

She growled under her breath, spell broken, and trudged after him.

She eventually reached the car, where she got in and started the engine.

The drive back to Roseford Aged Care consisted of her staring ahead and refusing to look at Orlando. Not that he seemed to mind. He spent his time gazing out his window, flashing an occasional dumb grin from the corner of her eye.

When she did pull up to the home, she counted the seconds until the infuriating man would open his car door and leave.

But he didn't leave.

"Sophie." His voice held a gentle quality, the low rumble adding intimacy within the tight confines of her car. "Look at me."

She blinked ahead, fingers tightening around her steering wheel. "No. We've done more talking today than in our entire time knowing each other. Let's call it a night."

A heavy silence drew out. Perhaps he waited for her to change her mind. But he'd already referred to her as indecisive and passive and naïve, and she'd prove him right in falling for yet another of his attempts to embarrass her. She wouldn't give him that chance.

He blew out a loud breath, and his seatbelt clinked as he released the buckle.

"Fine." His door popped open, but he still failed to leave, the bite of cold air hitting her side. "The thing is, I know I don't have what it takes to be what you need." Next came the rustle of movement, and in her peripheral vision, he stepped out—only to lean in and poke his head through his open door. "But I would if I could, too."

# Chapter Seventeen

Sophie dipped her brush into the orange watercolor paint, her movements scaled down to avoid any accidental clashes with Orlando. They sat side by side in the home's common room, a photo of a farmhouse backed by sunset clipped to the easel, a photo she and Orlando were tasked to reproduce on canvas together.

"So how is it that your mum lives in town, but she never takes you out anywhere?" She focused on the painting—on the pink and orange hues—anything to avoid looking directly at *him*.

"Trust me, she's tried." He dabbed green paint at the farthest edge of the canvas, seeming equally invested in maintaining his space. "I told her not to. Everyone in town already knows I'm an invalid. I don't need to parade myself through the streets with my mother clutching my hand and crying at the sight of me."

Sophie's heart squeezed, and she looked about to see if any of the many fellow residents or volunteers overheard Orlando's cruel description of himself. *An invalid.* A deeply derogatory term meaning literally *not valid*. Which Orlando was anything but, especially to her.

She frowned, lowering her brush half an inch. She understood why he wanted to shield his pride in public, but Marcella loved her son, and raw emotion had flowed in thick waves off the woman whenever she discussed him. And then there was his clear protectiveness over his mother, so maybe he cared as much about safeguarding her pride as he did his own.

"Your mum loves you." She collected more orange from the pallet, while considering how Orlando might benefit from redefining his relationship with his mother. "And why do you care what anyone in town thinks?"

"Sophie, my mum is in her mid-seventies. She should be looking out for herself. Besides, she's not all that good in an emergency." He let out an exasperated sigh. "One time she thought someone was breaking into her house, and she called me, who lived hours away in the city, to ask what to do."

"I mean, that's not completely unreasonable. Many people call those close to them in an emergency. Not the best course of action, but understandable."

"The point is, she should have called the police first, and she wasted precious minutes panicking on the phone with me. I don't want to put her in a position of having to manage me in an emergency."

She shifted her hand to the canvas, just as he moved his to paint a patch of sky beside her sun. Their knuckles nearly touched, but he redirected his movements, guiding his brush back to the pallet between them. For a man who'd boldly declared *he would if he could*, he sure was being skittish today.

Sophie glowered at her portion of the painting, unsure what to make of his current evasiveness, while also miffed he'd limited his mother's involvement in his life over one mistake.

He cleared his throat, perhaps a distraction from the literal near brush of his hands. "The point is, she worries enough. If something went wrong, she'd spend her remaining years blaming herself."

Sophie gave a gentle nod, and a steady silence drew out, her heart plodding under a slew of conflicting thought.

Maybe she should come right out and discuss what he'd said the other day. Wasn't it best to deal with issues of impossible attraction in a direct manner? Maybe in a clinical sense. But the human side of her, the side that maybe did feel something for Orlando—as a man, not as a *project*—couldn't find the courage to broach the subject.

She glanced sideways, to his occasional downward gaze at the paint palette, that gaze giving him an air of sadness. Her energy dipped in response. She recalled his heavy tone as he'd told her he didn't "have what it took to be what she needed". The way his eyes had grown darker, as if the brutal honesty pained him as much as it had her.

"You never talk about your parents." He spoke low and warm, but the abrupt sound of his voice jolted her focus back to the canvas.

"There's not much to tell." The cold creeping through her body begged to differ. "My mother lives in York, has done all her life. Now all her kids are grown, she spends most days in her garden or social-izing with her lifelong gal-pals. And Dad… He…" Her words snared on a sudden lump in her throat. She took a long breath, allowing her emotions to settle. "He died a few years ago. A bad heart. You know. Kind of sudden."

Orlando paused and turned to her, her gaze momentarily fusing with his, before she got too overwhelmed and peered back at the emerging artwork.

"It still hurts even when you know it's coming."

She gave a quick nod. "You speak from experience?"

"My dad died seven years ago. If you ask Mum, he worked himself to an early grave."

He began painting again, and she joined him, the light from the wide window behind her reflecting off the wet canvas. "Why does she believe that?"

Orlando let out a rough laugh. "He did everything he could to keep the farm running, but a few bad years and a shaky economy overshad-owed his efforts. The house and the lake you saw the other day are just a small portion of the original land belonging to our family. My parents were forced to sell off two-thirds a couple of years before Dad died. And Mom's right. The stress and disappointment did kill him."

She willed her eyes to stay pointed forward but failed, her wobbly tone also taking on a life of its own. "I'm sorry."

Her focus trekked down to the dark, thick stubble over his strong jawline, his full lips commanding her attention.

A shock wave of need quaked heat through her body, and she yearned for the days where she saw only hard scorn and denial in his eyes. This new, softened look, along with his sudden ability for candid conversations, felt impossible to ignore. He should have shut her out after he'd learned of her digging; instead, he opened to her even more.

*I would if I could, too.*

*Arggh.* Her heart fluttered, nerves unsettled. Would she? If she could…

She turned away from him. From answering that question. The pressure of his stare too much.

*Even if she could…* Orlando's defensiveness served a purpose. At the least, it helped him survive. And then there was Candice's warning…

Strain constricted the muscles in her throat, but even then, speaking in that moment sure beat thinking. "It must be hard on your mother. You know, living alone."

From the corner of her eye, Orlando dipped his chin, as if taking a moment to consider his words. "A lot of Southern Europeans of her era weren't overly welcomed in Australia. My parents had a hard enough time relocating from post-war Europe, without the decades of blatant racism and being shunned by some folk here. I guess times changed, and most people in these parts got to accepting us eventually, or maybe they look out for us now out of guilt for how they treated us back then. Who knows? Either way, my parents had each other through it all, and they had a bond only death could break. Which it did."

He dropped his brush into the cup of water designated for cleaning off paint, and slumped back in his seat. "The ending was bad. So yeah, Mum pulled the short straw, but she got more love from my dad than a lot of people can ever hope for. I doubt she'd take a refund on their time together just to spare her the grief of that ending."

Sophie sank deeper into her seat, too, twisting the end of the brush between her fingers. Orlando's resignation from their task zapped her own desire to paint, much less that the deep tragedy in his words hinted he would be one of those people who'd never have the chance or the decades to experience the relationship his parents had shared.

That sentiment alone made it hard to forget the phone call she'd received that morning—an answer to a few enquiries she'd made before spilling the truth to Orlando about looking into his past.

He wouldn't be happy if she told him about the call, he'd accuse her of more meddling. But to look at him and do nothing? To know that one way or another, his days might be numbered, or at the very least, he'd likely never regain all he'd lost. Maybe she had a duty to tell him either way.

Her attention shifted to the rustle of other volunteers standing and packing up. A wall clock to her right signaled an ended to their time together for that day. She needed to decide whether she should tell him. In order to do that, she needed distance from this man. So, she stood, her purse strap already halfway up her arm.

"Don't leave yet."

She startled at the gentle command, her gaze catching his. The depths of his eyes were endless, and they swallowed her whole, keeping her in place.

He grinned and sudden lightness ruptured whatever tension lingered between them. "I like having more than octogenarians for company. Stay, please. Or if you have plans, take me with you. Just don't leave yet."

She flicked her attention to the tiny stampede of volunteers filing out into the parking lot. Her brain yelled to turn him down flat, but where he'd once forced her out the doors, now he finally invited her to stay. She couldn't find it in her to reward this hard-won acceptance with rejection.

"It's nice out, and I'd planned on enjoying the good weather." She refocused on him, her heart in an inexplicable flitter. "I've been meaning to visit the beach along Manna Gum Grove. I wouldn't have to go alone if you joined me."

Orlando's smile stilled, and his gaze drifted over her face, like he saw her fraying nerves and her heavy doubt. Like he too understood the risk in prolonging this visit.

"I know Manna Gum Grove well." Stern tension marked his

features, as if avoiding any sudden move that might awaken her ability to say no. "I can show you the nicer sightseeing spots."

She gave a tight nod and turned on her heel, drowning her misgivings with a rapid-fire response. "Grab whatever you need to take with you, and I'll meet you by the doors. It's almost lunchtime, so we'll swing by my place and fix something quick to take with us."

Her cheeks burned; thank goodness she had her back to him. Not only had she signed up for an impromptu beach adventure, but she'd just invited Orlando to her cabin.

～

Sophie leaned into the open door of her fridge and searched for what was left of the lunch meat she'd bought yesterday. The muscles between her shoulders burned under the stare she envisioned Orlando pinned her way. *Envisioned* because she'd struggled to look at him from the moment she invited him to the cabin.

The lunch meat lay wrapped in thin, white deli paper at the back of the top shelf; she pulled it out and ferried it to the kitchen island.

"I hope you don't mind sandwiches." She spoke down to her hands, unable to get her mind around the rough-edged man propped against the far wall in her kitchen, or to come to terms with her stupid plan to feed him.

He didn't respond, which only added to the twitchy sensation in her gut. This was ridiculous. This was her place—at least for the time being. He didn't get to make her feel uncomfortable in her home.

She reached into a drawer and peered up at him as he gave her a slow head shake. His lack of words and full attention caused her fingers to fumble, and she dropped three teaspoons whilst searching for a butter knife. The high-pitched, metallic ting shattered the painful quiet.

She huffed out a groan. Annoyed at him. Annoyed at herself. "Will you please say something? You're creeping me out."

She had two brothers. Had just come out of a long-term relationship. She'd been around plenty of men and performed a great many medical assessments on them. Why did this particular one bother her so much?

A smile broke across his face, as though he'd been only half-aware of his leering, and her admission cracked some unspoken barrier.

"Sorry." His focus switched to the wood-paneled walls around him. "Quaint little cottage." He refocused on her and shrugged, as though the simple observation was the best he could offer.

She paused her bread buttering and glared at him, before gazing around the small, but light-filled kitchen—black stone bench tops to her left, cutesy paneled windows above the sink behind her. "This is my brother's cabin. Luke runs a successful tech business. He's somewhat of a star." She returned to the sandwiches. "So go-figure, he has a spare house or two. Me, on the other hand…"

"Let me guess." Orlando's rich voice came as a warning for her not to peer up, in case the look in his eyes matched his tone. "You've racked up years of student debt so you can learn important skills to help others. There's nothing wrong with your career choice, Sophie. The world would not function if we were all businessmen."

She warmed at his genuine defense of her career. A job he'd given her hell for earlier. A job where she witnessed the best and worst of people, and often had to deny her humanity in order to work fast and avoid becoming overwhelmed.

She dared to look up, to his softened smile. If he truly did hold respect for her job, perhaps now was the time to tell him about her earlier call. That she'd nabbed the assistance of a specialist willing to look into his case…

She opened her mouth, ready to blurt out what he'd see as her latest misdeed, but he pushed himself away from the wall and sauntered toward her, drying her ability to speak.

"Let me help you." He picked up a tomato from the bench. "It's only fair."

She snapped her jaw shut and handed him a serrated knife. His powerful hands enveloped the slim handle, and he went to work slicing the tomato—drawing her focus to the ripple of muscle in his thick forearms.

For a brief moment, she had a sense of standing outside of her body. Like none of this was really happening. Orlando was making sandwiches in her kitchen, and somehow, they managed to hold off on the fighting long enough to have a normal conversation. *Much less* his presence felt easy and pleasant—even though her nerves remained set to fluster.

She buried her confession about the specialist. *Perhaps another day.*

For now, she'd settle with maintaining the *nice*.

"I don't know how you do it." Her heart sank the second the words fell from her lips.

*So much for maintaining the nice.*

He peered up at her, and his direct stare signaled he understood her reference.

"Neither do I." His jaw muscles strained a moment, before finding release. "Most days I don't want to."

She nodded, heartsick at the toll of his daily battle with his condition. "I kind of figured that much."

He drew in a loud breath and put his knife down, before he curled his fingers into tight fists and pressed his knuckles into the kitchen island's rustic wood top. "I feel bitter most days. I can't go back to what I had before the episodes started. I can't find hope in any kind of future because I simply don't see one ahead of me. The last three years have been me trapped in the middle of a raging storm with no escape. Every day is incrementally worse. Every day takes me further away from what I used to have. But something's changed."

His chin tilted down, but he lifted his grave focus onto her. "Lately, I get glimpses of calm within that storm. I'm trapped, but sometimes there's this new kind of stillness. Moments to breathe within the panic. Does that make sense?"

Her eyes prickled, but she gave a weak nod. She'd weathered storms too. Personal ones. Ones that engulfed her whole and spat her out, aimless and afraid. And even though his admission unlocked her own painful memories, she held her emotions together. For his sake. For his willingness to include her.

"You're accepting your circumstances." She offered a soft smile designed to reassure. "The limitations. The inevitabilities."

"And I've found someone that makes my days a little more bearable."

He held her stare. Immovable.

His open vulnerability came with a purpose. Or more precisely, a challenge.

Clear thought ran from her mind, leaving her deficient in words, though his resolute gaze demanded an answer.

She'd come to admit an interest in him, at least to herself, but she'd never once considered marring this semi-professional relationship with something more personal. She'd also never imagined he'd be the one doing the marring.

Her ability to speak wore down to a rough rasp. "You're supposed to hate me."

He straightened and loomed over her from across the island. Elbows locking. Brow flexed and stern.

"I never hated you. I recognized your ability to ruin the neat solitude I'd built for myself." Hard tension pulled his shoulders wide, making him appear broader than ever. Finally, she could see the man his mother had described, the one quick to run into burning buildings, the one confident with women. And that same confidence took him around the kitchen island. He drew near, and his close proximity coupled with his swarthy features made her pulse race and breaths short. "You don't give up, and for all your prodding, I've learned one truth. The only thing I hate about you, is the hope you bring, when hope for me is dangerous. But hope doesn't keep me going, Sophie. Your visits do. Each day you're not at the home is just time between when I get to see you next."

She needed space to breathe, space from him, and took a step back. "That kind of dependency isn't fair to you."

"Incorrect." The word shot from his mouth, fierce and certain. "I'm not in control of where my condition takes me, but don't let that confuse you into thinking I'm not in control of my mind. Not once has my competency come into question. You can ask Candice about that one. I know what I want. The question is, do you?"

She dug her fingers into the rough counter, his iron resolve rendering her momentarily speechless. "What I want is irrelevant."

He stepped forward, disallowing the space she'd claimed. "Maybe to you, but not to me. And what you want is written all over your face. Every time I look at you, I see your mind ticking away. I bet you wish you could make that ticking stop, huh? Maybe break free of yourself just long enough to live a little. Isn't that why you left London?"

Her muscles locked. He seemed to know at least some of her reason for being in Australia. But she needed to save herself now. Needed to redirect him. Anything to keep Orlando from digging out more truths or setting any more challenges. God help her if he articulated her desire for a short-term lover.

She eased her shoulders down, attempting to conjure a sense of calm. "My precise job as your volunteer is to help make your life more bearable. It's understandable you'd look to me for an escape."

His gaze darkened. "That's one piss-poor attempt at deflection. If you truly want what's happening here to be fair, then I sure as hell wouldn't mind shaking up your world the way you've shaken up mine. And I dare you to tell me that *your job* is the only reason for all this energy pinging between us."

Her mouth fell open, ready to throw forth a quick rebuttal. But nothing came. All she could do was stare. She couldn't lie. She also couldn't admit to her feelings—no matter how much his all-encompassing presence made her want to. And even then, her lack of confession wasn't just about her job, so much as a literal inability to speak her mind when it came to anything that mattered. When it came to *him*.

From the moment she'd met Orlando, she recognized his capability to shake up her world. And part of her deep-seated concern had always been about whether she could withstand anything he had to offer. Maybe he was right. Maybe her status as a volunteer did present a poor reason for deflection. And maybe, in many ways, her state of mind was just as fragile as she'd assumed his to be.

Her focus shifted to the low-scale commotion of a gusty wind outside, and the creak of windows.

He drew near, as though she'd run out of time to fight the tug-of-war he'd extended, her heart clenching in response.

"I see."

What exactly did he see? And why did she feel like some newfangled discovery under a microscope?

He stood close enough that his heat touched her, the front of her body enlivened, caressed with warmth. His palm engulfed her left cheek, and the challenge faded from his eyes, replaced with a new kind of tenderness. Somehow, her heartbeat settled.

In all her confusion, two things remained indisputable. This man had innate power over her, and for all his brooding, she trusted him. She felt safe.

"If you don't want this." His arm locked around her waist, and he tugged her against him. "Just say so." His voice dropped to a whisper, as though for once he wanted to be the one to comfort her. "I never sought you out to help me, Sophie. I'm not your patient. I'm a man in my own right, and I want you. Do you understand?"

Her mind struggled with the reality he unfurled around her, and she produced just about the only action she could manage—a slow, dumbfounded nod.

He drew his face closer still, and a small smile tugged at his lips. "Then I'd like it if you didn't try to distract me this time."

Blood rushed her veins. Her skin prickled under an attack of nerves. He'd seen through her blurted confession at the lake when he tried to kiss her. And still, her every muscle burned with sparks of desire. The touch of his hand to her cheek and his spoken certainty settled her into following his lead.

His lips closed the space between them, and before long, his full-bodied kiss commanded hers, overriding and inescapable—as if he'd decided her chance to protest had passed. His movements mirrored the man himself. Dark. Hot. Powerful. Somehow robust and gentle all at once.

She should have said no, should have pushed him away, but already, he'd taken her too far. His tongue swept her mouth, claiming her. His strong hands held her pressed to his large frame.

And even as he kissed her, she wanted more. His touch intoxicated and left her no choice but to melt against him, to relish all he gave, and for once surrender to losing control.

Seconds passed, and she unearthed the courage to kiss him back.

He rewarded her with a growl. His hands swept down her body, wild energy coursing from his fingers as they curled around the backs of her thighs, and he hoisted her off the ground.

She cupped his face and pulled him in for a deeper kiss. He carried her across the room, then pushed her hard against the wall. An exhilarating burst of air escaped her lungs. Her body responded with a burning sense of recognition. She ground against him, hoping to sooth the needy ache tearing through her body.

As much as she wanted to blame herself—to call this moment a lapse in judgment—Orlando was right. He *was* a man in control of his mind, and he proved it every time he set her in her place. She'd never once questioned his self-awareness, never once doubted his ability to know what he wanted.

She clung to him, her fingers raking through his thick wavy hair, whilst vividly aware he was right about something else. She had used her position as a volunteer to run from him. To run from herself. But now, for once in her overly-controlled life, if just for one fleeting moment, she wouldn't shrink away from what she desired most.

# Chapter Eighteen

Orlando had learned that anyone in his predicament could not waste time. And after weeks of watching Sophie blush and stumble through every exchange, he wasn't about to lose this chance.

He'd also once read that what people missed most after a big loss was the mundane. Things like: a favorite meal, a parent's hug, a much-loved book lost through the years. What he missed most was the assumption he had any kind of future. He missed fitting in. Stability and direction. But Sophie in her kitchen, carrying out the mundane tasks of making sandwiches and dispensing with easy talk, had brought another thing simmering to the surface. Something he thought he'd never have again. *Connection.*

The scorch of her lips now tore open a space in his heart, a pain he chased, despite settling for less than what he truly wanted with her. That ever-elusive future. He couldn't imagine her desire for him running as deep as what he held for her, but at least for this moment, she was his.

A dull ache bore into him from her fingers clinging hard to his shoulders. He relished that pain too. A reminder of her need, as he held her lifted and pinned to the wall. For once, someone *needed* him. He was more than a compliant patient doing what he was told.

She pulled her lips away, panting. "This is the most absurd thing I've ever done."

"It's not my brightest move either, but making good decisions hasn't gotten me all that far, so…" He slid his hands over her thighs, pushing her loose red sundress until it bunched around her waist, his touch an incentive for her to stick with him. He'd be damned if he let her overthink this. "Let's forget about using our brains for a while and focus on our bodies."

She shuddered, sucking in a sharp breath. His blood surged at her uncontrolled reaction, but seconds later, her hazel eyes clouded in seriousness. "I'll regret this."

"No." He held her gaze, dismantling her stern approach. "No. You won't."

"You'll regret it too."

The pain in his heart vibrated through his body, another hint he couldn't let her back out. "I can't think of anything I want more."

The throb in his chest deepened into a sharp needling, the truth in his confession a surprise even to him. A part of him prepared for yet another of life's rejections.

"You're okay, aren't you?" Her gaze searched his, the darting movements betraying more misgivings. "You'll be okay?"

Her question left him momentarily speechless. Never had a woman he planned to sleep with asked if he'd be okay. He couldn't imagine why it was so important to her, but he nodded. "You?"

She nodded, too, hand rising until her knuckles skimmed his jawline.

"I'm scared, but I still want you." She let out a staggered laugh. "Or maybe I'm scared *because* I want you. Or maybe it's how much I want you that's the frightening part."

Her touch and words ignited a flame. Based on what he'd witnessed of her personality, she'd probably never done anything quite this spontaneous before. Compared to him, she was sweetness personified. But then there was her courage, compassion, and quick intellect. And the gleaming truth that she was too good for the likes of him.

But still, she wanted *him*.

And yes, he saw her wide-eyed fear. This situation had her lost, but for a change, they shared equal standing. Or maybe he had the ability to help her here and, therefore, had the upper hand…

Little Miss Neat and Nerdy was about to get a lot less "Neat and Nerdy", and as for him, he hadn't been with a woman in years. Yet, the constant panging in his chest told him this one time with Sophie wouldn't be enough. If there were more time, he'd do so much more. Take things slow. Lay her down. Explore every inch of her. He'd taste her. Repay her for all the ways she got to him.

But there wasn't enough time. Not for her. Certainly not for him. And he needed to get Sophie Tindall out of his system.

Her fingers shifted to the nape of his neck, and she pulled him closer, initiating the next kiss. Hunger and passion mixed with force, and her lips unleashed an untamed desire. A wild fire allowed to run free, or a woman held back for far too long.

He pressed his body to her, allowing her to feel him—all of him. Matching her intensity. Encouraging her bravery. He wanted to strip her naked right there and then, but as ready as he was, she needed a moment to warm up.

He pushed his tongue into her mouth, his lashes slow at first, then more commanding, mimicking what he wanted to do to her at the lower point where their bodies pressed. Her gentle whimper prompted his hands up her ribcage, and she ground against him, escalating his need.

His palms found her breasts—rewarding her courage, rewarding himself—kneading her small, firm, perfection through her dress.

She ripped her mouth away, her gaze failing to meet his. "I know you prefer a woman with bigger breasts."

Her pupils were wide and truly apologetic, the comment a reference to his ribbing weeks ago at the biker bar, back when he'd teased her with a potential trip to a non-existent strip club. Of course, his assholery would come back to bite him now.

He touched his forehead to hers until her gaze met his again. How could he have done anything to make this woman doubt herself?

"The only breasts I can think about are yours." He brushed his thumbs over her dress's thin fabric, the hard pebble of her nipples prodding through whatever equally thin bra she wore underneath. "They're flawless, and so are you."

Her eyelids fluttered closed, her body sinking against the wall, though her cheeks lifted with a small smile. "What about my potato sack clothing and uptight personality?"

A low chuckle broke free of him. "Potato sack or not, I'd prefer you with no clothes on. So if you'll let me get back to it, I was about to help you with the uptight thing."

She gave a soft laugh, but he nipped at her neck, where the scent of spring daisies floated off her smooth skin, and the laughter she held turned into a needy gasp. He wanted to devour her, to purge himself of his intense need for this woman. At the same time, he'd only just started and didn't want to let her go.

His mouth found hers, and he slid his hands under her dress until he felt the rasp of her lace underwear. Tongues meshed. Breaths drew heavy. One need rose and then another. He needed to be inside her. Needed to feel her gliding over him, and watch her come undone at his touch… But not just yet.

First, he shifted her underwear until his thumb met with her slick center. She gasped again, inching higher and away from him, like even that amount of stimulation was too much.

He drew light circles over her flesh and soon she relaxed, her keening cry calling for more.

The brush of her breath to his neck brought on his own excited shiver. He claimed her mouth, swallowing her moans. She bucked against him, gathering speed, until he buried his fingers within her, and her climax exploded.

Not waiting for her to finish, he freed himself; before he slid his length into her, having to stop halfway. She clenched around him. Resistant. Seconds passed as he gave her time to soften and relax. When she did, he entered her fully.

Her eyes closed. She called his name. And he nipped her plump lower lip, losing himself in a kiss, before he moved within her.

Her head tilted forward, and he buried his face among a cascade of exquisitely soft, sable hair. She gave another moan and tightened. His heart soared, and he plunged harder, deeper, faster, putting himself to work until he found a solid rhythm. She wanted this. Wanted *him*. Never before had he felt so needed. She was perfection—too perfect for him—but he'd take her. All of her.

He increased speed, and with each of his thrusts, small puffs of air escaped her lips; her body trembling beneath his until she gave out a long, great cry. Every corner of the tiny kitchen reverberated with her beautiful sound—the call of her unrestrained pleasure—of his victory and pride. Neither of which he'd had in years.

He picked up speed, made way for his impending release, only for a heaviness to settle in his heart.

No. Not heaviness. *Fear.*

He teetered on the edge of losing control—so similar to what occurred during his episodes—the dizzying sense already building. Would he be okay? Would letting go with Sophie induce an episode? Would this be yet another moment stolen from him?

Her eyes flung wide open, and she gasped with continued need. She wanted him to join her, to see him tumble too. But uncertainty battled lust as he threw himself at the mercy of whatever happened next.

He buried his face into her free-flowing hair again, his orgasm building with more intensity than he'd ever experienced and way too fast to stop now. He'd have to trust her. He didn't trust himself. But she'd seen him crumble before. *Sophie. Perfect Sophie.* She'd forgive him. Surely, she'd forgive him.

Pleasure struck—a million shooting stars racing past him faster than a freight train. He dug his fingers into her hips. Trying but failing to maintain control.

*I can't control this. Trust her. Just trust her.*

And, oh, how he trusted her. Maybe a little too much. But he trusted her all the same.

This was about more than mere sex or finding validation as a man. *This* was something he thought he'd never have again. *This* was something other than his usual daily grind of life within the same walls. Something beyond the same battle between soul-crushing routine and the agonizing uncertainty of what his condition would do next.

A guttural groan tore from deep within him, the sound disappeared into her hair and the wall behind. He poured himself inside her. Literally. Figuratively.

Long minutes passed before he found direction again. He'd lost himself, yes, but not as much as he could have. Fear had held him back. He'd trusted her, when maybe he shouldn't have. She'd looked into his past after all. Though even in her more dubious decisions, she always meant well, and what he trusted in most was her goodness.

His racing mind settled, as did his body. He leaned back to search her gaze. Her focus held his, pupils wide and directionless. *At least he wasn't the only one.*

She stroked the scar along his hairline, as though even now she embraced his imperfections. He blinked down to his own fingers tracing the edge of her chin, the room so impossibly quiet, save for the sounds of ragged breaths and his blood pumping loud in his ears.

And with that silence, clear thought descended like slow settling snow. He pulled his face farther from hers, a shock of realization flooding in.

Yes, he'd taken an unwise emotional leap, but then there was something else he'd just done. Something far more reckless.

# Chapter Nineteen

Sophie grabbed his collar, halting his escape. "No. Don't."

Her attention skittered over his ashen complexion, and his gaze settled down at where their bodies met. The moment she'd felt the heat of him spill within her, she'd known what seemed to only dawn on him now.

They hadn't used protection.

"I'm so sorry." Even as the words fell from her mouth, she couldn't say what she apologized for, just that her thoughts raced in an attempt to make sense of all that had just occurred.

He withdrew and lowered her to the ground, hot wetness clinging to her thighs. She focused on his sunken cheeks, confirming his shared alarm.

Her chin wobbled, and she let go of his collar, grappling to control her emotions. Orlando shook his head, expression firm as if his usual defenses had kicked in. "This is my mistake. I'm the one who messed this up, you got it?"

She gave a small nod, lips parted, though no words escaped. She'd loved every second of being with him, had traveled halfway around the globe seeking this very encounter. Well, maybe not this *exact* encounter…

Tears stung her eyes. Her heart drummed now for a very different reason. How could she have gotten so carried away?

Because *Orlando*. Of course.

The man stole all logic and turned it into pure and unavoidable impulse. Not that she really believed this was all his mistake. There'd been his ability to short her logic, sure, but her inability to control herself when it came to him was also to blame.

She turned toward her kitchen and paced in small circles, patting her open palm to her forehead over and over again. *Stupid. Stupid woman. The same mistake again?*

And even in her panic, she knew better than to fall apart. He didn't know her story. Nor did he need to know. Moreover, she refused to give him another reason to feel worse about his life.

"No. I'll handle this." The platitude broke from her, weak and reedy. "It's okay."

"To hell it is." His harsh tone cut across the room. "It won't be *okay* if we've just produced another freak like me."

Her hand slipped down to her chest, and she rubbed the heel of her palm over her boney sternum, choking back a sob, thankful that at least she made no sound. As much as she wanted his support, she knew better than to expect any.

"I'm just as responsible. I wanted this. The heat of the moment got to me, that's all." She kept her back to him, cheeks so hot she needed to obscure her face in an attempt to buy time until she could escape. "And we don't know for sure there's any genetic factor to your condition."

Even though her body still pulsed and hummed from the most arousing sex of her life, her thoughts jumbled and flew at her fast. She had no space to worry beyond just how stupidly carried away she'd gotten.

His hand landed on her shoulder. "Look at me."

She jolted at his touch. "No. I need to go."

She shrugged him off before he saw whatever pathetic expression marked her face and stormed toward the bathroom. He stayed silent in her wake, though in all truth, she was thankful she couldn't hear much beyond the pounding of her feet on the wooden boards, minus the sounds of him following.

She got to the bathroom and plonked down onto the closed toilet seat, where a heavy sob tore through her chest and echoed within the small enclosed room. She wriggled free of her underwear and wiped away all evidence of sex. She must have made one pitiful sight.

Her muscles vibrated, weak from adrenaline, but she forced herself up to the mirror, where splotchy marks covered her face. Her eyes were puffy, and her cheeks were red. She'd achieved her goal. Gotten laid. But the spontaneity and frosty outcome proved far more than she'd ever planned on.

She should have been happy—and in all truth, for a brief moment, she had been. He'd made her feel so utterly alive. Given her a profound experience she'd likely never match. But all that was before she realized their grim mistake.

She peered down at her hands, uncertain what to do about the shaking, much less her splotchy face. She'd have to deal with him. He'd take one look at her and know she wasn't handling this "slip up" as well as she pretended.

*Would it kill him to see I'm human?*

Maybe it literally would. And any resulting hurt would be her fault.

*Stupid. Stupid woman.*

She turned on the tap and cupped her hands under the running water, attempting to hold back a great need to vomit the lunch she hadn't even had the chance to make, much less eat.

Even as she washed, new tears sprung free.

*Wait. I'll cry all I want once he's out of this house.*

So, she pulled in a slow breath and tried to forget that she'd jumped in without thinking—made herself vulnerable—jeopardized her fledgling life improvements and sold herself short professionally.

Even though what they'd done wasn't off limits. Even though he said he didn't see anything wrong in their attraction. She had her own limits, and she'd broken them with this exchange.

*What a terrible fall.*

She splashed her face one last time and did a simple calculation.

She was midway through her monthly cycle. The timing was right. Or more precisely, wrong. Either way, she could very well be pregnant. The morning-after pill might have been an option—if she could find a local drug store. But given her past, she just couldn't go down that path. How would she explain an unplanned pregnancy to her mother? Much less her brothers who'd warned her of exactly this? And how would she finish her studies as a single parent, or practice in her chosen field?

Goodbye holiday.

Goodbye clear and easy life plan.

Goodbye to her last throes of youthful spontaneity or freedom.

God, she couldn't think. Had to get out of this room. Get some air. She'd sure as hell made a mess of *spontaneity and freedom*. Maybe she should just fly back to the UK and cancel any final *adventures* in this country.

A light knock sounded at the door. She paused, still not ready to face Orlando.

"Are you okay?"

She squeezed her eyes shut and shook her head. No. No, she really wasn't. And even his question got in the way of her need to hate him right now. He had his hang-ups too. And rightfully so. He deserved a moment to blunder his reaction, his comment about creating "a freak" case in point, but she didn't have the ability to handle him and whatever fevered thoughts entered her head.

She snapped the faucet closed and took one last steadying breath, then opened the door to him standing before her, his espresso-dark eyes dulled slightly. "I've called a taxi. I'll get myself back to the home."

"I can't let you do that." *Though she wanted to.* Not because she thought less of him, but because she simply wanted to hide. To have many, many hours to get her head around what was the second most confusing moment of her life. Her fingers curled tight around the door handle, her tone about as flat and hollow as her heartbeat. "What if something happens to you?"

His attention danced around her face, assessing her, no doubt filtering in the signs of her devastation. His mouth wavered, as though he wanted to say something, but seconds passed, and eventually he frowned. "I'm not totally useless. The center is ten minutes up the road. You have the look of a woman whose life has just ended, and it's my fault. So, I sure as shit don't expect you to drop me off at that pathetic place I call a home."

He turned, and she failed to find it in her to insist on the lift. At the very least, she'd call the home in twenty minutes to ensure he got back safe.

He took only a few paces from her before he spun back around. The tiny muscles in his cheeks softened. "I'm sorry, again. We both need time to think things through." She glanced down at his hands curled into fists at his side. Maybe he too held something back. "The only upside to this whole disaster is I've had every test under the sun. Aside from the potential 'freak factor', you can at least rest easy you haven't caught anything from me today."

She winced at his second reference to his contribution to a child as the freak factor, but she gave a shaky nod, still unable to speak.

He gave her one last long look, and then walked away.

# Chapter Twenty

Orlando pinned his focus on his hands clasped together on the table in the common room. Fifteen minutes had elapsed since the beginning of the volunteer gathering, all while his fellow residents and their volunteers surrounded him, and Sophie was nowhere to be seen.

*Idiot. Isn't this what I wanted?*

And if that wasn't the case, then Sophie leaving to get on with her life sure as shit should have been. He'd made the biggest mistake, and of course she wouldn't want his baby. Then again, maybe everything would be fine. Maybe he hadn't burdened her. Maybe she'd decided to do the smart thing and stay away.

He lifted his gaze, to the room's entrance, where Candice Olsen powered through, pulling a tear-stained Sophie by the crook of an arm.

Candice stopped before his table and nudged Sophie gently forward.

He zeroed a glare at the director, but her expression pinched in equal warning—an uncharacteristic gesture for a woman dedicated to all things compassion and healing.

"Watch your step, Orlando." She turned away, then shot him one more scowl from over her shoulder, leaving Sophie seated across from him.

His heart strained at the red around Sophie's eyes, her face unusually pale, even for her. "What is this? What's happened?"

She pulled her body into a poker-straight stance, shoulders raised and hands squeezed between her tight, blue-denim-covered knees. "I told Ms. Olsen everything. I quit the volunteer program."

His gut churned. His breath momentarily stalled. She really was leaving him. And then, his old friend anger struck like a lightning bolt. "Why the fuck does Candice need to know anything?"

Sophie startled, only for an eerie calm to wash over her. "I'm worried about how what happened between us might affect you. Believe it or not, Candice is on your side."

He glared at her, wanting to get to the real issue here. They had a lot to sort through. Or maybe they didn't. Maybe that's just what he wanted to believe in order to delay letting her go, even though letting her go was the inevitable thing. The best thing.

"I pay Candice to be on my side."

"I feel that in light of what's passed, and this being our last meeting, I should explain myself." She took a shaky breath, as though she held back more tears. "I'm sorry. I just can't escape the feeling that I've used you in some way. I came to Australia with a goal of getting some life experience. For myself, for my work. And one of my goals included meeting men, for..."

She held a hollow look and stared out the window to her right, face crumpled, clearly unable to finish that sentence.

"Well, if it weren't for the disastrous ending to our last encounter..." He gestured down at his body, meaning to lighten the mood, though probably doing the opposite while looking ridiculous. "I'd say, 'use away'."

He narrowed a glare to the wide-eyed gape she lobbed back. He didn't feel used, but his blood near boiled at the mention of other men. That he'd been wrong in his assessment of Miss Neat and Nerdy being somewhat rusty.

Maybe there'd been others directly before him. Maybe she'd leave this room and move on to someone else in her quest for "experience". What she did with her body shouldn't have bothered him. But it did.

His hands clenched, and he struggled to accept the forlorn expression on her face as being anything real. Once again, life and another person were leaving him behind.

He damn well wanted to punch a hole in the nearest wall.

She cleared her throat, as if resetting her composure. "I know why I found myself attracted to you, and I was wrong. As to why you were attracted to me, there's a good chance my therapeutic role has caused something called erotic transference, and—"

"I know what transference is." His voice snapped out, and the sick sensation in his gut turned into a rolling ball of white-hot anger. "I was a fireman, remember? I have a basic understanding of psychology. I know about hero worship. How people get romantic delusions and attachments to those administering assistance. And for the record, that's not me."

She blinked at him, either to gain a moment to regroup, or to provide him time to calm down. Which wasn't about to happen. "Yes, but—"

"I resent you implying that I lack the self-awareness to know whether I have feelings for an idolized version of you or not." The raspy strain in his voice rose. "That I'm a passive victim who can't see who you are beyond how you meet my needs. I know you. I know exactly why I did what I did. We talked about consent and how cognizant I was, remember? You're taking the coward's way out. You're leaving now because whatever passed between us has you scared."

Her mouth fell open, but no words came. His cheeks burned, and he had a sudden sense that everyone was listening. Well, if they did, he didn't care. He'd alluded to having feelings for her, when in reality, he was falling in love. What a shit of a moment to realize *that*.

For the first time in a long time, shame sent tingles down the back of his neck. Shame. An emotion afforded to those with something to lose in the first place.

*But I do have something to lose now. Don't I?*

Heavy silence settled between them. Her mouth wavered, while his heart seemed to stop altogether. If she asked him to elaborate on his feelings, he'd deny everything and claim a slip of the tongue.

Did he really love Sophie Tindall?

She took a sharp breath, as though her senses returned. "I just want to know you'll be okay."

The way her gaze flittered around his face, brows pressed together, complexion pale. She knew something.

Maybe she sensed just how dark his thoughts got at times. He'd been stupid enough to admit to her that her regular visits gave him something to look forward to. Clearly, the unintended shift in responsibility weighed heavy now she planned to leave.

Then again, anger wouldn't help here. It never had where she was concerned, and he didn't want anger to be his parting gift.

"You know my story doesn't end well." He softened his tone, willing his taut muscles to release. "Given your career choice, you should get used to bad endings."

He'd seen enough death and tragedy to know. Poor Sophie had little idea just how much her career would change her. How others' pain could seep into her bones, and she'd wear that pain wherever she went. One day, much of the hope and innocence he adored about her would be replaced with cold reality, like a bitter poison winding through her system. And one day, she'd wake to a sense of merely passing through, a sense those outside of her job wouldn't understand. They'd call her pessimistic. Tell her to lighten up. But then she'd learn to build her own defenses against it all. Just as he had.

*And everyone would always assume she was okay, when maybe she wasn't.*

She gave a shaky nod, and a tear spilled down her cheek. The first actual tear she'd allowed him to witness. "This is for the best, isn't it?"

"Yeah." He gave a weak smile, though the lump in his throat made speaking hard.

He drank in every last detail of her face. The ill-deserved concern dilating those mottled brown, gold, and green eyes. The downturn of her peach-pink lips. The wisps of hair kissing her cheekbones. It hurt to look at her too long, to know she'd soon turn and leave.

She bit her lower lip and nodded again, her hands unfolding to reveal a piece of paper tucked within her palm. "I have something for you."

She slid the paper over the table toward him, the table itself an unnecessary barrier between them. A barrier he wanted to push aside so he could take her in his arms one last time. But even that would send them backwards, when he really just needed to be thankful for the physical distance and let her go.

He scowled down at the folded page, unwilling to touch it lest it be another thing to draw him to her. "What is it?"

"I figured since this is goodbye, it wouldn't make much difference to reveal the extent of my meddling." She jutted her chin out toward the page. "These are the contact details for Professor Faith Bandara, a neuropsychopharmacologist. I pulled some strings with my professors back home, and they recommended her above anyone else. She specializes in the effects of drugs and various chemicals and compounds on cells. She's brilliant and practices in Melbourne, and she's willing to dig deeper into your case."

His shoulders drew together, and he pushed the paper back toward her. "You're right, this is meddling. It's also patronizing. I don't want your professor."

She frowned and pushed the paper back. "Keep it anyway. She's only willing to look into your case with your consent. If you change your mind, she'll start out with an assessment and some initial pathology, but it's really up to you to get the ball rolling. I can't do anything more."

"I never asked you to do a damn thing for me in the first place." Though he did want things from her now, things that were more important than chasing down another dead-end doctor. "In fact, I expressly told you I've been through all of this with a million other doctors."

Her new frown dragged deeper than the last. "I might be leaving your life, but there's no reason you can't still get help. Please don't make this an ugly ending."

He reached out his hand and slapped it over the piece of paper on the table, then dragged the page back toward him, closing his grasp to scrunch the page. An immature, childish, and dismissive gesture, sure, but she'd been right about him not appreciating her meddling, much less that this ruined what could have been a heartfelt goodbye. "Happy now?"

Another flash of pale displeasure streaked across her face. "Since you're set on ending things this way, maybe you can answer me one last question?"

He released a grumble, suddenly wanting her to put him out of his pain and just leave already. "What?"

"If getting better were an option… If tomorrow you woke up with a different future ahead of you… What dreams would you have for yourself?"

He reeled back. "What sort of a fucked-up question is that?"

"You had dreams once, yes?" She merely returned his glare with a weak smile. "They were enough to make you strike out of this town and embark on a life of your own making. What were they?"

He raised both hands and pointed out the room. "Look around you, Sophie. Look at how I live. Look at *where* I live. The only dream anyone in this place has is that the end comes soon, and it isn't too painful. Whatever dreams I had are moot, now."

He leaned in and summoned all the ice he could into his stare, raising his hand with the paper still crumpled in it. "And if your conversation on dreams is a lead-in to tell me that this scrap of paper here is the answer to all my prayers…" He shook his head slowly. If he was going to let her go, then he'd make damn sure she had every reason to leave and zero reason to come back. He owed her that. He owed it to himself too. "Then save the bullshit and do as I ask. Just go."

A few seconds passed before his abrasiveness hit its target. She gave a single, solid nod and launched to her feet. "You're a hypocrite. You accuse me of being condescending, Orlando Piras, but you're the king-of-all-things condescension. And I'm almost certain that was the case before you ended up here. I've only ever tried to help you—to do exactly what I promised the day I walked through those doors and got lumped with your sorry ass."

She pointed to the main doors, doors she'd any minute now walk through, never to return. Her hands curled at her sides, and her cheeks glowed a furious red.

"And you, I might be carrying your child, and all you can do is grumble and sulk and attack. You want to fool everyone here into thinking you're some unshakeable tough guy, but I've seen you ruffled.

As much as you think you know me, I know you too. You're really just chicken-shit scared, so much so, you can't make one easy phone call in a final effort to save your own life." Angry tears streamed down her cheeks. "I might not be the worldliest person ever, but unlike you, I try. And I don't give up on people. I tried here. I really did try. Your mum was right. At some point long before your condition, you decided you weren't going to let anyone in. So, bravo, Orlando. You've made a fool of us both."

Her voice ricocheted off the walls, and the common room lay inordinately silent. All eyes had turned to her. She swiped at her tears with the heel of her hand. Only then did her glare break from him long enough to take in the room.

But her watery expression didn't waver, and for the first time ever, she seemed unaffected by what others thought. She gave him one last crumpled glance and turned in a marching gait for the exit.

The sight of her back made her leaving more real. Instinct took control, and he launched to his feet. "Sophie."

She swung around. Eyes wild and demanding he not stop her. "I'll be in touch if there's any news about our slip-up the other day, but you're right, we're better off not knowing each other." Her face scrunched, indicating another wave of hurt took over. "I was an idiot to believe I could make a difference here."

She clapped her hand over her mouth, and her shoulders shuddered. And just like that, she turned and raced out the door—a woman holding back her cry long enough to leave him.

# Chapter Twenty-One

"Put the phone away."

Sophie followed Agathe's order and pressed the hang-up button on her phone. "I was just about to—"

"Nope. It's not enough." Agathe sat across the table at the harborside bar, chin dipped low, the reflective light from the water behind her illuminating her brown skin a lustrous gold. She outstretched a hand. "I need you to hand the whole phone over. Now. Otherwise, we have no chance of enjoying this weekend."

Sophie groaned. "Fine. But I want it noted that Hannah called me, and your phone hasn't stopped dinging since we left Melbourne."

She slapped the phone into Agathe's hand. Impromptu weekend in Sydney or not, nothing could distract from all things Orlando.

Agathe held her giant, multi-colored purse agape and dropped the phone inside with extra ceremony. "What can I say? Luke's a stresshead, and he wants to know every detail about how me and this baby are doing. Besides, Hannah's call was merely my tipping point. Whatever redemption you're looking for is not gonna happen on that little device. He's gone, Sophie. In fact, you're the one who did the leaving. Remember?"

"I know." Sophie peered down at the bright yellow mocktail—a fancy word for fruit juice and soda water—the one she'd ordered under the pretense of supporting Agathe on her alcohol-free weekend. She hadn't found the strength to break it to her new friend that she might not be the only pregnant woman at the table.

"Anyway, since I've had to marvel at the harbor view alone while you wrapped up that long-winded conversation, maybe you can tell me who Hannah is." Agathe's deep-brown eyes sparkled against the midday sun. "Oh, and Randal, and Hector. I had no idea Miss Sophie Tindall came with a past."

*A past?* Sophie's breaths tightened. She didn't just have a past. For a time there, she'd had a whole other existence few knew about. Not even Hannah. And history seemed set on repeating. She swatted a hand in dismissal. Yet another thing she couldn't get into with Agathe.

"It's not as exciting as you think. Hannah is my best friend and housemate. Hector is my ex-boyfriend. He's a nice guy, but our relationship fizzled. And Randal Berry—" She let loose with a strained laugh. How could she have ever been so silly? "Randal lives in my building. I had a mini crush on him, and Hannah likes to give me updates on his love life, but…"

Sophie pressed her lips together, not quite sure how to finish that sentence.

Agathe stabbed a straw at her drink, ice cubes clinking. "But let me guess, you forgot he existed the second you met Orlando?"

Sophie's heart slowed to a heavy, plodding beat. She frowned at the severe accuracy in Agathe's guess, thinking deeper on her time in Australia thus far. How she'd assumed Orlando's lure had crept up on her, but a closer look revealed an attraction had existed from day one.

"And Hector too. I forgot about him, too, despite how long we were together and how much I sympathized over the way that relationship ended. It's as if I met Orlando, and everything else faded." She buried her face in her hands. "Urghhh… I'm such a wooly-brained idiot."

She lifted her gaze to Agathe's reassuring smile. "It happens to the best of us."

"No, this stuff never happens to me. The vast majority of my adult life has been dedicated to study. To making one well-thought-out decision after another." She lifted her hand to her face again. Her cheeks burned, the pleasant, midday sun suddenly too hot and muggy on her skin. "The more I think about what I did, the more I uncover just how much damage I've inflicted on our lives."

Agathe shook her head through an uncomfortably long silence.

"What?" Sophie frowned. "What is it?"

Agathe shrugged and picked up her glass again. "This is going to be one long and dull weekend if you don't loosen up quick-smart, especially since there's not a drop of alcohol between us." She held her glass higher, inspecting the near glowing contents. "And since I'm the one who's engaged, I'll need you to carry the baton for us both. So, I have just one question for you…" She lowered her glass to the table and shot Sophie a sly grin. "Which one do you prefer, Blondie or Mr. Tall, Dark, and probably Loaded?"

Agathe gave a small nod toward a blond, surfer-looking waiter and then an immaculate-looking businessman, with deeply tanned skin and a navy-blue suit.

Sophie felt her eyes pull wide, and she hunched over the table to whisper, "You don't seriously expect me to hook up with some stranger while wallowing over Orlando?" She peered over at the men, her stomach flipping at the mere thought of approaching either one of them. "Besides, you make it sound like they don't even get a choice."

"Nooooo." Agathe's smile broadened, eyes sparkling anew. "I said nothing about hooking up, though I won't tell anyone back home if that's what you do." She wiggled back in her seat. Too cool. Too confident… Or at least for Sophie's liking. "Just give one of them your number. The sole benefit of me having to endure your long chat with Hannah was that I got to watch both dudes checking you out. So, don't you worry about their choices. Hell, give both of them your number, if that's what'll pull you out of this slump."

Sophie crossed her arms and leaned back in her chair. "You can't be serious."

"Serious about us having fun this weekend? Hells yes." Agathe patted her tiny baby bump. "I'm on borrowed time here. So as much as I want to support you, you better believe I intend to enjoy my last shreds of freedom before this little one arrives. And I'm certainly not going to let you kill the vibe with your broken-hearted act. You need this just as much as I do. Maybe more."

Sophie stared down at her abandoned drink, and mumbled, "It's not an act."

"Whatever." Agathe swatted a hand. "So, here's step one of my plan. You go over to one of those gorgeous men and slip them your number. You know, just to prove your heartsick little self can do it and that a world of men still exists beyond Orlando, Hector, and Robert—"

"Randal."

"Whatever. I'm pregnant, and my brain can't keep up with you." Agathe swatted her hand again. "Anyway, you can slip those two hotties your number, *or* you can spill the beans to me about your Orlando drama. I know you've been holding out on the details. I figure if you release some of those icky sads holding you back, you'll start enjoying yourself again."

Sophie tucked her chin in and scowled at Agathe through her lashes. "Everything I know about mental health tells me your ultimatum is a really bad idea."

Agathe pointed a finger, smile still firmly in place. "Yes, but it's better than whatever you're doing now, right? And judging by the color in your cheeks, I'd say you're already feeling a tad better. So, what's your choice?"

Sophie huffed out a weak laugh, her focus falling to Blondie and then Mr. Tall, Dark, and Probably Loaded. For a long moment, she contemplated saying nothing—that perhaps the simplest course of action would be to hand out her number and deal with the potential calls later. But a new sense of guilt flared, green-lighting the probability she'd be surrendering to easy escape; in other words, keeping quiet to avoid speaking on what bothered her most about all that had passed between her and Orlando.

A tight band squeezed around her chest, good old guilt rearing again. Afternoon sunlight passed through the glass before her, reflecting rainbow fractals across the table. The vibrant colors helped to distract, ever so slightly, from the tension in her body. Would Agathe judge her if she knew everything? Maybe. But there was at least one thing she could say for herself.

"While I sit here with you in a different city, lapping up a beautiful day on the harbor, with plans for a civilized night at the ballet, Orlando sits within the same stale walls he's been in for the last two years. The same walls I left him in. The walls he now can't escape because I'm not there to help." A lump formed at the base of her throat, the surrounding muscles seeming to swell further, while no amount of swallowing erased her discomfort. "There are so many unfair things about his world, and for a brief moment, it was my job to bring some kind of happiness to his life. I failed him. Not only did I fail him, I was the one who always had the privilege to walk away. And I did. I walked. I practically ran. I added to his burdens, and then I ran."

Her chin trembled, but she clenched her jaw long enough to regain composure.

Agathe reached out a hand and placed it over Sophie's. "But it sounds as though you did improve his life. He accepted your help when at first he wouldn't. It seems he changed a little for the better. And then you found that professor willing to help him, right?" She gave a half smile as if to offer reassurance. "He made progress, and that's easier said than done. I put up one heck of a fight when Luke urged me to get help. Hell, we busted up over it too. You have no idea where your influence will lead Orlando. Maybe his life will continue to improve from having known you."

Sophie shook her head. "I don't think so. Orlando was right when he said the referral to the professor is a long shot. And if that's the only thing I helped him with, it's not much. I expended so much energy defending my interferences when he really just needed support."

"Okay, sure. Let's say you screwed up, which I don't entirely think you did." Agathe shrugged. "But what more can you do now? You offered him the professor, and he threw that idea in your face. Meanwhile, you're twisting yourself in knots over a bust up with no remedy, which by the way, I'm still unclear why exactly you two are fighting to begin with."

Sophie felt her hairline prickle with sweat. Though Agathe knew she and Orlando had had an encounter, Sophie still couldn't bring herself to share the whole story about her potential pregnancy. "I know. I know. And the silliest thing is, I'll have to deal with combative patients like him in the future. So, the fact I'm struggling so much to let this one go—the fact I couldn't even carry out a volunteer position without getting things so incredibly wrong, only makes me think I've wasted all my years of study on an ill-suited career."

Agathe scooped up her drink and toyed with it. "Yeah well, I mean, I'm sure the whole getting it on with a patient is a huge no-no if you're their actual psychiatrist, but that wasn't the case here, right? There was always a personal element to your work with Orlando, though maybe neither of you banked on just how personal things would get." She paused to sip on her drink. "You're not the type to make rash decisions, Sophie. And almost no one is immune to being swept away, not when there's someone they truly connect with. I was so angry and forcibly alone for years before I met Luke, and as much as I fought to stay away from him..." She smiled, sudden light entering her expression. "We ended up together, anyway."

Sophie's mind filled with the sounds of people talking and the rumbling of a passenger ferry on the harbor. She wanted to give in to Agathe optimism, but just couldn't. "That's not going to happen with Orlando and I, even without factoring in his condition. I love living in London. I want to finish my studies. Either way, I'm returning home when this holiday ends."

Agathe scooted closer, brows pulling down in clear sympathy. "Sure, but my point is, Orlando is a bloody gorgeous man, close to your age, with an incredibly sad story. You'd be a lacking human being if something about the people you encountered didn't affect you from time to time. And"—she pointed a finger as if to demand more attention—"he voiced a clear attraction to you from the very beginning, before you ever knew his deal or became his volunteer. You know, when he tried to set up on that bogus date. Don't forget that. And you felt the same attraction for him, otherwise you wouldn't have said yes to that same bogus date." She dropped back into her chair, point made. "Accept this experience for what it is and find a way to forgive yourself. Take it from someone who knows, second-guessing your past will only swallow your future."

Sophie drew small circles with her fingertip on the white-linen tablecloth, as an even sadder realization settled in.

When it came to Orlando, she simply wouldn't get the closure she desired. No ballet or fancy bar would save her from knowing Orlando was right. His life would have no happy ending. With or without her in it.

And maybe he'd been right about another thing. Maybe her meddling did come with an ulterior motive—her wanting to avoid the cold, hard truth that someone as vivid and vital as him could still meet a cruel and early end.

There'd be no silver lining. No absolution for what he'd endured.

Certainly nothing for them as a couple.

Now, all she had left was uncertainty over her immediate circumstances, and a sickening sense this whole holiday had turned out to be far from the fun "shake up" she'd wished for.

"There's that sullen look again." Agathe huffed out a sigh, "Clearly, this talk has done nothing to improve your merry-making abilities."

Agathe dug around in her bag, the coin fringe tinkling, her phone in her hand within seconds.

Sophie frowned, her heart entrapped. "What have I done now? What are you doing?"

"First, I'm putting out a social media post asking if any of my Sydney-sider friends want free tickets to the ballet tonight." She tapped away at the screen, a bright and mischievous smile pulling at her cheeks. "And then I'm going to find out what's shaking over on Oxford Street."

The heat returned to bother Sophie's cheeks, and her stomach roiled in protest. Despite her mood, she'd been looking forward to the ballet. "Oxford Street? What's on Oxford Street?"

Agathe's dark eyes glittered as if she'd morphed into some kind of evil genius. "Drag queens. Male strip shows. And since I can't drink, and you won't, watching other people get absolutely obliterated." She returned to her phone, shimmying her shoulders in a little dance to go with her monologue about drag queens and male strippers. "You'll love it."

≈

Orlando lay in bed while the not-so-muffled murmurs of a volunteer meeting traveled down the hallway. He let out a heavy sigh and rolled his eyes, fixing his stare to the beige ceiling.

He'd missed two volunteer meetings so far, with zero interest in joining another, not since he'd finally succeeded in driving Sophie away. He didn't want a new volunteer. He'd learned his lesson. Never again.

And even if his budding psychiatrist did return, his condition and inability to offer more than a few good times and a bucket load of regret meant he couldn't speak to her again. He'd done enough damage. He needed to let her move on.

A hard knock came at his door, but he made no effort to respond.

The door handle squeaked, and soon the whole thing swung open. Candice Olsen stood over him, hands fisted on her hips. "Ignoring me won't make me go away."

"What if I outright *told* you to go away? Would that work?" He turned his attention from her searing judgment and back to his neutral ceiling.

"Oh, hahaha, Romeo." Her dull and stagnated tone held no real humor. "It's been more than a week since you and Juliet put on your woeful, *star-crossed-lovers* act. Are you going to hide in this room forever?"

"I'm not hiding." He ignored her dig at his last-ever encounter with Sophie—an encounter that had indeed been woeful and way too public for his liking.

"Really?" Candice leaned over and stuck her face in his line of sight. "Then what are you doing? Meditating?"

He let out a sarcastic laugh, eyeballing her back. "No. I'm giving up."

A long pause filled the room. Sure, his words were dramatic, but they'd sure as fuck mess with Candice.

Her small flinch indicated he'd achieved his goal, but judging by the twisting pain in his chest, maybe his lie about giving up did hold some morsel of truth. That he'd given Sophie a piece of his heart without even knowing.

He raised a brow, a gesture designed to throw Candice off the topic of his wellbeing. "Sophie told me you know everything about our time together. Don't tell me you want a recap of the gory details?"

Candice leaned back, expression flat. "Funny. I can't say I'm happy about the extra drama your showdown brought around here, but you're a grown man, and not the first resident we've had pair off with a volunteer. Though the last couple to do that got married rather than fall just short of clawing each other's eyes out. Despite your condition, Orlando, you're hardheaded enough to leave no doubt you were a willing participant in whatever relationship developed between you and Sophie."

He kept his flat stare trained on her, pretending her less-than-professional description of his personality didn't bother him. "It wasn't a relationship, Candice. It was fucking."

She grimaced, before settling on a pinched glare. "Yeah, sure. I saw the look in your eyes when she asked what your dreams were. The woman got to you. Even blind Mr. Larson up the hall could see that. And now, I'm left with the sole job of diverting your crusade to spend the last years of your life moping over her."

"Is that why you've come to bother me today?"

She lowered her chin, as if to say, *What do you think, dipshit?*

"Right." He returned his focus to the ceiling, ignoring the fact Candice was right and so was Sophie. That his injury was not the sole cause of his isolation. That he didn't want anyone getting too close to him. And he truly hadn't. Not until her. "What I do with my 'last years' is none of your business."

"Wrong." Candice pointed a finger and leaned forward enough to loom over him. "What you do is precisely my business: mine, my staff, and every poor sod who has to deal with you. And we're all worried about you. We've been worried for a long time, way before Sophie happened. We've all jumped hurdles to keep you here and help your family, you're just too knuckleheaded to see it. We thought you were making great strides with Sophie in your life. She was the best volunteer we've had for a long time. But of course, just like all the others, you had to push her out the door. So, call my presence right now whatever you want. Me, I'm calling this an intervention before we all do truly give up on your sorry ass."

*Intervention?* A cold sensation ran down his body, but he refused to let her see how much her intervention bothered him. As if losing Sophie didn't hurt enough. He'd let her leave, believing she'd made no difference to his life.

The biggest kicker? Sophie Tindall *was* the difference. Even just the fact he'd allowed her enough access to his world to *make* that difference…

Now he just wanted to be alone. To wallow in his loneliness. Striking up more concern would not help his goal.

"Aren't you supposed to be on my side here? You know, offering me warm milk and cookies in light of me getting dumped and all?" He gave Candice a hard glare, the untruthful kind that mirrored everyone's impression of him being *knuckleheaded*, pretending he'd be just fine.

She let out a sigh, like she saw through his act. "I would if you made an attempt to show you cared. We've tried being on your side and look at you." She held a hand out, gesturing at his supine position on the bed. "So, have it your way, Orlando. I'm cutting you loose from the volunteer program. I'll stop trying to convince you to interact with the outside world. If you want to stay in your room and brood until your last dying day, who am I to stop you? But if you really did ever give two hoots about that poor woman, then the least you can do is call the number on the paper she left for you." She pointed to the torn page still sitting on his bedside table. "Call the last professional willing to put themselves out there to help you."

"And why would I do that?"

"Because you love Sophie."

"I told you." He put on a snarky grin. "It was just fucking."

Candice merely blinked at him and held a short silence. "You think a few swear words will throw me? I hear worse from Mrs. Boyle when I demand she take a shower, and that's on one of her more pleasant days. Save your energy and stop wasting everyone's time."

She gave him one final death stare and shook her head as if to say, *I can't believe what an asshole you're being.* "If you really didn't care, then you wouldn't still be holding onto that piece of paper. And now that you've had a chance to mope over the loss of your girlfriend, maybe you could help us all by trying to get better for a change."

Candice turned and left, falling just short of slamming the door behind her. He stifled the urge to yell out. To make some joke about how the paper only remained at his side because of the center's shitty housekeeping.

But genuine pain swelled deep beneath his ribcage and pulled him up short.

He looked about him. At the empty room. Symbolic of everything missing in his life. For weeks, Sophie's unrelenting presence had urged him on. But now, he had Candice and her all-too-clear message. He'd disappointed everyone. He was a man-sized vacuum sucking up all the air wherever he went.

And somehow, he now had even less than before.

Sophie had offered change. She'd offered hope. That day in her kitchen, she'd given him back a piece of himself. Not just because of the sex, but from the way she'd looked at him. Her unwavering stare. Her open vulnerability. Her trust. Like she saw him as a man, not a problem.

And then there'd been something more, a kind of acceptance, as though she didn't just see him as a man, but she saw *him*.

He turned his head toward the torn page and pushed down a desire to skim his finger over her handwriting for the millionth time.

A rip ran along the page's edge. A rip he'd caused while losing his temper, as well as the unmistakable anguish that had filled her eyes as she'd run from him.

But despite what anyone insisted, he had no business in messing with change or hope. And because he had none of either, he'd dashed her hopes, too.

He dragged at his next breath, and sadness burrowed ever deeper. Maybe he couldn't have her, but he did still owe her for the differences she had made. And maybe, just maybe, he owed himself.

He'd spent decades denying it, but he did have a dream. A dream of finding someone like Sophie.

And now that he'd found her, maybe it was time he imposed on her life the way she'd imposed on his.

# Chapter Twenty-Two

"Your volunteer gig went bust two weeks ago. Why are you still living Roseford? Come back to Melbourne with me."

"You're right." Sophie peered over at Luke in her kitchen, one hip leaned against the counter, a beer in his hand, while she constructed a salad for their lunch. "I have no reason to stay in Roseford, it's just—"

"Let me guess." The silver kettle dinged behind her, and he disappeared for a moment to pour hot water into a waiting tea cup. "You're hoping things will turn around with that Orlando guy?"

She frowned and pointed at her brother. "That was *not* what I was going to say."

He gave her a silent look, one that hinted at disbelief.

"I enjoy having my own space." She focused on seasoning the salad, careful to use chili instead of pepper like Luke preferred. "What with two rowdy brothers growing up, and then nosy Hannah as a housemate, this is the first time in my life I've had an entire house to myself."

"Hey." Luke stabbed a teaspoon in her direction. "I wasn't 'rowdy' and as I recall, I was off on active duty those last few years you were at home. You should have had heaps of peace there. And I thought you liked Hannah, so what makes her so nosy?"

"Sorry, you're right. I do like Hannah." A slow grin pushed at her cheeks, and she shook her head at the emerging salad, as if it might somehow understand what she'd meant. "But I enjoy having a crack at a life where I have to navigate all challenges for myself. You know what I mean?"

He offered a gentle smile, one that showed just how much her older brother had changed in the years since he'd left the British military. He'd checked out a hardened and confused man, only to start a successful tech company and find love in Australia. "Yeah, I do. And if you really want to continue the self-discovery thing, I'm happy to set you up with a place of your own in the city too. You're not limited to Roseford."

Now that things had ended with Orlando, and they'd had zero contact in two weeks, perhaps the time had come to spend her remaining weeks in Australia closer to the action in Melbourne.

She washed her hands in the sink and returned Luke's smile, truly grateful to have someone to count on. "Thank you, I'll think about it."

"Listen, Soph. I didn't drive here just to nag you into coming back to Melbourne." He added some milk to the teacup and placed it beside her, then stepped back, a slight rosiness spreading across his cheek. "Agathe told me about how broken up you are over Orlando. I wanted to check you're okay."

She held back a chuckle at her brother and his clear discomfort in addressing his little sister's love life.

"I knew that free trip to Sydney would come with a catch." Despite the subject matter, she couldn't resist the chance to have fun at his expense. "Did Agathe also tell you about our exploits at that club on Oxford Street? The drag queen show, the male striptease act, our invitation to hang out with the guys backstage afterward..."

Luke's expression sagged, his brilliant green eyes turning dark. "No, she didn't tell me any of that. She's smart enough to understand there are limits to how much I want to know."

She laughed, impressed with her brother's ability to ignore the wilder details of his wife and sister's interstate adventure. Her time in Sydney helped with her goal of learning to loosen up, whilst gaining a break from all the Orlando drama. And she wanted a break now more than ever.

She'd was due to take a pregnancy test in the next few days, though she tried not to overthink that detail or what she'd do if she turned in a positive result.

Every small churn in her belly, every instance of exhaustion, played on her mind as a possible sign of early pregnancy.

Luke took a sip of his beer, his gaze not once leaving her. "But let's make one thing clear. I don't like Orlando." She flinched at the bold statement—exactly the words she didn't need to hear in light of her predicament. "He's damaged, and worse, from what I hear, he's been cold toward you. I don't see any future in whatever you two shared."

Her body felt hot and her mouth dry. Luke meant well, but he overstepped with his criticism of Orlando, a man he'd never even met. "That's a patronizing statement if ever I heard one. And who decided I was looking for a future?"

He paused his beer bottle at his lips, half-choking in a loud spluttering cough. He placed the bottle on the counter, whilst pressing his rolled-up sleeve over his mouth.

"If your defense is that you were just looking for a good time, you could have had that with anyone other than your volunteering resident." He cleared his throat, still struggling with the aftermath of his wayward mouthful of beer. "And despite your shock tactics, you don't fool me. You're much too cut up about this whole thing ending."

She shrugged a shoulder and went about prodding at the salad with a pair of metal tongs. "Fine. Maybe Orlando was a little more than a 'good time', but who are you to talk about damaged? Weren't you the one who went off the wall after your military service? And then there's Agathe. You said yourself she had a lot to work through when you two first met."

"Off the wall?" Luke let out a derisive laugh. "As a would-be psychiatrist, I think your terminology needs improvement. And as for Agathe, I'll be the first to admit working through her stuff nearly ended us." His voice tapered off, gaze slipping from her and over to a vase of plastic sunflowers on the counter. "It wasn't an easy time. I don't want the same for you."

She dipped her chin and inspected the ground between them. "I know. But despite all of that, Orlando's still a good guy dropped into a terrible situation. Before things turned sour between us, he'd displayed genuine change and lost that coldness you mentioned. He was funny and playful and would have had far more in common with you than you think. He's the type of person to throw himself on the line if called to do so. I'd appreciate it if everyone just took a step back and cut him some slack."

She lifted her gaze to her brother, his bottle-green stare searching hers. "Sure, I get it, but by the time I met Agathe, the worst of her damage had already occurred. Your guy is still drowning in the thick of it." Luke towered over her, so tall despite her being related to him and a total short stack. He sidled up to her, his hand patting her upper back in a seeming attempt to soothe. "Just tell me you'll be careful."

She gave her brother a quick nod, her throat contracting over her ability to form words. No matter his blunt approach, he only looked out for her.

"Neither of us have anything to worry about, okay? I haven't spoken to Orlando in two weeks, and I don't plan on changing that. And I have every intention of returning to the UK. I'm not giving up on my studies for anyone, 'damaged' or not. I've worked too hard and for too long."

She took the salad to her kitchen table and sat. Luke must have been satisfied with her assertion, because he said nothing else and followed to take a seat across from her.

They ate in comfortable silence, while she contemplated that perhaps his instincts to protect her were right, even if he hadn't been there to witness the full impact of her past. His work overseas had left him unable to save her from her bad choices back then, both when she'd been younger and in more recent years with Hector. Not that it had been his job to save her. But his concern now felt like a loving hug softening the crush of all things hurtful.

If only there'd been less of an age gap. If only she'd had him around all those other times she needed help.

Her phone rang, and she pulled it from her jeans pocket, still chewing as she answered. "Hello?"

"I got a call from Professor Bandara."

Adrenaline rushed her body. Her heart swelled within her chest—medically impossible given the circumstances—but something felt awry in there all the same. She regretted having been too lost in her thoughts to check her caller I.D.

"I need to show for an emergency appointment this afternoon." Orlando's unmistakable gravel pulled her from further analyzing the strange workings of her heart. "I'm not going alone. You're coming with me."

Her chin wavered, and involuntary tingles washed over her skin.

Eventually, she managed a breathy, "What?"

"Your professor had me do some blood tests. She wants to see me about the results." The matter-of-fact tone. The one with the slightly annoyed edge. *So, Orlando.* She wanted to dance. She wanted to cry. "You got me into this. I'm sure as heck not going alone."

Sophie squeezed her eyes shut and shook her head, the shock refusing to recede. "I can't go with you."

The desire was there. But she just couldn't.

"Why not?" His voice rose. Hard. Angry. Abrupt.

Luke tilted his head and mouthed, "You okay?"

She waved a hand—a sign for him to not worry.

"You know why not." And with that first bit of reasoning, her rational thought flowed smoother. "We can't see each other. Why don't you get your mother to go along?"

Luke lowered his cutlery to the table, denoting he'd figured out who she spoke to.

A terse laugh cracked into her ear. "Because your professor has either good news or bad news, and Roseford Aged Care doesn't keep hard alcohol on hand to help me deal with whichever type of news this is. Plus, someone in my position can't be expected to also deal with whatever my mum's reaction might be either way. It has to be you."

"Well… what about one of the nurses?" A small tremor worked its way into her fingers holding the phone, though she couldn't pinpoint if from Orlando's insistence or Luke's now-seething scowl. "Surely, they'll have to organize a car to drive you to your appointment in the city, anyway?"

He released a heavy sigh. "Look, I'm not getting any staff to take me. You're the one who pushed for this, Sophie. The one who found Professor Bandara. I would have thought you'd want to see this through. Call it part of your research. Aren't you interested to know how this all ends?"

She bit the inside of her cheek, holding back from pointing out she'd already *seen things through* two weeks ago by ending whatever volatile relationship they'd shared. Hadn't passing on the professor's details been her parting gift?

But then again…

She'd also done a lot of legwork researching Orlando's past, visiting Aero Syntech, finding the professor, and then getting her onboard. And Orlando was right. She *was* interested in how this would all play out… In her role as a medical student, of course… Not as someone in any way still attracted to Orlando Piras.

What if she encountered another patient like him one day?

Plus, she'd never met a neuropsychopharmacologist before. Especially not one as esteemed as Professor Bandara. She'd be giving up a hugely unique chance at gaining more knowledge.

And despite the strained relationship, whatever news the professor had to share might have big implications. She couldn't leave Orlando to deal with this alone.

"Okay, fine." She ground the words out, already certain she'd made the wrong choice. "I'll go with you."

"Great." A loud knock sounded at the front of her house. "Let's go."

She startled, her attention shooting to her front door. "You're not outside already, are you?"

"Yep. Like I said, let's go." His voice projected in stereo, his warm timbre rumbling through her phone and again from outside.

"What? Right now?"

"Right now. Open the door."

She shot to standing, and her focus hit Luke. He gave her a side-long glare.

She turned and marched across the room to the front door, her brother's thudding footsteps close behind.

By the time she opened the door, Orlando had his back to her and his arm raised, waving off a taxi. He spun around, and her heart gave a painful palpitation against the ache of seeing him again—of knowing in that moment just how much she'd missed him. Even though she most definitely shouldn't have.

"I'll wait here if you need a few minutes." His tone softened along with his gaze.

Rigidity ran across his shoulders and along the strained and ropey muscles at the front of his neck—like he hadn't forgotten what had transpired the last time he'd entered her house. Like he wanted to avoid making that mistake again.

His impossibly dark gaze flicked to a point behind her. She turned to Luke standing over her shoulder, glaring at Orlando, jaw muscle ticking and cheeks taut, and a burning glare that said, *You broke my sister's heart. I want to break your face.*

But she'd been just as much to blame. Probably more. And Orlando didn't deserve any retribution. Only Luke, in all his loyalty, didn't seem to care. She couldn't leave these two men alone. So, she presented her brother with a beseeching look and gave up on the idea of finishing her lunch or taking a moment to change her worn jeans and faded black t-shirt.

She offered Luke a weak smile. "You'll be okay to lock up, won't you?"

# Chapter Twenty-Three

"I've been thinking about the end." Orlando eyed Sophie, her fingers white-knuckled around the steering wheel. They'd been driving for twenty minutes, and still neither had said anything. "This isn't how I want to go."

His throat constricted even as he admitted that, but he needed to show her he was trying.

She glanced his way before refocusing on the road. "I need you to define what exactly 'this' is?"

He looked ahead, ignoring the pit opening up in his stomach. From experience, specialists only ever took emergency bookings when they had news—good or bad—not to share they'd merely found nothing. The importance of his fast-approaching meeting with Professor Bandara weighted heavy on every breath he drew.

"I mean freezing people out, giving up, making rash decisions. I want to stop doing all of that." He swallowed at the knot in his throat, voice thick and syrupy as he tried his damnedest to hold on to his thoughts; all while he searched for the words to explain himself to this woman he'd tried so hard to shut out. "And you. More than anything I regret how I've treated you."

A short laugh shot from her mouth. "And forcing me to drive you to the city after I ended things doesn't count as a rash decision?"

"No." He thought of all the things that had brought him to this moment. Candice dressing him down. His subsequent call to Professor Bandara. The phone assessments, blood tests, and then the call this morning. And of course, now, him taking this chance to rope Sophie in on a city-bound road trip. "Me calling you wasn't rash, it was a tactical decision. Walking out on you after we'd made love, losing my cool when you decided to ditch me, now *that* was rash. Trying to make things right, isn't."

Her attention stayed on the road ahead. Nothing about her still demeanor revealed much of her thoughts. "I'm not sure I'd call what we did *making love*. And you walking away that day didn't hurt me so much as my own lapse in judgment. And I'm not totally sure I regret ditching you."

Strain compressed around his ribcage, and he pulled at the car's seatbelt that suddenly sat too tight, or maybe it was his shirt. But he didn't wear tight shirts, so it must have been just him. He didn't want to believe she had no regrets. Because he sure as hell did. And he missed her. Not just the physical attraction, or even the outings, but *her*.

Then again, maybe he'd moved this conversation along a little too fast. Perhaps he needed to lighten up.

Isn't that what he did best? Lighten up or take the mickey out of someone or something until they either laughed or left him alone. But he definitely didn't want Sophie to leave. He'd tried that and hadn't liked it. Now he wanted to learn to live with what little he had, but in a new way. And having Sophie at his side would, if even for a short while, make that transition into a new way of living a heck of a lot easier.

"If what we did wasn't making love…" He smiled, while the light floral scent of her skin drifted over him and tugged at his memory. "What would you call it?"

A deep blush rose up her neck and blossomed over her cheeks.

He chuckled to himself.

She turned to him with a startled gaze.

"What?" She switched her attention back to the empty country road with golden grass plains on either side. A reluctant smile wobbled and then broke fully across her previously hard-set lips. "Some of us aren't as free with the colorful language as you. That wasn't a fair question."

He turned to his window. Whatever she called it, she'd loved what he'd done to her. He could still recall the heavy sigh of her body as he'd had her against that kitchen wall. And he'd loved having her too. More than loved it. At least for one heavenly moment, before all hell had broken loose.

She cleared her throat, drawing his focus back to her. "If I had to call what we did anything…" She held a tiny whisper, as if speaking to herself, yet that whisper cut loud enough to overcome the rev of the car's engine and the road's rushing winds. "It was the most thrilling moment of my life."

He stared at her, silent, her honesty slapping the smile right off his face. She stared ahead. Silent too. Not acknowledging what she'd just said.

Meanwhile, sparks of joy danced through his body, and goose bumps prickled his skin. Even though the lack of protection had marred what they'd done, maybe she didn't hold all that much guilt after all.

A smirk pushed at his cheeks. "You might be able to trade in the whole sweet and prudish act now."

He meant it as a joke, but she returned his smile with a sadder one of her own, then shifted her gaze back to the road. "I never was a prude, Orlando." She wrung her hands over the steering wheel, knuckles pointed as a result of her tight grip. "I keep telling you. You don't really know me."

The downward tilt to her voice, along with everything else about this whole encounter, was a precious stolen moment. It begged him to absorb every last detail of her. Because no matter how hard he worked to find a way to get her to see him, no amount of time together would be long enough.

"I know. I'm sorry."

She gave a small nod to his husky whisper, and another unreadable expression washed over her face. "Since we're being honest, I don't think I can take any more of your belittling. You really hurt me when you scrunched up the paper with details I'd worked so hard to get, and the way you barked barked at me to go… I get why you did it and that I was wrong too, but I didn't come to you that day aiming for an altercation. If you insist there's nothing professional between us, then I can't say I'd endure any friend or lover lashing out at me like that."

The slight waver in her voice suggested her stoic energy had more to do with protecting herself than shutting him out. His mind spun from what she'd said. In one breath, she admonished him for hurting her; in the next, she referred to him as a lover.

She glanced his way, and her lower lip momentarily tucked between her teeth. "In other words, it was one painful encounter too many. So, if one of your goals today is to instigate a reconciliation, I'm not sure I'm ready to forgive you."

It was his turn to look away. Witnessing what he'd done to her, that he'd given her multiple reasons not to trust him, raked nails over his heart. He'd inflicted one cruelty after another, yet only now did he compute the magnitude of his constant moods. Heck, and not just on her. Everyone.

He'd taken all the toxic energy whirling around in his heart and passed it on to anyone who dared cross his path. According to Candice, even the staff and residents at Roseford were on the verge of being done with him. These same people who endured thankless tasks day in, day out; and he, the antithesis of brilliance, had driven each and every one of them away.

He needed to deal with his mess. *But how?*

Maybe he didn't deserve Sophie's forgiveness. But he wanted it. More than he wanted anything. Despite the complete irrationality in that desire.

He was a man condemned, and she was everything he couldn't have. What he'd failed to achieve in his former life.

She was bright and beautiful. A gentle soul with an iron edge. A woman with a whole life ahead of her. A woman who dredged up every hope he'd packed away. And every wonderful thing about her delivered a messed-up reminder he had nothing to offer in return.

Nothing except maybe love. And maybe even that would be gone soon, too.

Who could say how long his malfunctioning mind and body would hold out? After all, the appointment they barreled toward now would either solidify or refute his death sentence.

But he needed to know this woman still thought him capable of redemption, because if someone as pure-hearted as Sophie couldn't see it, then maybe his life really had been worth nothing.

He blinked at the road, feeling hollower with her beside him than in all their weeks apart. As always, more his fault than hers.

"I'm sorry." He stared off into the distance, and the sound of his voice seemed to come from way down deep in his belly. "I've been a real asshole."

But she gave no reply, so he looked at her with her attention still pinned ahead.

Slow and silent minutes passed where she merely clenched her jaw, and visible tension dug shallow ridges along her forearms. "What you don't seem to factor in when you're being an asshole, is that everyone has their own hang-ups and pressure points." A tear rolled down her cheek, and she swiped it with the heel of her hand. She whipped her attention at him in one quick, hot, and angry stare. "You've all but admitted in the past that you know what pressure points are, but you press and press until those around you buckle and break. I know you just want everyone to leave you alone, but we're trying to help you. Have you ever considered the toll administering that help takes on the people in your life?"

The air chilled his skin, and he found himself speechless. He did often think about the constant effect he had on others. The price of his illness. How achingly dependent he was on others. How his bad attitude wore everyone down, including himself. But then, honest anger took less energy than faked happiness or groveling gratitude.

His heart hurt as the toll of knowing him played across Sophie's taut face, with its streaming tears, and the dent under her cheekbone from her gnawing on her inner cheek. The sight of her twisted a knife in places he'd assumed long numbed.

"Thanks to Candice, I'm starting to," he whispered. His learned hostility had become rooted in his very being. He could try. He would have to show her. And though words and promises were as helpful as using a sieve to catch water, he offered more words. "I wasn't always like this."

His inclination to bargain now made him wonder if he'd been mistaken in roping her into this road trip. Maybe his continued presence would only damage her further.

She drew out a long silence, followed by a sigh. "I'm sure you weren't. Time and circumstance changes everyone, Orlando. I've seen pictures of you from back in the day. You used to smile on occasion." The jest didn't lighten her voice. "You say there's nothing impulsive about pulling me back into your orbit, but you can't know that. Not without really knowing me. And you don't know me, Orlando. You don't know the first thing about me. You certainly don't know why I'm 'prudish' or have a deep need to avoid risk. You seem to assume that's just how I'm made. But you have no idea how much that day together cost me. All you have are a bunch of assumptions, when I'd bet my life every one of them would be wrong. You're so wrapped up in bitterness, you don't know how wrong you are."

He stared at her. "I want to know you."

A dull, soulless laughter broke from her. "Why? So you can use the truth against me? You've done just that with every other sore point, observation, or insecurity up until now. I return to the UK in mere weeks, and according to you, you're a 'lost cause'. So, why would I ever trust you? Why would I put myself through the wringer of recounting anything that might hurt me?"

He frowned, again drawing a blank. "I don't know. You're right. I haven't earned anything from you."

The hollow laughter returned, like her anger kicked up another notch. "You know, I hoped you'd return to my life, but now that you're here, I'm only just realizing how mad I am. The fact that you've already given up on getting me back only adds to my mistrust."

Her raised voice and palpable fury spoke volumes. He'd done enough. She was right. He didn't deserve her. What on earth had he been thinking?

"You should stop the car. I have my wallet. I can get myself to

Melbourne." The countryside flicked by, and he tried to gauge where exactly outside of Roseford they were. "Go home, Sophie. I've only made things worse."

"Oh, for fuck's sake." The enormity of her swear ricocheted around the car's tiny cabin, and she lashed a hand out and grabbed his wrist, as if she figured he'd throw himself out of the moving vehicle just to get away from her. "You're the one who reopened the wound here. You don't get to wriggle away so easily."

This scene, with her yelling and latching onto him, losing all control, while insisting he not wriggle away, held a comical edge. His earlier words about not ending his days as someone who gave up returned to haunt him.

The need not to give up tethered him to this car. He didn't just owe trying to *her*. He owed it to himself.

So, he tried.

He turned to her, pushing his usual resistance down, and attempting a different approach. An approach that required something other than defiance. An emotion he hadn't touched in years.

Empathy.

"Sophie." He eased his tone and allowed his own vulnerability to shine through. He needed this possibly more than she did. "Let me help. Tell me what I need to know."

Each of his days in more recent years had been about survival. His own survival. And everyone else's needs had ceased to exist. When for a large part of his life, being of service to others had been his entire world.

She peered over, eyes glistening and cheeks sunken, as if she didn't know how to respond. "You won't see me the same way." Her voice was small, reedy, her shoulders rounded. "I can't."

"You've supported me through an episode and a flashback, and neither one sent you screaming away into the night. Give me a chance to repay the favor. Besides, maybe me not seeing you the same isn't such a bad thing. As you said, you're going back to the UK, and I'm a lost cause, so what have you got to lose?" He offered a strained smile, his head aching from all the extra energy this sincerity drew from him.

She blinked ahead, posture slumping another degree. "More than you know."

He reached out and touched his fingers to her upper arm, where her muscles bunched beneath his touch. "Try me. Please."

She lashed her gaze his way before her focus returned to the road, and she blew out a heavy breath, as if needing time to weigh up whatever she had to say next. "I'm not 'Neat and Nerdy' by choice. It's a learned behavior. A survival technique. I haven't always been a 'prude', and the one time I did step out in the name of adventure, I learned a painful lesson."

She grimaced ahead, as though she'd already said too much, when in reality, she'd revealed very little at all.

He kept his attention on her, not wanting to miss a single detail, despite her not looking his way. "What lesson was that?"

"That every decision has a price. And that price can impact everyone around you."

# Chapter Twenty-Four

Sophie stopped the car at an empty intersection and waited for a lone light to change. The ensuing quiet between her and Orlando made the tick of the indicator seem inordinately loud. She took a long and shaky breath, using the silence to build her courage. *Oh God, am I really about to admit this to him?*

"I had my first boyfriend when I was sixteen. He was eighteen. I was always a model student with top grades, but I wanted out of that stereotype. Having a boyfriend, along with the things we got up to, made me seem so wild to all my friends. I could sense the amazed jealousy every time we talked. It was more admiration than I'd ever experienced, as if acting out justified greater rewards than being well-behaved ever had."

She turned to Orlando, a concerned frown gracing his face, as though he already didn't like where this story was going. Why? Why was she telling him this?

*Calm down. Maybe he's right. What do I have to lose?*

She'd carried this secret for so long. Even those who knew the truth did their utmost not to speak about it. But she needed Orlando to understand. So, she pushed on.

"Of course, my parents didn't know. I feel like such an idiot admitting this now, but he lured me in with his ability to sneak me into clubs, buy me alcohol. He had a car when all my peers were walking. Stepping away from the 'wholesome' role, regaling my friends with things none of them were doing, it was one big rush. Besides, Luke was off on active duty, Max was busy training for his swimming comps, and I was the reliable quiet one in the family. So, my parents didn't think twice about me coming home late. They assumed I was studying at a friend's house. I didn't even have to lie, beyond omitting the truth and letting them fill in the missing details."

Her stomach churned, a hot sensation burned her from the inside out.

She'd thought herself clever, lying, spending time with people who were older but not all that invested in her wellbeing. "I knew that boy was using me. He didn't really love me. But then, I was using him too."

"Sophie…" Orlando's voice dipped, pleading in a way that said he knew where this story went, but hoped for a different outcome.

She gave a weak smile, one that would only confirm his misgivings. "You already see me differently now, don't you?"

The muscles over his face hardened. Maybe he disapproved of her ability to read him. Maybe he already thought less of her. Maybe he regretted chasing her out of her house and into this car. But all he gave her was his continued stare and a simple demand. "Tell me what you're getting at here."

She let out a sigh and sunk back against her headrest. *Here goes…* If he wanted to reject her over this, so be it. She'd condemned herself to losing him two weeks ago, anyway.

"One particular weekend got way out of hand. I can barely recall what happened beyond us taking the train from Scarborough to London and crashing on the floor of my boyfriend's friend's flat. Well, that's where we left our stuff, anyway. We didn't spend much time there since it was an all-weekend clubbing event, and we proceeded to get completely wasted. The only other thing I remember is having one drink after another and spending the next two days paying for it with the headache from hell." Her chin trembled. The headache and fatigue had been minor consequences. The worse stuff came not much later. "I treated my body like a dumping ground. Except, what I didn't know was… It wasn't just me I was hurting that weekend."

Orlando's clothes rustled against the car's leather seats, and he shifted his torso toward her. "What do you mean exactly? Tell me what happened."

She couldn't bring herself to return his stare, so she blinked at the road—her head shaking a silent and numb denial of his request—though she knew she had to finish this story.

"Two days later, I was at school and I started getting these cramps. My lower abdomen and back hurt more than anything I'd ever experienced, and I was doubled over in pain during math class. It was completely surreal. My best friend kept rubbing my back and asking if I was okay. And I kept saying, 'Yes, yes, I'm fine', and bargaining that it was just unusually strong period pain. Maybe just a result of dehydration from my big weekend. But the minutes kept ticking by, and in my heart of hearts, I knew something was really wrong." Her lips took on a life of their own, forming the words to a tale that sounded strange and unfamiliar out loud, even though it was her story.

She turned to him for a second, her eyes stinging, cheeks cold as though her circulation had lost the will to flow that high up her body. "The teacher eventually sent me out of the room, and I was about an hour into lying in the nurse's office when the worst of the bleeding started. About an hour after that, my mum sat beside my bed at the nearest hospital and a doctor stood before us informing me I was experiencing a miscarriage. My heart shrunk. I wanted to curl up and stop existing. I hadn't even known I was pregnant and I'd drunk myself to oblivion just days prior, I'd done this to myself. I'd been so foolish."

Her throat felt drier than a scorched field, but despite the pain of delivering her words, she focused ahead and rasped out her final sentiments on the matter. "I'd done this to myself, but I'd also ripped a potential new life out of this world, too. It was all my fault. For being so blasé. So naïve. I can't ever for a second forgive myself for that mistake."

A heavy hand landed above hers on the steering and wrenched the car into a sharp swerving motion off the road. She screamed, instinctively slamming her foot on the brakes and working to pull the wheel in the opposite direction.

"Let go. Pull over." Orlando's hand fought hers again, and she did as he asked since fighting him held the strong possibility of directing the car into a tree.

The car swung into a dip at the roadside; she planted her foot on the brake again, and the tires crunched the vehicle to a stop.

Her body flung forward, inertia running its course until her shoulders flopped back into her seat.

"What about your appointment?"

Her question sounded ridiculous against the panic of swerving all over the road.

"Kill the engine. We can spare ten minutes."

She killed the engine, and the churning in her gut gave way to a hollow sensation.

What now? Had she waited all these years to talk about her past, only to find she'd picked the wrong person? As much as she wanted to deny it, Orlando's opinion mattered. His harsh tone still rung in her ears, along with the engine's soft tick, tick, ticking, as though it too needed a moment to recover.

"Jesus." He pressed the heels of his hands over his eyes. "Sophie." Her name came out on a low growl, and he dropped his hands to his lap and pinned her with that dark, inescapable glare. A glare that always saw too much. "Please don't tell me you've been beating yourself up over that for all of twelve years. What happened was a tragedy, but how many other sixteen-year-olds lie about their age so they can hit the clubs and get wasted? Too many to count. Hell, even I was into the same shit at that age. You made a mistake. An inexperienced, never-been-out-in-the-world, sixteen-year-old mistake. And there were two of you involved. So, as much as I understand your guilt, you can't claim full ownership of what happened."

His words hung in the air, slow to filter through. She peered down at the steering wheel while her shoulders rounded. She felt small. Exposed. Completely vulnerable in the worst kind of way.

Forgiving the past wasn't as simple as admitting to a mistake.

"Logically, I know that. But people beat themselves up for less."

How could anyone love her knowing what she'd done? Who she'd been? If even for the briefest time. Perfect Sophie Tindall didn't exist. In fact, she was so fatally flawed, her actions had quite literally cost the life of an unborn child. "Over the years, I've had so many reminders of just how wrong I got it. Of just how much I need to make sure I never make those same impulsive decisions again. Except—"

"Except you made almost that same exact mistake with me." He frowned, eyes darkening as he made the connection to that afternoon in her kitchen, where they'd had sex but hadn't been careful, and her frantic escape from him minutes later.

"I had no idea." His tone softened, but his eye contact remained. "I'm sorry."

"Please don't apologize, I don't deserve it. And like you said, you didn't know."

"Not knowing isn't an excuse. I was selfish and so wrapped up in my own dilemma after we..." He reached out a hand and placed it over hers. "I own every bit of my part in all of this. Including the part where this has reopened a wound for you."

She squeezed her eyes shut and drew in a breath. Somehow his compassion hurt more than the disgust she'd expected. "There are people like Agathe, people who have lost a child, or people who have tried over and over and over again, only to never get the baby they so desperately want. Then there are monsters like me. I could have had a child, and I not only ruined it, but I also felt a sense of relief that one never eventuated. Whenever I think about that day, every thought is worse than the one before it."

She leaned her head to the steering wheel, spare hand pressed to her middle. Even though Orlando sat less than a meter away, she felt so alone. He might have shared responsibility, but no one could wear her pain for her, and she deserved every last bit of it. For being so cold. For spending all these years running from something she'd so recently and carelessly repeated again.

His hand squeezed hers. "That first time, you were a kid playing at being an adult. You weren't ready, and you have no idea how you would have adjusted had things turned out differently. And you can't compare yourself to Agathe. I doubt she'd want you owning hers or any other person's hardship." He kept his tone low, as though coaxing her away from a proverbial ledge. "I don't know much about her story, but I'm guessing you were in very different stages in your lives when you both fell pregnant. What's right for one person isn't right for the next. You had things to sort through and a heck of a lot of growing up to do back then."

She turned to him, a rise of panic sweeping through her body. "But if I'd only stayed home that weekend. What was I thinking? I was only sixteen."

"Sophie." His insistent tone, along with his exasperated sigh, commanded she listen. "You're the one with the medical degree. You know more than I that some pregnancies survive much worse than what you did, and some don't. You also know that the human brain isn't fully developed until the mid-twenties. Teens are hardwired to make idiotic decisions, to rebel sometimes. I should know, I've pried far too many young bodies out of smashed-up cars as a result of drunken joyrides gone wrong. And just like pretty much every other teen, you thought you were invincible and older and had more control than you really did. Some people just get through those years more unscathed than others."

She opened her mouth, ready to argue, only to snap it shut again, her mind racing. "You're taking this way better than I thought."

He huffed out a laugh. "Yeah, well. Let's just say I also have first-hand experience talking people off ledges, and I've heard some pretty crazy-ass stories. Though yours does still surprise me."

She gave him a lopsided smile, her level of brokenness still high but not as stratospheric as before. "Well then, there you are, I'm not as innocent as you thought."

"No." He reached out and touched her cheek. "You're even more so."

"You can't believe that. I've repeated the same mistake, and I'm older now. I didn't enter your life as a lover. I was supposed to help you. I should have known better."

"And you're also human." His frown returned, more severe this time. "Listen to me, I'll never consider what we did a true mistake. And I understand why you're cautious. Why you were keen to break away and that what we did brought you close to that confused sixteen-year-old you once were. I'll always regret getting so lost in my own shock. No wonder you didn't want to see me again."

"I understood you were fighting your own demons."

"That's not an excuse."

"It kind of is."

They watched each other in silence, and sense of mutual understanding passed between them, offering the one positive out to this whole ordeal—they at least knew each other a little better.

Orlando broke the silence first. "I'm just starting to realize that both you and I have complementing needs. We've been so caught up in trying to protect each other that we kept missing the mark. I didn't give you enough credit to manage your life. I assumed you wouldn't be able to handle disappointment or my condition, much less my general shitty attitude. And you"—his hand squeezed gently around hers—"you decided I'm too psychologically fragile to handle anything beyond a volunteer-resident relationship. And that's not fair, either."

She kept her mouth closed, knowing she should reply; for the most part, agreeing with him but unable to commit to where she stood when it came to this relationship.

He offered a soft smile, perhaps his recognition of her struggle. "Regardless of what the doctor has to say today, I want to continue knowing you. On one condition."

She quirked an eyebrow, falling just short of a genuine laugh. "You're the one trying to convince *me* right now, remember?"

His eyes took on a joyful gleam, his gaze flitting over her face with a new kind of lightness. "I remember. But you're going to forgive me, anyway, I know you will. You're just as intrigued about where this will all go as I am."

She gave him a sideways glance, reminding him she thought he was full of himself. But he was kind of right, and she wanted to hear what he had to say all the same.

"Whatever happens, I promise to do my best to shut down my cagey-bastard act, but you have to promise not to mess up your life for me."

She gave a nervous laugh. "Don't worry, I never had a plan to mess up my life for you."

He rolled his eyes, the *cagey-bastard* making a minor appearance. "Whatever. Just promise not to get swept up and forget why you came here to begin with. Got it?"

"Sure. Whatever you command."

Somehow, she'd missed this man's cockiness.

A distinct shadow clouding his eyes indicated he wasn't impressed with her snarky answer. "Promise me you'll return home and continue your life as planned. You'll keep studying. You'll keep living. No matter what. Whether I live or die, Sophie. Promise me you won't stop being you, and you won't break with your goals."

His hold on her hand tightened again, and his strong tone sent cold fear rushing through her body. All his talk about dying, she didn't want to think about that. Whether he spoke of dying naturally or taking matters into his own hands, she wanted him to share in her denial. Or better yet, share her hope. To reassure her everything would be okay.

"Orlando..."

But his dark gaze held firm. "Promise me."

"Fine." She gave him what he wanted, surrendered to the knowledge he would never offer her the benefit of sugar-coating his future. "But I'm still not convinced us knowing each other is a good idea."

He shrugged and let go of her hand, as if pleased to have her agreement either way. His suddenly relaxed demeanor seemed contrary to what she expected of a man about to learn his fate.

"We'll iron out the details later. For now—" He jutted his chin toward the empty road ahead. "We have an appointment to get to."

Orlando sat on one of the five maroon fabric chairs within Professor Bandara's waiting room. Sophie sat to his left, her fingers interlaced with his. A middle-aged, female receptionist sat behind a high counter, tapping away at her computer, the *clack-clack-woo* of her printer breaking whatever small calm existed within the room.

He counted all the purple shapes on the massive abstract painting on the right-hand wall. Twenty-five. When that was done, he moved onto the green. Seventeen. His palms grew sweaty, and his grip around Sophie's hand tightened. She wriggled her fingers, like maybe he'd cut off her circulation.

"Sorry." He loosened his grip.

She shifted sideways to face him. "Are you okay?"

He opened his mouth to admit that maybe he wasn't, but the door at the room's farthest corner opened and a woman with South Asian brown skin and chin-length black curls stepped out. She held a small smile and looked to him with eyes as dark as his own. "Mr. Piras?"

He nodded and stood a little too fast, his heart already racing from the wait.

He took the longest walk of his life into the professor's office, all the while refusing to let go of Sophie's hand. And while he walked, he made a promise to himself and the universe at large. That regardless of what the professor said, he'd spend whatever limited days he might have supporting Sophie and adding value to her life, rather than thinking about himself and his bitter existence for a change.

Professor Bandara lowered herself into her black leather chair and dispensed with quick pleasantries. "I'll get right to the point and spare you the technical jargon." Her eyes glittered and the corners of her crimson-covered lips crept higher. "You are the proud owner of an enzyme I'll affectionately call ACRUNase. It was an ordeal for myself and my team to find, hence why we required so many blood samples from you, along with your past MRIs. Sorry about that."

He blinked at the professor's sympathetic cringe, his mind spinning out of control, while completely blank at the same time. He wouldn't have cared if she'd asked for half the blood in his body and access to his dwindling bank account, as long as he got some answers.

When he failed to offer any reply, the professor gave a tight smile, and continued with what she'd been saying. "So, the thing about ACRUNase, it's incredibly rare. For certain people, it has the potential to alter nerve, muscle, and general brain function when exposed to particular influences. Do you understand what I mean, Orlando?"

Her chin dipped, and she stared up at him, as if she considered he might be a bit slow. To her credit, they'd only ever spoken on the phone, and he'd so far only managed a tight, "Hi," on his way through the door.

But her words did filter through, and his muscles and thoughts froze in place, his cheeks cold and sagging as though all the blood had drained from his head.

What the professor had just described sounded like the answer he'd always searched for—and nothing—all in one.

"Influences?" His throat prickled and lumbered as he forced the question out. "You mean, the TL-20 at the Aero Syntech fire site?"

"Yes, exactly." She nodded. "I tested your blood samples against separate compounds from the TL-20 ingredient list Sophie supplied and got a definite reaction out of one set. Though I suspect the accumulation of some third element, maybe something such as stress or viral exposure or anything really, might explain why your episodes are intermittent and differ in duration."

He turned to Sophie, the only other person in the room with a medical degree, hoping to decide how excited he should be. She held a gleaming grin, cheeks lifted and eyes aglow, signaling perhaps he could afford to lighten up too.

He refocused on the professor, not yet ready to cash in years of crushed hopes on a premature chance to celebrate. "What does this all mean for me?"

"It means what wouldn't affect most normal people, messed with your brain like an over ripe banana in a blender. The day you put out that fire, you walked into a perfect storm, and all hell was unleashed on your body and your brain. Our job now is to try to find a way to switch off the hyperreaction your body has been stuck on since that day—which is what your episodes essentially are, a hyperreaction."

He frowned at the word "hell". Hell was what he already lived in. What he needed most, was for the professor to confirm he'd finally earned his way out of hell and had something a little more like earth to look forward to. "Can you fix me?"

The professor shrugged. "Maybe."

"Just maybe?"

He got a sly smile back from the professor and turned to Sophie.

"As Ms. Tindall can confirm, we doctors don't like to give guarantees." She gazed back at him, the smile hardening, and a sterner look taking over. "I'm confident I might be able to customize the right combination of drugs to block the ACRUNase production in your body. If I can pull it off. If my theory is correct. Then you'll be okay."

He held onto his frown, his long-time safety blanket, unable to find it in him to believe her. "You mean there'll be no more episodes and this nightmare will be over?"

She gave a silent, but steady nod.

He slumped back in his chair, the air knocked from his lungs.

His attention fell to the ground and the swirling, teal patterned carpet below. Years of pent-up hopelessness slipped from his body. He shook his head, face hot, eyes stinging, unable to form proper words.

*I might be healed one day. I might return to my former life. I might actually have a future.*

But it couldn't be true.

Good things like that didn't happen to less-than-worthy people like him.

"But Mr. Piras," Professor Bandara called for his full attention, and he whipped his focus back to her. "I need to be very clear. This will be a process. A potentially very long process. Next to nothing is known about your condition, so you'll be a guinea pig of sorts on this, do you understand? I'll need time to adjust dosage, medication, and my approach, depending on how you respond."

He heard her words. Nodded to say he understood. Yet no warning would put him off trying to get what had eluded him for years. And there wasn't much this doctor could do to him that others hadn't done already.

"Whatever you need." His voice came out a rough croak.

"I have another warning." Her jovial smile from earlier seemed long gone, but he cared little for her gloominess. She held the keys to his cage. Nothing else mattered. "Even if I do cure you, there's no promise this won't happen again. That means you need to steer clear of as much chemical exposure as possible. That means you won't ever return to your former job as a firefighter."

His ribcage compressed, and his body felt suddenly heavy, but he nodded all the same. He'd never expected to live beyond the next few years. Any dreams of returning to his old job had been long packed away.

The professor's eyes sparkled anew, and she grinned, a woman whose natural default expression might be a permanent smile. "I have a good idea of where to start with your treatment." She spun her office chair to a set of cupboards behind her, and very soon a white plastic pill bottle rattled within her palm. She slid the bottle across her desk and waited for him to grab it. "You won't get this stuff from your run-of-the-mill pharmacist. I had two of my best underlings compound these for you. We'll adjust dosage and mix based on your feedback and reactions."

He examined the pill bottle and expected it to glow, like some kind of beacon or the holy grail. But no, it was just a little white bottle with his details printed in black across the label.

Still, he turned to Sophie, the sudden lightness in her eyes prompting him, for the first time in years, to envision a whole new world ahead of him.

"This must be a lot to process." Professor Bandara's voice turned his head toward her again. "You can, of course, contact me with any concerns or reactions you might have to your new medication. Just know, this whole left-of-field discovery is very exciting for me and my team. We're not going to let your case slide by without giving it our full effort. But before I let you go, do you have any final questions?"

He flicked his gaze back to Sophie and nodded. "This enzyme, is it genetic? Will it affect any future children of mine?"

A heavy weight seemed to bear down on his chest as he awaited the professor's reply.

"Yes." The professor held a strong tone, one that didn't hide from the truth. "But here's the good news. Like anything of this nature, now we know you have it, we can help any affected future offspring. Again, whatever switches this enzyme on, appears to be very specific. Quite often with these types of disorders, one can be a carrier and live their entire life without any reaction. That would be true for any children you have." Professor Bandara sank back in her chair. "Your earlier assessment questions stated that no one else in your family has presented with this issue. So, I'd say that, up until now, you've just been one really unlucky guy."

~

Orlando stood beside Sophie in the elevator on the way down to the hospital lobby. A dumbstruck silence stretched between them, though they'd shared a few skittish glances before continuing the status quo of watching the shiny metallic double doors ahead.

"I'm not going to say I told you so, but..." Her low, yet sing-song whisper echoed around the tiny space.

"Really?" A small laugh bounced from his chest. "And I guess you're also still not convinced us knowing each other is a good idea?"

She released a stifled chuckle. "Shut up."

He gave her hand a gentle squeeze, and said nothing, glad that for once worry didn't underscore either of their moods.

She turned to him, so he returned the gesture, only to find her smiling up at him. "Just don't you forget, I said yes even before the professor offered her glimmer of hope."

# Chapter Twenty-Five

"Your brother, Luke. He wants to kick my ass, doesn't he?"

Sophie stood outside her open car door and smiled at the unique sound of Orlando initiating the conversation for a change. "Probably Max too." She swung the door shut and laughed, fawn sandals crunching over the sandy gravel in the parking lot at Lacey River—a stretch of thick bushland half an hour from Roseford. "But Luke has had his fair brush with complicated relationships, and as intimidating as he seems, I think he'd be willing to give us the benefit of the doubt."

Orlando slung her black backpack, containing their lunch, over his shoulder. "So that means we're an 'us', now, huh?" He grinned back, the expression uncharacteristically light. "I don't blame your brothers, really. I'd want to kick my ass too. Then again, I have zero regrets over storming the cabin."

She made a show of raising a brow, a folded picnic rug clasped in her right hand. Orlando led her down a track; his palm on her lower back sending a soft wave of heat throughout her body. "I missed your friendship, Sophie."

She leaned into him, despite the churning in her tummy, as if the roles had reversed, and she'd become the skeptical one.

Professor Bandara had unleashed her surprisingly positive diagnosis just days ago, and already Orlando exuded an air of bright new hope. Candice reported a marked ease in his attitude, though that change had started days before Professor Bandara's appointment, as if he'd made a sudden decision to invest in himself.

This shouldn't have been a bad thing, but Sophie needed to know he'd be okay. That he'd genuinely improve, both physically and mentally. But she couldn't pinpoint what would cause him to reawaken from the slump he'd been in.

His quick change scared her. Like his enthusiasm might burn out, and his sudden rise would lead to an equally sudden fall.

What would happen should the professor's treatment fail? Should Sophie's *own* relationship with him fail? Or he not be as accepting of her return to the UK as he'd claimed?

"Have you noticed any improvement yet?" She spoke with the echoes of Candice's warning in her ears. "I mean, with the medication."

She held her breath, not easy given the quick pace he kept down the gnarled bush track. All the while, she awaited his reply, afraid of yet another regret to haunt her through the decades.

"Not really." His broad shoulders took up the limited space on the path, his torso far taller than hers. He turned to her, lines scoring his cheekbones. "I can't imagine a day where I'll feel totally out of the woods. I'm not buying into hope just yet. I've been down this road too many times."

On a surface level, she wanted to believe him, to ease her guilt about just how deep she'd pulled him into trusting her, but his change alone signaled he wasn't quite as disengaged with hope as he claimed. "What hope exactly aren't you buying into?"

He twirled a thin gum leaf from a nearby tree through his fingers, then tossed it back to the ground as he walked on. "That a man who's lost everything can still have a future." He gave a tight laugh, as if the gesture alone could erase the heavy expectations pressing down on both their shoulders. "That he could have..."

His husky tone tapered, as though he fell short of uttering his dreams out loud, or at least lacked the heart to finish the thought.

Her own heart beat faster, cresting on a sharp ache. She wished to know what a man like Orlando wanted, and yet, given how temporary her presence would be, maybe she had no right to pry. He'd said as much the day she left him at the care facility.

The rushing of water pulled her attention, and the track thinned until a wider clearing opened up, one that revealed a great, brown river with white caps smashing over protruding rocks along the banks. She paused a moment to watch, to catch her breath.

Everything about this place invited contemplation. From the glaring midday sun, to the joyful kookaburras and white cockatoos in the nearby gums. Cheery wattle trees dotted the landscape with bright patches of yellow. Across the river, a gigantic sheet of flat, gray rock made up the steep mountainside, and a mass of tall trees battled to grow from between the cracks.

She'd taken time to learn a little about the Australian bushland as part of her travel experience, but she wasn't all that confident in her powers of identification. She pointed to a small, dark bird, darting and circling the water's swollen surface. "Is that a willie wagtail?"

The same bird swooped closer, and Orlando's gaze followed its path. "No. That's a welcome swallow. Notice the red chest? The local indigenous people watch for its appearance as a sign of the start of a new season." He turned to her, squinting against the sun. "I guess we'd call it spring, but they have about seven seasons and their own way of tracking things. Their weather calendar is more accurate to the area than the four European seasons we all follow."

She couldn't help it; she let out a small laugh. "I'm beginning to think you calling me 'nerdy' was more a case of self-recognition."

He smiled and turned back to the water. "A lot of firefighters in these parts have a basic understanding of indigenous seasonal change. Plus, I grew up running wild around places like this. The first people have been here for over sixty thousand years, and they know the land better than anyone. So, when those same people forecast a season high in heat and wind, and you're the one slated to fend off any resulting fires, you'll take any bit of help you can get."

She watched the bird a while longer, the scent of the damp ozone rising from the river's edge. The alien landscape differed so greatly from dreary London or the oak-and-birch-dappled forests around her hometown of Scarborough. She could never dream of asking Orlando to leave this place. To uproot himself from everything he knew. *Again.* And for her this time. Even if the professor's plan miraculously worked...

She sucked in a breath at her runaway thoughts, far too dangerous considering the limits on this relationship.

"I don't want to be your friend." The words slipped from her mouth, and she regretted them instantly. Her statement could be easily misinterpreted as her not wanting to know him at all.

"I don't want to be your friend either, Sophie." He reached a hand out and stroked his thumb over her chin. "You and I could never be just friends. We're all or nothing. When I said I missed your friendship, I only meant it as an entry into picking up where we left off."

His hand slid down her arm, and he interlaced his fingers with hers. His dramatic statement was more truth than she could deny. They'd tried to maintain distance, in a number of ways, but failed every time. Still, she needed to be clear.

"You know I can't stay. We have no choice but to accept less than *all.*"

"I know."

"Then what *are* we? Not friends. Not lovers. What?"

"Are you looking to name this?" His attention dipped from her eyes to her lips. "I have every plan to have you again, multiple times if you'll let me, but—" He captured her gaze, deep-brown eyes drawing her in. "I'm never going to call you a fuck buddy, Sophie. You're more than that. You're... You're my spark." He frowned, before an easy smile lifted his cheeks. "We burn bright and hot, but not forever."

She laughed, nudging at him, skin tingling at the hard and heated feel of his ribcage. "Nice firefighter analogy." But then her laughter wobbled under a swell of broken emotion. "And you're okay with that? Not forever? Because no matter what happens, there'll come a day when we won't know each other."

The swell grew, overwhelming and taking up an inordinate amount of space within her chest. If she didn't get hold of herself, she'd turn into a blubbering mess. She couldn't do that. Not in front of Orlando. He'd contended with so much misery already.

His hand tightened around hers, as though he saw her struggle. "Want to know how I get through one day after another? How I survive the knowledge that things will probably only get worse?"

She gave a shaky nod, peering down at their joined fingers because she'd lost the strength to look at him.

"My survival depends on not thinking about the future. Any chance of me enjoying anything depends on not thinking about what's coming next. So…" He lifted her hand and brushed his lips over her knuckles. "Stop thinking about the day we won't know each other. Think about now. Think about how *this* feels." He pressed a drawn-out kiss to the back of her hand, and her skin responded with instant heat.

Her eyes closed to the skim of his breath, his words already sinking in. The hurried *whoosh* of wind through the trees added to her drunken feeling. "You make escaping reality sound simple."

"For now, it is." He pulled her hand away from his lips and cradled it in his palm. "It won't be for much longer. I know that."

She peered back up at him, an empty feeling opening inside her, a hollow she instantly recognized only he could fill. That knowledge alone meant she would collide with disaster if she didn't get some other details straight.

She'd always been one to have her life planned out; as long as she played things safe, things tended to work. But this situation was far less than perfect. The only thing that did work was how well they got along, which seemed enough for her.

When he looked at her, her former obsession with leading an ideal life evaporated. So maybe she could be okay with the limits and just enjoy what they had, but first…

"I plan to stick to our agreement. I plan to return home. Just as I promised." She turned her hand so their palms pressed together. "But I worry about you."

"You shouldn't."

The importance of what she had to say formed a hard ball in her throat. This relationship's trajectory hung on whatever happened next. She couldn't go further with him unless she spoke now.

"I have to worry. I absolutely have to. And you have to understand my obligations both as a woman and as a doctor, just as you had obligations as a firefighter back when you were one. There's a duty of care here I can't ignore any longer. Even if our relationship has never been anything formal."

She lifted her gaze to his frown, perhaps he suspected he wouldn't like what she had to say, though right now he remained silent.

"I need you to let Candice line up ongoing psychological care for you."

He jolted, mouth open as if ready to protest, but she held up a hand and cut him off. "If you're allowed to stipulate conditions, then so can I. And this is my one condition. I can't shoulder the pressure of your wellbeing alone, especially knowing I'll be leaving."

"But I don't need a psychologist."

"Oh, come on, Orlando." Her voice rose, and she inched back, ready for a fight. "You're having flashbacks. If not for your condition and circumstance at the home, then get help with how to handle those. And if not for the flashbacks, then to help me feel confident I'm not crossing any line here as your sole place of support."

His gaze shifted away from her. On the surface it appeared he distanced himself, but the lax skin over his cheekbones suggested deep thought rather than rejection.

A fluttery feeling spread through her stomach. She needed an answer and that answer had to be yes.

He turned back to her, frown still set, forehead pulling at the middle. "Okay."

Her shoulders dropped as his gravelly agreement seeped through to her brain. She'd envisioned an argument—her storming off to the car, him storming after her, and a frosty ride back to Roseford Aged Care Center together.

"Really?"

He gave a short nod. "I won't add more doubt to your life. And… maybe you're right about the other stuff, too."

She held back a laugh. Partly because of his reluctant acknowledgement, but also out of relief. He'd gone a long way to elevating the huge burden she'd carried in the weeks since her talk with Candice. More than that, he'd be getting extra help.

She reached out and cupped his face in her hands, then landed a hard kiss to his right cheek. He reeled back a little, like her excitement surprised him.

Still, she had more to say, perhaps something closer to what he'd want to hear. "The one perfect thing about our situation is that maybe we can both get what we want here."

He tilted his head in questioning.

"I mean, you're worried I'll sacrifice everything I want in order to be with you. And I get it, I tend to help others, while failing to grasp at what I want. But you've forgotten something else." She gave a sharp smile, taking joy in the confused crinkling of his face. "This *is* me grasping for what I want. I want what you've already proven very capable of giving me." His scowl gradually lightened, a sign he'd read the subtext of what she got at. "Up until now, you've wanted to live, but couldn't. I want to live, too, but I don't know how. And I'm asking for your help. I don't do spontaneous, Orlando, but you've given me glimpses of just that. For once, fear didn't stop me. And as much as we fumbled that day in my kitchen, this is still something you could help me with. Because… because I trust you."

Her heart stammered at that last confession.

His eyes pulled wide; maybe she'd caught him off guard. Then his posture lifted, indicating he liked what he'd heard, that she'd handed him a ticket to something he hadn't had in years.

For a short time, he'd be needed. He'd have a relationship where he wasn't the only one requiring help.

His eyes glinted like polished onyx, if polished onyx could hide a brewing plan. "I'm sure I can arrange that, and with surprising frequency. But since you're after spontaneity, maybe you could be the one to show me what you want?"

Her jaw slipped loose. She peered around her, to the river with its forceful current. "What? Right now? Right *here*?" Granted, no one had walked past in the entire time they'd been talking, but still… "I think you're throwing me in a little too deep."

He let out an easy laugh before a devilish grin took over his features. The same grin he'd given her that first day he'd offered her a fake date. Though *this* devilish grin didn't mock so much as play.

"I'll help you." He drew nearer, voice low and rough. "Spontaneity starts with a kiss."

Those simple words shifted a space in her heart. A space that allowed room for the trust she'd mentioned. And she did trust Orlando. She couldn't quite define why, but she did. Completely.

Her heart pounded; her senses heightened, even the brush of a cool breeze on her sun-warmed skin grew her aching need for him. But he held still, just watching her, and it was then she twigged that he wanted her to initiate his mentioned kiss.

He leaned in, larger-than-life, as though he saw her grapple with the situation.

"You can do this."

His coaxing whisper suggested she could back out if she wanted to. She was safe if she changed her mind. But she *did* want this. She wanted him. She'd wanted him since that first meeting, even as he messed with her and left her running in anger.

And now here he was, wanting her too.

She stood on her toes and reached for him. And in an instant, their lips met.

He remained still, allowing her to find her way. To explore. She lifted her hands and stroked his neck, marveling at his play of muscles dancing beneath her fingertips. Her nostrils filled with the scent of clean skin and soap, of manly musk, all of which melted her further. His chest rose and fell, his body taut, the strain of a man holding it together for her.

She paused. Overwhelmed. Then pulled away, resting her forehead to his as she waited for her bearings to return.

Since when did any man make room for her?

*Since never.*

Not with Hector. His passionless love-making had been sparse but efficient. Not with the boy from her teen years. His hurried and selfish attempts couldn't even be called anything close to *love-making*. But both men had praised themselves as heroes. Heroes she'd been supposedly lucky to date.

And then there was Orlando.

He never praised himself. Not without a heavy dose of sarcasm.

He'd been the antithesis of a hero. Her villain. Someone who'd set out to block her dream of doing good things, even though in some ways he'd succeeded.

She opened her eyes, drunk on wonder and a man of total contradiction. A man fast becoming her undoing.

His eyes held humor, but his brow twisted in mild worry. "Don't give me that look."

She smiled, choosing to focus on the lighter side of his expression. "What look?"

The twist in his brow untangled, and his smile mirrored hers. "Like you're about to adopt me or something."

A quick laugh had her head swinging back. "Haven't you noticed? I've already adopted you."

"I know." He stroked her jaw with the pad of his thumb. "Come with me."

He took her hand and led her farther up the creek, over a small, stony cliff most people wouldn't bother climbing. They descended to where a large rock face and the cliff's base met with a thick line of weeping willows. From the smoky scent, she figured these willows were native. Long, leafy tendrils spilled over and brushed against the straw-colored tall grass.

He pulled her farther through the line of trees until he had her pressed against the cliff behind. "No one will see us here." He gave a curled grin. "But we'll need to be quiet."

She giggled, genuine joy mixed with nerves, as his hands traveled up her arms.

Warmth flowed from the rock behind her and into her back, turning her body languid in his hold. He tilted her chin up, kissing her again, his large body engulfing her in this intimate space where the trees served as a tent, the interior thick with river sounds and the *chirrup* of insects.

But his lips blocked everything, and suddenly all she sensed was *him*. Her hunger for him grew as they fought to explore each other, his hard length pressing to her belly and lighting a fire within her.

His hurried fingers bunched the hem of her dress, and she responded by fumbling at his pants until she freed him. Their breaths were rushed, ragged and raw, as though they couldn't get to each other quick enough. His hands moved to her shoulder straps, and he tugged them past her arms. She wore no bra and stood exposed all the way to her waist.

He leaned back, assessing her. A second of self-consciousness roiled through her. As much as she loved the open look of awe, he'd called this her show, and she meant to take control.

She gripped his shirt in her hand and pulled him closer. He smirked, rewarding her bravo. She ground her hips against him, her voice a tight whisper. "It has to be now."

He pressed his nose to hers, his fingers curled to the rock beside her head, the other hand curved around her bare waist, strumming her skin and sending electric shivers through her body.

Next, he crushed his mouth down on her until his tongue plunged deep, his long fingers traversing lower until they met with her hot, wet core. She let out a whimper, but he swallowed the sound, as if possessing her so completely spurred him on.

Her excitement had blossomed in the delicate moment he'd told her to kiss him, but things weren't so delicate now. Heck, she didn't want delicate. Not gentle. Or sweet. She wanted Orlando. Resilient and rugged. Simple and sometimes crude.

She found her voice, demanding once more, "Turn me around."

He pushed back and out of her hold. His lust-filled glare paused before he released a low growl and reached out.

He spun her as asked, and her face brushed warm rock, his breaths heavy, in sharp bursts against her ear. Next came the crinkle of a condom wrapper. And then the harsh relief of him entering her in one hard thrust.

She tipped her head back, reveling in the moment, hips tilting out of an instinctual need to deepen the connection.

His lips nipped and sucked at her shoulder, and he moved within her, low and indulgent glides, until her moan broke free, and she begged for more.

Sophie Tindall never begged.

She waited. Patiently. Without a word. And as a result, she *never* got.

His large hand snaked down her back, over her ass, and lower to her thigh. She clenched beneath him, anticipating his next move, only for his hand to reverse trajectory. This time over her waist and up between her breasts, his fingers stopping at the base of her throat. He moved within her and held her there, suspended in his tight embrace. Erotically trapped. She dug her fingers into the rock, her other hand joining Orlando's on her hip.

He pounded into her, rough but deliciously controlled. Her excitement grew, and each thrust sent new shock waves through her body. Her heart rate lifting. Blood heating. Her every cell and nerve alive and elated.

And just as her peak rose, his fingers entangled with hers, moving her hand to the front of her hips and between her thighs.

She sucked in a breath, flutters twirling through her body. His fingers met the electric juncture of her excitement, and his hold on her hand meant she joined him in touching her. Slow and strong, circling caresses kept her captive. The soft pressure of his hand at her throat and his rhythmic thrusts overwhelmed her body. She couldn't keep up, and her ability to hold together imploded.

His movements turned harder and faster all at once again, until her voice ground on a strained moan, one that morphed into a needy cry. She lost control and sagged in his arms—a state of total and inescapable surrender. He plunged deeper still and released his own groaning pleasure.

Minutes passed while the clouds of desire cleared. He spun her around, unleashing a torrent of desperate kisses on her lips.

Like he couldn't believe what they'd just shared.

Like he needed to make sure she was real. That this moment was real.

Her laugh broke through the anguished tension, and he gentled his hold, pulling back as they watched each other.

A lot went unsaid, and a new truth settled in. One that burrowed down to the depth of her bones.

She didn't need words. She didn't even need the mind-blowing sex. The one thing she did need would never be hers.

She closed her eyes and buried her head against his shoulder. Breathing in his musky scent.

She couldn't have him. Not forever. But she'd try to be thankful, just as he'd told her. Thankful for what they had. Thankful for the air in her lungs. Thankful for the sun through the trees. And for the beautiful man in her arms.

The man who—with touch alone—set her free.

ORLANDO

In the spirit of doing things we never do, I have one thing to say before you close your eyes tonight...

Sophie stood in her bathroom with its giant wicker baskets filled with lush towels under the wood vanity. She pulled the ivory towel already wrapped around her wet hair, her phone in her spare hand as she replied to Orlando's text message.

And what is that?

Her phone pinged.

I wish you were here now.

She smiled, instant warmth spreading through her chest.

That's sweet. I miss you too.

Wait. I wasn't finished.

She brushed her tangled locks cascading over her fluffy white bathrobe and waited for him to complete his reply.

...So I can get you naked and scare the bejeezus out of Mrs. Davy next door with the sounds of us boning.

Instant laughter echoed within the tiny, steam-filled room, and she scrambled to keep from almost dropping her phone.

There's NO way I'm agreeing to that!

She could imagine Orlando's smug smirk now, proud of his cleverness in setting her up for a dose of his smutty humor.

Sorry. Too much? Don't worry. The old folk's home is off limits anyway. Too depressing.

Too depressing, huh? Well, since we're being brave, and in the spirit of 'doing things we never do'...

She sent the message, leaving him to stew for a few minutes. Meanwhile, she leaned against the vanity, second-guessing her idea before forcing herself to stick to her vow of bravery.

Her black satin and lace slip, one of the pieces of underwear bought during her shopping trip with Agathe weeks ago, hid beneath her bathrobe. She stepped into the bedroom with its full-length mirror outside the wardrobe door and shrugged off her outerwear, letting the slightly cool air hit her skin.

She tilted forward, striking a pose with one hip popped to the side, lips pouted, and her hand in front as if blowing a kiss. The other held her phone, camera ready. And then she took a photo.

And then she hit send.

She tried her best not to hyperventilate in the seconds it took for him to reply.

HOLY SHIT!

She clapped a hand over her mouth, her heart racing. Maybe the hyperventilating would start after all. She needed more to go by than, *Holy shit!*

As if the man read her thoughts, her phone pinged again.

> Jeez, woman! Damn Mrs. Davy, get yourself down here now. Or scratch that, I'll be right over.

A hysterical laugh tore from her, and the panic truly set in. The last thing she needed was for Orlando to go missing from the home and a midnight search party to turn up at her door.

Her fingers trembled as she typed out a hurried reply.

> No. No. No! Don't you dare leave the home. I'll see you tomorrow, okay?

A few moments passed, and a message arrived.

> Okay. But please wear the black lace under your clothes when you visit. ;)

She laughed, heart beat settling. Still not quite used to Orlando's brand of excitement. Still not sure she'd ever get used to it, only that she savored every little encounter they had. For once in her life, she felt sexy, powerful, adventurous. She had a man who rewarded her small moments of courage. Someone who truly saw her.

Maybe, even if this did have to end one day, it wouldn't be all bad. She'd come out a stronger, more rounded person for having known him.

She typed one more message.

> Dream on, Lover Boy. xox

And got a final reply for that night.

> Thanks for giving me something to dream about. I'm not just talking about the black lace.

# Chapter Twenty-Six

Two weeks had passed since Professor Bandara's diagnosis, and now, Sophie stood with Orlando in Luke's spacious dining room, a sense of mild optimism bouncing between them. So far, Orlando had suffered no episodes. He'd also completed some sessions with a psychologist Candice had visiting the home, and even those progressed well.

Sophie had come to the city with him today for an appointment with Professor Bandara to assess how his new medication was taking. Luke had extended an offer for them to stay at his place before braving the long drive back to Roseford in the morning.

Now, Luke rushed past with a stack of white plates in his hand, his footsteps heavy on the high-polished floor. "So, how'd the appointment go?"

When Orlando didn't answer, she turned to find his gaze paused at Luke's impressive Jarrah dining table, a burgundy runner and crystal candelabras intersecting the middle. His attention moved across the room to the casual-but-still-expensive custom, designer, silk curtains.

She shrugged, deciding he needed a minute to settle in, so answered for him. "Right now, it's a case of *no news is good news*."

"And what do you think"—Luke stopped setting plates and focused on the man standing next to her—"Orlando?"

Orlando dropped his gaze from the equally custom, equally designer, and very arty light fixtures. "I don't like to get ahead of myself."

His short reply plunged the room into a lead-filled silence. The two men stared at each other before Luke shook his head and gave her a *what the hell?* side glare.

Orlando caught the glare, and his jaw set firm, leveling his own scowl of mutual loathing.

Her shoulders sagged, and she dipped her chin so she wouldn't have to look at either man. She'd wanted to show her brother that even if she could only have Orlando for a short time, he wasn't a bad bet and deserved acceptance. And she'd wanted to show Orlando a normal night out with her family—something he hadn't had in so long.

She'd thought she knew both men well enough to guess they'd get along. But neither was having it.

Luke, a man who was usually nothing but kind and welcoming, returned to placing the last dish, the dismissive gesture shutting everyone out.

"So." Agathe bustled in, smile in place. Max followed close behind. "Buy anything interesting while you were on Collins Street today?"

Sophie laughed, though the sound seemed to get stuck partway in her throat. "Does window shopping count? Most shops were closed by the time our appointment was done, and the theater crowd was already rolling in. We ran out of time."

"Oh, well." Agathe held a light smile and lowered some wine glasses to the table. "Hopefully you'll get other chances to collect more souvenirs. You know, beyond the ones we've already purchased." She gave Sophie a not-so-subtle wink.

Orlando cleared his throat, the following mild splutter concealing a poorly hidden laugh. He'd figured out what *purchases* and *souvenirs* Agathe referred to.

Luke's attention passed between his wife and Sophie. "What souvenirs?"

Sophie sent Agathe a wide-eyed glance, pleading with her not to mention the lingerie they'd bought together weeks ago. Her cheeks burned, but she infused an edge of low warning in her voice, "Agathe…"

Orlando's eyes gave a wicked glint. "Agathe's right. Sophie, you really should do more shopping before you head back. In fact, we should go first thing tomorrow morning. Examining your new purchases brings genuine enrichment to my otherwise empty life."

Agathe's mouth dropped open; she seemed to have deduced he'd already reaped the rewards of Sophie's lingerie shopping. Seconds later, Agathe slapped a hand over her mouth and a giggle shattered any notion she shared the same doubts as her husband about Orlando's ability to socialize.

"If that's the case, maybe *you* should be the one to buy her something tomorrow." Luke frowned. His rigid voice indicated he at least understood the conversation's sexual undertones, even if he'd been excluded. "Though Collins Street might be out of your price range, buddy."

The room fell silent. Luke and Orlando commenced another stare-off, while Sophie, Agathe, and Max peered between each other, uncertain at what might unfold next.

Luke understood full well neither she nor Orlando could afford much of anything—especially not anything from one of the designer stores on Collins Street. Not that either one of them cared. The dinging trams and the lively street buskers had been enough enjoyment for their evening, both of which had been free—and most importantly—something they'd experienced together. And then there'd been the clash of old-world buildings against modern skyscrapers and geometric art houses. Her days with Orlando were numbered, and time, more than stuff, was what she grasped for most.

But then, Luke's rude statement had nothing to do with his attitude toward money, much less those that didn't have it. Luke himself hadn't come from privilege. He was the last guy to care what any person had in their bank account, and far from a snob, despite current impressions.

That being said, her brother did seem trapped in some moronic protective-older-sibling act, enough to make it clear he didn't think Orlando was good enough for her. Not because of money. But perhaps because he'd hurt her before. Still, Luke's attempt to protect her was turning him into a grade-A jerk, and she wanted him to stop.

She took a small step, about to unleash on her brother, but Orlando's hand shot out and stopped her.

"Thank you for welcoming me into your home." He turned to Agathe, omitting Luke from his gratitude.

The subtle slap down was far more elegant than what she'd had in mind.

Agathe offered a gentle smile, her gaze narrowing at Luke. His jab about money was below him, and everyone knew it.

"Well." Max plonked himself down at the table and held up his knife and fork. "Looks to me like there's too much talking and not enough eating. I made the ribs, so I get dibs."

His lips split into a wide toothy grin, indicating pride over his rhyme.

Sophie led Orlando to the table, and whispered, "You'll like Max. He's the family clown, but there's more going on in his head than he lets on."

Orlando took a seat beside her and looked down at her from his extra height, his dark gaze dancing around her face. "You're worried Luke will make me feel bad. Don't."

She turned back to Luke, who chatted to Agathe. From the strain across her cheeks, Agathe wasn't ready to forgive him yet, and he wasn't ready to apologize. "He's not usually this obnoxious."

"I know."

She jolted back. "You do?"

He lifted his hand to grasp hers, all the while his smoothed-out features emitted a calm so different to the prickly man she'd first met. She'd only just begun to get used to this new and unperturbed version of him, occasionally wondering if his stillness had been a feature long before his health deteriorated, destabilizing his world.

Maybe he'd bought into the hope Professor Bandara offered.

Or maybe their blossoming relationship made all the difference. Not just to him, but to her too. And not simply because of the life-altering sex. He challenged her. Forced her to be okay with impermanence.

Because of Orlando, she'd be forever changed.

Because of him, her world opened to new possibilities beyond a life of meticulous control.

"Sophie." His softened voice returned her to the conversation. "I can handle your brother."

She offered a weary smile, his reassurance not enough to abate her concern.

He turned back to the table, his grip tightening around her hand, a signal for her to bear with him.

"Luke." The strident boom of his voice killed any and all chatter, and with that boom, a cold wave of reality washed over her.

When he'd said he could handle her brother, he hadn't meant to reassure her of his lack of offense, he'd stated an intent to literally *handle* her brother. As in, right now. In front of everyone.

Her skin turned instantly hot, and her insides quivered. Luke glared at Orlando, silent, expression rigid, as if anticipating what would happen next.

"I know you don't like me." Orlando's battle mask reappeared in the form of a lifted chin. "And I understand why."

Luke eased back in his chair, a seeming challenge to Orlando's direct approach. As a prominent CEO and former army man, Luke wasn't all that used to people being bold enough to confront him.

"You do, do you?" He kept a measured voice and his gaze steadfast. Her brother was a bright man, one who knew when to tread carefully. He'd recognize someone as well-lived as Orlando likely possessed the ability to hang him with his own words. "You're right, I don't like you. But more than that, I don't trust you."

Orlando said nothing.

"Luke." Agathe's voice broke past the silence, her gaze darting between the two men. "Maybe you could give Orlando a—"

"No." Sophie reached out a hand, though the hard demand surprised even her. "Let them talk. Luke doesn't owe Orlando any fake sympathy. And if I've learned anything first hand, it's that Orlando can stand his own ground."

Agathe threw a split-second, wide-eyed glare, as if to say, *Are you crazy? These two will kill each other.* Then she grumbled something under her breath and settled back in her chair.

"It's because I've hurt her before. And maybe because you think this—" Orlando gestured between him and Sophie "—isn't built to last?"

Luke scoffed. "I thought the whole premise of your relationship is that it's a temporary arrangement?"

Orlando paused, and the momentary silence squeezed a portion of life from her heart. She hated reminders of her inevitable return home. Her eventual life without Orlando.

"Sophie has much brighter days ahead of her without me, I know that. We both know that. And so do you." Orlando nodded toward Luke. "But our inability to be together long term doesn't cancel out what we have now. Sometimes, a few shared moments is the lasting thing you take with you, even if the relationship doesn't survive. Sometimes, there's no other choice but to accept the limits of what you have. And sometimes, those small moments are more than what many get in an entire lifetime."

For a moment there, Luke held an unnatural stillness, before his posture collapsed ever so slightly. "I appreciate that. But your sentimental motives aren't enough to make me trust you."

"But you trust Sophie, don't you?"

"Sure." Luke shrugged. "As much as anyone else close to me. She's family."

"Then your mistrust toward me is irrelevant. She's capable of making her own choices and living with the consequences."

Luke's gaze flicked over to her. The soft focus in his bottle-green eyes gave the impression his mind harked back to sixteen-year-old her and her subsequent decade of *living with* one particular consequence. Or more precisely, beating herself up over it.

But even Luke couldn't deny that she'd knuckled down and turned her life around, albeit by checking out of life and locking up her heart. But she *had* done her fair bit of living and *did* deserve his respect.

She sat a little taller. A dare to her brother. *Defy me and you'll pay.*

Luke turned back to Orlando and gave the smallest of nods. He understood. He agreed.

And in an instant, the room's energy changed—less prickly, with space for easy banter.

Eventually, Luke regaled Orlando with the tale of how Max, a co-founder of his successful tech company, Tiluma, had quit when it became clear he wasn't at all suited to working in an office.

"The breaking point came when he got the entire building shut down by fumigators on the same day we had a major investor visiting."

Agathe laughed and shook her head. "He not only almost ended Tiluma, but damn near ended Luke and me."

Orlando chuckled around a quick sip of his water, then set his focus on Max. "How did you manage that?"

Max gave a sheepish shrug beside her. He, Luke, and Agathe all replied in unison, "Bring your dog to work day."

Sophie seized the opportunity to draw out the crosstalk and chimed in. "Or more exactly, some flea-infested stray that Max invited into the office."

Orlando pressed his knuckles to his mouth and restrained another laugh. The extreme lightness in his mood made her heart dance.

This was the most laid-back she'd ever seen him. He and Luke got along just fine now. The tension from earlier long forgotten.

Orlando fit in. There were no episodes. No flash backs. She'd succeeded in providing him with a normal night.

"Yeah, well." Luke grumbled and he gave his brother a playful side glare. "That stray almost ruined the entire company."

Max pointed his beer bottle at his brother, eyelids flared in opposition. "Hey, I also managed to save the company, don't forget that. You have to admit, Brett turned out to be a much better fit as an investor than Ernest Schneider would have been."

Luke rolled his eyes and busied himself with a sip of his beer, rarely one to admit he was wrong.

Orlando jutted his chin to Max. "So, what do you do with yourself these days?"

A rosy hue spread across Max's pale cheeks, and he shook the shaggy blond surfer waves from his eyes. "Not much, to be honest."

She laughed and leaned into Max with her shoulder. "He enjoys the yearly profit share he receives from the company, while trying to 'find himself'. Isn't that right?"

A grin pulled at her cheeks, and she turned to gauge Orlando's response, but something about his sudden frozen stare made the smile fall from her face.

He lowered his gaze down to his hand on the table, the careful gesture imploring her to look. There, his little finger on his left hand trembled. A small movement. Barely noticeable. But uncontrolled. And a very, very bad sign.

She met his gaze. An ashen tone stole brilliance from his golden olive skin. He peered down once more. She followed his line of sight. And the tremor claimed his next finger.

A sense of alarm shot through her body, her own hands shaking, but for a whole other reason. She needed to take quick action and help him.

She glanced at the others. The conversation had already moved on, while she and Orlando had been left behind. His eyes now pulled wide in a silent plea. He needed help. He needed her to get him out in a way that didn't alert everyone to his problem. He'd made a point of notifying only her, sign enough he didn't want the others involved.

She had little time. Her one idea was a long-shot. It would have to do.

She dropped a forkful of pasta from the side of her plate, into the lap of her teal dress. A large portion of white-sauce clung to the fabric.

"Oh, hell!" She leapt from her chair, the pasta landing with an awkward splat between her feet. She kept her voice loud, dragging attention away from Orlando. "Oh, I've made a mess. I'm so sorry."

"Don't worry about it." Agathe stood, hand outstretched, waving her forgiveness. "You go get yourself cleaned up, and we'll take care of everything here."

Sophie turned to Orlando, twisting her voice to play up her panic. "Would you help me?"

He rose in haste, his chair scraping against the floor. "Get to the bathroom. I'll find you a change of clothes."

She sent him a pinched smile, one that hopefully portrayed gratitude and not alarm. He jammed his still-trembling hand into the pocket of his black pants and followed her out of the room.

# Chapter Twenty-Seven

"Is it another episode?" Sophie slammed the bedroom door closed and turned to Orlando. She pressed her hands to his cheeks, taking stock of two positives—he was warm and his pupils were even in size. At least his circulation and brain function weren't altogether shot.

"I don't know what's happening to me." He doubled past her and slumped back against the closed door, breaths loud, but shallow. "I don't know…" He shook his head, shoulders now trembling too. "No. This. This is different."

His words rushed out, and sweat trickled down his temples. Her own muscles turned weak at the signs of his alarm.

Any moment now she might lose him to that childish voice again, the one reserved for his episodes. Or maybe something else entirely would happen. If she couldn't get him to slow down, then she'd have no choice but to call an ambulance. Then her entire family would know everything, and goodbye to his wish to save face.

He peered down at his right hand, the shakes having spread wider, producing a staggered tremor to his voice. "I…I don't. I don't…" He glanced up, pupils blackened and lost. "Help me. I can't stop it."

She wrapped his hand in hers, offering the warmth of her enclosed palms, trying to distract him. Her insides set heavy like concrete. Her hope sank with every passing second. What if everything she did wasn't enough?

*Think. Don't give up yet.*

*What do I do if someone is having a panic attack?*

Okay. Good. If she proceeded under the assumption that his trembling might be psychosomatic, then maybe she could stop this thing in its tracks.

"Orlando, look at me." He continued shaking but did as asked. She kept her voice gentle, steady, predictable. Attempted to play the role of a buoy amidst his mind's raging tempest. "Tell me what you need."

His gaze skittered around her face. "I…" A frown weighed his twisted expression as he struggled to control his words, much less his face. "Breathe. Help me breathe."

She peered at his chest. His sternum was heaving up and down, so, actually, he could breathe, but perhaps not enough as a result of whatever he experienced.

She rose a hand and pressed it to his cheek. Another sensory distraction. Another point of contact to help center him.

"Okay. Let's slow down. I'm going to count to ten, I'll go slow and you just try to slow right down with me. One… Two…" She counted, while a play-by-play of all they'd achieved in the last couple of weeks ran through her head. Everything hung in the balance. Especially the ramifications of Professor Bandara's treatments perhaps not working. That maybe Orlando's death sentence would be back on the table. Perhaps all the lightness and laughter he'd recently regained would go…

She couldn't stand for any of that. Though the dart of his gaze down at their joined hands seemed to convey similar thoughts crossed his mind. "You're doing great. Five… Six. Let go of your muscles."

She shifted a hand lower and rubbed her thumb over the thick tendon at the side of his neck. His gaze jolted back to hers, as if searching for a lifeline. As much as she'd needed him, he needed her more.

"The damage is done, Soph." His voice wobbled, similar to a man neck deep in a semi-frozen lake. "I'm falling apart, and your family thinks I'm crazy."

"You'll be okay, and they haven't noticed a thing." She brought her body closer to his, hoping to keep his thoughts on her. "Now focus for me, please. Seven… Eight."

His muscles spasmed. "They know we've disappeared together. They're not stupid. They'll figure we're either getting it on, or I'm having a spaz attack."

She locked her arms around him, losing sight over which of them needed the other most. The room's soft light and warm plum and burgundy tones did nothing to heat the chill working through her body. "I'm having a problem with my dress and you're helping me, remember? Besides, it doesn't matter what they think. Orlando, please, I need you to focus on slowing down."

"No. It does. It matters." He rushed his words, overly loud and uncontrolled, hitching between phrases. He pushed back, his stare landing on her, a man grappling for what precious seconds his mind afforded. "As much as I didn't want to, I found a new home with you. I care what you think." An uncontrolled shudder worked through his body. He clenched his eyes shut and stopped, as if pausing to fight off his trembles. "I care about the people you care about—the same people who care about you. What they think matters. My being here will affect how they see you when I'm gone. I don't want to embarrass either of us in front of them."

Her chest caved at the mention of him being gone, and she worked fast to suppress a surge of tears burning the backs of her eyes. Again, Candice's warning played on her mind. Where before he would have lashed out in anger, now fear reverberated through those pleading dark eyes. *Fear and vulnerability.* Where was her brash firefighter? The man who unleashed more passion in one minute than most summoned in their entire lives?

His broken honesty broke her, too. She wasn't a miracle worker. She was at best a newly minted doctor. And whatever had a hold of him lay always one step ahead. Just out of sight. Just out of reach. A mystery taunting her from afar.

And this man had endured years stripped of dignity, years of choices pried from his hands. Just when he thought he might get his old life back, this new incident set him adrift again. That he might have to face her family in his rattled state, with broken edges exposed. Perhaps her family's potential judgment would be his limit, amongst so many already shattered limits.

Pure instinct prompted her to throw herself toward him. She had to turn this around. Had to give him some small win. "Hold me. And don't let go this time."

Where he once would have scoffed, he merely did as she asked. His arms enfolded around her, and he shook. The tremors passed right through him and into her. She could feel his need and his pain. Like one of her injured birds.

His violent storm picked her up. Transported her back to her childhood. Back to her mother's arms, where all things bad could be made good again.

And that's when, for some inexplicable reason, she began to sing.

A lullaby her mother had gifted her.

She sang and she swayed.

A song for a child afraid of the dark. A child afraid of the blind unknown. When darkness held all that might hurt, much like the uncertainty Orlando experienced in each episode.

She would not let him go. Not until the fear subsided. Not until he found his calm, just as her mother had done for her as a child, and again that night when a scared sixteen-year-old Sophie sat on the edge of her white hospital bed crying. When she'd willed herself to get up and continue on with life, while everything within her refused to move.

Her mother had held her. Allowed her to cry. Until fat tears darkened the shoulder of her mother's emerald green sweater.

That same lullaby guided her now.

A song about Scarborough. Her home. *Parsley, sage, rosemary, and thyme...* A playful song, with a haunting melody. A song that offered relief. Protection. A reminder of times gone by and how small she was against the scheme of all history. That maybe, because of that, everything would be okay.

If only she could erase Orlando's pain, and just like the song did for her, offer him a comfort.

She opened her eyes, her voice still carrying the sweet, ancient melody. Orlando's purposeful breaths now skimmed her neck.

His shaking had stopped.

He squeezed her tighter, then stepped back and let go completely.

Though his gaze met hers, it lacked its usual fire. His attention shifted sideways. Shutting her out. As if reality stepped in to keep him from her reach.

She offered a smile in the hopes he might need a minute to regroup. "You're okay? This one wasn't so bad, right? Maybe the fact I was able to bring you back is a good sign? Maybe the meds are still doing their job?"

His attention snapped back to her, though his face still gave nothing away.

"Yeah. Maybe... Thanks." He turned for the door, his fingers already wrapping around the handle.

She'd helped him, yet his shuttered demeanor now made her heart drop to a sluggish beat.

"Let's get back to your family."

Orlando found his place at Luke's table, the scuff of Sophie's movements trailing somewhere behind him. He knew he shouldn't have walked from her, not after she'd just pulled him back from the brink of whatever the hell had just happened. But tonight was a reality check. A *much needed* reality check. A reality check on just how much he didn't belong. Not with these people who were too undamaged, with too much to look forward to.

She took a seat beside him and from his peripheral vision, her stare burned into him. Understanding. Compassionate.

But a mess like him could offer no more than a tangle of humiliating outbursts on top of non-existent prospects. He needed to release her. Sooner rather than later.

"Seems Sophie didn't bring a change of dress after all?" Luke stared at him with a quizzical look.

"Oh, that." Sophie gave a tight laugh. "Everyone here knows me well enough, and I'll probably head up to bed soon, anyway. I figured I didn't need to do the whole outfit change thing."

She gave a playful shrug. A very fake, somewhat strained, playful shrug.

The muscles in Orlando's jaw bunched. She didn't need to cover for him. He wasn't a cyclone and she his clean-up crew. If anything, he'd come to Luke's house to support her.

He gritted his teeth, tempted to admit they'd left the table because of him. Him and his stupid condition. Him and the fucked-up dream that brought him to this home with her family to begin with. That maybe he could be normal. That maybe he could have a relationship with Sophie beyond their secretive outings alone together. That he could learn how to live again, if only for a short while. Well, clearly fucking not.

And all that, for what? He wasn't getting better. His attack just proved Professor Bandara and her magic meds didn't work.

He recalled the bargaining scrunch of Sophie's face, her unwavering stare, and the way she'd pleaded with him to breathe with her. And then how she'd sung him a song, trying to get him to stop shaking…

*Christ.* Watching her joy give way to panic had brought him as close to torture as the attack itself.

And something as close to a lullaby as anyone could get, of all things, had stopped his episode. No experimental science. No highly esteemed professor… No. *A song. A bloody song.* And one that might as well have been for a child.

In the early days of his episodes, he'd read all he could about neurological disorders—including how music could sometimes soothe patients with dementia. Music was apparently intrinsic to every human culture. Its effects were imprinted on even the most inaccessible parts of most people's brains. And Sophie, with her song, had played him like a fine-tuned fiddle. It seemed that, in the heat of an encroaching episode, his mind had been reduced to the base level of a baby.

*How fucking pathetic.*

He sucked in a quiet breath, allowing an inevitable truth to sink in;

one that acknowledged what he needed to do next. He couldn't keep bringing her down.

*I don't deserve her. Why can't I get that to sink into my thick skull?*

As hopeful as she'd been, he didn't share her hope. Sparing her from impending heartbreak would be his best parting gift. She was too good for him in so many ways. Her future too bright. And even in the best-case scenario, even if he got his life back, he'd be starting out all over again with nothing to his name.

She deserved better. She deserved more.

Agathe turned to Luke with a joyful spark in her eyes—a spark Orlando hadn't ever witnessed in Sophie—perhaps because, unlike Sophie, Agathe had more than just hard work and a bitter ending to look forward to.

Agathe turned to him next, beaming grin still in place. "Well, if Sophie's set on wrapping things up, before you both go, Luke and I have a question to ask you, Orlando. Would you like to come to our wedding next week? You know, as Sophie's plus one?"

Sophie twisted in her seat, her body angled toward him. Her hazel focus locked to his. Once again, no joy lit her eyes. Certainly nothing resembling the joy Agathe displayed. Only wide hopefulness. Wide hopefulness with a heavy edge of doubt. The same sad look she gave him every time she expected he'd say no. The look of a woman used to disappointment.

Or more precisely… disappointment *from him.*

A hard lump knotted within his chest, twisting and writhing, burrowing deep. He wanted to say no. *Of course, he did.* Tonight's near episode meant he couldn't predict what would happen at the wedding. But he owed Sophie. He owed her so much. More than he could ever repay. She held impossibly still, her face holding an optimistic glow…

His presence at the wedding meant the world to her, and without him, she'd almost definitely go alone.

So, he nodded.

A held breath hissed out of her. A hiss of relief.

And there it was, the glitter of joy now lighting her eyes, her sad smile momentarily gone. For that alone, he'd endure another night out. Or more precisely, one *final* night out.

He reached for his glass of water and downed a large gulp. Somehow, he'd have to keep his battered mind together and get through another evening without letting her down. Without turning himself into another burden. An evening a thousand times more important than this one.

Soon, dinner wrapped up and everyone said goodnight. He walked back upstairs with Sophie. The moment the bedroom door closed, she rounded on him, face pinched in concern. Or hurt. Or maybe anger. He couldn't quite tell.

"What happened after your episode tonight? You closed up on me. You shut me out."

He tugged his collar open, his neck itchy and all too hot. His gaze dipped to the white smudge of pasta sauce still marking her dress. A mess she'd orchestrated to bail him out of trouble.

"It's nothing." He turned away. *Turned from her. From his own lie.* Then distracted himself with ripping open buttons on his shirt and then pitching the light fabric onto the bed. "Whatever happened rattled me, okay? I'm fine now."

He couldn't tell her the truth. That he saw everything with her and his medical issues spiraling down and out of his control. The more he confided in her, the more she dug her heels in. She'd never leave him. Not willingly. Perhaps not even to fulfill the promise she'd already made. She'd sacrifice herself to the end. And the mere knowledge of her sticking around and ruining her future brought vicious pain to his heart.

She couldn't save him. *Shouldn't* save him. Saving him had never been her job. A job he'd specifically asked her *not* to take on. But she'd taken it on anyway.

And tonight's near miss only proved how much that misstep would cost her. She'd sacrificed enough. He couldn't let this continue much longer.

The soft padding of her feet neared behind him. He stifled a jolt, his darker emotions imploding, as her hands slipped around his waist. "Are you sure you're okay? Tonight worried me. I can't imagine how it felt for you."

His muscles tensed at the press of her warm cheek between his shoulder blades.

*Why did she have to be so damn compassionate all the time?*

He turned and gripped her wrists to his chest, exchanging his need to shield her for the open conversation she deserved. "Tonight was a warning, Sophie. Don't get ahead of yourself. Okay?"

She offered a gentle, knowing smile, and flattened her palms to his chest. Just as always, her touch seared into his skin, sparking an unavoidable need. "It'll be okay. You'll see."

"Sophie, you can't say—"

She stood on her tippy toes and pressed her soft lips to his. "I can. See…" She kissed him again, her sweeter, more playful way of silencing his doubts. "It'll be okay."

The scent of spring flowers and something uniquely her teased his senses. He groaned against another of her feather light kisses, clinging to an urge to warn and protect. "Sophie."

"Orlando." She lowered her heels, and her head leveled with his chest, her attention lifted. "It'll be okay."

She raised a brow. Challenging him.

Somehow, she'd found it in her to unearth a good mood—making him one heck of a giant asshole if he spoiled her optimism with his need for bleak predictions and caution. Besides, at least until after the wedding, they had more time. And she had the ability to turn his caginess into contentment. Doom and gloom could wait while love and affection shone a little longer.

Only she could deliver him from the shrieking pit of nothingness he lived in most days. He would have to end this soon. But not tonight.

Tonight, she was still his.

# Chapter Twenty-Eight

Sophie tucked her hand into Orlando's, her muscles relaxing at the live harp music drifting through the small, ornamental garden. A gathering of about sixty friends and family settled in collective silence, while Luke stood mere meters away from her out front, face pale and gaze glassy at the top of the aisle. The last bridesmaid swanned her way down, and the final murmurs died. Agathe appeared from behind the russet vine arch at the back of the crowd—her dress a gorgeous fairy tale puff, billowing ice-white lace and satin into the aisles. Her bouquet was a giant ball of burgundy roses, and a single large rose sat perched behind her ear.

The white dress glowed against her nutmeg skin, the bursts of red added extra drama and warmth. A charged quiet hinted at the gravity of what was about to take place—a ceremony of promises and forever, hopes and fears. A day to bind two lives together for eternity.

Agathe stopped beside Luke beneath the circular arch, another thick forest of burgundy roses framing her and her future husband.

The celebrant neared, and Max shifted into position just behind his brother.

Luke. *Oh Luke.* Gone was the pale skin and glassy gazing, his features lifted and eyes sparkling for the woman beside him.

Sophie's heart squeezed, and Orlando's grip tightened in sync around her hand. Did he feel it too? The sense of rightness in the world. A dreaminess. That maybe, just maybe, *they* might have this one day, too.

Tears prickled the corners of her eyes, and the muscles in her throat strained. She was being foolish and certainly getting way ahead of herself. All she really wanted was for him to enjoy this day. To forget the darkness of his near-episode last week. To adopt the professor's nonplussed attitude and focus on the positive. He hadn't escalated to a full-blown episode, and with his meds now tweaked, maybe a similar happy future awaited him as well.

Though maybe not with her.

She drew a strained breath and focused on the scent of red roses and how Agathe's deep crimson lips spread into a wide smile. Because of love. Because love had cured all. Or at least, that had been true for Agathe. Her life before Luke was far from any fairy tale.

She'd endured the senseless death of her child. The end of a marriage. And years and years of destructive behavior and isolation. And though her first days with Luke had been tumultuous, love *had* won in the end.

Sophie shuddered, an involuntary reaction against the subtle changes that had occurred between her and Orlando in the last week. More a change in mood and energy than anything she could put her finger on. He peered down, as if her shuddering caught his attention, but she shook her head, letting him know she'd be okay.

Not the best. Not what she wanted. But *okay*.

Just okay.

She pressed her hand to her lower abdomen, around about where her uterus would be, heart sinking further. Yet another portion of hope had slipped away. A last portion of hope she still struggled to share with Orlando, but a lost hope she'd have to tell him about either way. But how could she have held onto this particular hope without ever even knowing she'd cared?

She squeezed her eyes shut and crammed her rising guilt.

How would Orlando react?

*Hush. Everything will be fine. Orlando's problems will improve. He'll go on without me. And he'll never, ever again think about hurting himself.*

She opened her eyes to Luke sliding a plain gold band onto Agathe's trembling finger.

*Damn it.* She needed to focus, or she'd miss the whole wedding.

The celebrant rang off more sentiments, and then the happy couple shared a passionate kiss. Guests whooped and cheered, while tears rained down her cheeks.

She was happy for her brother, heartbroken for herself.

*I'm a losing bet, remember?*

Orlando's words echoed in her head, as if the man standing next to her remained that same, angry resident she'd met months ago. But he wasn't that man anymore. And he wasn't to blame for her heartache now.

She'd been the one with choices. The one who could always cut and run.

But she hadn't. And her pain now was all her fault.

Every day took her closer to leaving him. And something worse. To learning he might never recover. If that happened—if he hurt himself —a piece of her would stay forever broken too.

Orlando locked an arm around her waist, heat engulfing her hip where his hand lay. His smile beamed down at her in a look of happy sympathy. "Sucker for weddings, huh?"

She laughed and gave a quick nod, wiping away her tears with an open palm. "For some reason, watching my smelly older brother get married makes for a cathartic experience."

His smile grew, his glinting, brown eyes setting her heart to flutter before he pulled her into a tight embrace, her head tucked under his chin, her face buried against his navy-blue suit jacket.

The scent of freshly laundered fabric and woodsy-sage warmed her senses. He usually just smelled of soap and man, but this new fragrance turned her stomach hollow—simply because he never had reasons to dress up, much less wear suits and cologne. For better or worse, she'd changed his world. And he'd changed hers.

"Come on." He planted a kiss on her cheek and pulled back, her heart stumbling as his thumbs wiped away her last remnants of tears.

"As the groom's sister, you'll have to pose for photos, but after that, we're free to escape to the reception together."

~

From rag-tag country boy, to stupidly confident fireman. To now. The guy with nothing going for him except a limited life within the walls of an aged care facility... Luke and Agathe's wedding reception brought Orlando worlds away from anything he knew.

No expense had been spared, and everything about this place, from the orange light spilling from the chandeliers, to the scent of cinnamon and clove hanging in the air, screamed, *You don't belong here.*

But then, Sophie. Sophie was here. And therefore, so was he.

He couldn't have made her come alone. Not when she'd asked. Not when presented with the one thing he *could* do for her. The one thing guaranteed to make her happy, when so much about their union was constructed on the graveness of a ticking clock. And also because... well, frankly... he loved her.

*He loved her.*

He tugged at his collar, his shirt a discomfort after years of growing accustomed to wearing t-shirts and sweat pants. At one point in his life, a dressy shirt and tailored trousers had been his second uniform. He'd lived to go out. To put on a show. To pull in a new woman. The mere act of wearing a suit now made him feel like a fraud. Which only made him wonder how many people at this event knew his story and thought the same.

Did anyone here look at him and see a freak on display? Maybe. Or maybe no one did. Still, the whole suit charade, coupled with this reception and all its extravagance, only rubbed in just how much he could never compete with Luke or Max's financial wealth.

Even if his condition disappeared tomorrow, he had no money. No security. No means of providing for Sophie in the ways he wanted to.

And even with all the impossibilities and differences, he still managed to damn-well love her.

"Will you dance with me?" Her sweet voice pried him from his doubts, and he took in the details of her floor-length peach dress. The fitted cut matched her slender build and innate grace. A row of delicate glass beads circled the high collar, lighting her already glinting hazel eyes. How on earth would he let her go?

The woman belonged here. In a place as lavish as this. He didn't.

But then, she held out a hand to him, and he had no other answer. "How can I say no?"

She laughed, nudging him with an elbow as he took her hand. "You never had a problem saying no before."

"We wouldn't be together now if I'd made it easy for you." He led her toward the sparse dance floor. "We both know you prefer men who play hard to get."

He tugged her into him, and she laughed again. He relished the trilling sound and her soft warmth. He would have to say no to her *soon*. Would have to break it to her that their relationship needed to end. Though the precise word would be more like *goodbye* rather than *no*.

Her head came to rest on his chest, blessing him with her light scent of daisies, but then she pulled back enough to look at him, eyes glittering. "So that was your plan all along? Reel me in with angry glares and fake trips to biker bars?"

An ache unfurled in his chest, but he offered a lopsided smile, wanting to enjoy this exchange while he could still be the one to hold her in his arms. "What can I say, my sick idea of charm?"

She threw back her head and laughed once more, offering the concession that he'd made her happy. At least for tonight. "You definitely picked a riskier form of flirting."

*God.* That effortless laugh. Those flecked, hazel eyes. Her ability to make him dance with her in a crowded room when months ago he would have flatly refused.

She'd broken so many of his barriers, given him a last chance at being a man. He'd be forever grateful. But a woman like her belonged with someone else. With someone who had more to offer. And keeping her would be cruel, if not impossible.

She stared at him, her attention darting about his face as though she read his thoughts. "Orlando?" Her hand rose to cup his cheek. "I have news. I don't know whether to call it good or bad, or how you're going to feel, but…"

His heartbeat plodded, as if conserving energy for the shock of whatever she had to say. "Share it anyway. Let me decide."

"I…ummm…" Her gaze dropped to his chin; it seemed she struggled to hold a direct stare. "I thought maybe the outcome would be different. I mean, I was almost three weeks late, and I guess I was too scared to take a test, but I figured sometimes I'm irregular any—"

"Sophie." He frowned, wanting her to stop rambling and get on with the plain truth of whatever news she had to share. "What are you trying to say?"

Her gaze shot up to his, and she held quiet for a second.

"I'm not pregnant." She bit into her lower lip, like she hadn't meant to blurt the harsh truth. Her focus left his face and slipped down to his chest. "I got my period a few days ago. I'm not pregnant. And I thought you should know."

His shoulders sagged, and his hands ached with an urge to let her go—not out of rejection or judgment—but because of one biological truth. His last fleeting chance to father a child had just passed him by.

He pressed his jaw shut, unsure what to say. Unsure of Sophie's feelings, especially in light of her past. His potential for keeping this woman had just diminished even further. Or maybe, he'd been handed a small gift. Another opening to set her free.

*What poor child would deserve me as their dad?*

"Orlando?"

She frowned up at him. He shook away the thought. Somehow, he felt numb and on fire all at once. The news was sobering, painful, somehow predictable, yet too much to process.

He gave her hand a gentle squeeze, then pulled her close to land a kiss on the top of her head.

"I can't call this good or bad news. It's…" He swallowed back a need to say much more. "It's sad."

A couple just a few meters away gave a soft laugh, the clinking of champagne glasses complemented the mellow jazz quartet playing on the stage. The subdued light illuminated a defused halo of red around

Sophie's sable hair. Despite the heavy topic, a sense of intimacy danced around her.

"You probably don't want to hear this"—she looked down again, chin wobbling—"but I'm calling this bad news." She peered back up at him, eyes glistening as though she clung to a wall of emotion. "You know my past. And these last months with you, I didn't expect to feel this way." She gave a shaky laugh, trying, but failing to recover composure. "Getting knocked up right now would have been terrible timing. I'm still not ready to have a kid. Neither are you. God, I don't even know what to call this thing between us, but…" She squeezed her eyes shut and took a long breath. "But I'm still disappointed. And I can't help thinking, if things had been different, if I was pregnant, then I would have… I would have… I would have found a way to make it all work."

Her body shook along with her words, and he pulled her into him, tucking her head beneath his chin and offering a soothing, *shhhh*. She didn't need to explain. He understood. Though he couldn't say if he had the right to wish for a different result.

The sad sheen in her eyes. Her words of regret. So much about this woman dug an agonizing pit in his stomach. And with every encounter, she dug deeper into places and desires he'd had no idea existed within him. And then *this*. Holy hell, this moment did things to him. To hear she'd wanted *his* child all along. To know that if circumstances were different, he'd want the same. That he'd bundle her up and kiss away the pain and promise they'd try again someday soon.

But circumstances weren't different, and it wasn't safe to get any more attached.

His life was a twisted joke.

To find her.

To love her.

And after tonight, to do the humane thing and let her go.

She turned her head against his chest and obscured his view of her face. "Urghh. I'm sorry. I sound irrational."

He lifted her chin and cupped her face, forcing her to look at him, and then he pressed his forehead to hers. A million volts of electricity surged through his body, prickling his back and lifting the hairs along his arms. She was right. Her wanting his child was irrational, but then...

"Sophie, the only irrational thing about all of this is that I'm at a wedding with you tonight instead of at the home staring at my ceiling, alone, as I have been every day for years before you barged into my life. And of all the impossible things, that I get to hold you in my arms, and that you feel anything for me. At least for now..." He stopped to watch the concerned wrinkles on her forehead smooth and a slow smile grow over her cheeks.

The mere sight made his throat clog and his voice drop to a hoarse whisper. "You're beautiful. Unselfishly kind. You're more than I could have ever wanted or imagined. The only irrational thing about you is that you're with me. Do you understand? And for that reason, it's a damn good thing you're not having my child."

She moved to talk, but he shook his head, demanding she listen and stay crystal clear on just how much they couldn't be together. "The chemistry we share is enough to contend with, you don't need anything more forcing us together, certainly not a child. What you need is to be free to live the life you're supposed to have."

"But what if you're part of the life I'm supposed to have?"

His heart clenched with a desire to believe that. But he shook his head again, certain she was wrong. He'd let himself get caught up in her beauty and painful brand of gentleness long enough, and his love for her cleaved into his heart with more power than that of a steel axe. Their relationship should have been casual at most, but his feelings had long bolted far from his senses, and now they'd both pay the price. No matter how much he wanted to agree with her, he simply couldn't.

"We had a deal."

"Life isn't a linear plan, Orlando. Isn't that what you've been telling me all along?" Her body went tight within his hold. "Maybe our deal sucks."

He clamped his jaw shut to keep from knee-jerk agreeing with her.

The rise in her voice meant they needed to have this conversation somewhere private. So, he slid his hand down into hers and tugged her along, guiding her through the main exit until they stood to the side of the venue in the fresh night air.

The plan *did* suck, but…

"Our plan will save you, Sophie." She made eye contact, and her frown indicated anger, but he pressed on all the same. The night would be over soon, and he couldn't spare her this cold reality any longer. "This is the only thing I want from you. The only thing I've asked for."

She pushed her chin out, but the hardness in her eyes wavered.

"Why?" She didn't even try to hide the pained tininess in her voice. "Because you think my future is worth more than yours?"

"No." He inched his face closer, his tone now reduced to a strained whisper. "Because you actually have a future and I don't."

"You don't know that. Professor Bandara isn't fin—"

"I won't bring you down with me. Do you understand?"

He wanted Sophie to understand, but her sharp attention surveyed his face, features softening, as if her analytical mind worked to fit a bunch of new and formerly unknown pieces together.

"You could never bring me down. It's not in your nature. The mere fact you so adamantly protect me. I wish you could see yourself through my eyes…" Her voice trailed, and she peered at the ground, hinting she was lost in thought. "You're a good man, Orlando, with an unnerving stare and an uncanny stillness. There are moments where just being beside you brings calm to someone like me. Someone who needs to know the answer to everything at the smallest sign of uncertainty." She gave a heartier grin, her words competing with the rustle of wind through nearby trees. "I don't think I've ever felt as *me* as when I'm with you."

His chest drew tight, like his heart expanded in an attempt to bust out. "It's not enough."

"It is for me." She blinked up at him. "*You* are enough for me."

He stared down at her. Unable to say or do much else. Her eyes held open sincerity, which made his emotions war between pushing her away and holding on to her forever.

As if forever were an option…

He bit down on his burgeoning words, but he couldn't stop now. No matter how messy things got from here on out, he could at least give her this. He didn't want to be without her, but being with her was unworkable. Foolish. The most selfish thing he could do.

The best compromise would be not to let her go without hearing just how much she meant to him.

"If you could see yourself through my eyes, you'd see the woman who saved me." He paused, needing a second to find some stillness. "You'd see the first person to dig deep enough to really notice me. You've forced me to care. You've forced me to see myself and the good that still exists within me and around me. And for the first time in years, I don't completely hate what I see."

The spread of a slow and lazy smile etched small creases over her cheekbones. "What are you trying to say?"

The optimism on her face twisted a knife in his gut. But she had to know.

"Do you think when you first met me, you could have ever imagined we'd get along? That I'd be standing here with you now, immersing myself in your family and life?"

She released a soft laugh. "No, no, and no."

He reached out and stroked his thumb over her cheek, memorizing the velvet softness of her skin and the way the outer corners of her eyes lifted. "Then does that say enough about what I'm thinking? How I feel about you?"

She shook her head, her hand coming to rest over his heart. "Not nearly enough. So, if you've got something to say, say it now. We're at a wedding, right? The timing couldn't be more perfect."

Her glistening eyes, her look of hope, dumped more pain on his heart. She wanted him to say words he'd never said to any woman beside his own mother. Words he *did* want to say, but words that clashed with his need to release her from his life. And damn it. Words he wasn't sure he deserved to utter.

"This isn't easy for me."

"Please." She pressed to him, her small body adding warmth in the night. "Say it anyway."

An amplified voice broke through an outdoor speaker attached to the building's side. The overly loud sound ripped at his attention. Something about the bridal dance starting soon, and could everyone please gather on the dance floor. Next came the muffled scraping of chairs from inside, followed by the stomping of many feet.

He returned his focus to Sophie. To her hopeful stare and her request to hear his declaration of love.

Despite his planned exit from her life, he'd regret missing his one chance to tell her how he felt. To give her something to take with her. Maybe his admission would be as much for her sake, as his. He couldn't leave her wondering.

Her smile dropped, and she tilted her head sideways, her attention on him turning hyper-focused and narrow. Something was off. She looked perplexed.

He pressed his fingertips to his cheek, certain an involuntary tremor reverberated through his jaw.

"Orlando?" Her eyelids flared, and her hand locked around his wrist, hard, unnaturally commanding.

He peered down. His entire hand shook beneath hers.

"Orlando." Her voice rose to a yell. Why did she think he couldn't hear?

A sharp pain sliced through his head. Disorientating. Torturous. He jolted back. Away from her. Swatted at her. As if she'd been the one to hurt him.

"Orlando!"

Her hand beat at his chest. Fierce. Pleading. She wanted to get through to him.

*Didn't she know?* He could see her. Hear her. Feel her.

But then the world fell around him. Or maybe he fell.

Yes. A fall.

He'd fallen.

The ground was cold.

And then came black.

# Chapter Twenty-Nine

Sophie turned to the woman sitting next to her in the hospital waiting room, the one wearing sweat pants and a bedraggled lopsided ponytail. She peered down at her own peach evening gown, with its floor-length hem and glass beads. From her experience, people tended to show up to emergency rooms in all sorts of outfits. At least in that regard, her overdressed state meant she fit right in.

She dropped her head back against the cream-colored wall behind her and let out an exhausted sigh. The white fluorescent lights made her eyes sting and her skull ache. She'd been shut out. Relegated to this waiting room. While the honor of sitting by Orlando's side went to his mother.

Not that she protested Marcella's presence. Sophie had used his phone to call her during the panicked ambulance ride over, after all—moments before he'd woken up in some kind of altered personality state, freaking out at the strange environment, and as a result had been sedated into unconsciousness. He'd since woken up again but banished her from his side. And for the time being, he refused to see her.

She'd tried bargaining with a nurse to gain entry. Had even tried the *but I'm a doctor* card. Only to be told again to stay out. So now she sat here, alone, contemplating what it all meant. What, if any, future existed between her and Orlando.

She leaned forward in the gray plastic seat, elbows pressed to her knees. Too shaken to cry. Too worked up to merely sit and wait. So, she did what most people did when all they could do was begrudgingly cool their heels. She pulled out her phone.

Her social media feed didn't offer much more than videos of friends' babies laughing or various acquaintances holding up drinks at whatever party. None of it steered her thoughts away from the closed double doors ahead of her.

For the briefest moment, she'd thought Orlando had been on the cusp of declaring his love for her. Like maybe she could entertain a reasonable dream of extending her stay another month or two to see if maybe his health stabilized. To support him if it didn't. To perhaps plan an alternate future for her away from London.

Her studies wouldn't start for some time yet. Her professors would potentially let her commence the first few weeks of term online. Despite Orlando's protests, she might have even considered switching to an Australian university. But now…

Now everything lay uncertain.

Still, she had every intention of proving to him they could work through anything. No matter the damage from this latest episode. *They* would be okay.

She scrolled through her phone contacts, contemplating whether to call Hannah, only to decide that would be a bad idea. She still hadn't told Hannah about Orlando. She couldn't do so now. Not in a moment of crisis, with so much to explain, and in light of just how sick she felt at the thought of recounting all that occurred. And if she told Hannah none of it, and called simply to say hi, then Hannah would no doubt go on a verbal tangent about all things Randal Berry. And the last person Sophie cared about right now was *Randal Berry*.

Her insane, illogical crush on that guy might as well have been a million years ago. And in the wake of loving Orlando Piras, Randal Berry was a fresh-faced and bratty schoolboy, with zero substance beyond his last pub crawl and whatever girl he just happened to be dating.

No. She didn't need him. Or any other guy. Or anything else waiting for her back in London. All she wanted was the man she'd watched collapse in front of her some four hours ago. To know he'd be okay and that in spite of him telling her to leave, in spite of her stupid promise to return to the UK, all between them wasn't lost.

Instead of watching him collapse, she wanted to return to the moment just before that. The magical moment where he'd held her, ready to say the words she'd waited to hear her entire life… Even though she'd had no idea she'd been waiting to hear them.

She lifted her gaze to the emergency room doors, the eerie stillness another reminder of all that had been snatched from her. Watching him collapse put her feelings under a microscope. The ordeal changed everything. She was weeks away from leaving, but how could she leave when he needed her?

She simply *had* to be there for him.

Candice's earlier warnings played on her thoughts. Not just about his potentially fragile state of mind, but the sometimes-harsh severity of his episodes. What awaited beyond those doors? Would the Orlando she'd come to know be gone forever?

The air around her hovered at overly cold, and she rubbed her hands over the backs of her exposed arms, her attention dropping to her phone balanced precariously in her lap. A white notification panel at the top of the screen flashed, declaring she had an unopened message. She tapped the panel, and a profile photo of Hector popped up.

HECTOR

Times are tough here in London Town. How much is this photo worth to you?

She tapped the concealed attachment, only to be confronted with a photo of her standing in front of a mirror wearing nothing but her underwear. The same photo she'd sent Orlando weeks ago.

Her mouth dropped open, and her blood ran like ice water through her veins. And just as quickly, she launched into fight mode and typed back.

You've got to be joking.

Never contend with a man who has nothing to lose. Right, Sophie? :)

She scowled at her photo, lips pouted in a mock kiss, breasts barely covered in a thin layer of black lace. Not something she was all that ashamed of, but not something she'd want any future employers, colleagues, or patients to see should they run a search of her name.

As amicable as she'd thought the break up with Hector had been, she found herself somehow unsurprised he'd make his presence known in the worse kind of way and at the worst possible time.

He'd always had a buried vindictive streak. Always been somewhat peeved about the good things that entered her life. The few times she and Hannah had hit the town, he'd hounded her with text messages about when she'd be getting home, rather than just wishing her a good night and trusting her to make her own decisions. The fact he'd struggled to find a job in an industry usually falling over itself to hire, only deepened his bitterness. And that bitterness only deepened his dullness.

So, what's your plan, post the photo to your newsfeed and embarrass me in front of our mutual friends? Why are you doing this?

Why not?

Because I haven't done anything to you. This is beneath you.

What's beneath me is having to pretend it's okay that my girlfriend dumped me so she could jet off across the world. I thought there'd be a chance we'd work things out when you got back. But what's REALLY beneath me is receiving sporadic photos of you with your new boyfriend in our shared photo account.

*Oh no. Oh God. Their shared account. She'd forgotten all about that.*

Hector had always been the more technical one. He was a programmer after all. At some point in their relationship, he'd insisted on setting up an automatic back up of all photos taken with their phones. She'd forgotten, but Hector clearly hadn't.

> Go for it. You sad-faced little man-baby. You'll just come across as a vindictive ex. Of course, you decided on my behalf that we might get back together. You never did care to actually listen to what I wanted. And by the way, any rational person would have simply reminded me to deactivate my end of the account, not use the opportunity to keep tabs on me.

> Sounds like your new lover boy has turned you into a real bitch, you know that? And no, I won't be sharing anything to my feed. In fact, there'll be nothing linked to me at all. Can't say it won't turn up anywhere a future employer or patient might look though... :)

A ball of heat exploded in her belly. She wanted to scream. Or at least throw her damn phone. But Hector was right about one thing, she was being more brash than usual, and she had Orlando's influence to thank for that.

> What do you even want from me?

> I still need work. Your brother is a power player within the same industry. What do you think?

> So you want a job?

> Bingo. And a good one at that. And a positive introduction to other power players.

She grimaced at her phone. How naïve she must have been to have given this man so many years of her life. As if she'd pull Luke into this mess.

> Have you ever thought that maybe no one will hire you because they see everything you lack? The fact you're trying to blackmail me might be a hot tip on your not-so-charming personality…

> Whatever. I've decided to make my own luck and you're my ticket in. Call it a favor for old time's sake, if that'll make you feel better. You have a month, Sophie. Got it?

> No. I haven't 'got' anything. Why would my brother tarnish his reputation recommending you?

> Everything comes at a cost. Luke's a businessman, he'll know this. Maybe he'll decide your reputation is more valuable than his. Honestly, I don't care.

> You're an ass.

> Screw you. You have one month.

Sophie hissed out an expletive and switched off her phone, before tossing it into her clutch purse on the seat beside her. She didn't have the headspace to think about Hector or his ultimatum, but a new wave of nausea crashed within her. For the second time in her entire life, she felt completely trapped, like a scared rabbit in a cage waiting for whatever terrible thing might happen next. First with Orlando, and now her ex.

She peered up, and a small gasp broke from her at Orlando's mother standing before the emergency doors watching her. Marcella's washed-out blue eyes held no joy; she tilted her head to one side to say Sophie should follow.

The ashen tinge on Marcella's face indicated Sophie would detest what was to come. The nausea didn't abate. It solidified into a hard lump in her gut. Her feet were heavy as lead as they carried her to Marcella's side.

The older woman placed a hand on her shoulder and guided her through the corridors. "This one was bad. Maybe now you take my advice?"

Sophie nodded, her thoughts a soupy fog. *Please don't break my boy's heart. If you feel for him, let him go.*

A twisting maze of cream walls and nurses' desks flicked by, but eventually, she spotted Professor Bandara waiting outside a room, hands crossed over her casual red cardigan as if she'd been called in just for this.

Sophie paused. "How is he?"

"From what I understand…" The professor gave a mild, but telling, cringe. "It's the worst one he's had in over a year."

Sophie nodded and took a step toward the door, but the professor's hand shot out and stopped her. "I need to warn you. He's very unwell, Sophie. I'm talking minor mobility in his limbs, and similar to all his past major episodes, no one knows if or when he'll regain movement. He's not in the best mood, either."

"Is that why you're standing out here and not in there?" Sophie tried to ignore the tremble in her voice, the surge of prickling heat all over her skin.

The professor gave a slow and hopeless nod. She too had been banished.

Sophie envisioned Orlando unleashing his hot temper at Professor Bandara, the one he'd blanketed for weeks under the hope of getting the help he'd dreamed of. That hope and his dreams were now shattered.

She closed her eyes, steeling herself for what awaited through the frosted glass door.

In trying to help him, she'd betrayed him. In trying to know him, she'd knocked down walls built to avoid the same demoralizing blow he dealt with now.

She lifted her chin, as always, hunting for the last sliver of hope. "Does this mean your job is done? The treatment is an official failure?"

"No. Far from it." The professor shook her head. "This episode could be completely separate from my treatment. We're still in the experimental phase, and we may need many months to get his therapy right. But from what I just saw, I don't expect he'll invite me back to do any more experimenting."

Sophie pressed her hand flat to the door.

"There's just one more thing."

She paused and turned to the professor again.

The professor frowned, gaze downcast as she recommenced talking. "Orlando doesn't know this yet, but his lashing out in the ambulance prompted questions from a number of hospital staff. They want to know why he's in an aged care facility without being on behavior modifying drugs." Her expression dimmed, while her lips formed a hard line—perhaps over what she had to say next. "I'm almost certain someone will report this, in which case, there'll be major upheaval at the center. Orlando's might soon not have a home to return to."

# Chapter Thirty

For the longest time, Sophie just stared at Orlando, and he stared right back. A shocked silence ebbed and flowed between them—the moment alive with its own heavy pulse. He lay propped up on the adjustable bed, intravenous lines running from the back of his hand, while a fingertip monitor tracked his oxygen levels. She'd barely made it a meter from the door before she'd had to stop, too shaken at the sight of a usually vital Orlando laid out and vulnerable in this hospital bed.

He rolled his focus off her and sunk his head deeper into the pillow, his resigned gaze redirected to the ceiling. "Say something."

Her mouth hung agape. She opened and closed it a few times before managing a sound. "I...I don't know what to say."

He released a hollow laugh. "That's a first."

"How bad is it?"

"I can't move or feel my legs. Arms are limited. So, bad." Something about his flat delivery worried her more than his inability to move. "I'm thinking the usual months of daily rehab until I regain full function."

"Orlando." She stepped deeper into the room but not quite close enough to take a seat in the chair beside his bed. "I'm so sorry."

"I don't want your sympathy." He pushed out a jagged whisper. "I only asked you here to let you know we need to end what we have. Consider this early permission to move on with your life."

Coldness hit her, and her chest constricted as if fielding an almighty blow. A wild rush of burning tingles overtook her entire body. She said nothing. Just stared.

He spoke again, "You should go."

"I can't." Her tone seemed to come from a place low within, dull and disconnected, so far away someone else might as well have answered for her. "I want to help you. It doesn't have to be like this. Please."

He snapped his head up, his gaze finally rejoining hers, deep brown eyes dilating with palpable fury. "I wasn't suggesting you leave, I was telling you. I want you to go."

The severity of his farewell left her wobbling in place. His old defensive ways had kicked back to life, stronger than ever, a hot iron branding her with rejection.

"Maybe I'll do that, but first, I need to know you won't harm yourself."

He reeled back, as much as any bedridden man *could* reel back— eyes flaring, chin pressing down. "Harm myself? What the hell sort of a question is that?"

"If you're set on removing me from your life, I want to know you'll be okay."

Though her muscles felt weak, she couldn't let him give up. If not for him, then for her. She loved him. Wanted him to love her back. And after months of overcoming seemingly impossible hurdles, surely he could find it in him to fight again. To fight for her. He'd verged on voicing his love just hours before, hadn't he?

His eyes narrowed. "Is that really all it is?"

"Yes."

"How long have you been holding onto the idea I want to harm myself?"

A quiver worked through her muscles, but she forged on. "Just promise me."

"I don't have to promise you anything."

Her shoulders sagged, and the lack of assurance left her feeling sick. But then the silence dragged, and his scowl lost all energy. He turned from her with a sigh.

"Look, let's make one thing clear. I'd be lying if I said harming myself has never crossed my mind, but I'm not suicidal. I'm a realist. I know I'm not expected to get better. I know I'll probably die decades before my time. And in that case, my suffering would be drawn out and my final days difficult. I have no intention of hurting myself anytime soon, nor have I ever. But if I've given you that impression, it's only because I decided long ago that if things got bad enough, I'd go through the proper channels and use the state's assisted dying laws."

Her mind floundered to process what she knew of him against what he'd just said, plus all the various other perspectives given to her from those who knew him.

He turned to her again, seeming to lose patience with her lack of response.

"Do you hear what I'm saying? There'd be doctors and multiple legal hoops to jump through, a well-timed lethal injection, and even that would only happen under very specific circumstances. And if I did go down that path, it'd be with the goal of ending my life humanely, not through whatever gory plan you thought I was hiding." A muscle ticked beneath his now grinding jaw, suggesting the information he offered came under duress.

An iciness expanded in her body, though her cheeks burned with rising shame. Only now did she see just how she'd misjudged him. If things grew bad enough, he wanted control over his end. Not a completely unreasonable desire. She'd seen enough death and frailty to understand his stance. But to her own discredit, in her scramble to organize his life, she'd rushed and dived into a pool of assumptions, blindly accepting Candice's version of this man. She'd been so wrapped up in ensuring he had enough joy and distraction to keep him busy, she'd never once considered that his plans weren't quite as eminent or irrational as she'd decided.

*Stupid move.*

She cleared the thickness in her throat, her pride still clinging to the logic in her thinking. "But Candice said—"

"Candice doesn't know shit."

She jolted at his searing tone, opening her mouth to respond, but he squeezed his eyes shut and spat out an expletive.

"Candice is the one with the complex. Not me." He snapped his razor-sharp glare back to her. "Her son and I went to school together. We were in the same year level, but we weren't all that close. I know nothing about him except that at some point, years after I'd left Roseford and settled in Melbourne, he fell into a deep depression and decided to park his car on the train tracks ahead of the 6 a.m. express to the city. Me taking up residence at Candice's facility was the best thing to ever happen to her. She's been projecting her baggage over her son onto me ever since, including his issues."

Sophie's hand flew to her chest, and she once again struggled for words. Every time Orlando spoke, a new hole opened up under everything she thought she knew about him and his situation, much less his initial mistrust about her being an aspiring psychiatrist.

"I had no idea."

"Yeah, well. Both you and Candice would look a great deal less unhinged if you'd just bloody asked me. I guess that explains why you both took it upon yourselves to insist on me seeing a psych."

"You know that wasn't the entire reason. Your flashbacks and my unwillingness to carry the total weight of your wellbeing was part of it. I hope you'll continue accepting help, even after today."

His expression grew dark, colder. "Maybe I'll need it, now that I'm left to wonder how much of this whole relationship was one big act of charity for you. How much of my condition is your ticket to fulfilling a constant need to make up for your own regrets?"

The pain of his criticism left her winded, his growing resentment hinting that nothing she said would be enough to convince him this relationship was still worth pursuing. But for all her assumptions and missteps, he didn't get to use her past to hurt her. "This relationship was always more to me than just holding you together."

"I never needed or asked for you to hold me together, Sophie." He settled deeper into his pillow, narrow glare dismissing her in favor of the ceiling again. "I'm starting to think you never really saw me, that maybe I was just a means to make you feel better about yourself."

Her anger rose, bunching and pulling tight within her gut. She wanted to reach out and shake someone—and of all people, a helpless man in his hospital bed. Though even her temper was a sign of just how much he'd changed her. How important he'd become. How much of her true self, good and bad, this man unearthed.

And as much as she wanted to hate him, her better judgment guessed his scornful approach was the only way he could find to say goodbye.

A raw feeling swirled and spluttered within her, but she forced her voice out again, a voice that crackled with a need to do away with regret. "I'm not ready to let you go."

"You don't have a choice."

He still didn't look at her.

"You were ready to declare your love for me just hours ago. Remember that?"

He scoffed out a laugh. "Yeah, and thank fuck I didn't. If you haven't noticed, things have changed."

Her muscles held a dull ache from holding back her true range of emotions. The lights in this room were overly bright and bounced off the pale walls, and neither the lights nor the walls did anything to help with her overwhelming fatigue from an entire evening of great stress and uncertainty.

"You need me." Her tone twisted, loud and pathetic.

"I've lived thirty-six years without knowing you. I'll be fine. Well…" He peered down at his sheet-covered body, wires protruding and drainage bag hooked up to the edge of his bed. His mouth bent in a mocking smirk. "Maybe 'fine' isn't the right word. Let's just settle on me returning to 'business as usual', and you realizing you're not Mary Poppins and that no one asked you to be my nanny."

She'd tried to play calm. Tried to plead. But Orlando was a master at prodding her soft spots. Nothing worked on this man. Nothing. He knew how to hurt her. And maybe he was right. Maybe she was a martyr. Someone too nice for their own good and not so inclined to seize what she wanted. A woman cut off from herself.

But she could change that. Even good people stood up for themselves at times, and despite what he thought, selflessness didn't always equal manipulation.

She stabbed an accusing finger his way. "I'd ask why you're being so cold right now, but we both know it's because you can't stand to admit you're scared about your future and what my role in that future might be." She ignored his astonished jolt and stepped closer. "It's easier to be a crabby bastard than admit you think vulnerability is weakness. Even though we both know that's not true, and you're really offloading your shit onto everyone else—especially me—just so you don't have to work through any of your messy hang-ups. Stop offloading your shit, Orlando. Just bloody stop it. You're better than this."

His wide glare held hers for the longest time, his expression still and stunned, while the soft murmur of far-off conversations out in the hospital halls filtered in. Her words rung on repeat in her head, like the walls absorbed their impact and bounced those words right back at her.

She sounded like a real monster. She hated being so mean. Especially at such a low point in his life.

But harsh honesty had always been one of the few ways to get through to him, and maybe this was the extreme she needed to resort to for him to see that isolating himself and pushing her away—early and with so little tenderness—wasn't in anyone's best interest.

Soon enough, his stunned stillness morphed into genuine red-faced fury. "We both agreed this ending would happen, so what I'm *better than* doesn't make a lick of difference to you." He jutted his chin toward the door. "Go, Sophie. Go have the life a *crabby bastard* like me could never give you."

Her limbs shook, and she opened and closed her hands in quick, flicking movements. Whatever she said next would not be quiet, and everyone outside this room would hear. But for the first time in her entire life, she didn't care about how she looked or what other people thought.

"I've never asked you for anything but your time, so don't start on what you can't give me. And I care about what you're better than because of *how* you're ending us. You're flaking out on me, Orlando. I never thought I'd see the day Mr. Tough Bravado himself would turn into a fucking coward."

"Look at me." His voice exploded, and the veins in his neck protruded. "Fucking look at me." He gave a sharp nod down at himself. Even the scar on his forehead appeared raised, red, and angry. "Do I give the impression of a man able to take part in a relationship? Christ's sake, I'm involuntarily pissing into a bag. Running through burning buildings used to be nothing to me, but right now, if this building caught fire, I'd be at the mercy of whoever damn-well remembered I exist. So, the last thing I want to think about is how impossible it is for me to be with you. Don't you dare call me a coward. You have no fucking clue."

"You think I've never seen a man in a hospital bed before?"

"Think, Sophie. Think." He released an exasperated breath and clenched his eyes shut. "Think about all the conversations we've had over the last few weeks. How we were never meant to be just friends. How I was meant to be your thrill. That's what we agreed on, remember? Well, there's nothing thrilling about me now."

"If that's your way of pointing out that sex is off the table..." She released a tight and incredulous laugh. Her yelled response about sex had her struggling to believe that she—Miss Neat and Nerdy, Sophie Tindall—was embroiled in a semi-public yelling match. "We're both adults here, Orlando. We can choose to change the course of this relationship."

"Jesus—" He threw his head back and released an explosive growl. "That's only half the point. You're not that scared, sixteen-year-old girl any more, you got it? You need to be the one to dig yourself out of whatever rut you're stuck in. Stop using me and whatever we do together as a crutch to live, and start actually damn-well living. We had sex. Don't get me wrong, lots of great sex. But there's more to life than being holed up in the Australian countryside, getting it on with a man whose life is a complete and utter car wreck. Stop being a doormat, Sophie. A sad, misguided, and eventually threadbare doormat."

"A doormat?" She shook her head at him, mind throbbing from rage-filled offense.

"Yes. You can't do shit unless you look after yourself first."

She'd never once considered herself a doormat, but Orlando's dig, coupled with Hector's earlier ultimatum, cut deep. "What am I supposed to do, Orlando? Set a village on fire? Do a spot of shoplifting? Tell me. Tell me what would make me less of a doormat in your eyes?"

"You know what I mean." His voice tapered and lost steam, his head settling down again. But she wasn't leaving before she either convinced him to take her back or she at least got every last detail on why he pushed her away.

"No, I don't. Spell it out."

"You're too good, Sophie." He turned back to her, the words snapping out. But then his features slackened, as if he came to some final and illuminating conclusion. "And that's our problem. You have no place with me."

The statement sank heavier than a large boulder in a tiny pond. Dramatic. Final. The impact sending ripples that broke the banks in the space lingering between them. A space fast growing wider and pulling them apart. For the longest time, she just stared, her throat tight.

"Don't I get a say on where my place is? Wouldn't that make me less of a doormat?" Her voice lost its volume, her thoughts suddenly clear. She drew a breath, demanding his unbroken, yet reluctant attention. "Because ultimately, this is about self-worth for you, isn't it? About what you think you deserve." She leaned in, so close it was impossible for him to ignore her. "But Orlando, you deserve happiness. You deserve to live. Despite all that's happened, you're still you and there's still so much you can do. You have it in you to fight, but you won't."

He shook his head and turned from her. "Stop it."

"You have so much life in you, can't you see? There are adventures you can still go on, adventures we could share. If only you'd—"

"I said, stop it."

"No. You're pushing me away. You stop it." Her voice hissed, anger creeping back in. "Stop making this about me. Stop blaming me every time things don't go to plan. Do this for yourself. Regardless of what happens with us or however long you have. If you can't give yourself a decent shot, Orlando, then you'll never find peace."

"And maybe giving up is my way of putting myself first, have you ever thought of that?" The sharp edge to his gaze eased, opening a window of fragile intimacy. "Maybe not putting myself through the grinder over and over and over again is my version of self-preservation. And that having you and every other interested person coddle me is one of the most fucking dehumanizing things a person can go through. You have no idea how it feels to lead this life. So yes, I don't want to fight anymore. And when bitterness and vulnerability make up my everyday life, maybe getting by is about as much as I can manage. Maybe I've earned my right to give up. And who the hell are you to tell me I can't?"

His delivery stayed tender, pleading even, despite the cutting choice of words. He was a man truly resigned.

A man saying goodbye.

And that resignation, of all things, cut her deepest.

Tears welled and then spilled down her face—fiery, despondent.

He'd gouged a hole right through her heart, and worst of all, she understood why. She wouldn't ask him again to reconsider his stance on this relationship. Not for himself. Not for her. Not for a man who'd lost everything, multiple times over.

But his rejection still stung, and hopelessness hit her harder than a wayward gust of wind slamming a door shut on her last chance at loving him. Because in outlining his suffering, he'd also outlined that her love wasn't enough.

"You're right." She spoke in a hollow whisper, eyes hot, as she took in her final glimpse of him. "Who the hell am I?"

His brows flexed; a sign he grasped what she'd left out.

*Who the hell am I… to you?*

The answer to that question had been swept away the moment he'd collapsed at Luke's wedding. The answer lost in the words he'd come close to saying but would never admit to, now.

"Go home, Sophie." His tone fell flat, and he returned to staring at the ceiling.

The answer to whether he loved her was *no*. The answer would *always* be *no*.

"This is the best ending we're going to get."

# Chapter Thirty-One

Sophie stood outside the airport's ropes, doing her best to stall the inevitable—not so much because she'd miss Australia, but because she'd be leaving behind one man in particular.

A man she hadn't talked to in weeks.

Luke offered a soft smile, one that recognized her need to delay. "I'm going to miss you."

She returned his smile, at least grateful for the ride and that he'd come to see her off. "I really did enjoy myself."

He tilted his head. "Really?"

"Yeah, really." She patted him on the arm, savoring her last few moments with her brother in what would be an indeterminately long time.

Not everything about Australia had been bad, Orlando included. Despite her broken heart, she'd succeeded in finding pieces of herself. Pieces she'd sought when she first left London. She still had a lot to think over, but already had a few ideas about where she wanted her life to go next.

"Do you think you're about ready?" Luke handed the long handle of her suitcase to her. "Is there anything else I can help with?"

"No. Thanks for dropping me off though, I know how busy you

are. I would have been happy if you'd just spotted me the cash to catch a cab." She gave him a cheeky smile, knowing full well he was the sort of guy to roll up his sleeves rather than just throw money at a problem.

"You really are the best brother, you know that?" A wave of emotion rolled through her, making her voice wobble; she launched forward, flinging her arms around his wide shoulders.

He caught her and laughed. "I'll try not to tell Max you said that." He patted her upper back. "You'll be okay."

She nodded, chin digging into his shoulder, sudden tears soaking into his white t-shirt. She must have looked like a total cliché. An emotional woman clutching desperately to some guy at the airport entrance. But the whole experience with Orlando left her broken wide open. Her old rules of sensible control no longer applied. Barely a day passed where she didn't cry. But even that didn't seem so bad. For the first time in a long time, her emotions ran raw, and something about that left her feeling alive.

He'd given her so much in so short a time. She couldn't be angry at him. Not when she understood why he'd shut her out. Her main source of pain came simply because he *had* shut her out. Much of what remained now was longing and sorrow.

That sorrow gnawed at her, became part of her, and she wondered if its heavy presence would ever leave. Every day, she struggled to let him go. She'd even gone so far as to call Roseford Aged Care Facility. Twice. Attempting to get a surreptitious update on how he was doing. The first call garnered no news, but the second had been a true shock. She'd gotten hold of Shelley, who'd informed her Candice had resigned. Orlando had been moved too, though Shelley didn't know where. But Professor Bandara had been right. Orlando's latest hospital stint had prompted an investigation into his care at Roseford Aged Care.

Candice had taken all the blame, claiming she'd pressured staff and residents into accepting Orlando minus any behavior modifying medication. She'd blamed her decisions on the trauma of her son's death. Anyone close to the situation would know she'd sacrificed herself to spare the facility, as well as everyone else who'd more than willingly complied with having Orlando around.

The center's good track record and lack of internal complaints meant further discipline wasn't likely, though they'd have an increase in surprise checks from industry inspectors for the foreseeable future.

So now Sophie lived in the dark when it came to Orlando, and it had taken all her powers of self-control to rein in her natural compulsion to find out more and track him down. But at least she had something to take away with her. As weird as that logic would have sounded months ago, she now had the stuff that made mature, well-lived, *real* people. Experience. Hurt. A sense of just how convoluted life could be…

And hadn't that been why she'd come to this country?

Well. Yes.

And no.

She'd come to gain. Not lose. To accumulate experience. To take that experience home and become a fully rounded psychiatrist. But now so many former choices about her life no longer fit. Not with what she'd learned of herself. Not with where she wanted to go next.

And she hadn't come to Australia expecting to leave anything behind. Well, besides her naïvety or ideas about people. But not something tangible. Or something so utterly dear and unique. Or should she say, *someone*?

She let go of Luke, unwilling to allow her thoughts to wander any further.

He stroked her arm. "Are you sure you don't need anything more from me?"

"No. No. You've done enough." She dug into her small brown purse for a tissue and then dabbed at her eyes, just as a new thought entered her mind. "Actually. Yes. There's something you could help me with." She peered down at her feet, stomach sinking at thoughts of Hector's nasty ultimatum. "Is there any chance you have an overseas tech buddy that owes you a big favor?"

She cringed, Luke already giving her a sideways glare. "There might be, why?"

She told him about Hector and his plan to blackmail her.

"And you want me to help that slime ball out?" Luke's sea-green eyes blazed with fury. "Not a chance. I'd much rather crush any possibility of him ever working in tech again."

"No. Don't." She checked her phone and saw she'd have to rush if she wanted to board her plane on time. "Hector won't be getting any free rides. I promise. I'll call you when I land at Heathrow and let you know my plan."

"Okay." His scowl didn't abate, but he didn't protest either. He threw his arms around her. "You take care, okay? And remember, there's always a place for you here in Melbourne."

She gave him one final squeeze and held her emotions together. "Thank you. I love you. Goodbye."

She filed into the line of people waiting to get their boarding pass checked. Before long, she'd cleared security and sat aboard her plane. And as the wheels lifted off the tarmac, her heart squeezed and stomach roiled, and the finality of this exit hit her with great force. She was leaving. She'd really and truly given up on a future with Orlando.

She never gave up. Not on anything.

But what more could she do?

This was her farewell to Australia. A farewell to who she'd thought she was. Farewell to the first man she'd ever truly loved.

Her throat constricted, and she buried a sob. Perhaps if she'd known how things would pan out, she would have been more careful with her heart. But even as that thought entered her mind, her heart compressed, confirming it wasn't true.

She loved Orlando.

And even with all the missteps and wrong turns; her multitude of terrible decisions, she wouldn't trade one minute in his presence to be free of her pain now.

He was a broken man. Yes. Full of flaws and full of passion. If only his passion could extend to him crawling out of his all-consuming darkness, so he could find his fight without her help this time. Even if she'd never witness or benefit from his recovery.

She pressed her fingertips to her window's cold glass and closed her eyes, releasing her one silent yet impossible wish. That her heart would mend someday. That Orlando's body would mend, too.

And by some utterly and outrageous miracle, he'd find his way back to her.

~

Orlando peered down at his feet dangling over the edge of his bed, his blue veins protruding in small mountains and valleys under his skin, the familiar fawn carpet underneath. Four weeks had passed since his episode, two weeks spent relearning how to sit, another two just to shuffle his way into the bathroom alone. *Oh, how the already-not-so-mighty had fallen.*

Still, his recovery had been surprisingly quicker than usual.

If it weren't for the utter boredom or the sheer pain of lying down twenty-four-seven, he wouldn't bother with rehabilitation after each and every episode. He'd just give up. And even in the wake of banishing Sophie from his life, he wondered now why exactly he *did* bother.

*"You deserve happiness. You deserve to live."*

He spat out a laugh at her proclamation. *Naïve Sophie.* As if everyone in this world got what they deserved. Like some dirtbags didn't lead lives of luxury, and good Samaritans didn't die alone and beaten in gutters. He'd seen enough of both to realize the word *deserve* had no value.

But in the last two days, insomnia hounded him, and a permanent knot had formed in his belly.

Two days since Sophie would have hopped on her plane and returned to the UK.

*Far from him.*

*Where she belonged.*

But his more selfish desires hadn't lessened. His heart still ached for her to stay. His mind refused to let her go. And his mouth had lied the day he'd said he wanted her to leave… The same day he'd been seconds from telling her he loved her…

*What an asshole.*

He scrubbed a hand over his face and released a sigh. Her absence hurt like a bitch. Having met her, only to lose her, he was more alone than ever. Alone to do nothing but ponder her absence. Alone with his thoughts. Dangerous thoughts. Thoughts that reminded him day in and day out how little he mattered.

*All I do is take up space.*

Sophie would move on. In five years' time, she'd probably not even remember his name. And the knot in his gut grew yet again. The light inside his room dimmed, the sun through his window disappearing behind a cloud, as if to rub salt into the wound of just how much he didn't deserve anything positive.

*I should just end things.*

*Do it now.*

He slid his weight forward, feet touching the soft carpet, then lumbered his way toward the shower. A much harder task now that he lived with his mother. The bathroom lay some meters down the hall, a significant trip compared to the tiny ensuite he'd had at Roseford Aged Care. He had a walking frame and caregivers to assist him twice a day; they helped with his rehab, meds, made sure he was clean. But right now, he wanted to see if he could make the distance to the shower on his own.

He stood in the hallway, elbow leaned against a wall. His mother was probably out in the garden or off walking Nero; either way, he refused to bother her. He'd run shit out of luck the day he'd had his episode, not only losing Sophie, but his place at Roseford. His lashing out in the ambulance on the way to the hospital had been his undoing.

He'd been given a choice, ship off to another facility more dedicated to patients his age but farther away—and only *if* a place could be found for him—or stay at Roseford Aged Care. Both options required him to be drugged to the point of docility, rendering him something other than himself. Both were miserable options he didn't want. But then again, so was imposing on his mother.

He drummed his fingers against the wall and growled as he shoved his lump of a body onward. He needed to get away from his thoughts, his mind a murky soup from his already heavy meds and his rising depression.

Maybe he *would* be better to end his pathetic existence, just as Sophie had thought he might. Though maybe he'd wait until his current routine of drugs and fatigue eased and didn't cloud his thoughts so much. Maybe then he'd do things on his terms. Screw the plan. He didn't have much to live for, anyway. No future. No woman. No one cared. Not even him.

*"You're flaking out on me, Orlando. I never thought I'd see the day Mr. Tough Bravado himself would turn into a fucking coward."*

He got into the shower and turned on the faucet, hoping the gushing water would drown out the sound of her words replaying in his head.

Hot water spread over his shoulders, and he lowered himself into the white plastic chair he used because his legs could only hold him for so long. As he did, he mumbled through gritted teeth at the fatalistic ideas plaguing him. "Not yet, you impatient dickhead. Not today."

Water disappeared down the drain at his feet, and a sense of overwhelming hopelessness ate away at him. Maybe his stalling wasn't really just about wanting control over his end. Would such control even ever come? He sure as shit had been lacking in control from the first day his condition tore through his life.

*"You have it in you to fight, but you won't."*

Her voice again. He growled, shutting off the water with a sharp snap of his wrist, then leaning over for a towel on the nearby rail. He proceeded to pat himself dry. Maybe being alone in his room was where he'd gone wrong. Maybe if he rehired the psychologist Sophie had made him see, maybe then he'd get some reprieve. Maybe then the voices would stop hounding him.

Or perhaps all he needed was an hour of origami—or whatever the fuck they would be doing at the aged care facility right now. He wouldn't know though, because right now he lived with his mother, like a child... Which in itself was ironic because weeks earlier he'd been living like a geriatric.

Then again, even living as a geriatric trumped putting his mother in the firing line of another of his episodes. So maybe he'd have to go against her wishes after all. Maybe he'd have to pick being a heavily medicated vegetable over putting her through more trauma because of him.

He groaned and urged himself to standing, wrapping the towel around his waist as he did. He was halfway to his room when he paused at a figure standing inside the front door.

"Hello, Orlando."

Professor Bandara stared at him with her midnight eyes, her raven curls acting like some devilish kind of anti-halo.

His mother slunk out from behind the professor and gave him a guilty half-smile, before shutting the front door and then padding away.

He turned for his bedroom door and continued his silent journey back to bed. Unfortunately for him, being a slow cripple and all, meant the professor had no issues keeping up.

Once in his room, she stopped in his doorway behind him, as if waiting for him to acknowledge her. But just to drive home how little he cared for her presence, he turned his back and dropped his towel, showing her his ass.

"Nice view." She held an anticlimactic bored tone. "But I'm a doctor. Your ass cheeks won't make me blush."

He swiped up a pair of gray sweat pants from the end of his bed and tugged them on, followed by a white t-shirt, continuing to deprive her of any direct attention. "Pity."

"Well, I appreciate the effort, but I've spent half my day getting here, and I need just a few minutes of your time."

To his total annoyance, he caught the smile in her voice.

He stifled a need to send the professor an angry glare. He hadn't spoken to her in over a month, and he still didn't want to look at this woman. "Whatever you're selling, I'm not interested. I made that pretty damn clear the last time we spoke. Go knock on someone else's door."

The professor remained silent for a while, as if weighing up whatever hollow thing she planned to say next. "I believe we still have a shot at breaking your condition. I'm here because your mother invited me, and because I want you to reconsider your stance on stopping your treatment. I wasn't joking when I said your case was exceptional to me."

He plonked himself down on his bed, his legs weary and his

stomach queasy from his meds and the novelty of moving around. Frankly, he needed another nap. "No thanks."

She crossed her arms. "I'm offering you a chance to get better."

He nodded down to his less-than-spry body. "Look at me and tell me your last 'chance' was a roaring success."

Professor Bandara didn't reply; she didn't even take up his offer to look him over. She simply scowled. "You gave my treatments mere weeks to work when this stuff needs at least three months to accumulate in your body. Don't pin your failure on me."

His muscles tensed at the word *failure*, but he shuffled back on his pillow and interlaced his fingers behind his head. "Whatever. Unless you can give me a guarantee this time, I'm just going to assume you're dicking me around again."

His last attempt at stirring any sort of hope in his life had only set him up for one cluster fuck of a fall. He wouldn't go there so easily again. Especially now. He didn't have Sophie to motivate him. And as much as he'd despised Roseford Aged Care, he didn't even have that extra support to prop him up either.

Derisive laughter shot from the professor, and she rolled her eyes. "Oh, cut me a break, Orlando. Your demand is a load of total and utter bullshit, and you know it. If anyone should be disappointed here, it would be me. Well, me and Sophie. What happened to your commitment to your recovery? You had one big stumble, and you ran Sophie out of town and derailed your progress. Your choice to quit on both counts was less than what I expected from a former firey like you. So, tell me, why are you so freakin' eager to stick with the life you have now?"

He snapped his gaze at her, and an intense heat burst within the center of his body. "You think I want this life?"

She shrugged, a mocking gesture. "Well, do you? Because I'm offering you a chance—as slim as you think it is—to have a different life. And it seems to me you're set on wasting away at your mum's house."

"You're overestimating your ability to help me."

"Maybe." She stepped closer, her stare boring into him. "But even a slim chance is a chance. And frankly, your recovery isn't about you only."

"What are you talking about?"

"Well, your mother for one. Having spoken to her, it's clear she's been to hell and back for you. Looking after you at her age, watching you languish now, it's slowly undoing her. And then there's Sophie." The professor let out a heavy sigh and uncrossed her arms only to place them on her hips. "Do you think I'd be jumping through these hoops if it weren't for how much that woman campaigned on your behalf in the first place? Can you even see how much she so obviously cares for you?"

"Right, well, you can rid yourself of one guilt. Sophie and I haven't spoken in weeks. I'm certain her life is already improving without me."

And still, shame twisted the knot in his belly.

"You know that for a fact, do you?"

He thought about her initial goal of coming to Australia, in part to gain experience with men. The selfish bastard inside of him still hoped she hadn't resurrected that goal. It hurt too much to think about the alternative, that she'd maybe already moved on.

His throat burned rough and dry on the inside, and the speed in his reply sent a shiver through his body. "Do you know otherwise?"

The professor tilted her chin down like she'd figured she'd got him. "Why do you care?" When he didn't answer, she straightened. "Right, well, Sophie described you as strong-willed. She wasn't completely wrong."

"She said that about me?"

"She called you stubborn-headed, actually, but I padded the wording for you. And anyone with eyes, who'd seen you two together, would know you could call her tomorrow, and she'd fall over herself to get back here again."

He strongly doubted that but didn't contest the bit about him being *stubborn-headed*.

Professor Bandara looked around the room and shook her head, before taking a seat next to him on the bed and placing a hand over his forearm. "Listen, I get that you're as low as any person can get right now. But it's also really not that uncommon for a person to stay sick because they're trapped in a loop of believing their life is what it is. No matter the internal dialogue you've used to survive, Orlando, you don't belong here. Not when there are other options. Not just with regard to your treatment, but your quality of life. Let me do my job."

Her words, her logic, her compassion, sent a shock wave through his body, and some of what she said filtered in. Much of it made sense. It stirred a yearning in him to accept what she offered. Yet a greater part of him didn't want to separate from everything he'd come to know. As illogical as that sounded. Even to him.

So, he lay there, blinking at her, unsure of what to say.

Her brow dipped at the center and her expression implored him to believe her. "I wouldn't have squeezed in appointments to see you, stayed late to work on your case, or traveled out to this Hicksville today if I didn't think you were a good candidate to improve. Imagine, Orlando, if just for the next three months you turned the energy you've used to merely survive, and used it to save yourself instead."

Strain spread across his face, tightening the muscles over his jaw and forehead. Maybe she had a point, but skepticism was hard to let go of.

"How would a change in motivation be different to what I was doing one month ago? Before the last episode wiped me out. And who's to say another episode won't take me out again?"

"There's nothing to say you won't get more episodes, but I hear you're recovering quicker this time. A good indicator that maybe the meds I'd prescribed had some impact. Imagine the results you might have if you stuck with our plan." She offered a light smile, like she saw her encouragement affected him. "And if you do have another episode this time around, you don't stop taking your meds, do you understand? We push through together. We give this a proper go. And if I really, truly, feel the therapy isn't working, I promise to break the news to you early so you don't think I'm 'dicking' you around."

She paused, as if assessing his response. He gave her nothing, though he could already feel himself softening to her idea. If skepticism was hard to let go of, hope was even harder.

"And Orlando, there's more. If you make this commitment, I can secure patient housing for you through the university I conduct my studies through. They'll fund you on compassionate grounds, but also because you'll be a research subject. You'll be close by, so I'll be able to look in on you more. And even if it doesn't work, at least you'll be able to give your mum a break, which I know is important to you."

Her grin grew wide; the spark in her eyes belonged to a woman proud of her scheming. What the doctor offered was riskier than what he'd accepted the first time. She offered immediate escape. A significantly loftier hope to fall from. And more than that, a chance to unburden his mother.

And even though the offer stirred his desire for more than he'd been lumped with all this time, he couldn't fathom a future, much less freedom. Did he dare to grasp for any of it?

His heartbeat surged with a sense that something wasn't right. Risk and faith challenged him to find the *fight* Sophie had been so adamant he didn't possess.

Risk told him he'd been down this road before. That any attempt would only end badly.

But faith.

Faith said to take the chance. To believe in something. Or someone.

Professor Bandara.

Himself.

The meager chance he might have a future with Sophie.

With every niggling doubt, came the memory of her hazel eyes, her soft pink lips, her petite, silken body tucked against his... And then there was her constant determination. The same determination that, for the briefest time, had turned him into a better man.

He had a chance. A chance to recover. To press restart on his life. To piece together a new man and redefine who he was away from his condition. And if recovery didn't happen, he'd need to accept his life as it was.

As Sophie had put it, he needed to find a way to live.

To be happy.

# Chapter Thirty-Two

Sophie took the few paces across the tiny, but once familiar, cobbled street with its black and white pedestrian crossing. After six months in dreary London, the weather was warming. She turned her face up to the cloudless sky. Her attention caught on a building with bronze-colored bricks, or more precisely, to a second-story window. That window belonged to an apartment she'd been glad not to visit in almost a year.

Still, moving on in life sometimes required doing things she didn't want to do. Though in this case, at least, she wasn't the one struggling to move on.

She traversed a set of stairs and ran through her game plan. By the time she got to her intended door, she found the thing creaking open before she had a chance to knock.

"What the hell are you doing here?" Hector's eyes blazed from the other side of his mesh screen.

An empty pit opened within her stomach, and she eyed the landing from where she'd just come, willing herself to stay put. "Hannah told me your flight leaves today."

He shouldered his way past, a giant black suitcase dragged behind him. "Yeah, and? It's a bit late to pretend you give two shits about me. Besides, I got to get a hurry on, my taxi will be here any minute."

She stepped back, allowing him more space, reacquainting herself with her old *meek-and-mild* act. Six months of careful planning had brought her to this moment. "Oh, okay, sure. Just, with all that's happened between us, I wanted to make sure we're all good now."

"What you mean is, you want to know whether I'll still upload that photo of you?" He pulled his door shut with a loud thud and then patted her on the cheek, his eyes squinting with a mocking grin. "Don't worry, Hun. We're all good."

She followed his hurried steps down the corridor, giving her best impression of a lost puppy, giving him time to relish the power trip. "Oh, that's a relief. And you don't even mind that it took Luke a few extra months to line up the new job? I'm really sorry about the delay."

"Well, I guess an international career in Dubai and a tax-free income will make up for the wait." He marched on, not sparing her a glance, his suitcase bouncing as he pulled it down the rugged old stairwell with its army-green metal banister. He paused at the foot of the stairs, breaths puffing against the effort of lugging his stuff, his gaze sweeping her from top to toe, face crinkling in a show of disgust. "I'm definitely moving onto better things getting out of this shit hole, that's for sure. So why don't you fuck off, and let me get on with it, huh?"

His dismissive glare stung about as much as his rotten language. Maybe she was more sensitive to these things in light of her heart still being nowhere near healed from Orlando's rejection months ago. But even then, time had seen her grow.

She'd paused her studies to figure out what she wanted to do. Traveled to more countries—ones that scared her, ones that opened her eyes to just how lucky she was. Much of her travel had been sponsored in part by her university, in exchange for her providing medical assistance to remote villages in need of care. She'd learned from those people, her views on life challenged. And a single insult from a bitter man like Hector couldn't keep her down.

His cab was indeed idling at the curb outside, and she gave him an easy smile. "I'm glad you're looking forward to the trip. I'm extra glad Luke found a place worthy of you."

The cab driver opened the trunk, and Hector hoisted his suitcase in with a strained grunt. "What's that supposed to mean?"

"Oh." She broadened her smile, making sure her expression showed every bit of the vindictiveness she intended to portray. A cheap emotion, sure, but one that still felt good right about now. "Just that we worked it that way to get you out of my life. You know, for good."

He rolled his eyes, small footsteps trotting him closer to the front passenger door. "Whatever."

He got in, but his scowl dropped as she leaned in front of his window and waited for him to roll it down.

"I want you to know, my brother isn't an idiot. And neither am I. We dragged out your job offer just to make you suffer, and even then, we could have gladly made sure you received every other last punishment you deserved. You only got this job because it will give you something to lose." Cars squeezed past the cab in the narrow side street, but her attention didn't waver from Hector and his narrowed pupils, his face resembling that of a scared weasel. "You're right where we want you. This job will also take you far, far away from me. So just know, I've saved every one of your extortionist messages, and if that photo ever surfaces, if you ever contact me or make any kind of trouble again, Luke and I will make sure *your* employer knows. You *will* get fired. We *will* lawyer up. And good luck finding another tech job with a criminal record after that. You'll never work in IT again."

She straightened and backed away. The cab driver took his cue and rolled the car forward, while Hector pushed his head out the window, rewarding her with a bug-eyed gape.

His uncharacteristic speechlessness made her slow months of stalling worth the wait. She was done with Hector. Done with being anyone's doormat.

# Chapter Thirty-Three

Less than an hour later, Sophie mounted another set of stairs, these belonging to the small, double-story building where she and Hannah lived. She took one slow step at a time, nearing her top-floor apartment, her smile still lingering from her meeting with Hector. But the moment she reached the top of her stairs, her smile sank, and she stopped in her tracks.

A broad, muscular man, in a gray cotton long-sleeve shirt stood at her door. His back stayed to her, while the scent of woodsy-sage cologne wafted across the landing. A small gasp fell from her lips, and she nearly dropped her keys. That scent. She associated it with Luke's wedding, with Orlando holding her, so close to affirming his love.

Her mouth wavered in its open position, but she failed to produce any sound. The thought this man could be him… Surely not.

Orlando lived a literal world away, and she was the last person he wanted to see. This had to be a coincidence. Besides, this guy was slightly broader, his posture a little straighter. He carried himself with a certain confidence Orlando never had. Another stark difference was the sharp clothes he wore compared to Orlando's scruffy t-shirts, sweat pants, or, at best, jeans.

*I'm having delusions.*

What were the chances a guy that looked a bit like him, and certainly smelled like him, would be standing at her door?

She laughed to herself. *Silly woman.*

*Probably just someone wanting to sell me a new electricity plan.*

The man spun around. His espresso-colored eyes wide.

Tingles burst through her body in one giant, painful explosion of nerves. "Holy fuck!"

The expletive rushed out—so unlike her. Her muscles turned to metaphorical liquid, and she lashed out a hand to the nearby rail to keep from falling down the stairs.

It *was* him.

*Orlando.*

His expression eased; a slow exuberance lit his face.

*Since when would she ever have described Orlando as exuberant?*

Since now… apparently.

Meanwhile, a war of emotions clashed within her mind. She didn't know where to look, much less what to think.

"Holy fuck, indeed." His smile grew, eyes near sparkling. He looked so carefree, but somehow still him. Tidy. Strong. His thick hair was still soft and slightly scruffy, just how she liked it, only perhaps now freshly trimmed. "I want to believe I'm the one who taught you that."

She reeled back a little, face heating at the reference to her colorful language. In truth, yes, because of him, she did swear more these days, out of an expression of her increased confidence *and* her months of frustration.

"I—" Her voice caught in her throat. "What?"

His grin remained, and he took a step toward her. She shuffled back, only to remember she was standing on stairs. Her balance faltered, hand tightening on the cold metal rail, and she righted her stance, just in time.

His smile dropped, her tense reaction seeming to give him all the information he needed. She hadn't forgotten the trauma of their last meeting.

"I think you're trying to say, 'What am I doing here'?"

She gave a quick nod, voice still trapped. She wanted to launch forward. To wrap her arms around him. To congratulate him on looking so amazing and somehow making it all the way across the world to London. Yet, so many sadder memories held her in place.

He outstretched his hands on either side of him, gesturing down to himself. "I took your advice, or rather, Professor Bandara cornered me. It seems I recovered."

For the longest time, she merely stared ahead and blinked.

"You're better?" She gave a tiny, incredulous laugh, sounding manic. Light flutters filled her belly, and her hands shook, the rest of her still struggling to move.

He gave a slow nod, the gesture tentative and controlled, as if he'd decided anything too sudden might shatter her presence before him. "I recovered three months ago, but I waited before coming here, just to make sure. You were right, all I needed was a little more time."

She swallowed and took another look at him, making sure her eyes really weren't defective. "You mean… You mean, you got on a plane all on your own, and you found me here?"

Already her voice quivered, and her eyes stung, but she forced herself to hold her emotions together.

His lips upticked at the corner. The warm expression, the rare coyness of it, made her ache to reach out and touch him. "Luke gave me your address. He said you wouldn't mind."

Her brow grew heavy, and she contemplated that statement. Did she mind?

She didn't hate seeing Orlando, that was for sure. Her heart beat so hard and fast, her emotions clashed between excited, hurt, and confused. But some forewarning from her brother would have been nice.

"I…" She paused, unsure what to say, though she felt she should at least try to fill the silence. "I'm glad for you."

But the silence continued, and she found herself grappling with how much of herself she wanted to throw into this moment. She was happy for him. Genuinely thrilled. She loved him. Still. But she'd learned the hard way to hold on to her emotions, that unchecked love didn't work when it came to this man.

*He told me to leave. Even though I wanted to love him regardless of whatever his condition did next.*

His focus burned through her, her skin burning right along with it. And with that discomfort came another thought. He was trespassing on her turf. She was the one with the right to scrutinize. To leave him waiting in *her* dust this time.

Another shiver ran up her spine, waking her from whatever dreamland she'd disappeared to. She launched forward and right past him, her hand with the keys finding her front door.

"Sophie?" His deep voice echoed around the stairwell, seeming to find a home way down deep within her rage.

Her attempts to unlock her door weren't going so well, not with her trembling hand. The sound of scuffling shoes against the polished concrete floor behind her meant he intended to follow.

Her heart raced. She kept fumbling with her key, but the damn thing just made a series of sharp metallic tings and refused to fit the lock. "I don't know what you're doing here..."

"Sophie." His voice insisted she turn around, but she continued in her fight with her door, her key finally managing to slide into place. "Sophie. Listen to me."

His hand landed on her shoulder. She froze, her eyes slamming shut while her heart clenched from the pain of the connection.

"Sophie."

"Stop saying my name."

"Why?"

*Because it makes me want to turn around. It makes me want to listen. It makes me want to throw my arms around you and forget you ever hurt me.*

She took a steadying breath, her body already warming in response to his touch. "Look, I said I'm glad for you, and thanks for the visit, but you should go."

"Because I told you to leave?"

Her eyes flung open. A growl broke from her chest. Something dark and innate burst within her, and she spun around. His hand left her shoulder, while her muscles primed to lash out, even though her better sense stepped in before she managed to actually punch him.

"Yes." She half yelled. "You told me to leave, and I did. I left. And now you're here wanting to… to… what? Tell me I was right? Tell me you're better? Do you want my applause or should I throw a parade? Is that it?" Her voice rose even more. Any minute now her neighbors downstairs would stick out their heads to see what was happening. "I'm happy for you. Okay? I am. I really am. But what else could you possibly have to tell me?"

The echo around the vacant stairwell gave her blistering words a life of their own.

His cheeks fell slack, and his gaze searched her face as if he needed another second to digest her tirade. "Wow. I didn't think Sophie Tindall was capable of being so pissed."

She scowled at him, unsure of what else to do with her rage, so she kicked the brick wall on her left and regretted it instantly.

"Fuck." She stomped her booted foot to the concrete floor, as if that would take away the pain.

"And she really does swear now."

She snapped her gaze to Orlando again, his eyes lit up like a man impressed. Her complete reactivity confirmed that, yes, Sophie Tindall was capable of *being so pissed*. She was also more skilled at *not* psycho-analyzing every tiny decision she made, which was all part of the range of emotions this man pulled from her.

A wide smirk crept over his mouth, and his famous devil's grin made an appearance. "You must really like me."

She clenched her hands at her sides—about all she could do to keep from exploding—which in itself would make for a fascinating medical mystery, though one she'd rather study than be the victim of. His smug ability to bend a conversation made her want to kick the wall again. Though, in this case, she hated his conversation bending because he was right about her still really *liking* him, and she had nowhere to put that *like*.

"Sophie. Please, just listen." His soft tone hinted he was done play-ing. His close proximity, coupled with his change in tactic, left a small crack in the ice around her heart. This time when his hand connected with her shoulder, she merely stared up at him, less enraged and simply doing as he asked out of a hope she could soon disappear into her apartment. "I'm here because I like you too. I didn't come here just to tell you I'm better, or that you were right, even though both are true. I came here because I want you back."

Time seemed to stop and her heart along with it. "You cast me out. And you never once tried to contact me."

"You knew the deal when we got together."

She shoved at the hard wall of his chest. "And things changed. You *know* things changed."

"They did. And I'm sorry." He grabbed her wrist and rubbed his thumb over her pulse. "But I was in no place to have the relationship I wanted with you, and we needed that break. You have to know that." He smiled down at her, his gaze flitting around her probably red and fury-filled face. "And from the attitude you're giving me, I'd say you benefitted too."

She twisted her hand loose and smacked his chest again, though with a little less intensity now. "You hurt me. If I have an attitude, it's all your fault. I was willing to be there for you. I could have been there through your recovery. I *wanted* to be there. We lost months and months when we could have been together."

Just the thought made her hate him all over again.

He pulled her closer and pressed his palm to the side of her face, his other hand sliding to the small of her back in a gentle possessive gesture that kept her from any escape. With summer gearing up in London, her arms were bare, and already her muscles loosened against his warm touch; that same warmth flooded her body, even though she struggled against him.

"I know. I know I hurt you. I'm sorry. I'm so sorry." His hushed tone coaxed and comforted. He shifted the hand at her face, and his thumb stroked her earlobe. "But let me explain."

"Hey." Randal Berry's voice sailed up the stairwell, a loud TV blasting in the background of his now-open door. Of course, this would be the moment he noticed she existed. "Are you guys okay up there?"

She closed her eyes and drew a slow breath. "Yes, we're fine. Go back inside."

"Okay."

His door clicked shut.

She peered back at Orlando, lowering her volume. "Explain."

His gaze dropped to her chin, and he took a moment before speaking. "I don't want to get to the end of my life and realize I didn't show up, that I took one look at you and chickened out, that you were right about me not feeling worthy of putting up one final fight. But more than any of that..." His beautiful dark stare lifted to hers, and a pained expression pulled at his features. "Sophie, if I didn't try, then the end would have come with the knowledge I'd let you go without fighting to keep you. That, of all things, would be my biggest regret.

"I'm sorry it's taken me this long to front up. I understand if you can't, or don't want to, or if the damage is too great... but I'm sorry. I still want you back. Not an hour has passed in the last six months where I didn't want you. Even as I told you to leave, I wanted you."

No words came to her, though she knew it was her turn to speak. She merely stared at him, body rigid in his arms.

Could she let his honesty get to her? Could she say yes?

Maybe she was better off doing the smart thing and protecting herself from further heartbreak. They didn't exactly have a great track record of getting along for any extended period of time.

His gaze searched her face again. The steady shake of his head seemed an attempt to dowse her rising doubt. "Look, can we just go inside? We can talk about this. Properly. Without bothering your neighbors."

She stepped back and out of his hold, not ready to give in without a clearer explanation. She couldn't open her door for him, didn't want him in her house. Because judging by the sharp need burning through her body, and the way her attention kept flitting over to the scar along his forehead, lighting a deep need to kiss him right there, she still plainly wanted him. She couldn't let arousal get in the way of the biggest decision of her life.

"No." She pressed her hand to the cold brick wall beside her, as if that might stop him from getting past; as if borrowing the wall's strength to hold her up. "What happened to me being too good for you? To me having no place in your life?"

He winced, drawing out a pause, before he offered up an answer. "I lied, Sophie. I lied to myself when I said I wasn't good enough. I allowed others to tell me the same thing. I've been allowing it ever since I was a child, and getting sick only made that worse. I made it okay for others to treat me like I didn't matter, like I didn't fit in, to abandon me, to dictate where my life went. And even if my response was to tell them to fuck off, I still believed them. I still took their words to heart. I let myself be broken because I didn't know how else to be.

"I thought my condition would bring you down, when it was me and who I'd let myself become, who had the power to do that all along. I know that now. I know I screwed up. As a lover, as a friend, as a son... In every relationship, but especially with you. And I screwed myself over too. I told myself, 'this was who I am', and for so long, in the most dysfunctional way possible, it worked. I believed it. That belief helped me survive. Except then you came along, with your prying and bullheadedness, hellbent on adjusting my life—"

"I'll take that as a compliment."

He smiled, and the mere look of that smile provided all the healing warmth of a ray of sunlight to her broken and bruised heart.

"It is. And I wouldn't have come to any of those realizations if you hadn't forced me to get help."

A hard knot formed in her chest, followed by a sinking feeling. Or maybe the feeling was that of melting. It was hard to tell. Except that something had certainly shifted within her.

Here stood Orlando, a man of few words and the epitome of all things brooding, pouring his ever-loving-heart out about the inner workings of his mind, so far removed from his man-of-perpetual-mystery act.

She slumped back, shoulder blades connecting with her door. She wanted to believe him, though maybe the knotted, sinking, melting sensation meant she already did.

He drew closer, crowding her space with his woodsy-sage smell and masculine heat, both of which permeated right through her doubts and reawakened her need.

Her hand itched to reach out and touch the soft weave of his shirt, as if her fingertips remembered his beautiful form hidden underneath. *Which they did.*

"Sophie." His voice redirected her attention. Maybe he'd sensed where her mind wandered, but his furrowed brows said he had serious matters to clear first. "I get that my being here is a shock, and maybe you've moved on. God, I hope that's not the case, but I needed to be here. I needed to see you. To tell you how I feel. I needed it as much for myself as the outcome I'm hoping to get here."

Her throat constricted, and a choked splutter came out instead. "I… ummm…" A light sensation eased the sickness she'd been feeling in her tummy. Maybe she did understand a great deal of what he'd endured and why he'd done the things he'd done. How huge an achievement it was that he even stood before her. "You were right, too."

He tilted his head to one side, confused.

Her thoughts ran to Hector, to her last decade of taking shit she should have walked away from.

"You were right when you said your influence has changed me. I've allowed myself to run through mine fields for people who wouldn't even cross the street for me." And for that she'd misdirected a lot of her anger at him. Because she could. Because a part of her knew he'd take it without truly turning nasty. Because he'd told her to leave, when every other boyfriend had used and depleted her until she had nothing left. "You helped me see who I am, to clarify what wasn't working. You hurt me, but somehow, I'm happier for having known you."

Happier for all his pushing and stonewalling. His resistance had forced her to stand up for herself. His rejection had made her define what she really wanted. To grapple for what seemed worth fighting for. To connect with her aspirations and strike out on her own.

"Having known me?" His jaw tensed. "I'm not sure I like you speaking about me as if I belong in your past."

Despite her struggle to hide her amusement, a small grin managed to escape. "I haven't decided where you belong."

He inched closer, sandwiching her between him and the door. "Is that so?"

"Yeah." The word came out a broken croak, and she gave a quick nod, swallowing hard at her nerves as well as her desire.

Even though anger had seeped in over time, in truth, her feelings for him remained unchanged. But then, she couldn't let their problems lie. She wanted more than what she'd left behind in Melbourne.

"Okay, well." His gaze held hers, direct and certain. "Maybe it's time I told you where I think I belong."

She gave a small nod, wanting promises, wanting *him*.

"You can love me or not, Sophie. God knows, I haven't loved myself, and there are a lot of people who would do anything to never see my face again." He reached for her, pressing his forehead to hers. "But I love you. I love you with my whole heart. And that love still holds even if the next words out of your mouth are to tell me to go to hell. I make no apologies for saying what I'm saying now. I love you, and I don't want to lose you a second time. If I'm correct, then I'm certain I belong right here with you."

Her heart stilled at the ragged edge to his tone, and every muscle in her body turned slack. She would have fallen if not for the door behind her and the man pressed so firmly to her front.

Her mind raced to accept what she'd heard. That Orlando, of all people, could admit to an emotion as soft and fragile, as soul-baring, all-leveling, and ever-lasting, as love.

"You… You love me?"

He gave a small nod, and his molten dark gaze held firm to hers. Despite what he'd said, her first thoughts were far from telling him to go to hell.

"Go ahead." He leaned in, lips close to her ear. "Ask what my dreams are now."

She wanted to sink further. Maybe because his mouth didn't move from the shell of her ear, and she yearned for his kiss. Or maybe because he'd brought up a question she'd asked months ago. A question he'd thrown back in her face and refused to answer.

She cleared her throat, certain her voice would be husky when she spoke. "Tell me about your dreams."

He pressed a feather-light kiss to her ear, then whispered against her lobe. "The answer is simple. My dreams involve you."

She reeled back. "Is that it?"

"You want more?"

She nodded, heart thundering in her chest.

"You sure you can handle it?"

"I'll try."

"I want a family. That means children. But if you don't—"

"No." She swallowed, breath heavy, pulse straining because she too had thought about this and already knew her answer. "I want that too. I just… I want to wait. I want to finish studying and establish a steady career first."

He released a soft chuckle. Her rushed answer seemed to amuse him. "Don't worry, I'll need a good while to get established too. I'm starting my life from scratch, remember?" He paused, his smile dropping. "But, Sophie, there's something else. Before all of that, I want you to be my wife."

She jolted, though not as much as she would have preferred given the door pressing into her back. "You do? But… But we live in different countries. Where will you live, where will I? There's so much to work out."

He laughed again, louder this time, his tone rumbling and rich enough to send butterflies flittering through her tummy. "So, you're happy to have my children, but we need to iron out the details of you being my wife?"

"Well, no." Her cheeks burned, but a smile broke free all the same. "I've got this all a little bit backwards, haven't I?"

He pressed his forehead to hers again, falling just short of their lips joining. "My life is starting over, and I'm free, do you understand? I go where you go. We'll work everything else out from there." He paused, gaze searching hers. "So, what's your answer? Will you take me back?"

She allowed slow seconds to pass, giving the impression she didn't already know her answer. "Go to hell."

Orlando's face paled, before she let loose with a playful laugh. For once she'd had a turn at toying with him. "But if you do, take me with you."

# Chapter Thirty-Four

Sophie's smile dropped as tears gathered in her eyes, the weight of the future she'd just agreed to sinking in. Orlando leaned closer and pressed the lightest kiss to the corner of her mouth. So tender. So intimate. So unlike Orlando. "Invite me in, Sophie."

Every nerve in her body settled to a low thrum, and everything in her world seemed suddenly right. Her heart beat just for this moment, for him. How her life had changed in the brevity of a few minutes. She reached her left hand out to the side and behind her, until her fingers found the door handle and the door sprung open.

She stumbled back, into her apartment; but before she could get too far, Orlando caught her and swept her off her feet. Unrestrained laughter erupted from her, and she pressed her palms on either side of his face. "We should bolt the door. Hannah won't appreciate being locked out, but it's better than her walking in on us."

He planted a strong kiss to her lips and kicked the door shut, his gaze soon sweeping across the tiny living room, with its cluttered arrangement of second-hand furniture, brightly colored cushions on a violet couch, and a stack of textbooks teetering on the coffee table's edge. "Hannah will have to deal. She can always leave again. Now point me to your bedroom."

She jabbed a finger toward an open doorway behind her.

He gave a playful growl, and within a few wide paces, crashed through her door. Before she could take stock of what happened, he pinned her beneath him on her arctic blue, cotton bedspread.

The weight of his body offered welcome comfort and pressure, his lips raining down a firm fall of kisses, like he couldn't believe he got to have her again, like he would never let her go and that he feared at any moment she might disappear.

To be honest, she felt the same.

Her desperation came through on the hard press of her returned kisses, her fingers claiming the thick curls at the nape of his neck.

He pulled his lips from her, breathless, his hands buried in her hair. "Tell me there's been no one else."

The depth of his stare, the clench of his jaw, denoted a man held barely together, as though his next breath depended on her answer.

"No." She shook her head and swallowed back a rise of sadness. "I wanted to, but I couldn't."

She would have loved to have moved on. To pretend he hadn't hurt her. That his absence hadn't existed as a living, breathing thing in her day-to-day life; a dull pain piercing her heart every time another man hit on her, that pain saying she wasn't ready.

She'd loved her six months of freedom and hated it even more.

The muscles across his face relaxed, his broad shoulders easing above her, like he understood why she'd wanted to. "I'm sorry." His voice was a small, sincere whisper, his nose skimming hers. "I need to slow down with you, don't I?"

She gave a hurried shake of her head, the need gathering in her core saying she didn't need *slow* at all. "No. No, you don't."

His deep laughter rumbled through his body and against hers. "I'm going to anyway."

He slid his hand under the hem of her emerald blouse and farther beneath her matching lace bra. His large palm engulfed her breast, and she arched into him, his thumb brushing her nipple with a feather-light touch.

"You're going to kill me." She wriggled against him.

"Shhhh..." His lips landed on the side of her neck. "I've just found you again. I'll make sure you survive. Just let me adore you for a minute."

She bit back her need to shatter the stillness with more words. Bit back the uncertainty that she *would* survive whatever he had planned, especially if that plan meant going slow.

For months, she'd been starved of this man, but now his kiss claimed every one of her breathless moans, while he kneaded her flesh, and the bulge of his excitement dug into her inner thigh. His body overwhelmed hers with sheer size. But she'd never felt so safe. So content. So ready to break from uncharted passion.

He pulled her shirt away, along with her bra. His lips took over where his hand left off, palm grazing over her waist until his long fingers vanished under her white skirt and into her underwear.

She bucked against him, demanding more, but he held her down with the press of his thigh, insisting on patience.

Her nipple puckered under his lips, and she surrendered, sinking deeper into her bedspread, while she vowed to simply enjoy. He was only getting started, but already months of waiting morphed into a splintering need. Never once had she imagined he'd be back in her bed.

A moan broke free. She wanted him and everything he offered. She voiced as much as his finger slid into her, and she clutched around him working at her longing, his thumb drawing slow circles over her bud. Higher and higher her need for him grew, until her breaths turned ragged, and her head thrashed against her burgeoning climax.

He was still a devil of a man, still capable of setting her world on fire, only now he lacked his former bitterness, his wicked edge honed in on bringing her pleasure.

A rushing sensation seared through her body and she released a soft whimper. His hot kisses branded her shoulder, making a meandering journey back to her lips, her excitement rising with each gentle caress; his lips travelling farther, to her brow, and to her cheek, and then her temple. The soft intimacy undid her on a shuddering cry.

He pulled away, tugging at the last of her clothes, taking off his own, while her climax settled; and she watched him roll on a condom, her gaze flicking to the rest of his body to confirm an earlier observation.

"I see you've been hitting the gym since we last met." She quirked a smile, unable to keep from commenting.

He positioned himself between her bent knees, but paused, his eyes glinting, and his devil's grin returning. "Let's just say I'm working with increased energy levels these days. I hope, for your sake, you can say the same."

She wanted to laugh at his challenge and argue back, but he lowered his hips and entered her in one slow, long stroke; his eyes sliding shut, as he released a drawn-out hiss of pleasure.

She allowed her spirit to float with the warm, stretching feel of him; like his body converging with hers made her somehow complete, even though it was his undeniable love that held her most.

His elbows dug into the bed on either side of her shoulders and he watched her, as though invested in her every reaction and detail. His body pressed hot like an engine against hers, his movements building within her, while desire stole at her thoughts, holding her in the moment with this miracle of a man; his strong hands cupping her face, as a tender and completely physical conversation unfolded between them.

A steep avalanche of emotion seemed to roll through him and into her, his entire body claiming her; her breaths bursting with each of his euphoric thrusts, and each thrust growing harder, faster, more desperate to convey how the time apart had hurt him.

She couldn't hold on any longer and an urgent cry broke free from some place deep within. Blasts of light effused from behind her shuttered eyes, similar to sunshine cutting through crystal, bringing with it showers of color, and wonder, and radiant heat settling all around her —just as Orlando swelled and fell along with her.

For the longest time, she surrendered to being right here with him, to the languid sensation of time pausing, his embrace a reality that, for the first time ever, matched her fantasy.

Orlando wasn't leaving.

There would be no bittersweet end.

No fleeting exchange leading to a permanent split.

She could have him again. Have *this* again. And again. Whenever she wanted.

And that thought alone left her heart soaring.

His face hovered just above hers, and his thumbs stroked the edges of her forehead. The dreamy look in his eyes said he'd reached the same conclusion.

Seconds passed, and she sucked in a slow breath, her mind slowly overcoming the adrenaline still lingering in her body.

"Oh!" She smacked her hands over her mouth, almost taking Orlando out with her sudden movement. "I never gave you an answer."

He tipped his head to one side, brow raised.

She yanked his face back down to hers and kissed his lips. "The answer is yes. Yes. Yes. A million times, yes."

When he pulled away, his brows still hadn't lowered. "I love an enthusiastic yes, but Sophie, honey, I need you to elaborate."

A smile took over, and overwhelming joy scattered her thoughts.

Well… all thoughts except one…

"I mean yes to being your wife." A tear rolled down her cheek and she laughed. "Also, I love you too."

# Epilogue

Three Years Later

Sophie sat in the airport lounge, her fingers linked with Orlando's, the line of people standing at the boarding gate creeping forward. She never could understand why, the moment a flight was called, people rushed to line-up. She preferred to sit and wait. The line would eventually dwindle, and then she and Orlando would glide through to their plane seats with minimal standing, bumping, and shuffling. But then again, what did she know? This was her first flight in three years, so maybe there was some secret traveler's motivation she didn't understand.

So much had changed in those three years. Not long after Orlando had ambushed her at her apartment, she'd knuckled down on her studies, and now she found herself partway through the core component of her psychiatry training. One of the best parts being that she'd started getting paid for her work.

She and Orlando had been able to afford rent on a small apartment on the outskirts of town. Though she'd planned on specializing in old-age psychiatry, her experience with Orlando had changed her interests.

The transformative effects of his treatments meant she'd befriended Professor Bandara online, and with her encouragement, embarked on studies centered on research and finding new drugs to improve patient outcomes.

The work was fascinating and ever-changing, and she'd come to embrace her bookish tendencies more than ever, rather than run from them.

Meanwhile, the people of Roseford banded together to help Orlando restart his life in the UK. They raised funds and ran social media campaigns. His mother and brother also scraped together what money they could, and he'd gathered enough to live off while he picked up new skills and settled in with Sophie abroad.

In time, he landed a new career he cherished. A job that incorporated his experience and passion in fire risk minimization, as well as land management. A job that kept him outdoors and bouncing between acre upon acre of countryside. One that offered something so completely different to the life he'd endured at the care home.

He worked as a park ranger, a career that suited him to a tee. He'd even made an endless number of friends: from hikers to families, co-workers, and the occasional quirky tourist. So many people knew, loved, and accepted him. And every day he returned home to her, hands a little dirtier, but the rest of him smelling of fresh air and pine trees… along with undertones of sweat and hard work.

His world was a full contrast to her days viewing research papers in air-conditioned rooms. And he'd come to know all the beautiful places to visit on the weekends, and for that, she loved his job too.

Two years had passed since their wedding. A small country ceremony in York, with her mother and everyone they knew from Australia in attendance. Nova, Luke and Agathe's daughter, had only just started walking, but she'd toddled down the aisle, hand in hand with her proud mother, a picture of baby sweetness as Sophie's flower girl.

But the time had come for Sophie and Orlando to jump on a plane. To do the visiting. Her muscles shook with a spike of adrenaline. She half bounced in her boarding lounge seat, itching to have the marathon flight over, so she could see everyone again.

The boarding gate queue dwindled, and Orlando stood, his hand outstretched in an offer to pull her up. She took the offer, only for him to tug a tad harder than expected, causing her body to collide with his.

He engulfed her in a strong embrace, large hands wrapping all the way around her burgundy wool coat, before he gave her a fleeting kiss. "You ready?"

She swallowed at a lump of emotion, overwhelmed with the impending journey, but even more so, the swell of memories flooding back. The state of their lives was unrecognizable to when they'd first met. So many things had needed to go right just for them to be together now.

She nodded, relishing his easy smile, where at one point he'd been neither easy nor the smiling type.

He stepped back and slid his hand into hers, while the other hand dragged their carry-on luggage. They walked over to the now-empty boarding desk, and an attendant checked their tickets, soon waving them through to the plane.

Gusty winds and wild gray skies surrounded the open-air board-walk. Her fingers clung instinctually tighter around Orlando's, and she allowed her head to lull over to his shoulder. Three years and a different outlook had changed everything forever.

Risks and courage had brought them to a place of harmony.

For her, courage had come in the form of learning to stand up for herself, to risk failure. And with Orlando, she'd failed, big time.

But he'd returned to her life all the same.

For him, courage had meant the will to fight. To believe in his worth and find peace within himself and his condition. To know that, no matter what, his life held value. And regardless of what the future held, he would never be alone. He had love. He had Sophie.


THE END

# The Last in Line

LOVE AT LAST, BOOK 3

# The Last
# IN LINE

LOVE AT LAST **BOOK THREE**

## KATERINA SIMMS

# Description

**She's on the run from a horrific past. He's on the verge of a riches to rags nightmare. Until one chance encounter changes everything…**

Burlesque bar owner Freya Cortez, leads a razzle-dazzle life until she learns her mother has just weeks to live. Now she is forced to juggle a once-in-a-lifetime business opportunity with the torment of her far-from-perfect childhood.

Millionaire party-boy Max Tindall is facing financial ruin, even his most prized possession is at risk—his home. But a casual encounter with Freya gives him one last chance to turn his life around.

Though Freya has vowed to never fall in love, even she can't deny Max is the kindest person she's ever met, the one man to challenge her "no settling" rule. But how can a woman so sassy and independent ignore the fact that there's something gravely amiss with him? Something even he hasn't noticed. Something bound to destroy both their lives.

*For fans of heat with heart romance, and It Ends With Us.*

**Keep reading to curl up this unique romance like no other!**

# Chapter One

Freya Cortez bounced on her heels outside The Ruby Room's double doors; her sleeveless, sunny yellow dress, with its nipped-in waistline, doing a piss-poor job of keeping her warm. Late summer in Melbourne, Australia, could be fickle, and lately, the nights held a constant chill.

"How'd things go with the rep?" Crystal loomed to her right, tall, dark, and slender, dwarfing Freya's significantly shorter and rounder physique—probably a good thing, since she'd hired the woman as the bar's bouncer.

"Well enough."

Wednesday nights at the burlesque club weren't usually all that busy, but business had picked up. Freya looked over the small huddle of people still trying to get into her venue, despite the time nearing midnight.

"Just well?" Crystal's voice somehow still held a bored, dull edge, as if very little ever impressed her.

After years of being knocked back, followed by six-months of planning now that they were in, the bar's inclusion in the Live Wire Festival *was* reason for excitement. And that inclusion was what brought Freya to the club on her night off tonight. More planning. More prep.

"Okay, better than well." She shrugged, still downplaying things.

The festival rep she'd met earlier had been impressed with the weeknight atmosphere and the flow of patrons.

Now, four people waited in line, and she whispered for Crystal to admit these last patrons, then lock the doors to anyone new. Her voice held a subtle croakiness from much yelling over bawdy music while talking to that rep. Though with any luck, last drinks would be called in the next hour or so, and then it would be time to go home. She'd rest her voice soon.

A young woman in front of Crystal dug around in her purse for ID, only to drop the hot pink clutch.

Crystal's bored tone returned. "I'm not getting that."

To be fair, Crystal's skin-tight leather pants and five-eleven frame meant Freya was closer to the ground, and therefore the better person to help.

She crouched and began collecting stuff off the pavement, sparing Crystal the long, tight-panted journey down. That said, Freya had her limits too, like collecting the loose tissues floating about; though the rolling pink tube of lipstick and blue pen she could do.

Someone huddled down beside her, the warmth from their hand crossing hers in the cool night and drawing her gaze to a set of soft blue eyes. Varying shades of stone and sky held her attention for a beat too long; for some reason, she imagined gentle waves atop a wintery sea within those pupils. An irrationally dreamy thought, especially for her.

Her eyes narrowed of their own accord. She knew this guy. One of her regulars. Knew those shaggy, surfer curls kissing his brow, and those broad shoulders paired with his tall physique, a tad on the slender side.

Yes, she knew. Some sort of tech millionaire, or maybe that was his brother, or something along those lines… Unlike his queue of admirers at The Ruby—mostly her own staff—she pretended not to notice.

She gave him a small nod and extracted a case of mints from his long fingers. "First drink's on me. Just tell the bar staff the door woman sent you."

A smile pulled at his lips and sent a small thrill of electricity through her tummy.

Small, yes, but still enough to compel her back to standing.

She turned away from him, offloading the breath mints on to the bag dropper, catching the jittery movement of her own hand as she did so. *Screw that.* Surfer guy might have had an unintended effect on her, but she wasn't above flirting out of pure retaliation.

She turned back around, intent on delivering some witty one-liner, only to find someone else standing in his place. Someone who stank of sweat and cigarettes and had a dirty blond buzz cut. *Not the surfer guy at all.* This guy's blue eyes didn't conjure the ocean, unless she counted the turbulent sinking sensation dragging at her belly. No, all she got from this guy was a flat, leering stare.

She offered him a weak smile anyway, and then turned to go back inside the bar, pausing at the low grumble she *thought* she heard, one that sounded something like, "Where's *my* free drink, bitch?"

A distant whisper in the back of her brain warned her, a whisper that had saved her life once before. She'd owned The Ruby Room for years now, had worked other bars for years before that. She knew a creeper when she met one. The Leerer had positioned himself up against her on purpose. He'd wanted to touch her. Expected she'd shrink away.

Well, he wouldn't get what he wanted. Not from her.

She spun around, ready to ask him to repeat those words, partly so Crystal would hear and keep him out of the bar. But he spared her that trouble, already marching down the street, past the closed stores with their blackened windows, fists clenched at his sides, taking with him his downright *off* energy.

Or at least, so she thought.

She pushed past Crystal and back into the bar. This night was turning out too long and weird for her liking. Time to go home. She crossed the darkened space, with its red-tinged lighting and boisterous patrons, only to catch sight of one of her bar staff clutching his hand.

Blood poured from his enclosed fingers, a glass having shattered in his grasp. She picked up her pace and came at him with a clean wad of paper towels from the counter, ordering him and the bar manager to the back where the first aid kit lived. No way would that employee be returning for his shifts any time soon, so she tended bar till the manager returned, then stayed back even longer to rejig the week's roster.

By the time two a.m. rolled around, and like an idiot who didn't know better, she exited The Ruby Room alone, her attention buried on the stack of fresh messages on her phone. She'd already ambled a few meters from The Ruby's doors, when a sick sensation surged through her tummy, urging her to stop.

No.

The feeling was less *sick*, more *off*.

The feeling offered a premonition, or maybe a warning; she jerked up her chin, but too late. The Creeper from earlier stared at her from across the sidewalk, his back against a banged-up blue van. The super wide pavement meant she stood closer to him than the bar, too far to double back inside, with zero chance of anyone in The Ruby spotting her.

She could scream.

Would anyone inside hear her over the music?

That only left running forward, toward him. Sure as shit not an enticing option, nor was running to her car since she didn't have one. The Creeper didn't even bother to give her a typical, sleazy scowl or an uptick of his lip to spell out his ill intentions. What he offered was worse—a flat stare, soulless and as dead as a long-departed snake.

His hand rested over his crotch, its placement by no means an accident. She darted her gaze to the rusted blue van behind him, his foot pressed against the open door's edge. An aching silence made a coldness rush her body. The sharp night air cut down to her bones.

He would grab her. He would shove her into that van, and no one would see.

A sob broke from her lips. Any second now, the terrified tears would start—a big feat since she pretty much never cried. The Creeper pushed away from the van and took a step toward her, not even giving her the credit of being quick with this attempted kidnapping.

His slow and snake-like movements gave the impression he'd done this before. *Gotten away with this before.* He tipped his head to one side, and the wrinkles over his cheek bones settled, as if he savored the expression on her face. Her open fear.

A loud crash sent more ice through her veins, and she startled as The Ruby Room's doors burst open. The Creeper's expression turned hard, and his stare flicked off her to a point in the background. Modern jazz fused with dance, The Ruby's door always slow to draw shut. Next came the crack of laughter and a jovial male voice calling goodbye to his friends.

Her heart sprung to a wild and racing gallop, the sudden ray of hope twisting another sob through her chest.

*Fuck this guy.*

He wouldn't get her tears.

She spun around to whoever had just left The Ruby. The millionaire surfer!

The guy already powered away from her, his hands jammed in his pants pockets, his rapid and fading footsteps like claws digging into her heart.

*Well, fuck him too.*

"Hey, Marcus!" Her voice wobbled, but rang true enough; whether surfer guy liked it or not, she'd make him part of this showdown. "Where are you going?"

Her entire twenties had been spent yelling at people from across noisy bars, so she had friendly yelling down to an art form. Of course, surfer guy's name probably wasn't Marcus, so he didn't turn around, though for the literal life of her, she couldn't remember what his real name was.

"Hey, asshole!" She took a risk and ran after him. "Marcus, are you fucking drunk again?"

This time he did stop, and he spun around, a single brow raised, as if to say, *Who you calling an asshole?*

She caught up to him, plastering on her biggest fake smile and looping her arm through his. "You weren't just about to leave without me, were you?"

She fluttered her eyelashes, hoping the over-dramatic approach would tip him off enough to play along; though her frothy blond curls, Betty Boop dress, and their earlier eyeballing probably only worked to make her look like some kind of psycho-clinger, hoping to nab herself a millionaire pretty-boy.

Maybe when this whole thing was over, and if she got out alive, she would find a moment to puke at that idea.

Surfer guy frowned down at her arm on his. "Who's Marcus? My name's Max. What's wrong with you?"

His cool British accent caught her momentarily off guard, since she'd seen him so many times and never once swapped a single word. But now, she narrowed her eyes, a voice inside her head screaming, *Fucking catch on, you sun-affected doofus!*

But she held onto the charade, because her life depended on it, and gave a bright, air-headed giggle.

"Oh, shut up, you big dope." She gave Max's arm a playful smack, though the space between her shoulders burned with The Creeper's stare.

If Max dropped her, The Creeper would swoop in.

Her leg muscles felt weak, and a pain dug into her gut. Maybe it was time to lose the bimbo act. The man she clung to didn't seem all that quick on the uptake.

So, she rested her head to his bicep, making it seem from the outside that she might be his girlfriend, all while dispensing her situation's harsher truth.

"Please. Just play along, okay?"

# Chapter Two

Max regretted having rolled up his shirt sleeves the moment the woman who'd latched onto him dug her nails into his arm, dragging him into a brisker walk.

He tried to tug his arm free, eager to return to his luxury apartment for a decent night's sleep, before an ocean swim first thing in the morning, then his flight to Ibiza tomorrow night. But hell, for someone a whole foot shorter than him, this woman had one heck of a grip.

He peered down at her, her wide-eyed, chestnut-colored gaze meeting with his. "Play along with what?"

He swore she mumbled the words, "Just look."

Her suddenly pale cheeks sent a chill down his spine; he'd only ever seen this woman hyper-focused on whatever it was people who worked at bars did. The mere change in her, plus those mumbled words, made him peer over his shoulder in search of her problem.

Icy-blue eyes connected with his, that creepy-ass stare attached to a long, lean, somewhat scruffy-looking dude walking about ten paces behind them.

Instinctively, Max picked up speed. "Holy shit!"

On size alone, he'd probably smash the weirdo in a fight, but hell, there was no accounting for what kind of added strength or weaponry came with being a deranged kidnapper. *Kidnapper.* Was that even the right word for someone clearly more into stealing fully grown women?

*Focus. For once in my life, could I just bloody focus?*

Yes, right. Focus. Don't make this woman regret trusting him, even if he was the most unreliable choice for a hero in all of Melbourne.

His heartbeat thundered, and he lashed his hand around the scared woman's waist—a performative and real show of support. He wasn't clever. He wasn't *anything*. All his advantages came from pure, unexplainable luck.

Still, this woman's actions showed hard-to-match bravery and intelligence; at least for this moment, he'd try to level up.

He kept his stride long and fast, and she panted, her hips bumping into him as if keeping up wasn't all that easy. A quick glance over his shoulder revealed The Stalker in hot pursuit, albeit at an ambling, stalkerish pace.

Max held a hand out to the woman. "Give me your purse."

She frowned up at him but did as told.

"What the fuck are you doing?" The woman's voice came out as a low growl as he stopped and turned to face the screwball trailing behind them. "Are you stupid or something?"

Maybe he should have been insulted, but at least she said out loud what most people implied to him in silence.

The Stalker stopped ten paces away, his deadpan stare working over Max.

Max put on his best deranged smile but slipped a hand into the woman's purse, hinting The Stalker wouldn't like what might be inside. "Are you all right there, mate?"

The Stalker took the bait, his gaze flicking down to the purse and narrowing for a beat. He lifted a hand and scratched the back of his dirty blond head, grumbling something about, "Fucking hipsters," before turning in the opposite direction, literally stalking away.

Max held onto the woman beside him and made sure she didn't go anywhere just yet.

"That could have gone a whole other way." Her unimpressed tone fell short of the enthusiastic relief he'd aimed for. "What was your plan if he'd pulled out a knife or something, and all you had in your hand was one of my tampons?"

The Stalker retreated some more, and Max handed over her purse, turning in the direction of his car. "Yeah, well, he didn't. Aren't you lucky?"

"*Me?*" She followed beside him, a good thing since he wouldn't have to insist she do just that, anyway. "I'm pretty sure that nutter had plans for you, too, buddy."

He stopped at a corner and peered back in the direction they'd come from, seeing nothing but the flash of red taillights from the busy street, cutting through the quieter one they'd turned down. "Look, is your car nearby? I'll walk you over and wait until you drive away."

Her cinnamon stare darted across his face, and she shook her head, her thick, platinum blond curls kissing her light olive cheeks. "I don't drive. I mean, I know how to drive, I just don't have a car."

She jutted her chin forward, drawing attention to the line of her neck and a small tattoo on the crest of her left shoulder, one of a thinly drawn sun and a cat dancing beneath its rays.

He forced his gaze back to her challenging stare. That stare, daring him to protest her lack of car—even though her chest still rose and fell in the wake of her earlier panic—and he had no intention of making this moment any more difficult.

"Do you need a lift?" Cold tension spread through his muscles, the lingering set of her jaw making him fear she might say no. Then again, could he blame her? "It's a leap of faith, I get it, especially given what you just escaped, but I'm parked a couple of blocks up. If a ride is too much, then you can even just sit a minute and catch your bearings. We can leave the door open, if that would feel safer for you. Or, I don't know, maybe I could call you a cab?"

Her pupils grew darker. She didn't say anything, didn't even hint whether she liked his plan or maybe contemplated kicking him in the shin and running for dear life.

He rubbed the back of his neck with an open palm. Nothing he had to say seemed right. Yet another thing he should be used to, even though he wasn't. "I'm sorry. I just don't want to leave you here alone."

She pulled her attention from him and extended her hands with palms turned down in front of her, the ends of her delicate, red-tipped fingers shaking.

He tensed, his own hands curling into fists at his side. He wanted to step forward and pull her in for an embrace. But even he wasn't dim enough to think that a good idea.

*She doesn't know me. She can't know that not every man is out to hurt her.*

Over his last few months frequenting The Ruby, he'd watched this woman pour drink after drink with unbroken proficiency, never shaky or unsteady, but this… *this* was a story he'd heard his female friends recount far too many times. A story of being followed, harassed, and threatened.

He should have believed them. He *did* believe them.

Only believing and experiencing were two very different things, and he'd swum amongst their same fears tonight.

"I'll call the police first." Her crisp voice snapped his focus back to her face. "I got his license plate number, and I won't sleep tonight knowing he might move on to another woman."

He wanted to ask if she'd manage to sleep tonight anyway, but the question seemed too personal, so he gave a quick nod instead. "Yeah, sure. If you think you're up to it."

"The bar will have footage of me leaving with you. If something happens, they'll know who you are from your past visits. Do you understand?"

Despite her hard tone and warning, and the joyful scent of sunshine and tangy mandarin floating from her skin, she wrapped her arms protectively around her waist.

He gave another nod, slower and smaller now; his understanding of what he'd stepped into earlier, and what it meant to her, sinking even deeper.

"Good." She unwrapped her arms, a woman with a new mission. "Then show me to your car."

Freya ended her call with the emergency dispatcher under the reassurance a police patrol would be on the lookout for The Creeper. Hopefully they would find him. She couldn't imagine how she'd ever leave The Ruby alone until then.

She shot a quick message to Crystal, asking her to check the security cameras for anything that might be helpful to the police. Now that the immediate danger was over, as well as her phone call, the ache in her shoulders rose to the forefront of her mind.

She sank back into the soft leather seats inside Max's stationary car, succumbing to exhaustion and the need to let go, taking in her surroundings—the pristine white and wood trim, the crisp scent of pine and mint, along with an unmissable Tesla badge in the center of his steering wheel.

Yes, the guy had money. And he sat in the driver's seat, silent and staring ahead, as if maybe the whole Creeper incident bothered him too.

Well, she had kind of dragged this poor man into her nightmare, so his silence was expected. She cleared her throat, all of a sudden overwhelmed and needing distraction. "Umm… Nice ride."

He nodded ahead, eyes narrowed, before turning back to her. "Are you okay?"

She nearly flinched at how easily he disregarded her attempt at small talk. Still, she held eye contact, not wanting to lie about her shaken state while also not wanting to stir discussion about what had happened.

She wasn't okay.

Nowhere near okay.

But he'd been at risk back there too, and he'd done *more* than enough to help her out of a bad situation. Whatever she felt now wasn't his problem. So, she set about doing what she did best, what the performers at her bar did all the time, *faking it till she made it.*

"I'm sorry for taking over your night back there. For what it's worth, thanks."

His lips curled with a sheepish smile, a smile so unassuming, her own lips yearned to mirror his expression. "I was just a prop, remember? You mostly helped yourself."

"You could have refused to play along. You could have decided The Creeper was too creepy and ditched me mid-escape." She ran her attention over his fitted, light-blue shirt, a light blue that highlighted the turquoise flecks in his eyes. A thin, silver swirl peeked through his open collar, a pendant shaped like a wave, which made sense given his whole surfer deal. "So… umm… Honestly, thank you."

He held her gaze but said nothing, so she peered down and twisted the silver ring on her pointer finger—funnily enough, shaped like a swirly kind of wave too, though with a chunkier design and a deep-set ruby pressed into the center. The whole thing looked mysterious and witchy.

And speaking of witchy, she'd learned at a young age to trust her intuition—intuition born from having to predict who could be trusted and who would hurt her. Maybe that's why she'd had that sick sensation wash over her before she'd even spotted The Creeper waiting.

Why she'd taken one look at Max and known he would at least try to save her.

Her heart quickened a little, and a subtle warmth swept over her skin. Despite this guy's "innocent dope" vibe, she'd watched him in passing at her bar for months and had only ever thought of him as a "good patron".

He kept patient during delays and slow orders, all while his cashed-up friends got snappish. He never groped or harassed her staff, a bare minimum of respect, but one so many failed at on a regular basis. And then there was his habit of stacking the empty plates on his table, making it easier for her wait staff to clear the area, even as he thanked them for every small assistance, furthering his thanks with genuine and engaged conversation.

Every time he visited, the crack of laughter could be heard from across her bar. As much as she tried to stay out of employee gossip, it was near impossible not to notice how many of her staff held not-so-secret crushes on him.

If she had to guess, Max hadn't grown up with money; he sure as hell didn't act like it, anyway. And now, as much as she'd avoided any kind of adoration, she'd just become the latest member of his fan club.

"I'm ready to go home now." She flicked her gaze over his face, to the masculine cleft at the center of his chin, to those sparkling blue eyes; her breath settling with a strong certainty she hadn't just jumped from the clutches of one dangerous man and into another's.

*This one can be trusted. His small kindnesses add up.*

"You're okay with me driving you?"

His long fingers curled around the steering wheel, but his attention stayed on her.

She gave a quick nod, recalling the few times she'd watched him focus that attention on other women at the bar, before eventually leaving with those women on his arm.

The engine started, and a distinct flutter worked its way through her tummy. One she knew well. Most women would not do what she was about to do, not after the near horror she'd just escaped... but then... she wasn't most women.

Her back catalogue of fucked-up experiences ran deep and wide. Enough for her to know she'd eventually recover from The Creeper's attempt to destroy her.

Even though it was clear Max had an unintended way with women, he had something far more interesting going for him.

Despite how easy his life seemed from where she sat, he still had compassion, his emotions so clear she could pretty much reach out and touch them, a rare enough combination to make her want some of that. *Some of him.*

Irrational, right? But her childhood had taught her everything she needed to know about survival, while adulthood had pushed her to thrive, to take her pain and turn it into something amazing. She *knew* pain. She also knew how to make it go away.

She could overcome another person's attempt to steal her joy and find an escape, just as she had tonight. She'd find that joy again, and in this case, pleasure.

All she had to do was convince Max to help her one last time.

# Chapter Three

Max pulled his car over to the front of a double-story brick townhouse on a small lane just off the heavy trafficked main road of Brunswick Street. He nodded out to a giant mural of a man, fist raised high and dressed in head-to-toe white, except for a gold jacket. "You have Freddie Mercury painted on your house?"

For the first time since this encounter, the woman beside him broke into a brilliant grin, the ruby of her lips no match for her hickory eyes, shining with their own unique brilliance. "I painted it myself. And he's joy personified, so why not?"

Max laughed at her statement but also her reaction—and the way his heart jolted at the pure exhilaration in her smile.

He shut off the engine and slumped back in his seat. He'd gotten this woman to safety. All he had to do was walk her to her front door, and his night would be over. He could go back to his multi-million-dollar apartment and the moonlit ocean just outside.

But first, he'd keep her talking and double-check she was truly all right. "You know, I doubt many people get through 'We Will Rock You' without at least tapping a foot along."

She gave a shrug, the light bronze in her eyes still glittering. "It's a classic, but I'm more into the flamboyance of 'I Want to Break Free' or the layered harmonies in 'Somebody to Love'. Freddie knew how to be completely himself. I admire that. He was bad in the best kind of way, you know?"

"I have a feeling you wouldn't be far from that yourself."

She lifted a brow but didn't respond. To be fair, he wasn't all that sure where that response had come from or if it had been all that appropriate.

Still, he struggled to pull his focus off what seemed to be a constant light behind this woman's expression. Constant, now there wasn't some crazed predator hunting her down, anyway. That smile hid a childishness, an unrestrained radiance, like a sunbeam personified… or something.

He chuckled to himself, at the way in which he'd suddenly waxed poetic about a woman he'd only technically just met.

"What?" She narrowed a glare at him, though that smile still held, her thick platinum curls overwhelming her yellow polka-dot head-band and hugging her doll-like cheeks. "What is it? Why are you laughing?"

He chuckled again. First because he'd likened this *woman* to a child, then the sun, and now a doll, which, with her killer curves, sensuous red lips, and Marilyn Monroe-inspired attire—complete with off-the-shoulder, polka dot, vintage pinup dress—she most certainly was not!

But second, because he now had to deflect his true reason for laughing.

"Nothing." He brought his closed fist to his lips and cleared his throat, unable to pry his thoughts off how he'd now decided those curves were less "killer" and more "divine" like a goddess. A *goddess?* Jesus-bloody-hell, he needed to get his mind together. "Umm… I just found it interesting how you've clearly not overthought your feelings on Freddie Mercury, that's all."

She beamed again and twisted toward him, his heart panging hard. "You saying I'm weird? I'm *not* weird."

"You totally *are* weird." He jabbed a finger at her house. "I bet you're hiding a Freddie Mercury shrine in there, complete with a life-sized cardboard cut-out and preserved finger you probably scavenged right out of his grave."

She threw back her head and gave a full-on witch's cackle, hands clapping as though she attempted to stem the laughter. "Hiding? You're more than welcome to come inside and have a look for yourself. I have no shame about my altar."

"You're joking, right? You don't actually have an—"

His shoulders locked under a suddenly rigid posture. Surely, she wasn't really inviting him in? But damn it, he wanted to throw himself at the offer either way.

*Get a grip. The woman just had the fright of her life. She's being friendly. She doesn't want me. Now open her door and let the poor darling out.*

He shifted in his seat and pressed a button on his door console, the one that released the locks on his car. "Well... good to know. I bet you're tired. I should let you go."

But she didn't move, and neither did he.

He just stared out to the cobblestones edging the lane and the black asphalt center bathed in pale-white street light.

"Max?"

He turned at his name, her dark lashes rising and falling, her gaze moving around his face in a way that made his heart want to throw itself against the front of his ribcage.

Like she, too, wanted to stay for a moment longer.

*Piss off, you dope. She probably just wants to say thank you, then be on her way. Go on then, just say goodbye already.*

And still he said nothing.

As much as he wanted to congratulate himself on his heroics tonight, he deserved a hard kick in the groin for also having noticed the way her yellow dress supported her ample breasts, or how the nipped-in waist didn't hide the slight bump of her tummy, a bump he found inordinately feminine and fucking sexy.

Hot lust burned through his body. Well, maybe he deserved to burn. Or maybe he was just human, and she all raw and unabashed woman made for physical worship in any other circumstances.

*Dude, these are the bleeding circumstances. Say. Good. Bye!*

"Seriously"—her light jovial smile returned, albeit a little slower this time and tinged with an unreadable focus—"do you want to come inside?"

His jaw slipped loose, and he tried to coax out words that just wouldn't come, his mind working double-time to decide what her invitation might mean.

Eventually, he decided to cut his lumbering brain a break and just ask. "You mean, as in…"

"As in, I'm not ready to be alone, and I figure I at least owe you a drink."

*Righto, then.* His posture dropped, and he couldn't decide whether to be disappointed or relieved, but he shook his head and pushed on with the farewell either way. "You don't owe me anything."

He wanted to jump at the offer, to at least grasp at some kind of connection with this woman whose name he'd stupidly forgotten to ask. But what he'd done for her tonight, not leaving her to fend for herself in the face of trouble, didn't deserve a reward.

Or a drink.

Definitely not a chance to heat up his dating life.

She extended her hand to her door and pulled the handle, only to fall short of actually leaving. "If it'll make you feel better, consider it another favor to me, but you're coming in for that drink."

He frowned, prepared to argue with her, but by the time he opened his mouth to do just that, she'd already slipped out, her keys jangling in her hand.

His hand worked on autopilot, unlatching his seatbelt, while his moronic legs chased after her. He waited. She punched in the code to a barred gate leading to a small courtyard and her front door.

He followed her into her house where she flicked on the lights. Beyond the entrance, a cozy, white kitchen with a gray marble counter greeted him.

"So…" He made a show of peering around the bright dining area just up ahead, this woman's home all "urban arty", with its white walls and various indoor plants, and in a trendy part of Melbourne. Whereas he'd invested almost everything he owned into upgrading his multi-level apartment into the eco-efficient apex of city-coastal living. "I might have been mistaken when I decided you were one of the bar staff at The Ruby Room."

"What gave me away?" She dropped her purse on a tiny table by the front door and sauntered into the kitchen. A giant painting of a half-naked lady—little more than a thick, black outline and a few solid splashes of color—graced the side wall.

He forced his attention from the semi-nude and back to the *actual* woman standing before him, a small knowing smile twisting her lips. "Even if you rented, this place isn't exactly within a bar worker's budget."

She gave a light shrug and pulled a tray of ice from the freezer. "Maybe I have five other house mates hiding upstairs, and we share the costs. Or maybe my money is inherited. Or maybe I have a more lucrative side-hustle, and bar work is merely a passion project."

"Or maybe it's all the money you save not driving a car?"

She laughed at that one. "I don't *need* a car. Not in this pocket of Melbourne. I have trams and buses, trains and cabs. Plus, this house is just blocks away from the bar."

She turned her full attention to him, but he stood silent, not sure what to make of her evasive reply.

"Fine." She rolled her eyes and went about ripping a handful of mint from a plant sitting on the white marble counter. "I own The Ruby Room. Now, I'm having a mint gin and tonic since I've damn well earned one tonight. What'll you have?"

He paused, still trying to get his head around the fact she owned The Ruby, one of Melbourne's more eccentric but cool venues, much less that she threw the fact out there with zero celebration; unlike his friends, who loved to harp on about everything they owned or achieved.

And maybe that's what he liked about this woman because, despite what his friends thought and his own tendency to blow money on travel and parties and renovating, his bank account wasn't a bottomless pit. He had money, yes, but unlike most of them, his was new and not inherited. He had no "bank of mum and dad" to fall back on. Since ceasing his work at Tiluma, the tech company he co-owned with his brother, his financial flexibility wasn't as crash hot as it used to be.

"No gin for me. I have to drive home soon."

"Right."

She turned to a cabinet behind her and pulled out two short

glasses.

Both landed on the counter with a loud clink, followed by the bottle of gin. She gave him an upturned grin. "You sure it's a no for that drink?"

He moved closer to the mint plant, its cool and peppery scent helping to ground him. And goodness knew, he needed all the grounding he could get to escape the familiar sense that, as always, he was just a few steps behind everyone in the room. Or in this case, the one other person in the room.

"Okay. Yes, to the drink." Anything to distract from the sinking knowledge that, as little as he knew about this woman, she seemed to have so much more going for her than he did. "Business must be doing well."

She dropped a slice of lime into each glass and slid one over to him, her direct stare seeming to see right through his mindless prattle. "How do you figure that?"

"It's a Wednesday night, and the place was busy. In fact, The Ruby is always busy lately. And then there were the new posters for the Live Wire Festival and the "Help Wanted" sign in the front window. Things can't be too bad if you're hiring, right?"

She tilted her head to one side, her luminous curls shifting to expose the long tendon down the side of her neck, as well as that delicate sun tattoo. "Oh really, you noticed I'm hiring?" Her gaze made a show of looking him up and down, hinting she'd caught him admiring her neck. "I wouldn't have picked a flashy guy like you to be interested in a bar job."

A broken chuckle slipped from his lips, and his heart jolted. *Damn.* He couldn't tell if she was giving him attitude or flirting, or maybe even both. He'd always been terrible at picking up these things. Case in point? This woman embodied all that he found attractive, and he had no clue how to move things along with her... or even if he should.

And because he wasn't exactly the smoothest guy ever, he often waited for women to approach him. And the women who usually did approach him, the ones who assumed he'd be interested, were similar to him, in that they were all tall and athletic and with decent access to "the bank of mum and dad".

When it came to hooking up, he didn't often get what he wanted. But given the way his nerve endings tingled, he sure wanted this woman.

He sipped at his drink, suddenly thankful for the liquid courage in his hand. "Me, work in a bar? That wouldn't go well."

"Why not?" She leaned a hip against the counter, seeming far more comfortable in his presence than he was in hers. "People seem to like you. That's more than a decent start."

He tipped his glass her way, heartened she'd noticed his presence in the past. Then again, she had no idea about his people skills, or lack thereof, and how his odd-ball behavior had gotten him booted from the company he'd helped start. "*Some* people like me. My former co-workers would say otherwise."

Since he'd left Tiluma, all he really had was travel, parties, and working on his apartment.

She raised her drink to him in a playful *cheers*. "Well, Max, consider me *some* people. Suddenly, I seem to like you, too."

Her attention flicked down his body again and back to his face, her cheeks maintaining their subtle blush, but nothing more than that. Like she had no qualms about checking him out or the potential repercussions of her words.

His mind snapped to the painting of the topless woman again, then the loud mural outside, along with her adoration of Freddie Mercury's ability to be completely himself. Except perhaps, her adoration had more to do with recognition. A recognition of who she was. A woman completely herself.

And this woman was *not* the damsel in distress he'd assumed, though true enough, she had needed him at least for a few minutes there. She was someone with an innate ability to survive, not the type to fumble on tough decisions. Someone who ran headlong into conflict and, unlike him, didn't bungle the hard stuff with her weird sense of humor.

In other words, she was his complete opposite. His perfect kind of woman. And probably why this encounter wouldn't lead anywhere.

He drew a steadying breath. "You know my name. What's yours?"

The least he could do was to stop referring to her as *this woman* in his head, perhaps even say hello the next time he saw her at The Ruby.

She smiled and placed her drink down on the counter next to his, the action drawing her closer to him. "Freya. Look, I'm not going to lie. I'm still shaken up about what happened earlier, so I'm not likely to get any sleep tonight." She rounded the counter and paused just in front of him. "So if you're in any way interested in staying here tonight, I'd like that. I'd like that very much."

Heat crept through his body, starting at his chest and filling up space from his head down to his toes; all while his skin prickled, the hairs along his arms and at the nape of his neck standing on end.

There she went again, running headlong while he scrambled to keep up.

He wanted so much to believe she meant that she wanted him, but he'd read so many people wrong in so many other scenarios, not just the sexual kind, and he wasn't taking any chances. She'd already met one creep tonight.

"I'm happy to crash on your couch if that'll help you feel safer."

Though maybe he should just stick to his original plan and go home, get a decent night's sleep, jet off to his holiday, and forget any of this ever happened.

Freya's eyes glittered, and she drew closer, bringing her scent of tangy, sweet perfume wafting over him, her body's full curves just dangerous centimeters away.

"I don't want to feel safe." She pulled the sheer yellow scarf she used as a headband from her hair, shaking out her curls. "I want to feel *you*."

Her hair, her scintillating words, that low and husky whisper, eviscerated his already unstable ability to keep his thoughts in check, drawing from him a desire to reach out and bunch his fingers through her wild locks.

But even with his compulsion to touch her, she was the one to reach out first, to touch *him*, her palms landing on his chest, only to slide up his pectoral muscles, finding a home at the side of his neck. "And I sure as hell don't want you sleeping on my couch, Max. I want you in my bed."

＃ Chapter Four

Freya's not-so-subtle seduction landed right on target, Max's breath catching in sync with his dilating pupils. Watching his reaction sent an electrified thrill up her spine.

He'd given all the signs that he wanted her—his lingering stares, his long pauses hinting that he played his advances carefully—when she didn't need careful. While toying with him had been fun, she preferred to get on with things and put the poor guy out of his misery.

A comforting heat radiated from his neck into her hand, and she extended her thumb to stroke the edge of his well-defined and only slightly stubbled jawline. The tips of her fingers curled instinctively, and she pulled him down to her, his lips parting a split second before their mouths collided.

A small blaze took light in her lower belly, and his hands found the small of her back, dragging her in, as if his body awoke right along with hers. The possessive gesture made her press into him more, her lips drinking him in, the tension from earlier draining from her body. *Just what she'd wanted.*

It'd been a hell of a long time since she'd felt this enlivened at a man's touch, and it wasn't as if she didn't have access to men. Max's kiss made her heart pound and her mind clear. She was supposed to be the one leading this thing, but he left her feeling needy and weak.

A sigh rolled through her throat, and her hands balled at the thin blue material of his shirt. She pulled him back with her a few paces before his movements stiffened, and he pried his lips away. "What are you doing?"

She peered up at him and gave a sweet smile, stroking her knuckles over his front, hoping to offer more reassurance, only to feel the distinctive brush of hard, rippling abs.

A manic laugh threatened to break loose at her indiscriminate good luck—at the joy of her senses returning to her body after a particularly shitty night. Though dealing with the occasional creeper was almost part of her job description, the one she'd encountered had gotten closer and creepier than most.

But a night with Max would fix her woes. She was almost certain of that.

"Let's take this upstairs." She took his hand and turned to leave, but he tugged her back, halting her journey.

"You had a scare tonight. One that involved a man trying to kidnap you, and God knows what else." Max frowned, his attention dropping to the floor, the blue of his eyes turning stormy. "And now you have me, another man, in your house and—"

She gave him a narrow side glare, a warning that he sounded painfully close to judging her decision-making skills. "Are you planning to kidnap me?"

"What? No. Of course not!"

"And are you saying no to having sex with me?"

He went still for a beat and then shook his head. Quiet.

"Good. Then let me decide how I feel about tonight, okay?"

His shoulders eased down a couple of inches, and he gave a steady nod. She reached out and grabbed his hand again, commencing the journey through her house. The stairs creaked as she pulled him along, catching a glimpse of him through a mirror at the top, his attention snagging on yet another of her painted nudes.

She hooked her teeth over her lower lip and held back a smile. Perhaps now he'd pieced together just how much the human body didn't faze her. She owned a burlesque bar, for hell's sake, and had zero shame about giving or receiving pleasure, with no time for any judgmental asshat who expected *any* woman to hide her general enjoyment of sex.

*And she loved sex.*

She loved that sex could defuse almost every form of stress she encountered.

She loved the play between connection and power, how sex made her feel about her body, so alive, so free, so divine and human all at once.

Her bedroom door lay open, and she got within stepping distance before her world spun and tilted. Max pushed her back to the wall, only to rain down a whole storm of kisses on her. Like he'd wanted to do that all along but only now found the courage.

*Well, welcome aboard, handsome stranger.*

She laughed at the pleasant surprise, at him stepping up and taking charge. Maybe her provocative paintings had stoked his enthusiasm, or maybe he'd just needed time.

His tongue brushed over hers, hot and demanding, a rush of adrenaline cascading through her body so that she gave in to his direction, allowing him to back her into her room.

She pushed into him, alerting him to the expanding need within her, making it clear she would give as hard as she got. Even if her lips hurt from the force of their kisses, and her limbs already trembled. She still wanted more. Wanted to taste him. To run her nails over every inch of his body.

A light thud sounded from his foot hitting her bedframe, he stumbled back, dragging her down with him onto the mattress, her forehead crashing forward and into the bridge of his nose.

"Holy shhhh"—he whipped a hand over his face and hissed—"my eyes are watering."

She couldn't help it; knew she should ask if he was okay, but burst into laughter all the same. He lowered his hand and pressed his forehead to hers, continuing the rain of kisses while laughing hard himself.

He now sat on the mattress's edge with her on his lap. Occasionally, she'd pull back to witness the sweet, lop-sided smile tugging one corner of his mouth higher than the other, the innocence in that look making her heart surge.

She began releasing his shirt buttons, opening all but the last before he pushed her hands away, his long fingers entangling the thick dress straps at her shoulders and pushing them down over her arms until her dress bunched at her waist.

Her breasts overflowed her black lace bra, and he sucked in a loud breath, as if for a moment there, he forgot to breathe. The reaction filled her belly with a million dancing butterflies and the shock of never before feeling so desired.

And because of his reaction, she decided to take her fill of visual stimulation too, trekking her gaze over his open shirt, to the valleys and mountains of pecs and well-honed abs.

*Holy Mother Goddess!*

*His body was remarkable.*

The man was built like an athlete—lanky, toned—as close to a living god as she'd ever seen. From his brilliant blue eyes, to his golden waves, once again she couldn't believe her good luck. That and, how the heck had she missed all that gloriousness whilst walking past him every other week at the bar?

Her next words fell from her mouth, breathy and unplanned, "Holy fuck!"

"Yes." He gave a slow nod, his stunned blue gaze catching hers, like he too needed a moment. "Holy fuck."

His "Holy fuck" seemed aimed at her body more than his own, so she shuffled back, resolved to put on a slow show of stepping out of her dress, holding his attention until she stood before him in just the lower part of her underwear.

The act of watching him watch her lit sparks of pleasure throughout every nerve, igniting heat between her legs, her body wanting more. More touch. More action. More *him*.

And as if he knew, he slid off his shirt, where a thick scar sat at the top of his shoulder, one that only added a sense of intrigue, strength, vulnerability, stoking her desire.

She wanted to know how he'd gotten the scar, wanted to press her lips right there since he was physically perfect in every way except for this small chink in his armor, which somehow still increased his perfection.

*Holy fuck again.*

He removed his pants, revealing narrow hips balanced by strong-looking thighs. He *was* a god. A Nordic one, probably capable of launching lightning bolts from his magical pecs or something. Kind of ironic since her name, Freya, came from the Nordic goddess of fertility, love, and beauty.

Maybe this guy was made for her after all.

Well, just for tonight, anyway.

She copied his initiative and took off the last of her clothes, her underwear finding a place on an armchair next to her bedside table, before she reached into the top drawer, seizing a condom in its silver packet.

She handed it to him, his long and seemingly dexterous fingers curling around hers, while his gaze held hers again for another beat, drawing that same strain on her heart as earlier.

She pushed at him, pushed at that feeling, and made him sit back down on the bed's edge, straddling her knees on either side of his powerful thighs.

He rolled the condom down his length and things moved quickly from there, his hands finding her hips, guiding her so very slowly onto him. Her head lolled back while he became incredibly still and released a low groan.

Exquisite pressure grew within her. Despite the lack of lights in the room, the soft, white glow through the sheer floor-to-ceiling curtains was enough for her to witness his pupils expanding.

She couldn't help but trace a finger over his cheekbone, marveling at the way his eyelids fluttered shut at her caress. He leaned in, giving in to her a little, kissing her neck, while hot, heavy breaths brushed her skin and lifted his broad, powerful shoulders.

Fingertips dug into her hips, rolling her over him in a steady, rocking motion, the gentle rhythm fueling one desire after another, forcing her eyes closed until she lost herself to the rising swell through her chest and the heat swallowing her every fiber.

This was a celebration. Of bodies. *Of her body.* Of being alive. Something she'd learned never to take for granted.

She'd survived. When surviving hadn't always been a given. And yes, she had more curves than mainstream culture deemed acceptable since there was less money to make from women who simply loved who they were. But she'd long ago decided that mainstream culture could suck eggs. She had a body made for indulging in, experiencing, one that functioned for her every day and deserved gratitude.

And oh, speaking of gratitude...

She pressed her palms to Max's shoulders and gave thanks for this beautiful man, too. For the way he held her in place and let her take her fill of him. For the awe expressed through his eyes, like maybe a total stranger could truly see her.

A moan broke from deep within her chest, and she allowed the light waves of tingling to rise and spread from the place where their bodies joined, the room thrumming with energy. An energy so electrifying it effervesced from her toes, all the way through to the very tips of her hair.

Oh yes, she did love sex. Always had. *But this man.* He was something else.

Another moan tore from her, and she clenched around him. His hand slid over her hip, over her tummy, fingers soft until he cupped her breast, his thumb abrading her nipple enough to steal her breath.

He bucked against her, rewarding her loss of control with further pleasure, taking their exchange up another level. A rich chuckle rumbled through her, betraying just how much she enjoyed this unexpected end to her night.

She cupped her palms to his cheeks, allowing him to kiss her through her slow and shuddering climax; her long curls falling forward and acting as a curtain of intimacy around them.

His fingers bunched the hair at the back of her head, and he deepened the kiss, grinding into her, obliging her to ride him harder; her breaths turned ragged, heart near bursting. His tongue lashed hers, hungry, hard, until he swelled within her and found his own release.

# Chapter Five

Max nudged the door to his apartment open, ignoring the ring of his phone and humming to himself, as the first refreshing glimpse of the ocean greeted him from his floor-to-ceiling living room windows.

He glided onward into his kitchen, the view opening up even more. Patricia and Tom, the married couple he hired to clean his apartment each week, stood at his counter, a red bucket of cleaning equipment beside them, blue wiping cloths and frosted spray bottles in their hands.

"Hey, Max." Tom folded his cloth and dropped it into the bucket. "Don't mind us, we're wrapping things up now and will be out of your way in a few minutes."

Max opened his fridge and pulled out filtered water in reusable glass bottles, extending one to Patricia and Tom. They both shook their heads.

Patricia dusted her hands against her checked work shirt. "Thanks for the offer, darl, but can't chat today. We've got to hurry off to pick up a present for the soon-to-be ten-year-old. Thanks to those extra clients you got us, we were able to scrape enough money together to get her that electric piano and lessons she's been begging for."

An instant smile hit Max's lips, and he leaned against the fridge. Honestly, his day just kept getting better.

"Oh hey, that's great." He took a sip of water, glad a few of his well-placed recommendations succeeded in getting Tom and Patricia some extra work. "And if you're stuck for things to do for her birthday, you just let me know, and you guys can host something here. Pool party on the deck, maybe?"

Tom's mouth dropped open, eyes lighting up, and he wrapped his arm around his wife's waist. "Thanks, mate, you're a good egg, you know that? We might just take you up on that offer, but in the meantime, we'll leave you to your day. Have a good one, okay?"

Tom picked up the cleaning bucket and led Patricia out the door. Max waited for the couple to leave before heading for his bedroom, eager to pack for his flight out to Ibiza tonight.

Unlike most of his friends, he packed his own suitcase because, sure, he *had* money but not enough to call his bank account a bottomless pit.

From the few years he'd worked at Tiluma, as well as the profit share he received each year, he'd dropped four-million on his apartment, not just the purchase but the renovation too—complete with upstairs energy-efficient gym, eco-friendly theater, and an indoor spa. Then there'd been his balcony. Meters upon meters of sparse terracotta tile transformed into a lush entertainment area, complete with two different garden areas, high-end furniture, and a solar-powered, heated pool for when he couldn't get to the ocean.

But still, he had to be careful. Since leaving the company four years ago, the yearly profit share was all he had, and so he needed to temper his spending, to live on, to keep up with his loaded friends—most of whom were "old money". So while he lived well, he couldn't afford a full-time maid or someone to pack his suitcase.

He had his apartment. He had his cleaners. He had his meal delivery service. And just enough left over to live and travel with.

*And still far more than most. Remember that.*

Yes, he appreciated that much, even if he did wish he had more to attribute to his last few years than tinkering on his apartment and bumming about on the beach. He did *want* a purpose, but finding one, much less committing... Well, that's where the spokes fell off all his nonexistent plans.

His phone rang again, and he pulled it out from his crinkled pants pocket—crinkled because those pants had spent the night crumpled in a pile on Freya's bedroom floor. His reflection in the window now showed his mussed-up hair and slightly puffy, sleep-deprived eyes. He looked about as crumpled as his pants. Crumpled, tired, but lighter than he'd felt in a very long time, despite his carefree reputation.

*If only people knew the truth about me, huh?*

He peered down at his phone, at his account manager, Elaine's, name on his screen, which only made the muscles on his face turn lax and his smile disappear.

He pressed the call-reject button, refusing to talk about money today. Not when he'd just returned from an amazing night with a beautiful, bold woman—a woman he wanted to reconnect with once he got back from his equally amazing holiday.

Hard pass on anything even remotely boring.

Elaine could call him when he got back from his trip.

He stuffed his phone into his pocket and strode over to his walk-in wardrobe, stretching to reach his suitcase perched on the highest shelf.

He set it open on the giant, cushioned bench in the room's center. There wasn't all that much to pack. Ibiza would be warm enough that he wouldn't be wearing much beyond swim shorts and maybe a light shirt during the days. Other than that, he really only needed a couple of outfits for the clubs at night.

A few clothes, followed by some toiletries, a phone charger, and some shoes went in his case. He wasn't all that careful about how he arranged things. Whatever he forgot to pack, he'd just buy when he landed on the island.

His phone rang. *Elaine again.* He hung up and abandoned his suitcase, distracted by the swim shorts in his hand and the ocean calling him less than a hundred meters away.

He threw the shorts onto the steel-gray, silk cover of his double king bed. Perhaps he'd eke out some time for a nap later, but right now he got changed, his stomach grumbling. There'd only been time to share a coffee and a light chat at Freya's before she'd taken an urgent call, one that stole her former brightness, and she'd pretty much shoved him out the door after that.

He'd left confused, concerned about whatever bad news had found her this morning. Heck, he hadn't even had time to get her number or ask about seeing her again. Still, he *would* see her again.

Maybe he'd find a few minutes mid-trip to order something nice and have it delivered to The Ruby Room, then check if she was okay or wanted to talk when he got back. He'd stay fresh in her mind, despite his absence, and lay the foundations to get close again when he returned.

He glanced at the clock on his nightstand, nearly midday. Breakfast could wait a little longer. The summer sun called outside, the water likely beautiful and warm.

He dipped into his linen cupboard for a towel, then went to the kitchen to refill his water bottle. The whole time, his damn phone kept ringing, making it clear it wasn't just the sun calling him today. Chances were, he wouldn't get any peace unless he spoke to Elaine.

"Hello?" he answered in the most droning, bored voice he could muster.

"Max, I'm glad you finally decided to pick up."

He frowned at her snippy reply, the hard tone not fitting for someone he was paying to keep track of his money. Then again, he had been giving her the run around all morning.

"Okay. Fine. I'm sorry." He rubbed his fingertips over the bridge of his nose, just wanting this call to be over already. "What do you need to tell me?"

"Oh, Max." She released a loud sigh. "Are you sitting down?"

"No." He dropped his hand, a sudden pit opening up in his stomach. "Why? What's happened?"

"Let's put it this way. If you're not already sitting down, do it now." She paused as if she expected he would do just that, but he didn't. He mostly froze, almost like what someone might do the second before a car ran them over. "Your life is about to change, and you're not going to like it."

# Chapter Six

Freya's shoulders sagged at the scent of chicken broth from the food trolley some kitchen worker left parked beside her. That smell. The salty-savoriness. It made her heart twist and plummet. Not because she sat in a hospital per se, but because in her younger years, she'd preferred her hospital stints to her dispiriting daily home life with her mother and brother.

"How long has she been having problems?" The words grated through her throat, and she turned to the young female doctor sitting on a chair before her.

The quaint furniture in the small alcove and upbeat floral arrangement on the coffee table hinted that this place existed for the express purpose of delivering bad news.

"From looking at Ms. Branner's chart, years." The doctor peered down at her notes, her sandy blond bangs skimming her brow. "It's often the way with cirrhosis of the liver. A patient can hold on for quite some time until other organs also begin to fail."

Freya swallowed at the dryness in her throat. She'd always expected this day to come but never expected she'd care when it did.

From past, very brief conversations, she'd known her mother had health issues. As socially inept as her mother could be, she'd known better than to make a big deal of health stuff around Freya, much less expect any kind of sympathy.

"She's not going to make it this time?"

The doctor gave a slow shake of her head. "No. I'm sorry. That's why we called you."

The doctor's hushed tone and the deep wrinkle between her brow suggested she'd made the wrong assumption about how devastating this news would be; the only devastating thing about all of this was that it *should* have been devastating and wasn't.

When it came to Kerry Branner, the only emotion Freya had left was apathy. Apathy and a pure and necessary need for self-protection.

She sat a little taller, the reminder about self-protection kicking in. "Right. How long does she have?"

The doctor leveled an unmoving stare, almost like she needed a second to decide how she felt about Freya's flat tone and lack of tears. "We don't like to give predictions, but my general guess here would be weeks to months."

"So..."

The doctor drew a deep breath, then released a sigh. "From my experience, I'd guess about a month on the shorter scale, but the really stubborn ones—"

Freya scoffed out a jagged laugh, cutting the doctor off, even as a tear pricked the corner of her eye.

*Hang on a minute, aren't I supposed to "not care"?*

She dropped her attention to the flared hem of her moss-green dress, a dress she'd made herself because growing up poor meant learning to sew her own clothes. Something she mostly still did with her vintage-inspired wardrobe. Something her mother had taught her to do.

See, even bad relationships weren't bad all the time. Not all bad people were bad all the time either, which was one thing that made leaving them behind all the harder.

And while her mother had been busy turning Freya's younger years into a living nightmare, there'd also been evenings where she'd tried to help Freya with homework, even though she'd had so little education of her own to draw from. Or sometimes she'd slip Freya candy, or a five-dollar note for getting a good grade, or sometimes just because…

But even then, those moments never held long.

Which was why she and her mother didn't share a name. Miranda Branner, the name Freya had been born with, had changed to Freya Cortez.

She'd wanted little to do with her mother, even in name. She'd picked a new first name simply because she liked it, then kept the surname of the people who'd eventually come to raise her, her grandparents.

She closed her eyes for a second and pressed her fingertips over her sockets, her heart a mad flutter, while tension bunched the muscles at the back of her neck.

"I'm getting the feeling you don't want to be here?" The doctor's softened voice cracked through Freya's racing thoughts. Perhaps reluctant relatives weren't all that uncommon after all. "But Ms. Branner listed you as her next of kin."

Freya dropped her hands from her face. Even after living out the remainder of her childhood without her mother, a harsh breakup with a boyfriend in her late twenties had sent her searching for a sign that perhaps the world wasn't so bad. That horrible people changed. That redemption could happen for anyone.

And to some extent, when she did reconnect with her mother, things weren't as deplorable as she'd recalled. Only because she was an adult now, and her mother couldn't hurt her in the same ways she used to.

"I guess I would be her next of kin." In that she checked on her mother occasionally and had spoken with her long enough to track down lost family members rarely spoken of. She'd wanted to uncover how monsters were made, and for better or worse, she'd found her answer.

Her gut tightened and churned, but she forced a casual shrug. "My brother lives overseas, so that makes me the only one to deal with this stuff."

This stuff?

More like, "end of life" stuff.

Which was ironic really.

"Ms. Cortez. I understand if you truly can't do this, but your mother will need someone to be there for her, if for no other reason than to settle her affairs and handle the funeral arrangements. The state can step in with government appointed contractors, but that would complicate matters, not just for your mother but for you, too."

She took a moment to kill her desire to walk away now, nodding instead.

Despite what her mother had done to her, or maybe because of it, she'd developed strength, even when she didn't want to be strong, to compartmentalize her pain and get through the hard stuff.

Her involvement now was way more than her mother deserved, but still, some indecipherable force kept her in her seat.

Could she handle her mother's final affairs? *Yes.*

Did she want to? *No.*

Would she do it? *Yes, again…*

*Fuck!*

Because even with all the poison lingering between her and her brother, Clay, she didn't want to give him more things to worry about. His life hadn't panned out to the success he'd been groomed for, and his life in America wasn't something he'd be getting away from anytime soon. Besides, any bad blood between them wasn't his fault. Not really, anyway.

She urged the muscles in her face to relax and forced her attention back to the doctor. Her mother was the last and biggest piece of her past to shed, and as it stood, mere months would pass and then that shedding would occur whether she liked it or not.

She could do this. She knew she could. She would push through as always.

"It's okay. Just tell me what to do."

Max plonked himself down at his kitchen table, his gaze pinned to the azure sky outside his wide windows, his phone pressed to his ear. "Listen, Elaine, I appreciate you have a job to do, but could we hurry this along? I have important things to complete before my flight out to Ibiza tonight."

Important things, like go to the beach, have a nap…

"Yeah, about that." Her tone went flat, unimpressed with his spiel about his important things, like she maybe knew his things weren't all that important. "You're not going to Ibiza, Max. You're not going anywhere any time soon."

He reeled back, his shoulder blades pressing into his chair. "What? Why not?"

"So, remember that thing I warned you about months ago?" She let out a heavy sigh, the kind that gave the impression he'd worn her last nerve, and she thought of him as some kind of simpleton or something. Maybe she wasn't all that off-base. "Unless you have some cash squirreled away that I don't know about, there's no way you can afford Ibiza. It doesn't matter if your flights and accommodation are already paid up. Just the daily costs, while making no money, will truly ruin you."

"Oh come on, that's a bit dramatic, don't you think?" He let out a sound that resembled a scoff and a light-hearted laugh rolled into one.

"No, Max. It's reality. If anything…" She paused as though she needed a moment to weigh her next words. "You don't know, do you?"

The softer edge to her normally bristly voice had his pulse racing. He searched his brain for whatever it was he didn't know, but of course, as usual, he drew a blank. "What are you talking about?"

"You have no money, Max." Her voice rose across the receiver, almost as if she'd decided to just spit that bit of news before she chickened out. Either way, an instant coldness hit him square in the chest, and his entire world seemed to tip sharply to one side.

"In fact," Elaine's voice lowered again, "you have less than no money. Your account is overdrawn by five grand."

"Wait." He planted his feet to the ground and shot to standing, trekking his gaze around the room—at the bronze-embellished and designer furniture, the pristine white walls and clean modern design, as if any of those might hold the clarity he needed right now. Meanwhile, his fingers clawed into the edges of his phone. "I have no money? How? Why? How did this happen?"

"Let's be real, you knew this was coming. You knew, Max. I've been telling you for years to moderate your spending, that your profit share from Tiluma wouldn't maintain your habits forever. I told you six months ago the overblown budget for your apartment renovation was a bad idea. You've also been on five luxury, international holidays in that time, and your partying, with all the costs that come with it… Oh, and of course, there was the hundreds of thousands you spent on your car prior to that. This isn't something that comes out of nowhere, it's a pattern of behavior with you. I mean, it's only January, and your next Tiluma payout isn't until June, but you're already five-grand in debt. What's your plan? Because I'm not a miracle worker. There's nothing I can do for a client who won't take my advice."

Her takedown seemed to reverberate through the silence, as he took one full, long breath to keep from being sick. This wasn't *just* about the money. Elaine was right, this was about him, and why he made the decisions—or more precisely, indecisions—that he did.

All his life, he'd dodged trouble simply by waiting for problems to settle down on their own. Only occasionally did his dodging culminate in any actual consequences. And *never* this bad.

He raked his fingers through the front of his hair, tugging a little before letting go. The mild pain brought him back from the feeling he might dissipate into a billion tiny pieces and disappear altogether. Though, maybe that wasn't such a bad thing given how monumentally screwed he was. "So, what do I do? How do I get myself out of this?"

"I don't know, Max. Maybe for once in your life consider moderating your behavior like pretty much every other person on this planet?" Her joyless inflection returned, offering zero silver lining.

Then again, she *had* been warning him for years, but just like those final months at Tiluma, every warning in the world didn't stop him from messing up all the same. Really, he didn't deserve any silver lining.

"You're going to have to find another means of topping up your income. You know, get a job, sell off some assets. I see here your apartment is now worth four million, so sell that and downsize to something modest. Even then, you'll still be doing better than ninety-nine percent of the population."

Her dragging tone held an edge of condescension and a lack of sympathy, like his fall from elite-client status meant she no longer had to be quite as nice to him. Or maybe she judged him for screwing up something ninety-nine percent of the population would give anything to have.

He put the phone on speaker and laid it down on the table beside him, needing a minute to bow his head and cup his hands over his eyes. The sudden darkness matched the colorlessness of his mood because, right now, all he truly wanted to do was hide.

Yet again, he'd failed, and above all else, he really didn't want to give up the one thing he held any pride in, his apartment.

He'd poured his body and soul into renovating this place.

*His sanctuary.*

A thudding pain overran his brain, making thought nearly impossible, to imagine a life different to the one he loved and lived now. It sounded shallow, oh he knew that much, but without his money, he had little else going for him, his identity nonexistent. And if he had to fail, he didn't want it to be as ridiculous as this.

He wasn't regimented like his brother, which had no doubt landed him in this mess to begin with, and nowhere near as book smart or cautious as his sister, again, more qualities that would have helped right about now.

And the saddest part was, he hadn't always been so aimless or clueless.

And speaking of his sister, Sophie and her husband Orlando would be flying in from the UK to stay at his apartment in mere weeks. Where on earth would he put them if he lost his home?

He cleared his throat. The least he could do was end this painfully hellish phone call and let poor Elaine off the hook. "Thanks for the call. I'm sure breaking the news to me wasn't easy for you. Leave this with me, okay? I think I know someone who can help."

# Chapter Seven

Freya stood in the hospital-room doorway, the semi-drawn curtains not allowing enough light in, while the cream-colored decor lacked in personality and somehow added to the weight of what she was about to step into.

She ran her fingertips over the emerald glass beads at her neck, stealing a moment for courage and not bothering to cover the nervous tell, even as she pressed her shoulders back and strode forward.

Four beds filled the room, though only two had people in them. Her mother lay in the farthest corner, her gaze lost on the cityscape through the window to her right. Her washed-out sandy hair sat in tangled waves around her head, and her blue veins glowed through now pale, thin, skin stretched over bony arms.

Freya paused, maybe holding onto some unlikely but persistent hope that her mother's dying days might have changed her; that Kerry Branner might find a sudden ability, or *willingness*, to be kind and accepting. To maybe apologize…

*Get real. That's never going to happen.*

Her mother's head turned, and her whiskey-colored gaze, a couple of shades lighter than Freya's, made contact. For the longest beat, her mother didn't react, her face an unreadable mask, though even that remained only half true.

The lines on her mother's face told their own story, scoring gouges along her cheekbones and deep trenches across her forehead. Those lines had existed for as long as Freya could remember, as if her mother had aged long before her time, the result of a lifetime spent trapped in mental warfare with herself and her demons.

"Why are you here?" Her weak voice held a distinct croak.

Freya's muscles pulled with instant tension, thoughts running through a list of appropriate replies any normal dying mother would offer a child. *"Oh honey, this must be hard for you too," "Come here for a hug,"* or maybe just a simple, *"Lovely of you to visit."*

"Your doctor called." She bit the sides of her tongue, vetting her usual need for brutal honesty. "She said you're not doing so well."

She didn't want to mention death, or that the doctor had in fact said her mother wasn't going to make it; because sure as rain, her mother wouldn't want to hear that, much less admit to being a mere mortal like everyone else.

In all her mother's years of using poor health as a means for attention, she'd also maintained the contradictory facade that death was for *other* people. Weak people. Certainly *not* Kerry Branner.

Her mother spat out a hollow laugh. "So what, you've come to look after me, then?"

Freya shook her head. As much as her mother couldn't confess to being susceptible to death, Freya wouldn't openly admit to caring. "Why, do you want me to look after you?"

She lifted a brow, daring her mother to acknowledge wanting help, but Kerry merely trekked her gaze down to Freya's exposed collarbone, right where her sun tattoo sat, before returning that same pointed stare over to the window. "No man wants a woman with scribble on her body."

The barb about Freya's tattoo left a dull ache in her belly, but she rolled her eyes, deflecting any signs of hurt. "Then you'll be glad to know there are an abundance of men who still want me."

She bit her tongue again, her thoughts flicking back to last night and how one particularly desirable man had wanted her numerous times, even going so far as to direct some of his kisses right onto her tattoo.

Her mother's attention stayed pinned on the outside, extending a sentiment that Freya was undeserving of any direct attention. So, nothing new really. "Don't be disgusting, Freya. Mark my words, no man will ever marry you." This time she did turn, but of course her eyes held a harder, darker edge. "And let me guess, you still pour drinks for a living?"

Freya clenched her toes in her black, leather ballet flats, mostly because her feet had a sudden and understandable urge to march her the fuck out of this room.

Hot emotions burned and bubbled through her abdomen and into her chest, like a rise of lava taking up more and more space, threatening to explode. She wanted to lash out, despite this being a quiet hospital ward, but her mother's slower movements and gray complexion came as a sign of physical fragility, and that too held Freya back.

*Not long. Not long. I just have to grin and bear her. I've gotten through worse.*

Easier said than done, though. Her mother knew full well she didn't just "pour drinks", that she owned The Ruby Room outright, and enjoyed a level of independence her mother would never know. Not that pouring drinks should have been a source of shame. But even in that sudden verbal demotion, her mother ran home one undeniable truth.

*Nothing Freya did was ever enough.*

Over the years, Freya had hoped each success would finally convince her mother to ease up a little and admit her daughter had done something incredible with her life. But those were her more irrational moments, and maybe the fact she'd crawled away from her shitty childhood and started her adult life with nothing, only to found a hugely successful business, could be reward enough.

"Not every woman wants to get married." She drawled on the words and took slow steps forward, her way of sticking her mother's rudeness back to her. "Certainly not me."

And certainly not since doing so would be dancing to the tune of her mother's fiddle.

Her mother dragged her cold gaze down Freya's body, like she hated the way her daughter showed an inappropriate lack of fear. *Good.* That hadn't always been the case. Far from it.

"You're over thirty. When are you going to grow up, Miranda?"

"My name's Freya. And the answer is never."

Her mother's dismissive laugh returned. "You're still going by that ridiculous name?" She shook her head in mock pity. "You just watch, Miranda. You'll regret not having children. You'll die old and alone and used up by every two-faced man you let touch you."

Freya's lip curled with her scowl. She wanted to point out how her mother was old and alone and very much dying, but even with all her mother had done to her, she refused to be dragged down. "Can you honestly say having kids turned out to be your dream come true?"

Her mother's gaze froze and then dropped, before a flash of fragility stole away the harsh lines from her face.

"One day you'll see, Miranda." She turned her head toward the window again. "I did the best I could."

"And that's why the state took us away from you?"

"You had more than I ever did."

"You think just feeding us every day makes you Mother of the Year?" Freya's tone rang flat, not from sarcasm now, but from the weight of her memories pressing down on her words. "And then there was the other stuff."

"Your father left. What did you want me to do?" Her mother's focus lashed back to Freya with an all-too-familiar look, her eyes watery with her barely contained temper. "Why don't you ever cry to me about him, huh? No one ever cares where the dads go, only that Mother Dearest keeps on going like she doesn't need the help. And then you were sick all the time—"

"Oh, don't you even start with that." Freya's heart clenched hard, the skin over her face suddenly too tight.

After all these years, she still couldn't relax around her mother, that and any mention of the past from this woman's lips sent her into a quick, defensive rage.

Actually, it wasn't even the mention of the past, so much as her mother had just fucking lied. *She'd lied.* She'd taken advantage of Freya's youth and innocence and blind willingness to trust, and now she tried to pass off all that horribleness as a figment of Freya's imagination.

Now she would never know what was more lies or another ploy to manipulate her. Or maybe her mother was just so damaged she believed the fabrications she spat forth.

Freya hiked the black, studded strap of her handbag higher onto her shoulder, her stomach churning because she wished at her age, after all these years, she didn't still want the kind of relationship most kids had with their parents.

A relationship where maybe she could say something and get a kind response back. Where maybe, just once, her mother would show proof of accountability; something akin to having evolved beyond blaming others or playing the victim.

Something where she acknowledged the hurt she'd caused.

Freya's phone rang, and she pulled it from her bag, glad for the distraction, though only so long as it took to answer the call and learn it was someone from the police.

She asked the person on the other end of the call to hold, taking a moment to refocus on her mother.

"I have to go. I need to take this call." She reached out and snatched her mother's house keys sitting on her bedside table. "I'm going to need these; you won't. And I want you to know, I'm only here to help settle your affairs and only because Clay can't do it. I won't burden anyone else with you."

She jangled the keys in the air and caught the sharp movement of her mother's face turning slack, startled, hopefully hurt. Freya turned for the door, taking the call and hiding a small jolt of satisfaction.

A cold consolation prize for the acceptance she'd ultimately always wanted and never received.

# Chapter Eight

Max strolled the familiar halls at Tiluma, the Edwardian building's open-air design the same as when he'd first viewed this place with Luke so many years ago. The same could be said of the bare brick entrance and modern gray carpets. Only now, a sickening, roiling feeling overran his former positive associations.

Since he wanted to believe he'd changed in those last four years, he refused to ask Luke to bail him out of trouble. He'd offer something instead, the one thing he still contributed to this company, the one thing he was truly good at besides swimming. *App ideas.*

For each idea the Tiluma board accepted, he got a nice pay out in exchange for signing over his intellectual rights. A pay out for just one or two good ideas would be enough to settle his current debt and then some. It wouldn't be enough to get him fully out of trouble, but it would buy him time.

He crossed the main corridor, thankfully not encountering any familiar faces, and took the elevator to the top floor. The building was no more than three stories, and the metal doors slid open with a happy ding way too soon for his liking. Still, he stepped out and turned left, anything but happy about being mere moments from his brother's office.

The air was a little too hot for him, and he rubbed a hand over the back of his neck, pausing before a frosted glass door. He didn't want to admit he'd messed up. *Again.* Didn't want to lose his home. Didn't want to add more to the overwhelmingly big pile of evidence already damning him as Luke's flaky little brother.

Losing his money had to be his biggest mistake yet, especially since Luke had handed him his wealth, and he'd screwed it up.

Still, he couldn't keep this news to himself forever, so he lifted his hand and tapped on Luke's door, thankful he'd at least had the rare foresight to call ahead.

"Come in."

He obeyed the muffled voice and twisted the door handle, entering to the sight of Luke at his desk, glowering at his computer and his fingers drumming over the keys. "Sorry, just one moment."

"Intense email?" Max smiled at his brother, but Luke typed for a while longer, silent, before clicking at his mouse and lifting his hand away with a certain kind of finality.

"Yeah, something like that. Anyway, what's up? I can't remember the last time you came all the way to the office to meet me."

"I've… umm…" Max peered around Luke's office, at the clean, white design, punctuated with the rich browns from his leather couch against the side wall and his walnut desk.

This company was born from Max's failure and Luke's guilt, a guilt Max would bet on profiting from once again. "I've, um, been toying with some new app ideas, and I wanted to pitch them to you."

Luke narrowed his green stare. "We're only coming to February, and the first lot of this year's apps are still in early development. You know it's way too early for us to take on new ideas."

"Yes, yes, I know." Max swatted his hand and half-flung himself into a chair opposite the desk, trying to appear casual in the face of Luke's deflection—trying to avoid having to admit the extent of his trouble. "But I have two cracker ideas that I'm really excited about, and you're going to love them. I thought, why not give you the early jump on what I have?"

He extended a giant smile, playing into his role as "flaky brother" once again, trying to throw Luke off asking too many questions.

Luke's eagle-eyed stare swept over him, before the skin over his cheekbones settled. "I mean, I'm happy to listen to what you have, but my hands are tied until the other team leaders are ready to field new ideas."

"Right…"

Max slumped back in his chair, veering his attention to his right, to a black bookcase filled with leather-bound tomes and a small array of healthy-looking indoor plants. For some reason, he wondered whether Luke took care of those plants himself or if he had his assistant do it.

A frowned dragged at his face, since he found it hard to imagine his six-foot-four ex-military brother taking the time to tenderly water what looked like some rather finicky plants. But then, Luke had a knack at being nearly perfect at everything, so maybe the possibility wasn't all that far-fetched.

Max cleared his throat, suddenly aware he'd gotten distracted. "Is there any chance we could expedite the new ideas thing, just this once?"

Luke blew out a hard breath and leaned back in his chair. "Max? Is something wrong?"

"Nothing I can't handle." He stared at the gray carpet, his chest prickling with heat.

He really didn't want to say more than he already had. Didn't want to hear the disappointment in his brother's voice or for him to interpret this meeting as Max asking for yet another bailout.

So, Max plastered on a smile and gave an easy shrug, holding his brother's gaze. "Though, I guess if you're really not interested in my new ideas, I can always pitch them to Ben Fink over at AmaziCorp. Maybe come back to you with whatever other ideas I come up with between now and when you're ready for me?"

"Now hang on a minute." Luke swung his weight forward, his elbows pitched into the desk. "Why would you go to AmaziCorp?"

His hardened facial features gave the impression of a man who'd just learned his wife had cheated on him, but Max shrugged again, muscles eased that at least, for this rare moment, he had the upper hand. "Why not? I have no exclusivity contract with Tiluma, and

AmaziCorp does joke apps too. You've said often enough that it's past time I find my niche in the world. Maybe this is it?"

Luke raised an eyebrow, though the tension in his jaw remained.

Max hated making stuff up, much less that this lie hurt his brother. But Elaine had been right too; he needed to put his finances first, which also meant utilizing what little skill he had. Maybe limiting himself to Tiluma alone wasn't in his best interest.

"You're right." Luke scrubbed his hand over the darker stubble on his chin, all while shaking his head. "Bouncing from one tech company to the next and shopping novelty app ideas is about as niche as you could get."

Max drew his eyelids into a tight scowl, holding silence over Luke's dismissive response, until a jolt of energy zipped through his body. He pushed his hands into his armrest.

"Well then." He shot to standing. "It was nice chatting, but—"

"Sit back down." Luke's voice boomed across the room, and he thrust a pointed finger at Max's chair. "I'm not done here."

Max startled before a firm rigidity took hold of his every muscle.

"Well, I am." And even with that, even with the compulsion to cuss and walk away, he didn't take a step. "I have things to do before my flight this evening."

"Sit. Down." Luke barked the order, remnants of his military past coming through. "I know something is wrong here. While I admire you not outright asking for me to help you out for a change, you need to damn well sit yourself down and start talking. *Now.*"

But Max couldn't find the ability to sit, maybe because sitting would mean talking, and for once in his life, he didn't want to do that.

"Okay, then." Luke stood, his stare piercing the space between them. "If you don't sit, I'm coming over there to shake the information out of you."

Max's knees buckled, and he plonked himself in his chair.

Luke gave a tight smile and followed suit. "Good."

In that moment, Max hated Luke, even though he couldn't recall ever hating his brother. Even in the months following the accident. An accident Luke, in a lapse of his usual perfection, had caused.

But right now, he did hate Luke.

He hated his ability to strong-arm every meaningful conversation they had.

Hated himself because, as always, he'd allowed his predictable pattern of life-wasting behavior to continue; as always, Luke saw right through his attempt to save face.

Hated his brother again because he couldn't simply let him save face, just this once.

"I overextended myself, okay?" The admission slipped from his lips, weak, hollow, and somehow still sharp enough to tear shreds through his insides.

The strain on Luke's face fell. "How?"

The lack of a judgmental glare shed a layer from Max's hatred.

"I…" Max tore his attention from his brother. "I don't know…" He released a sigh, and his entire posture sagged, taking with it his last remnants of anger, as if he'd run out of steam to hold on to it any longer. "I lost track of my spending. The apartment renovations ran over budget. I forgot about a few big bills that were due to be pulled from my account, and—"

"And let me guess"—Luke dipped his chin and sent forth a knowing look—"you also did a hell of a lot of partying, picked up the tab for your grifter friends a few too many times, and that flight you have to catch tonight is another luxury international holiday. Am I right?"

Everything about his brother, from his forward-leaning posture to his pointed stare, dared Max to lie, but they both knew Luke had a knack for finding shit out. So, Max peered down at the gray carpet and gave a silent nod.

Luke released a loud sigh and flopped back in his chair. "Jesus Christ." More silence, while Luke seemed to mull over what to do. "You're only halfway to your next profit share. How much do you have to last until July?"

Max cringed and hung his head lower. "Negative five grand. And… and there's a chance I might lose my apartment."

Luke sat bolt upright, the sharp sound of his movement sending Max's attention back to him. "How the hell did you manage that?"

"Like I said." Max shrugged. "Surprise bills…"

"Damn it. Max…" Luke's hands clenched in tight fists on his desk. "How long have I been telling you to set yourself up with a backup plan? You and I didn't exactly grow up loaded. We have no safety net. There's no excuse for frittering away money like you do."

"I know, Luke. I know." Max wrung his hands together, his shoulders rounding.

"But do you really?" A quiet moment passed while Luke's attention bore into Max in a lingering manner, suggesting he took a moment to piece together a game plan. "I can't help you out this time. I just can't."

But the softer edge to his tone said he wanted to.

Max blinked at his brother, absorbing the deep worry lines across Luke's forehead and the downturn of his lips.

"You know I'd still like you to." He grimaced, realizing with every passing second how unfair it was for him to keep asking for help.

"Life as you know it is over, Max." A rueful smile pushed at Luke's mouth. "I just hope one day we'll both look back and say this moment changed things for the better."

The words hit Max like a door slamming shut in his face. He couldn't conjure any kind of reply. Could no longer find it in himself to blame his brother, maybe because a deeper part of him knew just how right Luke was.

Max couldn't keep playing the victim game, even though he failed time and time again to find any other way.

His life *was* about to change, and the thought alone seemed to open like a gaping chasm inside of him. He wanted to be sick. He wanted to run. But with his finances tied up, even running wasn't an option.

*Shit!*

"Do you remember when you left Tiluma?" Luke's cheeks turned pale. "You promised you could survive well enough without my help. I thought you were doing okay. I thought…"

Max nodded to himself. He remembered that promise; had meant it at the time.

If only he hadn't been born the "dreamer" child in his family. The one with the wandering—or maybe empty—mind.

He had dreams, yes, but no way to see them through.

"I don't know how to get myself out of this mess, Luke." *So, I'm here hurting you instead.* "I don't even know where to start."

Luke pressed both hands to his face and growled into his palms. He either held himself back from his natural inclination to take on his brother's problems, or from a new tirade of swears in relation to Max's cluelessness.

"Okay. Let's start with your flight tonight." Luke dropped his hands, his voice settling into his no-nonsense CEO tone. "Knowing you, you bought the premium tickets, yes?" Max nodded, and Luke's shoulders dropped an inch. "Good. That means they're refundable."

"But—"

"No." Luke held up a finger, indicating Max should shut up and listen. "No, 'buts'. It's time to enter the real world and clean up your disaster. That means no holidays. No extra expense. Not for you. Not for a very goddamn long time, you understand?" Max opened his mouth to reply, but Luke just barreled on. "You call and cancel your holiday the minute you leave this office. Get back whatever you can from the airlines and hotels, got it? The money from the holiday alone will be far more than most people have when they fall on hard times. I'll loan you the five grand you owe, just so you don't get into any kind of legal trouble, plus an extra grand to tide you over. And that money is just what I called it, *a loan*. You will pay me back, understand?"

"But what if I can't?"

Luke crossed his arms and dipped his chin, peering up in a way that said, "You can't be serious."

In the next beat, he stood, and then wandered over to his office door, a sign this meeting was over and Max needed to leave.

"You want to know how you'll figure this out?" Luke opened the door and pointed to the hallway outside. "Because this time, Max, you have no other choice."

Chapter Nine

The returning tide crashed over Max's feet as he watched the twinkling body of water, his apartment building positioned behind him and across the street. He'd pulled himself out of the turbulent sea not fifteen minutes earlier, while thick gray clouds rolled in and the sun dipped lower in the sky. The wintery image wasn't all that unusual for Melbourne, the city known for its "four seasons in one day", including during the summer months.

With his hair plastered down from his swim, the occasional droplet slid over his temples and cold wind kissed his damp skin, that skin tightening and bumping in response. This day couldn't end fast enough, though the discomforting elements offered him a sense of camaraderie.

"You going to get sick sitting there like that." Miroslav, or Miro, as he preferred to be called, laughed and sat down in the sand beside Max; the man's thick Ukrainian accent so distinctive, Max didn't even need to turn to see who it was. A good thing really, since he couldn't find the heart to move much now that he sat here thinking.

He plucked a minor smile, mostly for Miro's benefit. "This is what we call tropical weather where I'm from."

Miro made a low *tsking* sound. "And where I am from, where you are from might as well be the Caribbean, and still, we call people crazy who sit wet on a cold day."

Max chuckled and tore his attention away from the waves, finally willing to look at his friend with the jovial dark brown eyes reflecting gray clouds ahead. "Inland Ukraine doesn't have any beaches."

"This is true, but beach swim or river swim is still a bad idea in cold. Anyway"—Miro jutted his chin at Max—"something is wrong with you, huh? You sometimes act like you have rocks in your head, but today you act like you got boulders."

Max scowled at his friend, his chest aching because he should have laughed at that joke, but instead he drowned in the painful truth. Maybe he *did* have boulders in his head, entire quarries and cliffs, even.

No matter which way he thought to spin the story of how his day had gone, he sounded like a bumbling and entitled fool. One who'd wasted a chance most people would do anything to have. How would he explain that even selling his apartment tomorrow wouldn't get him any real money for months?

And sure, he could get a bank loan against the apartment until then, but he really didn't want to do that, as much as he didn't want to ask his friends for help. Not if he wanted any chance of ever returning to his current social group.

Bad enough he'd cancelled the holiday, which might go unquestioned, but pair that with asking for money…

He'd never be seen the same way again, and social exclusion would be the only possible outcome. And if admitting his failure to Luke had sucked, well then, doing the same with Miro would be much, much worse.

The man had escaped the fall of the Soviet Union minus everything he'd ever owned, the teaching credentials he'd worked so hard to achieve virtually useless in a new country, unless he planned to study all over again.

He arrived in Australia with nothing but a small suitcase of personal belongings, suddenly unqualified and reduced to working multiple odd jobs, scrubbing dishes and as a factory hand. The professional loss had been nowhere near his fault. Yet, he'd worked himself to the bone until he'd scraped enough money to start his own café—the café attached to the ground floor of Max's apartment building.

Max peered down at his sandaled toes covered in grit and sea. Of all people, he had no right to complain to this man about cancelling a holiday, much less the stupid way in which he'd lost his money. "I'm just having some money issues. It's nothing to worry yourself about."

"Ahh." Miro clapped Max on the back, but the encouraging gesture didn't make Max feel any more deserving of sympathy. "You are worried, so now I am worried. You are my friend for a long time, and you teach me how to swim, remember? Now you tell me what is wrong."

"Nothing major." He straightened and stared out to the hazy horizon, pretending he was okay. "I just had to cancel my holiday, that's all."

"Oh yes, that would make anyone sad. But why exactly did you cancel? Your hotel double booked?"

The man had one of those sometimes useful, but hard to hide from, analytical minds.

"You're not going to let this go, are you?"

Miro threw back his head and laughed, the gathering wind whipping at his thick brown hair. "No. You are not giving the whole truth, so maybe now you could put us both out of our misery and talk?"

"Fine." Max scrubbed his heel in the sand, adding a shallow dent in the shoreline, the action a poor buffer to him sharing his lame story of woe. "I cancelled my trip because I made a stupid financial mistake, okay? Actually, that's not true either, it wasn't just *one* stupid mistake. I've made many. Over a long period of time. With a boatload of warnings in between… I just got back from negotiating a loan with my brother, just so I can pull myself out of debt for a few weeks. A loan I have no idea how I'll pay back. Even with his help, I'll probably still run out of money and have to sell my apartment."

"*Ouuff.*" Miro shook his head, blinking in an exaggerated fashion. "That is one mess you are in. Why did you not come out and tell me?"

"Because of all the people I know, you have the greatest right to take one look at my stupidity and call me a big, bloody moron."

"Ha! Because you know my story, yes?"

Max nodded, but Miro shook his head again. "No. My story does not mean I wish bad things for you. It does not make me not sad for your problems. If anything, maybe I am the best one to talk to, yes? I know what it is to start again."

"Thanks, but I don't expect you to fix this."

"Ha." Miro used the back of his hand to slap Max's arm. "You think I give you hand out? My head is not one full of boulders, remember?"

"That wasn't what I—"

"No, what I am saying is you give up too easy. You used to be a champion swimmer. A long distance one, too. You not give in easy then, but now you acting like a big sack of potatoes someone throw down stairs."

Max gave Miro a side glare. "What? Dude, you come up with the strangest analogies. Why would someone throw potatoes down a flight of stairs?"

Miro laughed. "I don't know, but my strangeness at least got your attention, yes? What I mean is, you need to pick yourself up, think of your life like you did your swimming."

"But I haven't competed in years."

Miro rubbed the heel of his hand between his brows, before using that same hand to smack Max playfully upside the back of his head. "You act dumb, but you really just making excuses, maybe because what you really are is scared."

"I'm not scared. It's just..." Max turned away to gather his thoughts, kicking more sand with his foot, the heavy weight of his past and current problems pressing down on him. "I watch everyone around me go about their lives so sure of what they're doing. They have *purpose*, while I have no idea what I want. All I know is that since I quit swimming, my passions consist of travel, parties, sex, and dipping into the ocean at any chance I get. That's all. And as much as anyone might yell at me, 'Just get on with it', I have no freakin' idea what 'it' is for me. Much less how I'm supposed to just pick any old vocation and find the will to invest my energy into a life I don't actually care about."

"Confused. Scared. Confused because you're scared. It is all the same thing. And maybe the boulders in your head are not so big that you cannot see you do nothing because you can. Well, could." Miro's eyes widened, and he leaned in slightly, pressing his point. "Your life is not normal, Max, and now you are closer to normal, you don't have luxury to hide behind. So now you do what normal people do, yes? You start something and hope it works."

Max stared at his friend a while, the advice sinking in, even though his mind drew nothing but blanks. "Where do I start?"

"*Yedrit' tvoyu...*" Miro followed his mumbled Russian with a smack of his palm into his forehead again. "I have to think of everything for you?"

"You're the one acting like my personal guru. Give me something to work with at least."

"Fine, since I am your guru." Miro took a deep breath and stared out to the ocean, his eyes squinting against the glare. "You already give me a list of your passions, so let's start there. First, I think probably you are too ugly to ask any ladies to pay for sex, so this option is not good."

Max squeezed his eyes shut and cringed at Miro's idea of humor. Meanwhile, Miro's lips split into a giant smile, before he near fell backward with laughter.

"Okay, I am sorry. Serious time now." Miro straightened, still chuckling. "Let us start with your other passions. What about swimming? You teach me, now you teach others."

Max's mouth fell open with an instant need to dismiss the idea, but then he forced himself to pause, to take a slow breath, and let the idea roll around in his head for a while. He wasn't exactly in a position to be choosy, and perhaps it wouldn't hurt him to "start something and hope it worked".

"I'm not sure beginner swim instructors make enough consistent cash to cover my current troubles, but maybe you're right, maybe it's a start. What else have you got?"

"Hmmm..." Miro frowned out to the bay. "I have no other ideas just yet. Maybe I take some time to think of more, though you the one who knows a lot of business people. Maybe someone is looking to hire?"

Max leaned sideways and nudged Miro with an elbow. "You, maybe? The café always looks full. Are you hiring?"

"You, work in the café?" He shook his head, slow and serious like. "No. No. No. You are fun for the customers, but I do not trust you with hot drinks."

Max actually found it in him to laugh at that one, and Miro shrugged, not even trying to cover his act of clear rejection.

The rushing ocean tugged at Max's focus, and he set about making his first decisions on how the rest of his life would go. Miro was right. He needed to start somewhere. And for the moment, that somewhere would be the site of the lowest hanging fruit—or in other words—jobs he could nab *right now*. Jobs to tide him over until he had a more permanent plan.

And Miro was right about another thing. Max *did* know a lot of people. In fact, he had a knack for making connections, but he didn't want to ruin those by asking for some entry-level job. Because again, social exclusion was something he wanted to avoid.

But there was one person he could *maybe* turn to. One encounter last night that had brimmed with potential, perhaps now in more ways than one.

He lifted his gaze to the darkening sky, the first star breaking through the city haze and a gap between the clouds. Any minute now, The Ruby Room would open. Not only would it open, but since his holiday had gone bust, he would be free to visit the one person he'd wanted to see all along. A person who exuded indescribable calm. A person he seemed to just *click* with.

A person who also just happened to be hiring.

Freya.

# Chapter Ten

"Sorry, you what?"

Freya stared in wide-eyed silence as she took a moment to decide whether she'd heard Max right.

When he first walked into her paper-crammed office, she hadn't noticed him, her mind buried deep in completing this week's payroll—her best attempt at forgetting her encounter with her mum and then the call from the police right afterward. Not only had Max's sudden appearance blindsided her, but the first few words out of his mouth outright short-circuited her brain.

"The job you have advertised in your window." He gave a weak smile, his blue eyes dimmed to gray. "I want to apply."

"Why? Why would you want to do that?" Her thoughts reversed to this morning and how she'd practically shoved him out the door. Not because she hadn't wanted him to stay, but because she'd heard the news about her mother and lost all ability to be any kind of decent company. "If this is your way of trying to make last night a regular thing, you don't—"

"That hadn't even crossed my mind." The muscles over his cheekbones stilled, and his color drained. "I mean, last night was amazing, and I did want to see you again, but no." His focus fell to the floor.

"Seems I really do need a job."

She slouched in her vintage, brown leather office chair, none of this making any sense. "But you have money, right? I mean, you drive a Tesla and your watch is a Rolex, and"—she leaned in and squinted at his black hoodie—"I'm pretty sure that's a Ralph Lauren logo on your top there, buddy."

"I *was* loaded." His gaze reconnected with hers, before dipping to the ground again. "At least, until this morning."

"You've got to be shitting me!"

A pink tinge rose on his face, and the twist of his brow in turn twisted something within her gut. He looked utterly devastated, like someone had stolen his favorite shoes from right off his feet, or keyed his car, or like, all his money had disappeared overnight or something.

"Oh my God." The words slipped from her lips in a soft whisper. "You're not shitting me, are you?"

He shook his head.

She stood, genuine sorrow for him hitting her square in the chest. "What happened? No, wait, you don't have to tell me that."

For a split second, her body warred between throwing herself forward in an offer of a hug or staying put and simply unleashing yet more questions. Thankfully, her jaw knew better and remained shut.

"So." His weighty stare broke her avalanche of thoughts. Sure enough, he wasn't all too eager to be here asking for employment, but that direct stare said he needed her to wake-the-fuck up and focus on what he'd come here for. "Can I apply for that job now?"

She wanted to say no. Actually, *hell no*. She wanted him in her bed, not working in her bar. Plus, she never canoodled with staff, even though Max hadn't been staff when they'd canoodled.

And still, what stood before her now was the prospect of a mighty awkward work situation.

She took a deep breath and crossed her arms, her sky-blue dress crumpling thick cotton against her bust. Only his reluctant presence kept her from giving him nothing more than a cold, hard rejection.

The slow bob of his throat as he swallowed, the unblinking strain in his eyes, the last thing he wanted to do was stand here and ask her for help—that much was clear. Which made turning him down flat impossible, even for someone as no-bullshit as her.

Strain slipped from her shoulders, and she lowered them by a couple of inches. She couldn't help but imagine what it'd be like to go from being a god in her bedroom last night, to standing here before her asking for work.

The very least she could give him right now was a chance to prove himself.

"All right." She strode forward, then took a seat on the front edge of her desk. "Let's start with your experience. Have you ever worked at a bar?"

"I've been to many bars, does that count?" One corner of his lip ascended into a grimace, the look in his eye something akin to a puppy who'd been caught chewing a prized heirloom. "Dive bars… high-end luxury bars… international bars… Bars made out of ice…"

He scrubbed the front of his shaggy hair with the tips of his fingers, perhaps a nervous habit, and his grimace changed to an apologetic smile.

"No. None of that counts." She jutted her chin and paused. If this had been anyone else, she would have booted him from her office for being a smart ass by now. The fact that she didn't, brought instant stiffness to her back. "Do you know how to mix a drink?"

"Not really. I might own fancy cars and watches, but I'm not into fancy when it comes to drinks. I'm more of a beer and water guy, you know?"

She exhaled, a low growl traveling up her throat, one that rumbled and sent forth a warning.

Did Max really want her to help him or did he just want to waste her time? Surely a person in his situation wouldn't pick the playfully stupid approach over at least *trying* to prove some kind of suitability to work at her bar.

She'd assumed he'd be nothing like his rich, clueless friends—the ones who thought it was cool to flit through life without knowing a goddam thing about anything. Now he had her questioning her judgement. And unlike him, she'd started with less than nothing and worked doubly hard for all she had.

The last thing she should do was let him mess her around or trash her bar's reputation just to throw him an undeserved line.

"I don't care what you drink." She gave him her flattest tone, along with an equally flat stare. "You know, all my job applicants come with a Responsible Service of Alcohol accreditation as a bare minimum, and often a bunch more years of actual bar experience. Is my livelihood a joke to you or something?"

*Oh no.* Her ribs felt suddenly too tight for her lungs, and she worked hard not to lean forward. Maybe last night had been his rich guy version of "slumming it on the wrong side of the tracks".

But then he pitched a wounded expression, one that seemed to melt her skepticism all over again.

He stepped toward her.

"Look, I'm sorry." His voice was soft and smooth as butterscotch, and a little flutter replaced the churning in her tummy. "I'm not messing with you. I promise. I'm just screwing this up like I seem to do most things. I wouldn't be here if I didn't really need the help."

"You do understand I'm running a business here, not a charity?" She cleared her throat, her cheeks warm from the obvious gravel in her tone. Even in this weird-as-hell encounter, his near proximity had an effect on her. "I'm not going to hire someone with no ability to earn their keep. Besides, up until yesterday I didn't even know your name. So even though last night was fun and all, given what we did, you working here would be a terrible idea."

She looked him over with his blond waves and baggy hooded sweater, albeit designer. How different he appeared now from last night. Gone was his clean-cut shirt and scent of fresh mint and sandalwood. Still, his mussed-up appearance added an air of vulnerability, unearthing memories of him and her intertwined in her bedsheets.

And aside from the hot-as-hell sex, he'd been easy to talk to, and just hours earlier, she'd learned his help with The Creeper last night had spared her from certain torture and death.

Her chest constricted against a cascade of emotion, a new lump taking space in her throat. She wasn't ready to think too much on what the police had shared with her on the phone earlier. About The Creeper and his known violent history.

"I can't have you working behind the bar." Her voice held a rasp, and she prayed Max didn't notice.

His chin dipped, and he gave a quiet nod, like he understood. The fact he didn't argue produced an ache around her heart.

"Look, there's no way you'll be able to work the bar without upsetting my customers." She gave a heavy sigh, set to once more pay her dues. He'd helped her. He'd saved her. And even if he didn't know all the details, she wanted to thank him either way. "Much less my staff, but I can offer you another position, if you really are that desperate."

He snapped his chin back up, a new light entering his eyes. "Honestly, I'll take anything."

"Good." She pushed her weight off the desk, heading for her office door and gesturing for him to follow. "You do a four-week probation period as part of my clean-up crew, all going well, then your position here becomes official. And then. *Only* then. If you're consistent and fit in well with my staff, and you get your RSA accreditation, I just *might* consider letting you serve behind the bar. I hope you're ready because you start tonight."

# Chapter Eleven

Max pushed his wheelie bucket and mop through a heavy crimson curtain and into the cleaner's nook, a tiny area separated from the main action at The Ruby Room. He'd changed the bucket water not fifteen minutes ago and already it held a murky gray-brown color that made the mop head disappear at the bottom. The nose-wrinkling smell wafting from the surface was stale and bitter.

He peered down at his white-gold Rolex, not exactly fitting with his black, grime-stained cleaner's apron. And if that wasn't sign enough of his faded lifestyle, right about now, his plane to Ibiza would be coasting down the tarmac at Melbourne Airport, mere hours from sunshine and paradise. *Without him.*

He lowered his wrist and rested his chin atop the wooden mop handle, the sound of yet another dropped glass shattering what he'd hoped would be a few seconds of sulking peace.

Two hours of hellish mopping and he'd had no break from the stomach-churning stenches and the sweeping of broken glass, much less the customers who insisted on giving him their orders, even though waiting tables wasn't his job.

He let out a resigned sigh and grabbed his new friends—the

dustpan and brush—from a hook on the wall, his grimy water-filled bucket coming along for the ride out into the bar again.

He'd been warned to be quick with cleaning up spills, something about broken glass, patrons getting injured, blood everywhere—which he'd have to clean up—and the potential for lawsuits.

A wall of joyful chatter engulfed his re-entry, coupled with people perched on red velvet couches along the back wall. The Ruby Room's iconic ruby-colored chandelier hovered high and center, pear-drop crystals dangling above black glossy tables. A burlesque trio danced on stage—a curly haired redhead and a brunette woman, along with a stocky guy in a black sequined corset, all belting out a '70s diva number.

A girl seated a few tables down waved him over, her cherry-red bob swinging with her movements. She pointed down, indicating she'd been the one to drop the glass.

He nodded and wove his way through furniture and people, the flash of disco lights and loud music muddying his senses.

This time yesterday, he'd been one of these patrons, enjoying an evening with his friends and spending money without a second thought for how much actually remained in his bank account. *What a dream that had been!* Now he mopped floors, tinkering with the real chance he would lose his home.

The cherry-bob lady leaned forward in her seat, lips curled into an equally cherry-colored smile. "Well, aren't you a handsome one? Sorry about the mess."

The glint in her dark brown eyes, and the way she used them to glance down his body, said she wasn't at all sorry.

"It's fine," he mumbled. "Seems to happen a lot around here."

He crouched down and started sweeping broken glass into the dust pan, avoiding eye contact with Cherry Bob's fishnet covered calf, the one she not-so-subtly stuck out beside him, swinging her black stiletto-covered foot pretty much right under his nose.

"I'm from Adelaide. Only here for the weekend."

He peered up to Cherry Bob talking to him, her voice low and rough like maybe she smoked about ten packs of cigarettes a day. "Is that an accent you got there?"

"Yes."

He stood and passed the mop over the miscellaneous red puddle on the floor. Wine, maybe? No doubt Freya would be disappointed he couldn't identify which drink exactly. Then again, Freya would probably want him to play friendly with the customers, even though he just wanted to get through this night.

A stray piece of glass sat inches from the woman's foot, and he bent down to pick it up. That's when her cold fingers latched onto his jaw.

He jolted his attention up to Cherry Bob smiling down at him, her clammy fingers holding a stink that confirmed his theory of her probably being a ten-pack-a-day smoker.

"I have a little secret." Her eyes glinted again, like she assumed he cared to hear what her secret was. She leaned in closer, more cigarette stench, her lips way too close to his ear. "I've been watching you all night, and I broke that glass on purpose just to get you here. What do you think about that, honey?"

The nauseating smell of red wine—at least he got that bit right—and bitter nicotine had him reeling back, just as Cherry Bob aimed her lips at his.

A sharp tug at the hood of his sweater pulled him off-balance so his butt connected with the hard, polished floor.

"What the hell are you doing?" Freya bent over him, her eyes narrowed.

He stood, almost head-butting her in the process, before dusting his hands over the back of his pants.

"This lady here"—he stabbed his thumb toward Cherry Bob and held back an urge to dry retch—"was just about to jam her tongue down my throat."

A crosshatch of wrinkles spread across Freya's brow. "Are you looking to get fired on your first night?"

"What? Why would you fire me?" He turned and scowled at the woman who'd assaulted him. "It's not like I *wanted* her to kiss me."

The tension on Freya's face dropped. "Wait. What? You didn't?"

He shook his head.

Her expression turned hard again, though this time she shot a searing glare at Cherry Bob. "You. Get out."

Cherry Bob's mouth slipped open. Freya ignored her, waving over the security guard standing at the front entrance.

Cherry Bob mustn't have moved fast enough, because Freya hooked her hand under the woman's armpit and jerked her up, barking, "I said, *out!*"

The security guard moved Freya aside and took over with Cherry Bob, the cigarette-infused woman peering over at Max like she expected him to save her.

*No freaking chance, lady!*

He pressed his hand over his stomach, holding back a need to heave.

Freya turned to him, gaze narrowed like he was a puzzle she wanted to work out. "Are you okay? I'm really sorry I assumed…"

"I mean, yeah?" He took a second to consider the softer glow to her eyes, perhaps a sign of genuine concern. "Though I'm not sure your reaction just then was proportionate to the lady's offense."

Her raised shoulders contradicted any sense she might be amused. "Why? Because you're a guy? You think if any man in here tried to make out with one of my staff, male or female, it'd be cool if I just let it slide?"

The muscles on his face turned lax. Frankly, he'd never thought of unwanted sexual attention like that. In truth, he'd always figured that as a man, not a small one at that, he was supposed to handle himself or any woman who tried to accost him. Hell, women accosting men wasn't even a thing in the world he grew up in.

He was meant to just laugh that shit off, right?

Or parade the attention with pride, a man desired, a "man's man".

He'd certainly never had anyone step in and save him.

"You have a point." Now the churning in his tummy had less to do with Cherry Bob's smell and more to do with the boatloads of times he'd shrugged off similar unwelcome moments.

She reached out and grabbed his hand. "Damn right I have a point, but that's not the only reason I asked if you're okay. Looks like you've sliced your thumb on some glass while trying to escape the mouth leech."

He peered down at his hand. Sure enough, a thin trail of blood snaked its way down his wrist, the piece of glass still clasped between his fingers. Well, at least he was up-to-date with his tetanus shots, probably the only good thing about cutting his foot open on a piece of coral while surfing in Hawaii a few months ago.

*Yeah, also another reason why I'm broke now!*

Freya instructed a fellow staff member to take him back to the cleaner's nook and the first aid kit before she disappeared to do whatever it was bar owners did. Max had orders to get a plaster on his cut, then get right back to pushing his mop bucket around.

Though the cut itself was small, the stream of blood remained consistent. He hunched in a seat at the back, waiting for the blood to stop, his heartbeat heavy and a sense of loneliness taking over.

Though he appreciated Freya stepping in before, she hadn't offered to help patch him up, hadn't jumped at the chance at some alone time with him in the musty, dark cleaner's nook, which could totally transform into a romantic hiding spot if only for a few minutes.

Heck, she hadn't even thrown him a lifeline and bailed him out of mopping floors. She'd merely sent him on his way and gone back to work.

Thick-skinned. No-nonsense. Caring, but not the sort to dote. Maybe this was typical of her? He could just hear the words, "Suck it up and get on with the show" coming out of her mouth.

Maybe she had more in common with his brother Luke than she did him?

A familiar laugh broke through the nook's heavy curtain. A quick glance confirmed his suspicion; the laugh belonged to Adele Maslow, snuggled up against her long-term partner, Cedrick Pascal, at a nearby table.

Max slinked back. The bleeding on his thumb slowed enough for him to stick down the plaster. Adele was the second to last person he wanted seeing him in his new role as bar cleaner, with Cedrick being the absolute last. Adele came from a family of high-profile lawyers and surgeons, while Cedrick's father owned a century-old business, his surname synonymous with a well-known brand of preserved foods.

Also, Cedrick was a prick. A mean drunk. Everyone knew it. Even

Cedrick. He showed zero cares about hiding the fact, especially when it came to Max.

Not after Max dated Adele for a short time about a year ago, back when she'd tried to break away from Cedrick and his ham-fisted ways. Cedrick had taken a huge enough exception that he'd stalked and harassed her until she caved and went back to him.

Though sweet and maybe a little timid, Max had liked Adele, but not enough for a strong connection to ever grow. He hadn't pushed the issue when she'd ended things, though maybe he should have, since it seemed even money and a good education didn't spare someone from a bad relationship.

He twisted his watch to find he still had another forty-five minutes on the clock. Somehow, he'd have to survive his shift *and* avoid Cedrick, the douche lord of the century, who'd no doubt blab to everyone in their shared circles about Max's fall from grace.

He'd been so desperate to get the ball rolling on earning some money, he hadn't really considered this particular complication before asking Freya for work. If only she'd given him a job behind the bar, something semi-cool he could spin as an easy way to pick up women while hiding the fact he had money. A rich guy's eccentric idea of having fun.

His friends would have thought him a bonafide genius.

As it stood, there wasn't much he could say that would glorify mopping floors and collecting empty glasses. *Shit.* He really didn't want to go out there.

"What are you still doing in here?"

He blinked to find Freya staring at him. *Shit again!* There were genuine disadvantages to the height difference here, namely, that she had a knack for sneaking up on, or more like, *under* him.

She snapped the velvet curtain open wider. "We have ten minutes till closing and a bunch of empties on your side of the room. The tables are filthy, and Edward says you've been hiding back here since you sliced your finger something like twenty minutes ago. You need to get out there."

She grabbed the front of his black apron and dragged him a couple of yards forward, out into the bar, and to where his "friends" waited.

# Chapter Twelve

"No! I'm not going out there." Max planted his feet and refused to move.

Freya stopped and turned to him, eyes blazing like she had a boatload of other things to do right now and wouldn't stand for his rebellion. "Fine then, you're fired."

His gaze skittered to the curtain again, the quiet seclusion so close but so far. He wanted to disappear again, but not as much as he wanted to keep his apartment. "Look, please don't fire me. It's just, there are some people out there I'd rather not see. People I haven't told about my situation yet."

The skin over her cheekbones eased, and a sudden laugh cracked past her lips. "And you want me to ask Ed to shoulder the entire floor, all so you can save some face?"

He gave a cringy sort of smile. "Would you?"

"*Pfft*. No." She jerked her chin back, expression twisting. "And what's with you? Do you not understand the subtleties of sarcasm? You can either get your butt out there and do the job you came here to do, or go home right now and deal with your financial woes without my help."

"You'd really fire me?"

"Dude. You think you'd be the first?" She barked out another incredulous laugh, head tilting back to display her glowing neck and that sun tattoo he loved. "Besides, this is a trial, remember? I haven't even hired you yet. And right now, you're letting a pack of judgmental assholes keep you from getting the job you practically begged me for a few hours ago. So yes, you have less than three-seconds to get back to work, or I'll give you the grace of slinking through our back exit at the expense of this job."

He darted his gaze around her face and narrowed his eyes, trying to decide how serious she was about kicking him to the curb after they'd spent last night all over each other.

"Right." She spun on her heel and took her first storming steps away from him.

"Wait." He thudded after her, wrapping a hand around her forearm, keeping her close. "You can't mean that."

"You haven't paid much attention to me or how I run The Ruby, have you?" She gave a slow shake of her head, her lips pressed in an expression he knew all too well. She was just another person on the long list of people he'd disappointed. "Go home, Max. You're not cut out for this place."

Despite what Freya said, his feet stayed rooted to the floor; for a multitude of reasons, he couldn't let her get rid of him so easily.

He'd be failing all over again. Something he'd done far too much of. Something he refused to do now. Also, he liked her and wasn't all that ready to burn this relationship for the likes of Cedrick Pascal.

He lifted his attention to the sea of people again. *Screw Cedrick.* He'd never liked the guy anyway, and Cedrick sure as death didn't like him either. Heck, maybe the opportunity to pound Max's reputation into the dirt would bring an actual, genuine smile to the asshole's sour and ugly face.

Either way, up until this point in his life, Max had blown far too many chances, which brought him to this predicament now. He couldn't afford to keep making the same mistakes.

"No." He stepped back into the cleaner's nook and grabbed a scuffed-up tray from a counter, then fronted up to Freya again. "I'm staying."

He pushed past her and went about collecting glasses, starting at the tables farthest from Adele and Cedrick. As brave as his snap decision might have been, he needed time to gather his courage. Or perhaps one small corner of his soul hoped the couple would leave before he got to their section.

Thankfully, because of his stalling in the cleaner's nook, a lot of empties needed collecting. His tray kept filling, and he made three trips back and forth between tables before he had no place left but Adele and Cedrick's table. The whole time, Freya stood in front of the cleaner's curtain, arms crossed and brow raised, as though she half expected he'd lose his nerve and run. Not an unreasonable expectation given the loud rush of blood roaring in his ears and the sweat prickling on the back of his neck.

For as long as he could, he pretended not to notice them, his face turned to some point across the room. And they didn't notice him either, not until his "non-looking" got the best of him and his hand fumbled, knocking over one of many beer bottles on their table. *Damn it.*

"Max?"

He'd already turned his back, set to flee to the next table, but Adele's light trill held him in place.

"Is that you?"

He squeezed his eyes shut, fingers straining around the edge of his tray. He could ignore her, move on, pretend he hadn't heard. But Adele had never been anything but kind, and he figured she probably had enough cold reality in her life just dealing with Cedrick.

He spun around and plastered on a smile.

"Oh hey, Adele. Oh, and Ceddie." He tried not to vomit in his mouth or throw the tray at the asshole's pinched face. "You're here too. How brilliant."

Adele's pale green stare took him in from top to bottom. "What are you doing?"

He let out a forced laugh, one that sounded like a choppy *ha-ha-ha*, just as his brain and mouth shorted, and the next lie slipped past his lips. "I'm. Ahh. I'm helping a friend."

To be honest, he hated lying, but a light tingle of relief zipped through his body at this lie. Maybe he could save face *and* keep his job all at the same time.

"Oh really?" Cedrick's voice was its usual bored drone. "Which friend?"

"Well, you probably haven't met *her*. Actually, I only met *her* last night." Max sent forth a wide smile, his emphasis on the word "her" an overt suggestion he only did this because a woman was involved.

"Hey, Max."

He jolted. Freya's stern voice was a solid smack to the back of his head.

She sidled up to him, her unimpressed stare pinned to his face. "The MC has already called for everyone to clear out. I'm not paying you to stand around holding my patrons up, so get these glasses to the bar, then hurry up and wipe down the tables. After that, you have chairs to stack and a final mop to do before you're good to go. Got it?"

Her lips curled, her not-so-subtle hint that she'd heard him use his connection to her to worm his way out of this uncomfortable exchange.

Cedrick looked from Max over to Freya, a rare light glinting in his eyes. "She's paying you?"

Freya gave Max a gentle punch in the arm and peered up at him with that same deranged smile. "Of course I'm paying him. The Ruby is an ethical employer. We certainly don't make anyone work for free or favors."

He narrowed a glare at her and bit the insides of his cheeks. She had good grounds to correct his insinuations, though lucky for her, he also had enough class not to point out that they *had* in fact slept together. But more than any of that, given the conversation from moments earlier, he was pissed she didn't back him up whatsoever.

He turned back to Adele's now gaping face and offered a light shrug, though his limbs felt heavy. He refused to stomach whatever snide-smug look Cedrick pinned his way. "The boss is right. I better get back to work."

# Chapter Thirteen

Max rested his hand on The Ruby Room's exit door, ready to leave a good hour after closing time. But a burning unease kept him from moving, a hard knot of emotion settling deep within his tummy, that emotion being one he so very rarely experienced. *Anger.*

Anger at his situation. Anger that his money was gone. Anger that he would likely lose his home, even though he'd had everything going for him and still screwed up.

But right now, his greatest anger lay with Freya.

He turned on his heel and brushed past the super tall security guard, Crystal.

"Hey, where are you going?" Her voice sailed across the venue, but he ignored her. "I'm trying to lock up here."

He didn't care. All he cared about was charging through the door marked EMPLOYEES ONLY and up a short flight of stairs where a single fuchsia door waited. Freya's office.

He barged right in, since any niceties would be wasted on a woman who, not an hour earlier, had smiled as she'd thrown him into a social bonfire.

She stood ahead in the arms of a tall, bronze-haired man, his fingertips caressing her jawline.

Max startled, the knot in his tummy turning into a lead-filled balloon, one that burst and sent shards of disappointment in all directions.

*Maybe he should have knocked.*

She turned her attention to him, before turning back to the man holding her, her hand squeezing his navy shirt-covered arm. "Go. I'll see you tomorrow."

The guy narrowed his brown gaze at Max. "You sure?"

She gave a light smile and nodded. "I'll be fine."

*Well, at least that made one of them.*

The guy's stare burned into Max as he passed; since Max was in his own bad mood, he had no problems returning the dude's venom.

The door clicked closed, and he nudged his head toward where the other guy exited. "What was that?"

"None of your business." Freya spun toward her desk and went about flicking off a couple of lamps. "What do you want, anyway?"

He had no place feeling jealous or possessive. They'd spent one night together and made no promises, but in light of all he'd lost today, his fading hopes over Freya just added to the sting.

He glanced past her fuchsia painted office, with its giant Picasso and Frida Kahlo prints, and over to the scene outside her double windows, white street lights disrupting the black night sky. The subdued atmosphere deepened his loneliness and offered the sense that this day and his run of bad news would simply never end.

"What you did out there wasn't cool." He turned back to her, his earlier anger not enough to stop his heart from shrinking.

"No, what I did out there was a stroke of genius, and you should count yourself lucky that I'm so forgiving." She punctuated her statement with a stiff clench of her jaw. "You implied to one of my regular customers that I'm paying you in sexual favors, or at the very least, you're working here in the hopes of receiving sexual favors. *That's* what's not cool, Max."

The mild heat in his chest turned into a sharp prickle, one that worked its way up his neck and into his face. He could have pointed out he'd already gotten "into her pants", but that was too crass, so he took another tack. A highly immature, blame-fueled one.

"I played along so you could lose that creep last night. You could have helped me when I needed it, too."

"What did you want me to do, dry hump you on the dance floor?" She snatched up her purse from atop a filing cabinet, an embroidered black silk-looking thing with bamboo handles, and began throwing things from her desk into it.

"Cut me some slack, maybe?" He strode forward. She wasn't even looking at him. "Heck, you even threw me right back to work after I sliced open my thumb."

"It's hardly 'right back to work' if you hid in the cleaner's nook for a good portion of your shift." She thrust her chin up, gracing him with a glare. "And did you stop to think about how your rumor-slinging tonight might affect my business's reputation, much less my personal safety? For someone so willing to bring up your heroics last night, you sure are quick to undo your good deed. And for what? Just to impress a couple who don't seem to care all that much about you, anyway."

He scoffed, a distinct and totally uncharacteristic stiffness entering his tone. "Well, you made sure there was no chance of that. So, thanks."

He turned to leave.

"Really?"

He spun back around. "Yes. Really."

She lifted a brow. "Really?"

"What are you getting at here?"

"As far as I can tell, I'm the *only* one helping you right now." She strode closer, honey-brown eyes blazing as though at any moment they might ignite like glowing molten gold and lock him in with some kind of enchanting spell.

And truth be told, it was impossible not to stand here alone with her and not think about what it had been to spend an entire night in her bed.

"I have help." The words sounded weak, even to his ears.

"Right, but not enough to stop you from coming here in search of a job? And I helped you, didn't I? I offered you a chance at employment, a decision you've made me question numerous times already, by the way."

She stopped just shy of actually touching him, even though she stabbed a finger forward. He yearned to have her hands on him all over again, even in retaliation. Even though he'd seen another man holding her just moments ago.

*What is this madness? What has she done to me?*

He opened his mouth ready to apologize, but he didn't know if he actually meant it or if his raging hormones merely held him hostage. Then again, this day wouldn't be so bad if he got to end it buried deep inside her.

Her gaze danced about his face, her posture and expression softer now, like she had dropped the boss-lady act and slipped into being the woman who'd taken him home last night.

"You realize most normal people don't get to just dip out of their job, don't you? That a non-emergency room accident doesn't result in an instant day off? Most of us don't have the luxury of hiding when someone we know enters our place of employment. We own it. We get on with our job. We have no other choice. Besides, your social set has been frequenting this bar since it opened five years ago. You can't tell me you didn't think you'd get a job here and never bump into someone you know."

A tiny smile curled the crimson corners of her delicate but teasing mouth, like holding a grudge didn't come all that naturally to her.

He dropped his attention to the floor, wanting to believe that something about him drew out her good nature, but not quite arrogant enough to truly accept that.

"Actually, that's exactly what happened. I was in shock over losing everything, and I just kind of raced to the first friendly face I knew might be hiring."

*Hell, even when I don't look at her, my mouth with its stupid words won't play cool.*

He gave a shrug and tried not to cringe. Her shoulders sank, and she stared at him a moment longer before turning away to lean against her plum-draped window frame.

The look she shot him was wide and incredulous, like she either couldn't believe someone could be so impulsive and shortsighted, or that the vulnerability in his mistake stunned her a little. Maybe both.

Eventually, a deep sigh fell from her, and she crossed her arms over her chest. "Can you see how what you did out there might make me question your character?"

A beat passed before he gave her a reluctant nod. Right about now, he felt as worthy as a blot of mud marring her dainty sky-blue ballet flats.

"Max?" Her gaze held him, unwavering, like maybe she wasn't all that done with her questions. "What is it about mopping floors that you find so shameful?"

He took an impulsive step forward, only to stop in his tracks. "I don't, it's ju—"

"Have you been frequenting my bar all this time, silently judging my floor staff? Perhaps their job, as necessary as it is, makes them inferior, somehow?"

His spine snapped to an involuntary straight position, a harsh coldness zipping down his arms. "What? No! I—"

"Then why hide from your friends?"

He parted his lips and tried to force an answer, but nothing came.

Her gaze dropped to the ground, as though she gave up on him having an adequate reply, probably a good thing since he still didn't have one. "Some friends you have if they'd ditch you for falling on hard times. *They're* supposed to offer you help, not some woman you spent one night with and who just happens to own a bar."

Her dark eyelashes flicked up, her knowing stare slamming into him; so hard, he could practically feel a solid indent forming in the center of his ribcage. She didn't seem annoyed at helping him. No. But she had succeeded in summing up his social support—or lack thereof —to a T.

Yes, he had family, and they'd helped him in the past.

But even they had limits and were sick of his shit.

Miro. Well, he was a genuine friend. Really, he was. But not one Max would ever ask for a bailout. Especially when he didn't trust his ability to pay anyone back.

And everyone else? Well, the best he could call them was entertainment, fun as long as the drinks flowed and the cash kept coming. Though, the one thing he could bet money on was that his exchange with Cedrick would come back to bite him at some point and probably soon.

"I'd rather work for my money."

And that much was the truth. At least then, if he failed to come up with any decent funds, he'd only be disappointing himself. This time, anyway.

"Max?" Her voice pulled him back to her again, husky and low, and way too compassionate for what he deserved. "I don't know how you lost all your money, and it's not my place to ask, but as a business owner, the prospect of going bust is a risk most of us juggle every day. I'm the last to hold it against you, so you want to know what I would do?"

He nodded, somehow believing what she had to say would be the most useful thing he'd heard all day.

"I'd go home. Give my ego a little time to heal. Then get back up and learn to find some pride in where I am now." Her throat bobbed, her pause suggesting she maybe needed a second to consider her next words. "You know. I've been where you are. Not in the sense that I've lost all my money, but that I had none to begin with. You have to dig yourself out of the hole you've fallen into, do you understand? Even if that means mopping floors and taking shit from people who know you. And while you're at it, as long as you're keeping up your end of the bargain, you've got a place here at my bar."

Her soft smile now offered the same kind of uncomplicated acceptance he'd found in her bed last night.

His heart kicked, and a dull pain spread beneath his ribcage, somehow buoyed and ashamed with how much his trampled spirit clutched at her offer of having somewhere and someone to rely on. That maybe he wasn't so alone. At least while he mopped floors, anyway.

"Thank you." He offered a wary smile.

If not for the dude he'd seen her with earlier, he might have stepped closer. Not so much because he begrudged her life away from him, but because she'd pointed to his arrogance and entitlement. Maybe working on that meant not presuming every encounter with her would lead to intimacy.

Plus, she had a point about him having a lot to think about. Trying to make things happen with her would be a bad idea. And didn't he have years of bad ideas to atone for?

Gone were his days of assuming everything would work out no matter what risks he took. He'd taken risks. Gotten too comfortable. Now his future lay more uncertain than ever.

As much as he wanted to believe he'd already hit rock bottom, a whisper rebounded within his head, one that said things could always get worse.

# Chapter Fourteen

Gideon Faber was one of the most attractive men Freya had ever met. With his thick caramel waves, tawny eyes, and full, European lips, he was downright gorgeous, and he knew it.

But Gideon had more going for him than just being beautiful. He was also her best friend, and maybe more than that, he was also one of Australia's top cabaret performers.

No matter what persona he wore—man, woman, or something else entirely—he rarely failed to garner a double take from those who encountered him. For the longest time, she'd lived in a weird kind of jealousy and awe, ever since he'd used his natural free-spirit to guide her from her dark early beginnings.

The Ruby Room's success in its first few months could also be attributed to his involvement, and once again, she counted on his immeasurable talent to lead her bar through the Live Wire Festival.

Now, she scowled at Gideon in his sky-high stilettos, certain she'd have zero chance of walking in them, much less keeping up with the two equally perfect female dancers either side of him, shaking and singing before the urban-chic rehearsal room mirror. Just the way he belted along to the horn-heavy music and filled out his tiny black booty shorts made her want to be him when she grew up.

The music stopped, and right on cue, so did Gideon and his dancers. Freya brought her hands together in an excited clap. Gideon strutted over, while the two dancers rushed to their gym bags in the corner, like they had somewhere else to be.

"Hey, Frizzle!" He winked and nudged her with a hip, Frizzle being his nickname for her. A play on the days she hadn't been so skilled at taming her curls, curl-taming yet another thing Gideon had helped her with. "Finally not too busy to talk to your old friend, huh?"

"Sorry about last night." She lifted her arms and wrapped them around her friend, hoping to goodness he wouldn't read too much into Max's interruption in her office. "Work dramas."

"Oh, forget about it. I'm just glad I finally got my hug." He squeezed her tighter, patting her on the back. "Missed you, Sweet Cheeks."

She laughed, and tears prickled the inner corners of her eyes. They stood there for a long time, swaying and laughing in the firm embrace, before she finally pulled back to get a better look at him. "Tell me about the Europe tour. I can see you've been working on your tan."

He threw back his head and closed his eyes with a sigh, just as the final dancer left.

"The shopping, the fashion, the nightlife, the shows, the beaches, the food"—he patted his washboard tummy as if he'd gained some weight, which was nowhere near the case—"heaven. The whole damn continent was heaven."

"And Prague?" She reached up and cupped her hands to his face, sending forth her biggest smile. "Amazing, right?"

"An art nouveau lover's fantasy." He reached down from his six-foot-two height, plus heels, and cupped her cheeks back. "But my goodness, I'm glad to see you again."

He rubbed his nose to hers. She laughed, so glad to have him back.

"Come on." She pulled him toward his white sports bag, with its hard-to-miss Chanel logo. "I assume you've got something other than booty shorts in there. Let's get you changed and go for that coffee."

He went about digging in his bag. "Yes, I have more than booty shorts, and why wait for coffee? There's nothing stopping us from chatting while I change."

"Actually, you're right, and there's something I did need to clear with you first." She joined him in the bag digging, though she riffled through her own giant, yellow, cotton handbag. "I have the flyers for your stint at The Ruby Room for you to approve. Helena, my event manager, had someone put them together."

He paused, wiping off the dusky rose-pink lipstick he often said helped him feel in character, even during rehearsals. "Oh, great. Give us a look."

She handed him a large white envelope. "If you like these, we'll do some minor tweaking and produce larger posters for around the bar and nearby alleyways."

He tugged off his thick false lashes, as if that would help him see better, and slid his gaze over the poster, its glossy, black layout accentuating the magenta font and a central photo of him in his full-drag glory.

His brows tensed for the shortest second, before a mega-watt smile broke across his mouth. "I love it. Especially the line, *'Come for the eye-candy, stay for the showwomanship'*. That's me in a nutshell, right?"

"Really? You love the flyer?" She gave him a sidelong stare. Gideon Faber almost never simply loved something. His exacting standards were a huge reason for his success.

He handed back the envelope, then ripped off his skin-tight black singlet and replaced it with a less-sweaty white one, his impeccable six-pack abs just one more perfect thing about him. "The flyer is fine, Sweet Cheeks."

He pushed his shorts down and then rolled his fishnets off, kicking them with precision into his open bag on the floor. "Though I hope you finally fixed The Ruby's manky old stage. That thing is a death wish."

He smiled at her from over his shoulder, fastening his pleated gray slacks.

She let out a growl and sank back. She should have known better than to get too comfortable with his praise. "I have some tradesmen booked to pull up the boards in two weeks. We've even closed the bar for a day to get it done."

"Brilliant. I'm not breaking my ankle in front of my home crowd. I don't even care who you are or how long we've been friends, I'll sue your ass. You hear me?"

She let out a laugh. "You're the genius who named their show, 'Shockwave'. Maybe a broken ankle would help the show live up to its name."

He snapped his attention away from his image in the giant rehearsal room mirror and on to her. "You know I don't need help in that department. You think I can't deliver the goods?"

"Maybe I should be more concerned you will?" She dipped her chin and gave him a look of mock suspicion.

"Damn right." He turned back to the mirror and used his long fingers to run styling product through his thick curls. "The Ruby won't know what hit it."

To be fair, in an odd way, his ever-present pressure forced her to keep her own business in order. Gideon had been the first person to ever expect anything much of her.

For so long, she'd thought herself insignificant and incapable. A shadow to her mother's criticisms.

Why would Freya ever try when everything she did was wrong?

For some inexplicable reason, a mental image of Max popped into her head, one of him holding the mop at work, refusing to step out and face his friends. As much as she could relate to how he felt, she frowned and shoved the thought away.

Gideon had changed how she felt about herself. A survivor of his own critics. He'd worked his literal butt off earning his place into a highly competitive performance degree, then built an incomparable reputation in the industry. And through it all, through high school to now, he'd taken her along with him.

She owed him, even if he never demanded repayment, and the least she could do was give him a great show every time he graced her venue. Because every time he did grace her venue, the crowds packed The Ruby Room just to see him. Festival lure or not, his shows sold out fast, though this time the festival did add extra pressure.

Gideon gave a dramatic turn in front of the mirror, checking out his gray pleated pants and loose white shirt with the first two buttons undone. He looked every bit a carefree and classic English gentleman, even though as a pre-teen, he'd escaped the refugee camps fresh from the Bosnian War, minus any English.

"All right, let's go." He swept up his bag from the floor.

She followed him down the dark staircase and into a side street leading to Chapel Street, one of Melbourne's major café hotspots.

"So—" She paused, using the advantage of being behind him as he entered the busy flow of foot traffic. "I… umm… I saw my mother again."

He stopped, just as a young woman striding toward him almost slammed face-first into his chest. He ignored her and spun around, eyes wide and focused on Freya. "What? You did *what?* Why would you do that?"

She stiffened her spine, ready to pretend she'd made peace with her decision, when in reality, the tense interaction with her mother still played on a loop in her brain. "I didn't really have any other choice. She's in a bad way."

"To hell with that. Or should I say, to hell with her? Don't tell me you can't remember how things turned out the last time you reconnected with that woman."

Yes. She did remember. How she'd sought her mother out again, expecting… what? Maybe some kind of remorse for the hell she'd inflicted, only to have to listen to a stubborn monologue about her mother being a blameless victim.

That stubbornness had sent Freya down a spiral of apathy, her old mode of survival kicking in, followed by a phase of soul-wrenching depression.

But she'd matured since then. She'd learned to use a detached perspective to view people, events, and various attitudes. At the very least, whatever her frail mother had to pitch at her now would never come close to eclipsing what she'd done to Freya as a child.

She swallowed at the strain growing within her throat. "Yeah well, either way, this is the last time. I can handle one last time."

Gideon hooked an arm over her and patted her hand, guiding her through the open double doors to an expansive café with large, gray-scale artworks decorating the back wall. "You mean, she's in a bad way, as in, she's dying?"

She plonked herself into a seat opposite him, nodding her silent confirmation.

"Wow." He paused, a reflective sigh breaking from him as he stared at her. "And just your luck, Clay isn't around to help. Your mum never made any secret of him being her golden child."

Golden child. A big, fat understatement.

Her mother had downright abused and neglected Freya, while worshipping Clay.

The overt favoritism obvious to her, even as a child, and she'd spent her entire younger years lost, unloved, and wondering why her mother had ever even had her.

And it wasn't as if she could just ask her mother why. Kerry Branner was the master of giving no straight answers, especially when the question meant holding her accountable in any sort of way.

"Yeah." She gave a hollow laugh. "On the golden child count alone, Clay deserves to be the one dealing with this mess. But as much as our relationship isn't the best, I can't blame him solely for where he is now."

Gideon toyed with the lid on a short glass jar filled with light-brown crystals of raw sugar. "And what exactly will 'dealing with this mess' entail for you?"

"Helping with final decisions if needed, organizing a funeral home, tying up lose financial ends, selling her house."

"Oh, please don't tell me you're about to organize a lovely send off for that mad witch." Gideon's face took on an uncharacteristic hardness, while she honed her lifelong skill of internalizing her dislike for her mother. "I can't imagine her having any friends who'd want to show up, much less you standing out front of an empty funeral home, sharing sweet memories that sure don't exist."

She peered down at her forefinger drawing small, invisible circles on the white table top, her heart straining because she didn't see her mother as a "mad witch", even though she maybe should.

Gideon was right. Chances were, her mother didn't have any friends. The fact that she didn't, and that her life had never expanded beyond the same cage of mistrust and fear she'd grown up in, only tightened the vice-like band around Freya's heart.

Her mother had endured things no child should endure, but worse, she'd tried to force that same existence onto Freya.

"I probably do owe her a visit." She mumbled the words, maybe out of a misplaced desire to make up for her mum's lack of friends. *Who knew?* She sure didn't.

"You don't owe her shit, and you know it." Gideon stabbed a finger her way. "Don't you start feeling bad, now she's the one in the hospital bed. I bet she didn't even ask how you were when she saw you."

Pain burrowed deeper into her chest because Gideon had called it; her mother hadn't asked anything meaningful. She'd just hacked and complained, and as usual, Freya's life and choices were never good enough.

She raised her hand, intent on rubbing at her sternum, only to think twice about making her pain all that visible to Gideon; so, she pushed her hands onto her lap, nails digging sharp and distracting points of pain into her palms.

"I know, it was just a turn of phrase." She veered her gaze, searching for any nearby waitstaff, anyone who might make eye contact long enough to bail her out of this conversation. "Is it time to talk about something else yet?"

She didn't like this topic, but he knew her whole story, and she didn't want to lie to a friend. Not with what would be coming up in her life. *Her mother's death.* He'd find out eventually, anyway.

Gideon didn't speak right away, which drew her attention back to him and his head tilted to one side, golden brown stare perusing her face. "Oh, honey, her problems aren't your problems, you know that, right? I just want to hear you'll look after you first."

"I know. I know." She took a deep breath and leaned back in her chair. "It probably doesn't make much sense to me either, but I just can't leave her to die alone."

"I think if you dig deep enough, you know exactly why you don't just give up on her." He sent a pinched, pitying look her way. "Still that little girl waiting for Mumma to be less messed up. For her to care."

*Well, mothers are supposed to care. Aren't they?*

And what if they didn't? What did that say about the child?

Her stomach lurched, but she ticked one corner of her lip up, still acting like nothing about her situation hurt. "I guess some dreams never go away."

"Well, speaking of dreams"—he reached out and pressed a hand over hers, as if he saw her pain and chose to make good on the topic change—"I hope your ruby chandelier is in top shape. I have big plans for that thing for the show."

She spluttered out a tight laugh and gave him a side glare; even for Gideon, the comment on her club's semi-famous chandelier seemed an odd thing to say.

"Why does my chandelier have to be in top shape? Please don't tell me you plan on swinging from it?"

"Ha!" He rolled his eyes and gave another snort of laughter. "Like that ancient roof would support my weight. No, just like the rest of the world, you're going to have to wait until the show to see what I have planned."

# Chapter Fifteen

Max adjusted his tie and climbed the stone stairs stretching between two old columns that led to a set of ominous black doors. The Morris mansion loomed giant as ever with its large stone bricks. Others walked ahead of him and into the great foyer, the family's annual charity ball already in full swing.

But as ridiculously glamorous as this setting was, something felt off.

Maybe it was just his fidgeting, coupled with the hard sensation nestled in his belly since long before he handed his car over to the valet.

In the foyer, he swept his gaze over the white-marble double staircase and gilded handrails, his thoughts snagging on how someone usually would have spotted him by now and approached to say hello.

"Max." Diana Morris, the reigning monarch to the Morris fortune, glided over, her pale pink sheath dress floating in her wake. "So unexpected to see you."

He gave a small cautious nod. "Yes, I should be on holiday, but there was a change of plans."

She lifted her chin before her lips pulled into a graceful smile, one that only slightly accentuated the wrinkles over her cheekbones. For the most part, women in her social set weren't allowed to age, something Max never understood, but he put Diana to be somewhere around her mid-fifties.

"Yes. That's right." She extended a hand and shifted side-on to let him pass, the strain in her smile hard to miss. "Very well, then. I'll have the staff seat you at Antonio Fiorei's table. As I recall, you two got along quite well at last year's event."

"Thank you." He moved past, but not without catching Diana's tense gaze holding on him for a moment too long.

He spotted Fiorei's table soon enough, and waited for the staff to add an extra table setting, before wandering over.

"Hey, Max." Antonio Fiorei held up his beer glass in his version of a wave; the nine other guests at the table all fell silent. "Been a while, hasn't it?"

Max huffed out a laugh, a portion of strain slipping from his shoulders, though he did peer down at his clothes. Surely, they hadn't gone out of style in the mere week since he'd become broke?

"Not since November and Jackson Morelli's thirtieth birthday. Ingot Nightclub, as I recall." He ran a hand over the front of his shirt. Maybe the others could tell he'd done his own ironing?

Antonio offered a knowing grin. "That was a hell of a night. Though I don't expect you'd remember much since you got so tanked, we had to fold you into one of the cars and have a driver ferry you home. You always were a wild one."

Truth be told, Antonio was right. Max didn't remember much about that night… Or many nights out, really.

He sat at the table now, all gazes still pinned on him and every one silent. For a moment there, he had a compulsion to vow he'd changed, but even that felt like admitting defeat, as though his situation had won out and his nights of fun and no consequences were forever over.

Besides, he hadn't come here to advertise his problems, even though his peers might notice he wasn't buying any drinks. Alcohol was usually covered at events like this, but the proceeds from tonight's bar were meant to go to a charity, so everyone was expected to drink and spend up big—something he couldn't afford to do.

Heck, one reason for his showing up was that he'd already paid for his ticket months ago, and a meal *was* included in the price, so one less thing to add to his list of bills for this week.

And maybe Freya had a point. These people were meant to be his friends. Educated, philanthropic, worldly. Surely his bank balance wasn't the only admission price into their lives?

He passed his attention over the table and made eye contact with Sadie Williams and the deep blush darkening her narrow cheeks, before she spoke. "Is it true?"

A collective "shhh" broke across the table, and the girl next to Sadie gave her a light elbowing in the ribcage.

So, there it was. Everyone *did* know.

Sadie gnawed into her lower lip. "I'm sorry. It's just that Cedrick said he saw you mopping floors at The Ruby Room, and I thought… I thought maybe that was just him being a salty dickbag, you know. Especially since that night when he threatened to kill you cos you had the nuts to go on a few dates with Adele and everything." She gazed around the table, cringing in awkward apology to the others. "Surely he's lying about your money though, right?"

For the briefest time, she and Max held a silent stare. Sadie was a good fifteen years younger and still had a lot of maturing to do—not that he could talk. Either way, her question now seemed more a genuine need to check in on him than pure and hollow curiosity.

Still, a cold wave washed over his body, and he did his best to hold his head up high as if his lack of funds didn't worry him. Maybe if he kept up that facade, he'd somehow recover his money and manage to keep his friends in the meantime. "Yeah, it's true."

Sadie's expression sank, and her gaze fell from him, skittering to the side, while her straight blond bangs covered whatever reaction flashed across her gray eyes. For the next hour or so, her gaze failed to meet with his again, as did many of the others around the table.

He excused himself after dinner and escaped to the courtyard, needing fresh air and a break from the tension.

His world had just shrunk.

"Don't take this the wrong way." Antonio pulled up alongside him and pressed a hand to Max's shoulder, like he meant to console him; though given how this evening was going, Max couldn't be all that sure anymore. "But these events are pricey and maybe your time would be better spent getting your affairs together. No one in here knows what to say to you. No one here wants to cause you any embarrassment. Heck, the charity auction is about to start, and we both know you won't be bidding on anything. Wouldn't it be easier if you just left?"

Max frowned, holding back from pointing out he'd paid for tonight's ticket months ago, back when he had money, so his being here cost him nothing new. "That's it? After years of knowing each other, I'm booted?"

"No mate, nothing like that." Antonio staggered out a laugh. "We all want to see you back on your feet. What I mean is, talk to your numbers guy, or whatever, and once you're back on track, come and regale us with how you did it. I'm sure being here doesn't feel all that good to you right now."

He stared at Antonio and worked against a compulsion to tell him to "fuck right off", even though something like that really wasn't his style, no matter how out of line a person's words or actions might be.

Antonio had been born into money. He had no idea what he talked about. In his world, failure was impossible, and there would always be plenty of money to bail him out, no matter how badly he screwed up. Hell, the only time anyone in a family like his ever claimed bankruptcy was when they wanted to fold a business without paying their debts.

Money was a game to them.

Not the difference between having a home or not.

And maybe Max's situation wasn't as bad as most, but he'd at least grown up in a world where something like poverty waited only a few missteps away.

Then again, maybe Max *did* need to take the hint and leave.

Maybe he no longer belonged and needed to let this place and the people inside it go.

But where would he go?

To the apartment he was set to lose? No. He didn't want to go there. Not alone, anyway.

He wanted somewhere he could escape to. Somewhere he felt accepted.

Only one place came to mind, but whether he'd be welcome was another issue.

*Only one way to find out.*

He patted Antonio on the upper arm, putting the man out of his misery, and accepting the truth. When it came to these people, he no longer belonged, and he would have to deal with his losses alone.

"I'll see you around."

Though Antonio's shoulders sank, the hard lines on his face eased. Max turned away, his world off-kilter.

He strode through the mansion, past the tight gathering of happy people, and down the outside steps. The arching black gates loomed ahead, and he waited for the valet to return with his car, all while wrestling with an image embedded in his mind from the last time he'd spoken to Freya. The image of another man holding her in her office.

Her social life shouldn't have mattered. She wore her free-spirit clear enough for anyone to see, and unlike him, she knew who she was. Far be it from him to expect her to alter her life over one encounter, even if something more drew him to her than simple base attraction—the obvious difference between her and him.

She'd never in a million years let the Antonios of the world hold her back or bother her.

So maybe Max was right to feel something for her. To need more of that. *More of her.*

Because heaven knew, right about now, he didn't have much, and he needed to get out of the rut he was in.

Freya's elbows dug into her desk's turquoise timber top, her fingertips pressed over her closed eyelids. Loud jazz music clanged from The Ruby Room downstairs, clashing symbols and piano-heavy rhythms so different from the fat bass and club bangers played at the bars she'd once worked at. Though she'd long ago learned how to block out loud sounds, the day's exhaustion had set in, and she fought to stay awake.

"You look wrecked."

She pulled her hands from her eyes, blinking against the assault of lights in her office, not taking note of who spoke to her.

*Nope, still too bright.*

She returned her hands to her eyes, splitting her fingers slightly to buy her time to adjust. "I had a brainstorming session with Gideon earlier. We came up with more ways to outshine the other venues in this year's festival. I've spent the rest of the day researching and implementing those ideas. I want us to make a splash, you know?"

Empty silence followed her answer, and it was then that she took a second to really look at who stood before her, instead of just assuming it was one of her managers.

A beautiful, blond surfer dude waited at the end of her desk, his fists jammed in his pockets, his irises a stormy gray. The mere look of him held her next breath hostage.

"Who's Gideon?" His lips pressed into a hard line.

She frowned. "He's our star performer for the festival."

"Is that all?" The stiffness held in his jaw. "Is he the same guy I saw touching you the other day?"

She jerked her chin back and then barked out a laugh. Was Max pissed? Jealous?

"That's still none of your business."

"We slept together."

"So?"

He opened his mouth, as if ready to protest, but then he closed his lips just as quickly in a sort of nonverbal, "Never mind."

"Look"—she let out a sigh, her brain too fried to continue this inane debate—"you weren't helping me cheat on anyone, if that's what brought you here on your night off."

She'd run from one disastrous, long-term relationship already, one involving five years of emotional and psychological manipulation because she'd been too messed up from her shitty childhood to expect any better.

A good chunk of her twenties had been lost to just learning she could do better alone. *And she had.* She wasn't doing that again. Not ever.

That's not to say she held a grudge against men. Her best friend was a man, and the man standing before her now proved she very much appreciated them on a physical level. What she hated was commitment and the prospect of losing even just the tiniest bit of herself to any one person. She wanted freedom more than she wanted another relationship.

She took a moment to look Max over—to notice his tailored, navy blue shirt with white detail on the collar and his fitted dove gray pants —so much dressier than the jeans and hoodie he usually wore to mop the club's floors.

He looked like the man she'd passed in the months before they'd ever even spoken a single word to each other. The man who'd saved her, then come back to her home long enough for her to make love to him, though with one marked difference.

"Are you done working?" His ragged tone spoke volumes yet again, as did the shadows under his eyes and the raw vulnerability flowing off him.

"Max, are you okay?"

He stared, barely blinking, his stillness making the hairs at the back of her neck prickle. "I asked you a question first."

"Fine. Yes, I'm about to head home." She stood, but didn't yet round her desk. "Now you answer my question. Are you okay? You look—"

"Don't go home. Come back to my place instead." His hyper-focused gaze didn't shift off her, and he squared his shoulders, as if bracing for rejection. Meanwhile, cheerful music busted through the floorboards from downstairs, only adding to the disquiet.

"Why?"

"I don't know." He released another heavy breath and stared at the ceiling. "Maybe because I'll probably lose the place soon enough, and you might as well come and see it."

A pitchy, deranged laugh broke free of her, and she glanced at the blue-framed clock on the wall behind him, with its painted, retro black cat. "It's past midnight and you want me to come to your place to appraise your decor?"

His face paled from fatigue or stress, or maybe both, like perhaps something had happened tonight. Either way, it took him an age to answer.

"Freya. Don't make me beg."

She wanted to laugh again at his dejected tone, as though a gorgeous man like Max really would get down on his knees and beg her to come home with him. But the sadness in his eyes pleaded to her in a different way—a way she simply couldn't mock.

He begged her not to play obtuse, to put him out of his misery with an answer either way. And she knew that look. Knew what it was to feel down. Knew what he *really* asked for. And maybe with all the things happening in her life, he had the right idea, that tonight neither of them needed to be alone.

She grabbed her sand-colored purse from beside her and tossed the long strap over her shoulder, rounding the desk and striding toward him.

"Okay, but"—she smiled, trying to lighten the mood—"just promise me you won't fall in love."

# Chapter Sixteen

Freya turned at the click of Max's apartment door closing behind her. He'd already spent the elevator ride up undoing buttons down the back of her dress, and now, the crimson polka dot material hit the carpet with a light thud.

Between Max devouring her lips and tugging away at the silk scarf she used as a head band, she laughed at her incoming weak joke. "I can't believe they cut off your electricity already. It's so dark in here, how am I supposed to fulfill my promise to check out your decor?"

"Shush, you." His tongue lashed hers, and she tried not to moan as he spoke again. "Things aren't that bad yet, but I can switch on the lights if that's what you're into."

She cupped his face and kissed him back, shaking her head.

Truth be told, she'd half forgotten how good he was at this whole "getting it on" thing. *And, holy fuck!* She'd forgotten how damn solid his body was pressed against hers.

Even as he guided her in a backward march through a doorway she presumed led to his bedroom, she wanted to melt into him, the space between her thighs bursting to life like an out-of-control fire.

Her back cooled at the kiss of crisp silk sheets suddenly beneath her. Seconds later, his naked torso pressed to hers, his weight a welcome reminder of what was to come.

"You're beautiful." He kissed the side of her neck.

"Umm… thanks?"

She tried not to frown into the dark, his touch arousing.

The kisses continued, and he whispered against the shell of her ear. "Like you don't already know you're beautiful."

This time she smiled. With her short stature and rounded curves, even the general lack of women like her on any mainstream cover didn't obscure her agreement that Max was right. She did know.

She loved the way she looked and the feeling of being alive, and strong, and able to sense every touch this man unleashed on her body. Her confidence wasn't one-hundred-percent bullet proof, but she'd begun to believe her act, her bravado, something adopted to help her get by in the world.

People liked her better when nothing seemed wrong, when she put on a good show, which meant they also asked fewer questions.

"Okay then, rather than tell me." She arched her neck, hinting his next kisses should extend there. "You really should show me."

He obliged with the throat kisses and hummed at her directive, a man willing to accept a challenge. And even as he did, even as he entered her and gave her just what she wanted, she couldn't keep from directing the play.

At times, she asked him to slow so she could savor the feeling of him inside her; at others, she demanded more when she wanted the thrill of him working at her pleasure. Harder. Faster. She relished being the sexually assertive one in this pairing. And bless his heart, Max seemed to relish it too.

His long fingers brushed her outer thighs, his thumbs hooking beneath her knees and pushing her legs higher so that he buried himself deeper within her. She sunk into the pillowy duvet, delighting in his increased thrusts, her breaths ragged along with his.

He wasn't like the others, intimidated or judgmental when it came to an insatiable woman. A woman unwilling to waste time suppressing her desires. *No.* His gaze fused with hers, and he studied her, as if taking in something only he could see. She felt free. Excited. Affirmed.

If only his life wasn't a mess. If only she wasn't allergic to relationships.

Actually, scratch that.

She liked being allergic to relationships. Her apprehension kept her life consistent, easy, trouble free, though she would miss Max when all of this ended.

She lashed her hands out so her fingers locked behind his neck, and she pulled him close, savoring the hotness of him—not just his beautiful aesthetic, but his literal hotness—the burn of his skin against hers and the heat of him within her.

His thrusts intensified, as though he lived for her reaction to his touch. She let go, giving in to what he wanted, allowing her peak to rise so that one pleasurable wave engulfed another. The swell of satisfied need shot through her body, and her arousal broke in a series of soft moans and uninhibited pleas for more.

He responded each time, driving into her with impossible force, his usually restrained strength now unbridled. She pulled him down and seized his mouth with hers, his pace unbroken when he did reach his own climax.

Soon after, the room filled with nothing more than the sounds of panting breaths as he collapsed forward, burying his face in her hair. Something about his near silence conveyed more than just a man who'd found pleasure. Like he'd searched her out in need of an emotional release and found it.

Blood rushed her body, rumbling and pounding in her ears, while something light and totally worth ignoring danced within her chest.

Joy. Maybe?

Max rolled and positioned himself beside her. Again came the silence, so she turned to him, her heart clenching at his pupils dilated and focused on the ceiling, only the smallest sliver of cerulean visible.

He turned to her, the action hinting that he sensed her concern, while the look on his face made her stomach sink. Even the room's limited light didn't obscure the sheen to his eyes, his whites tinged a pale pink. The thick line denting the space between his brows indicated a man overwhelmed and in need of comfort—but too afraid to ask. A man without an anchor and in need of someone to hold him through the turbulent weather.

She didn't want to be that someone, but her heart pulled rank, just as it did every time she saw the cracks growing across another person's soul.

She'd been where Max was now, many times alone, a child with no one to share the weight pressing on her tiny shoulders. So yes, her heart pulled rank. Even as her brain yelled for her not to get involved.

Her life had its own shadows to chase away, and yet, she rolled to her side and rested her hand on the furnace that was his bare chest.

The sharp rise and fall didn't belong to a man sated and unwinding. His untamed heartbeat pulsed through his ribcage and into her hand. And of course, her mouth pulled rank too, betraying her better sense and crossing the healthy space she'd put between them. All because she shuffled close enough to see the water gathering in his eyes.

She pressed her lips to his high cheekbone and whispered a sappy affirmation she knew better than to offer. One she'd wished to hear in her dark hours. Words he too probably needed to hear.

"You're going to be okay."

He gave a small nod, and his Adam's apple bobbed with a sharp swallow. Though he remained silent, she hoped he caught the subtext in her statement.

Nothing lasted forever, not even the bad stuff, even when things got so hard that it was impossible to see through to the other side. And as much as she didn't want to tie herself to this man, she did want him to be okay.

# Chapter Seventeen

Freya woke to the moon shining in her eyes. Okay, not the literal moon, but a lamp about half the size of her head that did a convincing impression of looking like the moon, gray shadows, craters, and all.

Now, she blinked at the lamp's "mooniness", those shadows and craters unnoticed last night when Max switched the thing on in passing, with her focus too busy ogling his beautiful nakedness.

She glared at a split in the curtains and the stinging sunlight creeping in, that sunlight aiding the moon in bathing the room in brightness. Years of working the bar scene meant she had a hate-hate relationship with early starts.

"Good morning."

She sucked in a breath and snapped her attention to Max smiling at her from the doorway. "Holy shit. You're awake?"

His wide grin grew and melted a small degree of rigidity in her body, even though his glittering blue eyes betrayed one poor and unfortunate truth.

Max was a morning person.

Her gaze slid from his face to the breathtaking view of toned pecs and perfectly naked abs above a pair of teal-blue board shorts. "You're too chipper for a Saturday morning, and why are you out of this bed?"

He laughed and strode over, taking a seat next to her on the bed's edge. "I wake early. Old habit."

She grumbled. She would ask about that old habit, but only after she caught up on more hours of sleep. Wanting to block the light, she pulled the bed cover over her face.

"I made breakfast." Max tugged the sheet down.

"Sleep first. Food later. Hang on a minute"—she gave up her attempt to wrangle the cover off Max, and for the second time in this incredibly short conversation surprise made her abandon sleep—"you cook?"

"If you call scrambled eggs on toast cooking." His smile made her skin go all tingly and alive, like he saw something in this moment that she couldn't.

That should have been her cue to drag on her clothes and get the hell out of his apartment. For some unexplainable reason, despite all his shortcomings of early morning wake-ups and all, she couldn't stay annoyed at him, much less leave.

Bailing on someone as likable as Max was like kicking a sweet-fluffy kitten, something she just would never do. Maybe his coming to her last night had something to do with her softening to him. He'd clearly been going through something. But the fact he picked her, of all people, again, should have sent her packing.

There wasn't any making sense of this, so she sat up and put on a dramatic groan. If they ever did this again, she'd make it clear that sleep-ins were her jam, and *no one*, not even Mr. Irresistible over here, messed with her sleep.

She nodded to the little moon, failing to recall any other time she'd seen anything similar in a grown person's bedroom. "What's with the nightlight?"

He shrugged, his smile easing to something wistful. "It reminds me of being a child again. Not because it's a nightlight but because it's a moon, and I spent way too much time sleeping under the stars."

She frowned, unable to identify with that memory.

He worked his attention over her face, as if maybe her confusion showed. "I mean, who wouldn't want to bring the moon inside with them?"

Who wouldn't, indeed?

She smiled at the innocence in his rhetorical question. "I'm going to take a not-so-wild stab here and guess you were a camping kid?"

He pressed his hand over hers on the bedspread, his palm and fingers so much longer than her own admittedly small digits. "Only the very second the weather warmed up back in Scarborough. I have a brother and sister, and we lived near the forest. If my dad was too slow to bring us out there, we'd take matters into our own hands and pitch a tent in our yard."

She caught the renewed light in Max's eyes, and a tight band squeezed around her chest.

"Your dad sounds like a great guy."

Whereas she'd barely known her dad.

Still, the mere stroke of Max's thumb over her hand sent a soothing warmth through her body. At least there was that.

"Yeah, he was." Max's gaze dropped from hers.

*Was?*

Her muscles locked, and she slipped her hand from his, fingers now pressed over her mouth. "Oh shit, I'm sorry."

He shook his head. "Anyway, Luke and I would sneak out to the forest on our own sometimes. Sophie was too chicken to join us half the time, but we still had fun."

She raised a brow at the sudden redirection, but let the change in subject go. He wasn't her boyfriend and she didn't need to delve into his problems, and he didn't need to tell her everything.

He stood, taking her hand with him. "Come have breakfast. You look like someone who needs coffee first thing in the morning. Besides, I have something exciting to tell you."

She wrangled her hand free long enough to drag a sheet off the bed and wrap it around herself, all the while grumbling because he'd not only gotten her up, but he'd also gotten her coffee-fueled "type" correct.

The moment she reached the bedroom door, she stopped, her mind freezing on her first glimpse of Max's apartment in full daylight.

To her immediate right stood a black stone kitchen island, with white embossed cabinetry behind. Four giant, bronze, hanging lanterns dangled over the counter, and ahead of that stood a ten-seater table, complete with a huge crystal vase filled with lush tropical flowers.

To the kitchen's left, a round black glass coffee table took up a reasonable amount of space in the huge living room, positioned in front of a giant white, L-shaped, leather sofa.

If her jaw didn't already hang open, it might as well have detached and fallen off the moment she focused on the wall-to-wall windows and the balcony outside.

Except, balcony was a gross understatement.

A wall of greenery backed an expansive red-wood terrace, banana lounges surrounding a small swimming pool, and a tall rusted-metal abstract sculpture nearby. And then there was the spa and slate stone tiles. Dark, woven chairs gave the terrace's other side a more intimate contrast, complete with an outdoor dining area comprised of Moroccan lanterns and a glass and bronze table.

She took a few silent steps forward, allowing the view to draw her in, even more than the terrace. Cool blue morning sky reached down, making contact with a teal Port Phillip Bay below, the ocean stretching out in calm, sparkling waves.

Melbourne could be so many different things depending on who and where the city was being witnessed from. Bustling and grimy. Sleek and professional. Boisterous and festive. But right now, all she saw was tranquility.

"Holy hell, Max." She took a few more steps and touched a finger to the cold glass window, not brave enough to splay her whole hand out and ruin his pristine windows with her handprint. "No wonder you're busting ass to keep this place."

Soft footsteps padded behind her, and soon, his warm body pressed to her back, hands sweeping around her waist, before he turned her to face him. "Yeah, about that, as much as I enjoy busting ass at The Ruby Room, I have another idea."

"You're leaving me already?"

Her stomach sank, even though she'd always figured he'd find something better.

Just not this quick.

"Ha! I wish." His cheeks creased either side of his full grin. "No, just something to add to my workload. Something more along the lines of my passions."

He led her forward, toward the kitchen; her gaze caught on a glass staircase along the living room's back wall.

*Holy mother fruitcake, there's a whole other level to this place.*

She squeezed her eyes shut for a second, reminding herself to stay on topic. "Let me guess, since you're a morning person, you want to be a professional alarm clock?"

"No, though the early morning thing does have something to do with what I'm passionate about." He deposited her on one of the four bar stools and then wandered around the counter. "Before I did the tech business thing, I was set on a career as an open water swimmer. Granted, it would never make me much money, but I loved it, and I want to return to it."

"Aren't you, like, thirty-seven?" She paused to drag her attention over his immaculate body, one part of the whole swimmer story checking out. "Wouldn't that make you too ol—"

"Old?" He narrowed his eyes at her like she was a bit slow in the head or something. "And I have a bung shoulder, yes. But I'm not looking to compete, I'm looking to coach."

She tipped back her head, rolling her eyes at the ceiling and feeling like a total idiot. "Right. I should have figured you meant coaching."

"Let's just blame the lack of caffeine."

"Thanks. I appreciate your understanding." She waited while he went about pulling cups out of a top cabinet. "Okay, so talk me through what becoming a swim coach entails."

"Well, from what I gather, there's an online component and two full days of training. I also need to do a first aid course and get a working-with-children check. I'll start with teaching smaller kids first and take it from there."

"Do you have the money to get all of that done?" She jutted out her chin, just as he grabbed a carton of milk from the fridge. "I'm dairy intolerant, by the way. I like my coffee strong and black."

"One black coming up." He gave her a wink, then pressed a button on his coffee machine, his voice rising over the whirring noise. "And if you mean, do I have money to spare, that's a definite no, but sometimes you've gotta spend money to make money, right?"

"Right. Why did you ditch the swimming for tech, anyway?"

He slid a tall glass filled with liquid black gold her way. She took a first sip and tried not to groan at the deep, bitter, wonderfulness.

"It wasn't by choice." He shrugged, leaning one hip against the counter opposite her, his own white coffee in his hand. "I got a shoulder injury falling off a cliff."

She choked on coffee and slammed a hand over her mouth, trying not to splutter all over his beautiful counter. "You fell off a cliff and survived?"

He gave a slow nod. "All one-hundred or so feet. Totally my brother's fault, though I don't like to remind him."

"Holy shit!" She stared at his shoulder and the jagged, raised scar running across it. "I guess that explains your scar."

His attention fell to the counter, and any light in his expression dropped, too.

She offered a smile, even though he couldn't see it. "This is where I make you feel better by admitting I think scars are hella sexy."

His gaze rose. "Really?"

She gave a steady nod, her heart pounding with just how much she wanted to breach the counter and press her lips to that scar, maybe rekindle a re-enactment of what they'd shared last night.

His mouth curled at the corners, yet another spot she wanted to kiss. "Good thing I *did* survive, then."

She peered down at her coffee and a vague reflection of her frowning face mirrored back at her on the shiny surface. "How did you fall off a cliff and live to tell the tale, anyway?"

"My brother, Luke, was going through something at the time, struggling with re-joining the normal world after his military stint. He asked me to come rock climbing on a day when conditions weren't exactly great." He rounded the counter and took a seat beside her. A low tug pulled within her gut, one that made her want to lean over and kiss him, to distract from her rising sympathy. "And after the cliff face gave way, I just happened to land on a stretch of earth without any rocks.

The fall smashed my shoulder, but I lived. I was lucky and unlucky all in one."

He rested his elbow to the counter and took hold of her wrist, rubbing his thumb over her pulse and sending an instant and delicious tingling sensation throughout her entire body.

She didn't know what to do, except to watch his hand stroke her wrist while she contemplated why on earth anyone would go rock climbing to begin with, much less anywhere near some pointy-ass rocks.

"What do you think about my swim coach idea?"

"Will it pay enough to save your apartment?"

He drew her hand toward him and kissed her wrist, the gesture sending a surge of electricity down her spine. "Probably not, but it might tide me over until I can figure out something more permanent."

They watched each other for the longest time, sipping coffee through the silence. A part of her wanted to point out that many normal people worked jobs they didn't love just to keep a roof over their heads, that maybe losing his multi-million dollar "roof" wouldn't be all that disastrous. But then, maybe her version of bad wasn't the same as his version of bad, and it wasn't her place to judge the series of shock changes he'd been through.

Her stomach growled, a reminder she hadn't eaten yet. Before she could open her mouth to ask him to feed her, his lingering blue stare caught her off-guard.

Once again, the innocence in his eyes struck her, and her thoughts switched to what he'd told her about his outdoorsy childhood. How he'd developed a love for ocean swimming, participated in rock climbing—not the controlled, indoor, abseiling type—but the actual "someone could fall and break bones" sort.

His life was so different from hers. His childhood alone was light years away, simply because he'd had both parents, though she suspected he'd enjoyed way more than that.

He'd had forests, and moonlit nights, and siblings who seemed to mostly get along; meanwhile, she'd endured lonely nights in hospital beds and a miserable home to return to when she did recover.

Even if her life was mostly awesome these days, the sinking feeling in her belly reminded her of her recent misfortune of being lumped with her mother, of Gideon's warning about having an association with that woman.

The sinking in her belly turned into a hot, bubbling sensation, one that prodded at her anger. Anger that her childhood had been so fucking miserable, that both parents had taken advantage of her vulnerability, wasting the magic of her younger years while making her feel so small and unimportant.

And instead of merely raging, she'd taken revenge and become everything those two staunch Catholics hated. Everything they'd said she couldn't be. Unique. Independent. Brazen.

There'd been her bartending, her friendship with Gideon, all her solo travels to dangerous and exotic countries, her tattoos, her unwillingness to settle down, and the scores of men she invited into her bed.

She brought her focus back to Max and surrendered to her sudden need to break free once again, perhaps what she needed in order to deal with all the new stuff complicating her life.

"Take me camping."

Max laughed, but she answered him with silence.

His exuberant grin slipped. "What? You're not serious, are you?"

# Chapter Eighteen

Two weeks passed, and in that time, Max completed his online work and two days of practical swim coach training. He'd also obtained a Working With Children check card. Now he waded in the warm waters at Little Sharkie's Swim Center, a school a few minutes' walk from his apartment. His uniform consisted of an unmissable bright red swim shirt, complete with a giant, smiling, cartoon shark over his chest.

Like the other two trainees either side of him in the pool, this was his fourth session today; but unlike his fellow instructors, he didn't look fresh out of high school. In fact, he looked truly ancient and totally out of place; though, at least he could count life experience as an advantage.

Little Sharkie's had been willing to fast-track his teacher training in light of his competition past. With any luck, they would bump him from babies' classes to training the more advanced children over time.

So now, he hung back with his peers in the section designated for babies and toddlers, the lead instructor, Melissa, out front waving baby-laden parents into the pool.

He tried to smile and wave too, tried to give the impression he was here simply because he loved swimming and working with children, not because he really needed the cash and would lose his home if he didn't find more ways to make some money.

A stack of utility bills waited on his kitchen counter, adding to his mounting expenses, and as predicted, he wouldn't have a whole lot of money left over from his deal with Luke.

So, while he truly *did* love swimming and had never really analyzed his feelings about kids, the dull ache in his chest made him wonder if the whole swim coach thing really was the best idea.

Melissa explained to the parents that he and the other trainees were there to observe but would help out when needed. Unlike at The Ruby Room, he was expected to interact with people here, and even just smiling and waving made his nerves prickle.

Smiling and waving would lead to talking, and he had a way of stuffing that up, especially when paired with the pressure to keep things professional. After all, his runaway actions had cost Tiluma a major investor and caused his exit as the Chief Technical Officer. People had quit over his involvement, and his stupid ideas had almost destroyed the entire company.

If he couldn't hold it together in an adult environment, what chance did he have with a bunch of parents and children? No doubt, he'd end up offending someone.

Class started, and the parents held their children at chest level in a circle. Melissa sang a version of "Wheels on the Bus", instructing the parents to dip their babies in and out of the water, encouraging them to splash or blow bubbles on the surface. Next came counting to three, then dumping cups of water over the babies' heads, all while saying, "blink" in an attempt to train the babies to close their eyes when submerged.

Much shrieking followed, and by this point, Max's face hurt from his fake smile. One kid in particular was not loving the class. He appeared to be around eighteen months, and things didn't improve when the same boy's dad thrust him into Max's hands, citing a need to take the boy's older brother to the bathroom.

Max's mouth hung open as the dad waded toward a four-year-old doing a cross-legged wriggle on the pool's edge, the scrunch-faced toddler in Max's arms escalating from shrieking into slapping Max's chest in clear terror.

He tried to join the class in the dad's absence but had no idea what to do to calm the kid lumped onto him, so he followed his instincts and made a little *sh-sh-shhh* sound.

The shrieking stopped, and the blond-headed toddler stared gape-mouthed into Max's eyes, as if fascinated with his unfamiliar face, as well as the shushing. Well, at least until the little blighter widened his eyes, perhaps finally clocking that his dad was gone.

The kid let out his biggest screech yet and swung a fast right hook into Max's chin. Max reeled back, pain radiating from his jaw to the rest of his face.

Despite his young age, the toddler weighed about as much as a small bulldog and had the meaty build to match. The strength of his punch suggested he had a promising future in swimming. Or shot put. Or ring fighting…

Max wanted to rub at his still-throbbing jaw but couldn't because of the gigantic toddler in his arms.

"Max, would you and Alfie be the first to go through the arch?" Melissa smiled sweetly, though the strain of her cheeks told him to focus and get his shit together.

She held a large, flexible flotation board, about the size of a small mattress, against the pool's edge until it bent upward in an arch. From watching previous classes, he knew he'd have to walk backward through the arch, floating Alfie on his back, all while Melissa sprinkled water from a toy watering can onto the child's upturned face.

"Sure can." Max glanced at the other parents, doing the expected thing and hooking his fingers under Alfie's armpits, ready to lean him back so his head rested on Max's shoulder.

Except the kid seemed to know what was coming, because he flailed around, gripping at Max's shirt and scratching at whatever exposed skin he could dig his little talons into. It was a near miracle Alfie didn't draw blood, which would have forced Max out of the pool, though that would mean an instant escape.

So much for Alfie's bright swimming career.

A mum with tight red curls leaned closer and whispered, "Alfie hates floating on his back. The best his dad manages is to cuddle him and walk him through the arch instead."

Max nodded his thanks for the advice, before doing just that and turning Alfie in for a cuddle.

The toddler stopped beating Max up, opting to push away with his chubby arms, his head flopping back, like he decided Max stank of trash and garlic—or maybe garlic-infused trash. Either way, Max had no idea what thoughts ran through this kid's brain, except he was glad when they finally made it through the arch.

Alfie snapped out of his flop pose and swung his massive head forward like an airborne boulder, his forehead cracking into Max's nose.

Instant agony seared through Max's face, and he stumbled back, almost tossing the child in the air but catching himself just before he did that.

He pried a hand free and clutched at his nose, certain there'd be blood. Okay, no blood, but a strong pressure built in his sinuses, and before he could stop, a loud sneeze broke free.

Alfie shrieked, startling Max. Mostly because, for once, this shriek involved laughter.

"Oh." Max smiled at Alfie. "You like that, huh?"

Alfie tipped his head forward, attempting another head-butt.

Max ducked out of the way and gave Alfie a pretend sneeze instead.

More laugh-shrieking. Max kept sneezing and Alfie kept laughing —so much so he didn't notice when Max hooked his fingers under the boy's armpits and maneuvered him onto his back.

Every time Alfie looked around, threatening to cry, Max simply sneezed.

They got through the arch a second time, and all the other parents smiled in silence, as though cautious any cheers might break the magic Max and Alfie had going.

Max passed Alfie through the arch again and again, and eventually, Alfie didn't need the sneezes to distract him. He just simply floated, his head supported on Max's shoulder and Max's hands around the boy's ribcage. Melissa even sprinkled water on the toddler's face, and he merely gave an appropriate giggle, spraying the droplets that landed on his lips with a noisy *"brrr."*

Alfie's dad re-entered the water, and he patted Max on the shoulder, his expression lifted in a big smile. "That was amazing. I've been trying to get him to float on his back for months."

Max handed Alfie over, unexpectedly sad to let him go. "I guess I took a beating, and he decided I deserved a little pity."

Alfie's dad laughed, giving the kid a playful nudge on the chin. "That sounds just like Alfie."

Melissa threw Max two thumbs-up and moved the group onto a new exercise. For the first time ever in a professional setting, he enjoyed the light sensation of having not messed up.

After the class ended, he took a quick shower and got changed, soon heading to the exit to find Freya waiting for him. For once, she didn't wear one of her flare-dresses and instead donned a pair of sweat pants. Lumped at her feet was a huge camping bag.

# Chapter Nineteen

Freya trudged over the wet ground, the tall gumtrees around her emitting a smoky-damp scent, the earthy smell from the soil strong and strangely calming.

She turned to Max beside her. "Is it true that male kangaroos can be really territorial and attack anyone who crosses their path?"

"I don't know." He shrugged, his breaths a light pant from the effort of lugging the majority of their stuff. "You're the Aussie, you tell me."

She tugged her backpack higher onto her shoulder and walked farther in silence.

The Ruby Room would be closed for a couple of days while her promised stage repairs occurred. Meanwhile, Max would be exposing her to the supposed joys of camping. Though given the current conversation, she wasn't so sure this whole camping thing was such a good idea after all.

"So, ah, tell me again why your brother has a spare block of bushland in Roseford?"

Max's eyes squinted against the glare from the pale gray clouds. "It's not a block per se, more like… an estate. Impressive, right? There's a main house and a smaller cabin just down the road from where we parked."

A flash of lightness spread through her body. "Ooh, does that mean we can spend the rest of the night under an actual roof if I pike out of this whole 'sleeping under the stars' business?"

Then again, Luke had already done so much to accommodate her camping dreams, lending them the use of these grounds, as well as his four-wheel drive since Max's Tesla probably wouldn't cut it with all the rough roads and needing to be charged and all. Maybe seeking to use Luke's house would be pushing her luck.

Max gave her a sidelong stare, his brow pressed into a straight line, as if to say, "You're joking, right?"

No, actually, she wasn't.

Just because she'd grown up in Australia didn't mean the bush didn't scare the absolute hell out of her. If not for the fact that nine out of the world's top ten most venomous snakes lived here, then because the venomous spiders weren't much better. And then there were those ill-tempered kangaroos.

And if not for the snakes and spiders and kangaroos, then for the creepy-as-fuck local folklore, from ghosts to indigenous bush spirits who gobbled up children who ventured too close to the rivers.

And if not for snakes, spiders, kangaroos, and freaky-ass ghosts, then because ever since she'd blurted out her desire to go camping, she'd doubted whether Max was the right man for the job.

Not because she didn't trust him to wrestle a snake or kangaroo for her, but because there was something indefinable about her connection with him. Something that made her believe this trip wouldn't end well. If for no other reason than they were at different points in their lives, and perhaps it would be safer to keep their relationship purely casual.

*I should have just stayed in the city.*

She turned to him again, with his backpack on his shoulders and a long, foldable tent strapped atop that pack. He also held a duffel with supplies in one hand and a rolled-up mattress in the other; his face tilted down, shoulders rounded, his shaggy blond waves spilling over his eyes.

"You know." She smiled as she spoke, her heart surging at the ambition of what she planned to admit. "I caught the end of that swim class you were in."

His head flicked up, his gaze locking to hers. "Oh, yeah?"

She let her smile grow, recalling his quiet air of vulnerability just seconds ago. "You did really well with that gigantor toddler."

He let out a laugh. "The scratches on my shoulders from that 'gigantor toddler' tell a different story. My nose is still recovering from his headbutt, too."

"Well, I don't see any bruises, so all's well that ends well."

A laugh bubbled through her, and she thought it best to let him know the truth of her observation. Ever since he'd come to her for a job, self-doubt seemed to be his default emotion, and she wanted to give him something to be proud of.

"I mean, for a second there I was sure you would pitch the kid across the pool, but you recovered well and won him over. Max, you have a knack. You made that kid adore you."

*Really? Just the kid?*

*Shut up brain, just shut up!*

She made a point of watching Max, his attention still on the ground, though she swore his posture straightened just a little.

"Thanks."

"I mean." She toyed with her ring, the one with the swirling silver and deep-set ruby, unable to hold back a joke at his expense. "He also looked like you, so that was weird."

He turned to her with a quizzical look. "Weird? How?"

"Well, it was like a freaky glimpse into your future."

He shook his head as though he didn't understand.

She groaned, sorry she'd said anything. Suddenly the joke seemed on her. "As in, if you ever had a kid, they'd look a lot like the one you were tossing about today. In fact, they'd probably act like the one you were holding, too. No doubt you were a knockdown, drag out toddler back in the day."

A new light entered his eyes, his expression lifting along with his smile. "I wish I remembered that far back, but you're probably right. Just like that kid, I had an older brother to rough house with, too."

The sounds of a rushing river, made fat from the recent rain, grew louder, and he swung his attention forward, his long strides making it hard for her to keep up. "And what were you like as a child?"

Her muscles seized for the briefest moment before she forced them to relax, and her well-tuned ability to save face kicked in.

She dug out a wicked tone. "Trust me, you wouldn't want to know."

Max laughed, hopefully fooled into thinking her statement had more to do with her getting up to all kinds of childhood silliness, and not because she'd been too terrified to engage in much childish *anything*.

The only upside to all this talk about children was that he hadn't yet grilled her about whether she wanted any. For some reason, she decided he wouldn't like her answer.

He stopped and dropped his duffel bag to the ground, the river bed about twenty feet away. "Right, this looks like a good spot to set up."

She peered about her, unable to find a full breath.

There were no signs of civilization nearby. She had no idea what a "good spot" looked like. All she had was her limited trust in the man beside her and that he'd get her through the night in the wilderness alive.

She let go of her bag, and it made a dull thud at her feet, her silence a sign of something she rarely gave willingly. Compliance.

Over the next few hours, Freya endured a crash course in outdoor living, and to her credit, she adapted well enough. She helped Max set up the tent, which wasn't all that hard since the thing pretty much popped up the second it was pulled out of its bag. And since there'd been rain, he insisted on trekking to the main house for dry firewood and kindling.

Of course, she flat out refused to let him go alone, not when she'd have to stay at the tent on her own. So, she followed him, making a concerted effort not to stray more than a couple of meters away, lest some snake or kangaroo jump out at her, or worse, a snake-flinging kangaroo. *Ekk!*

She shuddered at that possibility now, the flickering campfire before her lighting up the night, her belly full from the sausages and chili beans Max had cooked. He'd even gone to the effort of bringing a bag of marshmallows so she could have her first ever campfire toasted marshmallow on a stick… Not that she'd let on it was her first.

Her initial attempt fell into the fire, her second burned to an inedible crisp, but she got the hang of toasting marshmallows by the third try—the hot, sticky treat a comforting contrast to her cold, murky surrounds. She didn't even mind that Max switched between laughter and soft lingering stares throughout her entire awkward experience.

"It's probably about time we got some sleep." He slapped at a mosquito perched on his bare forearm, but the wily insect escaped. "What do you think?"

She nodded, silently refusing to move until he did.

With night here, and this being an unfamiliar and isolated location, her hands had already turned clammy. Getting a full and easy breath proved impossible. "Do we just leave the fire on?"

He turned for the tent. "Yeah. It'll burn itself out."

She shot up and chased after him, wondering if he noticed her extra clingy reactions.

Once inside the tent, he switched on a dim battery-powered lantern, which helped to slow her heartbeat a little. Not enough to quell her dashed hopes over not finding the peace she'd expected within the tent's cozy confines.

Max lay down and held his blue wool blanket open for her. She didn't waste time scrambling in next to him, his arms soon encircling her again; her racing heart slowed another degree.

He switched the tent lantern off, and her pulse shot to an instant gallop. Slow moments passed, while she tried to find calm, but the silence and darkness suffocated. Her skin prickled at every unidentifiable sound from outside.

She cleared her throat, deciding the best remedy for silence was talking.

"Have you ever noticed how in space sci-fi TV shows, no one ever wears shorts?"

She barely recognized the stiff and hollow tone she used, but just like her clinging, hopefully Max didn't notice.

He slid his hand to her tummy and rubbed a spot just above her belly button. The gesture should have comforted, but for some reason she found herself stifling a need to shiver. "What do you mean?"

"Like"—she shifted against him a little, trying to play casual—"no matter how warm it is on these other planets, no matter how advanced these supposed space travelers are meant to be, they haven't worked out how to make themselves comfortable on a hot day. What's with all the turtle-neck sweaters and pants? It's pretty much neck-to-toe clothes everywhere."

Max chuckled against her ear, the soft rumble producing the smallest bloom of warmth within her. "Maybe they evolved some kind of internal cooling system. Or their full-length clothes are made of some advanced cooling fabric?"

She blinked into the darkness. So much for her stalling. In one quick statement, he'd killed her attempt at keeping him awake.

"I don't want to have children."

The words shot from her lips before she could stop them. Where the statement came from, she had no idea.

She scrunched her face and mumbled a frustrated, "fuck."

In her hurry to think of something else to say, she'd picked the one conversation she didn't want to have, much less with someone she most definitely didn't want to have kids with, largely because he wasn't anything more than her current, casual sleeping partner.

"Ahhh…" Max pressed his fingers to her arm and tugged back a little, rolling her so he could talk to her face-to-face, even though the tent was pitch black inside.

She locked her muscles, refusing to move.

"Why are you telling me this?"

She blinked into the darkness and shook her head. "I don't know. Forget I said anything."

"Freya." He nudged at her arm again. "I didn't want to say anything, but you've been jittery all day, and you're acting even weirder now. Are you scared of the dark or something?"

Oh hell, he *had* noticed. Now she'd have to threaten to break his legs, so he wouldn't tell everyone at The Ruby that she was a huge wimp.

She shook her head again, denying her fear, the pillow beneath her rustling, just as a human-meets-animal screech broke through the night.

She sat bolt upright. Her blood rushed fast in her veins like it wanted out, all while a sharp pain grew in the center of her chest, making her want to cry from sheer, overwhelming terror.

Maybe more than most people, she hated being afraid. She'd had enough fear to last her five lifetimes, and she couldn't bear this, couldn't bear the powerlessness and the sense of some unknown danger just waiting to hurt her.

Max crawled forward and reached for the tent zip, the one leading to the outside world where vicious night creatures stalked and roamed. "It's probably just a possum. I'll go outside and have a look, if—"

"No. Don't," she yelled, lunging after him, her fingers latching to the back of his t-shirt while she pulled him back.

In her head, some mythical river beast with lion's feet and pointy bull horns waited out there ready to gore Max's guts out. And when that beast was done with him, well, it'd no doubt turn its beady, red eyes on her.

"Please. Just. Don't go out there, okay? Turn the damn lantern back on and don't you dare leave me here alone."

# Chapter Twenty

Fear ran like ice water through Freya's veins, and her high-pitched scream for Max to stay reverberated through the tent, unrecognizable from any tone she'd used before. Worse still, she had no idea where this fear came from, only that this uncontrollable environment did not agree with her.

"Freya, what's wrong?"

Max's question made her skin outright burn, while sweat trickled down her back. She wanted to answer, but her thoughts refused to slow long enough for her to find a reply. Even just the idea of telling him her real problem made her tongue dry and her words dissipate.

The lantern came back on, and Max sat beside it. As much as the light soothed her, it surely also made the fear on her face even more visible, too.

There'd be no way to cover this up. She would be forced to admit to being a victim of her emotions.

"Freya?" His tone held a husky edge, one that opened a pit in her belly and rocked her resistance even further.

She slammed her eyes shut, pressing her hands to her face. "I've never done this before, okay? This whole camping thing. I really wanted to enjoy it, but I... I don't know why. It's just too overwhelming and weird, and that overwhelm is playing mind games with me."

"Okay."

His voice slowed, so soft and gentle, and something light fluttered in her tummy. Whatever that fluttering was, it pulled her nerves closer to snapping, like maybe she'd handle it better if he just called her a wimp and told her to suck it up and go to sleep.

"We don't have to stay. We can head back to the hous—"

"No." She waved her hands out in front of her, subjecting this poor man to yet more erratic behavior. *Damn it.* Why couldn't she get her body and mind to calm the fuck down? For someone who dealt with feral drunk people on a regular basis, her current meltdown didn't make much sense. "No. I'm not going out there again and neither are you, got it? You stay here. Right here."

Not only did she not want something to happen to him—like an encounter with a lion-footed, bullhorn beast—but she figured she'd probably self-combust from pure terror if she stepped outside and tried to trek to the house.

And even if she did give up and go back to the house, there'd still be the awkward drive home tomorrow. She couldn't pike out and let fear win, even if that meant holding Max to ransom in this tent.

She turned to him. "I'm such a fucking idiot. I'm so sorry."

His gaze shifted about her face, like he worked double-time to understand her. "Everyone gets scared some—"

"No. No. You can't honestly say my reaction right now is normal." And sure thing, she didn't deserve his understanding because, even as she spoke, she struggled to control her wildly animated hands, as though the active movement kept her from flipping out completely.

"Well, no, I gu—"

"Because while little kid Max Tindall was off pitching tents and getting over his fear of night creatures, I was… I was…" She paused a second and a cold shiver ran down her spine. "Let's just say I wasn't doing that."

His pupils grew into expansive black pools surrounded by cerulean blue; a picture of innocence, or maybe ignorance, since he'd lived a charmed life far different from hers. "What do you mean?"

His innocent-ignorance had her teeth clenching, and a renewed heat seared through her chilled veins. "As a kid, I never went camping, okay? Hell, I barely even made it to school."

His jaw went slack, and his cheeks hollowed as a result. She swore the color drained from his skin, while his unblinking stare seemed to say, "I hear you, but I don't understand."

A growl formed in her throat, and she shot to standing, as much as one could stand in a small tent. So really, she just hunched, while hot tears stung the back of her eyes.

"Fuuucck!" She pressed her face into the nook of her arm, damned if she cried now, resorting to the next best thing that would keep her from tears. *Swearing.*

"Fuck. Fuck… Fuck. Fuck. Fuck."

She spun around to find Max's mouth even more agape, his attention darting around the tent and giving the impression he wanted to be anywhere but here.

"I'm sorry. This is only getting worse." She smacked her palm to her forehead over and over again, waiting for a clear thought to surface.

*Should I tell him about what happened to me? What would I lose if I did? What would I gain?*

Nothing. The answer was nothing.

Speaking up was a bloody stupid idea.

She gave Max her direct stare, certain of one thing amongst all this havoc. "I'm not talking. You don't deserve the misery of my sob story."

"Well, that's a bit harsh." He tucked his chin in and frowned, his inquisitive stare making her feel as though even just alluding to her tragic backstory made her look erratic. "Besides, maybe now that you are talking, I want to know whatever it is you don't want to tell me."

Stillness took her over, and her hands dropped to either side. The reality of this conversation and why she didn't want to have it hit her.

"It'll change things between us."

Her voice sounded small even to her ears. She couldn't seem to pry her attention from the beautiful man seated before her, his expression open, and his whole demeanor way too quiet and accepting of her rant. "What if I promise not to let it?"

Her adrenaline from earlier fled, and her knees turned weak. She plonked down onto the air-filled mattress.

"I don't think that's possible. You'll backtrack away, or the truth will kill pretty much all excitement in this relationship. You'll start acting weird and feeling sorry for me. Or you'll get all strange and mushy, or worse, the second things aren't going well, you'll use the truth to hurt me."

Her gaze fell to the blue wool blanket all crumpled in the space between them, her thoughts sticking on the times she'd experienced every one of those scenarios. One of so many reasons why she rarely talked about her childhood.

"I'd like to think I wouldn't do any of that." He dropped his attention to the same blue blanket she'd been eyeing, his hands resting on his knees like he took a second to think. "I don't know what I'm dealing with here. You know, I'm fine with you not telling me." He peered up at her, a tiny smile curling his lips. "I understand."

His barely perceptible smile lingered, which only seemed to deepen the ensuing silence. She crossed her arms over her chest, and her muscles stiffened from the uncertainty of what to do or say next.

The silence should have helped. While it did buy her a minute to think without suffering through further bouts of verbal diarrhea, the lack of sound coiled the growing tension within her tighter and tighter.

Maybe she didn't owe him an explanation.

No, not maybe. She *definitely* didn't owe him one.

Her past struggles weren't just difficult to retell, they were downright exhausting.

Traumatic.

But then, he'd seen her rant and rave and accepted both. He handled her nonsensical reaction way better than she expected.

Maybe he would be different from most people…

After all, he'd let her drag him all the way out to the bush, just so she could enjoy this one normal thing pretty much every other kid experienced. Only she wasn't enjoying herself, and certainly not in any kind of normal way.

And now, the poor guy just sat there with a twisted smile, a tortured soul unsure of the reasons for his torture.

She threw her hands into the air and released a growl. "Okay. Fine. I'll tell you, but if you can't handle this in any kind of decent way, we're off, okay? You go back to being an employee at the bar. We definitely don't keep sleeping together. And we never, *ever* speak of this again. Understand?"

<h1 style="text-align:center">Chapter Twenty-One</h1>

Freya waited as Max sat taller and his eyes brightened, offering her a quick nod to continue, to share the details of her past and the reasons for her fear right now. His swift reaction hinted relief because she'd decided to trust him, but she wasn't quite done with setting her rules.

"Regardless of what you think of me next, you can never tell anyone a word of what I'm about to say. Got it?"

He gave another easy nod.

She eyed him a beat longer, no burning suspicions creeping in. So, she crossed her legs beneath her and readied to tell her story.

"I've never been camping because I was too busy just trying to survive my childhood." She scowled down at her red-tipped fingers caressing the wool blanket. "There was my mum and her issues, and then there were the years I spent in and out of hospital."

Max shifted in front of her, but she refused to look at him.

"Wait. You were sick?"

She shrugged like what she had to say meant nothing these days, but then she couldn't make eye contact, so maybe that was one massive lie. "Sort of. My dad left us when I was six and my little brother, Clay, was three. He left to be with another woman, and my mother blamed us more than she did herself. And I, being a girl, bore the brunt of that blame. My mother was raised to believe that girls were always the lesser of two options, an expensive burden, so of course she doted on my brother."

Wind howled outside the tent, flapping and pushing the walls in slight arcs toward her. She paused her story to flick her gaze at the rippling fabric, her stomach giving a sick flutter.

"Clay, he got the best of everything, while I was lucky to get whatever was left. I don't recall Mum ever freely giving me a single genuine hug, much less buying me clothes that weren't already well-aged from a second-hand shop. Meanwhile, Clay got all the brand new, branded stuff. And as often as she could, she pitted Clay and I against each other. School grades, popularity, looks, sports… You name it. Everything except chores, which were all mine, because boys don't need to know how to clean a dish or do a load of laundry, right?"

"Freya."

Max's voice dipped, but she frowned, glaring down at her nails again.

"Mum's temper had always been wild and unpredictable, and I'd already learned to moderate my behavior based on what mood she woke up in—play if she was happy, run and hide in a cupboard if she wasn't. And mostly, she wasn't. But something truly broke in her after my dad left. The shame consumed her so much she couldn't even admit to what happened, that he'd found someone else, so she deflected all that anger onto her children. Or should I say, me? Dad's leaving was all my fault."

She took a second to peer up at Max, at the two deep lines scoring the gap between his brows, his stare unwavering. She wanted to crawl forward, to land in his arms, but then she'd have no hope of finishing what she had to say, so she cleared her throat and pressed on.

"I recognized from an early age that Mum was damaged, but after Dad left, it was less about her inherent need to dominate and more about her reports of constant poor health. All she ever talked about to other adults was her doctor's visits and how she was dying. I don't know, maybe that just deflected her having to talk about the divorce. As messed up as our relationship already was, because of my mum's unwillingness to shelter me from her medical stuff, I developed a genuine fear that at any point I could lose the only parent left to me.

"I mean, sure, sometimes we'd get to visit Dad, but still, those years came with the sense that at any moment my mother could die, and my world would come crashing down. I lived on permanent edge. Except back then, I never accounted for how important my dad's occasional presence was. Not until I was ten, and he and his new wife died in a car accident."

Max parted his lips and then closed them again, as if he wanted to say something but thought better of it. She gifted him a few seconds of her direct attention.

"It's okay, you don't have to come up with anything insightful."

She smiled at him, and his shoulders sank by an inch or two, like maybe he appreciated her observation over his struggle to find the right thing to say at times.

"Anyway, after that, the wheels truly did fall off my childhood. Mum knew she had all the power and control over my life, and very little accountability. There'd be few close relatives to interfere or check in with us."

She paused to take a big breath and close her eyes, a dull ache growing in her chest, those old memories pressing on her shoulders. Only the outside river sounds and Max's mere presence brought her any calm.

"I don't understand." His gentle tone cut her like a sharp blade. "What did she do?"

Freya opened her eyes and went back to staring at the blanket, fingertips shifting the tiny, soft fibers while she weighed up how much to reveal.

Whatever she did say wouldn't come easy, and pangs of pain and humiliation clawed at her insides, reminding her of all she'd endured and escaped.

*Not that someone with a story like mine ever truly escapes.*

There were all the lies she'd been raised to believe. The ones about herself. That she was unlovable and the source of everything bad in her mother's life.

Those lies bubbled up to haunt her, doing their worst on the days she felt her lowest, and sometimes on good days, when a hard-won victory could fill her mouth with bitterness and the dreadful sense that she might one day return to her old hell.

No good experience felt real, not for long, anyway. And the scars she sought to cover sat exposed for all to see.

And then there were the times she wished she had a different story.

That she had a family like Max's.

One with two loving parents and siblings on equal footing.

The kind of family that acknowledged each other's specialness. That each person mattered.

The kind of family that went on camping trips.

She tugged at her black woolen sweater sleeves and pulled them over her hands, releasing those aching thoughts.

"I started getting sick. Just like my mum, but worse." Her tummy churned, maybe a form of muscle memory from her days of unrelenting illness, or maybe the roil of pure shame over how bad things had been, much less having to relive that story now. "I couldn't keep my food down most days, started losing weight. Sometimes I'd throw fevers, and this would go on for weeks and months at a time."

Her focus broke at a small screech coming from outside, perhaps some kind of bush rodent. Max reached out a hand and patted her knee, his thumb stroking warm circles through her cotton leggings.

For the sake of getting on with her story, she decided to let this screech go.

"This all lasted two years, and no one could figure it out. I just kept getting sicker and sicker, and new symptoms would appear. All in all, I looked skeletal and lacked energy, I barely ever made it to school. Not that my absence mattered much. I'd lost all my friends from poor attendance, and as someone entering their teens, the gray and bony look took a sledgehammer to my confidence. I didn't feel attractive. I wasn't social. I was behind academically. Even when there were phases where I'd be fine, I still had nothing and no place I belonged.

"Home was depressing, school was a place to feel stupid, ugly, and lonely. Though strangely enough, during that time, my mum's happiness improved. Clay would be at school, and it would be just me and her at my hospital appointments. She was super doting, and when it came to her, it felt to me like the sun had finally come out from behind a cloud. For that short time, she really seemed to care. I thought that maybe—just maybe—she really did love me."

She gave a tight laugh down toward Max's hand on her knee. "I guess, what with her losing her support payments after Dad's death, only for my illness to gather extra help from charities and government payments for her as my carer, she no longer had to continue her job as a dental assistant. So for that reason alone, I gave her a lot to love."

Her grim smile slipped, and she replaced it with a deep frown. "At one point, I saw her talking to the hospital chaplain. She was dabbing at her eyes with a tissue and making plans for my funeral arrangements. You know, what coffin to pick, which funeral home to use…"

A sharp pain stirred within her, and she snapped her gaze back to Max again, needing to break from that memory, only for his pure physical beauty and undivided attention to rip a hole through her all over again.

"Before I tell you anything more, you should know about my mother's childhood. She grew up in an isolated, rural area during the fifties where the abuse she encountered was easy to hide." She cringed to herself, that same shifting pain in her turning even more distinct. That a child could be born into the life her mother had. "She was beaten regularly, left hungry, her education patchy at best since she'd been mostly taken out of school to work on her parents' farm. Again, because she was a girl, no one saw a point in her having an education. She had eight other siblings, and although she was put to work at an early age, she was also just another mouth to feed.

"I've done a lot of reading up on psychology over the years, trying to understand everything that happened. One thing I've learned is that children's brains can be like cement, and you only have so long before their idea of 'normal' is set forever. Neither of my mother's parents held or kissed her. No one told her she was loved. From the moment she was born, she had no chance. Abuse and neglect were her normal, and her parents slowly but surely destroyed her spirit. I think about that little girl. I think about her a lot. Someone so small and in need of help, only for that help to arrive far too late."

Max's hand tightened around her knee, bringing her attention back to him. His open expression said that he hung on her every word.

"Freya, what are you telling me?"

"That when I say my *grandparents*, I mean the ones who adopted my mother, not my piece-of-shit biological ones who sent her and three other siblings to an orphanage when she was thirteen. That by the time she was adopted, the damage was done. That those same adoptive parents, the ones I consider my real grandparents, were the ones who saved me, too."

# Chapter Twenty-Two

Freya took a deep inhale and tried to use that breath to cushion the hollow sensation opening up inside her, the fire's strong, smoky scent permeating the tent walls and filling her senses. She wanted to stop talking, to keep the rest of her story to herself, but speaking about her past was too rare and validating, the pressure of what she constantly carried easing a little inside.

"That being said, long before I was born, my grandparents had stepped right out of my mother's life. She'd taken a toll on them too, and they really only managed a few occasional visits, and by occasional, like, every few years. And one of those visits fell around about the time I turned twelve."

She peered down, twisting the blue blanket laid out beneath her, that twisting somehow representative of how she felt about that day; her attempt at distraction not enough to make her forget Max's presence, as though she never needed to see him to feel him nearby.

"I guess they must have taken one look at me in my bed and suspected something I hadn't, because my grandad kept my mum busy in the kitchen, while my grandma talked to me alone in my room. I was old enough to notice the leading questions she kept asking: Whether my mother was giving me anything the doctors didn't know of, whether my mother hit me or had maybe scared me into covering for any lies. At the time, I denied everything because truly I'd never witnessed anything outside of my mother's usual yelling and mean-spiritedness. And again, I got more attention compared to my earlier years, so in a messed-up way, I thought my life had improved."

The muscles in her throat grew thick, and the heavy and familiar sense of shame over that day crept in. How she'd been so protective of her mother. How she'd been annoyed at her grandmother's persistence and what she implied…

"And even if those questions did make me think twice, I'd never known any other kind of love. And though I now know what my mother gave me wasn't actual love, at the time, I loved her fiercely enough to not want to let go of the more even-keeled mother I'd gained while I'd been sick. I simply figured she thrived away from her former job and, as my caregiver, that was what our relationship had needed all along."

"You were like a seed in need of water."

She flicked her gaze up to catch his softened smile, one that bent at the corners, not exactly happy with where this was going, but offering support all the same.

"Your mother essentially left you outside, in need of rain, so of course you drank up whatever she gave you."

She pulled her focus off him and back to the blanket, trying hard not to blink because his words cut her to the core and gathered tears in her eyes. Max Tindall wasn't meant to be insightful, but here he was, absolutely right.

She'd so wanted to believe her mother's heart had changed. That she'd really come to love and care for her daughter. That her sole motivation hadn't been the sympathy and attention she received as the mother of a seriously sick child.

But sympathy and attention *were* love to her mother, a woman who'd received neither, as well as no love.

And while a young Freya had thought her days of being ignored and discarded had ended, that belief had proved near fatally wrong.

"Anyway." She cleared her throat, wanting to get through her story, somehow feeling lighter and more damaged at the same time. "For the next two weeks, I made sure not to eat the food my mum prepared for me. I snacked on crackers hidden at the back of my wardrobe and snuck raw vegetables from the fridge into my room. I ate all those when she wasn't looking. Of the food she did prepare, I'd just pretend to feel too sick to eat, or I'd only take meals in my room where I could later flush them down the toilet under the guise of having thrown up. Some meals I secretly buried at the bottom of our trash can."

A jagged laugh broke from her lips. "I started to improve after the first week, and by the second week I felt pretty much normal, all while I pretended to feel as bad as ever. And then one Wednesday, my mum left for her usual trip to take Clay to school, her weekly shopping trip always after that. I knew she'd be gone for a while and searched the house until I found a mortar and pestle tucked in the back of a top kitchen cupboard. Nestled in the bowl was a blister-pack still half-full of pills."

The hard muscle over Max's cheekbones fell, and his posture deflated right along with them. "Freya. She was poisoning you? I can't—"

*Believe it?*

She held up a hand, shaking her head. "Please, I know, but let me finish. This story gets worse before it gets better."

Despite the forewarning, she still didn't want his sympathy. Still felt small and insignificant every time that day entered her mind.

She'd been a child. One who hadn't known better, and still, she felt shame.

"I didn't see her walk in behind me. I was too busy reading the pill packet, trying so hard to memorize the bloody long name, when the stool I was standing on gave way beneath me. Well, 'gave way' isn't the right term, more like my mum kicked the stool out from under my feet."

She lifted her hand and rubbed a spot within her hair, where the ancient tile counter had cleaved into her head a couple of inches from her hairline.

"I lay on the ground, blood gushing from my head, but she didn't care. Every lie she'd sold to the world about my illness had just unraveled. I'd ruined that lie for her, and so she flew into an intense rage.

She beat me with closed fists while I was down, blows landing on my ribs and tummy, like even in her rage she knew not to leave injuries in any visible areas. I tried to curl into a ball, to make myself small. I was so stunned, and I struggled to breathe. I couldn't even find the space to cry."

A tremor took over her hand, and not from the cold, though she pressed her fingertips to her cheek so she might ease the shaking.

"She… she just kept yelling about how I'd ruined everything. How I'd destroyed her life just by being born. I was nothing to her but the money my fake illness brought in. Her words and her rage hurt more than the blows. That rage terrified me, and I can still remember the foam forming at the corners of her mouth as she yelled and yelled."

Freya stopped to catch her breath, to allow a moment for those last words to sink in. *Again.*

"I thought she'd kill me."

"Freya. Take another second." Max scrambled forward, pausing a moment to grab a flask of water from beside the bed, which he then unscrewed and extended her way. "Here, drink."

She accepted the flask and sipped at the cool water, the strain in her body lightening if only just a little. Her gaze fell to Max, and the painful shiver playing havoc with her nerves turned to a warm and settled appreciation.

"Are you okay to continue?" His pinched gaze skated over her face, cheeks slack in clear concern. "You can stop if this is too much."

He reached out, as if about to cup her cheek; but she caught his hand, having reached the limit of sweet gestures she could take right now.

"Just as quickly as my mother had flipped into a rage, she stopped and fell to her knees on the floor before me. She started shaking her head over and over, rambling and rationalizing everything she'd just done. How seeing me up on the stool had scared her. How now I had a choice. I could destroy our family, destroy the money I brought in, or I could continue to play along, and everything could go on as normal.

"She stared at me, the pill packet in her hand, and that's when an explosion went off where my heart should have been. Like something finally broke inside. Something I'd spent years attempting to hold together. I started sobbing then, so hard, I couldn't stop. The jerking added more pain to my already bruised ribs, and the tears fell so fat and fast down my cheeks, watery pools formed on the beige linoleum floor. It was this suspended moment of just her and me, and of course, the choice she expected me to make."

# Chapter Twenty-Three

Freya couldn't blame Max for the ashen hue overrunning his cheeks, his pupils wide like he absorbed every word but struggled to believe any of it. She wasn't the kind to wear her heart on her sleeve—had built her life around fun and quirkiness—on being the epitome of lavish femininity and independence with nothing dry or serious to drag her down. So of course, her grim confession didn't fit with the woman he knew.

The rustle of leaves rushed from outside the tent, the tall and spindly mountain ash gumtrees emitting their dark scent, while cicadas chirped in all directions.

She gave a shrug and recalled her mother sitting across from her in that kitchen, her hard stare cold, unmoving, and demanding an answer —Freya could keep the pills and her guaranteed sickness a secret, or rat her mother out and tear her family apart, along with her mother's happiness.

Freya squeezed her fingers around Max's larger palm and forced herself to maintain eye contact, once more owning the decision she'd made all those years ago. "I chose the pills."

Max sucked in a low breath, his pale cheeks somehow paling even more.

She'd given the answer he didn't want, but it was her truth, and since she still sat here alive and well, her story clearly wasn't over.

He scrubbed a hand over his face. "I'm not sure I want to hear what happens next, but I know I need to, anyway."

She frowned and nodded. Perhaps more than his desire to know what happened, she wanted to finish what she'd started.

"Aside from dealing with the wound on my head and the agony from the beating, Mum made me take some pills. The vomiting and weakness started within the hour, and not long after that, I couldn't stay upright. So, she called an ambulance, and I lay on the couch while we waited. The whole time, she paced the living room, rambling about the story we'd use to explain my cuts and bruises—something about me feeling sick and fainting and falling down some stairs. Our house didn't have any stairs, but whatever, right?"

She gave a wobbly laugh, but Max just blinked, seemingly frozen in a state of shock. She went on, hoping to put him out of his misery.

"Anyway, at some point she looked at me with this flat stare and demanded I remember how many pills she'd given me. I didn't know. I'd numbly swallowed whatever she'd passed me. It was then she mumbled something about the pills not usually working so quickly, and maybe she'd given me too many."

Max's jaw dropped open, and his hand tightened around hers. She couldn't tell if he offered support or needed it.

Her hand clenched his right back, the action also helping to keep her from touching the small scar near her hairline again. A scar almost no one ever noticed since she covered it with her thick hair and signature headbands. Occasionally, she'd had to answer to those who did notice, always providing a fake story about needing surgery as a child.

But even now, the hot prickling through her body and sinking in her belly reminded her she'd never forget the moment she thought her life really over.

Sure, with her years of precarious health, there'd been many such moments. But it was one thing to face death at the hands of a slow and nondiscriminatory illness, and another at the hands of the woman who'd brought her into the world in the first place.

Mothers were meant to protect and nurture. To love without condition. *Not Freya's.* Her twelve-year-old self had just registered that her mother had never once loved her.

And that's when she came to think of her mum as less "Mum" and more "Kerry". Just a woman. Not a mother. And a fundamentally broken woman at that. Irreparably damaged. Even though Freya would spend years hoping that one day, maybe, just maybe, her mother would develop the ability to care. To love.

That day, watching Kerry rant and pace, Freya made her first ever truly selfish decision. *She would save herself.*

"The doctors and nurses were waiting for us when we got to the hospital. A few already knew me from all my past visits, so soon enough, I had my own bay in the pediatrics emergency ward, my mum glued to my side giving her award-winning rendition of a devastated mother. Of course, she was really just following to make sure I played along."

Freya pulled her hand from Max's and wrapped her arms around her waist, missing his touch, but needing space to get out the rest of what she had to say.

"I peered up at her, weak and in excruciating pain, and she had the balls to say, 'You'll be okay, darling. Mummy will make sure you'll be okay.' And something about that made me so angry, that I might die without anyone knowing what had really happened, that I could never rely on her telling the truth. I started to imagine my funeral and my mother using my death to garner more attention. She'd turn my memory into a farce. I had never been the rebellious type, always sweet and stupidly trusting, but right then I knew, if nothing else, I couldn't give her that final win."

Max's brows rose and a small light entered his expression. "So, you outed her?"

"My mum was busy filling in forms in the waiting area just outside my bay. A nurse I'd met before held my hand, trying to attach some kind of monitor, and I just came right out and whispered, 'Keep my mum away. She's poisoning me. This whole time she's been poisoning me.' I remember the pause, the way the nurse's expression turned slack. I hoped she'd believe me; that she'd understand. That she'd help. My whole life up until then had involved no one caring enough to make any real difference to my shitty existence."

She paused and gripped her hands around her ribcage even tighter, holding back a swell of emotion, one that took up space in her chest and threatened to break out in the form of an untamed cry.

"But this one time, this one time when I needed it most, that nurse squeezed my hand and gave me the softest smile, one that said she would keep me safe."

Her eyes prickled now, and she forced a deep inhalation, her breath shaky and undoubtedly betraying fragility. That nurse had cared enough to kick-start the beginning of Freya's life free from abuse.

"Everything happened so quickly after that. The nurse whispered something to another nurse, who went on to keep my mother busy until security, and then the police, came to take her away. At some point that same day, she confessed to what she'd given me. I later learned the police had threatened to add a murder charge to her list of offenses if I didn't live. I've had lots of therapy since, but one thing that helps is to think of all the people who gathered around me that day, the hospital staff, police. When I eventually recovered, my grandparents took in me and my brother. We didn't have to go into the system."

"And what happened to your mother?"

"She was given a diagnosis of what used to be called *Munchausen by Proxy*, likely influenced by her troubled childhood. The newer name for her condition is now *Factitious Disorder Imposed Upon Another*, but me, I prefer to call it medical child abuse."

"And did she go to prison for what she did?"

"No." She shook her head, Max's shoulders sinking like that wasn't the answer he wanted. "She avoided the maximum prison term in exchange for four years of good behavior and extensive psychological treatments."

The bulk of her story now told, for the longest time, Max merely stared at her, his face mostly still, as though he took time to process everything she'd said. To be fair, she'd shared one hell of a long and harrowing story.

He frowned, his gaze dipping to her hands still around her waist. "Did you ever see your mum again after that?"

She compressed one corner of her lip and gave a small shake of her head. "Her contact with us after that was heavily supervised and mostly only via phone. After the first six months, I guess the novelty wore off, and she'd maybe call once a year."

He nodded, his energy in the tent's close confines so still and quiet. "I can't imagine what living out that childhood must have been like for you, much less sharing it again now. Thank you."

"I don't usually like to tell anyone." The whispered admission slipped free without much thought, and she slumped back, hands releasing from around her. "Sometimes I'm not all that sure if the benefit of talking is worth the cost of dredging up those memories. I was taught I was the problem. My dad left. My mum was a nightmare. I spent years out of touch with my peers, wasting away in my sick bed. I believed there had to be something I couldn't see, something intrinsically wrong with me. Something to make me deserving of the hell I lived. I thought of myself as truly unlovable. And telling others, having them reject me because of my past, only made that unlovability more real."

"Please tell me you don't believe that any more."

She frowned down at her lap. How to explain?

She'd done all the work she possibly could, attended countless mental health appointments and improved greatly, but in the real world, not all honesty was rewarded with kindness. Rejection was a punishment unto itself. One that ingrained the hurtful things she'd been raised to believe.

"I *used* to tell people." She refocused on Max's pinched and imploring stare, feeling impossibly alone sitting within touching distance of him, fighting a desire to lean in and curl up in his arms. "I haven't for years, not since I learned that some less-than-brilliant people will use my past against me. I'd try to bring up an issue I had with them, and they'd use my trauma to label me oversensitive, like my past made me imagine problems that didn't exist, when I was really just asking for some basic respect."

The base of her throat swelled and turned her voice into a rough whisper. "Or worse, when people assume survivors of abuse are forever doomed to become abusers themselves, as if all the hard work I put in counted for nothing. Sometimes the unpredictable reactions just aren't worth getting into it with others, you know?"

Max's beautiful blue stare held hers for a while, and the strain across his face slipped away. He sat with his hand draped over his bent knee, those long fingertips pointed to the ground. "And why are you going there with me?"

His question sent an electrified shock through her veins, maybe because her "going there with him" surprised her, too.

Or maybe she'd hoped to get through this lengthy talk without analyzing her motivations at all.

She bent her head and took a few seconds for herself. As much as she wanted to think of Max as perfect, as much as she wanted to believe his life had thus far been immaculate and easy, that wasn't true.

She saw his everyday self-criticism, his struggle to figure out what exactly made him so passive, and his attempts to pull himself from the consequences of his passivity. She'd also witnessed others discard him and the resulting disappointment.

One key attribute shone above all else.

The *real* reason she liked having him around and why she'd just "gone there" with him.

"Because as much as you think you're a screwup"—a wobbly smile tugged at her lips, and the rigid strain pulling at her chest ebbed to a melting, warm sensation, one that brushed away her ability to restrain any praise—"you're not mean, Max. There's not a mean bone in your body, and to me, that's worth so much more than anything else not working in your life."

# Chapter Twenty-Four

Max clamped his teeth together, fighting his jaw's instinctive need to drop open. Meanwhile, Freya's lips parted, as though she too hadn't expected to say those words.

Her comment about him not having a mean bone in his body stood out as the most significant thing he'd heard about himself in as long as he could remember. The first compliment he sort of believed, one that acknowledged something inherent to his personality, transcending his money, reputation, and his current problems.

What she offered was a raft he could cling to. His first taste of *purpose.*

The only problem? He wasn't all that used to people saying nice things about him. At least, not things that weren't about his looks or his money, both of which he'd done nothing to earn.

He took in the details of Freya's golden-brown eyes, now a burnt treacle color against the lantern's dim light. Her kind words echoed in his head, and the one truth he'd held onto throughout her tragic story fell from him.

"I don't know how anyone could be mean to you."

Her muscles pulled taut for a few seconds, before falling slack, her unblinking stare pinned on him in stunned silence, before a sharp wave of broken laughter escaped her.

She turned from him, seeming to hide from his scrutiny, her flaxen curls obscuring whatever expression marked her face.

A dull ache grew low in his stomach, an ache that spelled hope over pain, suggesting he might have inadvertently reciprocated her gift of saying something she needed to hear, even if she too didn't know how to handle it.

"Thank you." She returned her attention to him, her voice a husky whisper, the whites of her eyes pink-tinged, and her lips bent in a frown, despite her words of gratitude. "The thing about abuse is, it doesn't end when the abuser leaves your life. That's just the start, and there are constant small reminders. Someone says something that's innocent to them but painful for you, or maybe an interaction doesn't go so well and scrubs at your damaged self-worth like a new abrasion over an old scar. And sometimes, even happy moments are drowned under a sense of looming dread."

Her fine-boned hand lay flat atop the dark blue blanket, her painted nails glinting in a contradictory happy shade of red.

He shifted forward and dared to hold her hand again, not all that sure if he offered comfort to himself or to her, only that his awe over her personal strength held him trapped.

"Do you mind if I ask you something else?" He gave an easy smile, hoping to lighten the mood and wanting to help her at the same time. Even if she did seem more than perfectly capable of helping herself. Even if he doubted his own level of grit to handle the intensity this woman carried with her, day in and day out. "I have a hunch, though my hunches do have a reputation of being way off target."

Not only that, he also had a justified reputation for screwing up important conversations. But she'd trusted him and voiced her struggle to talk about her ordeal, and he wanted to offer her some kind relief for sharing her story. He rubbed his thumb over the back of her hand, savoring the silkiness, until she gave a quick nod.

"That sense of looming dread you mentioned"—the muscles around his throat clenched, but he pressed on all the same—"has that been hanging around a lot lately? Is that why this whole camping trip has you spooked?"

Her gaze dropped from his. "Yeah. I guess."

"Has something happened?" He thought back to the first night she'd approached him. "Was it that creeper we dodged outside the bar? Has that experience set you off, maybe?"

"No. At least, I don't think so." She shook her head. "Though maybe at any other time he might have, this has more to do with that morning after you first came to my house. That call I got before I sent you away, was about my mum. She's sick. Dying actually. And I'm the one in charge of tying up all her loose ends."

"You still speak to your mother?"

"No, not really." She released a sigh and pushed her hair from her face, lifting her posture as she did so. "I've tried for a different outcome with her over the years, but each time, it's like holding my hand over an open flame and expecting it not to burn. I know this doesn't make much sense to most people, but I have a lot of guilt about escaping and taking my brother with me. About being the one who well and truly busted our family up. About surviving. About having a better life than her and Clay. I don't want to feel that way, but I do. Mum knows this, and she loves to poke at my guilt, laying the criticisms thick every chance she gets."

His brow turned heavy, and he frowned at Freya. "You didn't 'bust your family up'. *She* did."

Freya rubbed her palm over her forehead and squeezed her eyes shut. "I know. I know. There's not a lot that's logical about this. My only two comforts are that I'm not the only child of abuse to grow up confused, and at least my mum won't be around too much longer to continue this vicious cycle."

He waited until her attention returned to him. "I'm trying to understand. Why put yourself through it all again?"

"Because what was done to her was, to a different extent, done to me and because of that..." She rolled her eyes, her expression more sad than sarcastic. "I understand her."

He wanted to ask her to explain further, though he already had a small hint of what she referred to. So, he stayed quiet, allowing room for her to offer what she wished.

Her attention stayed on him for a beat longer, and she dropped a heavy sigh, shifting in her spot, as if to get comfortable to unleash her reasoning.

"Look, it's the irony of abuse, okay? The crushing of another person's spirit until they believe all the things the abuser imparts. No matter what age or background, no one is immune, as much as some of us would like to believe we are. Manipulation is what my mother does best, what she was inadvertently programmed to do to survive. So was I. Though maybe I turned out differently because I had access to people outside of my messed-up family, at school and in the hospital. I had glimpses of what 'normal' meant away from hearing I was *less*. Less than my brother. Less than my peers. Worth no more than a fortnightly government payment and the attention my mother could get from parading my misery. And want to know the most fucked up thing about all of that?"

She lifted a brow, as if assessing his focus, before her expression faltered and crumbled altogether. "An abused child will love their parents despite the abuse. Any hate is turned in on themselves. The abuse is all their fault. They are not good enough for kindness and love. And those beliefs filled my mum's childhood. They're what she passed on to me. She took her hurt and hurt me, all the while believing my life was an improvement on what she'd had.

"I've experienced first-hand how someone like her is created. And I sit somewhere between wanting to punish her for what she did, and acknowledging she has a mental illness she didn't ask for. Even if it sounds to others like I'm making excuses. Where I sit is my choice. What I know for certain is, she doesn't know any other way, and maybe, the only difference between us is that her experience broke her and mine didn't."

Max's heartbeat plodded under the weight of his inability to know what to do with her words; meanwhile, the muscles over her face hardened, and she spoke again. "Max, unless you've lived this for yourself, you really can't know."

His stomach sank, and the dark truth of that statement pulled him under, a genuine ache surrounding his heart.

He *didn't* know. Which made him want to beat his chest and promise to strip away the layers of confusion and contradiction blanketing this otherwise steadfast woman. To save her.

But she wouldn't want that, would she?

To have someone take on her burdens. To surrender her control.

The least he could do was check she'd be okay.

He pressed on a strained smile and lowered his voice, hoping his tone would match the level of care she deserved. "Have you got anyone looking after you while all of this is happening?"

She remained silent for a while, her focus landing on some far-off point beyond the tent's close confines. "My best friend Gideon knows, but I don't need anyone looking after me. It's not fair to lump my wellbeing onto my friends when I can pay a professional to listen to me if I'm feeling overwhelmed. To be honest, therapy has been the single most useful thing I learned to lean on after they first took me from my mother. I'm lucky to have access to basic mental health care." Her gaze landed on him again, and she gave a light smile. "I'm at a point now where I think I can compartmentalize my relationship with her and dust off any venom she spits my way during the short moments I have to see her."

And still, in spite of her statement, the precariousness of her situation with her mother had his spine stiffening. Like one misdirected push would send that whole relationship tumbling down, and more alarmingly, taking Freya's wellbeing with it.

He schooled his face as much as he could, working hard not to betray skepticism over whether she truly believed even half of what she said. Could she hear the level of mental gymnastics she performed in order to justify her contact with her mother?

Then again, she *had* explained this was one of those things only someone on the inside could understand. As much as he wanted to jump to her defense, he most definitely wasn't "on the inside" when it came to Freya or her past.

"You're right." He took a steadying breath, resigned to giving her the next best thing he could offer outside of his unwanted advice. "It's no one's place to tell you how to handle this, but if you do need someone to look out for you, to help you in any way, you can count on me."

Her stare burrowed into him, her lips curling slightly at the corners. "And who's looking out for you, Max?"

"What do you mean?"

"I mean, you've got a heck of a lot happening in your life, too, and I don't see many people jumping in to help."

He let go of her hand and slumped back, quashing a hot swell of anger over the truth in her observation.

"The problem is, I've had too many people looking out for me, which is ironically why some of the main players in my life have stepped back."

"No person is an island though, right?" Her stare held firmer than ever, as though she analyzed his every nuance, bringing a wave of electricity to his skin. "You need *someone*."

He scoffed, dipping his chin in an expression he hoped denoted sarcasm. "Are you volunteering?"

She threw back her head and gave her first genuine laugh in way too long, the throaty richness bringing levity to his dampened spirits. "Definitely not, but maybe the *real* problem with you is that you've had people helping in the wrong way."

It was his turn to laugh now, though the sound had a decidedly taut delivery. "And you've burned way too much energy analyzing what's *wrong* with me."

Despite his half-hearted jab, her eyes glittered with good humor— the sort of humor that came from years of working at a bar and learning not to take people's shit-talking too seriously. To that extent, maybe he did need to believe her when she said she knew how to compartmentalize her dealings with her mother.

"Don't flatter yourself. I'm just good at reading people."

He smiled, not for a second doubting her claim.

Unlike him, this woman had the art of *"knowing thy self"* down to a precise skill. "Is that your way of saying you have psychic powers? Because *that* would be very useful to my situation right about now."

Her shoulders shook with a chuckle. "Yeah, I wish. I'd use those powers on my own problems first."

"You sure? Because if you could just slip me this week's lottery numbers before I drop you off tomorrow…"

She laughed again, deeper now, and grabbed a pillow from atop the camping mattress, throwing it at him.

"God, I'm exhausted." She lay down, soon tucking the pillow she hadn't thrown under her head. "We've been talking forever, and I feel like my eyes are going to fall out."

He opened his mouth, meaning to point out how her eyes dangling from their sockets wouldn't exactly be her most attractive look, that she was the reason they'd been talking forever. But then she peered over and patted the empty spot on the bed beside her, drying his words.

He crawled on over, the thrown pillow in his hand. He settled next to her, and she shifted closer, tucking herself against him so that her head rested on his shoulder.

In that moment, with the smallest hint of humor-induced tears in the corners of her eyes, and in the wake of her painfully honest story, something within his world stopped.

He took a minute to figure out what.

Maybe it was the constant whirring sense he might get things wrong.

Maybe it was the nonstop race of his heart whenever this woman was close.

Or maybe the never-ending knowledge she had her life so much more together than him.

He could never hope to measure up, but in that brief second, he also knew one undeniable fact. He'd succeeded at *something*. For one fleeting moment, he'd made her feel better, been someone she trusted enough to confide in. Added value to her life.

She blinked up at him and pressed her palm flat to his chest as though she heard every one of his thoughts and wanted to reply.

"You have something missing in here, Max. Most people have figured that part out. But your unease, it didn't start in your heart. It only exists because there's something off-kilter in your head."

As much as he wanted to pry his eyes from her, to rein in his wild thundering pulse, his voice was what ultimately ran from him in a raspy and way too serious tone. "So, you're saying I'm not right in the head?"

"Your head works fine, Max, or at least your brain does, and though you seem to have decided otherwise, you're not inherently lazy. What I mean is, there's a sadness buried inside you, and until you figure out where that sadness comes from, you won't get rid of that lost feeling."

His focus lingered on the finer details of her small and alluring lips. She was probably right about his buried sadness and how it was the root to all his issues, but as much as he should have zoomed in on her big reveal, his mind snagged on something else entirely.

On just how much she recognized parts of him no one else did.

"I'm really lucky to have met you." His voice came out strong and way more certain than he expected, maybe because he meant every word.

She was his silver lining in what remained an extra-horrid period in his life.

He crossed an arm over his body and ran the pad of his thumb over her cheekbone, his forefinger brushing away one of her silken ringlets. "Up until now, I've been plodding through life, but you're one of the few people to demand I lift my game without being condescending. Somehow, your approach makes me want to do better, Freya. It's like you know me better than I know myself."

Her gaze dipped to his collarbone, and a slow smile crept across her face. "Maybe that's because we share something in common. We're both stuck in less-than-perfect situations right now."

He kept stroking her cheek, admiring the way the lantern's warm-yellow glow added extra radiance to her skin. "I don't need my life to be perfect to know we might just be perfect for each other."

"Max..." She all but whispered his name, and her attention flicked back to him. "This is what I meant about certain conversations changing everything. You promised me that wouldn't happen."

His lip tugged at one corner, and he gave what was likely a bitter, lopsided smile. Though his heart shrank from her rebuff, the dull pain in his chest wasn't enough to keep him from wanting to prove her wrong.

Besides, the intimacy in this tent had him feeling bold.

"What you told me about your past hasn't changed *everything* for me, it only changes how much I know about you. Your past doesn't change what I like about you most, which is who you are right *now*. I like your laugh. The way you don't make excuses for anyone, especially me. How, when I stuff up, your jaw gets all stiff, like you want to throw me into heavy traffic, even though you still give me a chance to get things right the next time."

She gave him a sidelong glare, new light entering her eyes, like maybe he'd given her a pleasant surprise.

He took her new lightness as a chance to move his fingers down her face, to that stubborn jawline of hers. The one that spoke volumes of what went on in her head.

"You had no reason to give me a job at The Ruby Room, but you did anyway. You helped me because you knew I needed help. And for some reason, you accept me as the lolloping fool that I am."

He gave a soft chuckle, hoping to provide at least a glimpse of what he saw every time he spent time with her. "I don't think you appreciate how rare your brand of acceptance is, or how much it means to me. What's more amazing is how you continued to accept me after you learned I was broke, even though you barely knew me. I'm not the brightest man ever; I know you could do better than me, I get it. But I am smart enough to acknowledge my gratitude for you. I'll *always* be thankful for you, Freya. I'll never forget how, when my life turned into a steaming mess, you were the one who cared enough to be there for me."

# Chapter Twenty-Five

By the time Freya crawled from the tent the next morning, the sun and azure sky hit her with a glare that stung her eyes. She squinted at a frying pan beside the newly re-built fire, the savory scent of fresh cooked bacon and eggs being what had pulled her from the tent in the first place.

She perched on a toppled log also beside the fire; wary over being alone with no sign of Max nearby.

A high-pitched screech came from high up in the trees. Try as she did, she couldn't see much, though she knew enough to recognize that the call belonged to a cockatoo.

Then again, bugger the bird, all she really wanted was Max.

Her heartbeat picked up pace, and she peered behind her, shrinking at the idea of having to venture too far from the tent in search of him. A loud snap came from up ahead, and she flinched, her startled focus landing on an overgrown clump of trees.

"Good sleep?"

Max stepped out of the clump.

The snapping sound must have been him treading on a fallen branch.

She swore under her breath and stiffened her expression, wanting to hide any not-too-happy glower. Then again, she could at least be grateful that Max stood before her and not some giant, murderous kangaroo.

She gave him a weak nod and tried to forget how her crippling fear last night had led to an outpouring of her life story, followed by hours of fitful sleep in his arms. No sex required, no need to prove there was nothing wrong with her in light of her past. All this, despite previous bad experiences divulging to others, much less deep conversations generally being off-limits in casual relationships such as this one.

*Stop it! He's just a nice guy, and we had a nice conversation. It's no big deal.*

Right. Maybe that screaming voice in her head had a point. Best not to overthink this.

He bent to the fire and went about serving bacon and eggs on a white, tin plate. "I made food for you. It's still warm."

Her stomach churned in spite of her hunger, the day's gathering heat not enough to keep her from tugging her khaki jacket closed over her chest. Even as she reached for the plate, she pressed her tongue to the roof of her mouth, stemming a new rise of emotion.

"Thank you." She cleared her throat, refusing to look directly at him. "My first ever fire-cooked breakfast."

And he'd let her sleep in. Hadn't prodded her awake so he could get some early morning attention. He'd merely woken when he wanted to, and made food.

Simple.

But she wasn't used to simple.

She took a nearby fork and began picking at her breakfast, her thoughts nagging her to hurry up and eat so they could end this whole camping thing and go home.

Maybe she'd been wrong to share so much of herself.

Maybe she'd ruined the one good thing they had going for them, casual sex with no touchy-feely emotions swirling in-between.

Besides, he might have handled her story well enough last night, but Max still had so much soul-searching to do. It wasn't right for her to stick him with a potential sense of duty to stand by her.

Maybe his words of adoration last night only supported her idea he might be needlessly attached.

*Don't lie. I'm scared he'll hate what he sees and then abandon or control me, just like the others… mother, father, pretty much every boyfriend…*

She shoved a piece of bacon into her mouth and chewed with way too much enthusiasm. Max sat on the log beside her, elbows resting on his knees and his attention burning into the side of her face from her periphery.

His stare made her skin sting and her mind race. *What was he thinking?* He liked to play the fool, but there was a certain intuition there, one not even he seemed to know he possessed.

"I got a bit bored waiting for you to wake up." She turned at his voice, one corner of his lip hiked in a bashful grimace. "So, I made you something."

She tried not to choke. "The food wasn't enough?"

He chuckled and reached behind him, pulling out a bundle of brown twigs and white twine, his forefinger hooking on a loop, before the whole bundle fell and dangled from his fingertip.

The crisscross of knots and twigs resembled a five-pointed star.

A tight giggle broke free, and she extended a hand to tap the star so it spun in the air in front of her. "Thank you. I can hang it on my front door to ward off evil spirits."

And still, there was something so childlike about his gesture, which only added to the guilt already pressing on her ribcage.

"I was aiming for a Christmas tree ornament." Max's wonky smile grew. "But whatever works for you."

He handed the star over, and to her surprise, she clutched the bundle of sticks against her unnecessary jacket.

His gaze lingered on her hand for a moment too long, and a flood of conflicted emotions grew within her. She turned her attention to the campfire, the lack of new wood reducing the whole thing to little more than a pile of hot glowing embers.

"When do we head home?" She pressed her lips together, regretting the question.

"I thought we'd go for a walk first."

"I know you're Mr. Fitness and all"—she gave a light-hearted shrug, hoping to dampen his pain—"but I actually enjoy doing nothing on my days off. I'll pass on the walk."

"Okay, well, we could just pull out a blanket and spend some quiet time by the river." He jutted his chin toward the tent. "I noticed you brought a book with you. Why not kick back and make the most of being out in nature?"

She stared at the embers backed by a tranquil bush and the river, and tried to remember the last time she'd just "kicked back".

With all the chaos of festival planning, her mum on her death bed, and whatever the heck this thing was with Max, maybe delaying her re-entry into the real world wasn't such a bad idea.

"And if I were to pull up a blanket and read my book"—she sent a playful scowl his way—"can you promise there won't be any overly friendly snakes trying to cuddle up to me?"

"Do I count as a snake?"

"Hey." She kicked a plume of dry dirt his way. "I'm serious here, I need to know I won't become some creature's new chew toy."

He gave a sly grin, his crystalline eyes sending sparks across the space that illuminated her grim mood. "I don't know how Australian snakes select their chew toys, so I can't promise anything, but if it'll make you feel better, I'm happy to keep an eye out while you get a few pages in."

"I can live with that." She shifted her plate off her lap and placed it on the ground, before dusting her hands against the rough spun denim of her jeans.

"Good." Max stood and headed toward the tent. "In the meantime, I'll try not to get in the way of your time with 'Taming Mister Trouble'."

She sputtered and coughed, pounding a closed fist at her chest.

"Jesus… Max." She coughed again, pain shooting through the base of her throat. "You've been gawking at my books?"

"Just one book." He held the tent flap open and laughed, deep wrinkles scoring the corners of his eyes, which only served to make him even more annoyingly attractive, despite his mocking. "Have you seen the cover? Abs galore and the guy's zipper is wide open. There's no way I wouldn't have noticed that."

Her belly shook with new laughter, her next words hard to form. "Screw you. Why are you checking out some guy's abs and open zipper, anyway?"

She picked up a handful of dirt and tossed it at him. He shielded his eyes with his forearm, then disappeared into the tent, his laughter still painfully clear even from inside.

"My masculinity isn't so weak that I can't acknowledge a fit-looking dude when I see one." He stepped out, the blue blanket from last night tucked under his armpit. "Actually, I'm so confident with my masculine prowess, I'd be happy to borrow the book from you when you're done."

She fisted another hunk of dirt and threw it at his back. He hunched, laughing again and deflecting the small explosion of dust and tiny stones.

"Leave the blanket. I'll set up for myself. Just go. I'm banishing you to the tent."

"But you need me to ward away the bitey snakes, remember?"

She shook her head in a slow and calculating way. "Not if you're going to shame my reading choices."

"Actually, I love your reading choices, especially if they mean changing your mind about heading home."

His attention lingered on her again, but she couldn't for the life of her figure out why.

Or maybe she just didn't want to.

The heavy silence following all that laughter, the pointed way his pupils narrowed and trained on her, held a certain grave significance that caused her heart genuine pain.

He turned away and spread the blanket out on the ground, soon abandoning it and taking himself to the riverside. Meanwhile, her mind worked over what had just happened.

Laughing with him had been so easy.

And his jokes at her expense didn't sting like the backhanded criticisms her mother, or any other man she'd dated, flung her way.

Maybe some of those criticisms had been her fault. Maybe she had a broken barometer for sensing who was good and who would hurt her, so she'd made a few misjudgments when it came to picking who she allowed in her life. Either way, she'd come to a point where she'd given up. On everyone. Except the couple of people who'd proven time and time again they wouldn't hurt her.

And now there was Max.

With his jokes about her and her reading material, his kindness and gratitude over the chances she'd given him, the fact they could talk, and that their times together were always just plain fun.

She rubbed the heel of her hand over her sternum, embracing the dull ache, as she tried to massage hard at a niggling unease.

The truth skirted the edge of her mind. Even as she got up and went into the tent in search of her book. Even as she found her book and stepped back outside, settling down on the blanket, the bright day failing to offer any extra comfort.

If anything, the sight of Max standing with his back to her—a giant gray gumtree to his left and the brown rushing river ahead, meters from his feet—only increased the tight sensation deep within her gut.

She couldn't just sit here. Couldn't ignore what was happening to her. So, she stood, the thick, dry tall-grass crunching under her feet while she trudged toward him.

Honestly, she should have just sat her ass back down on the blanket and opened her stupid book, but she moved forward all the same. At least until he spun around and a wide silence stretched between them.

"There's more to us, isn't there?" She jolted at her own words and prepared to deliver an unequivocal denial of what she'd just said, only to snap her mouth shut because she simply couldn't do it. *Not to him.* Not to a man who'd only ever worn his heart on his sleeve.

A muscle twitched at his jaw. On any other man the reaction might have intimidated, but on Max it only gave insight into the raw emotions circling within him. "And you don't like that, do you?"

Once again, she was incapable of lying, so she did the only thing she could do and gave a tiny nod. "Neither of us are in the right place."

"I know."

She allowed the silence to take over once again. He advanced, bringing his body mere inches from hers. "I just want our time together. That's enough for me."

He lashed out a hand and pulled her to him. Before she knew what was happening, his lips met hers. He unleashed on her a lingering, sweet kiss, so slow and gentle, he made it impossible to miss the suggestion of things she'd always figured weren't for her.

What it would be to have someone fall for her. Really fall for her.

To have them consumed with her every detail, and her with his…

A small chuckle worked past her lips, and she broke loose of his hold, mostly because she refused to fall for her ridiculous thoughts.

A shadow of a smile drew at Max's lips, and his eyes glinted with the welcome return of his trademark mischief. "Can Mister Trouble do that?"

She gave a small laugh and shook her head. "Not even close."

His eyes glinted again, this time with seemingly genuine pride.

"Come with me then." He slid his palm down her arm and hooked his fingers with hers. "Reading is cancelled. I'm giving you a few new positive associations with tents."

Max steered Luke's four-wheel drive off the country road and into the heavy flow of suburban traffic, Freya silent in the passenger seat beside him, her attention lost somewhere through her rain-covered window.

He depressed his foot onto the accelerator, the car picking up speed on the wet road and keeping up with the other vehicles all around, his mind still toying with his time alone with her in the bush.

He frowned at her, and then refocused on the road. "What are you thinking?"

Personally, all he could think about was her tragic childhood and the sometimes confused, sometimes broken, sometimes overwhelmed looks she kept giving him all this morning.

He'd never been great at reading a room, but he sensed he'd gotten closer to her now than before they'd left for Roseford.

She gave him an easy smile, appearing totally relaxed and content, while he had to remind himself to keep watching the road.

"Actually, I was just wondering if we could go camping together again sometime. It's a pity the rain rolled in and forced us home early."

He laughed, chancing another quick glance her way. "Really? I could have sworn you were ready to bounce out of Roseford the moment you opened your eyes this morning."

*What changed?*

With the heavy pounding of rain on the car's windscreen, he wrung his hands over the leather steering wheel, waiting for her to say that *he* was the reason for her shifted opinions on camping. That the time with him meant something to her. That he stood out from any other man she'd ever dated, even if she insisted that this thing between them remained temporary.

He thought back to that first night he'd worked at The Ruby Room and the man who'd been holding Freya...

*Oh hell, what if I'm still not the only one?*

His nostrils flared. He tried not to glare at the road, even if his fingers hurt from clutching the steering wheel, and he battled against emotions he wished didn't exist. *Envy. Entitlement. Misery.*

"Max?"

He didn't answer right away, instead focusing on the silver hatchback ahead, all while pretending he didn't hang on her every word.

Even when he'd wanted more, he'd never had a relationship last longer than a few months, but his flighty relationship history wasn't enough to obscure the huge warning signs that putting too much importance on this woman would leave him broken-hearted.

His phone hung mounted on the windscreen, guiding him back to Melbourne and now ringing as if the tech gods heard his need for distraction.

He glanced at Freya again. "Do you mind if I put the call on speaker? It's Luke's wife, Agathe."

Freya shook her head, and he pressed a button in the car to answer the call. "Hey, Agathe, you're on speaker. What's up?"

"Oh, okay, no problem." There was a long pause, as if Agathe was stalling. "Do you happen to be near the airport? There's been a change of plans."

"We're maybe twenty minutes from there. Why? Did Sophie and Orlando's plane land early?"

"Yeah, like twelve hours early. Their stop in Abu Dhabi was shuffled around, and they're waiting at Tullamarine Airport right now.

Only, you've got Luke's car, which leaves only my car with Nova's giant child seat taking up a bunch of space in the back." Agathe gave a tight chuckle. "I don't think we'll be able to fit all the luggage, Sophie, and a big guy like Orlando. Rather than sending them over in a cab, it'd be so much nicer if one of us turned up."

"Right."

Max peered over at Freya, her hand pressed over her mouth, her complexion paled like a woman realizing she was minutes away from meeting her casual lover's family.

He wouldn't have borrowed Luke's car, except that it had so much more room than the Tesla for camping equipment and did better on rough country roads.

He mouthed the word, "Sorry," to her, but she swatted a hand. The situation wasn't ideal, but she'd obviously bear it either way.

"Can you do it?" Agathe's voice dipped with an air of uncertainty. "Can I let Sophie know you'll be right over to pick her up?"

# Chapter Twenty-Six

Freya hung back just barely inside Luke's South Melbourne home, her body jammed between Max and the front door, while she tried to be as invisible as possible.

Sophie ran out across the foyer's high-gloss floorboards and into Luke's open arms, a similar scene having played out less than an hour earlier when she'd first seen Max.

Sophie slipped out of Luke's hold, tears streaming down her face. Orlando, in all his beef-cakey glory, stepped forward to give Luke a strong slap on the back, thanking him for taking them on as guests since everything was up in the air with Max's place.

Freya switched focus to a little girl bouncing up and down, clearly excited with all the commotion and adding to it herself. This had to be Nova, Luke and Agathe's three-year-old daughter.

Freya had barely heard of Luke, and she'd only learned of Nova whilst listening to the conversation in the car ride over. Now she stood awkward in this home, her hands clasped at her elbows, a definite thickness coating her throat over how this happy reunion was totally foreign to her.

The Tindalls consisted of siblings and spouses genuinely excited to be together. A functional family, with a child loved and unafraid of her parents.

Orlando grabbed Nova and swung her around, the little girl squealing in delight as he informed her that the closest they'd ever come to meeting was when she lived in her mother's tummy, and that it was "so cool" to see her now.

Freya's heart hurt at the display of clear affection, and she struggled to pry her attention from the cozy scene, though she also didn't want to look like a total weirdo for staring.

The excitement ebbed, and everyone shuffled deeper into the house.

With its dark-brown polished floors and giant abstract paintings on the walls, the only two people not heading forward were her and a woman she assumed was Agathe—her wide grin and nearly onyx-colored eyes glinting at Freya.

"You must be Freya." She extended a hand. "I'm Agathe, and I'm sorry we highjacked your journey home."

Freya accepted the hand shake and opened her mouth, ready to say it wasn't a big deal, even if it kind of was, since she was way exhausted and hadn't had a warm shower since yesterday morning.

But then, Agathe tugged her hand, dragging her toward where the others sat, amidst a cluster of cream leather couches and armchairs. "Sit with us. You must be exhausted."

Freya closed her mouth, shocked at her uncharacteristic lack of words and that she allowed this woman to pull her into something she wasn't all that sure she wanted to be part of.

Sure, none of this impromptu meeting was Max's fault. Flight plans changed, Sophie and Orlando needed a ride from the airport. But none of that dulled the overriding sense that she didn't have a place in such an intimate setting.

She wasn't Max's girlfriend. She couldn't even call them firm friends. Or that their association would survive much past the physical stuff inevitably dying out.

Not that she necessarily wanted this relationship to survive past then. And she still remained the odd person out at this close family gathering. Besides, what with her shitty childhood, she wasn't exactly experienced with how to handle displays of affection between loving family members, which only made this whole thing awkward as hell for her.

She dropped onto the end of a couch, the end closest to the front door, resigning herself to mostly just skirting the edge of this reunion until she could wrangle Max away long enough to get a ride home.

If only she didn't have so much stuff to haul from the camping trip, then she'd just excuse herself and catch a tram home. Maybe she could still call an Uber? All she had to do was ask someone to open Luke's car, and she could unload her stuff.

*No. Just, no. That would be weird, and rude, and antisocial. I'll just sit quiet for a minute. They've already forgotten I'm here, anyway.*

Agathe stepped in front of Freya again, a warm smile on her face. "I'm no bartender, so please don't expect too much in terms of drinks, but could I get you a glass of wine or something?"

A subtle heat spread over Freya's cheeks. Clearly, Agathe knew at least something about her, the part about her bar, which meant Max *had* mentioned her in some shape or form.

She and Max had just returned from a night camping together; no doubt everyone here had the wrong idea about just how involved this relationship was.

Max raised a brow at his sister-in-law. "Shouldn't you offer her tea? Isn't that your entire schtick?"

Freya frowned at Max, oblivious to what he meant.

"Oh, that's right, you don't know." He nodded to Agathe, with her bronze skin so flawless it almost hurt to look at her. "Miss Tea Obsessed here owns a tea shop in the city. She specializes in all things tea cups, teapots, and actual tea."

"No way." Freya turned to Agathe. "Not 'Pekoh Boo', near the corner of Elizabeth and Little Collins?"

Lightness entered Agathe's eyes, and she nodded.

Freya shifted her entire body to face her new acquaintance. "I stop by there every time I make it into the city. It's the cutest boutique in the area, and the tangerine and gold packaging is luxury in box form."

"Well then, next time you're in, ask the sales assistant for me. We also do wholesale orders if you're ever looking for something for the bar…" Agathe winked, then inclined her head to one side. "So, can I get you a tea after all?"

Freya ran her gaze over the room and let out a loud sigh. "Given that I went from the seclusion of the bush, to a giant family reunion of people I don't know, maybe a straight whiskey would make more sense."

Agathe cracked out a laugh, already turning away. "I'll hunt down some of Luke's nicer stuff and send out a family order for everyone to go easy on you."

Tendrils of warmth moved through Freya's body, and a portion of her doubt slipped away. Just because she'd had the exact opposite of a happy family, it wasn't fair to begrudge Max his. What's more, no one fluttered an eyelid at her presence. Both Sophie and Orlando, and now Agathe, had welcomed her. Maybe she needed to stop trying to find fault here.

She settled back, allowing her right shoulder to sink against Max, vowing to simply enjoy this glimpse at an untroubled family. Perhaps absorb some of the tranquility for herself, as well as the knowledge that people like this actually existed.

"How was the camping trip?"

She lifted her gaze to Luke, his moss-green stare on her.

She gave a shaky laugh, not really wanting to recount her near meltdown last night. "It was an adventure. That's for sure."

"Well, I have to hand it to Max." Luke jutted his chin at his brother. "I didn't expect you'd both come home in one piece."

"Ha. Ha." Max scowled at Luke, though the slight curl in his lips said the fake laughter was mostly playful. "I might not be G.I. Joe, like you, but I do well enough."

"G.I. Joe?" Freya glanced between the brothers. "What's that about?"

"Luke here did a few years of military service before becoming a CEO extraordinaire. And yes, he is the family's overachiever."

"And aren't you glad?" Luke grabbed a couch cushion and threw it at Max.

Max caught the cushion with a laugh, just as Luke snapped his mouth shut in a way that hinted he'd been about to remind Max of his struggles over the years. How Luke's help was the only thing keeping him afloat in that time.

Agathe swanned in between the brothers.

She rolled her eyes at Freya, extending a short glass with whiskey, a tray of nibbles in her other hand. "I'm sorry about these two. Brothers, right?"

Luke straightened and redirected his focus to Freya. "And what about you, do you have any siblings?"

"Don't answer that. It's a trap." This time Orlando intervened, his attention switching to Luke. "Vetting the potential new family members again, are we?"

Her heart beat faster, not liking the line about "potential new family members", still remaining quiet so she could hear what Luke would say next.

He shrugged, nothing more than a light smile on his face. "Does that sound like something I would do?"

Sophie flopped back in her seat on an adjacent couch and clapped her hand over her mouth as she laughed. "You mean you've forgotten how you gave Orlando a hard time when he and I first got together?"

"Well, look at him." Luke gestured to Orlando. "Doesn't he look like a guy deserving of a hard time?"

Freya peered over. Orlando, with his big frame and broad shoulders, golden skin, dark stubble, and a thick scar along the top corner of his forehead, looked rough and handsome all at once—a complete contrast to Sophie's sweet, bookish looks. Luke kind of had a point.

"I have a brother." The words flew from her mouth, perhaps because the mild tension in the air, particularly when it came to family discord, set her nerves on edge. "He's in prison."

*Fuck! Did I really just say that?*

Everyone's gaze switched to her, before looking to each other in dumbfounded silence. She couldn't quite meet Max's eyes; didn't want to read anything there that hinted at displeasure.

*Nice first impression, genius!*

Orlando reclined next to Sophie, his elbows raised on the couch's back, his beer bottle dangling loose from his fingers. "Yep. Told you it was a trap."

Luke nodded to her drink, a not-so-subtle suggestion she should take a sip.

"You know, I couldn't care less if it was." She let go of the tension in her shoulders and started on her drink, allowing the rich warmth to settle her. "I have no control over what other people do or what they think of me, my brother, and everyone in this room included."

Agathe sat next to her, her hand finding Freya's forearm. "Hey, you'll get no judgment here. I'll make sure of it."

"Thanks." Freya smiled at Agathe, then returned her attention to everyone at large. "But since imaginations have a way of doing more harm than good, I'm willing to explain what my brother did to get locked up."

"Freya. No." Max grabbed her hand, the one without the drink. "You don't have to."

"It's a simple story, and I have nothing to hide." She shrugged him off. "My brother, Clay, went to the States hoping to become a corporate big shot. But he's my mother's creature, idolized to the point of having to reflect everything she said he should be. Handsome. Rich. Popular. But the money wasn't coming in fast enough, not for the crowds he wanted to break into, so he turned to running online scams, which brought in the money sure enough. At least until he caught a four-year prison sentence."

"I bet there's more to *that* story."

"Luke!"

Agathe reached out and smacked his knee.

"No. I don't mean it like that." He squeezed his eyes shut and shook his head. "I mean, as much as we siblings have our squabbles, we still have a bunch of positive memories to lean on when times get tough. I'm not prying. I just figure, to have a brother and not really have a relationship with him, which is what I'm getting from her story, must be a hard thing to contend with."

Freya stared at Luke for a while, her cheeks slack, and her skin suddenly cold, like he'd traipsed through her brain and uprooted hidden emotions she made a point of hiding.

Even as the "loved" child, Clay still paid a price for their mother's brand of love. He'd been hyped up and deemed undeservedly special for nothing more than being born a boy. That love had destroyed his ability to develop his own self-image, leaving him to waste years trying to prove his mum's theories about him right.

He played a role. A role that damaged him in more ways than one.

And just like she understood their mother, Freya understood Clay, too. She just refused to hurt herself trying to maintain any kind of involved relationship with him.

She took a deep breath and directed her next question at Agathe. "Does Luke do that often?"

"You mean the psychoanalyzing thing?" She grabbed the nibbles plate and pushed it closer to Freya in some kind of peace offering. "You have no idea, but on a positive note, it usually means he likes you, or at least considers you a possible regular fixture in our lives."

Freya brought her glass higher, pressing its cool surface to her cheek, all while deliberating over whether she should break it to everyone that she and Max were only slightly more than fuck buddies.

Thankfully though, her phone rang, so she took herself a few meters from the group to answer the call.

"Hello?"

She didn't recognize the number calling, but the quick-fire response of a female voice had her staring dead-pan at the kaleidoscopic reds and yellows of an abstract painting up ahead.

She gave a numb, "Yes. I'll be there," and ended the call, her light-ness from this morning completely gone. She turned a quick glance to the group of happy people behind her, her heart plummeting at the vision of something she'd never have.

As if sensing her change in mood, Max leapt from the couch and drew near, stopping just short of touching her. "What's wrong? You look gray."

"I need to go." Her throat swelled from the inside, and the audible rasp in her voice betrayed the rising tension in her body. "Mum's had a violent outburst in the hospital. The nurse said it's a normal, end-stage reaction. Something about toxins building in her brain, but they've had to sedate her. She's refusing to wear a hospital gown and wants her pajamas from home. I need to go to her house and retrieve her paja-mas. Maybe then, they can settle her without more drugs."

Max ran his fingers through the scruff of his hair before he gave his family a quick glance. "I'll say goodbye to everyone here, and then I'll take you. Don't go alone, okay?"

"That would be a bad idea."

His brows slammed together, more insistent than offended. "No, it's not. You don't have a car, I do. You're already visibly tired, and it'll take you hours to get everything done without my help."

"That might be true." She crossed her arms over her chest. "But I'll manage all the same."

"I never questioned whether you could manage."

"I can't ask you to leave your family when they've only just arrived."

"You're not asking, I'm offering." He twisted his torso, nodding at Sophie and Orlando. "Look at those two, they look even more wrecked than you do. The quicker we get out of here, the quicker they can wrap up the pleasantries and get some showers and a nap. Heck, same goes for us. Besides, there's some hardworking nurses dealing with your cranky mum right now, just praying you'll hurry along and end their misery."

She narrowed her stare, allowing a burning silence to drag between them, but the mere sight of his kind, star-filled eyes shifted something.

Even as his gaze slipped from her and to the ground between them —a sign his conviction waned—she couldn't deny his reasons.

"Fine." She dropped her arms, already heading for the door. "But wherever we go, you wait outside."

# Chapter Twenty-Seven

The moment Max's pristine Tesla pulled up to Freya's childhood home, Freya sank deeper into her seat, the house a tattered, old weatherboard in the thick of Melbourne's northern suburbs.

This house looked even worse than when she'd grown up there. Bad enough to call it a headache-inducing eyesore—the peeling paint an unappealing shade of custard yellow, the window frames and dented gutters a gag-worthy shamrock green. Even the exterior door appeared ready to fall off its hinges, while the fly wire hung loose, torn at one top corner.

As much as the sight made her queasy, staring at the house beat meeting Max's gaze, especially since they'd arrived to this decaying hovel fresh from Luke's lavish home. Even if she did trust Max not to judge her on her poor upbringing, she still couldn't understand why she'd agreed to let him witness this bleak part of her past.

"The thing is." She squinted at the quiet street ahead, at the lack of trees lining the grassy nature strip, her words a chance to delay the inevitable. "This is probably a shitty thing to say, but I can't help but second guess whether this errand is really just Mum manipulating the situation again. You know, she spent so many years using her health, and then mine, as leverage. I can't tell what's real and what's not anymore. I can't escape the idea that this is one final attempt to gauge what hoops she can get everyone to jump through before she drops."

Max frowned down at the steering wheel. "You think she'd go to the extreme of getting sedated, just to watch everyone dance to her tune?"

She let out a sigh, flopping her head back against the headrest. "Honestly? Yes. The woman drugged her own daughter just to fill a void, so…"

She eyed the Tesla's see-through roof while a long silence dragged out. She didn't need him to acknowledge her point to know that now neither of them knew what to make of this mission to collect pajamas.

Her resentment toward her mother grew in her abdomen, a hot, hard knot taking up space and bringing pain to her lower ribs. She closed her eyes, absorbing the ache, only for Max's long fingers to slide through hers rested on the center console.

"You sure you don't want me to come with you?"

The sweet gesture cooled her anger and made room for another, more frightening, emotion. *Affection.*

She sat bolt upright and pulled her hand away. "Fine, let's get this started."

Maybe if he came face-to-face with the evidence of her childhood, he'd get scared and stop messing with her long-term dream of being alone forever. The fact she'd caught Luke's lingering frown as Max ushered her out of his front door, like Luke too could see this relationship getting way out of hand, and that Freya would, sooner rather than later, crush Max's way-too-kind spirit.

She dug through her backpack and retrieved the keys she'd collected the last time she visited her mum at the hospital. Even as she exited the car, and Max followed, she found herself thankful for his silent and unquestioning compliance.

With every hurried step toward her mother's front door, her heart rate climbed, and a thin sweat clammed up her hands, forcing her to cling tighter to the keys, at least thankful she'd packed deodorant in her camping bag.

She stepped over the fat cracks on the veranda's concrete slab, refusing to make eye-contact with Max. When she tugged at the flimsy fly screen's thin metal handle, the springs made a sharp metallic *twang.*

The solid front door behind wasn't much better; the thing refused to budge open, and she had to jam a shoulder into the cream-painted wood before she finally stumbled in. The shambles of a small living room greeted her, sinking her mood deeper.

There was the cheap, blush vinyl couch, with shadows of hibiscus flowers embossed all over, the sand-colored carpet stained and uneven. Her trauma-loaded brain protested the imprinting of any more memories of this place.

So, she marched ahead and took a left into the short hallway, assuming Max would follow despite his uncharacteristic silence, her mind settling into some kind of blinkered, protective mode.

She came to her mother's bedroom at the end of the corridor, the bed still unmade and a collection of clothes strewn across the mattress and floor.

Her mum had never been all that neat, but this scene suggested she'd given up entirely. Maybe she'd figured this place was for her eyes only and that no one visited, so why bother?

Except right now it wasn't just her mother's eyes taking it all in, and all Freya could think about was how the state of this house embodied her mother's inner world.

*Apathetic. Disorderly. Chaotic.*

A chest of drawers along the room's back wall stood with most drawers still open. She strode in and made fast work of digging through each drawer, unearthing multiple pairs of pajamas.

She bundled the clothes in her hands and took a moment before turning around.

One day soon, she'd have to pack this house up, its mess and horrid memories filling each corner of each room. She'd have to enlist a real estate agent and sell the place, even though she preferred the idea of burning the entire goddamn house down, just erased from the earth altogether.

She turned and lifted her gaze to Max standing in the doorway, his long frame blocking the already limited light in the crammed space.

The look of him brought more pain to her heart, his continued silence still unnerving.

She marched forward and squeezed past him, her steps quick, but not quick enough to block out her heightened awareness or her imaginings of how this all looked to him.

The disarray. The lack of luxury. Her former life of decay, solitude, abuse, neglect. That people lived like this. That *she'd* lived like this...

*God, my list of contrasts to his life don't end, do they?*

The linoleum floors out in the corridor were a scuffed and depressing shade of beige, the whole thing printed in a pattern resembling fake tiles. Not even the thin plaster walls, in a misleading bright cool blue, hid the dented and bowed panels.

Still, she powered ahead, set on getting out of the place as fast as she could. Just two quick turns and she'd be back out on the veranda, reunited with the fresh air and the outside world's sweet civility.

Only another door lay straight ahead. The final obstacle. The door she'd ignored on her way in. The one leading to the kitchen.

Her feet came to a dead stop, and a heavy stone seemed to drag down on the inside of her stomach, all while a voice in her head screamed to turn right and get the hell out of there.

Staring back at her was the same, old, green table she'd eaten at multiple times a day for years, a significant amount of those meals poisoned. She took another step where dirty and crooked white tiles drew her in, her gaze falling to the stained brassy yellow sink along the left wall, a rickety, wooden breakfast stool beside the adjoining counter.

A wave of sickness rolled within her stomach and hit her with a painful vivid memory, one of a small, frail girl, pale and bony, her head full of ratty blond curls...

That girl balanced on the wooden stool—weak of body, but ultimately, not weak of mind—her bare feet stretched so that she stood on her tippy-toes, her wiry arms reaching high into the cupboards.

The girl shifted and adjusted, accommodating for the stool's uneven feet, but no amount of adjusting compensated for a cold-hearted mother determined to cover up her self-serving and evil schemes.

Freya's lungs drew a sudden sharp breath, and the memory collapsed like a weak house of cards, all while her skin prickled and her nails dug into her palms.

"Are you okay?" A pair of large hands pulled her in so that warmth soon lapped at her back. *Max.*

His voice delivered a gentle whisper, one that hurt her far more than his silence.

She closed her eyes, and emotion swelled in her chest, taking up too much space.

He'd caught more than a glimpse of what she'd lived through, and now he asked if she was okay, his concern not strong enough to quell the shame swallowing her whole. A shame that made her shoulders hunch and her cheeks burn.

She reopened her eyes and made room for a cooler, more collected, Freya to return. Sure, Max knew her story, and now he'd seen where she'd lived. If that didn't drive him away, meeting her mother would.

Kerry Branner's eyes crinkled at the corners, quite a feat given the woman was dying, the strain of her forced smile directed at the person she'd already deemed the most important in this room. *Max.*

Freya ground her molars together, dreading the inevitable questions to come.

"Thank you for the pajamas, honey." Even now, addressing Freya as "honey", a term of endearment her mother never used, all while neglecting to give her own daughter any direct eye contact. "Who is this handsome young man you've brought along with you?"

Max stepped forward, at least refraining from any reward laughter at her mother's attempt at charm. "I'm Max. I drove Freya here."

Her mother's attention slid down to his hand around Freya's. Sluggish and slow, she raised a brow, before finally focusing on Freya. "You never told me you had a boyfriend."

Freya did her best not to growl at the brightness in her mother's fake-nice tone, sending forth her own words on a flat delivery. "I heard they had to sedate you."

Her mother giggled and gave Max a weak shrug. "Oh, that. They don't understand what it's like in here. I only wanted a little comfort from home."

The giggle turned Freya's cheeks rigid, much less the not-so-subtle victim act she'd already witnessed far too much growing up.

There wasn't anything comfortable about her mother's home either, though any actual discomfort had more to do with the cold woman who lived there than the shambolic conditions or her mother's lack of funds.

Besides, her mother's glib response now, in light of Freya and Max's journey across town, only added more weight to the suspicion that this whole pajama fiasco was yet more manipulation.

Max tightened his grip on her hand, pulling her attention from her anger and onto the slow circles his thumb drew in the center of her palm. "Well, hopefully you're feeling much better now. Apologies for the quick visit, but we really should go—"

"Oh, such a sweet boy." Her mother purred over the gravel in her age-worn voice, though the hard set of her amber eyes failed to match her saccharine delivery. "Tell me how you met my Freya? You look so unlike someone I imagined my girl would date."

Freya glared at her mother, every muscle in her body clenching in protest. "You've never met anyone I've dated, and—"

Max squeezed her hand again, perhaps a reminder not to fall into her mother's trap. "I met Freya at her bar. You must be so proud to have such a successful daughter. She's excellent at what she does."

Kerry swatted a hand in Max's direction, her narrowed stare fusing on Freya. "I couldn't give her the best things growing up, but I did my job and gave her everything I had. I didn't raise soft children. I taught her the world is a hard place, and because of me, she knows how to survive, even if teaching her meant she abandoned me in the end." Kerry's eyes filled with frost, a frost that melted as she turned back to Max and gave an unconvincing shrug. "And you're right. Just look how she turned out."

Freya's shoulders sagged at her mother's reference to parenting as a "job".

If that were the case, her mother would have only ever made a great, sadistic army drill sergeant or maybe the heartless matron of an 1800s orphanage.

Not only did her mother take credit for how Freya had turned out, she also claimed "abandonment" while Freya quite literally stood staring her in the face, as death slowly but surely crept close.

No Clay in sight. Just Freya.

*Here, right now.*

Hand delivering pajamas, when she had every right to never look her mother's way again.

And the most ass-end-backward of all statements? That preparing Freya for a "hard world" counted when it was her mother who'd been the sole source of all that hardness.

"Anyway." Her mother spoke to Max now, again leaving Freya to think she should have just stayed in the damn car and let Max drop off the pajamas. "What's a man like you doing at her club? You don't look tattooed, drunk, or scruffy enough to be in that place."

Freya spat forth a manic laugh, her gaze lifting to Max's pinched expression.

Lucky for her mother, he jumped in and replied before she could. "Not that tattoos are any measure of a person, but I started out as a customer at The Ruby Room. Freya was kind enough to offer me a job when I really needed it."

"Well. Well." Her mother let out a croaky chuckle, ending on a spluttering cough. She turned her venom-filled gaze to Freya again, as if Max's value had just plummeted. "You're screwing the *help* then?"

Her mother popped the "p" in the word "help", then flung her head back into her pillow, a series of rattly laughs and coughs breaking forth.

Freya's spine turned rigid, and she bounced on her heels trying to work through an emotional onslaught. Anger. Shame. Anger again. Her mother found ways to make her feel small at every turn, always insinuating she'd been put together wrong—doomed to be a screwup, no matter what she achieved.

She quashed a desire to lash out, clinging to the distraction of the gray cityscape outside the hospital room window, mostly because lashing out would only feed her mother's habitual need to stir people's temper.

Freya wouldn't lower herself to unleashing on someone slumped at death's door, wouldn't waste her energy defending herself against a woman who would never be convinced to change—even though holding back felt like losing, like Freya sent forth the idea she didn't mind the disrespect.

*Disrespect from a dying woman. There is that.*

Yes. And her mother's impending death was one point of relief.

In the scheme of things, letting her mother have this one shallow win meant little. So, Freya forced a half-smile and let go of her clenching muscles, relief soon sweeping over her body. "It was something to see you today, Mum."

Her mother's laughter stopped, her silent stare holding Freya, as if she didn't know what to do with the lack of retaliation.

Despite the shitty meeting, and maybe because Freya had taken a bit of her power back, she leaned in and kissed her mother's forehead. "I love you."

From the outside, and in light of all the abuse, that statement seemed like a weird thing to say, but for all Freya knew, this would be the last time she'd see her mother.

Then there was Freya's other coping mechanism—seeing her mother for the tortured child she'd been, not the damaged woman she'd become.

Her mother ripped her attention from Freya and blinked out toward the window, her sudden quietness causing an ache in Freya's tummy.

This wasn't her first declaration of love to her mother, though she'd learned long ago never to expect the sentiment returned. The way she saw it, at least she tried. At least she could say that she didn't hold back and that she hadn't inherited her family's inability to show affection. And whatever her mother did with that affection was her own damn problem.

Freya turned to Max and nudged her head in the direction of the door, only for her mother's cracked and hollow voice to halt their exit.

"Love?"

Kerry continued to blink at the window, her stare soulless and the flickering movements of her eyelids picking up speed. "I don't know what that is. No one ever taught me."

Freya spun around, ready to leave; only Max tugged her back, a stern stare fixed on her mother. "Freya just did."

# Chapter Twenty-Eight

Not quite ready to start the engine, Max paused behind the steering wheel, the hospital parking lot several levels high, densely packed, with sharp corners that would have made maneuvering even a small car a tight squeeze.

"This day just doesn't want to end." Freya scrubbed a hand over her face, the skin under her eyes darker than usual, her cheeks pale like the interaction with her mother had totally drained her.

"Come back to my place." He clenched his jaw, not having intended to speak his wishes out loud. Though on further reflection, he had zero regrets about the offer.

Freya didn't need to be alone tonight. Heck, neither did he, and he also didn't want to see her go.

"I can't." She spoke down to her lap, her voice muffled by her hands still over her face.

"Sure you can."

"No, I can't." She lifted her head, and the sad distance in her stare left him deflated. "You've done enough for me today. I'm sure you want a little time to yourself now."

He reached out and put his hand over hers, hoping she'd appreciate the extra support and connection. "I'll waste whatever time I have to myself, anyway. Come back to my place. Let me look after you. It'll be good for both of us."

He offered a weak smile, biting back an urge to say he'd found nothing likable about her mother, and that she'd been manipulative and mean. That he hated the toll the woman took on her daughter. Hated how Freya continued having anything to do with her mother, when even one short encounter zapped all signs of her innate happiness.

But this was Freya's life.

Her story.

He'd respect her desire to work through her mother's last days in her own way.

Her stare skittered around his face, her lower lip disappearing between her teeth as if she took a moment to weigh things up. "You sure? I mean, *I'm* not sure. Aren't we stepping beyond the whole casual limits of this relationship?"

"And spending a night in a tent together is something normal work colleagues do?" He allowed a short shot of laughter. "Look, I promise I won't overthink this if you don't."

The guarded sheen in her eyes melted. "Okay, fine. Let's do it."

He started the ignition. "Good, my house it is."

The late hour made the drive to his apartment a short one. He soon pushed open his front door, the heavy camping gear and bags clanging together over his shoulder.

"Feel free to throw your stuff in the washing machine first." He held the door open and side-stepped to make room for Freya to pass. "Unless you'd prefer a warm shower first?"

"More than you could know." She groaned, squeezing past him, her own giant bag trailing behind. "I've been dreaming about a shower for two days now."

He laughed and closed the door behind them, then took a few steps deeper into the apartment. A wave of cold air hit his face.

"Just a moment, I'll crank up the heat before you jump in. No one likes a cold bathroom."

Melbourne weather tended to shift through temperatures faster than a Formula One driver shifted gears—even at the tail end of summer—that and he made a habit of shutting down his climate system whenever he left his apartment for any extended time. His apartment's location at the edge of the bay only made the evening chill-factor worse.

He dumped his bags by the kitchen counter, then found the touch-screen control for his climate system. He fiddled around for a bit, but the usual start-up "beep" didn't come.

Freya sidled up to him, peering over his shoulder as much as someone significantly shorter could peer. "What do you have there?"

He frowned at the tablet and pressed the start button three more times. "Still trying to get the heat to work, but this thing is glitching out. I need a moment to restart the app."

Except, even when he did restart the app, over and over, nothing happened. He growled under his breath and restarted the whole device, the screen turning black.

He'd spent crazy money on the best climate system available, one that would heat and cool his apartment, whilst being as eco-friendly as possible—this system just one of many additions he'd gone literally broke installing.

Surely, a climate system that damn-well worked was the least he could expect for all the money he'd spent!

His skin tingled, and his heart rate picked up. The device finished rebooting, but no amount of app tinkering worked. To make matters worse, his funds sat dangerously low, so even with his work at The Ruby Room and the new swim instructor job, he probably wouldn't have enough cash to pay for repairs.

Freya tapped him on the shoulder, but he was too busy glaring at the tablet to look at her. "Hey, there's a note on the kitchen counter."

He continued stabbing wildly at the blank screen, the back of his neck prickling with sweat because he was sure his system was about a year out of warranty now. "Just read it out to me."

"You sure?"

"Yeah, go for it." He shook the tablet, as if that would get things working.

"Hey mate, thought you should know, seems your heater and air conditioner are on the fritz. Tom and Pats." She dropped the note to the counter and gave a light shrug, like she didn't understand the severity of that news. "Well, that sucks. Who are Tom and Pats?"

He ran a hand through his hair and headed back toward Freya, his face and fingers cold and void of blood. "Tom and Patricia. They're my cleaners."

Her eyelids flared. "You *still* have cleaners? Are you crazy?"

"It's highly likely," he mumbled, not exactly in the mood to have his poor life choices dragged out at this very moment. "I haven't found the heart to fire them."

He waited for Freya to spill with her tough "Boss Lady" advice, but she reached a hand out and stroked his arm. "Oh, Max."

He dropped the tablet onto the counter alongside Tom and Pat's note, not quite able to take her look of sympathy, even though he did appreciate it.

The problem about splashing out on expensive things was they weren't supposed to break all that often, but when they did, they were painfully expensive to repair.

He let go of a loud sigh and sank back on his heels. "This is probably going to set me back a couple of thousand."

"Do you even have a couple of thousand?"

"No. No, I definitely don't." He whispered an expletive, staring off into space. "This is embarrassing. I wanted to look after you, not freeze your ass off and bore you with my problems."

She drew closer, stroking his face, her touch undeservedly soft and warm. "I've bored you plenty with my problems this weekend. You're welcome to bore me with a few of yours."

Despite the warmth sweeping over his skin, he fell short of reminding her that her offer to share problems probably went beyond the casualness she insisted on maintaining in this relationship.

"Fine." She dropped her hand and released a sigh. "Maybe you having a few problems makes me feel normal about my own issues, okay?"

"Way to make this sound like a fair trade."

"It is a fair trade. Tell me, do you need help with your problems or not?"

"If you're offering to loan me money, then no. The whole point of my downfall is I'm supposed to claw my own way out. At least, that's what everyone keeps telling me."

She shrugged. "Well, yeah. They're kind of right."

He rubbed the heel of his palm against his chest and accepted her bitter truth.

One way or another, he'd find a way to keep his apartment, preferably without going broke or the place falling to pieces due to his inability to maintain repairs.

Freya leaned back against the counter behind her, though her gaze dropped to the floor. "And you don't need to worry about me tonight. You heard my mum, she built me tough. We didn't have heating or cooling growing up. This isn't something a thick sweater and some sweat pants can't fix."

She peered up from under her lashes and sent him a rueful smile— the sensually sweet look spreading heat through his belly. But in the next beat, his insides churned at the memory of her unkempt child-hood home, its dilapidated, weatherboard exterior and thin plaster walls. There'd been nothing warm there. Not anything the world's most sumptuous woolen sweater could fix.

Comfort had been yet another thing lacking in her life, and the fact she'd been through so much, only to have more unpleasantness in his home, sent a sharp line of shame snaking through his body.

He stepped forward and dropped a hurried kiss to her lips—a kiss he hoped conveyed everything she didn't want him to say out loud.

That he wanted her to be his.

That he wanted to give her far more than what her past entailed.

But for any of that to happen, he needed to get his life together.

An easy task, right?

He pulled away, logic stinging him to the core, even as her mouth twisted up in a sly grin. "Well, there *is* another way to stay warm."

He paused a second, before quick laughter broke free. Trust Freya to take a bad moment and turn it into something else. *Something wicked.*

Her grin widened, and she kicked off her shoes, at the same time grabbing hold of his hands. "Come on. Let's check if the shower still works."

The playful trail of her voice, the new sparkle in her eyes, the high lift of her cheeks from her smile; he couldn't and didn't try to stop himself from getting to her again, from scooping her up with a light growl so he could transport her to the shower as suggested.

And even as he worried about how he'd fix his life, even as their clothes hit the pewter gray tile and their mouths meshed together in a series of deep and hungry kisses, his heart clenched at the knowledge she once again accepted him despite his shortfalls. Despite his dwindling money, shitty friends, and nonexistent heating.

Steamy water spilled from the shower down his back. He held her to the wall and entered her quickly, taking all the comfort she offered, accepting her ability to turn any sucky situation good. That as always, she wouldn't leave him to deal with his problems alone.

# Chapter Twenty-Nine

The Ruby Room buzzed with way more commotion and music than usual, quite a feat given this was a Wednesday morning, and the bar should have been closed.

But this was no normal Wednesday morning, and butterflies danced within Freya's tummy as she nursed a hot cup of golden chamomile tea and planted her feet under the small table to keep from wriggling. The reporter sitting across from her had a tall glass of local craft beer, the woman's near six-foot frame intimidating, even though she'd been nothing but kind.

"The Ruby Room is already a well-established underground live arts venue." The reporter leaned forward, her black cowboy hat shielding her eyes, her looming question hanging partway between Freya and the cell phone recording this conversation. "What prompted you to put The Ruby forward for the festival?"

Freya pondered the question, allowing her gaze to shift to the stage, not having to imagine Gideon up there since the dim houselights and open stage curtains showcased a bright spotlight shining right on him. His two dancers stood on either side, and they ran through an abridged dress rehearsal, a photographer snapping photos from ground level.

"Honestly?" She turned back to the reporter, conscious that whatever she replied would likely appear in one of Melbourne's most widely distributed newspapers ahead of Saturday night's first show. "The fact you use the word 'underground' is exactly why I'm doing this. I want to pull The Ruby Room out of the shadows and make live performance art accessible to all. I didn't grow up with much, and I understand what it's like to be locked out of certain experiences. That is why we partnered up with The Walk with Pride Foundation to raise money and awareness of their wonderful work. I want everyone to know The Ruby Room is a home for all. A place where everyone is accepted. A place that tries to be different, as well as make a difference."

"As someone who's been to a show here, I can definitely say The Ruby Room embraces all things avant-garde, while being a safe space for anyone who walks through the doors. And then there's you, an enigmatic and bold woman who runs this whole thing, which only makes a night at The Ruby even more exciting. Has starting and growing The Ruby been a long road? As a female business owner, do you find there are different pressures on you?"

"You mean, aside from certain people asking when I'll settle down and have some babies?" She gave the reporter a mock cringe, her thoughts switching to her mother and how no amount of success or work would ever be enough.

Maybe if Freya had forced her past relationships, the ones that weren't working, and gotten herself needlessly pregnant, maybe then her mother would be happy.

Another pitchy laugh broke free from her. *As if!*

A baby would only please her mother for all of two seconds before she found fault. So, Freya sure as hell didn't regret putting her uterus on permanent hiatus.

She straightened, having only partly answered the reporter's question.

"And yes, the road up until now has been long and grueling. I've been looked over for promotions or refused additional training simply because of my gender. Don't get me started on the colleagues or patrons who assume their drunkenness and your close proximity entitles them to grab or jeer. These hurdles put a lot of women off this industry, which is one reason why I started The Ruby. I stopped waiting for an invitation to get ahead and set my own place at the table. And wherever possible, I help those who have been in a similar situation."

A wide smile spread across the reporter's face. "Thank you. I have everything I need. I'll call if I need anything more, but in the meantime, our photographer will get a few shots of you when he's done with Mr. Faber." She tipped her chin to Freya's direct left. "Also, I think there's a gentleman here who wants your attention."

Freya thanked the already departing reporter and turned to Max looming over her left shoulder. She jolted at the sharp flex of his brow, as though she'd interrupted him in deep thought.

Her heart thundered, his attention making her insides burn in a *good* way, a way that made her feel like she'd been caught doing something she shouldn't.

"I wanted to double check the tables are positioned as you wanted them." His gaze slid over her body in a slow, up-and-down motion, his concentrated frown bending into a delighted grin. "Before I go to the effort of arranging all the chairs."

She gave the room a quick glance and nodded, then dropped her focus to his chest, not all that sure she should have invited him to help today.

Aside from juggling the reporter and photographer, she had staff prepping the bar for tonight's press and society preview—The Ruby's chance to gain early reviews before Saturday's first show—as well as providing something for the arts industry "who's who" to talk about.

Besides, since her camping weekend with Max, she'd kind of spent her days brooding and burying herself in work. Work she needed to do, what with the whole make-or-break festival drawing near, though perhaps an element of her busyness had something to do with running from her bubbling emotions.

But then again, Max did need the money, and she couldn't find it in her to deny him the chance of some extra work. The money wouldn't be near enough to fix his problems, but he'd still jumped at the offer of a double shift.

"If you don't mind..." She turned away from his frown, her eyes stinging at the glare of the returned house lights now Gideon was done with his rehearsal, all while she pretended her hands didn't burn with a need to touch Max. "The photographer needs me."

And she didn't touch him. She didn't even offer a smile. She merely mumbled something about the layout being good and then brushed toward the bar, denying any chance of anything "touchy feely" playing out at her place of work.

She didn't want any overly familiar exchanges of looks. No displays of affection.

Not here and especially not in front of her best friend or the press.

She ran her attention over the venue edged in crimson curtains and mirrored walls. A venue *she'd* created, despite her hellish childhood, the years it had taken for her to claw her way out and her soul to recover... And the myriad ways it still hadn't.

Gideon crossed the room and took a seat with the reporter, Freya still hanging back since the photographer fiddled with his camera.

In that brief pause, her mind slipped to a series of thoughts plaguing her from days ago. To the stuff she'd told Max.

There'd been her childhood abuse and her decision to take on her mother's current needs, and how maybe Freya's existence so far away from her horrific childhood made up one big reason why she'd agreed to help her mother.

She'd lost count of how many people had called her lucky over the years—because of her thriving business, or her carefree spirit—but what they didn't understand was that luck had little to do with anything she'd gained. Attributing her success to luck denied the hot coals she'd dragged herself over.

For her, freedom hadn't come without a cost. There'd been years of believing she wasn't good enough. That good things only came to those with a good start.

Those from a supportive family and no murky past.

Then she'd had to overcome the lies. That she was stupid and incapable. That she was still just little Freya, unlovable and born to bear the consequence of other people's neuroses.

For so long, her mother had guided Freya's internal dialogue, though the day Freya had spilled the truth to that nurse had changed everything. That day became the impetus to her own voice finally breaking through.

The Ruby Room *was* hers. *She'd* made this place. Not luck.

Her efforts afforded her a beautiful home in her favorite suburb and provided a steady income to scores of employees. The Ruby was a sanctuary for artists, staff, and patrons alike, especially those who didn't have anywhere else to go.

And The Ruby provided her most valued asset. *Freedom.*

Freedom from her past. Freedom from ever having to rely on anyone else. Because, despite her self-made reputation for having an unbreakable heart, her heart *wasn't* unbreakable.

It was more fragile than most.

Her heart knew pain and wanted nothing more to do with it. Her heart knew abandonment and betrayal, all on a literal and excruciating level. She would never, *ever* let herself be hurt like that again.

And so, she'd become a master of defenses and hid those defenses with an air of playfulness and deflection, just like so many other abuse survivors.

But oh, how those defenses were wonderful, soul-protecting things. They operated every moment of every day, squeezing her heart at any minor sign of impending disappointment.

And that was her problem with having Max around.

She could see herself falling for him. *Deeply. Completely.* And that fired more painful reactions, unleashing the prospect that her heart might never bounce back should things go wrong, and all because her instincts warned her of something else. Something downright undeniable.

Things *would* go wrong. This relationship would not work.

Not with the messy way he conducted his life. Not with how little he knew of himself. Not with her desperate need for consistency, despite her "fun and carefree" persona.

Even if Max wasn't moody or violent like her mother; even if his growing affection shone undeniably. Freya's stomach hollowed at the possibility of once again living on tenterhooks with someone else, which gave life to a special kind of anxiety. One she didn't want to address but would have to anyway… Sometimes, love really wasn't enough.

"What's with you and Mr. Cute Face?"

She blinked and tried not to appear shocked at Gideon standing before her. "Sorry, Cute Face, who?"

"The man I'm guessing you were just daydreaming about." Gideon dabbed at his forehead with a white sweat towel, stabbing his gaze toward Max. "Shouldn't you be drowning in thoughts of how to make my show shine brighter for the festival, if that's even possible? And don't play stupid with me, lady. Spill. Who's the hot blond fellow over there with the bed-ruffled hair? Why does he have you blushing like a Catholic school girl?"

She touched her knuckles to her cheeks, which had in fact gotten warmer at the reference to Max. "He just works here. And yes, he's admittedly attractive, but otherwise nothing worth mentioning."

"Well, I really only came over to get your feedback on the show, but since Mr. Cute Face 'isn't worth mentioning', I most definitely am going to need you to start mentioning."

Gideon crossed his arms and tapped his foot, waiting.

An awkward silence dragged out. Well, silent except for all the noise of furniture shifting about and Gideon tapping his brown Oxford on the black wood floor.

His unwavering stare said he wasn't moving on from this conversation, so she better get talking.

"Fine. I confess." She rolled her eyes in an impression of a bored teenager. "I climbed aboard Mr. Cute Face's train a couple of times, that's all. I mean, look at him, can you blame me?"

Gideon jerked his chin back, doing a poor job of suppressing a smirk. "Really now? What happened to your whole 'I don't mix business and pleasure' rule? How many dreamboat men have walked through The Ruby's doors, and you've never 'ridden their trains'?" He leaned way in now, eyes narrowing mere inches from her own. "Tell me, what's changed?"

She forced herself not to look away, even though her eyes stung, and she wanted so desperately to peek down at her shoes and escape this standoff.

Gideon might have spent way too much time over the years away from her, studying and then touring, but Goddess-damn-it, he knew her too flipping well.

"What do you want me to say?" She shrugged, keeping her small show of defeat low-key in the hopes it would be enough for him.

His smile softened just a little. "You like this one, don't you?"

The invitation for honesty coiled her muscles and brought nausea to her stomach.

"We're a bit more than friends with benefits, but still nothing more than friends. It's hard to explain." She crossed her arms and gave herself the treat of looking away and escaping Gideon's scrutiny for just one second.

"He knows. Doesn't he?"

She nodded, catching on that he meant Max knew about her past and mother now being ill.

"I let him meet her. I don't know why I did it, but I let him meet her."

Gideon's fingers curled over her shoulders, and he turned her to look at him again. "He met The Dragon?"

"You know I don't like it when you call her that."

And still, an unavoidable chuckle broke from her.

"*I* haven't even met The Dragon." Gideon pressed a hand to his chest in mock offense. "Sorry, I mean, Ms. Dragon."

She narrowed a silent glare at him. In truth, she'd never let him meet her mother because Kerry would take one look at Gideon and unleash untold cruelty on him based on his sexually. Gideon didn't deserve that. No one deserved that.

"What?" He raised his hands in a gesture of innocence. "The name fits. I mean, I'm sure a dragon would totally eat their young, which is only one step worse than what your mother—"

She squeezed her eyes shut, a wordless warning for him to just stop.

"Sorry." The apology prompted her to look at him again, while Gideon flung his sweat towel over his shoulder. "Okay, so tell me how the meeting with Mr. Cute Face and Mother went."

She dipped her chin and mumbled, "Not well."

"And let me guess, you thought you'd present this stunning tall drink of a man to Mama Dearest, and she'd finally give you some love in return?"

She opened her mouth, ready to tell Gideon to shove his theory, *that* wasn't what she'd intended at all, but then silence swallowed her reply.

She hadn't used Max to gain approval from her mother; rather, she'd wanted support *against* her mother, but Gideon would take any explanation as an admission of guilt and forever heckle her for using Max as mother-bait.

So, she cleared her throat and set about giving him nothing. "Anyway, so feedback on your show, it's brilliant. Thank you again for using The Ruby as your premiere venue."

She offered a giant, cheesy grin, daring him to return to the subject of her and Max.

"Of course, you know flattery will get you everywhere, including off the hook." Gideon gave her a side glare, his features brightening, as he jutted his chin toward the stage. "It looks like the photographer is ready for you. I'll let you go for now, but I'll need way more than flattery before I drop this whole Mr. Cute Face scandal."

# Chapter Thirty

Gideon's show began with a flash of blinding yellow light and a blast of jazz horns, but for the longest time, the man himself didn't appear. The audience mumbled. Why wasn't he on stage? Only the soft ding of a bicycle bell turned everyone's attention all the way to the back of the venue.

The curtain belonging to the cleaner's alcove flew wide open, and Gideon pushed through on the back of a bicycle; his outfit a super tight, aqua blue unitard. A bushy, horseshoe mustache overwhelmed his upper lip, and a white sweatband stretched over his forehead.

He pedaled through the crowd, spraying water from a drink bottle in all directions, yelling at the audience to get out of his way and to stop looking at him. Melbourne traffic had supposedly fucked him over, and now he was late, and everyone would know what he looked like without his makeup and heels.

Howls of laughter filled the room. The impact of his entrance was more amazing when he leapt to the stage and began his first song, his immaculate voice and instant stage presence cutting clear across the room.

In that moment, he proved without a doubt he'd never needed his innate beauty or the glam costumes to grab a crowd. Not even garish spandex and a hideous mustache obscured his talent.

Freya worked the bar, feverishly helping her staff fill the endless demand for champagne and red wine, all the while stealing glances at the show and trying not to ogle Max.

*Max.* As much as she tried, she couldn't wipe him from her mind. More to the point, as cruel as it seemed to push him away, doing so would be inevitable.

Even with someone who wasn't a great person, walking from a relationship was never easy. But Max was better than great; he was amazing. If not for a couple of fatal flaws, he'd be her perfect man. He didn't deserve the distance she had already put between them, using her work and the festival as an excuse to pull back.

Then again, leading him on wasn't right either.

She giggled at Gideon seated on a man's lap a few rows from the front, the man somewhere in his fifties with a gray-streaked red beard and a bunch of laugh lines creasing the corners of his eyes.

Gideon had changed from the aqua spandex to a short, under-bust corset and his iconic skin-tight booty shorts over black fishnets. His bike shoes were gone, too, and his signature black suede heels covered his feet. Now he rested cheek-to-cheek with the other man, crooning a sweet serenade into a cordless microphone.

Freya smiled at his unabashed freedom, at his effortless command over a room filled with been-there-done-that press and society notables, but even this wasn't Gideon's true self.

She'd grown up with him after all.

She knew his stage face when she saw it. His alter ego.

Together, they'd fought to figure out where they fit in the world. Her personal challenge all about sorting through her past and where to go next; Gideon's struggle spread over a series of things.

There'd been his fight for his place as an artist, made worse in a family and world set on devaluing art, despite the daily consumption of movies, music, and books.

Then there'd been his coming to terms with his sexuality and identity, the biggest tragedy being that he'd had anything to come to terms with. For some, acceptance was a given, while others, like Gideon, had no such luck.

He'd been forced to choose between buckling to the pressure of becoming something other than who he was, or developing a thicker skin, shedding family and friends who'd refused to make good on their promises of unconditional love.

And as much as Gideon had gotten tougher, he'd taken a real hit some years ago when the entire country engaged in an unnecessary survey on whether gay people could marry.

Bad enough there'd been a vote, but then so many in his community were left to process the huge betrayal of having forty percent of voters—people they interacted with on a daily basis—choose *against* something that had little-to-no impact on their lives.

And surprise, surprise. In the years following, the country hadn't collapsed, and life went on as normal.

"I'll have a scotch on the rocks."

She startled at the familiar rumble, her attention lifting to Max on the other side of the bar.

She gave him a side-glare, and his lips split into a mischievous grin. "As if I'm letting you drink when you're not even halfway through your second shift. Besides, you're more of a beer guy."

His blue eyes twinkled in the venue's golden light, and she swore her breath caught in response. "You've been watching what I drink?"

"Don't get too cocky." She busied herself wiping down a nonexistent spill on the polished black bar top. "I've poured drinks for as long as I've been legally allowed to. I have a mind for orders, and if you don't believe me, I can tell you what the lighting guy drinks."

His grin fell by a degree. "You mean I'm not special?"

"I mean, if you're looking for some kind of undying declaration while we're both working"—she flicked a curl from her eyes, dismissing her desire to prop him back up or comfort him—"it's not going to happen."

"Well then, I am working." He nudged his head toward the stage. "I'm here bothering you right now because the show is about to finish, and Gideon asked me to find you during his last song."

Her nerves fluttered into high alert. "What do I have to do with Gideon's last song?"

Just because she had a venue that hosted shows didn't mean she wanted to be *in* them.

"He told me to pass on a message."

She swore under her breath, her leg muscles jittery with a sudden need to run. "What's this message?"

Gideon danced across the stage, too busy being a star, while she calculated there was no way Gideon picked Max at random to be her messenger of bad news. He wanted to meddle. Or at least, invent a reason to talk to Max.

Max pointed a finger. "See that gold cord running along the wall back there?"

She spun around. A gold rope was, indeed, camouflaged amongst the equally gold-framed mirrors behind her. She turned back to Max, the heavy bass and brass in Gideon's song overly loud, the deep vibrations playing havoc on her insides. "What about it?"

Max's cheekbones lifted high, a man proud to be part of Gideon's shenanigans. "The music will slow at the very end of Gideon's song. He'll hold a really long note on the word 'love', and that's when you pull that rope."

"And what's supposed to happen?" She snapped her attention to the stage. There stood a solid chance she'd fuck this up for Gideon.

She narrowed her glare and tuned into the music—her glaring a nonsensical reaction to intense listening. The music slowed, and Gideon winked to her from across the room. Her eyelids flung wide. No doubt she looked like a terrified rabbit.

"Oh God, is this it?"

Max shook his head and held up a hand, gesturing for her to wait.

"*Loooooooooooooooooooooooooove.*"

Gideon's voice filled every corner of the venue, the crowd whooping in support of his perfect pitch and the high and prolonged execution of what he called "a money note". His ability to pull that sound off quite literally paid his bills.

Max nodded at Freya. She sucked in a breath and lunged back, pretty much falling over herself to pull the damn rope.

A shriek of excitement broke from the crowd. She turned just as an avalanche of fuchsia and electric blue sequins fell from an aqua silk canopy Gideon had stretched under the iconic ruby chandelier.

Three child-sized, inflatable bicycles floated from the fray of sequins, the crowd dusted in sparkle. The bikes bounced, audience members swatting them between each other, like a game.

Gideon melted away behind the velvet curtain, everyone in the crowd too busy to notice, his exit as enigmatic and as "Gideon" as an exit could get.

Max smiled, his eyes giving off a soft sheen, as though the crowd and commotion faded and all that mattered was her. "I guess Gideon thought I deserved advance warning since I'll be the one cleaning up the glitter bomb."

Her stomach clenched at how it felt to be the center of his attention, a man as beautiful and well-meaning as Max. In all her years, she'd never been one to attract beauty *or* goodwill, not without a decent amount of hard work on her part. Mostly people treated her more like an afterthought, and that said a lot about her headspace during the years just following her escape from her mother.

She'd surrounded herself with new people, but most of those new people still held too many similarities to the family she'd known, her sense of familiarity completely askew when it came to those people she allowed in her life. The themes of coldness and dysfunction repeated.

Gideon had been the only exception. One person to truly look out for her.

Even now.

So Max, with his sweet brand of innocence, had decided this whole rope-pulling spectacle was about Gideon's need to forecast mess, but Freya knew better. That wasn't the case at all. Gideon had wanted to meet Max. To vet him. To make sure he could be trusted with Freya's heart.

Points of warmth radiated through her chest. Her friend cared. Even after years of managing herself. And despite knowing her days with Max were severely numbered, his stare on her now forced her to consider what life would be like attached to someone like him.

Someone who noticed her.

Someone who cared about the smaller details like the cringe-worthy books she read or her aversion to dark tents. Someone who accepted her completely, from the tattoos on her body to the scars from her past.

And more than any of that, she questioned whether she had the stamina to *pick and stick* life with someone. Anyone.

That thought left her mind and a new one entered. The memory of her parents' disastrous marriage and how quickly people turned into monsters.

Would she one day turn into a monster like her mother? Would Max?

Because her experience of monsters was a real thing, something even the fictional type could not rival. Knowing what she did, how could she ever truly trust anyone?

"Max, maaate!"

The bellowed words yanked her focus toward a man standing yards away, his bloodshot eyes and flushed cheeks hinting he was drunk or perhaps even high.

Max pivoted and stared at the man, too, before turning back to her and whispering, "Why does my old crowd insist on following me?"

A smile tugged at her lips, and she couldn't resist her next comment. "They're not following you. You work where your old crowd hangs out, remember?"

"*Pfft*"—he swatted a hand—"details. Anyway, I'll fob this one off and get back to work. Catch you later."

He gave her a lazy salute and slunk away, but her years of dealing with nasty people reared up to warn her. One look at his friend's twisted sneer told her this particular guy wouldn't be easily "fobbed off".

# Chapter Thirty-One

"Hey, Cedrick. Sorry, can't chat. Got to get back to work."

Max gave Cedrick an obligatory wave and brushed past, but not before catching the demented joy fading from the man's eyes.

Unwilling to pretend Cedrick was anyone he wanted to talk to, Max gave the equivalent of an internal shrug and headed for the cleaner's alcove.

Perhaps the biggest benefit of being booted from his former social circle was that he no longer had to pretend to like certain people. The farce was over. He had no money. Therefore, no value. Now he and his old "friends" could move on.

He grabbed the large broom from the farthest corner of the cleaner's alcove and went back out to the dance floor, detouring away from Cedrick.

Loud applause rolled across the room as he went about sweeping sequins, glad that less than a couple of hours remained of his long shift. He peered up to find Gideon prancing down the stage steps and into the crowd. He now wore an eye-catching, royal blue blazer embroidered with tiny gold stars, thrown over his plain black shirt and pants.

Max couldn't remember the last time he'd met someone so skilled at drawing attention, all while somehow maintaining so much class and mystery. Gideon's elegance made everyone want to be his friend—a funny observation coming from a man who'd lost almost all his friends.

*Only the ones who never really counted.*

Right, well, the loneliness still sucked, and as much as he knew nothing of performance art, a small portion of jealousy grabbed at him. He begrudged Gideon his natural born showmanship—the type that looked simple but that no normal mortal could achieve.

What Gideon did wasn't by any stretch easy. Max had watched the man rehearse, and he worked hard for his perfection, that work ethic and drive a puzzle to Max.

Why couldn't he just get his act together and be more like Gideon? What was with the constant aimlessness?

"You think you're too important to talk to your old friends?" A hand gripped Max's shoulder and spun him around. "Now that you're sweeping floors."

Cedrick smirked through an unfocused gaze.

Not wanting any trouble, especially not on an important night for Freya, Max turned away and went back to his work. "I saw Adele around here somewhere, why don't you guys just enjoy your night, okay?"

He eyeballed Adele standing by the bar, hoping she'd do something to draw her control-freak boyfriend away. Only, she just pressed her glass of complimentary champagne to her lips and averted her gaze to the floor, denting any idea she might one day find the courage to stand up to, or at least leave, Cedrick.

Since Max had forgotten to bring out the giant dust pan, he pushed the glittery pile of sequins across the floor with his broom and toward the cleaner's alcove, the task a legitimate reason to walk away.

By the time Max came out again, Cedrick seemed to have forgotten him. So, he hauled away another pan of glitter, then came back out to start clearing tables since the crowd had thinned out.

He passed Freya on his way to the kitchen to get an empty tray, a huge relieved smile on her face as she served out last drinks.

He sidled up to her and used his elbow to offer a nudge of encouragement, even though what he really wanted to do was pull her into him and kiss her senseless. "Gideon was brilliant. I hope you're ready for The Ruby Room to be at capacity for the rest of its existence."

She slid a drink over to a patron, giving a little shoulder shimmy as she did. "I can't believe it. Now I've seen the show, I'm so excited for what the next two weeks will bring."

He waited for a pause between patrons, and for her to turn and look at him, before he spoke again. "I'm really happy for you, you know that? And I'm happy I could be part of that happiness, even in the tiniest way, such as sweeping your floors."

Her lips parted, and her stare lingered on his for some time, like maybe she hadn't experienced much of anyone being glad for her. For a microsecond, his thoughts revisited all that he'd learned about her childhood, but rather than pity what she'd endured, he felt pride.

She'd pulled through. Even as a child, she'd stood up for herself, forging ahead with her life—two things he still struggled with as a grown man. And somehow, he'd been lucky enough to meet her. To be part of her world. She'd confided in him. Included him. Surely, that meant something?

"So... err..." She blinked and shook her head, as though snapping out of a trance. "What's with your friend over there?"

She tipped her head toward Cedrick.

"To be honest. I have no idea. I'm counting down the seconds until he leaves, or we can at least close and I don't have to look at him anymore."

"Well." She gave a seemingly casual shrug, though the downward bend of her lips told a different story. "He keeps glaring at you, and he doesn't look all that sober. My guess is he's ready to cause trouble, so I'm seconds away from getting Crystal to boot him."

"You don't have to do that." Max backed away so they could both return to their work. "Cedrick and his crowd are regulars here, and I don't want his problem with me to get in the way of business for you. Let me handle him, okay?"

He winked at Freya, an untruthfully light gesture given the invisible weight pressing on his shoulders. He couldn't opt for his usual tactic of ignoring and avoiding the problem, since Cedrick seemed disinclined to go away, which meant Max needed a plan to deal with the guy. Again, not great, since Max had a zero-percent success rate at dealing with anything, much less people in tense situations.

He went about collecting a new tray of empty glasses, waiting for courage and a game plan to surface.

His tray was half-full by the time a wide palm hit him square between the shoulders, pushing him forward so he stumbled. He wobbled, trying to correct his position, every small effort consistently too late.

The glasses slid to the front of his tray, and as if by slow motion, toppled one by one over the edge. One by one, those glasses smashed to the hard wood floor. A high-pitched shattering filled the room.

Patrons gasped and leapt out of the way, a sudden clear circle opening up around him... Well, him and the man who'd done the pushing.

*Cedrick.*

Max peered down, first to the broken glass across a large expanse of empty floor, then to his shins, his long pants having saved his legs from an encounter with any flying shards.

But then he lifted his focus to a woman a yard away who hadn't been so lucky.

Blood dotted the yellow hem of her knee-length dress, and a steady red stream gushed from her knee. Her gaze darted around the room, only to land on him in a wide stare.

A cold prickle washed over his skin. He was meant to do something, but he stood frozen and unable to make sense of what had just happened. He glanced to his left and found Cedrick glaring back, the knuckle dragger having stooped to pulling innocent people into his grudge.

Max strode toward the woman, but the double thud of footfall followed.

Again, his world spun. He found himself wrenched back by his shirt until he caught sight of Cedrick for one brief second—a brief second before the man's meaty fist connected with Max's left cheekbone.

*Holy shit!*

A sickening crack filled his ears, and the crowd gasped again. Sharp pain sliced through his face, and he stumbled to the floor. Cedrick bounced on his heels, shaking his hand in the air, swearing, yelling… Something about his "broken fucking knuckles."

Maybe the cracking sound had come from Cedrick's hand more than Max's face?

Still, the only thing Max could really focus on was the way the room wobbled and his thoughts jumbled. Really, he had no focus at all, and his head bloody hurt! And still, he tried to push off the ground, not wanting to fight, but needing to stay upright so that Cedrick wouldn't get on top of him.

Cedrick wasn't much bigger, but he wasn't sober either, and there was no telling what a person in a bad state of mind might do. Plus, Max didn't want to leave The Ruby in the back of an ambulance.

"I don't know what your problem is." He held his palm to his throbbing cheekbone and clenched his eyes mostly shut to keep them from watering. "But you need to leave."

Crystal stepped in through a hollow in the crowd. "Actually, someone's called the police, and he's coming with me until they get here."

"Fuck you both." Spittle flew from Cedrick's mouth, his glassy stare holding Max. "And you don't tell me what to do. Do you think you can waltz on in and get what you want, *who* you want? No, you fucken' can't. You're just a piece-of-shit nobody. A sad, pathetic, broke-as-fuck loser!"

Well, Cedrick was still pissed about Max dating Adele for all of two minutes. That much was clear.

Crystal took a step forward, only for Cedrick to spin around and clamber onto a glossy black table, the ruby chandelier looming just above. Crystal's next step prompted him to kicked a beer-filled glass at her. She ducked out of the way, but glass and amber liquid exploded at her feet.

Screams cut from the crowd. Some yelled for Cedrick to get down. A few fled through the venue's front door, though most stood in wide-eyed morbid fascination. Meanwhile, Freya stood in a spot a few feet ahead of the bar, her mouth open, seemingly frozen.

Crystal kicked beer from the hem of her black jeans, using quick, shifting eye movements to signal for Max to help tackle Cedrick off the table.

Max nodded and ran forward, only for Cedrick to kick another glass.

This time, glass bounced off the floor and struck Max's shin, his pants no match against the projectile's velocity. Though pain radiated up his leg, he didn't have time to dwell on the ache since Cedrick jumped into the air, and in the most idiotic move ever, grabbed the chandelier's brass spokes.

A loud ripping sound cut through the space and a huge crack opened up in the white ceiling. The chandelier jolted. Cedrick held on, his face turning pale like he finally saw how asinine his plan was and didn't know what to do.

Plaster and paint fluttered down like tiny snowflakes, and once again, the chandelier moved, the whole thing dropping by a couple of inches.

Another rip split the air, and this time the entire chandelier fell, taking Cedrick down with it. His ass hit the table first, while the giant chandelier landed on top of him, the table legs snapping and then collapsing.

Dust sailed out in a billowy, white cloud from the epicenter of the fall and across the room, followed by eerie silence.

Max didn't dare breathe. He didn't move. Save for mumbling, "Is he still alive?"

Crystal lunged forward, soon tugging at the chandelier, only to stop. "Hang on a moment, are we even meant to move this thing?" She spun around, glass crunching under her shoes, as she stared at Max. "Won't that cause more damage?"

He'd only just completed a first aid course for his swim coaching job, so the information sat fresh in his head. The chandelier's wires were completely severed, so electrocution wasn't a risk.

"He doesn't seem impaled on anything, so we'll pull the chandelier off, but not move him in case of possible spinal injury."

Besides, copious amounts of glass lay all around and moving Cedrick might mean inadvertently slicing him up. That wasn't something Max wanted to do. Even if the guy had just caused everyone a world of pain.

Max stepped forward, half contemplating whether he could just give up now—go home and have a cup of tea—maybe leave the snot-nosed-bastard under the chandelier where he couldn't bother anyone anymore.

At the same time, his stomach churned at the dystopian vision surrounding them. The Ruby Room's gaping roof, the iconic chandelier a twisted mess atop Cedrick and a now scuffed-up floor.

Freya would have seen everything unfold. And yet he lacked the courage to turn and acknowledge her since he'd played a part in whatever heartbreak would come out of tonight.

He leaned down and wrapped each hand around one of the chandelier's brass spokes, nodding to Crystal to lift along with him. Though nowhere near as heavy as he expected, the chandelier groaned, and a hard tug freed Cedrick enough to have him rolling and shoving clear of his entrapment.

He soon sat coughing and spluttering, a tirade of swears coming between each involuntary noise. Spots of blood seeped through his silver gray shirt, his face a busted and weeping mess.

Even through the blood, Cedrick's glare turned glacial, and he pinned it to Adele standing nearby. "Did you film that? Did you fucking film that? I want a copy for my lawyer."

He made no attempt to rise from the floor, which made Max wonder if he actually could.

Cedrick stabbed a finger at Freya. "Your pathetic club is over, do you hear me? I'll sue you, and I'll fucking win. I'll have this place shut down."

Freya shuddered as though trying to awaken from this entire nightmare. "Has someone called an ambulance yet?"

One of the bartenders waved her hand from across the room, a phone pressed to her ear. "I'm on it. They're already on the way."

"Good thing the hospital is just down the road." Freya spoke in a dull mumble, as if a large part of her had already left the building.

Meanwhile, Cedrick became weirdly silent, his head lolling forward, the heel of his oxford pushing at a pile of red glass before him. There was something ironic about that image—a man, who moments earlier had kicked beer glasses with no regard for the damage he caused—now soaked in blood, the self-inflicted victim of the mother of all glassing incidents.

Freya's focus flicked to Max, her pupils dilated and jaw still loose. Heavy seconds dragged until slowly, but surely, the muscles over her brow hardened, and her eyes formed a razor-sharp scowl.

He'd promised to handle Cedrick, shutting down her offer to get Crystal to eject the guy long before he caused any problems. Now The Ruby Room lay in ruins, as did this monumental night. The entire festival was now likely a lost cause, too.

And of course, there was the bleeding woman and Cedrick's injuries, plus his threat of a lawsuit. Worst of all, the countless employees, performers, and technicians now out of a job with the bar in its current unworkable state.

There'd be no positive spin to bail Max out of *this* disaster. Nausea swirled in his gut. Guilt and yet more failure lay heavy on his heart.

The bartender from earlier sidled up to Freya, phone still in hand.

"Honey, there's a call for you." She extended the phone with a grimace. "Saint Vincent's Hospital. It's your mum. It sounds urgent."

# Chapter Thirty-Two

Freya's heart beat so hard and fast her chest hurt from the unstoppable effort, her muscles so weak they trembled and felt as if they were made of water. She sat in the passenger side of Max's car, wringing her hands, hating that she hated him right now, while still needing his help to get her the few blocks to the hospital since she wasn't anywhere near stable enough to make it there alone.

She opened and closed her hand, her elbows down to her fingers numb from the unforgiving adrenaline filling her muscles, and she tried to get back some sort of sensation. She didn't know what to think. *Couldn't* think. Her thoughts were out of control and incapable of slowing down.

Her mother's last moments loomed.

Heck, so did Freya's time with Max.

Or any man.

Regardless of what had just gone down at The Ruby, she couldn't see herself wanting to date for a long time. Something not easily defined was about to happen, something uncontrollable. No matter what, death waited for no man or woman, and her life balanced on the edge of a major change.

Her throat hurt from the labor of holding back tears. Her stomach

held the heaviness of someone seconds from lunging off a bridge—
even though she'd always imagined she'd feel nothing on the day her
mother's reckoning finally rolled around.

The car stopped at a set of lights, and she gnawed at the inside of
her cheek, her focus glued to the pedestrian crossing and a smiling
couple walking hand-in-hand on the other side of the windshield.

To them, this was just an ordinary night. They had all the time in
the world, and life held no hurry. But not for her. Certainly not for her
mother.

She pressed the heel of her hand to her sternum and rubbed, the
rapid beat of her heart refusing to abate. There were things she had to
say. Things she'd held on to for far too long.

She'd tell her mother that although she could never forgive the
abuse, she understood how she'd ended up the way she had. That
wherever death took her next, she really did hope her mother would
finally know peace from the hurt and hate gifted to her as a child.

If death were a fair place, perhaps her mother would get a replay. A
new family. A new life free from abuse, neglect, and childhood trauma.
A permanent escape from the war that had raged in her mind every
day for decades.

And maybe one day Freya would get a new childhood too…

A tear spilled down her cheek, but she swept at it before Max could
notice, breathing deep to still her runaway mind—a mind for some
reason grappling with the concept of reincarnation.

*What the heck is that about?*

Just once, she wanted things to be okay. To think that maybe, just
maybe, in her final moments with her mother, she could see a flash of
something more than judgment and manipulation.

A sense of love. Apology. Acceptance…

Max's car plunged into a stretch of deep shadow, and she blinked at
the concrete gray walls of a multi-level parking lot, one packed level
flicking by after another level, an available spot seeming illusive.

She needed an escape from the rising panic that she wouldn't make
it in time, so she rehearsed what she would say, all while questioning
whether she could really execute this final conversation.

Then again, even if her mother failed to budge, at least she could say she'd tried her best, that she'd done all she could to fill in the final missing pieces and have the one talk she and her mother had never had.

Maybe she'd get closure, before the opportunity was lost forever.

Max parked, and she pulled at her door handle, her bag already slung over her shoulder.

She raced for the bank of elevators, leaving him to catch up—or not—because at this point, she didn't care.

Soon, she dashed across the asphalt to the hospital, then into another elevator, and up eleven floors to the palliative care unit, where she burst across the blue-carpeted corridor and right past the nurses' station.

Her breath exploded through her lips and cream-colored walls flickered by, her gaze darting from one door to the other until it landed on her mother's room number.

She bolted through an icy-blue curtain surrounding the only bed in the room. Her feet ground to a halt, her body jolting at the sight of a nurse—a woman in her forties, with short salt and pepper hair—standing over her mother, hand stroking her sandy-blond fringe, thumb rubbing tenderly at a forehead no longer quite so scored in wrinkles.

Freya's muscles turned rigid. There were no more monitors. No more drips. No needles feeding pain meds into her mother's arms. A rolled-up towel sat tucked under her mother's chin, keeping her slack jaw from falling open.

Freya's knees unlocked, and she forced a few tiny steps before she fell to the ground yards from the bed. Her attention locked on her mother's eyes.

*Closed eyes.*

Freya jerked her chin higher, catching sight of the nurse's lips pressed into a thin smile, one that conveyed sympathy and apology.

"I'm so sorry." The nurse held a soft tone, one that somehow sounded like glass shattering in a silent room. "She's gone."

∿

Freya's body took over, and she stumbled the few steps to her mother's side, collapsing at the bed's pillow end, a great wail breaking free of her. The deep-within sound wasn't like anything she'd ever known herself capable of making. It embodied all-consuming grief and knowledge that an invisible cord had just been severed. The link between mother and daughter. A link that existed regardless of where the relationship stood.

She reached out and stroked her mother's forehead, the warmth in her skin still present as if her mother only slept. And now the tears came thick and fast. Tears she hadn't let herself cry in years, but which she worried would never stop.

Her tummy cramped, pained and hollow, as though someone had taken a shovel and scooped out her insides, and even as the tears fell, a new and more depressing understanding grew.

That this was the first time. *The only time*, she'd ever been able to touch her mother with any kind of tenderness, except for that ill-received kiss on her mother's forehead last time. The one chance she'd ever have to voice any of the thoughts that swirled within her mind for as long as she could remember.

"Oh, you poor woman." She leaned forward and pressed a kiss to her mother's head. No one would understand this. That *she* would feel sorry for her mother. Her abuser. Her tormenter. But no single journey through life was the same, and this was her particular mess to untangle. "I hope you know what peace is now."

Another sob broke out, along with more fat tears. She crumpled forward and rested her head on the thick hospital pillow beside her mother's. The room and everyone watching—the nurse, Max—all disappeared.

It was just Freya, her mother, and a heavy, uncontrollable grief.

That final conversation, the one she'd planned during the ride over, would never happen now. All she had was *this*. And the ability to touch her mother. Her *dead* mother. Along with the engulfing sense she was forever alone.

A filling breath forced its way into her lungs, as though she'd failed to breathe the entire time she'd been sobbing, which maybe wasn't all that untrue.

So, she sat back and took more breaths, dedicating herself to memorizing the details of her mother's face one last time. For once, Kerry Branner looked calm, her wrinkles eased, and her skin inexplicably glowing.

Even growing up, Freya noted the permanent creases between her mother's brow; her jaw always fused and strained. She'd wondered if her mother even had the ability to just let go.

As an adult, Freya knew different. Her mother had never had an easy moment in her entire life, the ghosts of her past continued to haunt, and that alone was something worth crying over.

Freya extended her arm and pressed her hand to the top of her mother's sternum, wishing her heart still beat in there. "You never had a chance, did you?"

Another wave of grief rose through her chest, culminating in another thick downpour of tears. They slid to her jawline, hitting her forearm, the room's cold air adding a chill.

Her mother's golden lashes extended down in their closed position, sprinkles of gray highlighting the rarity for Freya to really observe. Never once in her life had she felt comfortable enough to really look at her mother. At least, not in a way that didn't involve staring each other down.

She jerked back, the space between her shoulders taut, while a new heat flared in her belly. She swiped at her face with an open palm, sniffling, her eyes narrowed at her mother's peaceful face.

Except, now her expression appeared less restful, more mocking.

Amazing how a motionless face could still portray so many emotions.

When Freya had received the call to come to the hospital, she figured she'd have a few minutes alone with her mother before she passed away. But no. Her mother had blindsided her.

"You couldn't wait just a moment longer, could you?" She laughed and shook her head.

*Am I really talking to a dead person?*

And of course, her mother hadn't waited.

Even in this last thing, she denied Freya.

A daughter she'd never wanted and used all the same.

*Fuck.*

Freya rubbed at more tears. Even in death, her mother confused her.

Unlike any normal child from a normal family, this experience couldn't be as simple as knowing she was going to miss her mother. Just the fact that this moment hurt so much seemed truly unfair.

*Why? Why do I care?*

*Because her life is just one giant pity, now isn't it?*

A ruined childhood. A ruined child. A damaged woman who'd only known how to damage others. She'd passed her wound on to her children. A generational wound that dated who knew how far back and kept on giving, or more precisely, taking.

Nothing and no one could help Freya climb out of the hole she'd been born into.

No one would truly understand. Not even her brother.

She'd always been alone, her latest involvement with her mother an attempt to get the inflictor of her wounds to provide the healing, and that ploy had always been doomed to fail.

Maybe she'd brought this pain on herself.

Gone was any chance of an apology, any chance her mother might express any feelings of love. Freya would find no resolution here, that much was clear.

A large hand landed on her shoulder. She slammed her eyes shut and sucked in a breath. *Max.*

"Is there something I can help you with?"

His gentle tone made her want to fold forward into a ball, his kindness more jarring than if he'd been mad at her for shutting him out. She shook her head and withdrew any verbal response, continuing the sham of being mad, when she really just didn't want to hear her own grief-affected voice.

"I just spoke to the nurse." His strong fingers massaged her shoulder, and her heart sank. "The hospital needs to know which funeral home will be collecting her body tomorrow morning."

She tilted her head toward her handbag, which she'd thrown onto the ground on her way in. "There are papers in my bag. Can you call and tell them? I just... I can't..."

She sucked in another shuddering breath, rustling filling her ears. How was it possible to have so many layers of pain? Pain for her mother. Pain for herself. Pain at Max's presence.

She launched to her feet. "Wait."

She faced him for the first time since entering this hospital. She had no idea how much of her grief he'd witnessed, and she didn't really want to think about it. All she knew was that she was glad she hadn't been completely alone.

His attention snapped from the handbag and back to her, and within seconds, he stepped forward and wrapped his arms around her. She sank against him, burying her face in his black cotton shirt, the boozy scent of The Ruby Room and his cool mint cologne infiltrating the emotions already swallowing her whole.

A new set of claws dug into her heart. The pain of having someone take her weight, both literally and figuratively. This should be a relief, but for a broken woman like her, the support hurt more than she could handle. A sob tore from her, and she shook in his embrace, more tears spilling forth and soaking into his shirt.

And he just stood there, silent and holding her, as if he knew words couldn't help.

He held her for as long as she needed, until she took a step away and said, "Thank you."

The weak gratitude was the best she could muster. She slunk back and stared at the ceiling, the top of her head hurting from all the crying and having to process so much all at once.

The totality of her mother's life.

All the missed opportunities and wasted years.

The sheer lack of love.

And the coldest, hardest truth of all?

Sometimes, no matter what, there was no apology, no heartfelt goodbye, certainly no happy ever after.

While she'd been running for years, trying to escape her past, working double time to gain all she'd missed out on, her mother's death came as a brick wall telling her to stop and just be sad. To say goodbye to all the things she'd never had and the things she'd never wanted in the first place—the abuse, the permanent emotional scars.

She refocused on Max and his soft smile, his brows raised in an expression of hope, like maybe she might tell him the worst was over. But the pain in her head said the worst had just begun, and the ache in her heart would likely never leave.

"Come back as soon as you can." She paused, taking a second to appreciate her even voice that time, vowing that for once in her life she'd hit stop on the treadmill and finally step away. Things were going to change. "I want to go home."

# Chapter Thirty-Three

A mixture of gray and white filtered in as Max lay on the couch, blinking at the heavy floor-to-ceiling drapes in Freya's living room, the tiniest slip of light spilling in through a break in the center.

Having slept there overnight, he huffed out a sigh and interlaced his fingers over his belly trying not to breathe in the smell of clothes still worn since the beginning of his long bar shift yesterday morning.

Every so often, the light from the curtains flickered with the soft plod of people walking by in the street outside. People just starting their day. Occasionally, the plodding came with the sound of chatter, another reminder of just how long he'd lain here, awake and alone.

Last night, within seconds of arriving home, Freya ran upstairs, and he'd stayed in case she needed anything. In case she needed *him*.

So far, she hadn't.

He let out a groan and sat up, his head aching from sleep deprivation, his back sore from his night on the couch. A dull click came from upstairs, followed by the creak of floorboards. *She was awake.*

He shot up and made his way to the curtains, not wanting a dark, depressing room to greet her when she came downstairs.

"Oh, you're still here." Her tone croaked, flat on delivery.

He spun around, his ribs contracting painfully at the sight of her bare feet on the bottom step.

He slid his gaze up to her lopsided, white silk robe and her frizzy, misshapen hair. The unkempt look didn't bother him so much as the soullessness in her eyes, the surrounding skin red and puffy, her small and fragile stance adding to her overall shattered look. Like all the spark he loved about this woman had left.

He swallowed at the thick sensation in his throat and stepped forward. She slipped past him, veering to the right and into the kitchen.

"I wanted to make sure you'd be okay."

She poured herself a drink, an *actual* drink, tequila splashing around in a flare-rimmed shot glass at seven in the morning.

She pressed the glass to her lips and tipped back her head, gulping the straight liquor, before straightening and staring at him. "I'm not okay."

She poured another shot and tipped that one back too, catching his gaze as she placed the glass soundlessly to the white marble counter. "It's best you leave."

His mouth turned dry, her speech slow and calculated. Couldn't she just get angry and lash out at him? Give him something more than dull apathy? If she'd lost all spirit, then that meant he'd lost something else altogether. Something he still grappled to understand. Something irreplaceable.

He opened his mouth ready to speak, but his jaw just wavered and nothing came out.

His natural inclination in a bad situation was to find the sunny side, but this was way beyond a *bad* situation. Her bar had been trashed. Her mum was dead.

Maybe she was right.

Maybe she wasn't okay.

Maybe more went on in her mind than she let on.

He forced a smile, though the thick knot grew in his throat, his heartbeat drumming loud in his ears. "Is there anything you need me to do for you today?"

He paused, not sure he should mention The Ruby Room, though

the situation there needed urgent attention, too, largely because of him. "Anything you'd like me to handle at the bar?"

She dipped her chin, her fingers twisting the faceted shot glass so that a rainbow of reflective lights danced round the counter.

The prettiness of those lights did nothing to hide her numb reaction.

She shook her head, messy bed-curls flopping about her face. "Burn the bar for all I care. Your friend half-demolished the place, anyway. I don't have the energy to fix any damage before the festival tomorrow night." She lifted her chin, her red-tinged stare meeting his. "Leave me alone. Please."

The lower rim of her eyes glistened with burgeoning tears, and her pitchy tone drove a knife through his heart.

This wasn't Freya. His strong. Upbeat. Self-assured. Freya.

This was someone else entirely.

Or maybe it *was* her. Some long-buried version he only met now.

What he *did* know was that he wanted to bundle her in his arms and take her upstairs to bed. To hold her and kiss her until all signs of palpable pain melted.

He stepped forward, seeking to do just that. "Let me—"

She slammed her eyes shut, a tear breaking loose. "You might like people to clean up your messes, Max, but I don't. Go!"

Her voice reverberated around the room, casting a tight wire net around his heart, but leaving no doubt of just how much she meant what she said. When her eyes flung open again, the fire in her glare sucked the air straight out of his lungs. All he could manage was a numb nod, before turning for the front door.

His hurried steps didn't distract from the pain filling his chest. The pain of being discarded. Of having his flaws once more thrown in his face.

His association with Cedrick, however unwilling, meant he'd contributed to Freya's hurt, and for that alone, he'd never forgive himself.

He stepped outside and squinted at the bright morning light, the crisp breeze nipping at his cheeks. He stood on the wrong side of her closed door, breaths faster and harder than he could handle.

He leaned forward and placed his hands on his knees, the wild beating in his ribcage battling against the mad churn of his belly because maybe, just maybe, she'd finally had enough of him. And even though he'd never thought too deeply on their relationship, now that he did, he simply couldn't bear to lose her.

*So, this is what heartbreak feels like.*

That couldn't have been it, though. He and Freya had nothing more than a casual thing, right?

*Wrong.*

Multiple people had ditched him over the years, especially of late, but the thought of losing Freya overshadowed any fear of having no friends, money, or his apartment. Her sudden dismissal shone a giant spotlight on something he'd never known he wanted but now clearly needed. A sense of belonging. More precisely. Belonging to *her*.

He peeled away from the wall and strode toward his car, his phone lighting up with a message the moment he pulled it from his pocket. In fact, there were a number of missed calls and voice messages, all from the same number.

He slid into his car and settled behind the steering wheel, glowering at his screen and flipping through the messages.

He had no idea how this person—the last person he expected to be sending him a slew of sweary, demanding messages—had wrangled his number. But they had. And each message read more urgent and heavy-handed than the last.

# Chapter Thirty-Four

Max pushed through The Ruby Room's doors, only to stop in his tracks. Apart from this not being somewhere he wanted to be right now, his pulse still ran high at having watched the spark fade from Freya's eyes, only for her to cast him out moments later.

And now *this*… The carnage from last night.

A massive pile of rubble and glass sat in the center of the bar's floor, and his mouth filled with a bitter taste at the sight of it. In the stark light of day, everything was so much worse. If not for Gideon's convincing that fixing the bar was the one and only chance for Max to make things right with Freya, he wouldn't be here.

"Oh, this isn't going to work." He tapped his forehead with his open palm, turning back to eye the door.

Not only was the chandelier shattered into a million tiny pieces, but the floor itself sported major dents and scratches. If he squinted hard enough, he was almost certain spots of Cedrick's blood still dotted the place, too.

His stomach churned, not only at the blood, but that Gideon had to be out of his mind to genuinely think he'd be putting on a show tomorrow night.

Gideon strode across the room from the cleaner's alcove, some stocky woman Max had never met keeping pace beside him. "Oh yes, it will work. I don't quit, and I certainly don't cancel shows. So, wipe that frown off your face and start with the positive thoughts, you got it?"

Gideon stopped a few paces away, his narrowed gaze tracking up and down Max's body. He made a show of sniffing the air.

"Holy Rollers!" He swatted at the air and made a show of coughing and spluttering. "You might be hot, but right now you stink like a moldy shoe."

The woman behind Gideon puffed out her cheeks, face turning a quick red, before she doubled forward in a fit of laughter.

Max peered down at his clothes, the ones he'd indeed been wearing since yesterday morning, all rumpled from sleeping on Freya's couch. "I haven't been home yet."

"Lucky for you I have more friends coming in to help." Gideon rolled his eyes. "I'll get someone to bring clothes. The bar has no showers, but I'm sure we can hunt down some soap. Just freshen up in a sink, or something; whatever it takes to put us all out of our misery."

Max gave a lopsided smile. Despite the dig at his unintended lack of personal hygiene, the more he spoke to Gideon, the more he liked the guy. At least he could take comfort that Freya had one decent friend, someone she could rely on since she'd kicked him to the curb.

"You really think we can do this?" He ran his fingers through the front of his hair, needing every last bit of hope he could get, no matter how hollow.

"That's what Cynthia's here for." Gideon gestured to the woman beside him. "She's a Jill-of-all-trades who can fix anything."

Cynthia shrugged and gave a sheepish wave, perhaps embarrassed about her loss of composure just moments ago. "It'll be a last-minute throw together, and we definitely won't get a replacement ruby chandelier in time, but I have an alternative plan that should work. Freya can always get the original fixed or replaced if she doesn't like what we do."

"Okaaaay." Max switched his gaze between Gideon and Cynthia, unsure how he felt about the whole "thrown together" aspect. "Where do we start?"

Cynthia cringed. "We can't do anything without money, and we're talking thousands of dollars of damage here. I need materials and plenty of extra help. I have some buddies who'll pop around for free though, so I guess that's a start, yeah?"

Gideon whipped his phone out of his pocket and waved it around. "I've started an online fundraiser and pitched in what personal money I can, but other than that, it's a waiting game until we have some cash flow. There's definitely not enough time to wait on the bar's insurance to come through, that's for sure."

"So, until the fundraiser money *maybe* eventuates, we do nothing?"

Gideon shrugged. "I mean, for now it's all about cleaning up the mess. And then I guess we see what money we have to work with in the hours to come."

"That's not good enough. Your show is tomorrow night."

"Well, if we're lucky and my fans and friends feel generous, we'll have the beginnings of something to work with by the end of today." Gideon lifted one corner of his lip, cramming his phone into his black pants pocket. "Maybe we can get stuck into something tomorrow morning."

"There's no way you'll get everything done in one morning." He turned to Cynthia, shaking his head. "The plaster won't be in time, right?"

Cynthia nodded. "I mean, there's a beam the chandelier will be bolted to, but it'll still be a tight call. I'd say we'll be applying paint right up until showtime."

His pulse climbed, the seed of a non-ideal notion taking root. "But if you get the money straight away, you can start straight away?"

Cynthia rubbed the back of her neck. "I don't see why not. I have people waiting to start today, just in case there's a miracle, but I don't see how the money will be here any earlier."

He glanced around the rubble-cluttered Ruby Room and drew in a deep breath, taking time to reconsider before committing his new intentions into words.

There wasn't much to consider. His next move had been decided the moment Cedrick ripped the ruby chandelier clean out of the ceiling, and the numerous moments since, when despair marked Freya's face.

A distinct strain bunched the muscles around his ribcage, the repercussions of what he was about to do sinking like a heavy stone in still water. Last night's disaster jeopardized Gideon's career, along with Freya's bar, and the multitude of people relying on it staying open.

This was the right thing to do. The only thing to do.

"I'll pay."

The tightness around his chest disappeared the second the words came out, and he sucked in an easy breath. He'd not only done the right thing, he'd done the *responsible* thing, which was so contrary to his nature he had the inexplicable desire to dance.

Gideon merely stared, though his light brown eyes glittered with understanding.

The desire to dance faded just as he remembered this move would cost him his apartment.

*No matter what I do here, something sucky will happen.*

Yes, that much was true, but he could deal with something sucky happening to him, something sucky that he'd brought on himself. Freya and Gideon, The Ruby Room, were innocent victims to his years of recklessness, of bad friendships, of ignoring multiple warnings on multiple fronts. Cedrick included.

Besides, the apartment had turned into a ball and chain around Max's neck—albeit a nicely designed, eco-friendly ball and chain—though not so much more than a glamorous arrangement of bricks and steel attached to a nice view.

From the desperate attempts to dodge calls from his bank, to taking on any job he could get, while trying to fix things he could no longer afford, he'd been so stressed just trying to keep the place. *This wasn't the way he wanted to live.*

Maybe it *was* time to move on, to downsize like he should have the moment he lost all his money.

Gideon pressed his fingertips to his lips and gave a playful shake of his head. "I'm not even going to ask if you want to reconsider. We're taking that offer and running, regardless."

Max reached into his back pocket and handed his credit card to

Gideon. "Go make all the calls you need and get this thing started. I'll wait around until you need me."

Gideon fanned himself with the credit card, his expression aglow like a man already making plans and on a mission. "Trust me, we have *a lot* of work to do, and you won't just be sitting around here looking pretty. While I'm busy calling around and spending your money, you better be making a few calls of your own. We need all the help we can get. That means getting any and all of your friends and family down here to lend a hand."

# Chapter Thirty-Five

Over the next few hours, a small army of people Max didn't know arrived at The Ruby Room to help. Miro found someone to take over at the café; Orlando, Sophie, and Agathe also came by. Luke still had to work at Tiluma but would swing past at the end of the day.

At least Max had some familiar people here, even if he hadn't found the courage to tell anyone about his run-in with Freya that morning. Also, true to his word, Gideon found someone to bring Max a change of clothes, though, much to everyone else's amusement, a button-up shirt in an eye-watering shade of tangerine wasn't what he'd expected.

The roof repairs were well under way since one of Miro's first jobs when he'd arrived in Australia had been as a painter. He knew a fair bit about patch up jobs and turned out to be Cynthia's best assistant.

Orlando, being a former firefighter and now a park ranger, took on the physical tasks of hefting heavy items to and from the work site. Sophie sat cross-legged on the floor with a pair of pliers, attaching new crystals sourced from one of Gideon's costume designer friends to the old chandelier's frame.

Cynthia called a rest break, and Miro fired up The Ruby Room's coffee machine, going so far as to take individual coffee orders. Max, having resigned himself to losing his apartment, threw financial caution to the wind and put in a phone order to a deli down the road to provide sandwiches for everyone.

Though the coming months would be a financial challenge, he had no regrets about lobbing money at getting The Ruby Room ready for tomorrow's show. His contribution made a pivotal difference, and the sea of smiling faces today confirmed he'd taken a wise risk.

Even if she didn't know it, Freya would still get her dream of being part of the festival, of being part of something bigger.

The sandwiches arrived, and he took one to the cobblestone alley behind the bar. He'd intended to have a quiet moment alone, except Gideon beat him to the idea and stood with a gold-rimmed, black coffee cup and saucer perched in one hand, a sideways glance pitched Max's way as he sipped. His cheeks were ashen, like maybe the effort of appearing chipper for his friends had finally worn him out.

Max leaned against the opposite wall, ripping at the white paper around his sandwich. "Not what you expected for the day before your big new show?"

Gideon's posture sank, his gaze searching the silver clouds. "Expending my precious voice on a million phone calls followed by hours of hard labor?" He dropped his attention back to Max. "No. Not exactly. But then we do all manner of extreme things for love, don't we?"

Max returned Gideon's stare, not entirely sure whether to read into what he'd said. Did he mean his love for performing? Or maybe his love for Freya as a friend?

Gideon raised a brow, a sudden lightness lifting his features in a way that suggested humor, or maybe that the statement about love was meant for Max. As in, Gideon thought Max loved Freya.

An invisible fist slammed into Max's gut, and he clenched his stomach muscles against that suggestion's hard truth. Freya had only hours ago booted him from her house. And his relationship with her had never been more than anything casual. He'd played a part in her bar getting trashed. Her mother had died. He didn't exactly stand in the best position for falling in love.

A small smile curled Gideon's lips, as if his verbal sucker punch had landed exactly as intended. "You still sure about what you did in there? You know, giving away your money? Freya told me you're working at the bar because you need the cash."

Max peered down at his sandwich, not sure he still wanted to eat. "What choice did I have?"

"You and I both know you could have done nothing."

Gideon took another slow sip of coffee, perhaps drawing out a chance for Max to think over that statement. But Gideon was right, only Max couldn't bring himself to admit anything regarding his feelings for Freya. Maybe because he knew it was way too late for any of that.

"What happened last night is partly my fault."

Gideon set down his cup and closed his eyes, letting out a loud sigh. "You know, I don't like wasting my voice on pointless conversations. It's not your fault that assholes exist in the world, so maybe you could cut the bullshit and start saying something we can both work with."

Heat flared in Max's belly, and his fingers tensed, no doubt leaving an imprint in his still uneaten sandwich. "Fine then. I had to do this for her."

"Well, now. That's a different story, isn't it?"

Max straightened, the muscles at his spine drawing taut along with his jaw. "You would have done the same."

Gideon shook his head in a slow, deliberate, somehow mocking movement. "Uh-uh. Similar, but not the same. Intention is everything, and you, sir, have very different intentions. But then, who you are and what you intend don't always sync up, do they?"

Max slumped against the wall. He'd always thought of himself as the fun guy. The sociable guy. The one who everything worked out for, no matter what. But here he stood with a nearly empty bank account and all but one of his old friends gone.

He bit into his sandwich and tore off a chunk, the deli meats and grilled vegetables tasteless in light of where his mind went. The woman he potentially loved wanted nothing to do with him.

"I can't remember the last time I had any idea what I wanted for my life, but this sure isn't it."

This day had been a total rollercoaster, what with this morning's devastation, then the joy of having so many hands on deck at the bar, and now this—a demoralizing education on just how lost he'd become.

Gideon's stare lingered, and the center of his forehead crinkled with tiny lines. "You know, I'd be willing to bet money that somewhere deep inside that pretty-boy brain of yours, you know exactly what you want to do. You're just too chicken-shit to do it."

Max jolted. "Sorry. What?"

"All these years and you've used money and distraction to avoid taking any real risk." Gideon took another sip from his coffee cup, smiling over the rim. "I've been around a while, you know. I've watched a lot of artists sit about waiting for 'inspiration', rather than just getting the bloody work done. You're no different. I can even guess why you do it."

Max frowned, doubting Gideon would know anything more than he did about the inner workings of his mind, mostly because he'd mulled over this exact problem for years and always came up empty.

Gideon lowered his cup into its saucer ever so slowly, seeming to enjoy the way-too-long pause. "You're afraid of starting something and failing, which is pretty cliché and boring really, so I'll do you one better. Given your failed career as a tech mogul, as well as who your brother is and that he *didn't* fail, my guess is you feel the need to justify your existence and your choices with how much potential money you might make. You've decided that since you can't have guaranteed huge success on anything, you just won't try."

Gideon quirked a brow, as if awaiting confirmation, even though everything else about his face said he'd already decided he was right.

Max frowned at his feet and the slate-gray cobblestones beneath, his churning stomach continuing an assault against this new revelation.

"I don't know if I ever quite thought of it that way." He peered back at Gideon and shrugged. "But maybe?"

"I'm right about the fear of failure, yes?"

Max took another bite of his sandwich, the flavor returning, and the tension in his body inexplicably lighter. "Yeah, I guess so. Something like that."

"Then my question to you is, given you're likely to lose everything anyway, what's stopping you now?"

Max paused mid-chew. "I don't know where to start."

Gideon rolled his eyes, though the upturn of his lips signaled he meant no insult. "You don't need to know the where, you just start. That's all there is to it." He stabbed his cup forward. "Let me ask you something. What do you think people said when I told them I wanted to be a performer?"

"I don't know. Congratulations?"

Gideon threw back his head and barked out a thick laugh. "You are a sweet one, but no. They laughed and said an arts degree was a one-way road to homelessness. Maybe the career I have now is an exception to the rule, but even if I had never made it on stage, there were always other options. I have never regretted my choice. Unlike so many people, at least I'll die knowing I got to discover who I am through chasing my dreams. So as much as the ridicule and abandonment hurt, I'm still the one who lives in this body day after day, not them. I decide where my story goes, no one else."

Gideon's expression hardened. "You take whatever start you can get, Max. You don't have to do things right the first time, but you do have to work your ass off to build a life you're willing to smile about on your deathbed. Your only other option is to live an existence you've let others bully you into." He paused and eased his shoulders down, lifting his hand in a resigned sort of gesture. "And if you really want some cheesy motivation, then do it for love."

Max nodded to the ground, this time not even trying to escape Gideon's assumptions about his feelings toward Freya. Truth be told, he wanted more than what they currently had, though they currently had nothing, so the bar was set mighty low.

"You're right." He raised his chin, for the first time in ages relaxed and not totally discordant with his own body. "Freya won't want a man who's not successful in some way."

Gideon burst into laughter again, tipping forward as much as a man could while holding a half cup of coffee. "What sort of hideous 1950s rhetoric is that? Do you even know Freya? Jesus… If you haven't already noticed, she's about the last person to care what's in your bank account and is an old hand at looking after herself. The question is, can you do the same? Do you have the ability to survive without expecting other people, *especially her,* to compensate for the unglamorous mess you're so tangled up in right now? Because I can tell you, like any person with her backstory, Freya sees your issues from miles away. She most definitely does not deserve to deal with yet another person's problems."

Max winced, heart retreating at Gideon's morsel of truth. From the sound of things, he and Freya wouldn't be a couple for a long while.

And at his current rate of success, probably never.

"You're right." His voice dragged thick past the tension in his throat. "I'm not happy with where I am. I'm coasting through life and fucking things up as I go. What's the point of wasting these years being miserable and going nowhere? I don't want to pretend I'm okay with that kind of aimlessness anymore. I want my life back. I want something to look forward to. To work toward. And *someone.*" He peered back at Gideon, delivering his next heartfelt truth. "I want Freya, but I just don't see that happening."

"Max." Gideon twisted his lips in an expression of deep thought. "I would love to tell you to go out there and get your woman, but I can't. Freya is my closest friend. My oldest friend. When she hurts, I hurt too. She needs a man who can take charge of his happiness, who walks his own path, and doesn't expect her to always lead. You and I both know that's not you, even though you want it to be. And while wanting is admirable, I need to ask…" He downed the last sip of his coffee, the flatness of his stare not making him appear all that hopeful. "Do you honestly think you can become that man for her?"

# Chapter Thirty-Six

Another day passed, and Max pushed in the final chair at The Ruby Room. Gideon's show was due to start in four hours. He took himself to the farthest wall and ran his gaze over the space, the updated chandelier sporting less ruby glass and a little more rainbow.

For the first time in months, his skin tingled with excitement. The club's rushed repairs forced him to focus in a way that he hadn't managed in years. Not since his time as a competitive swimmer, staring down the challenge of a long-haul race, his perspective sharpened after Gideon's motivational talk.

Soon, Freya would be in to look over the repairs. He hadn't seen her since yesterday morning when she'd been a total wreck, demanding he leave. Though he wasn't stupid enough to think one day would change her mind altogether, maybe the club's quick renovation would lift her mood in some small way.

*"Burn the bar down for all I care… Leave me alone. Please."*

Those words knocked around in his head, and his lungs filled with a strained breath. He'd quite literally put everything into these repairs, but chances were, they'd mean nothing to her. Not after what she'd been through. Not when he'd contributed to making a bad situation worse.

But he'd needed to do something—anything—to increase her chances of finding happiness again, at least eventually, anyway.

So, he'd sacrificed the money he'd spent weeks saving and thrown his heart into the possibility that her outlook on the bar might change, that she might still want him around in some kind of way.

The club door creaked, and seconds later, she stepped through, her dazed stare tracking around the room, her cheeks pale, hair unkempt, and expression frozen on the room's center.

Gideon snapped the microphone into a stand on the stage, causing a loud pop through the speakers. She jolted, her lashes fluttering in rapid blinks, and her lips slipping open.

Gideon only now noticed his friend. In no time, he leaped off the two-meter stage and ran toward her, dodging a gauntlet of tables. Freya took two quick steps toward him, and he threw his arms around her.

Max's muscles turned weak at the sight, at Freya sagging into Gideon's embrace, her face buried against his neck.

There was something so intimate about the way they held each other, two people with a long history of supporting each other. He didn't deserve to feel jealous, but he did anyway, wanting desperately to be the one holding her, to sweep her up and hug away her pain.

Even if Gideon hadn't seen Freya since her mother had passed, and as unhealthy as Max's desire was, he still wanted to be her everything.

He closed his hands into fists and made himself stay put, watching the scene unfold, acknowledging Gideon's place as her comfort. For one, he'd never ruined her club. In fact, he'd only ever added to her success, standing alongside Freya throughout some of her worst years.

He also had his life together and had a heck of a lot more to offer than Max did.

Freya pulled away and said nothing.

He fought an urge to slink away and hide in the cleaner's alcove, far from where he'd have to witness yet more of his shortcomings when she finally did look at him.

But denial hadn't been his friend thus far, so he stayed and followed her line of sight to the new chandelier, no longer pure ruby

since many of the lost or damaged original crystals had been painstak-
ingly replaced to make a multi-colored chandelier.

The new chandelier wasn't inferior. It was an explosion of iridescent color. A surprising change fitting with the spirit of the pride
charity the bar would raise money for during the festival.

But then, his opinion didn't matter anywhere near as much as hers,
and right now, her unblinking gaze filled him with a weak ache.

At no point did her attention land on him, which brought up the
possibility that she'd noticed him but wanted to keep her distance just
like yesterday. And though he wanted to look away, to wallow in his
heartache, he also refused to tear his attention from her.

Her focus remained latched to the rainbow chandelier, the skin
under her eyes red and splotchy.

"It's nice. Thank you." Her husky, tattered voice traveled across the
room.

She gave Gideon a tight smile, like she acknowledged the effort in
getting the bar in shape but lacked the heart to dredge up any real
excitement.

Gideon wrapped his arm around her shoulder and squeezed her in.
"Honey, are you okay?"

She bit her lower lip and gave a quick shake of her head, wincing as
though she might cry. "I'm sorry. I have to go."

She twisted out of his hold and rushed toward the door, disappearing behind the black tinted glass.

Max's legs took on a life of their own, and he bolted after her, only
for Gideon to catch his elbow as he reached the door. "She's not well.
Let her go."

He held Gideon's furrowed stare but said nothing, the man's brow
twisting in an expression of concern more than a need to control
anyone's actions.

And perhaps Max *was* better off letting her go. Nothing about his
desire right now made any sense. But then, when had anything he'd
ever done made sense, much less anything to do with Freya?

The tension in Gideon's hand eased, and he released his hold, stepping back with a resigned sigh, as if conceding to Max's need to speak
with Freya. Max lunged forward and out the door, the stark contrast of

afternoon sun making it momentarily hard to discern the world around him.

He turned from side to side, searching for her among a throng of daytime window shoppers, her distinctive blond curls glowing in the distance, across the entrance of a narrow laneway.

He called her name.

She paused, her weight shifting forward in the inertia of her abrupt stop.

He bound after her, barging between two women chatting shoulder-to-shoulder, despite Freya's head dipping as if she didn't want to have this encounter.

He caught up and positioned himself in front of her, delaying any attempt she might make to walk from him. Her gaze flicked up; the mischievous affection she often held in his presence gone like it had never been there to begin with.

"How much did you spend on the bar?"

"How do you know I paid?" He took in the details of her face, his stomach clenching at the fact that even her characteristic red lipstick was missing.

"Gideon sent me updates. I only saw them this morning, otherwise I would have told you to keep your money and asked everyone to go home."

"So why did you come today?"

"To see if I could." She jutted her chin. "And I did."

"And?"

"And what?" Her voice rose, and she threw her hands out to the side. "I felt nothing. Absolutely nothing. Is that what you want to hear?"

His throat closed up, and his own voice dropped to a whisper. "You know it's not."

A fellow pedestrian bumped into him, breaking his stare-off with Freya. He hooked his hand around her elbow and pulled her into the nearby laneway.

She huffed out a heavy breath, her shoulders slumping on the exhale. "Just tell me how much you spent. I'm paying you back. The bar's insurance will reimburse me, eventually."

"It doesn't matter." He stepped in, wanting to hold her but falling short out of the fear of breaching some unspoken boundary. "My contribution is about more than what's between you and me. Everyone at The Ruby deserves for the festival to go ahead, and so does Gideon. It's partly my fault they almost missed out. Count my money as an apology gift."

"I don't want gifts. I just want to go home." She squeezed her eyes shut and shook her head, a growl breaking from deep within her. "Look. Whatever. Forget it. I'll ask Gideon and repay you via your payroll bank details."

"And I'll return the money each and every time."

"No." She paused, and a small muscle ticked at the corner of her jaw. "I won't let you. Not with where this relationship is headed."

Taut muscles throughout his body turned slack, a sense of foreboding settling in. And even though he didn't really want to hear the answer to his next question, he asked anyway, needing the truth out all the same.

"And where exactly is this relationship headed?"

# Chapter Thirty-Seven

"Nowhere, Max. This relationship is going nowhere." Freya dropped her gaze to his chest, not wanting to face the reality of what she was about to do to him. "We don't belong together."

"I know you said you don't want anything serious, but—"

She flinched at his words and glanced at his cheeks suddenly hollow and pale, his lips parted, as if he wanted to finish his thought but couldn't. Like he now recognized her aversion to the topic at hand.

Yet, barely a second of silence had passed before he replied, hinting that maybe he'd known this conversation was coming and had already planned his rebuttal.

So, she helped him out, making sure he would have no further doubts about what she wanted.

"You're right, I don't want anything serious. Actually, I don't want *anything*. I can't be in any kind of relationship right now. Do you understand? And… and it hurts just to look at you."

Her voice creaked, and now her eyes prickled. *Shit!*

She'd spent the last day bawling and hiding. The skin around her eyes still burned from the continuous outpouring of grief. She should have been done by now. The fact that she wasn't meant she really did need to get back to the painful solitude of her house. She couldn't do this whole "talking through their problems" thing. Not now. Not ever. Because to her mind, there was nothing to work through.

"Look." She compressed her lips into what hopefully looked like a regretful smile, once again burying the extent of her pain. "I know you feel guilty about the bar getting trashed, but I'm over it. You don't need to keep beating yourself up. You also don't deserve to be in the thick of whatever misery I'm in right now. And before you argue otherwise, let's be clear, I don't *want* you with me through this, either."

His attention darted about her face, and she cleared her throat, deciding to lay down the plan for how things would go now that she'd stomped out the romantic side of this relationship. She didn't want him trying to make her feel better. He had his own problems to sort through, and she couldn't deal with his circus as well as her own.

"If you think you can handle seeing me at The Ruby Room, I have no issues with you still working there. Otherwise, I understand if you want to work elsewhere."

Max's expression twisted. "That was the last thing on my mind. I don't understand. We're damn good together. Did I do something else wrong? Why are you dropping the axe on us?"

She ripped her attention from him and onto the bare, red brick wall to her right, her hand finding its way into her hair—hair she hadn't had the time nor care to style. She looked and felt like misery, and sure as hell didn't want to be standing around in public hurting a man who'd been kind to her in all ways that mattered.

"You know enough about my life to understand why there's not much good about what we have right now." She stared back at him, her voice rasping past her already raw throat. "I've got a lot of shit going on. As do you."

"I'm selling my apartment, so my life just got simpler. Please, let me help you."

He stepped toward her, but she backed away. "No."

"Why?"

"Your problems are much bigger than just selling your apartment."

He dipped his chin, attention falling to the ground, hard-to-miss sadness dimming those lake-blue eyes, adding yet more pain to her already overburdened load.

"Let's at least call this a break then." His gaze joined hers again, her tummy clenching and aching. "Until things settle for you, and I can take some time to sort myself out. Maybe then we can reconnect."

For a moment, she toyed with the idea of accepting his terms, but even a break wouldn't be enough to salvage this capsizing ship.

She let out a sigh and worked to piece together a coherent explanation. "Max, as much as I love my independence, I don't want to always be the strong one."

She caught sight of his wince. *Fuck.*

This conversation would only get worse, but for all he'd shared with her, she owed him a clear end to this relationship. She wouldn't take the ultimate coward's way out and simply fade from his life.

"Well before you and I hooked up, I decided I didn't need a man, not in any permanent way. I've been there, done that, and it didn't work. I'm at a stage now where I know *I*, on my own, am enough. I'm a woman with a past, Max, a woman who knows how to survive and thrive. *If* I ever do commit to someone again, I need to know he will add to the life I've already built for myself."

The frown on his face deepened. "You're saying I'm not enough."

She cringed. His description was harsh, but mostly true. Though she wanted otherwise, he wasn't enough, and dragging him into a relationship would hurt them both.

She stepped forward and looped her palm through his, his pain palpable through the tension in his fingers and the low tilt of his chin. All she could offer now was comfort and enough plain honesty to help him find his way without her.

"I never planned on meeting you, much less that you'd take up so much space in my life, but I'm glad you did." She gave him a weak smile and rubbed a thumb over his knuckles. "I don't want you to walk away today thinking I'm not grateful for our moments together. I am. More than you could ever know."

His jaw locked in a fixed position, a slight harshness filling his eyes. "So then tell me what you want from me and don't leave."

His plea filled the space under her ribcage, putting pressure on her next breath, so she tightened her grip on his hand, demanding that he understand.

"I need someone who can hold their own space away from me. I need someone with purpose and direction. Someone who can stand on his own two feet, so I don't have to worry about his survival, as well as mine. I don't want a one-sided love where I'm the only stable person keeping us together. And contrary to popular opinion, I don't want to be anyone's everything. The thing that keeps their world from imploding. I want to be an equal. Someone's something extra. And if I can't have all of that, I want nothing at all."

She stopped, feeling as though she'd said too much and not enough, like what she wanted didn't exist, as much as she'd come to learn she desperately wanted it to.

And wanted Max to be the one she spoke of, even though he clearly couldn't be.

"In other words." He loosened his hold around her hand, as if he too stepped away. Her heart kicked in protest, even though this was just what she'd asked for. "You want someone who's got everything I don't."

Exactly.

But at the same time, no.

She reached out, pulling him closer when she should have dragged herself farther away.

"If you could see yourself through my eyes, Max, you'd see an incredible light. You'd see the potential for everything I just described, and more. You'd know you are someone special to me, and that this hurts me as much as it hurts you. I don't let you go lightly. You've come to mean more than I ever expected. But I have to do this. I have to let you go. It's what's fair for both of us."

His muscles strained under her touch, hot and hard, a man rippling with wounded energy. "There's nothing fair here, and let's not pretend this is what I want, too."

Stiffness entered her body, and she let go of him. No matter how much she explained, all signs pointed to him not wanting to understand.

Maybe this wasn't the right time, but she had no other options. She wanted to leave knowing she'd at least tried to give him the closure he deserved.

"You and I both know you're more than a little lost right now, that me sticking around will just enable the same dependent behavior you've struggled with for years. I'll also be falling into my tendency to patch others up at my own expense. I can't date potential, Max."

Her voice competed against the bustle of foot traffic just yards away, even though she wished so much for quiet calm and control. "Believe me, I want you. And I want you to stay, Max. But I've learned my lesson too late with my mother. I won't make the same mistake with you. Sometimes the kindest thing to do is to walk away."

He jerked back, perhaps an outward expression of his internal pain, his mouth wavering before he found his words. "I've never felt for anyone what I feel for you."

A large group strolled past the alleyway's opening. She flicked her gaze toward the loud chatter of smiling people, repressing an urge to ask Max to expand on exactly what he felt for her.

In truth, she'd grown up in a house where survival depended on reading another person's mood, so Max didn't need to admit to anything. She understood within her bones what he meant.

His love showed in his fight for her now, his direct attention lighting a hyper-awareness in her own body. Getting him to speak on his feelings would only be cruel.

His gaze fell to his feet again, and his blond waves tumbled over his brow, obscuring his eyes and seeming to take him further away from her. "And the thought of you moving on to someone else... I know I have no right to limit you, but—"

"Trust me, I have no plans to replace you anytime soon."

The only thing she had to offer was this pathetic concession prize. For so many years, she'd considered herself a free woman, and now her heart shifted painfully at the idea of being with anyone else.

*What have I done to myself? I'll have to move on one day, but how?*

One day, yes, she would have to move on, but the emptiness inside of her said that wouldn't be for a very long time. Her heart had jumped from one kind of sorrow to another of late; she didn't need more complications or hurt.

When would she learn? She always did better alone.

Max moved closer, his fingers finding the side of her neck. "Walking away right now feels all wrong. You're hurting, Freya. You need me."

His thumb stroked her jawline, the depth of his stare prompting her to lean into his touch, even as she gave a small shake of her head. "Sometimes being alone is the perfect antidote."

*It sure as hell hurts less, too.*

She repressed the thought, afraid that pain would stir an inability to end this.

"I know you want to fix my life for me, and I appreciate the sentiment, but sometimes there's nothing to do but curl up in bed and cry it out. That's what I'll do, and I'll be okay. You know what I mean?"

A small line formed between his brows. "I'm not sure I do."

She frowned and trained her attention on the finer details of his face, his skin smooth and eyes relaxed in an open expression. "What did you do when your dad died? When that cliff fall ended your dreams? Don't tell me you never grieved. Everybody does."

"I don't know." He shrugged and offered a tight smile, the darting motion of his eyes hinting at evasion. "I just kept myself busy. Though, clearly not with anything all that productive."

He gave a stumbling laugh, and she shook her head at his deflection masked as humor. *A typical Max move.*

Even as his lips settled on an oblivious grin, a new thought took root in her mind. The reason for his aimlessness. Why he'd been so busy distracting himself with fun, money, and socializing and never dealt with the disasters that exploded all around him.

She pressed her hands to his cheeks, the pads of her fingers lingering over the soft prickliness of his stubble. "Sometimes those who laugh the most are the ones running the hardest and fastest from something."

He gave her a side stare. "I don't understand."

"It's just—" She bit her lower lip and second-guessed whether she should say something.

But the pieces fit.

And maybe. Just maybe. Her hunch would help him.

She slid her hand down and patted his chest, savoring the warmth —a warmth she would soon give up forever. "Max, have you ever considered that maybe you're depressed?"

# Chapter Thirty-Eight

Max stumbled back a step, so fast, he might as well have held his hand to a hot stove and not the softness of Freya's neck. He dropped his palm, his lips dragging heavy at the corners, no doubt sending forth one monster of a frown.

*Have you ever considered that maybe you're depressed?*

What an odd thing to say.

And in the middle of a breakup.

Besides, if it were true, shouldn't his supposed depression be another reason for her to stay?

*Only if I plan on having the overly dependent relationship she just said she didn't want.*

*No. That's not what I want at all.*

Her suggestion about his mental health knocked around in his head, the sounds of rushing traffic and pedestrians passing only adding to his confusion. He'd never considered that maybe there was more to his behavior than just him being him. Depressed? Was that true?

He opened his mouth, ready to scoff, to defend himself and insist that she was wrong. But maybe she wasn't.

He hadn't always been lazy. He'd had goals and a routine, and a ton of discipline and motivation—motivation that had taken him across oceans on the pure power of his own body.

The years after his accident hung over him like a black cloud, Luke's guilt the reason Tiluma had come about—a new project meant to pull Max out of his funk.

Except maybe he'd never risen from his low point. He'd just gotten better at hiding his pain.

His routine and motivation had transformed into impaired forward thinking and impulsiveness; the majority of his days spent living in a hard-to-clear fog, though at least those around him seemed less worried.

And what about his need to always have people around?

Well, maybe he'd learned he couldn't trust himself alone, because being alone meant thinking, and he didn't like the man he encountered when left with his thoughts.

*Oh hell!*

In his years as a distance swimmer, he'd spent long stretches alone —had loved the solitude of just him and the waves—a serene stillness he'd never experienced since.

*My mind is never serene or still these days.*

"Oh, now." He flicked his gaze back to Freya. "That's messed up." His cheeks turned cold and probably lacked color. "You might be right."

And even as the words left his mouth, an unfamiliar heat exploded in his belly. An angry heat—one that made him want to charge away and smash something—an uncontrolled energy so unfamiliar to him, he struggled to breathe.

Worlds of sound and sight sped impossibly fast around him. That expanding heat roared in his ears. It roared at Luke for his thoughtlessness, for pressuring Max into climbing that cliff in the first place. It roared at Max for never telling his brother how much he resented the unraveling of his plans. How that unraveling left him adrift, with years of hating himself for failing to recover in a way that Luke and everyone else saw fit.

And sure, they'd talked about the accident. He recognized Luke's remorse and that he'd been going through his own issues leading up to the accident. Maybe Max had deflected his real rage onto other things, perhaps offering Luke forgiveness long before he'd been ready to give it.

Freya stepped forward, her hand landing on his bicep. "Are you okay?"

"I'm not sure." A thousand little firecrackers went off inside his head, exploding at random intervals without any indication of when they would all stop. "What do I do about this?"

"Find the help you need, Max. Find a good therapist, a government-funded one if your money won't cover it, though I guess if you down-grade from your apartment, that won't be an issue." She gave a light squeeze of his arm, along with her gentle smile. "Simplify your life and take some time to figure yourself out. Once you do that, go about discovering what *you* want and where you want to go next."

Though her even tone hinted at wise advice, he struggled to take in much of it.

His fall from that cliff had stolen far more than just swimming. He'd lost the one thing he'd been unquestionably good at. *His dream. His passion.* His future disintegrated in one dumb move. And now he was losing Freya.

Seriously, how would he fix this?

All his friends had left. He had orders from Luke to sort his life out on his own this time. Even Miro had a family to look after and a business to run; he didn't deserve Max sulking around.

Max had been a mess for so long, with someone always around to lean on when things didn't work. With Freya stepping away, he had no one.

He bore his gaze into her and pleaded with his eyes, the gravity of his impending loneliness all too much.

He needed help. He needed someone. He needed *her*.

"Can I call you sometimes? Can we still meet, even just for a chat and nothing more?"

Her gentle smile slipped as did her hand. Still, he wasn't below looking and sounding desperate, much less asking the impossible.

"I'm sorry." Her chin trembled in a moment of prolonged silence. "I wish I could help you through this, but I'm not in a place to help anyone right now and would do you more harm than good."

He stared at her a moment, seeing her fragility, before breaking eye contact and taking a second to come to terms with this really being the end. He nodded at the ground repeatedly, a man truly losing his mind. And his home. And his first genuine shot at love.

"Max." She stepped closer, as though she sensed his dip in mood.

Where she normally smelled like sun-warmed mandarins, today only the soft musk of her skin minus any fragrance cut through, indicating again that she too wasn't operating as she normally did.

"I'm used to dealing with things alone, so please don't think for a second I don't care about you, it's just…" Her hand met with his arm again, and she remained silent until he lifted his gaze to her whiskey-gold eyes, the surrounding skin still dappled in a red reminder of her grief. "I don't think either of us needs any false hope. I can't give you the answers you're looking for. I can't do the healing and discovery work for you. You need to find your own place in life."

"But what if I've already found my place in life?" He hooked a hand around her, pressing his palm to her lower back. "What if *you're* my place and walking away is the worst decision for either of us?"

She startled, almost as if an electrical current ran through his touch. "That's not a healthy example of love. People leave. Things happen. All love fades eventually—"

"Maybe your examples of love, but not mine." He pulled her into him, grasping at his last chance to change her mind, to spare them the misery of going through their respective hardships minus the other's support. "My mum and my dad, Luke and Agathe, Sophie and Orlando, they all experienced love transforming and redirecting their lives for the better. Why not us too? Please. Don't leave, Freya. This isn't the only way forward."

Her stare pulled wide and searched his face, her lips parted in a hint she wanted to say something but didn't. She turned from him and took a few hurried steps toward the passing crowd at the end of the alleyway.

Perhaps this was her way of showing she could walk away at any given moment.

He reached out, only to stop. She'd already fled from his touch. Maybe his desperation would be yet another reason for her to say no, even if her demeanor said she'd already made up her mind to leave.

"Don't. Not like this."

He bounded after her, catching her elbow before she could exit the alleyway, throwing away his last desire to save face.

She swung around and stuck out her chin, a stubborn gesture that didn't hide the tears gathering in her eyes.

"You're making this harder than it needs to be." Her voice wobbled, the heat in her stare cooling. "Don't you understand? Sure, we gave each other moments of happiness, but as individuals, we're still one-hundred-percent responsible for our own contentment. Maybe the fact we see love so differently is a big flashing sign we were never going to work."

"Freya."

"No. Stop trying to convince me." Her pitchy tone spoke of pain more than anger. "I have to leave. I don't want to, but I have to."

An emptiness opened up deep within him, and his ability to reply dried on his tongue, an inescapable truth seeping in. She *did* have to leave, even when every fiber of his being pushed him to plead other-wise. He wanted this. Wanted *her*. When, for so very long, he hadn't wanted anything.

She'd become his only sense of purpose, the only sure thing in a world rapidly falling around him, but the tears in her eyes, the huski-ness in her voice... She was right. He needed to stop.

For once in his life, he'd put someone else ahead of his need to escape a few difficult feelings.

*And what a time to make that realization...*

He took a half-step back and let his hand slip from her elbow. "I know, but first, there's something I want you to hear." He paused, trying to slow time down. Trying to memorize every small detail of a moment he'd hold dear until his dying day. "I—"

"No." She slammed her eyelids shut, a tear finally breaking free and spilling down her cheek. "Please don't say it."

He pressed his lips together, fulfilling her wish at great expense to himself.

This was as sweet a parting as they would get.

She flung herself forward, leaning her weight into him, her arms folding around his shoulders in a tight hug. And he wrapped his arms around her too, lifting her off the ground, giving his all to this embrace.

Her hands rose from his shoulders and landed on his cheeks, her lips finding his, as though they were made for him, even if this would be the last kiss they'd share.

And the kiss was everything.

Everything he'd ever wanted and by far not enough—hungry and impassioned—a rush of need and despair. For all his doubts about life, he had none in relation to Freya. And still, he would lose her, anyway.

Of course, she was the first to end the kiss. So, he lowered her to the ground, his heart rate slowing to a weak plod. She swiped at her eyes, and her lips twisted into a half-smile, a smile that somehow both acknowledged and denied the pain in that moment.

She spun away, her steps taking her closer to the main street and the throng of passersby, all while his insides ached, like she'd wrenched away some vital part of him.

He'd meant to whisper the following words, to keep them for himself, but as always, even this he fumbled, his voice rising louder than intended.

"I love you."

She stopped in her tracks and dipped her head low, her hand coming to rest on the wall beside her, her fingers curling into the red brick as though she fought his words and took a second to decide whether to respond.

In time, she turned her red-dappled face and gave him her anguished stare.

"I know."

# Chapter Thirty-Nine

Freya's hair whipped her face, and her burnt-orange skirt flapped about her knees as she stood on the rocky outcrop. The start of Fall might have been evident in the sea's icy winds, but more than a week after her mother's death, that iciness matched today's bleak mood, and she appreciated the element's camaraderie.

A light-yellow cardboard box weighed heavy in her right hand, her mother's ashes nestled inside. There'd been no point in a funeral since Freya would be the only person in attendance.

She snapped her focus to Gideon. He reached out from beside her, wrapping his long fingers around her waist, holding her steady on the rocks and offering comfort. "Are you ready?"

Her throat pulled tight, her answer stalling, though she told herself the cold wind had swallowed her sound. "Just one minute more."

He gave an understanding nod and turned to the ocean with its glistening surface like a million twinkling lights. She pushed her gaze a little more to her right, to the sandy alcove pressed between another outcrop. A spot where she and her brother played as children in relative privacy, this particular beach a good hour and a half from where they'd lived.

Sometimes, *sometimes*, her mother had tried.

Even if those outings occurred only a handful of times, the briny smell and the lack of people took her back to one of the few magical moments in her childhood, the sea succeeding to tame even the savage beast within her mother.

Freya slammed her eyes shut and shook her head, wanting to break free of the memory. Those happier moments never lasted long.

Sometimes, even just the arrival home would result in her mother's strong, adult hands locked around Freya's tiny arms. There'd be nitpicking and blaming, screams in her face, her eyes scrunched closed to block out the tirade. It was as if her mother could only stomach so much peace before her demons grew too angry and retaliated.

A seagull cawed, and Freya leaned to her left so that her side met with Gideon's.

She sniffed, the salty air settling her nerves, though the cold wind made it impossible to hold back her tears, and her heart hitched at the stubborn hollow inside her from ending things with Max. At least she still had her best friend.

She'd come to this beach to release some of her feelings, to say goodbye to her mother, to let go as best she could. Maybe this wasn't the time to hold back on acknowledging just how much she hurt right now. That some things she would never truly recover from.

She could survive. Yes, that much was proven.

But certain scars became a permanent feature, and sometimes life threw up events that would never make sense—no matter how many times she rolled the same thoughts over and over within her mind.

Every breath now made her nostrils sting, and that sting affixed to the harsh memories threatening to hurt her anew—the pure evil of having her survival tied to someone whose purpose should have been to love and protect her.

All she'd received was years of neglect, pain, and shame.

And her mother knew what she'd done. Though how much she could control her actions was anyone's guess.

Freya had witnessed the cycle. The guilt, the apologies and pleading, those apologies making her search for her mother's softer side, giving birth to an obnoxious need to find a positive. For years afterward, she'd hated herself for even trying.

She peered down at her hand clenched around the yellow box, a lovely thing with silk lilac flowers on the outside and a matching ribbon. Everything sweet, and delicate, and feminine. Everything not her mother.

Freya hunched and tugged at the ribbon, willing all her hurt and the bitterness to go, attempting to replace it with something more productive. *Hope.*

For all she'd been through, she knew something her mother never had. She'd experienced peace, time and time again, and hope said peace would return some day. Maybe not for a while, but eventually.

She lifted the box's lid and already gray particles fluttered out. She raced against the wind, tipping the box upside-down and allowing the remnants of her mother's body to burst out into a plume across the sea.

Freya's life would be better. That was her vow to herself, and maybe to her mother.

Freya would be the last in her line. Whether she went on to have children didn't matter so much. She would not pass on her pain, even if that meant being alone forever.

The gray plume dissipated, her mother gone except for the reminder that actions and decisions mattered. They mattered a lot.

Freya would start over. She would pick herself up. And everything she did would grow bigger and better. Not just for her benefit, but for anyone who came to her in search of a livelihood or life, or simply a place to escape a world that often punished those who dared to break from their torments or to simply have a dream.

Max handed Miro the apartment's keycard and waited for him to embark on his trip out the door for more moving boxes. Meanwhile, Luke dropped something loud and metallic on the dining room floor, the sharp sound bouncing off the tile and down the hallway.

Max returned to the kitchen and made a hard right away from Luke, continuing the task of packing glassware.

"You're quiet today." Luke sat on the floor, a socket wrench in his hand—probably what he'd dropped moments earlier and now used to loosen the legs on the upturned dining table. "And something tells me your silence is about more than just the move."

Max lowered the glass in his hand to a box on the counter. "Because losing my home isn't demoralizing enough?"

The narrow of Luke's eyes seemed to question Max's blunt reply. "You have a point, it's just that—"

"Freya and I broke up."

He hadn't planned on blurting out that news, and now he pressed his jaw tight to keep from saying anything else unexpected.

There was so much he still didn't understand, and he hadn't told anyone about his last conversation with Freya, though Gideon's recent lack of any mention of her hinted he knew something had happened.

Luke lowered the wrench and straightened his stance, his full attention focused on Max. "I thought you two were just friends."

The man was a master of reading between the lines and making it near impossible to delude him. Max skittered his gaze to the glassware inside the box before him. He and Luke rarely talked about relationships, and nothing about this moment felt natural.

"We were just friends, and then at some point, we were more." He reached for another glass. "At least, that's what I think happened…"

He peered over to Luke shaking his head. "And let me guess, things got too serious, and everyone got their hearts broken?"

He gave a knowing smile, maybe because he'd experienced a similar breakup with Agathe, long before she'd become his wife. Not like that would be happening with Max and Freya.

"Yeah, something along those lines."

He didn't have the energy to tell his brother that two weeks had passed since his farewell from Freya, and maybe he'd been the one with the bigger broken heart. After all, he'd told her he loved her, while she'd left, not stopping to reciprocate.

And so, he'd worked the entire festival, really needing the money to pay for this move, while also not wanting to leave his co-workers short-staffed and in the lurch. At the same time, he constantly checked The Ruby Room's doors hoping to see Freya walk through them.

But not once had she shown up. Not once in all the nights her best friend, Gideon, performed—the show exceptional enough to whip up a kind of buzz never before seen at The Ruby Room.

She'd missed everything, and in turn, Max had missed her.

A long silence dragged, and the brothers pretended to be hard at work, but a hot, niggling sensation pulled at Max's focus. "You know, Freya mentioned something the last time we spoke, and it's bothered me ever since."

New wrinkles scored Luke's forehead. "Yeah?"

"She thinks my whole aimless thing started when I fell off that cliff."

Luke scoffed and returned to twisting the wrench. "Sure. You and I already knew that."

"It's more than that, though." His shoulders drew upward, and his throat felt tight, like he fought to keep his voice at a reasonable level, while very much wanting Luke to hear him out. "I've only now started to admit this to myself, but all these years, I've secretly resented you."

Luke peered up, eyes flared, and his spine snapped to a poker-straight position, as though Max had somehow punched him with his words.

But Max pressed on, vowing that if he didn't get this out, his buried rage would continue to eat away at him.

"We've never talked about this, but the fall from that cliff really bothered me. The actual fall. The belief that I would die. Then, there was the physical pain and the recovery, much less losing my swim career. All those years. All that training, pushing myself, working at something only to have it ripped away. All that effort wasted. Then trying to mentally return to where I was before all that happened…"

He frowned, the deepest part of this confession only now coming to him in the form of a sickening and cold shiver through his entire body. "I'm still nowhere near where I want to be. I still don't recognize my new life, even though it's been years, and I've tried everything I can to bury my feelings."

Max forced his gaze on Luke, even though he so wanted to look away and would almost certainly hurt his brother with his next brutal truth. "But denial and avoidance doesn't work, and if I'm truly honest, I'm miserable. And it's all because of you."

Luke sank back, and his shoulders rolled forward, his fingers curling tighter around the wrench. His stare fell to the floor, and he gave his head a small shake.

Max's face burned in the aftermath of his revelation, in watching his brother grapple with this new spin on the last years of their relationship.

He waited to hear what Luke had to say, whether he'd belittle this confession or try to deflect blame, and for some reason, the prolonged silence didn't seem to bode well.

Luke returned his direct stare to Max and pushed an incredulous sigh past his lips. "You know, I don't think I've ever been prouder of you than I am right now."

Max's chin jerked back of its own volition, and he gave his brother a side-glare, Luke's hushed tone and ensuing short, sharp laugh taking up space in the room.

"I've lost my home." He fought to make sense of his brother's reaction. "I've lost my woman, and I'm probably going to lose my job at the bar. My entire life is one big fucking disaster, and you're telling me you're proud?"

"Well. No." Luke leaned his elbow on his knee, the casual position portraying a level of acceptance Max hadn't expected. "But as much as you've said you've forgiven me in the past, it would be hard to bring this all up again now. And come to think of it, I always felt like you took the whole thing a little too well."

Luke lifted a hand and scrubbed at the stubble on his chin. "Look, I don't live in your head, but I can imagine how betrayed you must have felt back when you first fell off that cliff. And you're right, that fall was my fault. Everything about that day is one-hundred percent my fault. I can promise you I live with that guilt every day. I screwed up your life. Yet, because of how things panned out with Tiluma, I'm the one who's been laying down the rules, putting my foot down recently and attempting a tough-love approach. I'm the one who's had more of a chance to move on, both with my own issues at the time and the mess I created for you because of that." Luke's face drew in a pained expression. "Max, you deserve a good life, and I'm sorry I got in the way of that. I will do everything I can to help you. I only hope that someday you get to a place where you really do forgive me."

Max twisted a glass on the counter, a real smile tugging at his lips. "The thing is, to some extent, I already have forgiven you. It's just that, this whole thing with Freya and losing the house, I've had to look at my life through a different lens. I'm seeing things I never noticed before, while having to figure out what to do with these new discoveries about myself. So, I do forgive you, but I'm still mad at you. Does that make sense? And I won't be able to let go of that anger until I find a way to heal."

Luke nodded as though he understood, even if the strain across his jaw said he didn't totally love everything Max had to say. "Do you have any ideas on how you'll move forward?"

Max shook his head, still struggling to look Luke in the eye while admitting to how lost he'd become. "I'm way over my head here, and I don't think this is something I can fix on my own. I need help, Luke, professional help. I'm scared to imagine where I'll be in ten years if I continue down the path I'm on."

Luke frowned, turning the wrench in his hand. "You're right. This isn't something you have to fix alone. You have me and Agathe, Soph, and even Orlando's all right to talk to if you get him in a good mood." He lifted his attention, curling his lip at one corner and making light of Orlando's initial rough start in the family. "You're surrounded by people who want to see you succeed, even if succeeding is as big or small as getting out of bed each day and knowing that a lot of people love you. So, get all the help you need, we're here for you, and if there's anything you need from me especially, just ask."

That offer of help contradicted Luke's initial response to when Max first lost his money. Yet, as much as Max wanted to be pissed about the sudden change in attitude, Luke had been right to cut him off.

"Thanks for the offer." Max leaned against the counter, a quick lightness taking him over. He'd spent years hiding behind his brother's guilt, while Luke's over-compensating had stalled all progress. And even as Max's world disintegrated around him, he sensed that maybe something else waited just around the corner. The spark of a new idea.

All he had to do was sort out his mind so he could begin to unpack his future. Not a simple task, yes, but he had hope. And maybe that would be enough.

He returned his attention to Luke. "You know, I think getting help is something I need to do on my own."

"But if you're really not doing well…"

"I know." Max stared ahead, uncharacteristically silent, mulling over his situation.

While he appreciated the chance to open up, he wanted to prove to himself that he could, for once, be the one to put his life back together.

Luke returned to twisting the wrench over the bolts in the table, head shaking, as he released a soft chuckle. "You've made some hard decisions lately. I never thought the day would come where I'd see you sticking to them. It must have hurt a great deal to put this place up for sale, and all so you could help someone else out."

Luke stopped, sitting taller again. "And if that wasn't bad enough, I can't imagine how you must feel after letting Freya go."

Max set about adding more glasses to the boxes, but made sure to plaster on his flattest tone. "Actually, she let me go. But semantics, right?"

Luke's chuckle returned. "And somehow, for the first time in years, I'm not worried about what might happen to you next."

"Gee, thanks. I think."

Max pushed his chin higher and glared at his brother, whose eyes now glowed with clear humor.

"Hey, I'm not saying I don't care about you. Nothing could ever be further from the truth. I just see the changes you've already made, and I get a strong feeling you're going to be okay."

# Chapter Forty



Freya slung her scarlet-embroidered handbag over her shoulder, the coin fringe tinkling as she passed through her office door and into the crowd at her new club. Sweat clammed up her bare collarbone, and her amethyst dress clung to her skin, the discomfort evermore noticeable since she ran late again. Gideon would no doubt chew her out.

She whizzed past the long bar, the air a mix of sweetness and astringency from the alcohol and juice cocktails. Various gargantuan gilded mirrors hung behind her rainbow-vested bar staff, the back wall dotted with black and white portraits of past and present burlesque stars.

And even as she raced, her body took on a life of its own, turning her toward tonight's manager, despite how ridiculous this final check would look.

She should have been on a tram already, speeding toward the stadium and a super rare Saturday night out to watch an even rarer concert. Besides, Gideon had a surprise for her, something he'd apparently been planning for a long time.

But her new venture was only two months old and a number of high-profile groups were booked to arrive soon, and so far, the bar hadn't yet done a night without her.

After the Live Wire Festival, more and more people had come to know about The Ruby Room. The place hadn't been the same, the smaller space struggling to keep up. And though The Ruby's makeshift rainbow chandelier had been replaced with a new ruby one, an idea had taken root.

She'd run with the rainbow idea and used the bump in success to expand her empire to a much bigger venue, one situated in the heart of the city; a place that held a bright mix of childish wonder, juxtaposed against the dark, adult glamor of nightly burlesque acts. The Rainbow Room.

And yes, a rainbow chandelier hung in the venue's center, a giant white unicorn reared with wings outspread atop a podium, the venue's walls coated in candy pink carpeting and bubble machines timed to go off throughout each night.

Vowing to work on her ability to trust her staff, she sidled up to her manager, his lips trembling from a barely restrained laugh. After a hectic year of setting up The Rainbow, she really did need to start enjoying her downtime again.

The manager flicked a hand and gestured for her to go, that he had everything under control. Her face heated, but she turned away, point taken.

She was running late now, so she took herself to the dark stretch of street outside and sent for an Uber, the time for a tram well and truly gone. Her only hope now was that the gods of rock and roll would be extra kind to her, and that Gideon wouldn't disown her for being so invested in her work.

Max sat in his home office, a small LED lamp lighting his desk along with the dusky gray of the fading sun through his window. His eyes now ached from the glare of his computer and the hours spent poring over designs.

Starting a business had been a million times harder than he'd expected, and funding the whole thing using money from his apartment sale, as well as two annual payouts from his Tiluma shares, only made the process even more stressful.

And rewarding.

He'd gained a boatload of new respect for Luke and all he'd achieved in the early days of Tiluma. Especially since he'd most recently taken Max under his wing and taught him all about money management, as well as given him a temporary after-hours cleaning job at Tiluma.

That job had allowed him to quit The Ruby Room without eating into his apartment money. He avoided facing his old co-workers and Freya, giving him space to work on rebuilding his life without his morale taking a further beating.

And as much as Freya's absence hurt him, he'd used his pain and solitude to undergo regular therapy, to develop ways to deal with the trauma of his fall all those years ago. Doubt still plagued him, but he now had tools to manage.

He'd crossed the line into becoming self-sufficient, learned ways to reframe his limiting thoughts. And his most important lesson? That as much as those around him liked to poke fun, they really did want the best for him. Heck, they *loved* him.

But the thing about depression, sometimes no amount of love could break through the fog clouding a person's outlook. So, he had zero regrets about seeking outside help because it had been what he needed.

Oh, and because of that, there was more. He had a new home. A small two-bedroom townhouse in Melbourne's south-east, nowhere near as expensive or sizable as his apartment, but still somewhere to rest his spirits. There was a small patch of grass in his yard, a place to lay, feel the cool earth against his body, and watch the clouds move across the sky.

Which brought him to here, leaning back in his office chair and scrubbing a hand over his face, his brain tired and his eyes dry from a long day's work. He slapped a hand over his laptop and closed the screen. Time to give up for the day.

He raised his arms high in the air, stretching, only for the clash of loud instruments to pull his attention down to his phone ringing on the desk. He groaned, hitting the speaker option, hoping it was a spam call over yet another work issue needing urgent attention on a Saturday night.

"Hello?"

He waited.

"It's time."

The reply came from a super low, heavily American-accented voice, one Max didn't recognize.

He scowled down at his phone. "Time for what? Who is this?"

"It's your fairy godfather. I'm here to make your wildest dreams come true."

*What the hell?*

He rolled his eyes, his head already throbbing from the toll of his workload without having to deal with weird prank calls.

"Okay. Bye."

"No, wait!"

His finger hovered over the red X button, but he paused because the accent had disappeared, and a decidedly more familiar Australian one had taken over.

"It's Gideon. Hear me out. I have a plan!"

By the time she raced up the top of the stadium's stairs, Freya's lungs burned and her sternum heaved with labored breaths. She paused before the doors to her section, the heavy music and cheers pulsing from the venue, the warmup band already begun. But Gideon wasn't anywhere to be found.

She peered at the time on her phone. *Damnit!*

She was later than she thought. He must have gotten sick of waiting and headed in without her.

No point calling him, given the deep boom and the stadium's walls vibrating around her. She'd just end up having to yell down the phone so Gideon could hear, and he'd yell back, probably annoying everyone around him in the process.

She shot off a quick text letting him know she'd arrived. Her phone pinged with a reply almost immediately.

GIDEON

Great to know. Just go straight to your seat.

She did as told, climbing down some steep stairs, then pushing her way through a long row of people on a lower tier. Of course her seat was smack-bang in the middle. Less expected, though, Gideon's seat was empty.

What gives?

She typed feverishly, taking a pause to have another swift peer around.

Where are YOU?

She plonked down on her seat and waited, hugging her bag even though a lot of people were already standing and dancing to the warmup act.

Granted, the band was brilliant, but she needed a minute to settle in, to breathe in the stadium's cold air, though she figured the temperature would rise soon enough given all the hot lights and people packed in.

Her phone lit up with another message.

Sorry. Forgot to tell you. I'm sick. Not going to make it, hun.

What on earth? Her mouth slipped open, and she stared at the screen. She might have said an expletive too, but with the mixture of noise and shock running through her head, she couldn't be sure of anything.

She growled at Gideon's perplexing text, then punched out another reply, relaying her scramble to get to this concert and asking him what the fuck was going on.

Her brows drew heavy. Maybe she should have gone for a more compassionate approach. Maybe asked whether he was okay or if he needed help, given his claim of being sick and all.

Either way, there was something strange definitely happening here.

Another message appeared on her phone:

> Let's just say, I took one for the team. Oh and… SURPRISE!

She slumped back in her seat, trying to work out what the hell this all meant.

Took one for the team? How? By not turning up to a show they'd both been looking forward to for years?

How did that benefit anyone?

Just as the warmup band finished their set, another expletive escaped her lips. She'd been dreaming of this night for so long, of seeing her favorite band, but never had she imagined she'd be here alone.

A hush took over the twenty-thousand-person venue, and her heart sank anew. She had no one to share the rising anticipation with—an anticipation that washed over the stadium like an electric charge—invisible and palpable all at once.

Her skin tingled, and the tiny hairs on her arms rose with the mood.

*Screw it. I'm going to enjoy this night either way. Since when has being alone ever stopped me?*

Never! That's when!

She nodded to herself and stood, lifting her chin and refusing to mope through the night. She'd made it to her first ever *Queen* concert, and no one—no one—was allowed to sulk through a Queen concert.

Her attention dropped to her right, everything about the empty seat beside her downright wrong, but then the venue plunged into darkness, and she lost all reason to worry.

Soon, lights exploded around her in short-sharp bursts; sounds bashed and clashed. She bounced in her spot, alternating between clapping her hands and raising a fist in the air, screaming a loud, "Woo hoo!" before looking to her right to see if the person across the empty chair showed the same excitement.

"Hi."

She startled, almost losing her balance, a man having taken up the now not-so-empty seat.

If he hadn't spoken, she would have assumed he wasn't real, that he'd materialized or was maybe a figment of her over-exhausted imagination. But his gentle tone was impossible to mistake. And those eyes. Those soft, crystalline blue eyes… they could belong to no one else.

The lights flicked off, only to explode once more. She jolted at the sound—the pull of her attention in two different directions. At him. At the stage. At *him* again.

Despite all odds, she wasn't hallucinating.

"Gideon said he didn't want you to go to the show alone." Max smiled at Freya, her pupils wide pools that betrayed her shock.

"So"—her mouth wavered for a moment before her gaze flicked to the stage and then back to him—"so he sent *you*?"

He fought an urge to step back, to leave her be, while questioning whether he should have let Gideon talk him into coming here in the first place.

"If you want, I can leave." He regretted the offer straight away. Leaving was the last thing he wanted to do.

She parted her lips, as though ready to say something, but then more lights flashed, and an even louder chorus of voices cut through the air.

Her gaze ripped from him and back to the stage, a giant white sheet covering the deeper part. There wasn't much to see.

Given her clear hesitation, he'd been right not to expect much from this night, and yet, hope still sprang eternal.

Maybe they'd healed enough to at least be friends.

*What a lie.*

*I don't want friendship.*

*I also don't want to be rejected. Twice.*

He stared at her. Just stared. Waiting for her attention to return to him, dazed that he got to share the same space with her again and dumbstruck over what to do next.

The music deepened, like the lower end of a piano or something. She glanced back at him, a sad frown dragging at her lips. Maybe she shared his confusion.

This time, when the music kicked up, the same distracting lights flashing in his eyes, she didn't turn away. Her stare held, her gaze shifting over his face.

They seemed trapped in a stalemate, so he dared to ask again, "Do you want me to leave?"

She pursed her raspberry-painted lips and gave a quick shake of her head, turning her whole body back toward the stage without a word.

He stood there, staring at her for the longest time, perhaps hoping for more, but she didn't give him anything.

He might have tried talking again, but the loud music made that near impossible. Besides, she loved Queen, and he wouldn't ruin this show for her, much less give her a reason to rescind his permission to stay.

The giant white sheet dropped from the stage, revealing the band. Queen.

Well, Queen minus Freddie Mercury, of course. Still, her lips curled ever so slightly, and her eyes glinted.

Standing beside her like a silent fool seemed suddenly worth her clear display of joy, much less that he got to share this experience with her. So, he smiled to himself, too. Maybe Gideon had banked on the forced close proximity and inability to have a conversation all along.

Max turned to the stage and vowed to just let things be.

He'd waited this long to see her again and spent months upon months learning to be okay with failure. Maybe this would be another exercise in dealing with uncertainty. What choice did he have? All he could do was wait and see where tonight took him.

# Chapter Forty-One

The concert lights dimmed, turning the entire stadium black; the crowd roared in a final goodbye. Freya had danced her way through the rockier songs, and tears ran down her cheeks through the sadder ones. There'd been no way Max hadn't noticed. And still, this night was so much more than expected.

At one point, she'd bumped her hip into him, attempting to get him to dance along with her. He hadn't, but his burst of laughter and the connection of his stare made her heart near explode, igniting an awareness of just how much she'd missed him.

*But I broke his heart. Why is he even here?*

The house lights came on, the sudden brightness breaking the concert's spell. She cleared her throat and turned to pick up her bag from her seat, not quite ready to make eye contact with Max again.

He walked ahead of her into the aisle, their pact of silence continuing until they got outside and into the cool night air.

Honestly, what were they supposed to say to each other? Where did she even begin?

Her chest hurt just standing near him. The wisest choice now would be to say nothing and let the past eighteen months of avoiding each other drag into eternity.

Her cheeks tingled, and the cool air brought a slight chill to her exposed collarbone. The beautiful man beside her, with his looming height and her working memory of what it was to make love to him, didn't at all ease those tingles or chills.

She glanced up to find his stare fixed on her as if he wasn't sure what to do now. Well, neither was she. Though a greater part of her wanted to disappear for at least a minute just to catch her breath in privacy.

Or maybe disappearing altogether was better.

But as always with Max, her body had other ideas, and she patted the large, over-stuffed bag on her shoulder.

"Gideon made me bring after-show snacks. I'm pretty sure he wants us to eat together." Shaky laughter broke past her lips, the low pain around her heart prodding a contrary desire to cry, one she stemmed by nodding to a low concrete wall a few steps away. "I'm willing to sit and indulge in his scheme, if you are?"

Max's gaze flicked to the wall, as though he needed a moment to decide whether that was what he actually wanted. A throng of people filed past, their bright chatter and screeches of excitement scraping sharp nails over her already heightened nerves.

She wasn't all that sure about her invitation to sit and eat together either, though maybe sitting and eating would be less weird than sharing an entire concert and a few laughs with this man, only to send him home without so much as a parting word.

"I..." His brows furrowed before he blinked and shook his head. "Sure. Why not?"

Old habits died hard, even if those habits hadn't been used for a solid eighteen months. Even as her shoulders dropped with released tension, she still fought an urge to reach out for his hand and lead him to the wall.

She ambled ahead, refusing to touch him, her steps loping and casual, like this whole thing didn't set her pulse to an aching gallop or that she hadn't spent the last year and a half in a state of painful curiosity over what he'd been up to. That curiosity now screamed at her to cut to the chase and ask him how he'd managed in all the time apart.

*Oh, maybe I should just admit it. I want to know if he's been a wreck without me.*

She took a seat on the wide wall, tucking her legs beneath her and trying to bury the memory of how messy she'd gotten in the wake of their breakup.

"How did Gideon rope you in, anyway?" She pulled her billowy dress over her knees, creating an excuse to avert her gaze.

"He sold me some story about being deathly ill and not wanting to send you to a rock concert alone." His easy tone tugged at her, making her attempts to look away impossible.

She smiled up instead, Max still standing over her, while she pretended the mere sight of him didn't suck the air right out of her lungs. "And you bought that story? Have you seen where I work? I think I can fend for myself."

Max laughed, and her own smile widened in response. "Well, the real clincher was his line about you dreaming of going to a Queen concert for as long as he could remember, and that he thought you should have someone to share the experience with."

She couldn't hold back and barked out a totally ungraceful laugh. "And so, calling my ex-boyfriend seemed like the best option?"

Her smile sank.

As much as Max had meant to her, she'd never even given him the honorific of being her boyfriend, though perhaps her mind had fallen back to him so many times over the years that *boyfriend* seemed far more fitting than *casual fling*.

He didn't seem to catch the pain in her expression, or if he did, he hid his awareness well as he sat on the wall beside her. "To be honest, I'm pretty sure Gideon wasn't calling me from his sick bed. I heard loud music, and I'm almost certain someone flushed a toilet in the background."

She spat out another laugh, willing a rogue tear to stay in her eye. "I bet he went out clubbing with friends and was calling you from the toilets."

An easy silence settled between them, and she twisted to dig around in her bag. "I'm surprised you didn't have anywhere else to go on a Saturday night."

Her face turned hot. Had she really just dropped a not-so-subtle attempt at finding out about his life these days?

Yes, she had.

*Or is that, more precisely, who was in his life these days?*

"There might be a lot about me that would surprise you." The added pause and the husky bend to his tone asked for her gaze to re-join his.

Her heart hitched, making her regret she'd even asked, that the hurt in his voice probably had a lot to do with her.

*Oh God, please don't let his life be bad now.*

She obliged and offered her attention, her heart rate kicking up another notch at that sad blue gaze connecting with hers.

"I was at home. Working. It's pretty much all I do at the moment."

The muscles in her face sagged, and his unwavering stare seemed to say, *Can't you see, I've changed?*

She went back to fidgeting, to pulling out food containers and placing them on the wall between them.

What did she hope might happen to him, anyway?

That he'd find his place in the world? Find direction and somewhere to focus his once wayward energy? That he'd found a woman who recognized how special he was? And even if he had changed, what did he expect her to do about it?

She pulled at the container lids, pretending everything about this situation was fine and dandy, telling herself to keep her emotions in check, otherwise she'd be swiping away tears.

Maybe she'd long ago recognized how special Max was, but she'd never done a damn thing about it. In fact, she'd flat out rejected him and left him in her dust. And here she was, her heart threatening to bolt out of her ribcage, her face near on fire, like she had the right to feel in any way possessive about him.

They'd never shared any sort of official relationship, his presence now probably having everything to do with his deep-rooted kindness. Besides, even if she did regret them not being together, she'd never regret her reasons for instigating the breakup.

So what if he'd evolved, maybe become everything she hoped he would be.

None of that meant she needed to change anything about the state of this relationship.

"I think I can relate. I've been locked down with work too." She gave him a weak smile and gestured to the food so he'd eat. "God, we both sound kind of pathetic. Two workaholics with no life, right?"

He reached for a cracker and returned her smile with a smaller one of his own. "You know, actually, this is the least pathetic I've felt in years. I like what I do now, even if I am on a short path to crashing and burning." His smile grew, and he nibbled on the cracker's edge, drawing her attention to his lips and how much she wished there wasn't so much literal and figurative space between them. "This is the closest I've come to taking a genuine stab at failure, and for some reason, it feels amazing."

Her eyes stung from staring at him. Or maybe it was the staring combined with not blinking. Everything about Max was the same. Those same arctic-blue eyes. The same ruffled golden waves. His lips with their subtle fullness.

But he had something else now. A glow. His eyes weren't just blue anymore, they shone with distinct brightness, like sunlight through sea glass.

"It's not the chance of failure that makes you feel amazing." The mumbled words found their own way out, and she distracted herself with passing him a grilled cheese sandwich wrapped in tin foil. "It's that you're trying. I mean, I'm glad you've found something you enjoy. What is your work these days, anyway?"

He shrugged; his gaze cast down to his long fingers toying with an edge of foil. "You're not going to believe this, but after I left The Ruby Room, I sold the apartment and used some of my spare cash to enroll in a year-long, intensive fashion design course."

She paused, halfway through unwrapping a sandwich, thanking goodness she hadn't already started chewing because she'd no doubt be choking right now. "You what? I don't think I ever got the impression you were *that* into fashion."

"I wasn't, but I've been into sustainable living for years, and that's where the fashion thing comes in." His smile resurfaced, vibrant and sparkling against the stadium lights. "By the way, your reaction is almost as good as the change itself."

She turned her hand in a repeated circle, gesturing for him to hurry up with his news. "Enough about me, how the heck does the rest of your story pan out?"

"Well, I ended up getting so into my design course, I graduated top of my class and decided to try my luck at producing a surf fashion line made completely from recycled materials."

He bit into his sandwich, his demeanor about a million times less ruffled than hers. "I'm still very new, so I have other designers helping me, but Luke taught me how to use the money I already had to bankroll the whole thing. The business is six months old, and I'm at the point where there's enough profit to pay myself a full-time wage, as well as hire virtual assistants to help with customer service and online marketing. Our next goal is to expand into activewear."

～

"Holy shit!"

Freya's breathy tone ricocheted between them, and her mouth hung open. Max decided she searched for something more to say but couldn't find the words.

To be fair, he'd gotten used to that reaction from people who hadn't seen him in a while. "Bit of a surprise?"

"I mean, yeah." She blinked as if coming to her senses. "But when you put it like that, I guess the whole eco-fashion thing does make sense." Her eyes narrowed, like she inspected him anew, her gaze traveling down to his chest. He wondered what she saw.

Though he'd always held an unaffected air—the kind that came from denial—recently, he'd been told his brand of calmness had changed to the sort that came from someone who truly knew themselves. Maybe Freya saw that now, too, saw something more than his old jovial, surfer-guy act.

Because heaven help him, there was so much more to his accepting Gideon's challenge to show up tonight than the pretense of keeping her company.

"There were always hints you had an interest in that stuff, it's just" —her stare trained on him, like she took a second to come to terms with something—"I… I'm proud of you."

Her face relaxed, and she drew her posture up, the admission seeming to lighten something within her. He held her gaze for the longest time, feeling like a moth caught in candlelight—drawn to her, his twin flame.

Though she probably didn't see him in the same way.

She'd spent most of tonight averting her gaze. He'd been the one to bust in on her concert experience, so maybe she was just being nice, and whatever connection he sensed didn't exist.

*Hey hero, whatever happened to "not fearing failure"?*

Well, maybe his moth analogy wasn't far off the truth, but in a whole other way.

If he got too close, he risked being burned. Hadn't he done exactly that with her already, only to get epically dumped?

There was fearing failure, and then there was making an educated guess based on past experience.

*But look at her, she's not turning me away now…*

*Maybe she's happy.*

*Maybe she wants the same things, too?*

He drank in the warmth of her close proximity before time and reality ripped them apart again. "And what about you? What are you up to these days?"

"I… umm…" She swallowed, her eyes taking on a misty sheen.

*Was she about to cry? Surely not.*

"I have a new club. I mean, I still have The Ruby, but we've expanded."

He pitched one brow upward since he'd only ever seen her get emotional once before, and that had been in the wake of her mother's death.

Still, just in case, he tried to keep the mood light and offered a casual grin. "You mean, The Rainbow Room?"

Her forehead crinkled, her entire expression tensing into a focused scowl, like maybe she didn't totally love that he knew of The Rainbow Room. "You've been keeping tabs on me?"

# Chapter Forty-Two

Freya's eyes prickled just looking at Max, her heart straining that she got to share a little more time with him. If that wasn't a big enough sign she most definitely cared… And then there was his mention of The Rainbow Room, an indication he too cared, at least enough to find out about her, anyway. And he'd turned up tonight, hadn't he?

*Fuck her life.*

Lord help her if he called her bluff. If he asked to rekindle what they'd had, how would she even respond to that?

*My life is so different these days. So is his. Why am I still terrified of throwing myself into a relationship with him?*

Because he'd want more than last time. He'd want a knock-down, drag-out, no-holds-barred kind of love. No more meaningless booty calls. Just intimacy, and promises, and a whole lot of other messy stuff she couldn't control.

And the worst part? He deserved all that and more.

Maybe she did too.

But her reasons for walking away from him had been all about what he lacked. Now she would be forced to look at what *she* lacked, and what she lacked was any kind of working knowledge or experience when it came to healthy, long-term relationships. Not counting her friendship with Gideon, of course.

"I'm sorry." She pressed her fingertips over her closed eyelids. "Things ended so abruptly between us, I guess I can't blame you for being curious."

"I wasn't keeping tabs." He frowned, breaking eye contact. "Enough people knew about us that some felt the need to tell me."

"It's fine."

She gnawed on her lower lip, fighting a desire to reveal the truth that she too had experienced moments of looking into his life. Like how, two weeks after the breakup, she'd spent an entire day clearing out her mother's rundown house. The sheer labor involved, the overbearing memories, the act of throwing so much of her mother away, had left her in desperate need of comfort.

Gideon was out of town with his show, and she'd been alone, so before she had a moment to take stock of her actions, she'd made it all the way to Max's apartment. Even gotten so far as pressing his buzzer numerous times, only to get no answer.

It wasn't until she returned to her car, despondent and more heartbroken than ever, that she saw the big *For Sale* sign.

He'd already moved. She'd missed him. And it was the act of catching herself digging through her handbag, seconds from calling him, that brought up the reality that she'd been about to drag him back into her orbit.

She'd used that moment to delete his number altogether, to sever all ties and all temptation to contact him again, to wise up to the truth that she needed to stop.

Her desperate clinging would only break her heart all over again.

An internal shudder worked through her core now, and she lifted her gaze back to Max. Reconnecting seemed like a nice idea, but maybe they'd be better off leaving things as they were.

"You seem well. I'm glad." She lowered her gaze and gave a weak smile, busying herself with the task of biting into her sandwich.

He chuckled, a light staccato not one-hundred-percent joy-filled. "Meanwhile, Freya Cortez continues on her road to greatness. Maybe we're both not so pathetic after all?"

She paused chewing and stared straight ahead, at the long journey of descending concrete stairs and the tall flag poles either side, banners flapping with adverts for future concerts. Even as she vied for mental distance, Max's lighthearted approach bore a hole through her defenses and made her want to hold on to him even more.

"Freya?" His lowered voice pulled her from her thoughts and onto his deep frown. "Are you okay?"

She swatted her hand through the air, dismissing his concern. "I'm fine. Just a lot happening right now. You know, work stuff."

"No." His shook his head, his overly focused stare offering no room for escape. "I mean, the last time I saw you, you'd lost your mother, and you were about as broken as a person could get. Are you *okay*?"

His emphasis on the word *okay* implied that she might fold over in a devastated mess. To be fair, anyone with her past could be forgiven for doing just that. Besides, he was right, she hadn't been a picture of mental stability in the days leading to their breakup, so maybe his concern now was somewhat warranted.

She lowered her sandwich to the foil wrapper in her lap and directed a smile his way. "Yeah, actually, I am. I'm good."

The lines on his face eased, and he tilted his head to one side, the slight curl of his lips hinting at delighted surprise. "Really?"

She cleared her throat and nodded, hoping he'd accept her reply as genuine honesty. "Yeah, really. I've had a long time to think since we last met, and even if there'd been time for my mum to offer the dying-hour apology I wanted, it wouldn't have been enough. A part of me would always question whether the apology was her way of hedging her bets. You know, easing her guilt before skipping off to wherever people like her go when they die?"

She shrugged and frowned down at her lap. "The only thing that might have truly helped was if she'd done a significant amount of work on herself long before she died. If she'd sought ongoing professional help and put in the hours to repair our relationship. I guess what you saw was me in the throes of realizing that was never going to happen."

His fingers slid along the concrete space between them, stopping just shy of reaching her hand, like he'd meant to comfort her but figured that was a bad idea. "That must have been a hard realization to come by."

"There's been a lot of hoops to jump through, and a lot of *ifs* and *buts*..." A ball of emotion took up space at the base of her throat, her voice raspy and hard to control. "I feel ridiculous now thinking back on how much I expected from my mother in those final months. I'd been on the right path, doing things my own way already, only to put my healing in the hands of my abuser.

"I should have trusted myself. Should have just admitted some relationships are complex, and it's possible to love someone and hate them at the same time. That it was okay to understand *why* she was the way she was, but still not be okay with her decisions. There were reasons for what she did to me, but none of those reasons made a valid excuse. So really, my mum's death threw one big fucking spanner in all the good work I'd done prior to her becoming ill, and it—"

Her voice cracked, and she slapped her hand over her mouth because there was no way Max hadn't heard her emotions rise up to overwhelm her.

"Freya?" He leaned in, the subtle movement imploring her to go on.

She took her hand from her lips. "It also means I might have been too quick to end things with you than I probably should have been."

His posture sagged, and he angled slightly away from her, his gaze searching her face in the prolonged silence.

Pretty much everyone from the concert had gone, which only left her with this giant wasteland of concrete pillars and some twinkling lights; the only sounds being the scuttling of leaves and the rustle of a few nearby seagulls scavenging for food. The whole scene built a haunting sense that she and Max might be the only two people left in the world.

His gaze dipped, as if he took a second to think, before a heavy sigh fell from him, and his stare captured hers once more. "You're the bravest person I know, Freya."

Her mouth slipped open. She'd expected his criticism, not a compliment.

"If I'd been truly honest with myself"—his hand slid forward again, this time succeeding in landing on top of hers—"I would have admitted that us being together wasn't doing either of us a whole lot of good, which means that you took the brunt and the blame when you did end things. And all during a time that would have been horrible for you already. And *that* makes you far wiser and braver than me. I can see that you want me to hate you, but I don't. Not at all."

Her insides gave an aching twist, her heart somewhere between swelling and shrinking at his words. With one hand, he complimented her wisdom and bravery, two traits she'd earned through blood and tears; with the other, he ripped away something she fast realized she still desperately wanted.

*Him.*

The truth was, despite what he believed, she *had* gotten a great deal of "good" from being with him. In fact, he'd been the first romantic partner to truly support her, to listen, to not ask her to dim her light so he could shine brighter.

He'd been gentle and sweet and obnoxiously positive—her soft place. Hell, most of their time together had been just plain old fun.

So yeah, hearing him say their relationship hadn't done much good took a pitchfork to her insides. That pitchfork stabbed holes right through the hope that *maybe* there was more to this catch up than stupid-old Gideon getting a big laugh at her expense.

"I… ahhh…" She tugged her hand away from his and went about shutting food containers and then stuffing them into her bag. She swore under her breath, tears gathering at the outer corners of her eyes. *Stupid woman.* "It's… it's getting late, and I have work in the morning. I should go."

She shot to her feet and gave him a lame half-wave goodbye.

He peered up at her—two great, thick lines digging trenches between his brows—gaze darting about her face like her reaction perplexed him. "Freya, what's wrong?"

"Nothing." She offered a tight smile, one that probably wasn't all that unbelievable what with her jittery movements and sudden inability to look any higher than his chest. "Nothing's wrong. You're right. There wasn't much good in what we had, and seeing you tonight, I should be thinking less about rekindling what we had and more about why I set you free to begin with."

*Ouch!*

She pressed her hand to her roiling stomach. The act of saying all of that made her want to pitch her barely digested sandwich. She hadn't meant to use such harsh words, but maybe harsh was what they needed.

He jumped up and drew in close. "Wait, what's happening here? Were you really hoping for a *rekindling*? Because right now you're walking away again, and I can't—"

She flapped her hands in front of her and spun away from him, tears beginning to spill while her nerves burned at the sense of teetering on the edge of something big. "I don't know, Max. I don't know."

She had a decision to make. The rest of her life with this man or complete nothing. Her wild reaction was all about her renewed chance to fuck up the only real and loving relationship to cross her path in her entire thirty-three years of existence, and still, things weren't as simple as picking between two options.

"All I know is, the reasons for us not being together still hold true. I still don't want to always be the strong one. I still can't take yet another person letting me down."

Max gripped her elbow and turned her to face him, and his mere touch and the act of making eye contact sent instant flutters throughout her body.

*He isn't making walking away easy.*

He pulled her closer, and despite her reservations, she allowed him to. "I wouldn't be here if I didn't in all honesty believe I've changed."

She squeezed her eyes shut, trying to shut him out, trying to keep her head clear. "I don't have it in me to find the hidden blessings in yet another bad relationship. I don't want to have to search for the lesson in something that's just plain broken. If losing my mother has taught me anything, it's that sometimes pain is just pain, and things just hurt. There's no rhyme or reason, no greater good." She shook free and pressed the back of her hand to her forehead. "I'm not even sure what I'm saying here."

"I think"—he took a side step so he stood directly in line with her, despite her constant turning away—"what you're trying to say is that you don't want me to flake out on you. That you want more than what we had last time."

She moved to speak, but he shook his head, indicating he wasn't finished.

"You want what happened with your mother to end with you." His voice held an urgent strain, like his life hung on his ability to convince her, even though his sheer lack of needing to convince her was what scared her most of all. "For you, that makes avoiding bad relationship choices even more critical. I get it."

"It's more than that. The need to get things right also puts a lot of pressure on whoever wants to be with me."

He narrowed his eyes, as if attempting to read her thoughts, before a slow smile lit his face. He lifted one hand to stroke her cheek, a cheek still hot with tears. "My parents raised me to believe that kindness costs nothing, Freya. And being kind to you is the easiest thing in the world. It's what you deserve. What you've always deserved, all along, despite how others treated you. Have I ever been unkind to you?"

Her chin wobbled with the emergence of a sad smile. She shook her head, distracting herself from the wave of emotion taking over.

He'd always been good to her, even when he'd been not-so-great to himself.

"Then let's start there. I have no intention of ever hurting you, and I hope you've seen enough to know that's not part of who I am."

Her gaze fused with his, and she held silent. Her reaction to his statement was easy. She couldn't envisage him ever mistreating her, couldn't even imagine him having a malicious thought or raising his voice. But the past was a shadow near impossible to step out from, and sometimes she saw monsters where they didn't exist.

*But I still believe him. He's right; he's given me every reason to believe him.*

With every encounter they'd ever shared, kindness had always been his default.

Not just with her, but with everyone.

How could she not give him a chance?

She took a deep breath and gave him a shaky nod, allowing her wayward smile to sneak through just a little. "Your parents did a good job with you."

His fingers connected with her chin, and he tilted her head so her line of sight matched his. "They did, which brings me back to why you're far braver and wiser than me."

His lips curled into a cheeky grin. He was stroking her ego, no doubt about it, but the hurt little girl in her needed the encouragement all the same.

"You developed your kindness, bravery, and smarts all on your own. You held so much pain, and yet you knew not to push it onto others. You're a special brand of person, Freya Cortez. Look at everything you've done so far. You're already the changed woman you wanted to be."

She tensed at the reminder of her mother and the unacceptable wounds inflicted on Freya year after year. "And you're not scared I'll turn into her?"

She'd been forced to carry a stigma she didn't deserve, so many people having distanced themselves, already labeling her a monster in the making. Why not Max too?

*Because he's different.*

"Can you imagine your mother, at any point in her life, being anything like you are now?" He raised a brow, point already made, but he had more to say. "You gave me a job when I had nothing. You gave me your personal time and affection when others ran. You've never yelled at me or insulted me, even after I made the dumbest mistakes."

"You mean like losing all your money?"

His lips curved into another smile. "Exactly. You couldn't be any further from your mother if you'd both come from different planets. Hell, you even broke both our hearts so we could each get our lives together. You did it for a greater good, and as much as I wanted to hate you for that, I couldn't. You achieved things with me others tried but failed to do. You saw the core of my issues when even I couldn't, and you forced me to heal the things that were holding me back."

"Well, then. You're welcome."

Despite her joke, his eyes held a focused stare, his cheeks lax in a somber expression. "No. Not yet. I'm not finished."

Her heart lurched. He was being way more philosophical and serious than she'd ever seen of him. Maybe he *had* changed.

"I know I've been indecisive, but I sure as hell know what I want now."

She quirked a brow, not used to this new and more direct version of Max. "And what's that?"

"I'm going to turn around in the next few seconds and leave for home. But when I do, I hope I won't be leaving alone."

He let go of her and stepped away, extending a hand for her to take, his forehead wrinkled in a silent question.

*Would she take his hand? Would she go with him?*

# Chapter Forty-Three

Freya stared at Max's outstretched hand, everything around her seeming to pause and her world completely silent. She had a decision to make, less about whether she would take his hand, more about whether she could.

She lifted her focus to the warmth in his eyes, his expression pinched like his entire future rested on this moment. Maybe it did. Hers certainly would never be the same, no matter what she chose to do next. And still, with all the thoughts buzzing around in her head, her body was the one to make the decision for her, overriding years of careful and considered life choices.

She watched, powerless, as her hand rose and fingers extended, all too soon sliding home into the upward curve of his palm. Her feet moved, betraying logic, stepping her toward him.

"I can't tell if this is the best fucking decision I've ever made"—the statement fell from her in a rush of words and her heart drummed wild —"or the dumbest. So, start walking before I have any more time to think."

Max's lips split into a mega-watt smile, and he let loose with a soft chuckle. The sound worked its way through her chest and into her heart. The hard strained beating made her feel near ready to burst.

And the light in his gaze, cool in color but hot in every other way, made more tears well in her eyes and caused her laugh to escape too.

She was just so damn happy. Maybe stupidly so. She hadn't ever felt this carefree. The closest she could recall was that night in his apartment, after the heating died and they'd found other ways to keep warm.

But even now, she held back from kissing him because if she did that, they'd never leave this stadium. So, she took his lead and followed him down the long flight of stairs, all the way to the parking lot and his car.

Except, it wasn't his car. Not as she'd known it, anyway.

The Tesla was gone, the lavish vehicle traded for a more reasonably priced midnight-blue sedan, yet another hint of change, of the sacrifices he'd made to fund his newfound dreams.

The freeway lights soon flickered outside the car's windows, green overhead signs announcing each suburb as they passed. He'd clearly also moved much farther out from the city.

The knots in her stomach untangled more and more with each little sign of change, every one an indication she'd made the right choice in giving him a second chance.

Throughout the drive back to his place—wherever that was—they talked about the most mundane subjects. From the noisy cockatoo that had taken up residence amongst the red blossoms of a Firewheel tree outside her townhouse, to the massive dog who kept pooping on the nature strip outside his.

They laughed along the way, the whole casual exchange slipping them back in sync with each other, so contrary to the months upon months of no contact.

He stopped his car outside of a brown brick townhouse in the middle of suburbia and neither spoke as the locks clicked open on his doors. She should have felt nervous, but her heart pounded for a whole other reason. Pride surged through her since this man, who at their last exchange lived a shambled life, had come back for her. He'd worked hard to turn his life around, and now that work paid off in their favor.

He'd studied and excelled, then built a new business around a passion he'd struggled for so long to find. More than any of that, he'd dismantled the soul-destroying emotions that had torn them apart in the first place.

And somehow, she found the ability to accept him, to accept what would happen next.

She stepped out of the car, the night air still cool and filled with the sleeping suburb's relative silence. The short path up to his chestnut front door took seconds to cover, the stain across its indented panels slightly faded, indicating a well-lived-in house minus any true neglect.

From the outside, it looked like a *home*, modest and cozy, nowhere near as glamorous as his former apartment. This alone brought ease to her racing pulse.

Max pushed open the door, and they stood in his entryway, for a moment looking anywhere but at each other. To her left was a living room, one that blended with a kitchen; the entire area was small, with modern floating stairs scaling up the far wall.

"I know it's not what I used to have…"

She spun around to find his pupils wide in apology.

She pointed to her surroundings. "No. This is enough."

Her breaths drew tight at the notion he thought she might ever judge him for making a few difficult choices. Maybe others had, but not her. She'd come from far, far worse and understood he'd achieved something worthy of bragging. Not that Max ever bragged.

She fixed her stare right onto his and pulled him into her, making sure he understood too. "Max, this is *more* than enough."

The tension around his eyes eased, and an innate gleam returned before his lips crashed over hers, taking her by surprise.

Her bag slipped off her shoulder and fell to the ground. He swept her off her feet, his teeth nipping at her lower lip, as his long legs marched her across the room.

Stairs creaked beneath his footfall, and she held onto his shoulders for dear life, the living area's lights soon dimming as he entered his bedroom. He plonked her onto the bed and another giddy laugh broke from her lips, the ungraceful approach so very Max.

His laughter mingled with hers, and he pulled his shirt over his head, tossing it to the floor—yet more ungracefulness, though his slow crawl across the bed toward her caused any sound she might have made to disappear, her breath pausing for one quick beat.

He positioned his body over hers, covering her, as beautiful as ever, perhaps even more so because of the journey they'd endured to get to this point. Even in his absence, her affection for him grew, heart holding on no matter how much she tried to bury all her memories.

The sudden stillness of his face mirrored her emotions, like he knew the impact of this moment and how much it meant to her. This was more than any woman allowing him to fall in love with her. She was a survivor. One who knew how ugly the world could be. And that knowledge made all the difference. It raised the stakes for just how much trust she put in him now.

He leaned in so his lips met hers again, though a million times softer. His tongue caressed hers until she released an easy sigh and arched her body into his—this reunion everything luscious and luxurious—bringing her as close to floating as anyone could get, igniting a desire for him now... and fast.

His lips veered, trailing a maddening line of kisses to the side of her neck, his breath hot against her skin; and before she knew what was happening, his hand found her outer thigh, and he pulled away her panties.

Max smiled down at her, her dress's off-the-shoulder neckline the next to go. She wriggled, helping him slide the purple material down her body, all while extending her arms and tugging at his belt.

In seconds, his hungry kiss devoured her lips again, and he took her body with one swift thrust. She gasped, tensing around him, before curling her lips at the wondrous sense of connection. Maybe there would be time for slow and sweet later, but this time wouldn't be it.

He thrust into her again, unapologetic, demanding, her mind dizzying, while she didn't even attempt to stop her body's reaction.

"Max." Her voice came out soft, like a wish already answered.

She tightened her legs around his hips and dug her nails into the hard muscle at his back. There was more to come, and they were both set on making up for lost time, every one of her nerves catching light at having him inside her... and all around her... his body and heat claiming her over and over again.

An electrified thrill ran from her head to her toes, circling back, torturing her all over again. She laughed at the joy of it all. At having him again. At just how freaking good it was to feel him once more and hopefully forever.

None of this made sense. Not the building pressure or the trill of excitement spilling from her lips, but before she could control any of it, his movements grew faster still, and the pressure became too much. She threw back her head, muscles contracting, while a guttural moan exploded free of her.

She pulled him closer, wanting to feel everything, even though she feared she might black out from sheer exhilaration.

"Oh, Freya."

Her name fell from him with gentle endearment. He continued to bury himself within her until his body shook with his release. Her muscles eased, and she accepted him. *Accepted this.* That they were together now, and that from now on they would fight to *stay* together.

His climax eased and his head found a place at her neck, and he settled down beside her, his lips leaving yet more soft kisses on her skin. "Freya?"

She still floated from her release and his lingering touch, and she failed to find the energy to reply.

"Freya?"

She drew a sharp breath, forcing herself to look at him. "Hmm?"

His eyes glinted with his smile, like he might have something meaningful to say, only to utter, "If you had a choice—live on any planet, time travel, or know everything there was to know about everything—which would you choose?"

Her stare fused with the dark expanse of his ceiling. Before long, a rich wave of laughter broke past her lips.

He couldn't have given a more "Max" response to making love than that.

She shoved at his shoulder, still laughing. His cheeks lifted with a boyish grin.

"Time travel, you doofus." She leaned into him and rewarded his lovable silliness with a firm kiss.

Her life had been one sad and serious event after another. Maybe this man was just the light she needed.

He turned with his lingering smile, waiting for her to settle into the nook under his armpit. "Same. I would go back in time and see all the cool stuff we don't have anymore, then I'd go forward in time and find answers to stuff I want to understand." His eyes widened as though a new thought entered his mind. "Oh, and then I would go to a time with advanced space travel, so I could still tick living on another planet off my list."

She gave him a mock flat stare. "Except, it'd suck if you went ten years forward and found everyone was dead."

"Well, yeah." He frowned. "That *would* suck."

"Or you might succeed in visiting another planet." She shrugged and ticked one side of her lip upward. "Only to die at the hands of aliens who are smart enough to wear shorts in hot weather."

She pulled her mouth into an instant smile, while a slow chuckle reverberated through Max's chest. He too remembered that awkward camping trip where she'd tried to distract him with questions about nonsensical wardrobe choices in sci-fi shows.

His gaze caught hers now, and his fingertips combed loose curls away from her face, the rest of him falling still. "You know, I love you."

His low whisper, so intimate and sincere, traveled deep into her body and wrapped around her heart, giving life to a dull ache—an ache to last a lifetime because that's how long she'd wanted someone to say those words to her.

Though he *had* spoken those words before, only she'd been too broken from her mother's death to stay and say them back. Now things were different, her only fear being that life would find a way to take him from her once again.

*I won't think like that. He's mine now. I won't ever let him go.*

And so, she gave him a shaky smile, ran her fingers over the soft bristle of his cheek, and gave him the reply she'd so wanted to say the first time he'd uttered those words.

"Max, I love you too."

# Epilogue



*Three years later*

"You don't usually hold these things during the day."

Max waited as Luke's attention broke to Nova bolting past, the little girl tearing through the busy beachside restaurant, while a heavily pregnant Agathe ambled after her.

"Much less encourage us to bring the kid." Luke turned back, sporting a bemused grin. "Come to think of it, where's Freya?"

Max dragged out the suspense and waved at Miro, bustling about in this, his new restaurant. He'd closed down his Port Melbourne café and moved to a bigger operation in the outer coastal suburbs.

The invites to this event had stated they'd be celebrating the launch of Max's company's new footwear line, but Miro knew otherwise.

An easy smile tugged at Max's lips, and he spun back to Luke, happy to continue the lie for a while longer. "Freya will be here any minute. She's caught up with work."

Sophie strolled past, also expecting, but not quite as pregnant as Agathe. Orlando trailed behind her, his fingers interlaced with hers.

They too headed outside to the restaurant's mini-boardwalk edging the sand.

The lightness of yet another secret prodded Max into patting Luke's shoulder, before excusing himself outside to meet the subdued heat of the late summer afternoon.

His feet scraped over the slightly faded wooden deck, and he turned toward the ocean before him, inhaling the briny air and awaiting his fate. A fate he'd instigated, only for Freya to join him the rest of the way.

They'd taken what they started three years ago and built something special. Together. The money from the sale of their respective townhouses had bought a larger home ten minutes down the road from where he stood now. A place for him to be near his beloved ocean and a haven for Freya away from the hustle of her busy city venues.

A place to raise a family.

A gasp broke from the restaurant's far corner. He spun around, his chest tingling with the fuzzy spread of excitement.

Two dancers burst from the kitchen doors dressed in skin-tight, black, mime outfits, only to prance through a gap in the crowd. He recognized the dancers from Freya's club, and though she'd mentioned she'd be making a grand entrance, he had no idea what she'd planned.

The dancers made it to the boardwalk and lowered a rucksack from over each of their shoulders, unceremoniously dumping the contents onto the deck with a loud metallic clang.

A pile of rose-gold-colored tubes lay at their feet, and they went about connecting the pieces together, occasionally stopping to prance before the gathering guests in a tangle of dramatic arm and leg movements. Perhaps their comical way of drawing out the building process.

The kitchen doors sprung open again, and two more dancers came out, Gideon positioned in the middle with a thick garland of bushy green foliage and pale pink roses draped over his shoulders, his midnight-blue velvet suit peeking out from underneath.

Subdued piano music spilled through the venue's speakers, and Gideon whipped out a cordless microphone from under his leafy plume. Before Max could register much of anything, Freya's best friend prowled toward him, singing Queen's "Somebody to Love".

The lyrics to the song weren't romantic at all, and a chuckle escaped him, but somehow Gideon sold the performance like only he could. By the time he made it to the boardwalk, the first two dancers had finished their construction—a rose-gold arch.

Gideon's dancers took the garland from his shoulders and draped it over the arch, and just about then, more gasps broke through the crowd—all Max and Freya's closest family, friends, and work colleagues.

This wasn't just any arch. This was a wedding arch.

The gasps turned to glee-filled shrieks, and Max's gut flip-flopped inside him. He didn't need to turn around to guess what had instigated the crowd's reaction, but he did, anyway.

Freya stood just inside the venue's main double doors, a shimmering blush silk dress flaring out from her waist, reaching down to just below her knee.

Her signature blond curls were swept up into a loose style with free locks of hair skimming her face, her hands wrapped around a white-and-pink bouquet.

She glided toward him, the slight tremble of her lower lip betraying uncharacteristic nerves. *Holy smokes.* The mere sight of her—dressed like that. *His* bride. Walking toward *him*. The muscles on his face fell slack, and his heart pounded faster than any of his swim races had ever required.

She stopped at his side, and together they turned toward their celebrant, Gideon.

Even though Max had always secretly wanted a wife, he'd never really expected to get a wedding day. He'd also never imagined the event galloping by quicker than he could process.

He caught Freya's quick glances at him, always capped with a coy smile. The voluminous lace on her dress hid the fact that she was three months pregnant, probably a good thing since they wanted *that* surprise to wait until after *this* surprise.

He reached out and wrapped his hands around hers, and before too long, they exchanged vows.

As much as this day meant everything to him, it meant even more to her. To trust him with the rest of her life, the words, "I do" falling from her lips and sending a jolt of joy-filled adrenaline through his body.

Tears gathered in her eyes, only to trickle down her cheeks, a shudder of laughter working past her lips, as though a heavy weight shifted off her. And maybe it did. Everything about this moment seemed so unlikely.

And as the words, "I do", fell from him too, the beat of his heart settled like one last puzzle piece finally slipping into place, where it always belonged.

A temperate wave of calm washed over him. Freya and his child would have a home a million times different to the one she'd grown up in. There'd be no shouting. No anger. No explosive rage. There'd be no name calling or manipulations. No fear. No pain. Just warmth and laughter and constant safety. A family open about their love for each other.

He might have lost all the things he'd thought he wanted, but he'd found so much more and all he needed with Freya—a woman who'd pushed herself through hell just to ensure she'd be the last of her line and the first to make a change.

THE END

**GET A FREE NOVELLA AND EXCLUSIVE KATERINA SIMMS MATERIAL**

Building relationships with my readers is one of the great joys of writing, it keeps me from turning into a robot! My newsletters are filled with information on new releases, cover reveals, sales, giveaways, and news relating to my books.

**To claim your copy simply go to the "Free Book" page on my website.**
**www.katerinasimms.com**

# Also by Katerina Simms

The Love at Last Series:

The Last Heartbeat — Love at Last, Book 1

The Last Place You Look — Love at Last, Book 2

The Last in Line — Love at Last, Book 3

The Harlow Series:

Sapphires and Secrets — The Harlow Series, Book 1

Secret Surrender — The Harlow Series, Book 2

Second Hand Secrets – The Harlow Series, Book 3

Small Town Secrets – The Harlow Series, Book 4

**For latest releases, go to:**

https://katerinasimms.com/books

# About the Author

**Katerina Simms is a contemporary romance author, RWA Emerald Award finest, and International North Street Book Prize semi-finalist.** She was born on a sunny Mediterranean island, only to move to the weather-challenged suburbs of Melbourne, Australia.

Tea addict, nature lover, and terrible gardener, Katerina's novels feature vivid modern settings and heart-stirring characters, punctuated with the occasional good laugh. Her romances skirt the edges of women's fiction, and her favorite tropes are opposites attract, slow burn, and heat with heart.

www.katerinasimms.com

# *How about a review?*

Authors love reviews, and good ones help us make a living, and thus write more books! If you've enjoyed this book, please consider leaving a review on Goodreads or your retailer of choice. Just a line or two would make a wonderful difference!

Eternally grateful,

Katerina Simms

# Sapphires and Secrets

## THE HARLOW SERIES, BOOK 1

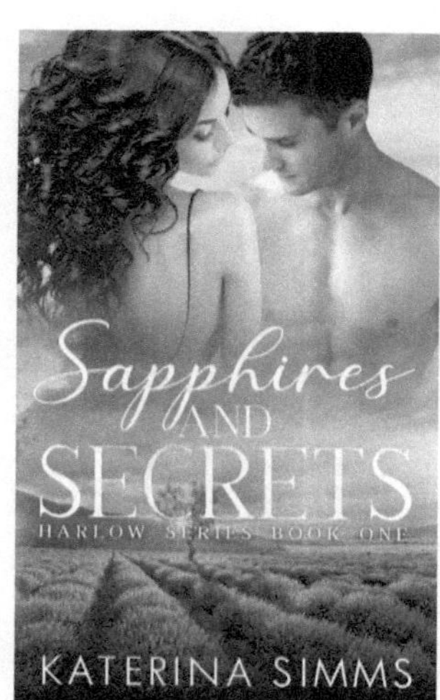

**Forbidden love in a town where danger lurks at every corner.**

Emilia Bonacci, introverted daughter of an overbearing jewelry tycoon. For one brief moment, she had it all. Now she's on the run from a family who wants to destroy her.

Small, charming, and picturesque. Harlow, Minnesota, seems like the perfect place to hide. Except a chance encounter throws her into the path of her forbidden first love…

Blaine Callaghan always had dreams of living in a big city, until he made the mistake of falling for Emilia. Her powerful family doomed him to exile in this small town, away from his family and future. Seeing her now unearths years of buried love and resentment. But this earth-shattering attraction is impossible to avoid.

Maybe they could be together this time. Except that anyone involved with Emilia will never be safe.

*If you enjoy Virgin River, slow-burn romance, quaint country towns, and a touch of suspense, you'll love Sapphires and Secrets.*

**A small town romance with a sinister mafia twist!**

**Buy link:** katerinasimms.com/sapphires-secrets/

Or use this QR CODE:

Copyright © 2023 by Katerina Simms

All rights reserved.

No part of this book may be reproduced in any form or by any electronic or mechanical means, including information storage and retrieval systems, without written permission from the author, except for the use of brief quotations in a book review.

This is a work of fiction. Names, characters, places, and incidents either are the product of the author's imagination or are used fictitiously. Any resemblance to actual persons, living or dead, events, or locales is entirely coincidental.

www.katerinasimms.com

www.ingramcontent.com/pod-product-compliance
Lightning Source LLC
Chambersburg PA
CBHW020237120726
47904CB00001B/3